Rolling Thunder

L. Erik Fleming

Strategic Book Publishing and Rights Co.

Strategic Book Publishing and Rights Co.
12620 FM 1960, Suite A4-507
Houston, TX 77065
www.sbpra.com

ISBN: 978-1-61897-047-3

Typography and page composition by J. K. Eckert & Company

Contents

1

FAM FLIGHT?

"Di vo'i tao"—Come with me, the young boy beckoned, waving his hand and smiling as he parted the thick, overgrown elephant grass. Overcome with youthful excitement, he moved quickly through stubborn vegetation that would slow anyone not accustomed it, and would lose anyone following. Every once in a while he'd have to stop and wait for the man to catch up and give him a reassuring smile to let him know that he was totally competent and wouldn't lead him astray. This was the only place the boy had known in his short life, and while he found it unusual that someone else, particularly a foreigner, thought his home was interesting, it made him proud.

The man smiled back. *"Tao se den,"* he said—I'm coming. He was trailing the boy by about ten yards, always reassuring him that he had total confidence in him. The man was sweating profusely from his fight with the tall blades that wrapped around his body and pulled him back, making for a more strenuous workout than he'd prepared himself for, but he continued his steady pace, making sure not to get too far behind. The man was an American in his late thirties and, like his guide, this wasn't the first time he'd hiked this way. He'd traveled this route countless times a decade earlier. For this American, today was the anniversary of his own personal Armageddon—a day of both a tragic end and a new beginning. He knew that occasionally throughout his life he'd have to revisit this place, whether metaphorically or literally. As always, there were the changes brought about by the passage of over a decade, but some things would remain unaltered, things that brought him here today and would surface in various details throughout his life.

1

As the American looked ahead, the boy had all but disappeared into the thick foliage ahead of him, leaving only the delicate voice to assure him that his young guide was still there. He followed the resonance of the song and the rustling sounds that filtered through the tall, green blinds and then said with a chuckle, "*Cho mot chut!*"—Wait a minute! He pushed his way through the blades that had momentarily stalled him into a clearing where the boy was waiting.

The boy then spread his hands out in a gathering motion as he said, "*Nhin cai nay kia!*"—Look at this here! He then walked toward the American and held out his hand when he realized the man was pleased, smiling as if to gain further approval.

The American reached into one of his pockets and handed the little boy an American dollar, which was worth about fifteen thousand dong at that morning's exchange rate.

The boy's eyes lit up and the smile across his dirty, sweaty face grew wider. He then said with enthusiasm, "*Cam on! Tao di duoc khong ngay?*"—Thanks! May I go now?

The American nodded with a smile and the young boy ran off with his treasure, again disappearing into the thick elephant grass. Alone now, he stared at his surroundings in shocked disbelief. He'd waited a long time to return here—it had taken him over a decade to find a reason and the courage to do so. He closed his eyes for a moment because what greeted his eyes today was far more painful than his memory of the place. Today he stood alone at the edge of a vast pond that was an island in a surrounding sea of rice paddies.

§ § § § §

Just a mile to the north was a small village, and off to the west sharp peaks rose from the relatively flat terrain. That was how he remembered it over the years. But today the smells and sounds drifting in the thick tropical air were different—harsher, more ragged, with no happy background chatter. He shut out the present-day stimuli and thought about how he remembered this place. He could hear the laughter, smell the food cooking, and feel the comforting welcome of the locals again. It was a time he'd never want to forget.

A smile spread across his face as he felt the warmth of his thoughts, just as real as the tropical sun drying the sweat on his face. He remained in this place until a bad memory crossed his mind, forcing him to open his eyes. He then stared blankly out to the horizon, until his urge to explore his surroundings made him walk. He hoped to find something that would bring him back to the place he remembered. He walked around the pond a few meters, then started toward the water's edge. As he drew to within a meter of the edge, the sole of his shoe scuffed over something hard, catching his attention. He took a step back and knelt, then dug around the object to free it from the muck it had been buried in for so long. It was obviously metal, but the mud still obscured its identity. When he finally freed the object and examined it closely, a sliver of its metallic luster caught enough sun to glint into his eyes. Curious, he scrubbed and blew on it until the mud was almost all gone, then polished it off with his handkerchief. When he unfolded the hanky, he saw an object that sent a shock radiating through his entire body. He'd come here to find something buried deep within his past somewhere in his thoughts, and he knew there was a chance that he'd stumble upon something like this—although not literally.

Maybe it was for this very chance that he'd come here to begin with. As he looked at the object more closely, his every muscle suddenly quivered and began to seize as a piece of his past rushed forcefully and unexpectedly through his mind. His head lowered to his chest, and from somewhere deep within he heaved uncontrollably. As unstoppable tears followed, he resigned himself to the fact that he'd have to, perhaps needed to, remember some of the things he'd so diligently tried to deny or forget for over a decade. As the tears continued, he unconsciously clenched the object in the palm of his hand so tightly that he drew blood, his knuckles now whiter than the handkerchief he'd used to clean it. He slowly released the object and cautiously turned it over in his hand, his curiosity at odds with the fear of what he expected to find. With the object now inverted, his eyes confirmed what he already knew was there—the tiny letters "N N" etched neatly in the corner. The object was a needle-guide plate from a sewing machine, and he knew exactly who they represented. His tears rained down on the plate and ran down his hand, diluting the blood that now dripped into the soil—and now his memories, good and bad, of this tiny Asian country on the Indochina Peninsula were not only gushing through his mind, but also deep within his soul.

§ § § § §

"I love you, Val. Hurry back to me. I'll wait until the end of time for you if I have to. Just be careful and return home safely to me—I can't imagine life without you. I could never even think of loving anyone else but you."

§ § § § §

Those parting words from his fiancée, Virginia, were etched in his mind. The whole scene that day was the most dismal in his memory, especially that last goodbye underneath the hulking shadow of the USS *Oriskany* at the docks in San Diego.

Everything before that moment was done as if it would be the last time, and even the most trivial things, always unnoticed or ignored before, were now suddenly significant. Ever since he got his orders to ship out, every minute detail of his life here at home was committed to memory, for while he didn't know what to expect, he had a nagging feeling in the back of his mind that he might need to recall these details some other time, when things might be worse. Some things he wanted to forget, but they too went with him, resurfacing time and again. All these would be melded with memories yet to be formed, and some of the ones he'd want to forget would also go with him. His own mind knew that he'd need all of them to complete the person he was, whether merely basking in good memories or resurrecting bad ones to help educate and moralize himself. One particular memory, the one of that last goodbye, was one that truly depended on the context of his situation at the moment for him to determine if it was good or bad, but it always left him empty, with a feeling of longing. The tears streaming down her face, that sinking feeling in his chest, the last seemingly way too short embrace, that final kiss goodbye—they all seemed to come back to him at the most inconvenient times.

§ § § § § §

He'd only been over here for two days, and now he sat in a sweltering cockpit under the gloom of an overcast sky, waiting for the engine-start-cart to kick in. Captain Valentine E. Jordan wiped the sweat from his face as he watched the gauges for signs of activity. Finally enough current ran through to move the needles, and he turned his attention to his plane captain and twirled his fingers, the engine-start hand signal, trying desperately to shake the images of the last haunting goodbye and get his head where it should be—on the task at hand. Seconds later the whine of spooling turbines filled his ears and blanketed the otherwise quiet Vietnamese countryside. He and his RIO (radar intercept officer), First Lieutenant Nathaniel L. Robinson, went over their respective checklists and BITs (built-in tests) as their great bird came to life. They were just supposed to go on a FAM (area familiarization) flight today, but here they were, going up with their squadron's CO and two other jets on a combat sortie to help a recon team trapped in heavy crossfire on some mountainside. Time was of the essence; the team radioed in that they were almost completely surrounded, and if help didn't arrive within fifteen minutes, not to even bother because they'd surely be overrun. To anyone trapped in a hailstorm of bullets, the whine of friendly jet engines overhead, if they can be heard, is as soothing as a choir of angels. To the opposing forces, it's the sound of the reaper coming for his due.

§ § § § § §

A nudge on the throttles and the flight of four were taxiing their F-4J Phantom IIs to runway 28 with priority over everyone, even an aircraft on short final. The squadron's commanding officer, Lieutenant Colonel Earl J. Driskell—call-sign "Papa"—was the flight leader on this sortie—and a living aviation legend. He was a two-time double ace, with fourteen kills in WWII and twelve in Korea, and was highly respected by everyone. Papa and his wingman, executive officer Major Chapman—call-sign "Chappie"—taxied into a staggered section departure on the runway, throttled up to military thrust, and held the brakes. When the control tower light turned steady green, they released the brakes, selected afterburner, and they went roaring down the runway. Val and his wingman taxied into position behind them and followed suit. They spooled their twin General Electric J79-GE-17 engines up to military power as they applied the brakes, the jets groaning in protest under the strain. When the light gun shined green at them, they released the brakes and selected afterburner, and the planes slammed forward down the runway. Even under a heavy bomb load, the planes accelerated moderately. About ten seconds later each pilot pulled aft on his control stick and the massive fighters leapt into the sky, with gear and flaps up. The planes continued accelerating and pitched up thirty, then forty-five degrees, disappearing into the gray veil of clouds. They were underway.

"Panama, Rhino Flight airborne. Flight of four Fox-4s with ten 500-pounders each and twenty mike-mike. We're at angels two-zero for base plus six on the Linh Thu two-two-zero for twenty -five." Papa's southern accent was smooth and unmistakable as he reported the position of the flight in compass azimuth and distance from Linh Thu, along with their altitude, to Panama, sometimes called Strike, which was the DASC (direct airborne strike control), similar to an air traffic control center in the states.

"Roger Rhino Flight. Radar contact. Contact the FACA (forward air controller airborne) on button blue, call-sign Watchdog Tango."

"Roger," the CO replied as he switched frequencies. The F-4 had twenty-four pre-programmed frequencies so that a pilot wouldn't have to fumble with the radio in an emergency or while maneuvering in combat. They were identified by stating the word "button" followed by a color: "Watchdog Tango, Rhino Flight on button blue, ready to copy mission."

"Roger, Rhino Flight." Watchdog Tango was a Marine OV-10 Bronco forward air control/reconnaissance aircraft. The "Tango" in his call-sign was the letter assigned to a particular pilot of that aircraft, which was changed monthly. "We have enemy troops hiding in two tree lines, one to the north and one to the south of some friendlies pinned down in an open grassy bald near the top of the mountain. Friendlies are taking heavy mortar fire from the south line and heavy machine gun fire from both lines. Both lines run east to west for approximately one hundred meters. I'll mark each with a Willie Pete. Drop four bombs each on the first run. Let's have a zero-five-zero run in with a right pullout at two thousand. Caution for low cloud bases and steep surrounding terrain, broken to overcast layer at four thousand, terrain peaks are about five thousand. Five second interval between runs. Call rolling in hot. Read back."

Papa read back the mission. "All right, gents—let's descend for a left-hand orbit at niner thousand. We're gonna earn our pay today, set for five hundred mils. We'll be flying a hi-lo-hi approach, on the deck and looking those bastards in the eye. Time to get down and dirty."

All four aircraft dove and leveled off at nine thousand feet AGL (above ground level) and began their orbit.

The peaks of the surrounding terrain poked through the low cloud layer in several places, and there were some breaks in the layer that allowed for visual contact with the ground, but for the most part the clouds obscured the target area.

"Watchdog Tango, Rhino 1. We are at angels nine, have limited visual on target area, no joy on you," Papa reported as all the RIOs checked their scopes for the FACA echo.

Watchdog Tango looked skyward and happened to catch a glimpse of a fast-moving dark speck through one of the breaks in the clouds. "Rhino Flight, I have you in sight. I'm beginning my run from the south; I'm now at your four o'clock." With that Watchdog Tango dropped to one thousand feet AGL, then sighted the south line by the mortar rounds being fired and fired a fan of Willie Petes at it. He then pulled up and performed a hard right wingover, after he had overflown the northern line and fired a second fan of Willie Petes along the length of it. "Rhino 1, do you have my smoke in sight?" Watchdog Tango asked. He knew that the jets most likely didn't, but he hoped they might get lucky and spot it through one of the breaks in the cloud deck.

All of the phantom pilots and RIOs began scanning the clouds below, searching in vain for the most part for any rising columns of smoke. "Negative, Watchdog Tango, but we'll see it once we punch through this shit," Papa said with a hint of resignation in his voice.

Watchdog Tango hesitated, not sure if it was a good idea for the jets to try that without a visual on the area yet, but he knew that the team on the ground couldn't hold out much longer. "Roger, Rhino 1. Make your drops behind and between smoke columns on both lines, moving northerly on the south line and southerly on the north line. You are cleared to attack, call rolling in hot." Watchdog Tango then quickly switched buttons to his low band FM channels to inform the platoon commander to get his team to lay low, the zoomies were rolling in.

The platoon commander had observed Watchdog Tango make his marking runs and was relieved to know that help was only moments behind. Once he got radio confirmation from Watchdog Tango, he had his men close the distance between each other and flatten themselves out so close to the ground that were eyeballing blades of grass. The deafening noise from the mortar rounds and machine gun fire would drown out the jets when they were on top of them, but the noise of their bombs would make the present din seem like a tomb. If the bombs hit their marks, a strange silence would descend, with only the distant gasps of sputtering flames to remind them that they still had a sense of hearing.

Papa and his XO broke off from Val and his wingman, deciding to hit the south line first in order to silence the mortars. Val and his wingman would follow, and would adjust their drops accordingly to the previous two runs.

"Dash 1, rolling in hot," Papa announced.

Five seconds later Chappie called out, "Dash 2, rolling in hot."

Val watched as the first two jets disappeared in the clouds, leaving only their swirling vortices behind to remind anyone that they were previously there.

"Dash 1, in sight. I have you leveling out. You look on line, you are cleared hot." Watchdog Tango was directing to help the jets make final adjustments for the desired effect. As Papa pickled off his first load, he called out, "I have four away, Dash 1. Dash 2 cleared for roll-in, in sight. Move slightly right of Dash 1's hits." A moment, then, "That looks on line. Dash 2 cleared hot. I have four away."

From his orbit five thousand feet above the cloud deck, Val could make out the brilliant flashes of the exploding ordnance fill in the breaks of the layer from the runs of his fellow Marines. He did notice, however, that those same breaks were suddenly closing as wisps of wind from the shockwaves and the convection of the heat of the massive flames swirled the layer into ever-tightening eddies. He queried his RIO for his opinion.

"Hey, Double-O, the cloud deck's tightening up. I see fewer and fewer places to safely punch through."

"Looks that way to me, too. I hope you studied up on the charts because you can see all the sharp rising terrain around us. The radar altimeter will be crucial when we penetrate the layer. It would make for a really short FAM flight if we tag any of these peaks."

"FAM flight? You got to go on a FAM flight? When do I get to?" Val replied with a smile, but he was quickly silenced when new instructions from Papa came over the frequency. The CO wanted the next two aircraft to attack the north line, since the south line had become relatively quiet. Then all four aircraft would mop up what was left of either line if required. Papa added that they were to commence attack directly from the east, moving west with a run in of zero-niner-zero with a left-hand pullout. The pullout was switched to left hand because of the terrain. This run would be a bit more risky than the first because both aircraft would now be on a direct collision course with the highest peak to the west, whose summit would be masked by the clouds once the jets were at the release altitude of their runs. Watchdog Tango added the safeguard of an earlier pullout, but that would mean high-g evasive maneuvering really close to the deck, which was little comfort to Val and his wingman, Dash 3, as they set up for their runs.

Val watched as Dash 3 rounded the westward turn in his orbit and called rolling in hot. He quickly faded from Val's sight just as Papa and Chappie burst through the cloud deck to Val's right. Val counted down a five-second interval, which would help ensure that debris from the previous bomb blast was clear by the time they were at the release altitude. When five seconds elapsed, Val looked at the reflection of his RIO in the right rearview mirror, took a deep breath, and very nonchalantly said over the ICS (intercom system), "Well, Double-O—it's time to get some."

"Ooo-rah, brother," was Nate's reply.

"Dash 4 rolling in hot," Val announced over frequency. He then moved the stick left and rolled his jet inverted and pulled gently aft on the stick until the nose was pointing straight at the clouds. The airspeed indicator's needle moved rapidly to the right, and the noise in the cockpit increased as the jet gained airspeed, building tremendous energy. The clouds that were once beneath them were closing at an incredible rate. He performed a half roll just before the nose of the jet touched the clouds so he'd be able to pull up quickly if he needed to. Instantly his entire field of vision turned into an opaque ghostly gray wall. The radome wasn't even visible now, as if a bed sheet had been wrapped around the canopy. Both his and Nate's eyes were glued to radar altimeter, which was showing that they were perilously close to the ground, but for some reason they still hadn't punched through the layer, which made them a little anxious. Just as suddenly as their visibility had vanished, the entire panorama limits of their vision flashed deep green as the ground and the peak ahead swallowed the horizon. Val caught a glimpse of the tops of trees rushing by in the outer reaches of his peripheral vision, exactly even to his own canopy. That meant that he hadn't broken out when and where he thought he would and that he was way too low! *Pull up, pull up!* his instincts screamed at him just as the jet scolded him with audible alarms. Without hesitation, Val yanked back hard on the stick as he dumped the jet into a left knife-edge bank and watched the earth fall swiftly away from him. Because it was in a bowl-like depression surrounded by high peaks, the target area offered poor accessibility for bombing with high-speed, fixed-wing aircraft. Slower aircraft would more effectively place the ordnance and deal with the surrounding terrain.

"Dash 4 in sight, very low. Pull up. You're at a good altitude now. Make your drops forty meters farther west of Dash 3's. You are cleared hot," Watchdog Tango gave his instructions with the same monotone voice, absent of excitement or concern, so as not to cause the pilots of the jets to get too nervous, doubtful, or anxious.

Val was breathing heavily from his close encounter with mother Earth, but quickly returned his focus to the task at hand and continued flying toward the rising columns of smoke. He had his pipper set where he wanted to release, then made a gentle dive and pickled off four bombs. He had to start his pullout almost immediately after release, and the first bomb exploded just as he rotated skyward.

"I have four away, Dash 4. That was a close one, Pal. Next run if needed on this line will have an even earlier pullout for better terrain clearance." Watchdog Tango was a little shaken by the sight of his fellow Marines almost auguring in, but he made sure he never let his voice give it away.

Just as Val was about to hit the cloud deck on his climb-out, Dash 3 came on frequency. "Dash 4, be really careful—there's one small area of sagging clouds in the layer, but it's so small, you should either miss it or be through it quickly."

"Dash 4 copies—thanks," Val said sarcastically, looking back at Nate in his rearview mirror. He could practically see the same sarcastic smirk through Nate's mask. "Dash 3's never been accused of being punctual. I can already tell," he said over the ICS.

Nate laughed. "First to go, last to know—that's us."

Watchdog Tango over flew both lines to see if additional runs were needed, and if it was quiet enough to send in the helicopters to extract the team on the ground. He began checking the south line first and could tell that there was still enemy activity on the eastern most part. Maybe the hostiles were just trying to slip away out of sight.

He conferred with Papa and decided that two west-to-east runs with a right-hand pullout should finish off the south lines, with Dash 1 and 2 each dropping their remaining six bombs. Val watched as Papa and Chappie swung around the eastbound turn of their orbits in front of the highest peak to the west. Then, established on an eastern heading, they plunged under the clouds. Dash 3 and 4 listened as Watchdog Tango instructed them on their adjustments, and the runs went flawlessly. Once again Papa and Chappie burst through the deck within minutes of their runs, and Watchdog Tango seemed to think that the south line had been completely destroyed. The north line seemed lifeless, so Watchdog Tango thought that now would be the best time for the helicopters to attempt the extraction after one more flyover to double-check.

Zippo 1, a flight of two UH-1 Hueys, had been orbiting low to the west, near the peak, awaiting Watchdog Tango's invitation to come in and get the team out.

"Zippo 1, Watchdog Tango."

"Go ahead Watchdog Tango, this is Zippo 1."

"Both lines seem to have been silenced. I contacted the platoon commander and he will release a smoke grenade at your landing zone. You should be outta here in minimal time. Go ahead and begin your descent."

"Roger. We're comin' through a small break about three klicks in front of the western peak. Have the platoon commander release his smoke when he has a visual on us."

"Wilco."

Zippo 1 descended quickly through the break and was under the clouds, heading east toward the grassy bald. When they were less than two miles from the bald, the platoon commander released the smoke, though he was still unsure that the enemy had retreated or was destroyed, and Zippo 1 instantly headed for it. When both helicopters were about fifteen feet above the ground, the platoon commander's suspicions were validated as the helicopters suddenly came under heavy machine gun fire from the north line. Zippo 1 had no choice but to pull out in order to save themselves from being shot down and stranded, just as the recon team was. "North line! North line! Shit! We're taking hits! We have to pull out! Are those fast movers still around? Get them down here now!" Zippo 1 yelled frantically over frequency.

"Affirmative! Affirmative! Get the hell outta there, Zippo 1!" Watchdog Tango barked back. Watchdog Tango had smartly positioned himself to the south to have a good visual on both lines if they were to start up again, so he quickly fired off a fan of Willie Petes that almost pinpointed the enemy's position. The high peak to the west prevented a run in from that direction, so any new runs had to come from the east. That presented a new problem in that the enemy had also moved farther west, knowing that it would be harder for the jets to pull out safely, much less begin a run on them. The terrain didn't allow for a long-enough run in from the south or north either. It was a real pickle. Watchdog Tango conferred with Papa once more to assess if such runs were too risky.

Papa quickly reminded Watchdog Tango, "We're Marines, dammit! This is our job! As long as those men down there need a hand and we can give it to 'em, they'll get whatever they want! Now give Dash 3 and 4 a goddamned mission to copy! When they run out of bombs, we'll switch to our guns and strafe 'em till we're Winchester!"

This run would be similar to the previous one Dash 3 and 4 had to make, except farther west. Both crews had a solid copy on what they needed to do, so they took a deep breath, knowing they had to really concentrate.

Dash 3 called rolling in hot and blasted through the clouds and performed the run without incident, but both crewmembers were breathing heavily and sweating profusely. Obviously the run was too close for comfort.

Val was instructed to wait until Dash 3 rejoined the orbit before making his run, and when 3 finally got back they muttered between deep breaths over frequency, "Watch out, Dash 4—don't try to be a hero. If you can't safely pull out, then what's the point? You can high-five the trees on this run."

"Roger," Val responded. Under his breath he added, "No sagging clouds on this one?" Over the ICS he sighed and told Nate, "Ready to soil your drawers again, Double-O?"

"I'm wearin' my best diapers. Let's do it," Nate said with a sigh.

"Dash 4 rolling in hot." Val knew he was going in even farther west and closer to the mountain, as Watchdog Tango had said. This time as his vision was obscured once again, he was better prepared to take evasive action as he planted his feet on the rudder pedals and tightly grasped the throttles with his left hand and the stick in his right.

This time when he broke out, what met his eyes was worse than before as the thick black smoke billowing up from the previous runs almost completely hid the mountain. His vision flashed green to black, green to black, as he punched through plume after thick plume of heavy smoke, making his speed through the air frighteningly apparent to him.

Watchdog Tango was orbiting low to the northwest when something unusual caught his eye. The enemy was now running as a group out in the open toward the west, which wasn't typical of the NVA. "Dash 4, make your drop about a hundred meters west of Dash 3's. I have visual on the Gooners. They are in a large group heading west for a tree line at the base of the mountain...I guess. You are not in sight. I will duck out to the south. You are cleared hot."

Val responded with a simple "Roger," then flew blindly toward the west, his vision totally obscured by the thick black smoke. He broke out to see a large group of about a hundred men running west about a mile ahead, all appearing to be firing at the recon team's position. It was unusual for Val to be able to actually see the human element of his targets. They were practically fish in a barrel, and he knew in the back of his mind that he would actually end their lives in a matter of seconds. Up until now, all he'd ever dropped bombs on were canvas targets during combat training. He'd never been on an actual combat sortie before, so all this was new and strange.

He also knew that late at night, when he was in his rack with nothing but his thoughts, he might have to deal with feelings he had not yet experienced in his lifetime.

Surprisingly, before he could close the distance, the men reached the tree line and were concealed by the foliage. The mountainside now loomed before him and it seemed like he'd have no choice but to pull out.

Watchdog Tango agreed. "Pull out, Dash 4! I'll set you up for another pass, plus I'll have their position marked. You're too close to the mountain." He was obviously disappointed by the thought that the enemy might escape.

Val was about to comply when something off to the right caught his eye. Just popping out of the north tree line were two light trucks, each with a .30mm machine gun on its roof, moving slowly south toward the recon team's position. As Val quickly gauged his distance from the western peak, he saw men on foot running east from their tree line toward the recon team. The enemy platoon wasn't retreating—rather they were flanking the team in an effort to drive them toward the trucks and toward annihilation. For their part, the trucks were trying to drive the team toward the enemy platoon.

Val realized that by the time he got turned around and set up for another pass, the team would easily be easily overrun, and all his fellow Marines would be dead! He wasn't about to let that happen. "Negative, Watchdog Tango. I've got to get those bastards now, and their trucks," he announced.

"What tru—" Watchdog Tango had to break hard right to avoid some tracers that raced by his canopy. "Shit! Where the hell were they hiding? Say intentions, Dash 4."

"Just remain to the southeast at five hundred feet or less. Clear the area, and stay out of my way. I'm gonna need a lot of room."

Papa overheard the conversation from his orbit but couldn't see what was going on, and he really hated not being able to see his Marines when he was leading them in combat. "Dash 4, Dash 1. I'm listening to this conversation, and I'm telling you now not to do anything stupid, like get yourself killed. I hate fucking paperwork. Get back up here and we'll figure something else out."

"Aye, sir—I promise I won't kill myself," Val said under the strain of g-forces as he pitched into a vertical climb. Just as his radome touched the clouds, he performed a half roll and, while in the clouds with his vision obscured, pulled back on the stick.

The rest of Rhino Flight looked to the west in time to see Val's jet barely break the cloud deck, only to dive right back into it in a tight, lenticular loop, all within the frame of a second and half. Val's jet then came blasting down the mountainside a mere five meters above the trees.

Val acquired a visual on the enemy platoon, which was still west of the recon team, and the closest truck, which was east of the recon team about a hundred meters in front and to the right of the second truck. The enemy platoon and the trucks had each now closed to within 150 meters of the recon team within the short time Val had begun his maneuver. He did some quick calculations and guesswork in his head and hoped for a touch of lady luck as he blasted down the mountain behind the enemy platoon. He waited a few split seconds, then pulled up as he released one rack, waited a microsecond until he was sure he had cleared the recon team, then released the second rack. The first three bombs slid in behind the enemy platoon, which was swallowed from behind in a vortex of fire. Two of the second group of three soared to the southeast and missed everything completely, but the third bomb landed fifty yards to the right of the lead truck and destroyed it. The second truck stopped dead in its tracks, the driver and gunner completely dazed from the blast of the three bombs. After a few seconds, the two men dizzily scanned the skies for the American jet responsible for their headaches, even as their entire bodies were still throbbing. The driver began to turn around and was going to drive back to the cover of the trees when his gunner spotted Val to the east.

Moments earlier the recon team's platoon commander had seen Val blasting down the mountainside toward the enemy platoon and his heart had stood still, thinking he was about to draw his last breath. After he heard the first explosion, he looked up in time to catch a glimpse of Val's Phantom streaking only a few hundred feet overhead and pickling off his second load. He realized then that he was still alive, but he couldn't believe what he'd just witnessed. He looked back to the east and spotted the second truck and Val's jet, and was even more shocked by what he saw next.

Val had pulled up, rolled inverted, and pulled back into a low altitude split-S, leveling off only two hundred feet above the ground. He didn't spot the other truck until his jet was greeted by clouds of tracers, like a swarm of angry fireflies, zipping by within mere inches of his canopy. "Big sky, little bullets. Right, Double-O?" Val said to Nate over the ICS as he switched to his gun, which had been pre-set before the flight to six thousand rounds per minute. Val put the truck, which was driving very intelligently at him head-on to present a smaller target, right in the center of the pipper. He squeezed the trigger and the 20mm M61A1 Gatling cannon growled as it spit rounds out of its muzzle. The rounds kicked up huge clumps of earth as they drew a straight line to the truck and then cut it in half, followed shortly by an explosion as some of the rounds sliced through the fuel tank. Val then looked up to see the peak rapidly filling up his view and yanked back hard on the stick and shoved the throttles to their full stops, stroking the burners, disappearing into the layer above, blowing by his fellow Marines in their orbit at nine thousand feet.

Watchdog Tango was speechless. He'd just watched a fellow Marine pilot do something he'd almost written off as impossible, all to save fellow Marines on the ground. "God *damn!*" he said with excitement as he flew over the area to see if Zippo 1 could safely extract the recon team now. "That was the craziest thing I've ever seen, Dash 4!" He looked down to the recon team standing up and cheering in elation.

Papa heard the excitement and at first thought something bad had happened as he saw Val burst through the layer and up into the sky above the orbit. Val had overshot by five thousand feet by the time he got turned around and rejoined. "What happened? Everything okay? Dash 4? Watchdog Tango?" After a few seconds of silence he said, "Will somebody fucking talk to me and let me know something?"

"Everything's fine, Rhino 1. Everything's really fine. You got a steady stick there in Dash 4. That crazy jet jockey single-handedly wiped out a platoon of Gooners and two of their trucks. I don't think there are any more NVA around, but hang around if you can for a BDA. Zippo 1 is cleared for extraction."

"Roger, Zippo 1." The Hueys once again dropped into the clouds to extract the team.

In the orbit, Val's fellow Marine aviators just flew around in silence, occasionally glancing over at the newest additions to their squadron with amazement. After a few minutes, the silence was broken by Zippo 1 announcing their departure from the area. Then on frequency everyone heard, "Rhino Flight, Zippo 1."

Papa answered "Zippo 1, Rhino Flight."

"This is Blue Fox Actual"—the platoon commander of the recon team. "I'd like to personally thank the crew of that last jet. You saved our asses. Drinks are on me, Devil Dogs." In the background everyone could hear the rest of the platoon telling the story of them taking heavy fire, and then watching the enemy disappear in a wall of flames only a couple hundred yards away, looking up to see a jet pass low overhead and taking out one truck, then swinging around and blasting the other with its gun.

Papa felt pride well up within him. This meant he got some quality newbies, and he was thankful for them having the guts to finish their job in true unselfish Marine Corps fashion. For Val and Nate, getting thanks from their fellow Marines for just doing their job was the best reward.

"Rhino 1, Watchdog Tango with a BDA"—bomb damage assessment. "Four mortar batteries, five machine gun nests, and at least 250 KBAs"— killed by air. "I'm impressed by your fancy flat-hatting down here, Dash 4. You're gonna fit right in. I'll pass along a full report later."

"We're about Winchester anyway. Thanks for the action today. It's sure nice to go on a scramble when it's for an important cause." Papa smiled as he glanced over to his wingmen, especially when his eyes came across Val's jet. "Rhino Flight, let's go home."

The Phantoms lined up in echelon right formation with Papa in the lead. As they got closer to base, Papa's voice shattered the silence, "For the FNGs, guess what—you just had your FAM flight. You gotta admit, that was a helluva way to get your combat cherries popped. Great job! Welcome to VMFA-2—you boys can stay."

2

THE BOYS ON THE FRONTIER

Ask any Marine aviator how they'd like being assigned to VMFA-2 and they'd say they would feel truly honored. After all, it was the most elite squadron in the entire Navy, if not the entire DOD. However, most would add, "As long as I'm not based at Linh Thu." Val and Nate had heard this sentiment many times before in their infant aviation careers, but they'd always dismissed it as scuttlebutt from someone who'd found out that they'd just bit off more than they could chew in terms of a career choice. However, after months of hearing so many stories about the mysterious base, they began to believe that some of them truly had merit, but at this stage of their careers; they both knew that they'd better take whatever assignment was handed them with a smile. It wouldn't be long before even they were on their way to finding out just how hard it is to smile at times in the most feared assignment in the whole of Southeast Asia.

Linh Thu. The name still sent shivers down the spine of men who'd served within her concertina wire fences in the past and gave the jitters to those presently stationed there. Just like the sword of Damocles, there seemed to be this looming fear that would be permanently ingrained into anyone who ever set foot there.

Originally intended to be a SATS (short airfield for tactical support) hot-pad, Linh Thu became a full-length base within a year of her inception and was the northernmost US base in Vietnam. Its very location put the people stationed there directly in harm's way. Located just five miles south of the 17th parallel and twelve miles from the Laotian border, it was just moments away from the infamous Ho Chi Minh Trail.

Rocket and mortar attacks were a frequent occurrence at night, and occasionally enemy troops actually entered the base during these attacks, causing much havoc. Even flying in and out of Linh Thu was dangerous as it lay under the southernmost tip of the umbrella of North Vietnamese SAM coverage, as just seventy-five miles to the northeast was the North Vietnamese airbase of Dong Hoi, once abandoned but now a SAM staging area. Besides the danger of the SAMs and MiGs, the terrain around Linh Thu made departures to and approaches from the west treacherous as a sharp rising ridgeline covered thick with trees towered over the western horizon only three-quarters of a mile away.

Thick jungle blanketed the remainder of the land surrounding the base, which provided excellent cover for enemy forces to attack and withdraw. The jungles also brought all its tenants to visit the base—rats, bugs, venomous snakes, and all the various ailments and diseases that accompanied them, things people who never experienced such a climate didn't take into account. The few buildings that weren't canvas tent living quarters were unpainted wood construction, partially sunk into the ground to give them a lower profile in a rocket attack—or that was the theory. The buildings bore the scars of skirmishes with enemy forces—bullet and shrapnel holes hastily patched up with putty. Around the base was stretched concertina and chain-link fencing, machine gun nests, and mud roads. Linh Thu was linked to the rest of the outside world in only two ways: daily COD flights, and one dirt road that led to Dong Hoi, which was the city east of the North Vietnamese airbase of the same name. The gate to the road was heavily barricaded and was often the focus of the raids at night. There were only two runways at Linh Thu—10–28 and 13–31, both made out of a special earth-toned concrete that, when viewed from a distance, gave the appearance of a wide dirt road. Overall, Linh Thu mimicked a prison camp in appearance, providing an especially drab and dismal setting for its inhabitants. Being so far into hostile territory is how the base got her name of Linh Thu—loosely translate, "frontier guard."

There were only two squadrons stationed within the concertina of Linh Thu—VMO-16 and VMFA-2. VMO-16 was a mixed bag of a squadron as far as the types of aircraft deployed. The predominant plane was the OV-10 Bronco, but there were three types of helicopters as well—UH-1s, AH-1s, and CH-46s. All VMO-16 pilots were trained to fly all four types of aircraft and rotated among them. The squadron performed a variety of missions—light attack, forward air control, reconnaissance, search and rescue, and insertion or extraction of troops.

Val and Nate were assigned to VMFA-2, a squadron famous throughout the DOD. They were nicknamed the "Playboys," a name they'd had since WWI. VMFA-2 pilots often got in heated debates with another Marine Corps squadron—VMAQ-2, which flew A-6 and EA-6B aircraft. They argued about who actually used the Playboys moniker first.

VMFA-2 flew F-4J Phantom IIs. They were currently the only squadron of F-4s in the Department of the Navy equipped with fixed 20mm Gatling cannons, serving as a test squadron to prove that guns were still useful on supersonic jets. But F-8 Crusaders were already proving that as they were killing more MiGs with their guns than with missiles, which were still largely in the infancy of their development. So after long debates and miles of red-tape, the squadron was granted the chance to mount the gun and validate their claims.

VMFA-2's missions were typically air-to-air superiority (air combat and interception), escort duty, medium to heavy attack, and close troop support. They were often asked for by name by the grunts because of their dedication to the mission and always putting the men on the ground ahead of themselves. Even Army units would request them, and all the ground troops knew that the Playboys were positioned way out in the forward areas and could assist quicker than other squadrons. The squadron was efficient and effective in an air combat role, with an outstanding record to back them up.

The squadron symbol was the rabbit's head insignia of Hugh Heffner's magazine of the same name superimposed on a lightning bolt. When Mr. Heffner first came out with his magazine in the 1950s, the squadron asked for his permission to use the symbol, to which he eagerly personally wrote his response, overflowing with enthusiasm for a squadron of Marines to use it. After all, servicemen were some of his most loyal subscribers.

The squadron had twenty-four aircraft, each with a pilot and RIO. Flight crews were on a rotation schedule, with four crews—eight men—would always be waiting in their flight gear in the "Shack," the only air-conditioned building on the base. The Shack was on the northwest ramp, or the hot-pad, where the crews' jets would always be fully fueled and waiting, and could be quickly armed with whatever ordnance a combat sortie require. They were known as Alert-5 crews because they'd be airborne within five minutes of a call, with priority over all other aircraft—including those on short final. Once a call came in, plane captains preflighted the aircraft and ordnance techs armed them, while linemen started the engines with start-carts and GPUs. All the flight crews had to do once briefed on the mission was to jump in the jet and go—just like the old saying, "Kick the tires and light the fires." Alert-5s would be the immediate response to any situation and buy the time needed until other aircraft could be airborne to assist, if needed.

Alert-5 crews were on duty for twenty-four hours, then replaced by another group. The rest of the squadron was often heavily involved in Rolling Thunder strikes—pre-planned, on call, or target-of-opportunity missions deep into North Vietnam. VMFA-2 was the perfect squadron for the Rolling Thunder strikes because of its location at Linh Thu.

Another reason VMFA-2 was considered elite was because of its personnel, especially its highly decorated CO, Lieutenant Colonel Earl J. "Papa" Driskell, whose combat record alone commanded respect. In WWII, he was drafted into the Marine Corps at the age of seventeen because he lied about his age, out of a small town in southern Louisiana and flew the super-fast inverted gull-wing Vought F-4U Corsair fighter in the South Pacific. He ended the war with fourteen kills in the air, just one shy of triple ace, and had many more ground kills, eventually earning the Navy Cross. He continued flying for the Marine Corps and after several years found himself in Korea. He started out flying F-9 Panthers and ended the war flying the Navy version of the F-86 Sabre, the FJ-3 Fury. Once again he became a double ace, with twelve air-to-air kills and many more ground kills. Again he switched between flying off carriers and land bases, and again he earned Navy Flying Cross. Many who knew him strongly felt he should have been awarded the Congressional Medal of Honor in both conflicts.

But that was just part of the reason he was so highly respected by subordinates, peers, and superiors alike. The main reason was how he carried himself, and his leadership style on and off the battlefield. Because he was a southern gentleman, he was laid back and easy-going, yet at the same time had certain expectations of each person under his command. He set a high example and expected everyone to do their part to help the squadron get the job done. On a more personal level, he was respected because he was a Marine who loved to fly high-performance aircraft. He led from the cockpit and not from behind a desk. He seized every chance to fly, and performed flawlessly every time— even under strenuous pressure. Passing up promotions to full colonel so he could keep flying earned him even more respect because it proved he wasn't focused on his personal career, as most officers were, but rather on his squadron and the men under his command. Because of his style of leadership he became affectionately known by all who knew him as "Papa."

Papa's wingman and exec, Major William "Chappie" Chapman had known Driskell for many years. They'd been wingmen since their early days in Korea, and Chappie was an ace himself with seven air-to-air kills and numerous ground kills. Both he and Papa had flown off the same carrier or were stationed at the same ground base. They would always return from sorties as the only two unscarred jets if their squadron got in a tiff with the enemy, and that completely baffled everyone. It was if they were being protected by an unknown divine force. Chappie was ten years younger than Papa and had learned almost everything he knew about leadership and combat flying from him. As long as Papa remained on active duty, Chappie wanted to serve with him. But as Chappie's reputation of being just like Papa became more entrenched, most believed he'd simply replace his mentor as CO when he retired. This earned him another nickname among the men of Linh Thu— "PJ," short for "Papa Junior."

There was one other officer who made VMFA-2 the best of the best, and that was the CO of aircraft maintenance—and Papa's best friend in the whole world—Major John M. Darrell, better known as "Big John." He'd known Papa since junior high school back in Louisiana, and was drafted into the Marines at the same time, but John's eyesight kept him from being a pilot. John decided the next best thing would be to repair the aircraft and keep them combat ready. He quickly became the best mechanic wherever he was stationed; with his uncanny ability to troubleshoot any problem and his resourcefulness when repairing things with limited supplies or equipment. When the age of RIOs arrived in the late '60s, John applied for a lateral transfer, but was denied in favor of younger men and the fact that the conflict in Vietnam was escalating. The Navy felt that they might not have enough time to train him, plus they'd be losing the best mechanic in the entire Department of Defense. Papa tried to pull some strings for John, to no avail, and many believed it was political retaliation against Papa for turning down what might have eventually led to a chief of staff assignment at the Pentagon. The best Papa could do was guarantee that he and John would serve their entire careers in the same squadron. John and Papa had similar personalities, both laid back and loving to joke around. Whenever they got to drinking, they were the loudest guys around and could out-drink any of the young men under their command. They were fun drunks, and people liked to be in their company—just at a distance.

Val woke up in a furious sweat. He glanced at his watch and saw that it was 0400. He rolled on his back to stare at the sloped canvas ceiling above him that would ripple under a strong enough breeze. Val never slept well here, and he didn't know why. The heat and humidity didn't help much, but he knew that in time he could adjust to that. It was clearly something that eluded his comprehension. Most nights the same thing would happen; something would interrupt his slumber and he'd lie awake until reveille, then be tired the rest of his waking hours. He'd never been a light sleeper, but now the least disturbance would wake him up and take a long while to wear off until he could fade back to sleep.

As he stared at the canvas, he began to wonder if it would get worse as his tour of duty progressed, and he wondered if anyone else had the same problem. He'd only been over here a scant fifteen days now, so he hadn't asked anyone yet—he wanted to give it at least a month before he did that. He felt that if it was affecting his performance, he'd address the problem immediately, but so far it wasn't showing.

It wasn't long before darkness gave way to the light of early dawn and it was time to get up and head to breakfast and then to the briefing room. Val, Nate, and their two wingmen on the past few sorties—RIO Jamie "Speedy" Sanders and pilot Frank "Notso" Wise—left their hooch and headed for the chow hall in the heavy morning air.

The chow hall was nothing more than a huge canvas tent the size of twenty hooches, and the dining area was a little larger, with see-through walls of mosquito netting, but it was the men's favorite place on base, after the pub. Every day presented new challenges on many different levels. One big problem was keeping rats and roaches away from your food. Both pests were fearless and would stay just out of arm's reach while you were cooking or eating, waiting for you to be distracted just long enough for them to make a pass at the food and dash away before you knew what happened. Life was stressful enough, but keeping pests at bay made it worse. Sometimes on slow days, the men would pass the time by betting on the pests in hot-tray races. The goal was to pick a captive roach or rat, whose owner had tied a colored thread to one of its legs, and place the critter on one of two metal trays that were slightly heated. The trays were placed side by side, and when the owners released their vermin, they would scurry across the tray in order to save their feet from being burned. The first critter across the tray won the race and its owner some money for the pub.

§ § § § §

The four aviators sat down to their breakfast of packaged scrambled eggs and crumbly pancakes and wouldn't speak until they swallowed the first forkful, which often required the assistance of juice or coffee to wash it down.

"What the hell were you dreaming about last night, Speedy?" Val said with a laugh. "You were clutching your cot like it was Marilyn Monroe. Your pillow was sopping up a lot of slobber." Val paused as he tried to swallow his chow. "You know maintenance is on the way to the briefing. Maybe we'll stop in and get you a mop this morning."

Speedy returned the laugh. "Hey! How you'd know it was Marilyn?"

"I know about them all, my friend," Val replied.

"Even the Playmates too," Nate added, "though lately you haven't been calling their names out as much. 'Brandy…Brandy!'" Nate held out his arms and kissed the air.

Notso joined in with a laugh. "Well at least he's not calling out 'Randy! Randy!'"

They were all laughing now as they finished their breakfast, knowing that there'd be few chances to yuck it up before the morning briefing. They were a bit ahead of schedule and took their time walking to the briefing tent, which was near Papa's office and the ready room, where they stored their flight gear. They talked openly about previous sorties while they could, knowing they'd have to keep their opinions to themselves while in the company of higher ranking officers. The second most common topic of conversation was sex. There was little else to talk out in the middle of nowhere but work and sex.

"How about those trees we leveled last night?" Val asked.

"Not as nice as the ones we nailed the night before," Frank replied.

"I wouldn't say that. These were a bit taller," Nate added.

"Wonder what it will be next sortie," Speedy put in.

"I don't know, but I heard we got a teletype from the lumberjacks' union telling us to stop because we're putting a lot of 'em out of work," Val replied.

"I just got an earful about wood and nailing things, and something about something being taller. Are we still talking about work, or have we moved on to sex?" Notso asked.

"I'm not sure. I haven't been around a woman in too long to know the difference—and Nate and I haven't been over here as long as you guys," Val replied.

Their conversation concluded when they reached the briefing tent. All four just took a breath as they opened the door and stepped inside.

The briefing tent was about half the size of the chow hall kitchen, and every nook and cranny was occupied by something—equipment, maps, easels, books, chairs, and so on. Because the men were squeezed in like sardines, writing on a knee pad was so difficult that the briefing tent was known as the "Cannery." Papa knew that such conditions reduced attention spans, even when a briefing was about a serious topic like an air strike, so he made sure everything was laid out as plain and to the point as he could. This would keep questions to a minimum and shorten their time in the cramped quarters.

Luckily for the aircrews, there wasn't a sortie every night, but there was one more often than not. The sorties were getting more and more detailed and involved with every passing day. Early on they mostly involved escorting other aircraft, but more and more often the Playboys were actually making the strikes themselves, and that trend showed no signs of slowing. Escort sorties required four to six aircraft at most, but the Rolling Thunder strikes involved at least ten or more aircraft. Sometimes the call would come on a night that had no previously planned sortie, and half the squadron would find them following the Alert-5s out into the blackness of the Vietnamese night sky. Occasionally the squadron would actually be returning from a sortie and happen to fly over some enemy activity or target and would be authorized to attack, though such cases were becoming more and more infrequent as authorization to attack targets of opportunity were rare—even though the target might have valid, even crucial, tactical or strategic value.

Val and Nate had only been on two Rolling Thunder strikes in their tour so far. Speedy and Notso had arrived in Linh Thu only a month and a half earlier, so they were still considered newbies, but they'd been on fourteen previous sorties. The enemy air defenses were intensifying with each strike, so returning with an aircraft unscathed was becoming a rarity. Val and Nate had had some very close brushes with SAMs on the two sorties they'd been on, and it was already making a firm impression on their minds. They thought of it as they tried to ingest the briefing being presented that morning.

Papa and Chappie always presented the briefings and always flew each sortie with their squadron. Chappie would give the basic rundown and Papa would fill in the details and accentuate all the really pertinent information that he wanted each man to know.

"Morning, gents. It's starting to warm up outside, so let's begin," Chappie said as he pointed to the image on the screen at the front of the room. "Our target tonight is this small complex suspected to be a truck park and ammo depot that supplies several of the larger NVA forces in our immediate area. It was found by a high-altitude reconnaissance aircraft, and the location was confirmed yesterday morning by one of Linh Thu's OV-10s on a low sweep. The OV-10 met heavy resistance, so there's no reason for us not to expect the same tonight." Chappie continued with the particulars of the briefing on times and directions to commence attack, ordnance used, what resistance to expect, lost com procedures, who'd be flying which sector, etc. Val and Nate noticed that the target was against a ridgeline, and they had flashbacks of their first sortie—except this one might be worse because it was at night and with anti-aircraft weapons—ack-ack. Both men wrote down everything they could while absorbing the images of the target and the sortie.

Papa finally took over the briefing but didn't have very much to add. He answered questions for the most part, and the men could tell he had a lot on his mind. Papa had a full plate, and envied him. Papa then sighed as he pulled a large envelope out of his briefcase on the table. This was the part of every briefing that he loathed. He pulled out some papers out of the envelope and had them passed around until every man had a copy. He sighed again as he said, "Gents, I hate this as much as you do, but it's just like a bad case of hemorrhoids—a constant pain in the ass that you can't ignore and even when you're done with one, there's a bunch more that just keep coming back."

All the men laughed briefly, then focused their attention on the paper and began marking on them with the pencils Papa passed around. The papers were a test on the Rules of Engagement that had to be administered before every sortie, and each man had to pass it with a perfect score. The test wasn't a challenge because the men knew that the answer that made the least sense or the answer that restrained the pilot the most would be the one the leadership back in Washington deemed correct. The first they had to take the test was the moment they knew that the leadership in Washington had no interest in winning the war. After all the steps set forth by the test were complied with in actual combat, it would be too late for a pilot to assist a fellow aviator or insure victory for himself in a one-on-one situation as the narrow window of opportunity would have already closed.

Papa scanned the room and saw his men shake their heads in disgust and disbelief, and he wore a sympathetic frown. It wasn't long before they all finished and passed the tests back up front. "You know the only freebie on this stupid thing is your name. Did anyone think they missed that one?" Papa smiled as he collected the last few tests. "You know, gents, I hate that you have to take these things, but I'm glad *when* you take them."

"What the hell for, sir?" Chappie asked.

"Well, they won't give us a damn fan in the Cannery, so the only time it gets cool is when y'all take this stupid test and you create a breeze when you shake your heads." The men laughed as Papa dismissed them, and they quickly filed out of the tiny briefing room into the hot mid-morning air.

§ § § § § §

Val always wrote a letter to Virginia after the morning briefing, a ritual he religiously followed. She was probably the biggest reason he couldn't sleep well. He thought about her in every imaginable situation. He'd look at his watch several times a day, do the math to figure out what time it was back home, and wonder what she was doing. He pictured her going about daily business and hoped all was well. It often took him an hour or more to compose even a short letter to her because he wanted everything to be perfect. Letters from her were the highlight of his existence here on the other side of the world. He always asked for her to send pictures of herself, which he'd tape to the canvas wall next to his rack. The pictures anchored his sanity when things weren't right and were the biggest motivator to avoid getting killed. He always kept at least one picture on him at all times, and when he was writing her a letter he'd take a picture out and glance at it.

Val returned to his favorite place to write letters—a small patch between the headquarters and logistics buildings, the only place on base where grass grew. The buildings shaded it from the morning sun, and a slight breeze added to the effect. It was sheltered from the noise of the flight line by the buildings and was one of the quietest places on the base. Some of the men with time off would stretch out on a few lawn chairs that had been smuggled in and read, drink a beer, or just sleep. Val sat in one of the chairs with his pen and paper and reached into his breast pocket for a picture of Virginia and another pen. He always had a spare in case the first one had dried up. Val clipped the picture to the paper and began to daydream a bit as he stared at it. She was truly beautiful, photogenic woman—tall and lean with long, flowing dark brown hair that faded to light brown at the very tips. She had large dark eyes and dark skin, and had a glowing smile that you noticed almost immediately. Val looked at her picture, then looked at his surroundings, took a deep breath, and began to write.

§ § § § §

Dearest Virginia,

I know I write to you every day, but it seems like an eternity to me between the letters. I hope you never get tired of me writing because it's the highlight of my existence down here. It's funny how I always took it for granted whenever I received mail back home, but down here it's really the only thing that keeps me sane. I've only been here two weeks now, and it already seems old to me. I'm flying on average once every other day, and once every other day fear chips away a small part of me. I've never known such a deep primal fear existed as what I felt on my last sortie, I can't imagine anyone ever getting used to it. I guess the only thing that balances it out is that some sorties are uneventful. Enough of this. I don't want to upset you with my day to day worries.

I hope you're doing well. I know that some of my letters are longer, better, and healthier sounding, but I just try to write something. I need to write you every day. You already know about how I like the people I work with down here, so tell me more about the people you work with on your new job. You said you were the only woman in that entire region, and that your boss was pleasantly surprised with your fierce hunger for your job that made you outperform everyone else last quarter. That's my girl! You're going to own the place soon! I guess I'm just rambling because I'm at loss for topics to write about since I haven't received a letter in a few days.

I'll just let you know as I always do how much I love and miss you. You're my life, you're why I live and breathe. Many people tell their spouses that their lives would be much easier down here if they didn't have someone so important back home to distract them from their duties, but I totally disagree. It's because I love you so much and think of you so often that it I'm inspired to do my job the best I can, and gives me the courage to fight through that primal fear so I get home and back into your arms. I think of you so much. Just simple things: what you're doing, how you're feeling, just in general hoping things are going good for you. Even if you're having a bad day, just remember there's someone down here who's always thinking of you and forever will be loving you. I think of other simple things that I miss, such as your voice, the smell of your hair and perfume, your smile, your laugh, your incredible hug.

God I miss you. I'd better just sign off because I'm just rambling. I love you so much.

Love, Val

PS: The guys are extremely jealous of me when they saw the pictures of you. You've got a lot of new fans down here at camp. Please send more pictures, I always keep a couple of them are on me at all times, so you'll always be close to my heart.

Val finished the letter and dropped it at the post office on his way back to his hooch. He needed to study up for tonight's sortie, so he and Nate went to the chow hall to compare notes. It wasn't long before Speedy and Notso joined them, and all four were studying. They liked studying together because when they felt they understood the mission they took some time to joke around. Free time was scarce, and the day always ate it quickly.

Before they could wonder where the day went, it was already sunset and time to prepare for the sortie. The ready room was silent as people strapped on their gear. Val was amazed at how much gear each man carried—almost ninety pounds of it. Every time they got together to inventory their gear and try to decide what to leave behind, they found themselves unwilling to sacrifice a single item in the name of comfort. Occasionally they would discard an item, but on hearing scuttlebutt about how some aviator used that very item to save their life, they'd find themselves burrowing through their locker or digging through the trash to recover it. There was an old adage that if you were comfortable in your gear, you either neglected to put in on right or you left something behind. Once the men got a last-minute briefing, they waddled out the door to the awaiting pickup truck that took them to their jet.

The night air was thick and heavy as it always seemed to be in Vietnam, whether day or night, but the night air was slightly cooler and was often stirred by a light breeze. Val and Nate started their preflight at the cockpit ladders and went opposite directions around the jet until they met at the right wing, where they would exchange discrepancies and have each other verify them. Along the way they pulled pins off bombs, and anything else they needed to do to prepare their jet for duty.

As Val met Nate at the right wing, he asked, "Got anything?"

Sometimes Nate would sigh, as if he wished he did find something. But tonight he just said, "Nope—she's ready to fly."

"All right—let's do it," Val replied as he and Nate locked hands with a firm grip at chest level. That was their way of letting each other know that they wouldn't let each other down. If they had a disagreement earlier that day, it was all forgiven and forgotten now; if one of them was feeling down, it had to be set aside for later. They had a job to do now, and they owed it to each other to be at their peak.

They walked around the nose to their ladders and climbed into the cockpits. Engine start and run-up were routine to them now, but they would never get complacent as they performed their BITs and checklists. Val looked up in one of the mirrors as he locked the ICS into "hot mike" and checked in with his RIO. "You up back there?"

"Five by five," Nate replied as he gave a thumbs up to his pilot.

They completed their checklists and had a minute to relax as they waited for Papa to ask for check-in. It was never very long as they listened over frequency for Papa's voice to come on, which meant it time to begin the mission.

"All flights check in," Papa called out.

"Dash 1's up," Chappie replied.

"Dash 3."

"Dash 4's up."

"Dash 5," Notso called out.

"Dash 6," Val called out.

After Val checked in, Papa called ground control to announce that Bunny Flight was taxiing out from the jet ramp to runway 31. As Papa throttled up and moved away, the rest of Bunny Flight followed close behind. As usual, they'd be departing in sections of two. Linh Thu was extremely dark at night. The surrounding jungle and ridgeline devoured all available light, and in the moonless sky only stars twinkled.

The pale glow from the instruments was almost immediately absorbed by the black veil of night just beyond the thick glass of the canopy. It was even darker for the RIOs, whose smaller canopy severely limited outside visibility. The aircraft were forbidden to use their taxi lights at Linh Thu. They were on only in emergencies, when an aircraft really needed them. It was actually the responsibility of follow-me trucks to lead aircraft down taxiways to the runway, or off runways to the ramp. Runway lights were only on when an aircraft was on approach or on its takeoff run or initial landing roll-out.

Once an aircraft rotated, the lights were turned off, and once an aircraft on landing roll-out had slowed down to just above taxi speed, the lights were extinguished, and it was up to the pilot to follow all markings with his landing and/or taxi lights until the follow-me truck intercepted them and led them to the ramp. Once they were intercepted, all exterior lights on the aircraft were extinguished, and they followed the dim row of lights in the bed of the follow-me truck, which contained a centerline hash the pilot lined up on. The light bar also told the pilot how far he was from the truck, and his speed on the taxiway. The reason for all this, in theory, was to make the base a more difficult target for mortar or rocket attacks from surrounding enemy territory. Whether it actually helped was open to debate. As the Marine pilots who'd served a tour on an aircraft carrier would tell the others, there'd been more available light on the carrier's flight deck than at Linh Thu.

It wasn't long before Bunny Flight was lining up and departing from the darkness of Linh Thu into the darkness of the night sky. The view outside the canopy remained unchanged; it was a steady veil of black until they were at a high enough altitude to make out the faint glow of Dong Hoi and Hanoi to the north and Saigon to the south, and that was if the sky was clear enough. It made each flight crew member settle into his cockpit even more, glad to be in a cramped space gently bathed in the glow of the instruments rather than outside in the black unknown. Rolling Thunder strikes were flown into designated route packs that were divided between the Air Force and the Navy. North Vietnam was divided into six route packs, with Route Pack II, III, IV, and VI-Bravo designated to the Navy and the others designated to the Air Force. It drove the flight crews from all three tactical air support branches crazy because they had to get permission to operate in another's route pack. At times it seemed as if there were more than one enemy—the Communists, and people from other branches of the US Armed Forces. Even if there was a valuable tactical target of opportunity in plain view, it couldn't be attacked in another branch's route pack without going through miles of red tape that often allowed the enemy to escape. These nightly strikes seemed meaningless to the crews as they attacked seemingly worthless targets while risking being shot down and captured or killed.

As Bunny Flight neared the target, Papa's voice came over frequency. "Okay, fellas, let's green 'em up." This referred to the light that indicated when the racks were armed and ready for release. If there were any mechanical problems, the troubled bird and his wing would then break formation and RTB. Soon TOT, time on target, had passed and Papa led his flight into their runs. Val saw him and Chappie break off and dive at a small hut illuminated by one pale light and appeared to have a small truck parked nearby, maybe twenty meters away.

Inside the hut, two men slept while another ate, completely unaware of what was poised to strike from the darkness above. The man barely got some rice to his mouth when he heard a whistling rustle from outside, causing him to drop his chopsticks and pick up his rifle. By the time he got to the door to take a peek, the sky seemed to fall on his hut as a deafening bang filled his ears. The world seemed to coming to a violent end as the hut collapsed around him. Somehow managing to make his way outside, he felt the ground shake violently again as another deafening roar rumbled from the south, just outside where his hut once stood. Soon he felt a pounding compression sweep around him and through his body from the shockwave of the blast, which pushed the truck five meters from where it had been parked. In great pain, he then heard a piercing whine and swish of air from above, and he looked up in time to see two bright purple cones of flame shooting out from a jet now illuminated by those flames. Then the thundering boom of another bomb landed even closer, spraying him with flying chunks of earth. He knew he had to get as far away as he could, but it was almost impossible to think. He tried to tell his legs to move, but they were sluggish. Each blast seemed to either be closer or originate from where he was trying to run in. Flames were raging in almost every direction, and it was getting harder to breathe as they sucked up all the available oxygen.

The target area was now clearly illuminated from the previous runs as Dash 3 and 4 began theirs. Val questioned in his own mind why such an insignificant target needed to be struck in the first place, much less by six heavily loaded F-4s, when an attack helicopter or an OV-10 could have easily done the job, but he knew it wasn't his job to question, just follow orders. Just as Dash 4 pulled up, Frank began his run with Val ten seconds in trail—"batting cleanup," as was his designation for being the last jet on a run. Val pushed his stick forward as Nate counted down altitude over the ICS. The flames were now so bright that Val had to switch to his red visor, and he still couldn't make out exactly what he was supposed to hit. The hut and the truck were no longer discernible, so Val picked out a spot in the middle of the flames that wasn't on fire yet and set his pipper on it. Nate soon announced that they were at release altitude and Val pickled off two racks and pulled up. The bright inferno gave way to the pitch black of the night sky as the nose of his jet pitched up into a climb. The target had not only been destroyed, but completely erased.

Moments earlier in the raging inferno below, the man realized he was hopelessly trapped. Feeling helpless and terrified, he struggled to breathe and keep away from the terrible heat. Filled with anger and a desire for vengeance, he realized his clothes were on fire and the skin beneath them was beginning to melt. In a final act of desperation, he rolled over onto his back and faced the sky, which was a tiny black wall at the end of a tunnel of fire. He grasped the AK-47 at his side that he'd dropped and nearly emptied the magazine at the black wall that was rapidly being swallowed in an orange haze. When he got to the last round, he stuck the muzzle to his chin and squeezed the trigger one final time.

As Bunny Flight climbed out to leave the area, each man gave one last look groundward to validate in their own minds if it was worth it. All of them were glad that they'd met no resistance on this flight. It made up for the ones that had aged them a bit from fright. Each looked toward Papa as he gave the order to RTB. Each man was looking forward to an early night, knowing that it was indeed rare to have it this easy. Papa asked all wings to check in and give him a damage report, and each crew replied that there was none. This always seemed abnormal to Papa. When things went too smoothly, he was left with the uneasy feeling that it would catch up with them on the next mission.

"Glad to hear it, fellas, but I always feel bad when absolutely nothing goes wrong." Papa then looked over to Val's jet and said, "For you FNGs, you'd better not get too used to this. Anytime we go on these types of sorties, it's usually some big cluster that ends in near disaster—always really fucking nerve-racking."

"Roger, sir. Guess we may be your new good luck charms, sir," Val replied.

"Great—you just fucked us now!" Papa returned sarcastically.

As soon as Papa unkeyed his mike, instructions came over from Panama that they'd just received a distress message from an A-6 shot down over Quan Lang. The crew had stayed with their wounded bird as long as they could but had eventually bailed out east of Vinh. They needed cover and their position pinpointed until the rescue helicopter arrived.

"See what I mean?" Papa sighed, then announced to Panama that Bunny Flight would assist after he got fuel status checks from his pilots. That done, each plane followed his lead as they turned northeast toward Vinh. Each jet was still armed with four 500-pounders each plus their guns, so they should have plenty of ordnance to provide cover for the downed flight crew and the rescue chopper. Papa knew in the back of his mind that if the crew landed close to the city, his flight could see heavy fire from ground defenses. The crews knew this had the potential to be an extremely dangerous recovery since Vinh had recently been identified as a SAM site, and that the surrounding area was mostly flat, open terrain. Flight crews liked having the natural cover of ridgelines and mountains to protect them from being tracked by SAM sites. But their primary concern was the recovery of the flight crew. They hoped that if they ever found themselves in the same situation, other crews take risks to help them.

Papa and the rest of Bunny Flight followed their DF equipment until they were in the area of the signal. The only rescue aircraft in the vicinity was King 02, an SA-16 Albatross amphibious aircraft circling off the coast, but he was too far away and unable to assist in this type of rescue, where a helicopter was needed, but he was able to provide some information since he was the first to pick up the Mayday call from the downed A-6.

"King 2, this is Bunny Flight 1, over," Papa called as he initiated contact.

"Bunny Flight 1, King 2."

"I'm leading a flight of six Fox-4s with four 500-pounders each and twenty mike-mike. We're overhead the downed flight crew with thirty-five minutes of playtime and will provide cover until recovery team arrives. Have not made contact with crew."

"Roger Bunny Flight 1. I have lost all contact with the crew twenty minutes ago, and do not know their condition. They should be monitoring guard. Their call-sign is Rattler 4. Chariot 1 is the recovery team and is inbound with ETA of twenty-five minutes."

"Roger. We'll orbit at angels niner so we can monitor all frequencies and will try to reestablish contact. Bunny Flight, throttle back to save fuel and descend to a right-hand orbit at angels niner."

Papa descended his flight to orbit at nine thousand AGL, then reached out for the downed crew on guard channel. "Rattler 4, do you copy Bunny Flight?"

An eerie silence mixed with the static was all they heard before Papa tried again. All the Bunny Flight crews were nervous, fearing the men may have turned their radios down for fear of being detected by nearby enemy patrols.

"Rattler 4, do you copy Bunny Flight, over?"

Again silence intermixed with static dominated the frequency for a couple of moments until finally a voice crackled over the static. "Bunny Flight, this is Rattler 4 Bravo"—which meant it was the bombardier. He'd heard the whine of jet engines above him, but couldn't see them in the blackness above.

"Say your status."

"I'm a bit banged up and have a sprained, maybe broken ankle, but otherwise I'm okay."

"Roger. Do you know the status of Alpha?" Alpha was the A-6 pilot.

"Affirmative. He landed about two hundred meters from me, but I'm beside him now. He's coughing up blood and is having difficulty breathing. We're taking cover behind an embankment at the southeast corner of a rice paddy in the elephant grass."

"Roger. Help is on the way and should arrive in twenty minutes. Lay low and report any problems to us. We're here to protect you fellas till you're recovered and headed home."

"Wilco." The bombardier looked at his watch and sat next to his pilot, trying to do whatever he could to comfort him. "Relax, Taylor. We got cover above and our ride out should be here in twenty minutes." Whenever his pilot violently heaved and coughed, he helped him sit up and tapped him on the back to help him cough up the blood that was slowly drowning him. "Stay with me—we're gonna be outta here soon."

Ten minutes passed uneventfully. The bombardier looked toward the vast, empty blackness above where his protectors could be heard, but not seen, then stretched aching muscles that had taken a heavy jarring during the ejection sequence. As he stretched his neck out, his eyes rested on something that made his heart briefly stop. Several dark shapes, human in size, were closing in on them from the west. They appeared to be about two hundred and fifty meters away. He squinted to make sure he was seeing what he thought he was seeing as he grabbed his .38 caliber pistol and also grabbed his pilot's pistol and tucked it into a fold in his G-harness. He grabbed the radio and quietly spoke," Bunny Flight, Rattler 4."

"Rattler 4, this is Bunny Flight."

"We've got a problem."

Papa knew this could only be urgent. "Go ahead."

"There appears to be a platoon of Charlie closing in approximately two hundred and fifty meters west of our position. Can you assist?"

"Consider it done," Papa replied, knowing that it could be trouble since they couldn't see the downed flight crew or the enemy platoon. It was just black everywhere—in the air, on the ground, out to sea. It was as close to flying inside of nothing as was possible.

Papa faced a dilemma because he risked giving away the position of the downed crew to the enemy platoon if his flight didn't eliminate them within the first couple of passes, and at only two hundred and fifty meters away the platoon could easily close the distance and kill the downed men before other passes could be set up. The platoon could also shoot down the rescue team if they were still around after a few runs. After a couple of seconds, Papa spoke. "Chappie, I want you fly a low pass from east to west about two hundred feet off the deck. Fire your gun once you think you're past our boys down there and see if you can draw some ground fire. I'll be close behind. The rest of you line up for sequential runs and note where you saw the muzzle flashes. I'm gonna drop one rack on 'em to make a barrier between them and our boys. We can finish 'em off with either our guns or our bombs, whatever it takes. Any questions?"

A resounding "No sir!" was the reply from the rest of Bunny Flight as they prepared to carry out Papa's orders. All the RIOs looked into the blackness below as Chappie set up for his strafing run.

"Dash 2's rolling in hot," Chappie announced as he dove toward the deck with his RIO calling out altitudes on the radar altimeter. Papa lagged behind eight seconds in trail, but remained at a higher altitude so he could hopefully see the muzzle flashes and would have a better angle to release his bombs.

Chappie leveled off when his RIO announced that they were at two hundred AGL. When he thought he was above the downed Americans, he blindly opened fire with his cannon. The 20mm Gatling cannon, with its exploding rounds, was more feared by the North Vietnamese than any other weapon in the entire US arsenal. It was so feared it was often referred to as "blinking death," and it was certainly no exception this time as the enemy platoon looked up to see a twinkling light in the sky and see tracers zip all around them, shredding the ground and sending small pieces of shrapnel flying. The entire platoon dropped to their bellies and tried to hug the ground until they heard the jet pass overhead. The older, more experienced soldiers were disciplined enough to stay still even after the jet passed, knowing there was always at least one more not far behind or coming from another direction. A few of the younger ones among them instantly jumped to their feet and fired their rifles in the direction of the roar of jet engines until their platoon leader scolded at them, but it was too late.

Papa had been watching as he began his dive, and the instant the troops fired, he knew exactly where they were. The other Bunny Flight crews instantly locked onto the muzzle flashes below and made a mental note of the location. Papa's plan had worked.

As Papa was in his dive, he gave the order for all aircraft to release at least one rack into the vicinity of the muzzle flashes, knowing the platoon would now either be in full retreat or moving to another position to attempt to get at the Americans on the ground. The bombs had enough power and range to easily compensate for any distance in any direction the platoon could possibly cover on foot. He released his first rack about five hundred feet AGL and began his pullout. The explosion completely whited out the next pilot's vision for a brief moment, but soon the surrounding terrain was exposed. Even the Americans' position was bathed in firelight after the third run from Bunny Flight.

It wasn't much longer before Chariot 1 checked on and was easily led to the downed crew's position with all the readily available light from the bombs. Chariot 1 was a single UH-1 covered by two AH-1 Cobras. During the rescue operation, Bunny Flight went back up to nine thousand feet and orbited with less than ten minutes worth of fuel to spare before they had to RTB. It wasn't much longer before Chariot 1 announced that they had recovered both men and were also returning to base.

Papa and his flight listened to the entire operation from above and breathed a sigh of relief when they heard from Chariot 1. Papa promptly ordered Bunny Flight to RTB and climb to angels eighteen for better fuel economy.

The fires from their bombs, to the southeast of Vinh, caught the attention of the CO of a SAM site, who happened to be outside smoking a cigarette when he heard and saw the explosions. He ran down and told his radar operator to turn on his Fan Song radar, knowing Americans were close by. The sleepy radar operator reluctantly turned on his radar and was pleasantly surprised when he immediately got several strong returns from Bunny Flight, who were still in their climb-out. The operator locked onto the strongest return and the commanding officer gave the order to launch.

Bunny Flight was near level-out when the audible alarm of the enemy missile warning rang in their ears, making every man's heart skip a beat. RIOs immediately scanned their scopes and pilots immediately began searching outside for visual clues. Val and Notso were looking groundward when the bright orange flame signaling a launch flared up at seven o'clock. It was immediately followed by another.

"Tally ho! Seven o'clock low! We've got a pair of SA-2s lifting off. Appears to be heading our way!" Val announced over frequency.

"Everyone spread out in loose deuce formation, make it approximately seventy-five meters between each jet," Papa ordered. He knew that SA-2s were often confused when aircraft flew this formation, usually passing between the planes, but the North Vietnamese would counter this by launching two or more missiles in succession. Papa also knew the missiles could be beaten by making a hard turn as the missile closed in, but the key was having a visual on the missile and keeping it in sight.

The missiles arced toward the closest pair of jets—Val and Notso. "Looks like we're the lucky ones, Notso!" Val said as he saw the missiles turning toward him. "I guess you can relax now, Papa, because it looks like you're gonna have your typical sortie glitch!"

As soon as Papa realized who the missiles were locked on, he ordered the rest of Bunny Flight to get down low and head to Linh Thu as fast as safe fuel consumption would allow. He stayed behind and lagged well below and behind Val and Notso in order to help them know where the missiles were. Val and Notso, meanwhile, began a shallow dive to the right to see if the missiles followed their general flight path, which would indicate they had a positive lock on the American jets.

Both pilots focused on the bright flame from the rocket engines to see that the missiles were indeed mimicking their flight path, tracking them both. The missiles were about a half mile apart from one another as they continued streaking toward the jets.

"First missile is now about four miles away, closing fast," Nate announced.

"Second missile is about four-and-a-half away," Speedy announced.

"Should we split up?" Val asked Notso.

"I don't know," Notso admitted, knowing that he and Speedy had only been over here two months longer than Val and Nate, and this was the first time his plane had ever been acquired by a SAM.

"Negative. Spread your formation out about ten meters more," Papa ordered. His voice was comforting counsel for both crews. "Now listen to me, gents. What I'm about to say will defy all your instincts to survive, but it will work, understand?" Papa reassured his newest aviators. "I've got both of you and the missiles in sight, so listen to me."

"Aye, sir," was the unanimous response from both pilots.

"Stay where you are. The first missile should pass between you. After it does, wait for my command and break in opposite directions. Then listen for my instructions for the second one, which will be only seconds behind, got it?"

"Yes sir." Again both pilots responded with nervous breaths.

Within seconds, the first missile was looming in both pilots' eyes, filling up their field of vision as it drew closer, streaking at them from below and behind, testing the nerve of each pilot to remain basically motionless.

"Here it comes, gents. Stay still."

Val and Nate looked outside to catch a brief glimpse of light zip between them and continue skyward, closer to Val's jet.

"Break now!" Papa ordered.

Both pilots responded immediately as Notso broke left and Val broke right. The second missile was now closing on Val's jet and was only seconds behind.

"Dash 6, reverse your turn and then immediately break back right in a steep diving turn!" Papa coached from Val's four o'clock.

Val responded and reversed into a sharp climbing left turn, as soon as he was in the left knife-edge, he rolled back to the right into an incredible energy building diving right break. The missile exploded just as Val was established in the right break, a mere seventy meters away. Both Val's and Nate's vision were still partially grayed out as the missile exploded, and its shockwaves buffeted Val's jet and almost forced it into departure as it began an accelerated stall. Val recovered his jet before it got any farther into departure, and his vision started to clear as he rolled wings level. He looked straight up in time to see the first missile explode high in the atmosphere.

"Excellent job, fellas! Are you okay?" Papa's voice was drenched in elation.

"Yes sir," Val and Notso responded.

"All right. Let's not hang around long enough to become targets for another launch. Let's get down to some cover and head home." Papa knew they were approaching the protective ridge lines of the west and would soon be out of the SAM site's range.

"Aye, sir, and thank you," Val said.

"What are you thanking me for?" Papa asked.

"For saving our asses, sir," Val answered.

"Don't thank me now—we're not home yet. You can thank me at the pub after debrief."

Val moved his stick forward and left so he could follow Papa and Notso back to Linh Thu, but his jet didn't respond as quickly as it normally did. Val tested it again by trying some gentle Dutch rolls, but the jet was extremely sluggish, and the stick required more and more effort to move it. Val's eyes immediately went to his hydraulic pressure gauges. The needles were dropping rapidly and soon a warning light illuminated on the panel. Val looked at the DME to see that they were still twenty DME from Linh Thu. When the last missile exploded, some of its shrapnel had apparently severed a line or punctured a reservoir. He drew a deep breath and reluctantly keyed up on frequency. "Papa, this is Dash 6. We have another problem."

"Go ahead, Dash 6."

"Apparently that missile got us after all. My instruments indicate I'm losing hydraulic fluid and my flight controls are sluggish."

"Roger—I'll have a look." Papa said as he rolled under Val's jet. As he pulled up close to the wounded jet, some drops of the red-dyed fluid splattered on his canopy. He could barely make out what appeared to be steady streams of fluid venting out from a few places in the fuselage and wings. "That's affirm, Dash 6. You have fluid spraying from several places in your wings and fuselage. We'd better get you on the ground quick. Lower you landing gear and tailhook now while you still can."

Val lowered the gear and tailhook and began mentally preparing himself for the challenge ahead. He'd only faced one real emergency before—the time he'd flamed out and had to dead stick onto a carrier at night during a thunderstorm with severe crosswinds and huge waves that rocked the ship. He knew that this time would be no less challenging. Although he still had his engines, he faced the possibility of complete failure of his flight controls and brakes, which would require that he and Nate do the one thing every aviator feared more than combat or landing on a carrier at night—eject from his aircraft.

Papa made the mayday call to Linh Thu tower, and fire equipment was now standing by runway 13 at various spots. The winds were light and variable so shouldn't be a factor, and the tower had the arresting gear locked into position should it be needed.

Val was flying hot as he turned an eight-mile final and the tower informed him, "Bunny 6, Linh Thu Tower, wind calm, runway one-three cleared to land, check gear down."

Val keyed up his response, "Bunny 6 cleared to land, three down and locked." The flight controls were extremely heavy now and inputs took a lot of physical force. The jet was even slower to react to commands from Val, so he had to stay several seconds ahead of the aircraft to anticipate where he wanted it to be whether than where it was now.

As he continued the approach, his muscles were starting to fatigue from the effort required to operate the controls, and he was drenched in sweat. The wings were now rocking, refusing to remain level for longer than a couple of seconds. Val kept the throttles at higher than normal settings in order to keep the plane airborne and hold the pitch and glide path steady. There was no chance for a go-around on this approach—it was either land or eject.

As he approached five miles, Val made sure as best he could that he was on centerline, for he had limited rudder control and most of his efforts and concentration was on controlling his roll and pitch. At two miles his airspeed and sink rate was faster than he wanted it to be, so he added a bit more throttle to bring the nose up and slow the descent rate. Adding power also seemed to stabilize the aircraft a bit more, but Val knew that any aircraft was more stable at higher airspeeds, so he didn't want to give up too much power until he was practically at touchdown. As he passed two miles, the oscillations of the wings had gotten bad enough that the jet sometimes banked as much as ten degrees, but Val knew if he tried to fight it too much he'd only make it worse. His jet was designed for neutral dynamic stability, so he could only contain the rolling slightly without the aid of having full flight control capabilities. Val planned to reserve his attempt to fully contain the rolling until just above touchdown, as he also knew his muscles didn't have the stamina to keep up this far out.

"Double-O, keep your hand on the ejection handle. I may not be able to keep up with this if her stability worsens," Val said.

"Just say the word, brother," Nate replied as he pulled his visor down in preparation for an ejection. He then reached down between his legs and grabbed the ejection handle, making sure he didn't grasp it too tightly in case a sudden jolt forced his arms up and caused an ejection when Val wasn't ready for it.

"Bunny 6, idle and boards," Val announced over frequency, his voice obviously strained as he quickly put both hands on the stick.

At three-quarters of a mile, he chopped the throttles back for a rapid descent at the numbers, knowing his jet, which was designed for carrier operations, could handle the jolt of a hard landing. He was able to contain most of the rolling, but some of it was too rapid for him or the flight controls to react to in time. The jet continued its rapid descent toward the runway, with the ground now rushing up at him. He knew the jet's airspeed was much higher than it should be at this juncture, and he hoped he wouldn't overshoot or float. The F-4 usually decelerated quickly at idle thrust, so there was also the fear that it would slow too quickly and stall. Val knew at this point that adding power might cause him to totally lose control. His strength was fading fast as he strained to keep his jet under relatively positive control, but he knew that relaxing his burning muscles wasn't an option. He'd have to endure the discomfort until the jet came to rest or until he and Nate were forced to punch out. With the runway now bathed in landing lights, Val buried the stick into his chest in an attempt to get his jet to round out and flare as it continued to roll.

When the jet was ten feet off the ground, it stalled, dropped, and slammed hard onto the runway in a steep nose-high attitude. Val kept the stick against his chest as the jet bounced off the ground and began porpoising down the runway, but rising lower with each bounce. The jolts from each bounce pounded the crew's bodies, even forcing Nate's hands off the ejection handle a couple of times. The jet completed its final bounce, then rolled swiftly down the runway with the tail-hook sliding along in a spectacular shower of sparks until it snagged the third cable, slamming the giant fighter to an abrupt stop.

Val, his harnesses tugging on his upper torso, looked up to see the glow of the instrument panel mere inches from his face. He then rose up in his seat, shut the engines down, and opened his canopy as he keyed up, "Bunny 6, boots on the boards, snag number three." He then queried Nate of his status and both men finally relaxed as they awaited the rescue crews and the tug to take them back to the northwest ramp.

It was a long, slow ride to the northwest ramp as the tug strained to pull the massive fighter across most of the airfield. Val and Nate didn't seem to mind as they tried to relax and savor in the moment, knowing that a slow, stress-free ride like this was a rare thing. The tug pulled the jet up to its parking space on the northwest ramp, which was in line with other F-4s, all parked behind a barricade of sandbags. Val and Nate were just climbing out of their wounded bird when they heard Papa's distinct voice as he walked toward them shouting, "Jordan! Robinson!"

They turned to the see their tall, slender CO, hands on his hips, his gray hair matted with sweat and his ice-blue eyes showing just a hint of concern. Papa smiled and said, "You boys have had a helluva first few weeks. Big John is gonna talk to you for a bit, then you fellas head to debrief." His smile widened as he added, "Then we'll go to the waterin' hole for a coupla cold ones on me! Course you know they're not actually cold. The only thing cold around here's the letters from my ex-wife." Papa laughed as he walked away.

"Aye, sir!" the young Marines said in stereo as they snapped a salute and returned the smile, then immediately went to their jet to inspect the damage. They found the underside still lightly coated with a thin film of the red-dyed fluid, but none of it was dripping from anywhere, which meant the reservoirs were bone dry. The Marines looked at each other with mouths wide open, then stomped down a couple of time to make sure they were indeed standing on solid ground and still alive. As they discovered the source of the leaks, they realized just how lucky they were to have actually landed the aircraft. They found five large holes, two in the left wing, one in the right wing, and two on the belly of the fuselage. Luckily, there were only punctures in the bottom half of the wings, but two fingers could fit in each. The holes in the fuselage were much deeper and larger—large enough to fit three, almost four fingers into both holes, and deep enough to jam their fingers into the holes up to their knuckles.

"Damn—that settles it," Val said as he jammed three fingers into the largest hole in the belly. "I'm suing the USSR."

At that moment, a big man about six-three and two hundred and twenty pounds walked up to jet, pushing a large tool box on wheels with "JOHN" stenciled on the side in large, black letters.

"Evening, boys," he said as he began to open drawers until he found a flashlight.

Val and Nate were a little awed by the size of the man and approached him to verify his identity. "You must be Big John," Val said as he launched into a detailed explanation about the SAM and the damage it caused. All the while the man listened with a smirk, waiting to get a word in.

By the time Val finished, he was a bit winded, and his jaw dropped when the man replied, "Pretty interesting, sir, but I'm not the one you need to tell all this to."

"Excuse me?" Val answered with a tone of surprise.

"You need to tell that to Big John, sir."

"What? You're not Big John?" Val said, surprised.

"No sir—I'm Little John."

"You're Little John?" Val said as he again took in the man's size.

"Yes sir. You know—like the guy in Robin Hood?" Little John patted the large tool box and explained, "This is Big John's toolbox. I was pushing it out here for him."

"Right. Well, where's Big John?"

"Here he comes." Little John smiled as he pointed behind Val and Nate.

Val and Nate turned around to see an absolute mountain of a man walking toward them—easily six-seven and three hundred and twenty-five pounds of solid muscle, with balding gray hair and blue eyes.

"Is that an earthquake or just King Kong's little brother over there headed toward us?" Nate whispered to Val,

"I thought the Incredible Hulk was just a comic book character. All this guy needs is green skin and a ripped-up pair of purple pants," Val whispered back.

Val and Nate froze in attention as the giant ducked under their jet to inspect the damage. He stayed underneath for a while before shifting his attention to the aviators standing beside it. He came out from under the plane and approached the flight crew with a furious look on his face, making both Val and Nate cringe.

"Evening, sir." Both aviators saluted the major as he stopped in front of them. His brute size combined with the angry expression was intimidating.

"Well, it would've been a nice evening if you boys hadn't ruined my poker game by waltzing in with not just one, but two fucking missiles. I was winning. That only made me slightly pissed off. I have a cooler of cold beers and a few hot local honeys waiting on me tomorrow night, so this plane better be an easy fix because I don't want to miss that. That would make me mad." Big John made his face cold and devoid of expression as he leaned toward Val and Nate and added, "You don't want to see me get mad, do you?"

"No sir," they replied in unison, avoiding eye contact with the giant towering over them.

"Good." Big John suddenly erupted in laughter. "Excellent, in fact, cuz the truth is, I totally suck at poker, and the only cold thing around here are letters Papa gets from his ex, which I'm sure he's already explained to you, and the only women around here are at the PX in the pages of *Playboy*."

Val and Nate breathed a sigh of relief and laughed with Big John, even though they were not quite sure if they should yet. Then the big major asked, "You're the new boys, right?"

"Yes, sir."

"You don't have to call me 'sir.' I hate being called 'sir'—makes me think I'm old or something. I heard about your very first sortie from Papa and the FACA pilot. Sounded impressive to me. Just don't do anything stupid and get yourselves killed.

"Listen to Papa and you won't ever go wrong. You boys'll fine here. You can go to debrief—Little John gave me the skinny on your jet. I'll have her up and flying in no time." Big John paused, then continued: "I don't know if you'd consider that good news or not. I'll see you gents at the pub later. Dismissed."

"Aye, sir," they responded as they walked away.

"Dammit—don't call me 'sir'!" Big John reiterated.

"Sorry. It's hard not to call a man of your stature 'sir,' sir. Oops—sorry!" Val said. Big John just smiled and shook his head.

Val and Nate walked into debrief just as it was being dismissed. They found it odd that it was over so quickly. Papa looked up at them. "Glad you strolled in. I want to thank you."

"Thank us, sir?" Nate asked.

"Yeah—for listening to me up there, as you should. Because you listened, we're having this conversation and I'm not writing a letter to your families about how you were killed in action. It's usually hard for young Marines to listen to anyone when they're first starting out; it's even harder for them to listen to an old fart like me. So I'm glad you do. I'm glad I get crews willing to hang it all out on the line, including their egos. I either get dedicated crews, or ones that're completely fucking nuts."

"Sorry we missed debrief, sir," Val said lamely.

"Don't sweat it, son. You'll listen to enough of 'em in time you might actually consider taking another hit so you'll get to miss another one. Anyway, I'll speak to both of you privately tomorrow at 0700 sharp. Why don't you boys head on down to the pub after you get out of your gear? You've had a busy night. Sit at my table, the staff already knows you're allowed to tonight."

The pub was another large canvas tent in the middle of the housing quarters, open to both enlisted men and officers—unlike on large installations, where there were separate clubs. Everyone was pretty much on a first-name basis there, except for when the brass made a rare appearance for inspections. The pub was where the men of Linh Thu got to know each other and simply relax after a stressful mission.

The only rule was that no shop talk was allowed, under penalty of a five-dollar fine that went into a mason jar at the corner of the bar. The money in the jar was used to buy special items for the PX that were usually unavailable to servicemen stationed overseas, thanks to supply officers with connections back home.

Nate and Val walked in and Big John slipped up behind them and directed them to a table that was reserved for Papa and himself. They were instructed by Big John never to sit at that table unless specifically invited by Papa or himself. Big John began to fill in the newest crew about everyone on base, including Papa and himself, and about the crew they shared their hooch with—Notso and Speedy.

Frank M. Wise was from Florida. His call-sign, "Notso," had become forever attached to him when he'd misspelled his name on a test at flight school—Frank "Notso" Wise.

Jamie Sanders, who hailed from Oregon, had earned his call-sign, "Speedy," when he'd gotten into a drunken argument at a party in the wee hours of the morning about whose car was faster—his, a Dodge Charger, or his buddy's, a Ford Mustang. Both men knew they were too inebriated to actually drive, so they did the next best thing—they had a foot-race down a hill, staggering and weaving a hundred yards down the empty street. Jamie won, but not before he flattened a street sign because he was too drunk to slow himself down in time. The next day he received a gag gift—a GI Joe parachute with the word "Speedy" on it.

Papa soon walked in and joined Big John and his newbies at his table, and after his first two beers he had them tell him the short versions of their life stories.

Nate Robinson was from Texas. He'd known Val practically his entire aviation career and they'd been stationed together in every assignment thus far. He spoke fluent Italian and French, and was extremely suave in his mannerisms. All these attributes added up to a man that never failed to attract women; they had flocked to him all his life. Nate never let that make him cocky or arrogant; he simply appreciated all the attention the fairer sex would shower on him and return the favor. James Bond was 007, so Nate became 008, since he seemed to be the real life version of the fictitious super spy. He'd known Val practically his entire aviation career and they'd been stationed together in every assignment thus far.

Valentine Jordan was from a small town in east Tennessee, where he'd lived until he was thirteen. He'd then moved to Hawaii to Ewa Beach, a small town on Oahu. His dad was a linguist for the CIA, and Val spent his youth traveling the world. An avid thrill seeker, he loved being a Marine fighter pilot and was always the best in his class. His got his call-sign, "El Tiburon," when he was at Guantanamo Bay, Cuba, on a cross-country flight. He and some other Marines had snuck out one weekend and somehow ended up playing poker in a shady, underground casino all the way up in Havana. He was winning consistently and ended up closing down the table. His aggressive playing style had the dealer calling him *El Tiburon*—"the shark." Val surprised the dealer by rolling up his sleeve to reveal a tattoo of a shark on his right deltoid. When the dealer asked him about the tattoo, his buddies explain that Val was a fearless pilot.

The men drank their warm drinks and shot the breeze for a couple of hours before deciding to hit the rack. The pub was the only place where the men of Linh Thu felt they shut out the world, which did its best to remind them that it was impossible to forget they were on a military base in the middle of hostile territory with a war raging around them.

Tonight ended up being no exception as a loud whistle silenced the conversation and laughter and replaced it with the thunder of a distant explosion. More explosions followed, accompanied by the rattle of machine gun and small-arms fire that intensified and drew closer. The lights suddenly went out and sirens sang out from various speakers. Linh Thu was once again under attack from rockets and mortars, and men scrambled in the darkness for their hooches and rifles. Because of the constant attacks, every man at Linh Thu was issued an M16A1 service rifle, war belt, and several full magazines. When the men reached their hooches, they loaded their weapons and took cover wherever they could find it. The only good thing about the attacks is that they seldom lasted more than twenty minutes, and the enemy normally never tried to enter the base.

Soon an eerie silence fell over the base, and the men just lay there in darkness, listening only to their heavy breathing and heartbeats, trying to pick up any rustle of movement that might warn of the enemy. After lying still in silence for ten minutes, most assumed the attack was over and relaxed a bit. They never knew for sure, so most would stay where they were for an hour before finally crashing into their racks to find the welcome peace of sleep—if that was possible when snuggled up to a loaded assault rifle.

3

Just Another Day

Val stepped out of his hooch and was greeted by the morning sun. He was already having a hard time getting a good night's sleep as it was, but after last night's attack, he knew it would be that much more difficult now. There was something unnatural about sleeping with a loaded assault rifle. The very fact that it was snug against his body invaded his subconscious, eliminating all chances of rest. Val felt even more uneasy with the thought that there was always the possibility that the occasion might present itself when he'd actually have to fire the gun.

Even though it would soon be unbearably hot, Val was always glad to see the sun because that meant he'd survived another day. It would soon be apparent to everyone at Linh Thu that thanks to the morning sun it would now be light enough to see the damage from the previous evening's attack. As he walked out of his hooch, he didn't notice anything at first, but within moments an awful smell reached his nose. Next his ears picked up strange noises, and finally his eyes were greeted with a scene of devastation.

He saw impact craters and buildings and equipment pock-marked by bullet holes. Smoke was still rising from fires that had long been extinguished. Sounds from bulldozers, hand tools, and trucks disturbed the normally still morning air. but the worst part were the smells that drifted in the dying breeze, one in particular.

What was that repugnant smell? As he passed several buildings and pieces of machinery that were burned, the nauseating odor almost made him pass out. Val continued on across the street, his face buried in the elbow of his

45

flight suit in a vain effort to keep the smell at bay, when the sound of a horn made him jump. He looked in the direction of the horn and quickly stepped back as a front loader bore down on him. As it approached, the smell grew stronger, and when he glanced into the bucket he saw that it was carrying the blackened, burned bodies of a number of enemy soldiers. Frozen on the face of one was an expression of fear and surprise—an image now forever etched in his mind, one he knew would visit him again and again. He dashed across the street and headed for the flight line, as he had some time to kill before he and Nate were to meet Papa at his office.

When he got to the ramp, he found Big John standing there, hands on hips, swearing at the scene before him. It seemed clear now that the flight line had been the primary target of last night's attack, and enemy troops had somehow gotten onto the base—a fact that diminished whatever feeling of security the base ever offered. Val saw that two UH-1s were substantially damaged, and farther down the line, in the spot where his jet had been parked, an F-4 showed a bit of damage. As he walked closer he realized that it was indeed his F-4—number 069. The right leading edge slat was punched in and torqued into a weave of bent metal for half its length. That definitely meant a longer repair delay for Val and Nate, a longer wait until the jet was returned to service and they could rejoin their rest of their squadron. Val cautiously approached Big John and said, "Well this can only mean one thing, sir."

"And what's that, young'un?" Big John replied as he looked at the young pilot.

"You're definitely gonna miss your cold beer and hot women tonight, sir, so I guess you're gonna be mad for a while."

Big John smiled as he looked at Val, then held up his right hand and looked at it. "Yep—guess it's just you and me again, ol' buddy," he said. "It's gonna take just a bit longer to get your jet back in the air. I'm still not sure how you feel about that, but if you're disappointed, you can personally thank the platoon commander from last night's raid. Here he comes now." Big John pointed to another front loader driving by with a couple of bodies in its bucket. He was gauging the young Marine's reaction to the whole grim scene, and he could see that Val wasn't quite sure how to feel about it yet. Big John placed his hand on Val's shoulder and said, "Try to get used to it, Kid. You're gonna see worse. Sad to say you'll be oblivious to it in time."

Val looked as the front loader drove by, wondering how it would be possible to become oblivious to such a hideous sight. Deep in thought, Val almost forgot that he needed to move along until the wind stirred the air. The stench again filled his nose and he gasped and coughed. It would never be possible to get used to that smell.

When he arrived at Papa's office, found Nate waiting outside the wide open door. "How long have you been waiting?" he asked.

"Since he told us we were expected here last night at debrief." Nate chuckled, then answered the question seriously. "About ten minutes or so."

"Did you knock yet?"

"No. I was waiting until you got here so I wouldn't have be in there one-on-one with Papa for too long."

"Gotcha. Ready?"

"Always," Nate replied as Val knocked on the door.

Papa invited the young officers in and told them to sit. Val noticed how small and cramped the office was, considering it belonged to a squadron CO. There was barely enough room for the desk and two chairs in front of it. It was another glaring example of how low a priority personal comfort was at Linh Thu.

Papa looked up from the papers on his desk and smiled at the Marines sitting across from him. "Morning, gents. Sleep well?" he asked.

Val and Nate looked at each other in confusion, not sure how they should answer. Finally Nate replied slowly, "Not really, sir."

"Brutal honesty. I love it!" Papa replied with a smile, pointing at Nate with his pen. "That's great. I'd be worried about your sanity if you did sleep through all that shit last night." Papa snorted and continued. "I'm sure both of you are well aware that your jet will down for at least a couple of days, maybe longer after last night, so until it's returned to flight status, I have some things I need you to do."

Val signed. "Great. If there's one thing I hate more than down-time, it's busywork, sir."

"More brutal honesty! Just do me a favor. When you're ready to express your opinion of me, make sure I'm there. Don't whisper behind my back like a little schoolgirl, okay?" Papa shook his head as the smile grew larger across his face. "I like you boys. I can count on you to tell it like it is. It's not busy-work that I have for you, son. You'll thank me. It'll be like weekend liberty back home." Papa paused as he shoved some papers across his desk. "But before we get to that, you gotta fill out a full report on last night. Most of it's already done, so just fill in the narrative part on the back."

Val and Nate began writing, and Papa went back to his work until he was interrupted by another knock. He looked up to see Second Lieutenant Fred Davis, the base supply and logistics officer.

"Just the man I wanted to see. Come in, young'un. You have some news for me?"

"Yes sir," Davis answered.

"Before you begin, this is Captain Jordan and Lieutenant Robinson, my newest crew. Gents, this is Lieutenant Davis, our supply officer. Be nice to him—he can get you and the rest of us all kinds of shit we can't normally get from HQ." The men shook hands, then Val and Nate went back to their papers and Lieutenant Davis continued with his report.

"I have some good news and some bad news, which would you like first, sir?"

"Just give me your report, son. Whatever order you wish."

"Well sir, all the construction supplies we had for repairing damage from raids like last night's were destroyed in the attack by a direct hit from a rocket."

"Damn! What's the good news, then?"

"Uh, actually sir, that was the good news."

"Brutal honesty, sir! You gotta like this guy!" Val interrupted with a laugh.

Papa laughed. "Well fuck me six ways from Sunday! What's the bad news then?"

"Sir, as you probably already know, COD flights to Linh Thu have been cut in half and the next one's not until the end of the week, so I get a lot of our supplies from our, um, neighbors, just to keep us afloat."

"So?"

"Well sir, the only bridge over the Nhat Le River in Dong Hoi collapsed last night after a runaway barge conveniently loaded with explosives hit it. I don't know how long it'll take to rebuild the bridge, but it was the only way to reach my source for supplies. To add insult to injury, the place itself was destroyed by a bicycle bomb."

"I understand. I know what you're trying to say in a round-about way, Lieutenant. "

"You do, sir?"

"Yeah. Basically you're saying we're fucked."

"Yes sir. I guess that's more direct."

"Not direct, Lieutenant—brutally honest," Nate put in with a smirk as he placed his paper on Papa's desk.

"See now? These boys are locked on," Papa said with a smile. Then he said to the young supply officer, "Well, I suggest you find out what we need the most of, then get your ass out to Dong Hoi and find a new supplier. Move it, son. We got a lot of patching up to do around here, and we can't wait until the end of the week."

"Aye, sir," Lieutenant Davis snapped back and left the tiny office.

Val put his paper on Papa's desk, and Papa collected both his and Nate's and placed them in a file. "Either of you fellas want a new billet? I'll give you mine for free. Now where were we?"

Val smiled. "You were gonna assign us some busy work, sir."

"It's not busy work, son." Papa then paused and smiled. "Aw, hell. You've been brutally honest with me, so I'll be brutally honest right back. Of course it's busy work, but it helps take a bit of the load off my back for a couple days at least. You're gonna help me plan and give mission briefings until your jet is fixed. Be at the ready room at 0900, and be ready to work. When orders come through, you *will* be busy."

"Aye, sir," both Marines replied in stereo as they were dismissed.

Two hours later, both Val and Nate were drenched with sweat when they opened the flap to the Cannery. "Good thing we started before noon," Nate said as he stepped inside.

Papa had handed them all the orders and explained what they needed to do and went off to another meeting, but he'd told them he'd check on them as soon as he was done and after checking on their plane with Big John. For a couple hours Val and Nate pored over the mountains of papers as they set up displays and prepared the room for the briefing when they were interrupted by Lieutenant Davis's voice, "Excuse me, sirs?"

They looked up from their work and Val said, "Yes, Lieutenant?"

"Do you know where the colonel is, sir?"

Val pointed to the building next to Papa's office. "He's in a meeting. He sent someone over to tell us he'd be back in about ten minutes." All the wood buildings on base stood out like a castles among the tents, making them easy targets for enemy attacks at night.

"Do you mind if I wait, sir?" Davis asked as he sat down in the first row of campstools.

"Whatever lifts your skirt, Lieutenant," Val said reassuringly to the young officer.

Val could tell that Davis was an eager, high-energy go-getter, chomping at the bit for a chance to impress the CO and wanting to be recognized for his work. The young Marine could barely sit still, and he began to nervously tap his foot against the metal frame of the stool he was sitting on, breaking the concentration of the other two officers. They both stopped what they were doing and glared at Davis, hoping he'd feel the weight of their stares and stop his fidgeting, but he continued on, unfazed.

Val finally spoke up. "Let me guess, Lieutenant—either you had too much coffee this morning, or not enough."

"Sir?" the young Marine answered with a puzzled look on his face. He sensed his superiors were annoyed, but didn't know why.

Val pointed to Davis's quivering foot. "Maybe you just have a nervous tic."

"Sorry, sir," Lieutenant Davis answered, flustered, and regained control of his foot.

"Thank you," Val said with a grin as he resumed. About a minute later, the lieutenant started tapping his foot again, totally unaware that he'd started again.

"I sure hope Papa gets here soon," Val said, his voice raised.

"Why's that?" Nate said with a smirk, knowing why.

"Because the lieutenant here is making me realize exactly how long ten minutes is," Val said even more loudly.

Davis withered under their cold stares and jumped to his feet. "Sorry again, sirs. I'll just stand."

"Not there, Lieutenant—over here." Val pointed to the open area between the first row of stools and the easels, screens, and blackboard at the back of the tent. Nate gave Val a curious look as the lieutenant moved over to the empty space. "There's nothing there for him to tap against." Val explained.

Both men returned to their work, but after a few minutes Val caught a picked up Davis out of the corner of his eye. picking up a pointer. "Clearly you have a grand sense of humor, Lieutenant," he said caustically.

"Sorry again, sir," Lieutenant Davis replied, setting the pointer down. Val and Nate both knew the lieutenant wasn't deliberately being irritating—he was just young.

Papa walked in ten minutes later to see Val and Nate working feverishly, and it made him smile. His smile immediately became a look of bewilderment when he saw Lieutenant Davis standing by himself in the far corner, his head hanging in apparent shame. "What the hell are you doing, Lieutenant?"

Val and Nate immediately looked up. Nate said, "Thank God, sir. I'm happier to see you now than when we ducked that missile last night."

"We had to put him in the corner until he was ready to quit fidgeting, sir," Val tried to explain without laughing. "He should be ready about now."

Papa smiled. "Are you ready to come out now, Lieutenant?" He was familiar with the young lieutenant's tendencies.

"Yes, sir," Lieutenant Davis said with a chuckle.

"You're gonna act like a grownup now, right?"

"Yes, sir." Davis explained to Papa that he thought he had two prospective suppliers. One was closed today and he hadn't seen the other yet because it was off the main streets somewhere, but both were in west Dong Hoi. Papa thanked and dismissed him. Papa then approached his aviators and looked over the work they'd done so far. After telling them what else needed to be done, he patted them both on the shoulders and said, "Gents, let's get lunch. Go to the pub and wait at my table—we've got a treat today."

"Twist our arms, sir," Nate said as he and Val dropped their papers and stepped out into the midday heat, which actually seemed cooler than inside the sweltering Cannery. It was apparent to both men just how busy Linh Thu usually was because the relative silence around them was so rare. If it wasn't the constant beat of rotor blades, it was the vibrating drone of the OV-10 or C-130 Hercules turboprops, or the ground-shaking roar of afterburners. Even in the dead of night there seemed to always be some sort of aircraft activity. When the night was silent of airplanes, mortar and rocket attacks filled in.

After lunch, Val headed right for his quiet spot to write another letter to Virginia. When he got there, all the lawn chairs were occupied, so he plopped himself down on the grass, pulled out his favorite picture of Virginia, and proceeded to write.

§ § § § §

Virginia, my love,

Hi again. I have some free time now since our jet is being repaired, and it's not expected to be ready for another two days or so. I finally got your first letter to me yesterday and I can't stop reading it. Every free moment I get I read it and look at that picture. It hurts me sometimes to look at that picture or read that letter because it reminds me of how much I miss you, but at the same time it keeps me sound, strong, and motivated because of how much I love you. I know it seems that I must say "I love you" every few sentences or so, but I really enjoy saying it and having someone to say it to. I can't say it enough; you are my life, you are what I live and breathe for. I'm counting the days until I can wrap my arms around you again.

Things are going good here, though this place can really test a man's character. I know when I get home there will be no obstacle we can't negotiate after going through this. We're gonna be the happiest couple in the world. You're gonna be the world's best wife, because you're already the world's greatest fiancée. I'm so lucky to have you in my life; I love you so much. I know this letter's kind of short, but I have to get back to work now. I love you, I miss you, I'll be seeing you again before you know it!

Love always and forever, Val

§ § § § §

"Hey buddy, be careful!" The voice shattered Val's daydreams of Virginia and made him look in the direction the voice came from.

"What?" Val asked.

"Look out, sir," a man said as he pointed to Val's left. "There's an anthill there."

Val looked down at his left foot to see that it was in the middle of a large mound that was now gushing ants. "Shit!" he said as he jumped to his feet, scattering the letter and picture in the wind while stomping his foot and brushing at his shin with his left hand.

"Don't use your hand—you might get bit," the man said. "Here—use this." He got up from his chair and dumped his canteen on Val's boot, washing the ants off.

"Thanks. I needed to change my socks anyway," Val said as they rushed around to gather his letter.

The man collected a page of the letter and picked up the picture. "Wow—she's gorgeous," he said when he looked at it. "I can now see why you didn't notice the ants. You're a lucky man. Is she your wife or girlfriend?" The man paused before adding, "Your single sister or cousin, maybe?"

"She's my fiancée," Val said, smiling, as the man handed him his letter and picture.

"Dammit! Well it was worth a shot. She's absolutely beautiful. Hold on to that one. Say, what's your name?" the man asked, holding out his hand to shake.

"Captain Valentine Jordan. You can call me Val," Val said as he shook the man's hand.

"I've heard of you—and tales of your beautiful gal there. You're the guy who dodged the SAM a couple nights ago."

"Yeah. How'd you know?"

"I work in HQ. I'm the intelligence officer—Captain Paul Overstreet?" Overstreet looked deep into Val's eyes, as if waiting for a particular response.

"Yes, Captain?" Val said, not sure what the intelligence officer was expecting.

"Waiting for the usual jokes about intelligence, Val," the captain said with a grin.

"Oh. Well considering how helpful your intel about the ants was, Captain, I didn't want to insult you with a joke."

Overstreet laughed. "Good one," he said as he turned and started to walk off.

"Do you keep a file of jokes?" Val asked, trying for a little sarcasm.

Overstreet turned back around to Val with a stone cold look on his face and replied, "Actually, yes we do." Then with a smirk he turned again and went on his way.

"And those guys wonder why they're never invited to parties," Val muttered as he watched Overstreet disappear. He then headed toward the Cannery to rejoin Nate.

§ § § § §

The day quickly gave way to night, and it wasn't long before Val and Nate found themselves helping Chappie and Papa with the briefing for that night's mission. The target once again seemed rather trivial—a wooden bridge and a couple of huts thirty miles north of Linh Thu. SAMs were considered to be the primary threat to the flight again, so Papa would spread out his flight in looser formation this time. Although SAMs were certainly something to be feared, AA weapons still presented a greater danger to aircraft and accounted for more actual kills.

At some targets, the ack-ack was so thick it was amazing to the flight crews that they got through without being hit. This was the age of supersonic jets, and the leadership in Washington was flabbergasted at the numbers of aircraft still being shot down by old-fashioned flak. The technique employed by the North Vietnamese was old fashioned, but extremely successful. They simply located the enemy aircraft and figured out what the target was. Then they filled the space between the two with a curtain of exploding metal. The laws of probability dictated that the aircraft would more likely take a hit than not. When the guns were guided by radar, their chances of success increased, no matter the weather or time of day. For all its horrors, anti-aircraft did have a bright side—literally. When it came up at night in steady fountains of light, it was easily seen and was actually beautiful, though no aviator would dare admit it while it was being deployed at them.

VMFA-2 attacked and destroyed the target with relative ease and all flight crews were surprised once again that they met almost no resistance. However, the RTB with Val and Nate hadn't been forgotten, and Papa made it a point to get his squadron to the cover of the ridges as quickly as possible, which he'd now do on every mission. The men breathed a sigh of relief as they closed to within twenty DME of Linh Thu, and the air was clear enough that the men could actually see the base until the lights were shut off after the helicopter on frequency was touching down on the northwest ramp. The flight of six flew a very loose formation with Notso and Speedy at Dash 6, where Val and Nate would usually be. The air was very still and everything was calm, including the flight crews, who were looking forward to an early night. As the flight passed twenty klicks, each man relaxed even more because they were basically out of range of the SAMs, and their low altitude made them too difficult to track anyway.

Each man was already thinking beyond the landing to the pub and a drink in his hand. Notso was looking over to his left at his wingman when he caught a very brief glimpse of a streak of light just underneath that was almost instantaneously followed by a thunderous boom and a brilliant flash that whited out his entire field of vision. The rest of the flight looked over to see flaming wreckage plummeting toward the ground and a black, empty space in the formation. Notso's wingman was gone—a jet completely destroyed in a split second. The rest of the flight was still looking to their right and saw another streak heading straight for the Notso's tail.

"Break hard left now, Notso!" Papa ordered.

Notso shoved the stick left and pulled hard aft to force his jet into a tight turn. The streak of light swerved and narrowly missed his tail, then disappeared into the blackness of night. Notso was still in the turn, feeling the g-forces pressing his body. When he turned his head to look at his instruments to check his attitude, they weren't there! He scanned in every direction, but couldn't find them. He could feel the jet going into a tighter turn and could hear the energy being built up as the aircraft picked up speed, but he couldn't verify what his attitude was now. "What the hell's going on?" he yelled as he fumbled around until his fingers felt the panel lights switch and cranked it up full. But it was no use—he still couldn't see his instruments. He grabbed the flashlight on his chest, clicked it on, and aimed it at the panel, but still nothing. He flipped up his visor and massaged his eyes, then reopened them—and that's when it registered. His view was the same whether his eyes were open or closed. He wiggled his fingers in front of his face but saw nothing. He was blind, probably from the brilliant explosion. He could hear Papa and other voices calling out, and could hear Chappie making the mayday call back to Linh Thu DASC, known to the flyers as "Panama."

"Smith, James—Dash 1. Do you copy?"

"Mayday-Mayday-Mayday. Panama this is Jackrabbit 2. Need immediate assistance. Send a rescue flight to the Linh Thu zero-two-zero for one-niner, over."

Among the other noises and voices, Notso heard Speedy chime in. "What's going on up there, Notso? You okay? Sounds like we're losing altitude and picking up a lot of speed."

"I can't see. That explosion must have blinded me. Can you see anything?"

"That's a negative. I've got bat vision too." Uncertainty seeped into Speedy's voice and mind as he realized how grave their situation was. They were flying over enemy territory at night and couldn't see—and therefore were unable to control their aircraft.

Notso keyed up to declare a state of urgency. "Pan-pan. Pan-pan. Break for emergency. This is Dash 6. My RIO and I were blinded by the explosion, request assistance."

The chatter fell silent for a second, then picked back up again as Papa said, "Dash 4, get on Dash 6's wing and help them out. In fact, you two take lead and RTB immediately."

"Aye, sir," Dash 4 responded as he looked to his right, then left, but didn't see Notso's jet. "You got Dash 6, Colby?" he asked his RIO, who looked outside into the black.

After seeing nothing, Colby went to his scope, where he picked up their echo. "Tally ho. They're at eight-o'clock low and descending fast"

"Roger." Dash 4 turned left and began a dive, but still couldn't see anything.

"Goddamnit! Someone talk to me and let me know what's happening!" Notso pleaded over frequency as he felt even greater g-forces push him harder and harder against his seat, signaling his turn was getting tighter.

"They're twelve o'clock and a half mile," Dash 4's RIO called out.

"No joy," Dash 4 replied to his RIO, then keyed up, "Dash 6, turn on your position lights, I still can't see you, but I'm on my way. I'm only a half mile away."

"Roger," Notso said under the strain of the g-forces as he blindly fumbled for the switch. The training on cockpit familiarity while blindfolded, which he once considered a nuisance, was paying off in a big way now as his hand, heavy and hard to move under the pressure of gravity, finally found the switch and flipped it on.

Dash 4 looked up to see his fellow aviators just ahead and to his right in a steep left graveyard spiral. "I have you in sight now, Dash 6. Relax. Move the stick steadily back to the right and get your wings level." When he saw Notso's jet rolling back right, he tried to anticipate when to tell him to stop. "Stop. You are wings level."

"Johnson—check altitude, we're getting close," Dash 4's RIO told him.

"I know. One problem at time, Bud." He glanced at his altimeter to see it was at fifteen hundred AGL. "Okay, Dash 6—gently pull aft on your stick. We need some altitude. I'm below and to your right, so relax." As Notso began a steady climb, Dash 4 chuckled to ease the minds of the blind aviators. "Hellfire, Notso. You turned enough revolutions that we're actually lined up perfectly with runway one-three. We're about fifteen miles out. Just try to relax. I'm sure your vision will return shortly." Dash 4 continued until both jets were about four thousand feet AGL. "All right, Dash 6—let's level out. That's good. We're niner miles out at angels four. How's your vision?"

Notso's vision was a black tunnel that was slowly opening up until finally he could see the instruments at full intensity. He reached over and turned them down to normal level and turned his flashlight off. His vision was filling up rapidly and registering the familiar view of his cockpit. "My vision's back now. Thanks, Dash 4. How's yours, Speedy?"

"It's back. Thanks."

"No problem, fellas. That's what we're all here for, to help each other out," Dash 4 said as he led the overhead break into Linh Thu for runway 13.

While Notso was having his problems, Papa was still trying in vain to contact the crew of Dash 5. Their jet was nothing more than burning wreckage rapidly twisting in a tight spiral toward the jungle below it.

"Smith. James. Do you copy? Dash 1—over," Papa said again and again. He was hoping that they'd somehow miraculously ejected, but he knew that they were dead. He made a wide sweep around the wreckage as it fell, and he could see that the cockpit was crushed and the empennage and radome were actually bent into where the crew would sit. Papa saw that he was getting close to the ground so he pulled up and watched helplessly as the wreckage fell away and exploded upon impact. He choked back the lump in his throat as and a tight feeling now began to squeeze his chest.

He heard Chappie still continuing his efforts to coordinate launching a rescue flight, so he keyed up. "Panama, Jackrabbit 1."

"Jackrabbit 1, Panama."

"Cancel the rescue flight."

"They're just lifting off now."

Papa repeated more sternly, "Panama—cancel the rescue!" It was clear that Papa was holding back tears. He'd never lost a single flyer in any squadron he'd ever commanded.

"Wilco, Jackrabbit 1." The controller realized there'd only be one reason a rescue flight would be cancelled.

The rest of the flight landed in silence without incident. Val and Nate had already heard what happened and were waiting in the Cannery for debrief. In the silence of an empty room, Val pulled out the chart he carried in his thigh pocket during a flight and marked the position and altitude that Dash 5 reportedly took the hit. As the Cannery slowly filled up with members of the flight, a thick cloud of depression hung heavily over everyone as each man now realized how swiftly and without warning they could lose one of their own. The debrief went by slowly with the look of defeat on the face of each man. Even though the sortie had successfully destroyed its target, VMFA-2 had lost two brothers in arms. Although Val and Nate had not been in the skies with their squadron, they felt the loss just as deeply as those who had been there when it happened.

After official debrief business had been completed, Papa wanted to discuss what had happened to Smith and James, even though it was a painful subject. "Gents, this is especially tough for me. I've lost fellow aviators in WWII and in Korea, and it's never easy, but I've never lost any of the men I commanded before." Papa was choking back tears with a shaky voice. "We need to try to piece together what just happened out there. Now, did anyone see anything?"

Notso slowly raised his hand, not wanting to answer, but knowing it was best that he did. "Yes, sir."

"Go ahead, Captain."

"Well sir, just before their jet exploded, I saw a faint streak of light just under the tail, close to the engines."

"I saw it, too, sir," Speedy chimed in.

"Yep—that's what I saw going for your jet, too," Papa replied.

"There was no audible warning, sir. No enemy missile siren—nothing to let us know any of us were being tracked," Chappie added.

"I noticed that as well." Papa looked around the room. "Anyone heard anything or got any theories?" After a few moments with no response, he knew his men didn't want to think about it anymore for a while, so he finished up. "All right, gents—try to shake it off for the moment. Go to the pub and we'll toast those fine young Marines. We'll have services for them sometime tomorrow after I speak with Commander Yeary."

The men slowly filed out of the Cannery in total silence with their heads hanging low. Val and Nate followed as the men headed for their hooches and then to the pub.

Papa walked slowly out of the Cannery about twenty minutes after the men left and headed toward the pub. As he walked, he held a "thousand-meter stare" into the silent blackness of the night. He then looked toward the heavens and took in the brilliant formations of stars, much brighter than he could ever remember back home. For a few moments he was transported back to his childhood, when he used to star-gaze from his boat while fishing on the bayous. The cosmos had always intrigued him—they'd even saved his life one cloudy, moonless night when he was a teenager, when he'd slipped and fallen into the bayou while trying to keep a lantern from falling overboard. His pockets, filled with weights for his fishing lines, pulled him deep into the water. The water and the sky were both black, so he was disoriented and couldn't tell which way was up. With his lungs burning for air, he still couldn't see or feel the bubbles he released, and no matter which way he swam, there was only water. Despite pulling off the jacket, he was near the point where his body would force him to take a breath, and he still had no idea where the surface was. He was about to give up hope when the clouds parted enough to reveal a single star that was visible even at his depth under the water. He immediately swam toward the star and expelled his last breath at the surface. As he plopped himself onto his boat, he heaved and vomited, then turned and looked skyward toward beacon that was his savior—the star at the left shoulder of the great hunter, Orion. The next day he went to the library to look up the star. He found out it was a red supergiant named Betelgeuse, one of the largest known stars. Later, when he was a young Marine aviator shipping off to the South Pacific to fight the Japanese, he got the name tattooed on his right arm after a night of heavy drinking before a morning deployment. He also named whatever aircraft he happened to be flying at the time after the star, believing it would not only give him the same protective karma he'd had when he was thirteen, but that it would also extend to everyone in his squadron. It seemed to have worked for the longest time, because even though his fellow Marines' planes might have taken hits, they always seemed to make it home. He even believed Val and Nate's close call the other night, was covered.

Now things were upside-down. His men were flying home one moment, and the next they were in a ball of twisted flaming metal spiraling toward earth—all without warning. They were supposed to be in the clear—only nineteen klicks and six thousand feet from home. What had happened? What caused them to crash? Did those streaks of light have anything to do with it? If they did, what were they? They were swirling in his mind until Chappie's voice broke through. "Papa? You all right, sir? We need you to join us for a toast."

Papa's gaze dropped to the door of the pub as he said, "Yeah. Yeah—I'm coming."

§ § § § §

The pub was filled with the noisy chatter of men telling stories about Smith and James, and several toasts were made about what fine young Marines and flyers they were. The drinking went on later into the morning than usual, but slowly people filed out until at last it was just Papa sitting alone at his table with his thousand-meter stare. He finished off the bottle of whiskey he'd been drinking and gazed at his watch. When his eyes focused, he saw that it was 0230. He stumbled to his feet, walked to the west wall of the pub, and flipped all the light switches, which turned off all but the lights near the entrance. Then he went back to his table, grabbed the empty bottle, and staggered toward the GI can against the wall behind the bar. Above it was a large picture of the members of VMFA-2 taken shortly before they'd shipped out to Vietnam. He focused on the smiling faces of Smith and James on left side of the second row, and it stirred up all the emotions he'd managed to suppress for a while.

"Goddamnit!" he swore as he slammed the bottle into the trash can, shattering it as it hit the bottom. "I feel like I just lost my sons." He buried his face into his hands and looked back up at the picture. "You boys did not die in vain. We'll get to the bottom of this soon—I promise. We owe you fellas at least that."

Papa took one last look at the picture, then stumbled to the door. He turned off the last row of lights, shut the door, and stepped into the thick night air and made his way back to his hooch. Along the way he made the quiet observation that at least the enemy did not add insult to injury by attacking the base tonight—at least not yet.

§ § § § § §

The next morning was grim as the base chaplain, Commander Edward S. Yeary, held services for Smith and James. It was difficult to create an aura of reverence as the padre had to compete against aircraft noise, but it was still effective under the circumstances. The men, wearing looks of mourning and relief, hoped there'd never have to be services for them. Val and Nate felt they owed it to the squadron by rejoining their fellow Marines in the air. After the services, they found Big John and asked him about their jet. He told them he'd get back to them by the afternoon.

Later that day, Papa was once again poring over paperwork when several trucks pulled up and stopped in front of his office. Lieutenant Davis hopped out of the first truck and walked into Papa's office without knocking, restless and full of energy as always.

"Sir, if you're ready for some good news, I'm happy to inform you that I got the supplies we need from the first new supplier I mentioned yesterday, and I got some from the second, which was harder to find, but they had more stuff and were a little cheaper."

"Good—great news." Papa sighed deeply as he sealed the envelopes going to the families of Smith and James, each containing a personal letter from their CO to console them on their loss. Papa then looked up at the lieutenant and said, "Get it done, Lieutenant."

"Aye sir!" The young officer snapped back as he hopped back into the first truck and the caravan followed him to his storage depot.

§ § § § § §

Val rushed down to the flight line full of hope when he got the news that Big John wanted to see him, especially since the major told him to bring his helmet and G-harness.

Val turned the corner around the last barricade of the ramp to see jet 069—his jet—on the ramp with both canopies open in a clean configuration with a start-cart hooked up to it. Val was about to ask one of the linemen what was going on when Big John came around from behind the jet wearing a helmet and G-harness himself. "She's ready, son. Let's take her out for a run-up and a test flight." Big John smiled as he began to climb the ladder into the RIO's cockpit.

"I need to run something by you first, sir."

"And that is?"

"First, where'd they get a helmet big enough to fit you—and second, how the hell are you gonna fit in the RIO's cockpit? I'm cramped back there, and I'm a small guy."

Big John laughed as he ascended the ladder. "I think they just glued two helmets together. I'll just suck in my breath and squeeze in."

Val laughed. "Hope we can get you back out," he said as he strapped himself in and set the ICS to "hot mike."

As Val's jet fired up again, a wave of excitement swept through him. He was impressed by how fast they'd repaired his jet, especially since it was the very complex hydraulic system that had been so severely damaged. Val called up ground control and was directed to the run-up area of runway 13 to perform all checks before trying to get airborne. A truck with a couple of other mechanics followed them out.

Once they got there, Big John had Val move the flight controls while the mechanics checked for leaks. Val also watched his instruments for any signs of trouble, and tested the brakes. He cycled the tailhook while on the ground, and would have to try the landing gear once airborne. After the ground checks were completed without a hitch, it was time to test the jet airborne. Big John loved doing maintenance flights—it was the closest he'd get to flying tactical jets since he was cheated out of an RIO slot years ago. Besides, he liked flying with enthusiastic pilots like Val.

Val taxied his jet into position on runway 13 and looked at Big John, who was filling up every inch of space in the cramped rear cockpit. "You ready, sir?"

"Always," Big John replied with a smile.

"We'll do the flight control and gear checks at high altitude, then return for a couple of trips in the pattern before we bring her to the ramp to be signed back off," Val said.

"Sounds good to me. Just give me a good military take off—that's all I ask. " Big John loved the thrill of a takeoff in a tactical jet.

"Bunny 1, Linh Thu Tower, runway one-three cleared for takeoff," the control tower informed them.

"Bunny 1's rolling," Val replied as he firmly pressed the brakes with all his strength and shoved the throttles to their full stops. When the brakes could barely hold back the thrust, he released them and the jet shot forward like a rodeo bull busting from the gate. In this clean configuration, the jet accelerated at a tremendous rate. At VR, Val gently pulled aft on the stick and the jet leaped off the ground. He then pushed forward on the stick and kept the jet in ground effect, flying along while still accelerating only a half wingspan above the deck. He then cleaned up his bird by sucking up the gear and flaps and roaring over the runway, rapidly closing on the numbers 1–3 at the end. When he was over the numbers, he pulled back hard on the stick and the jet pitched up into a near vertical climb, and the ground fell away as the jet rocketed skyward. Big John shouted his approval as the ground disappeared and was looking into the vast blue that was the sky. Val leveled out at sixteen thousand feet and began to go through a series of gentle Dutch rolls, turns, climbs, descents, and other easy maneuvers.

Big John then said something that made Val beam. "All right—we've done the test maneuvers, so enough of the sissy shit. Show me what you can do."

"I was wondering when you'd ask, sir," Val replied as he began an aerobatic series. He was happy to be throttling up in his jet again. He could only go so long without flying before feeling withdrawal symptoms. He performed breaks, loops, rolls, Immelmanns, Cubans, and other maneuvers he'd use in combat. Big John loved it all. "It's too bad our jets are not like the Air Force's, with stick and throttles back there for you, sir, because I'd gladly let you fly her."

"I know you would, Kiddo. Thanks. I enjoy that at least I can go along for the ride every now and then. Anyway, it's time to RTB. We'll do a touch and go or two. followed by one low approach and start it all off with the overhead."

"Let's do it." After Val performed the final maneuvers, he pulled up and chopped the throttles, then landed and taxied into his spot behind the barricades. As the engines spooled down, he looked outside and saw Nate standing beside the linemen.

When it was silent on the ramp, Nate approached the jet under Val's cockpit. "We gonna be good to go?" he asked as Val started to climb down the ladder.

"That's affirm. Big John's gonna sign our jet off when he gets back to his office."

"Where *is* Big John?"

Val pointed toward the rear cockpit as the hulk that was Big John stepped onto the ladder. He then climbed down and walked toward the young aviators. "What is it, son?" he asked Nate after noticing his expression of bewilderment.

"How the hell'd you fit in there, sir?" Nate asked.

"He holds his breath," Val said with a smirk.

"Good to know you're listening." Big John smiled as he handed a lineman his huge helmet. Then he looked at Nate and said before he could ask, "They glued two helmets together."

§ § § § §

The preflight briefing came and went, and Val and Nate were glad to be strapping back into their gear for a sortie with the rest of the squadron. To an aviator, even a short time on the ground seems like forever. Tonight's mission was considered more dangerous than any the squadron had flown in months. They were to fly farther north than on previous missions, to the very outskirts of Hanoi, but the target again seemed rather meaningless—a suspected supply depot. It wasn't long before they were again blasting off into the night skies over North Vietnam, with Val and Nate in their usual cleanup position.

The flight to the target area was surprisingly uneventful, considering that the squadron was flying over known SAM and AA sites. Papa finally broke the silence prior to TOT (time over target) when he said, "Let's green 'em up, fellas."

As soon as he unkeyed, the skies erupted with AA. Exploding flak was everywhere, forcing the aviators to pull down their dark visors. Papa knew his men were probably nervous or anxious, so he attempted to calm them over frequency. "Just fly as you normally do, gents, and we'll all be fine. We're at TOT, so let's begin our runs. Eight second intervals, mirror pullouts unless you absolutely have to do something different to avoid a hit. Rooster Flight's cleared hot."

Papa initiated the runs, and each jet followed eight seconds in trail, pulling out in the opposite direction the previous jet broke. Val was sweating on this flight as some of the explosions seemed to go off just outside his canopy. Nate announced "Roll in" when the time had passed and Val found himself doing the very unnatural act of diving his jet into the face of danger.

The AA gunners were equipped with radar, had figured out the pullout pattern, and knew Val was the last jet. They were disappointed that the other nine enemy jets had apparently escaped unscathed, so all guns were directed on Val as he dove steeply toward the target.

Val and Nate were simultaneously concentrating on the instruments, the target, and the intensifying curtains of flak. For every tracer there were eight to ten invisible rounds, and none of the shrapnel from flak was visible, even though the explosions were. It was the scariest fireworks show they'd ever experienced, but they stayed on target, even though they knew their run would probably have little effect on the mission's outcome. The black voids of the night sky were lit up in all directions by flak and tracers, and at times the light from the ordnance was bright enough to wash out the instrument panel's glow. The jet was buffeting severely in the eddies of disturbed and turbulent air. Nate began to call out altitudes as he fixated on the radar altimeter, which momentarily lowered his stress level because he didn't have to look outside.

About to hundred feet above the release altitude, a massive explosion about a hundred meters directly ahead rocked the jet, and luckily Val was looking under the center of the explosion, or else he might have been blinded just as Notso was the previous night. Both aviators heard flying metal ricochet off the canopy as Val fiercely fought to keep the jet on its desired glide path.

"Goddamn that was close. I think they almost got our position nailed," Val said as he pickled off his load and began to break to the right. As soon as he finished speaking, two more explosions barely missed them, and the tracers were noticeably closer.

"I think they do have us," Nate said as explosions rattled his body. "Reverse your turn!"

"Roger," Val said. Just as he broke back to the left, an explosion filled the empty space where they would have been. "Holy shit! How long before they adjust to us now?"

"Not long. I'm tryin' to watch outside."

"I'm gonna do some erratic maneuvering to try to keep 'em guessing."

"You don't have to ask for my okay."

The flak and tracers followed them until they joined up with the rest of the flight. When they fell in on Notso's right wing, the frequency was jammed with chatter between Papa and Dash 7, who'd apparently suffered some AA damage.

"Yes sir. We can clearly see a large hole in our right wing," Dash 7's pilot said.

"Any problems with hydraulics, flight controls, et cetera?" Papa asked, not wanting any of his men to go through what Val and Nate had a few nights ago.

"No, sir. Needles are steady and flight controls seem to be functioning normally."

"Good." Papa paused, then said, "All right, Rooster Flight—good job, but we better expect some SAMs, so keep your eyes peeled. RIOs, keep your radars scanning."

Rooster flight closed within twenty-four miles of Linh Thu before the first warning sounded that they were being tracked by a SAM site. Papa ordered the flight to dive for the cover of the ridges that were coming up. During the descent, the audible warning of a missile launch filled every man's helmet. Nate looked outside to see the flare-ups of two SA-2s lifting off to his seven o'clock.

"Tally-ho, Rooster Flight! A pair of SA-2s lifting off at seven o'clock," Nate announced over frequency.

All eyes went to their seven o'clocks as the pilots kept their jets in rapid descent. The missiles started to arch toward the flight, but just before Papa keyed up, they made a sudden right climbing turn away from them. They all followed them with their eyes as long as they could keep them in sight. Within a couple of minutes, they saw two large explosions high above them, with flaming debris plummeting toward earth from all directions. Apparently the missiles had self-destructed, and each man thought it weird that they'd suddenly changed directions when they seemed to have a lock on their flight.

Val saw that the DME showed fourteen miles and breathed a sigh of relief as he leveled off with his flight behind the ridges, with Linh Thu in sight. Papa told each crew to check their jets for flak damage once they were on the ramp. When they approached eleven klicks, a small flash appeared directly ahead of Dash 6, who didn't see it for a few seconds. When he did notice it, he saw that it was closing on him at an incredible rate.

Adrenaline and fear coursed through his veins as he stared at it. "Papa! That thing's back!" Dash 6's pilot called as he broke over the top of Dash 7 on his right wing. All heads swiveled toward Dash 6 to see the thing streak toward him, then suddenly turn right and slam into Dash 7, which exploded into a massive fireball.

It seemed as every member of the flight said, "Shit!" as they loosened up their formation. Dash 7 was nothing but flames burning in the jungle below, and once again it happened so fast that the crew had no time to react and eject.

"Goddamnit—not again!" Papa said in a rage. He looked up to see another streak whiz by him, then disappear into the massive flames that used to be Dash 7. "What the fuck?!"

"I saw it too, Papa," Chappie said, "but I don't have a clue either."

Val just happened to look at his DME, altimeter, and TACAN (tactical air navigation system). He grabbed his chart from the pouch on his thigh and marked the position, along with "Angels 9–5"—nine thousand five hundred feet MSL.

Papa was feeling helpless and devastated for the second night in a row at the loss of two more of his Marines—but even more than that, he was feeling fanatical fury.

"Goddamnit! Get on the deck, Rooster Flight! We'll do low-altitude breaks to bleed off speed to land!"

Rooster Flight approached the field low and fast, flying the length of runway 13 in the landing configuration, then performing a low-level, high-g left break at the approach end of runway 31. The break would slow the jet down with engines at idle and would allow the entire flight to land quicker than doing straight-in approaches. Once on the ground, the flight quickly taxied into their barricades and shut down, and the crews sprinted to trucks that took them to the Cannery for debrief. All personnel left their gear on, knowing Papa wouldn't be in very good humor.

The CO walked into the Cannery also still in his gear, pushing aside anything that was in his way. When he turned toward his squadron, the men could see his eyes were bloodshot with rage. He grabbed the file that contained the mission outlines and threw to the wall on the opposite side of the room. "Fuck the debrief right now, gents! We've got more important matters on our hands, like how we can land safely after a sortie. We lost Jones and Colby tonight—two more of our brother. This is unacceptable!" Papa simmered down a bit. "Any suggestions or observations?"

Val tentatively raised his hand.

"Go ahead, Jordan," Papa said.

"Yes, sir. I marked the location and altitude of tonight's, ah, incident, and I have the location and altitude of yesterday's as well." Val held up his map and continued: "If I may, I suggest that we don't fly directly back to Linh Thu when we RTB after a sortie. We should give the area I marked in red a wide berth and approach from a different direction. That may buy us at least a few nights without an incident." Val passed the chart to Papa and added, "If I may add another observation, sir, I noticed, as I guess everyone else did, that those SA-2s suddenly switched off us and self-destructed. It might suggest that there's some kind of communication between the SAM sites and this new weapon."

Everyone else nodded. Papa put Val's chart on the table in front of him and was impressed that Val had had the presence of mind to mark the exact position of the attacks. Papa studied the chart for a bit and then spoke. "I agree. Until we can resolve this issue, all aircraft on approach to Linh Thu from the north should swing out wide to the east or west and enter on the downwinds or use other runways if the winds are light, which they usually are. I'll have a copy of these positions for you tomorrow. I'll go with the captain's circle on his chart as zone to stay out of. We'll call 'Red Zone One.' We'll let all units in all branches know about it so they can steer clear as well." Papa paused with sigh as he looked over his squadron. They were all obviously trying to mask their pain. "Get out of your gear and head to the pub, gents. We gotta toast two fine Marines. Once again, I'll have Commander Yeary hold services tomorrow. I'll be down there in about half an hour; I have to talk to someone first."

The men slowly filed out of the Cannery and toward the ready room to get out of their gear, leaving only Papa and Chappie behind. Chappie gave Papa a look of concern. "Who're you gonna talk to, sir?"

"Someone who I think knows a lot more about this than he's admitting to."

Chappie knew immediately who Papa was referring to, but he wasn't sure if that man really knew anything. "What makes you think he'll tell you anything that we don't already know?"

"He'll talk to me. I can be very persuasive when I want to be."

"I'll back you to our graves, sir. If you need any help, let me know. I'd like to chat with him myself."

"Never doubted you, Chappie. Come along if you like."

Chappie and Papa changed out of their gear and headed for their offices, and as they were leaving they happened to see the very person they were looking for walking down the street toward the pub. Papa and Chappie picked up their pace and caught up to him, who looked over his shoulder to see who was behind him on the dimly lit street.

When Captain Overstreet saw Papa and Chappie closing in on him, he stopped and turned around. "Good evening, gentlemen," he said with a salute, which was discouraged at Linh Thu because it was so far into enemy territory, under the watchful eye of enemy snipers and artillery men.

"What could possibly be good about this evening, Captain? And get your hand down—you know better than that!" Papa scolded the intelligence officer.

"Well, sir—"

"You know what happened again tonight. Maybe you can tell me why." Overstreet was about to speak, but Papa abruptly cut him off and herded him on down the dark street, passing behind a building blanketed by shadow.

Finally Overstreet said, "Yes, sir—I know what happened, but I...I don't know why." Overstreet's response faded, which displeased Papa greatly, making him feel the captain wasn't being totally forthright. Papa reached around and violently jerked the young officer right off his feet and slammed him into the wall of the darkened building, pinning him firmly against the wall with his feet almost six inches off the ground. Major Chapman stood in silence behind Papa, staring into the startled captain's eyes.

"Goddamnit, Overstreet! What the fuck is going on? I mean really going on?"

Even in the darkness, the young officer could see the hurt and rage in both Papa and Chappie's eyes. He trembled in fear as Papa dug his knuckles deeper into his rib cage, sending sharp pain through his upper torso that was worse when he drew in a breath. "I honestly don't know, sir!" he wheezed. "All I do know is that this has caught the attention of the DIA, and they're dispatching a Marine Force Recon team to both sites tomorrow at 0500. I swear—that's all I know!"

"I bet you don't know any more, you little weasel! I *will* know what the recon team finds out. If they can't fix the problem, I guarantee you my squadron will. We'll have our own little special op."

"Sir, you've only lost two aircraft. It's hardly a problem yet."

That was the worst thing Overstreet could have said to Papa, whose just about lost control when the words reached his ears. Slamming the captain even harder into the wall and driving his knuckles even deeper when the captain's body, he replied, "One aircraft is too many, you wormy little jackass! Maybe you'd like to write their next of kin the letter—and by all means, tell them it wasn't a problem that their sons died. Now you'd better get on this like a duck on a June bug and report to me daily. This will be your number-one priority. I don't give a damn what other shit you have to do! Comprende?"

Even though he had no intention of following through, the young captain agreed. "Yes, sir. I'll be on it ASAP." However, he knew that if he didn't show Papa or Chappie some evidence that he was putting time into Papa's "request," he'd face dire consequences. He didn't want to be on Papa's bad side, and he knew the CO had some political pull up the chain of command.

Papa eased the captain to the ground, but kept his grip on his chest as he gave one last warning, "If I find out you've been hiding something from us, you won't have to worry about just me. I have two squadrons of Marines who'll eat you alive!" Papa drove his knuckles into the captain one final time, doubling him over, then he and Chappie walked off toward the pub to toast fallen Marines for the second night in a row.

§ § § § § §

Papa left the pub with everyone else around 0130. He walked to his hooch and flopped into his rack, knowing he'd have a very busy day again tomorrow. He thought of the men under his command as family, and he'd give his life to save theirs. He knew the only way to save lives was to find out what these streaks of light were—and more importantly, how to detect and counter them. Thoughts usually filled his mind every night when he hit the sack, so it always took a long time to doze off. He was just about to slip into sleep when an all-too-familiar whistling sound reached his ears. A massive explosion shook him out of his rack, followed by several more in quick succession.

"Goddamnit—not tonight!" he shouted into the darkness as he reached for his rifle and war belt. The explosions continued for fifteen minutes, but he crawled out of his hooch after the explosions ceased and it was quiet for a few minutes. He stood when he was sure the attack was over and walked out into the street to survey the damage, but it was hard to tell at night, especially when all the lights on base were out. Flames were flickering in all directions, but fire crews had most of them extinguished. Papa noticed the absence of gunfire on this particular attack, which meant the enemy had not rushed the perimeter or attempted to enter the base. After he was sure everything was under control, he went back to his hooch and again flopped onto his rack. As he set his rifle and war belt back in their locks, he muttered, "I get to deal with this shit tomorrow! Whoopee!"

§ § § § §

Papa got the full damage report when he went to the chow hall for breakfast. The control tower had slight damage from a hit, but was already repaired. Sick bay took a direct hit, but no one was injured and the ceiling was being fixed. The northwest ramp had some new small impact craters now that were being fixed. The services for Jones and Colby were even more grim than the ones for Smith and James, with the noise of repair work in the background making it almost impossible to hear.

Papa had barely caught up on paperwork and finished letters to the families of Jones and Colby when he got word he was needed at supply for another crisis. As he was walking to the depot, he passed a young lieutenant who'd just been assigned to Linh Thu. He asked the young officer as they walked along the road, "Wanna trade jobs? Mine sucks."

"No sir," the lieutenant replied as he headed off in another direction.

"Someday I'm gonna find some poor sucker who's stupid or crazy enough to take me up on my offer." Papa chuckled as he walked into the main bay of the supply depot to find several men perched on large crates, all partially open.

Lieutenant Davis looked up and said, "Oh good—you're here, sir. We have a problem."

Papa sighed and asked, "What's the problem, son?"

Davis reached into one of the crates and pulled out a large, black lacy bra. "I'm positive this isn't what I ordered, sir."

"Well I sure hope not, unless you got the women to go along with these things in these boxes, too," Papa said with a smirk.

"'Fraid not, sir."

"Well, just take 'em back and get what you really needed."

"Well that's the problem, sir—we have a language barrier. The last interpreter's tour was up two days ago. The owner of the place speaks broken English at best. I know your new RIO speaks French, but unfortunately the owner doesn't, or refuses to speak French."

"Of course," Papa replied sarcastically. "Why should we expect something to work out for us? Well I'll check around. Maybe Commander Yeary knows someone who can help. I'll get back to you by 1730. If you don't hear from me by then, just come by my office. Right now just pack this stuff up and load it back on the trucks." Papa paused briefly, "Just one thing before you begin, Lieutenant."

"Yes, sir?" Davis asked.

"Let me have one of those bras. It has 'practical joke' written all over it!"

§ § § § § §

Half an hour later, Val found himself sitting in front of Papa's desk, with Papa thumbing through his fitness reports and other personal files. "You needed to talk to me about something, sir?" Val asked as he eyed the folders.

Papa looked up and gave Val an inquisitive look as he pointed to one of Val's files on the desk. "This says you're fluent in Vietnamese."

"Yes sir, I am." Val was very nonchalant in his answer, as if it were normal for an American to know how to speak an Asian language.

"Well, two things. Number one—when and where did you learn. Number two—why the hell wasn't I informed sooner?"

"Well sir, number one—when I was a teenager in Hawaii years ago, and number two—because no one ever asked."

"Son, I had two, uh, three things on my mind when I was a teenager many more years ago—pussy, playing football, and more pussy. So where would that leave you, son?"

Val smiled. "Well sir, my neighbor was Vietnamese, I played football and soccer, and I fucked her daughter every afternoon after school when her mother was at work."

"Really? Anyway, here's why I ask now." Papa held up the large bra the lieutenant had given him earlier.

Val gave a puzzled look at Papa holding the large undergarment. "You need me to help you pick up a local gal, sir?"

"No. Well…yes, actually, but we'll get to that later," Papa said. "Our supply officer is having a hard time communicating with his new supplier. We needed construction materials, but we got these instead." Papa set the bra back down on his desk. "So now your new job when you're not flying or on Alert-5 rotation is to be his interpreter. You start right now."

Val sighed and replied, "Only if you'll give me an honest answer to one question, sir."

"Which is…?"

Val picked up the bra and held it to his chest, then looked at Papa with a goofy smile and said, "Think this'd look good on me, sir?"

Papa laughed as he waved Val out. "I don't have to tell you where the door is, Jordan!"

4

AWESTRUCK

The trip to Dong Hoi was long and tiresome, made worse by the heat and the poorly constructed roads that were often crowded with pedestrians, bicyclists, and beasts of burden. The first thing that got to anyone when they arrived in Vietnam was the intense, relentless heat. The air was already thick and heavy with humidity, but the sun beat down without mercy, draining all the energy from an unacclimated person. Even the dark of night failed to help as the air remained motionless and dense, becoming musty and stale until a gentle breeze stirred it around.

Val was riding with the windows down, but because of the slow speed it only brought brief moments of relief. Despite all the discomforts of the trek into town, the ride was made somewhat bearable by the picturesque scenery and how it drastically changed along the relatively short seventy-five mile trip. The steep peaks and dense jungles of Linh Thu gave way to long stretches of flat, open rice paddies divided by thin lines of tall palms and eventually morphed into the lush delta of the Nhat Le River that emptied into the pristine South China Sea along the large fishing town of Dong Hoi. The lone sliver of muddy road that Val was on twisted along until it joined the more modern National Highway 1, which ran north-south along the entire country. The two-truck convoy then had to take a switchback down a narrow dirt and gravel street to the new supply store, which was in a relatively accessible part of town just within the western edge of the city limits. It was actually easier to get to than the previous supplier, and it was surprising that it hadn't been discovered earlier. Though the main bridge across the Nhat Le

River was destroyed, there were a couple other places to cross, but what amazed Val was the temporary bridge made of bamboo poles that had been erected. The bamboo bridge didn't look very convincing, but Lieutenant Davis smiled at Val as he drove across it with the large 6x6, the bamboo groaning under the weight all the while.

"Relax, sir," Davis said. "These bridges can handle a light armored vehicle. I heard OV-10 pilots saying how they saw small tanks and trucks crossing similar bridges made with even smaller diameter poles and not even thinking twice about it. The amazing thing is how quickly they can build one of these. We could bomb everyone in the entire country and they could have them all fixed in a matter of hours or days."

"That's great, Lieutenant, but I'm not worried about the bridge—I'm thinking about how long I'd be on the shitter with toxic diarrhea if this truck went into the drink and we wound up in that nasty water down there."

Davis chuckled. "Yeah—looks more like chocolate milk than water."

"I'm sure it won't build strong bones and teeth, Lieutenant," Val said with a smile.

When the trucks rolled back onto solid ground, they made another switchback and finally turned onto yet another narrow dirt street. As soon as the convoy turned onto the street, they were greeted by thick black smoke from burning buildings, people running around them screaming, and the noise of whistles and sirens. The street was so thick with pedestrian and bicycle traffic going in so many directions that the convoy had to come to a complete stop. After sitting motionless in the chaos for ten minutes, Davis ordered a couple of his Marines to walk down the street and see what was causing all the panic. Val, bored sitting in the sweltering cab of the truck, joined the two Marines in their investigation. As they walked along, people eyed them warily, and when they'd walked about a hundred meters from their convoy, the smoke cleared enough to reveal that the very store they'd been heading for was burning, almost completely destroyed by a bomb blast of some kind. The three Marines quickly went back to their trucks.

"Well, Lieutenant, looks like you can cross that supplier off your list," Val said as he climbed back into the cab.

"Why? What happened up there?"

"Looks like a bomb wiped it out."

"Shit! Well, I hope the other place is still intact. Hopefully they'll let us exchange some of this stuff for what we need. It's a little closer to base and seems to have resources this one didn't have."

"Why didn't you go to that one first, then?"

"It's kinda off the main drag. I stumbled on it by accident when I got lost."
They did an about-face and followed a maze of narrow, muddy streets. The

locals once again gave them curious stares as they drove by, not used to seeing such large trucks on their streets, where even cars were a rarity. The convoy continued on through several small alleys that were tight fits for the trucks until they at last turned onto a larger but still narrow dirt street that widened as it approached a large pale gray building with two words painted on a sign in large black letters: *Tong-Hop*. The building wasn't much to look at—peeling paint in places and vertical cracks in the walls from the roof to the foundation. It gave no hint of the thriving business it actually was.

"Here we are, sir." Lieutenant Davis smiled with anticipation. "Maybe we can get things straightened out now."

Val eyed the building doubtfully as he mentally translated *Tong-Hop*. He said to Davis with hesitation in his voice, "You came *here* for construction supplies, Lieutenant?"

"Yes, sir?" Davis replied cautiously.

"That might be the problem." Val pointed at the building. "See that sign, Lieutenant?"

"Yes, sir."

"Roughly translated, *Tong-Hop* means 'department store.' Back home we don't go to a department store for construction supplies and hardware," Val said.

Lieutenant Davis was quick reply as he said, "Sir, normally I'd agree with you, but this place had everything in their warehouse—and I do mean everything. I'm talking lumber to typing paper." But Val remained doubtful.

Lieutenant Davis walked toward the door and tried to reassure Val. "Just follow me, sir—you'll see what I mean."

Val followed the eager young lieutenant into a small receiving area where an attractive middle-aged woman met them before a curtain with a smile and a barely understandable "Hello" as she folded her hands and bowed her head slightly. Though the room was small, reverberating echoes of female voices beyond the curtain suggested a cavernous space. Val gave the woman a warm smile as he too folded his hands and bowed, saying, "*Xin chao. Co choe kong?*"—Hello, how are you?

The woman's face lit up with a welcoming smile, apparently impressed that an American knew her language. "*Khoe cam un*"—Fine, thank you.

Davis was amazed at how smoothly his fellow Marine spoke Vietnamese. Val said to the woman, "*Ten la gi* Captain Valentine Jordan, *toi co hen vo'i ong Tong Giam-doc*"—I am Captain Valentine Jordan. I have an appointment with the general manager. He thought he heard a male voice among the female chatter and wondered if it was the manager.

"*Ten toi la Nghia Mau Nguyen*"—My name is Nghia Mau Nguyen. She then patted her chest with her hand as she struggled to say in broken English, "I manager."

Val almost flushed with embarrassment, though he hid it well from Nghia Mau. He had to be careful not to insult anyone, especially someone who could help him live a little more comfortably while he was in Vietnam. He bowed his head and apologized a few times, but she shrugged it off and took both men to the other side of the small room, where they sat and discussed business while having tea. Val and Nghia Mau talked casually for a while before deciding they each had the other's confidence and shifting to business matters. Nghia Mau laughed heartily behind the hand covering her mouth when Val told her of the mix-up with the bras. He let her know that they wouldn't feel the least bit insulted if she laughed openly. Nghia Mau paused in the middle of her sentence when she heard a particular female voice called out from behind the curtain. Nghia Mau smiled at her guests as she bowed her head and stood up, saying "*Xin loi*"—Excuse me. She then slipped behind the curtain, leaving the Marines to look at each other.

Val continued to taking in his surroundings, looking around the room, hearing distant conversations that echoed from behind the curtain, but- still not really expecting much to change the drab vibes he still had about this place. Val looked over at Lieutenant Davis, who was also taking in his surroundings while sipping on his tea.

As Val took in his surroundings, Lieutenant Davis said, "You're still having your doubts about this place, aren't you, sir."

"To be honest, yeah, but I've been wrong before."

"You told the woman what we needed and the mix-up in the other store?" Davis asked.

"Yeah. Surprisingly she said they'd take the bras and cut us a deal on the cost of the stuff we need. But I have to see her partner too. Apparently they make the deals together." Val sighed. "I'm not a businessman, so I hope we don't end up getting shafted."

"Most of the people I've dealt with in the past have been very honest, sir. I've never had any problems with prices. Besides, you'll be negotiating over fractions of pennies."

Val heard the conversation in the background quiet down and heard footsteps approaching from behind the curtain. "Guess we're about to find out, Lieutenant."

Nghia Mau parted the curtains and walked back to her customers with a smile on her face. She sat back down, pointed at the tea, and asked with her best English, "You like?"

Both men smiled and nodded. The three continued sipping their tea while looking at each other in silence. It was obvious to all that they were studying each other, trying to guess what they were thinking. After a while the Marines, a bit uncomfortable with the silence, started to fidget, but Nghia Mau was calm as she started writing on a piece of paper. She looked up and noticed her customers were becoming impatient, so she turned back to the curtain and said loudly, "*May den du'o'c khnong?*"—Can you come in here now?

A voice replied, "*Tao se den ngay*"—I'll be there right away.

The Marines perked up and glanced toward the curtain. A couple of seconds later, soft footsteps could be heard, and two small feet were quickly visible beneath the curtain. But before the owner of the feet emerged, she stopped to speak to someone else. Finally the curtains parted, and when Val saw the woman, his heart seemed to stop for a moment and he felt a tingling shock course through his body. She was the most beautiful woman he'd ever laid eyes on, and as she bowed her head and smiled, he thought, *She's not just beautiful—she's heavenly.*

"*Ten toi Nga Nghin Do'i Nguyen*"—My name is Nga Nghin Do'i Nguyen. She spoke with a soothing, angelic voice as she motioned for Val to follow her behind the curtain.

For the first time in his life, a woman left Val speechless. All his life he'd heard about how beautiful women from other countries were. He'd never given such opinions as credible since he believed American women could hold their own with anyone. But here was a genuine enchantress, quite possibly a siren luring him to his death. Val didn't care—he sprang to his feet, still in his daze and knocked over the pot of tea on the table, spilling hot liquid all over his lap. Val didn't care—he just followed the angel he met. Nghia Mau wasn't upset by the spilled tea—she just smiled, as if she knew that Val was under a spell, because every man who came into her store and met Nga Nghin Do'i fell under the same spell. Her business partner and co-owner just happened to be the most beautiful woman on the planet.

The small reception area gave no hint of just how huge the warehouse on the other side of the curtains was. He was led to a small office, and Nga Nghin Do'i pointed to the seat across from her desk. Finally regaining control of the muscles required for speech, Val pointed at his chest and stammered, "Captain Valentine Jordan."

Nga Nghin Do'i smiled and nodded as she retrieved her adding machine and a notebook from the desk drawer.

Val kept staring at the beauty across from him as she began to write and bang away on an adding machine, then he mumbled under his breath, "I bet you can rip off any man any time you want with that smile. I always believed in angels—I just thought I'd have to die first to see one."

She stopped what she was doing, looked back at the American across from her, and drew up straight as she blushed, her smile covered by her hand. Val was suddenly struck with an embarrassing realization. "Hey—you speak English!"

"And you speak Vietnamese, Captain," she retorted.

"So why do I even need to be here if you can speak English?" Val said.

"Why? You not like my company?" she asked with a smile.

Val backpedaled. "Well, uh, no…it's just that—"

"I not always here, Captain, so it's better if you come all the time. I go often to see my uncle in Hanoi, but I fix everything today."

"Hanoi?" Val asked.

"Yes. He live there," Nga Nghin Do'i replied matter-of-factly and returned to her notebook. She then leaned out the door of her office and shouted into the warehouse, *"Bat dau ngay gio, lam on"*—Let's get going right now, please!

At once a dozen young women came out of another room and went to the docks to unload Val's trucks.

Val was startled when he saw such small women walking toward the docks to move the crates. "They don't have to do that. We have six men who can move those crates."

"It is no problem. It is their…*viec lam*, uh…"—she searched for the right word—"Job?" She looked at Val for his reaction. She was glad to have someone to practice her English with. She enjoyed learning other languages because it gave her confidence.

"Yes. *Viec lam*—job," Val replied as he looked around her office and noticed all the books and documents, mentally practicing his Vietnamese by trying to translate some of the titles he saw. Then his eyes settled on a poster that showed the northern and southern halves of Vietnam shaking hands, with a hammer and sickle crushing the American flag. In bold black letters were the words *"Chong MY cuu nuoc!"*—Resist America for national salvation! Val was now curious why he was getting supplies in a store that displayed this poster. "You said your uncle lives in Hanoi?"

"Yes." Nga Nghin Do'i looked up from her work and saw Val staring at the poster. "We try to keep everyone happy, Captain. We have poster of America helping Vietnam," she explained as she pointed with her pencil to a poster behind Val with a photograph of US servicemen feeding infants at some village.

Val relaxed for the moment, but he understandably felt he needed to be cautious. As Nga Nghin Do'i went back to her work, he continued to watch her, knowing she could take his mind off anything. He noticed small details about her, like how gracefully she carried herself, how delicately she wrote in her notebook, how her brow furrowed when she concentrated on her adding machine, and how she carefully tucked her long, straight black hair behind her ear whenever it fell over her eyes. He also noticed how glossy and smooth her brown skin was, but he knew never to compliment an Oriental woman on her dark skin because they took that as an insult. As he gazed at her in awe, he realized something: "Your name," he said. "It means 'eternally beautiful woman.'"

She stopped writing again as she mentally translated his English, looked up at him, then looked back to her work and blushed. She tucked her hair behind her ear, flashed a coy smile and replied, "You don't like?"

"Yes. Yes I do like it. I like it a lot," Val said earnestly. "I think your name describes you perfectly." Val paused, then continued: "Those words were destined to harmonize with a woman perfectly. That woman could be no one else but you." Val hoped he wasn't laying it on too thick, but he was so taken by her that he couldn't help himself.

She stopped writing once again and her smile grew larger. This time when she looked up, she stared deeply into his eyes, searching for his true intentions. She sensed Val was trembling on the inside, but she was used to that; every man she met seemed to melt whenever she was around them. This time, however, for the first time, she started to tremble inside herself as she held his stare. Not even the sound of crates being dragged into the warehouse broke their trance. Finally she drew back, as if she'd found what she'd been looking for. She went back to her papers, and a long silence settled in.

Val finally broke the silence. "So, uh, where did you learn to speak English?" He wanted her to feel free to talk and not to think of this encounter as just a business transaction.

"My uncle taught my brothers and me, and I studied in school. My uncle used to go…" Once again she struggled for the English word. "*Nga-So.*" She snapped her fingers as she tried to think of the word.

Val's concern deepened as he glanced at the anti-American poster again. "Soviet Union?"

"Yes! So-vee-et Yune-yun," she said, sounding it out. "He was at US Embassy." It seemed coincidental to Val when she picked up the phone and spoke in Russian to whomever was on the other end. After she hung up, she looked back at Val and said, "*Ngay mai, may muon luc nao?*"—Tomorrow, what time is good for you? She wanted to confirm that Val really knew her language—she was still impressed that he spoke it.

When Val replied, "*Tao khong chac, may muon luc nao?*"—I'm not sure, what time is good for you?—they agreed on 0900.

Val was impressed by how quickly she got things done as she handed him Lieutenant Davis's purchase order. Then she asked the obvious question: "Where did you learn Vietnamese?"

"Please call me Valentine—or Val," he said.

She giggled politely and replied, "I like your name—it sounds sweet."

"I learned in Hawaii from my neighbor," he said.

"Oh." She smiled. "Do you know North and South?" she asked, referring to the distinctly different principal dialects of Vietnamese, though there were dozens of regional dialects.

"Yes, but I'm more familiar with the southern."

"Well North is more proper. You should learn it since you're up here." She then switched subjects. "See you tomorrow at nine?" She smiled again, and again it melted his heart.

"*Cam un rat nhieu*"—Thank you very much, Val replied as he bowed his head and walked out of her office to the reception area on the other side of the curtain. There he found Davis, Nghia Mau, and the dozen young women from the warehouse having tea.

Nghia Mau looked up at Val, then waved her hand around as she smiled and said, "*Cua toi con gais*"—My daughters.

As Val and Nghia Mau walked toward the door, she told him that the young women weren't really her daughters, but were orphans from all over Vietnam. She'd been seriously injured by a bicycle bomb as a young girl when shrapnel tore through her abdomen and destroyed her reproductive organs. Several friends who'd been between her and the bomb were killed, probably saving her life. For a Vietnamese woman, having children was considered the highest blessing, and Nghia Mau was denied that blessing. But she found a way to be a mother anyway, to children who barely or never knew theirs.

Most of her girls had been orphaned during the years the French colonized Vietnam or by American bombs, and some had fled from South Vietnam when their families were executed before their very eyes. It was fitting that they wound up with Nghia Mau, whose name loosely translated to "adoptive mother."

Val's respect for Nghia Mau grew when she finished her story. He bowed to her with a smile as he opened the door and said, "*Ngay mai, Nghia Mau Nguyen*"—Tomorrow, Nghia Mau Nguyen. He then looked at Davis, who was enjoying his time with the pretty girls, and said, "Let's go, Lieutenant."

When they got to their trucks, they found the other six Marines lying in the bed of one of the trucks, soaked in sweat. "Those gals work you men over?" Val asked jokingly.

A lance corporal said in between gasps, "Yes, sir. Those gals were amazing. They lifted all those heavy crates and didn't even break a sweat, while we thought we were gonna have multiple hernias and busted discs after just two of them."

"Maybe we should recruit 'em as heavy machine gunners or for Force Recon," Val said.

"No way. They might embarrass us, sir." The Marine smiled as he climbed into the driver's seat of one of the trucks.

The trucks fired up and the convoy headed home for Linh Thu. Val once again took in the incredible beauty of the passing scenery. He always tried to savor his surroundings, no matter where he was—even on a combat sortie. He was fully aware that he'd never know what the his last conscious vision would be, but he wanted it to be something tranquil and serene. Val thought to himself as he gazed upon the lovely countryside that it was truly a shame that the two countries were at each other's throats instead of working together to create tourism opportunities that abounded this place, especially along the pristine coast.

§ § § § § §

After Val and Lieutenant Davis briefed Papa about the supplies; Val went to see if he'd missed anything at mail call. Again he was disappointed because there was nothing from Virginia, but the clerk handed him a letter to take to Papa on the way to his hooch. Even though Val knew it was none of his business, he couldn't help but see the return address—Sophie Driskell. By the time he walked into Papa's office, he was shivering and blowing on his hands.

He tossed Papa's letter on his desk and said, "Here's a letter from your ex-wife, sir. If you'll excuse me, I gotta go warm up. The letter gave me a little frostbite."

"Dammit, Jordan! Get out of here, you clown!" Papa said, laughing.

§ § § § § §

About two hours before the VMFA-2 aviators were supposed to be in the Cannery for the briefing, they got word to join Papa on the northwest ramp. After five minutes, they found themselves on the ramp sans Papa, inventing reasons why they'd been summoned.

Finally Papa showed up and everyone quieted down as he stood on an ammo crate. "All right, gents. I presume you're pondering why I pulled you away from chow and free time, so I'll get right to the point." Papa looked toward the north and pointed to the empty sky, then continued: "In about five minutes, two Hueys will be landing here. What's on board is something very important to every member of this squadron." Papa paused as he looked at every face in the crowd.

"On those Hueys is the Force Recon team that's been investigating Red Zone 1. Hopefully they'll have something for us. I wanted all of you to be here when they arrived to show them how important their mission is to all of us. I'm good friends with the platoon commander's father. He and I served together, so he'll be up front with me and not try to hide anything. Just remember that we owe our fallen comrades this attention. Hopefully we can end this soon and not have to fear for our lives when we're on final to our base, that we can leave our fear back at the target area."

Papa never bragged, so they didn't know how he knew the platoon commander's father, that he was returning to his carrier after hours of combat when he overheard the desperate pleas for help from some Marines that were being mauled on an island by some well dug-in Japanese. Papa had checked his map and quickly found out that they were calling from a small atoll thirty miles from his present position. He was down to about a quarter of his fuel, but he radioed that he was on his way to assist. Papa knew he couldn't stay long, but he'd give them whatever help he could until reinforcements arrived. When he closed on the atoll, he found three Zeros strafing the Marines. He instantly engaged them and shot two down and wounded the other. Papa's Corsair, Betelgeuse II, had taken its own hits, including some to the fuel tanks. With precious fuel spraying out, Papa engaged the Japanese on the ground despite the hits, softening them up enough that the Marines could finally overrun them. Belching black smoke, he took on another pair of Zeros that had swooped in, wounding each plane. All the while the Marines on the ground had watched.

Finally a squadron of Corsairs and Hellcats arrived to finish the job Papa had practically handled by himself, so he and Betelgeuse II limped back to their carrier, dead-sticking his approach and trapping with a still prop. The Marines on that atoll were grateful to him and radioed the carrier to find out if the pilot who'd saved them had gotten back safely.

One of those Marines was Captain Ramone Torres, the platoon commander. He never forgot Papa's efforts to save them when he should have kept on going to the carrier, and no one would have blamed him for doing so. He looked Papa up afterward and their friendship continued after the war. Ramone's son, now First Lieutenant Alberto Torres, was the platoon commander of the recon team investigating Red Zone 1. The lieutenant believed he owed Papa for saving his father years ago. If it wasn't for Papa, he might never have gotten to know his dad.

Papa was responding to his men's questions when the steady beat of rotor blades could be heard in the distance, and at once the ramp fell silent. All eyes were fixed on the skies to the north until finally two choppers could be made out just above the treetops. The noise level steadily increased as they approached, and soon a wind stirred by the rotor blades gusted across the ramp as the Hueys set down on the tarmac. When the engines shut down, the platoon jumped out each side of both machines and clustered up behind their lieutenant as he walked out from under the whirling blades.

Overstreet appeared from nowhere and ran out to intercept the team, but the lieutenant stepped around him after a few words and headed directly toward Papa and his squadron. Once again Overstreet tried to cut the lieutenant off and divert him to a waiting truck, but the lieutenant simply sidestepped again. It was then that Overstreet made the near-fatal mistake of grabbing the lieutenant's shirt. As soon as his hand grasped a fistful of cloth, the Marine closest to his platoon commander ferociously jerked the captain off his feet and slammed him to the tarmac, then twisted his wrist into a painful joint lock. The Playboys immediately roared in laughter as they watched the event unfold. The Marine then released Overstreet, who scampered away to the truck where he'd wait until the platoon finished talking to Papa.

The platoon continued walking until they encircled Papa and Lieutenant Torres, with VMFA-2 surrounding them on all sides. Torres quickly snapped salute to Papa and Big John, who he respected deeply. Both men had helped his father him after WWII and Korea.

"I know you're not supposed to salute out here, sir, so I have my men surrounding us to shield us from any sniper's crosshairs," Torres said as he quickly dropped his hand.

"Not a problem, Lieutenant," Papa said with a smile. "Guess dipshit over there learned the hard way not to come between a platoon and their commander, huh?"

The lieutenant smiled back. "Sometimes you gotta speak their language, sir."

"Well, son, talk to me. What'd you find out?"

"To be honest sir, not much," the lieutenant said with a look of disappointment on his face, as if he'd let Papa down. "But no worries, sir. We're here at Linh Thu for the long haul. We're now permanently stationed here because this base is perfect for green side and black side ops. We'll get to the bottom of this, sir. I promise."

"Don't worry about it, son. Just tell us what you know so far."

"Well sir, the Vietnamese are very good at covering their tracks, so it's hard to find anything they don't want you to. What we know so far is that there's a very large platoon, maybe an entire regiment of NVA, operating in your Red Zone 1. We found a complex series of tunnels all through the area. Really impressive. They could move completely undetected any time they want."

"Have any clues as to what type of weapon is being used on my squadron?"

"None yet, sir. The only thing I can tell you is that it must be able to fit in those tunnels, so it's some kind of stowable or portable system. We will find it, sir. We *will* find it. Our priority after whatever mission we get sent on is to find that weapon."

"I know it is, son. Just let me know. If you need any help that we can provide, you have an entire squadron at your disposal." Papa looked over to the truck parked off the ramp and saw Overstreet stretching his aching wrist out. "I guess you need to go with the captain in the truck. Carry on."

"Aye, sir." Torres quickly snapped another salute and led his platoon to the truck, where they were quickly driven out of sight to HQ.

Papa looked back at his squadron and offered some reassurance. "Don't worry, gents—they'll find our problem." He dismissed everyone, and the squadron drifted back to what they were doing.

§ § § § §

The next morning, Val eagerly hopped into the lead truck of the convoy headed back to Dong Hoi to pick up their supplies. Now that word had gotten around about the pretty girls who loaded trucks, every man seemed really anxious to go on the detail. Val was already in a trance as intoxicating visions of Nga Nghin Do'i took control of his mind, like an endorphin rush. He'd actually experienced such a state many times before and wished he could bring one on at will, but it didn't work that way. Some event, person, or action had to initiate rush. Oddly, he'd never experienced it with Virginia.

When the brakes squealed in front of the store and belched the air in the lines, Val snapped out of it, and he and Lieutenant Davis jumped out and went inside to find Nghia Mau waiting for them with tea. To Val's disappointment, Nga Nghin Do'i wasn't in this morning, so the men wasted little time loading the trucks and heading back to Linh Thu.

§ § § § §

A month went by with amazing speed for everyone at Linh Thu. Rocket attacks occurred less and less frequently, night combat sorties were relatively uneventful, and word quickly spread that supply detail was the best thing going if you wanted to meet pretty local girls, or at least be near them. Val was finally starting to show signs of wear. He was sleeping a little better, but he'd only received one letter from Virginia since arriving in Vietnam. The stress was finally getting to him. Trips to Dong Hoi were infrequent since rocket attacks had trailed off for the time being—and even when he did go, Nga Nghin Do'i was there only one other time.

Val looked forward to seeing her because he'd enjoyed their conversations. It helped that she was a live, beautiful woman—something nonexistent at

Linh Thu. When he was on base, he was constantly called on to interpret intelligence information or to speak with South Vietnamese soldiers. He wasn't immune to callouts even when he was on Alert-5 duty, and people often came into the Shack and hassled him to interpret something. There was no such thing as peace for Val anymore, and he could now fully sympathize with Papa, who had to juggle so many responsibilities.

Val and Nate were sitting in the Shack on Alert-5 duty with two other aviators reading magazines, playing cards, and enjoying the air conditioning. Alert-5 did have its perks, one of them being that an aviator could actually catch up on sleep if they weren't called out. Val was sitting on the couch writing Virginia yet another letter that would most likely go unanswered. He made sure his return address was correct so there'd be no mix up in the mail, but he did this every time anyway. All four men jumped to their feet when the phone rang and the alert siren blared. They scrambled for their gear as Val answered the phone and copied their mission, which was also being relayed to the ordnance techs, who had to have the jets properly loaded when the crews climbed in. Val quickly briefed his fellow aviators as he pointed to a map, and then they dashed out the door to their jets.

A flight of Air Force F-105 Thunderchiefs was currently twenty-five miles northwest of Linh Thu returning to Thailand when a group of MiGs were spotted heading for them. It would only be a matter of minutes before the MiGs would be on top of the Thuds, and Linh Thu was the closest base for assistance. It would only take Val and his wingman a couple of minutes to reach the flight of Thuds to assist, but he felt as if something wasn't right as he fired up his jet. MiGs usually snuck in behind American planes, made quick passes at them, then fled for home, which made them harder to detect and react to, but these MiGs were acting weirdly, as if they wanted to get noticed. Their pilots were either extremely confident, extremely foolish, or they were trying to force the 105s to go somewhere they wanted them to go. Val and his wingman taxied at high speed to runway 28, then Val gave last-minute instructions as they positioned themselves and throttled up. The burners shot twenty-foot cones of flame as they thundered down the runway.

Once airborne, Val checked in with Panama to get the current position of the Thuds. Then he switched over to the frequency the Thuds were on and checked in with them. "Bowties are airborne off Linh Thu, thirty in trail. We'll be there in less than five," Val said. VMFA-2 Alert-5 jets off Linh Thu always used the call-sign "Bowtie" because of the bowtie the bunnies on their tails wore.

The Thud flight leader replied to Val, "Voodoo flight is on the Linh Thu three-zero-zero for the two-six-zero at three-three angels two-niner descending to angels two-five. We've got bandits moving in behind us twelve in trail. They'll be between us. We counted six, repeat six. Please move your asses."

"Both RIOs have got a steady echo. They're gonna disappear soon," Val said back to the Thud leader. All of a sudden, just as he unkeyed, Val's entire disposition was overtaken with uneasiness. He looked off to his left and saw nothing, then looked to his wingman off to his right. Everything seemed fine, but the feeling was still there. He looked back over to his wingman and saw an explosion under the engines separate their right wing from the fuselage, sending it over the jet. Bowtie 2 instantly spun into violent left snap rolls as half his lift vanished.

Val pulled his throttles out of afterburner and broke hard left to avoid a collision. Bowtie 2's roll rate was increasing dramatically with every rotation, and he was unable to hold altitude. "Get the fuck outta there, guys!" Val ordered. They were at a point where the crew could no longer be picky about waiting until the right moment to punch out—it was impossible to predict when that would be. They needed to just get out now.

"Mayday! Mayday! Mayday! Bowtie 2's hit and going down, one-niner klicks west of Linh Thu! Get a rescue flight out here now!" Val shouted back to Panama.

In a mere fraction of a second, Val saw the RIO's ejection seat scooting horizontally across the sky, indicating it had fired when the jet was knife-edge. Split seconds later, the pilot's seat fired off and rocketed away from the erratically moving aircraft, but was heading groundward. The pilot's seat fired off when the jet was inverted!

"I got one 'chute!" Nate announced relieved. "Charles is out!"

"Come on, dammit!" Val said as he saw the pilot still rapidly plummeting toward the ground, with only a few seconds before he'd be too low for his 'chute to work effectively.

Finally the controller drogue gun fired and deployed the drogue 'chute. As it filled with air, it deployed the stabilizer drogue, followed shortly by the seat falling away from the pilot. The pilot's personal parachute finally blossomed in the heavy jungle air.

"I got both 'chutes. Baker and Charles are both out!" Val called as he relayed his position to Panama. "Is the rescue chopper on the way?" he asked.

"Bowtie 1, Panama. Rescue 1 is airborne and will be at your position in one-zero minutes."

"Roger," Val acknowledged. When he looked back outside toward the parachutes of his wingmen, Val noticed a strange smoke trail in the air. It was thin and wispy white, and he wind was breaking it up. It was hard to tell now, but it appeared that it had originated in the jungles below. He made a mental note of it and put his mind back to more important matters at hand. He faced a serious dilemma now. Who needed him more right now—his wingmen or the Thuds? The Thuds would be seriously outnumbered and easy prey for the MiGs, but so would he without his wingman. He knew from reading other pilot's reports of encounters with MiGs that they usually scattered and retreated back to their base when they knew American fighters were closing on them. However, he also wanted to make sure his fellow Marines were safely aboard the helicopter and headed home. He orbited their parachutes until he had a visual on the helicopter, then deciding they were safe, he stoked the burners and screamed toward the Thuds.

"I take it we're going after the bandits?" Nate asked.

"Affirmative," Val said, adding, "I saw the rescue chopper. I think our guys are safe, so let's not lose any more Americans up here today."

"Roger. But something's weird. I got no returns on the MiGs. It's like they dropped to the deck and headed home. I'm tilting the radar down as far as it will go and nothing tagging up except our Air Force buddies up there."

Now within visual of the Thuds with no MiGs in sight or on Nate's scope, Panama called, "Bowtie 1, Panama. RTB. Your mission is cancelled. Voodoo 1 lost sight of bandits."

Val replied, "Voodoo 1, Bowtie 1. What happened?"

"I don't know. The bandits suddenly scattered and headed north, low level. Thanks for responding, you guys are the best. We'll be okay. Take care of your buddies back there, hope they're okay. What happened to them?"

"I don't know. They both punched out and the rescue chopper was nearly on them when I broke for you."

"Thanks again, Marines—we'll be okay. We're just worried about your wingmen."

"Roger. I need to head back there now." Val turned back, extremely angry now. He'd nearly lost his wingmen, and got no payback by splashing some MiGs. As he neared the crash site, he caught sight of the orbiting rescue helicopter, and once again he marked the position on his chart. It was similar in distance and altitude to the Red Zone 1 hits.

"Rescue 1, Bowtie 1."

"Bowtie 1, Rescue 1, go ahead."

"What's the status of the crew of Bowtie 2?"

"Haven't found 'em yet. We've been orbiting their 'chutes, but neither Alpha or Bravo has called us or has attempted to get on the penetrator. They're either injured or laying low for some reason. Maybe Charlie's down there. We're about to send a person down to check as soon as the door gunner's ready."

Soon Rescue 1 came under heavy gunfire, but they dropped a smoke grenade right on the position of the gunfire. The door gunner returned fire as he sprayed the area with his mini gun. After several minutes of heavy firing, the jungle fell silent again as a small column of smoke started to rise. When all aboard agreed it was pretty safe, Rescue 1 lowered a crew chief through the thick umbrella of trees to see if they could find anything. After a few minutes of looking around at smoke and thick vegetation, the crew chief climbed back onto the penetrator and was retracted up to his hovering bird. After another twenty minutes, Val was nearing bingo fuel and had no choice but to RTB. Rescue 1 stayed until they were at bingo fuel, but had no contact with the downed crew either. The feeling of uneasiness that had been a nagging after-thought for almost a month was now back.

§ § § § §

Papa walked into the Shack to talk to Val and Nate about what had hap-pened, though neither man was in a mood for conversation. "What brought Baker and Charles down? Did you see anything unusual?"

"Not really, sir. It happened pretty much at the same distance and altitude as the hits at Red Zone 1. After they ejected, I did notice a thin trail of white smoke in the air behind where they were hit. It was hard to tell because it was dissipating in the wind, but it appeared to have originated from the jungle."

Nate added, "I'm not positive, sir, but I thought I saw a faint echo on my scope a split second before the explosion. Something really small and moving very fast."

"Really?" Papa scratched his head. "Well, the recon team is being dis-patched there right now. Hopefully they can find our boys and some answers."

"If I can offer an opinion, sir, I felt something was wrong from the moment we got the call to launch."

"I'm listening, Captain." Papa was open to any of Val's theories because he had three aircraft shot down and no facts.

"Well sir, the whole scenario was fishy. From what I read, North Vietnam-ese MiGs don't fly the way those did. They were acting like they wanted to be seen. I think they were trying to draw us out, sir, almost as if they were setting a trap."

"Well that's an interesting avenue to explore, Captain. I'll keep it in mind. Right now let's hope we can get our boys back and that Lieutenant Torres's team can find some evidence about what's going on. Right now we have noth-ing but speculation."

§ § § § §

The squadron met again on the northwest ramp, this time to see the recon team off and wish them luck. Every member stood silent as spooling turbines followed by the beat of rotor blades filled their ears. It didn't take long for a camaraderie to develop between the recon team and members of both squadrons stationed at Linh Thu. The team was eager to help improve the lives of the men stationed here by trying to disrupt rocket attacks, destroying supply networks, or directly engaging enemy forces—and above all getting to the bottom of the Red Zone 1 mystery. The squadrons in turn would give the team all the air support they'd ever need and more. As the helicopters departed into the twilight, each man watching hoped for the safety of Val's fallen wingmen and a touch of luck that the team might find what so desperately needed to be found.

Luckily for VMFA-2, the mission they were supposed to go on got scrubbed because the original target was destroyed by South Vietnamese ground forces in a huge skirmish with the NVA The Marines had a rare night off and spent it in the pub. Val and Nate didn't get to join in the activities as they had another seven hours of Alert-5 duty, but they made the most of the quiet evening by turning in early and trying to catch up on sleep. Sleep didn't come easily to either man as the two other bunks, previously occupied by Baker and Charles, were empty. Val was sitting up in the darkness, staring at the empty bunks across the hooch, wondering if his comrades were able to get any sleep wherever they were. As he tried to doze off himself, he replayed the day's events and reflected on a few serious unanswered questions—most prominent the status of his wingmen. What was this mystery weapon that was bringing down their jets? Could he have reacted differently? Then he thought about Virginia. Why hadn't he heard from her in over three months? How was she doing? His thoughts even turned morbid. Had something happened to her? Something wasn't right, and he was beginning to panic. Val, now wide awake, had broken out in a cold sweat, he went to the head to splash his face with cool water. He stood over the sink for a few moments catching his breath and trying to gather his thoughts. Eventually he went back to his rack and looked at the clock—0215. But as tired as he was, he couldn't relax enough to sleep. He stared blankly at the ceiling, wondering how he could calm himself enough to get the sleep he so desperately needed.

But as his thoughts shifted to the beautiful and peaceful countryside of Vietnam, he started to relax. His breathing and heartbeat slowed, and his blood pressure dropped as images of lush green jungles and pristine beaches filled his mind. Before long he was in the town of Dong Hoi, caught up in the slow pace of life there, and it came as no surprise to him when the transcendent vision of Nga Nghin Do'i overtook everything else. Soon the soothing tingle of endorphins filled every cell of his mind and body, and then his dream-like state segued into the most peaceful sleep he'd had in over three months.

5

SOMETIMES SILENCE IS NOT GOLDEN

The jungle was black as a cave. Vegetation, like the ocean, had an insatiable appetite for light. The deeper in you went, the closer the darkness came, until the black clung to you like skin. And just like the ocean, the jungle at night was filled with noise. Insects and frogs and birds made their noises as they searched for a mate or food. Movement was sluggish at best in the thick vegetation, and each required care to ensure the proper footing for balance and silence. The air was thick, stale, musty, and motionless, stiflingly humid and dank. Intermingled was the lingering odor of smoke.

For humans, sweating was the body's way of cooling itself. There was no cooling effect here. Since sweat did not evaporate in the jungle, it either dripped from every exposed stretch of skin or saturated clothing and accumulated under straps and belts and inside boots. Even the cool metal of an assault rifle beaded with moisture, and in the silence following a skirmish, it would sizzle into steam.

As the recon team slowly crept in silence through the blackness, they were hoping to recover the missing aviators and find something that would help determine why they'd been shot down to begin with. They'd been searching for just over three hours now, but so far had found nothing. The team halted to review the situation as they closed in on the source of the smoke, which they knew was in the vicinity of the downed aviators' parachutes. It would be there that they'd be most likely to encounter the enemy or their booby traps. The source of the smoke was only a hundred meters to the north of their position, so the team spread out in skirmishers formation, which gave them the most effective use of their firepower if they met the enemy. Once in formation, Torres gave the go-ahead to his team by hand signal, and they slowly converged on the source of the smoke. It was on now!

While it was a mere hundred meters away, it might as well have been a mile. Each step had to be carefully placed, or else risk becoming entangled in the snares of a booby trap, or snap a twig or bump against some stump or tree and give away their presence. Sweat stinging their eyes, the team kept moving forward into the blackness, closing in to fifty meters from the trickle of smoke. Then, about twenty meters away, the ground was suddenly dry, warm, and devoid of vegetation, the surface dusty and covered in ash. The team slowed their pace a bit and finally closed in on the source of the smoke. There was no fire—it was simply rising off ground that was hotter than its surroundings. The men looked around and found nothing, not a sign that humans had been there—not even a footprint. The team then continued north, but in a tighter formation.

They'd barely moved another thirty meters when one of men felt something hard under his foot. He signaled the lieutenant, who approached quickly. The man held up a shell casing from a 7.62mm round, then fanned his hand across the ground to discover many more. With this many rounds on the ground, the team dismissed the idea that they came from a hill tribe or the Pathet Lao—Laotian communist guerilas. It was the NVA who'd been there after all, and apparently in a firefight with the crew of Rescue 1. The rest of the team spread out and found the ground ripped up, along with splintered tree limbs and torn vegetation, most likely from the door gunner's mini-gun. The men began to fan out from this location and found more shells, none of which proved anything new. One of the men off to the northwest, farthest from the platoon, passed over the spent ammo casings until he came across something that made his heart sink. He called the lieutenant over and showed him the aviators' g-harnesses. Then they looked up and saw both parachutes hanging in the trees some twenty feet off the ground. Not far away they also found torn pieces of flight coveralls, a couple stained black with blood not fully dry. Along the ground were .38 and a .45 caliber shell casings, both US-issued side arms. This was *not* good news because it meant the men had exchanged fire with the enemy.

The men collected all they could from the jungle, but had no luck getting the parachutes out of the trees. They then headed back to where the smoke was still rising as Torres radioed for the extraction. Since the vegetation was thinned out there, it was an obvious extraction point. The men waited in the blackness until they heard the distinct beat of UH-1 rotor blades in the distance. The helicopters would quickly draw attention if the enemy was nearby, so the platoon wasted no time in getting aboard. The Hueys, which were their lifelines, at times drew unwanted attention. At this extraction point, they were creating a maelstrom of dust and ash, and the men had to scale the ropes despite the downwash off the rotor blades. Lieutenant Torres waited on the ground to make sure all his men were safely on board before he prepared to ascend, a handkerchief over his mouth and nose as protection against the dust. His eyes were now watering up, and he lowered his head to shake some of the dust away and lost his balance for a split second, causing him to stumble. As he did, his foot bumped into something hard, and he looked down to see what it was. The downwash had blown away enough ash to reveal a long, narrow tube, almost four feet in length, unlike anything he'd ever seen before. It was apparent that it had been buried on purpose—something someone definitely wanted to hide.

When he bent down to examine it, he realized it was some type of weapon, like a bazooka or RPG. It was slightly burned, and one end was broken off, but the pieces were on the ground in front of it. When he realized what he'd found, he felt like he'd just beaten the house in Las Vegas. He grabbed the tube and broken pieces and carried it all with him up the rope. This had to be NVA gear, because their weapons were supplied by the Soviet Union and China, and they'd have more advanced weaponry.

§ § § § § §

Papa was asleep in his rack when a young lance corporal gently woke him up. He and Big John quickly awoke to see the young Marine parting the mosquito net in the entrance to their hooch, a look of urgency on his face.

"What is it, Lance Corporal?" Big John asked. "You're letting the bugs in."

"The commander of the recon team radioed in, sir. They're inbound, ETA twenty minutes. He said he had some important news."

"Did he say anything more specific than that?" Papa asked.

"No, sir. He did say that you'd definitely be interested in what he found."

"Fine. Wake up my squadron; tell them I said to wait outside the HQ building in one hour. That'll give us time to disseminate details of his findings. Have the chow hall bring coffee kettles to the front of HQ for my men to have while they wait. Get moving."

"Aye, sir," the young lance corporal snapped back as he jumped into his vehicle.

Papa jumped out of his rack as he and Big John stretched and headed for the chow hall for coffee, then out to the flight line to greet the incoming helicopters.

Papa, Big John, and Captain Overstreet were waiting on the ramp as the steady thump of the rotors could be heard in the distant darkness. As the Hueys approached, Papa was surprised to see that most of his squadron was already up and waiting behind him at the northwest ramp. Soon the choppers were overhead and touching down. The platoon jumped out and ran to the truck that took them and the waiting officers to HQ for the debrief. The rest of the Playboys ran to the area across from the HQ building and sipped coffee as they awaited word about their fellow aviators. They all knew that the longer they had to wait, the less likely the news would be good.

Lieutenant Torres sat his platoon down in the conference room across from Papa, Big John, Captain Overstreet, Chappie, and other high-ranking officers of both VMFA-2 and VMO-16. The lieutenant then walked up to the table across from the other officers and dumped all the contents he'd brought back on the table. Everyone looked closely at the various items and all realized the team's findings didn't look too promising.

Papa started the debrief, even though he was afraid of confirming what he already knew. "Well Lieutenant, tell us what your platoon has found."

"Sir, these items are all we found after an extensive search of the area, besides the 'chutes, which are still hanging in the trees twenty feet off the ground. We tried hard to retrieve them." Lieutenant Torres looked into Papa's eyes, hoping that he was okay with his decision to leave the parachutes in the trees.

Papa just lowered his head, certain the platoon had done its best. "Carry on, Lieutenant."

"Well sir, you'll notice everything is coated with dirt or ash because we had to dig for them. The Gooners tried not to leave any visible evidence behind." He then held up the g-harnesses of the men and the blood-soaked pieces of their coveralls. "We found these about twenty to thirty meters from their 'chutes—long with these…" He held up the shell casings. "They must've gotten into a skirmish with the Gooners. There were plenty of AK-47 shell casings around." The lieutenant picked up several of the 7.62mm shell casings and set them back down. "In my opinion, sir, I believe your men are still alive. They're probably being taken to the zoo or heartbreak hotel."

The "zoo" was a prison in the town of Cu Loc, on the southern side of Hanoi, where a lot of American POWs were held. "Heartbreak Hotel" was a section of the Hoa Lo prison in Hanoi, where new POWs were often taken. The prison had been built by the French at the turn of the century and was a dismal hellhole where many Vietnamese suffered under the colonization, and now American POWs were suffering just as badly within its dreary walls. Hoa Lo eventually became known as the Hanoi Hilton by many of the Americans who were unlucky enough to spend time there.

The lieutenant watched as the officers settled uneasily into their chairs as he presented the news. He continued, barely being able to look at Papa because he had to be the one to break the bad news about his men, but when he got to his most important finding, he caught Papa's eye as he said, "I'm glad to say I do have some better news." When all eyes were on him, he continued: "We may have a break in the Red Zone 1 mystery. Just as we were leaving the area, I came across this. Though it's burned, I think you'll find it enlightening." The lieutenant then laid out his poncho on the table. He unrolled it to reveal the long tube and its broken components. As soon as the object was exposed, Papa looked at Overstreet to gauge his reaction. The captain drew back and held his breath, as if he recognized the object.

Torres went on. "To be honest, I don't know what this is for sure, but it appears to be some type of projectile weapon." He began to point out various features on the tube that he felt confirmed his assessment. "This appears to be some type of power source. Here's the sighting system, and here's the trigger. I have no idea what this thing fires, or what it's meant to be used against." He paused, then looked over at Captain Overstreet and made a bold accusation. "I think someone knows exactly what this is, but is concealing that information from people who really need it."

Overstreet didn't appreciate that the lieutenant had drawn attention to him, and he felt a cold sweat break out as all eyes turned his way. He cleared his throat and was about to let the lieutenant know his displeasure when Papa cut him off. "Thank you, Lieutenant. You fellas did an excellent job. I'm sure you're tired, so be seated. We'll dismiss all of you shortly and get full reports in the morning."

The debrief continued for another forty-five minutes, then the platoon was dismissed. It was still early in the morning, so most of the officers filed out of the building and headed back for their racks a couple more hours of sleep before reveille. Soon the room was empty, and Papa forced himself to stop working. He knew his flyers were waiting to see him outside, so he stepped out onto the top step of the stairs. He could see that the entire squadron was still there. He figured they could tell from the expression on his face that his news wouldn't be good.

Papa paused for a moment as he stared at his men, then drew in a deep breath and spoke matter-of-factly. "I'm not going to sugar coat this, gents. Lieutenant Torres has given us his analysis of the situation, and no one in that debrief has no reason to disagree with him." Papa swallowed a small lump in his throat, and when he was about to continue he hesitated because he felt the hairs rise on the back of his neck. Something was amiss, but he wasn't sure what it was. He heard a faint swish in the air behind him just as gunfire broke out from every direction. He hit the deck shouting "Take cover!"

The instant Papa finished his warning, the back of the HQ building behind him burst into flames, accompanied by a deafening bang. Other explosions soon erupted from what seemed like every direction, and the air was filled with flying debris. Linh Thu was under attack again! All the men scrambled their hooches to retrieve their rifles while there was still light. Val and Nate jumped to their feet and ran toward Papa, who was lying face down and motionless in front of the blazing HQ building. When they reached him, they rolled him over on his back and both shouted, "Sir—are you all right?"

Papa opened his eyes and looked up at the Marines crouching over him, as distraught as if they'd witnessed their own dogs being hit by a car. He wiped the sweat off his face and said, "Damn! I could really go for a beer!" Then he raised his head, propped himself up on his elbows, and ordered, "Boys—get back to your hooches and take cover."

"Are you sure you're all right, sir?" Nate asked.

Papa sat up and let the question tumble around his mind before he answered, "I'm fine. Scratch that first order, fellas. Instead why don't you get your gear and *my* gear and meet me right back here. Those fuckers have some- how gotten inside the perimeter the last two raids, and they'll probably want to destroy whatever they can on the flight line. So we're gonna stop 'em."

"Was there anyone else in HQ, sir?" Val asked as he felt the heat from the flames. At that moment the lights went out, and the only illumination was pro- vided by the flames.

"I don't...aw, shit—I never saw Lieutenant Torres come out! I think he's still in there!" Papa looked down the street as he rose to his feet and saw a couple of dark shadows running toward them. Despite the quick glance, he could tell that the shadows were carrying rifles. "Let's get out of the open, gents," Papa said as he directed his Marines into black shadows nearby.

They crouched low in the darkness with all eyes focused on the rapidly approaching shadows, which were getting close enough to reveal more details. It was apparent that the shadows had several rifles, so the three Marines pressed themselves as flat as they could to the ground. The shadows then slowed, as if they'd seen Papa and his flyers, then disappeared momen- tarily as they moved in and out of the firelight. As the shapes moved into the black background, the Marines were now listening for footsteps amidst the explosions and gunfire.

All of a sudden, the shadows reappeared and were only twenty meters away, acting as if they were trying to figure out if they someone was hiding in the eclipse of the HQ building. All of a sudden, one of them stepped into the firelight and shouted, "Papa! Jordan! Robinson! Is that you over there?"

The three Marines jumped to their feet as they recognized Notso's and Speedy's voices. They had brought their rifles and war belts. "Yeah it's us, son! Damn glad to see you boys!" Papa replied.

"Gents." Speedy said as he handed Val and Nate their gear.

Val grabbed his gear, then set it on the ground as he remembered Lieutenant Torres and headed for the burning HQ building. "Where the hell are you going, son?" Papa shouted.

"If the lieutenant's still in there, we need to get him out!" Val shouted as he tied his handkerchief around his mouth and nose and charged through the door of the HQ building. The entire rear portion of the building was engulfed in fire.

"Wait for the firemen, son. It's their damn job and they have the proper equipment!" Papa yelled into the door.

Val dropped to his hands and knees and crawled around the dark front rooms, which were rapidly filling with smoke. The floor was getting hotter as he approached a partly open door at the rear of the room. Light from the fire at the back of the building was filtering in from cracks in the walls and floor, and the floor had gotten too hot to touch, so Val was now duck-walking. At the door, Val pushed it open with his elbow and was greeted by a wave of intense heat and thick billowing smoke. He strained his eyes for any shapes that might be human, then focused on a large dark object under one of the conference tables on the right side of the room. Val quickly waddled over to it and, to his surprise, found two unconscious men instead of just one. Grabbing a wrist in each hand, he began to drag them toward the front when a huge piece of the back wall and ceiling came crashing down from behind the table and partially buried all three of them under burning debris.

Val instantly jumped back to his feet as the flames clawed for his face with the ferocity of a wild animal. He kicked some of the largest pieces of debris off the men, grabbed their wrists again, and began to pull them out from under what remained. Suddenly they broke free, and Val stumbled and fell backwards into the door behind him, opening a large cut on the back of his head that instantly gushed blood. Dazed and running out of breathable air, his vision was beginning to gray when he finally made it to the door, only to discover that it had closed. Val tried to kick it open, but the heat had warped and expanded it. Val looked to his left and saw a window that had broken under the pressure of the heat. He picked up a folding chair that burned his hands as he grasped it and started to clear away any remaining shards of glass when all of a sudden the front crashed open as an axe punched through.

The firefighter saw Val standing over the two victims and charged in, with another right behind him. The second firefighter handed Val an oxygen tank and strapped the mask around Val's face as he and his partner grabbed the men on the floor. Then they motioned for Val to follow them out.

Outside, the normally hot, sticky night air felt cool and refreshing by comparison. The fire crew laid the victims on the ground and checked for breathing. As they gave both men mouth-to-mouth resuscitation, Val saw it was

Torres and Overstreet who were being treated. When both were breathing on their own, Papa thanked the firemen and ordered them to get both men to sick bay immediately. He then thanked Val and signaled to his aviators to follow him to the flight line.

The Marines walked cautiously and blindly in the dark toward the flight line, all ears alert for any whisper around them. Papa signaled for them to take a knee when the sounds of clanking metal, sloshing fluids, and words in Vietnamese words reached them from ahead. In the faint and brief light of a mortar round exploding in the distance, they could see two men dressed in black pajamas and sandals with AK-47s heading toward them up the street, throwing liquid onto every building they passed. When they were finally close enough for a clean shot, all five Marines opened fire and dropped the men where they stood. The Marines waited for a moment, then approached the bodies and realized the large cans they'd been carrying contained ether.

"This isn't a good sign," Papa whispered as he picked up a can and studied it briefly. "It can only mean that something else is headed this way."

All five Marines instinctively dropped to the ground as Val suddenly opened fire at five men approaching them from fifty meters away. Ten rifles answered back, indicating that there were more people behind the first five.

"Let's get behind that building!" Papa ordered his Marines as they returned fire. The Marines then dashed across the street as the enemy soldiers fired flare guns at buildings, which instantly ignited from the ether—but since the ether evaporated rapidly, the flames went out almost as soon as they flared up.

The Marines were breathing heavy as they lined up behind Papa, finding some security from the darkness and the building against their backs. "Fellas, we're gonna cut across this alley here to the flight line," Papa whispered as he pointed in its direction. "I bet there's a lotta Gooners snooping around there, and we can't afford to lose any more aircraft at this point."

One by one, the Marines rushed across the alley and crept up to the concrete wall that surrounded the fuel farm and faced the flight line on the other side. As they peered around the wall, they could see several enemy soldiers dropping satchel charges around various aircraft as they made their way along both squadrons' aircraft.

Val eyed the large hangar across from his position and said, "Sir, Robinson and I will go around to other side of the maintenance hangar and cut off their escape route while you pick them off from here."

"I will, huh?" Nate replied good-naturedly, knowing he'd never let Val go alone.

"Good idea, son. You boys get going. We'll give you one minute, then we'll open fire whether you're in position or not," Papa replied.

Nate followed Val as they quickly made their way around the perimeter of the wall. When they were almost halfway to their goal, Val tripped and fell face-first into the dirt. Nate stopped as Val picked himself up and saw the body of an enemy soldier who'd apparently died there after taking a round somewhere else, if the fresh blood trail was any clue. It didn't let it faze them as they continued to the other side of the hangar.

Papa glanced at his watch, then tapped Speedy and Notso on the shoulders and told them to fire on targets in the open area away from aircraft and to make sure to kill the soldier with the detonator switch. Val and Nate sprinted to the corner that as they heard the gunfire commence from the direction of the fuel farm. With the corner in sight, Val and Nate had just begun to slow down when Val collided head-on with the first of the enemy commandos fleeing the flight line. The impact sent both men to their butts as Nate opened fire at a few others running toward them. Val brought his rifle to bear and fired at the man he ran into, then at the men Nate was firing at. The enemy commandos fired blindly back at the muzzle flashes winking at them from the hangar, causing flakes of concrete and metal to buzz around the Marines' heads. The muzzle flashes from both side lit the dark in short bursts as a fierce skirmish broke out.

Across the ramp, another fierce firefight broke out as the enemy commandos smartly ran for the cover of the aircraft, hoping to flush the Marines out of their cover and force them to have to come over and pick them off one by one. Several of the commandos were already dead, including the triggerman, who was foolishly out in the open when Papa, Notso, and Speedy opened fire. The enemy saw their comrades lying dead in front of them and began to retreat for the cover of the hangar, knowing that the Americans would surely be calling for backup by now. Just as they began their retreat, Val and Nate opened fire, dropping more of their comrades. They were beginning to realize they were trapped.

All the Marines continued to fire until fewer and fewer and eventually no more muzzle flashes were seen opposite them. Everything fell silent and dark again.

Val and Nate relaxed a bit when the firing ceased, aware of the ringing in their ears from the close proximity of gunfire. Val walked over and tapped the soldier he'd run into with his foot, getting no response. Both men then stared blankly into the darkness of the flight line, searching for any hint of movement, when Val heard a rustling sound from behind him. He turned to see the soldier he'd just tapped with his foot standing behind them, raising his rifle to his shoulder. Val swiftly swung around and drove his rifle butt into the soldier's lower jaw and nose, sending him and his rifle flying through the air. Nate fired two rounds into the soldier's chest and Val added a couple more when the soldier finally landed on the ground. Both men exhaled a sigh of relief, then ducked when the soldier's rifle landed butt first on the ground and discharged.

Nate and Val looked at each other in disbelief. Then Nate let out a sigh as he whispered, "Now don't get me wrong—I like pajama parties, but only when they involve scantily clad coeds." He took a deep breath. "I'm tired of seeing these assholes every few nights, always coming over with no invitation."

"I agree, Buddy. It's fine if they want to come visit every now and then, but I think everyone'd be better off if we all just left our guns home," Val replied.

They didn't know how many commandos were still out there, hiding among the aircraft on the line. Not long after the muzzle flashes ceased, a jeep pulled up to the flight line. With everything eerily silent now, one of the men in the jeep played a spotlight along the planes. The commandos hiding under the aircraft knew they were trapped, and it wouldn't be long before they became desperate and did something that went against their natural instincts. As the jeep moved down the line, the spotlight closed in on their positions. They knew they had to escape or die trying. Unsure of how the Americans would treat them if they were captured, they were certain they'd rather die than give information to the enemy. Soon the enemy started slowly crawling behind the aircraft toward the hangar. They were almost there when all the lights came on as power on base was restored. They were caught out in the open now, and the jeep's spotlight illuminated them even more. They began to run for an open hangar door until a mechanic stepped out with his rifle and opened fire, dropping one of them. Meanwhile, the jeep was closing, also directing fire at them. The men returned fire as they ran south, the only direction that seemed open to them. When Val and Nate heard the gunfire, they turned their attention toward the flight line and added their fire to the mix. Now the enemy were trapped.

Fire from the jeep rapidly reduced their numbers until only two were left. Seeing they were hopelessly trapped, both enemy soldiers gave each other a look, then pointed their rifles at each other's hearts and squeezed the triggers, preferring to die than give the enemy the pleasure of a victory. Tonight's raid was finally over for everyone.

The aviators had never imagined anything like it. It was the first time they'd actually pointed a rifle at someone and killed them. They never stopped to think about it as it was happening; they simply saw another man with a gun. It was different than being in a jet and never seeing who was on the receiving end of their ordnance. There's was a cold, sobering realization that they were indeed in a real war, where real people were dying.

§ § § § § §

It took a couple of hours for the adrenaline to wear off. Each man lay in his rack staring blankly, their thoughts racing. For almost all of them, it was the first time they'd seen their victims die. They'd never forget the expressions of helplessness, fear and pain on the faces of their enemy, and hoped they'd never have to see anything like it again. Sleep would be elusive, but if it did come, it would be filled with strange dreams. The thing about adrenaline— when levels in the bloodstream finally crashed, the body seized and shut itself down from exhaustion practically without warning. One moment each man was staring at the ceiling unable to relax, the next they'd be in deep sleep with only nightmares to intrude on what should be a refreshing night's sleep.

§ § § § § §

The next morning Linh Thu was bustling with activity as the men once again began the almost routine task of rebuilding their base. Val watched as a couple of front loaders drove by with full loads of dead enemy soldiers in their buckets. Once they passed, Val could see Big John on the other side of the street. Big John shouted over, "See? I told you, young'un—get used to that sight. It's gonna be all too familiar."

"Somehow I'll doubt I'll get accustomed to it, sir," Val replied as he headed toward Papa's office.

Papa was standing in front of the burned ruins of HQ. Somehow the walls had managed to remain standing, even though the interior was completely destroyed. He'd just returned from a meeting with the other senior officers, where he'd insisted on a full-fledged investigation to determine how the enemy was getting on the base. He was frustrated because the items recovered by Lieutenant Torres's platoon were destroyed in the blaze, and now his already full plate was overflowing. Papa motioned to the operator of the bull-dozer, which roared as it pushed the shell of the HQ building, collapsing it onto itself.

Val cautiously approached his CO, not wanting to provoke him. "Morning, sir," he said.

"Morning, Captain." Papa took in a deep breath. "You already know what you gotta do, son."

"Yes, sir."

"Find Lieutenant Davis and get going. We have a long week ahead of us. We won't have another COD flight for ten days, so it's up to you boys to get what we need till then."

"Aye, sir!" Val snapped and hurried off to the logistics building, where he found six trucks waiting with several Marines in each, ready for the tedious trip to Dong Hoi.

Val had barely stepped into the doorway when Davis met him with a huge list. "Morning, sir. It's gonna be a long day. This is the longest list I've ever had to fill," the lieutenant said as he held up the pad in his left hand and flipped through the pages. "But our new supplier is our best chance to get all or most of the items in one place."

"What's left for the COD flight if we get all this stuff?" Val asked.

"I have a different list for them—only specialty items," the lieutenant said with a wink.

"Gotcha," Val replied as he and Davis walked toward the first truck. As they walked out into the sunshine, Davis gave the signal for all the trucks to fire up, and they rumbled to life as Val and the lieutenant climbed into the cab of the their truck.

"Let's go, Sergeant," the lieutenant ordered. The driver then stuck his hand out, signaling the others to follow as he put his truck in gear and started slowly moving down the base's muddy main road. As they drove along, men would stop what they were doing and wave, knowing that the trucks would bring back badly needed materials. Occasionally they heard shouts like "The hell with the supplies—just bring back the girls!"

The convoy pulled up to the heavily barricaded front gate and showed the guards their orders permitting them to leave the base. The gate was opened and the convoy rumbled through onto the muddy road to Dong Hoi. Val settled in and tried to sleep, but the incredible scenery was too distracting. There was an abundance of wildlife in the jungles along the infrequently used road—large lizards and snakes, birds and monkeys. The flat, open rice paddies and marshes were less interesting, but eventually the road led to the beautifully pristine coastline.

What enhanced the experience was the prospect of seeing the most beautiful woman on the planet. She hadn't been there on the last couple of trips, but it was still nice to see Nghia Mau and the other girls.

The convoy almost got lost again when the driver of the lead truck was forced to take an alternate road to avoid delays in Dong Hoi, but eventually they got back on track and pulled up to the store. Val and Davis hopped, then all six trucks backed up to the loading dock on the side of the building.

Nghia Mau came outside when she heard the noise of the trucks and the men. Val and the lieutenant approached her with a smile and folded hands as they bowed. She returned the gesture and invited them inside.

As Nghia Mau and Val talked, Val took every opportunity to glance toward the curtain, hoping that Nga Nghin Do'i was here today. From her office, Nga Nghin Do'i looked up from her work when she recognized Val's voice. Quickly she ran a brush through her long, silky black hair, tied it with a band with freshly picked flowers in it, and headed for the reception area.

Seeing little movement from behind the curtain, Val assumed Nga Nghin Do'i wasn't at work today. Disappointed, he showed Nghia Mau the list, then waited as she looked it over. Lieutenant Davis, who was sitting behind Nghia Mau sipping on tea, looked up and jumped snapped to his feet, nearly knocking the teapot over. Val looked crossly at the lieutenant, but tightened up himself when he heard the angelic voice from behind him.

"Captain! Good to see you!"

Val turned and was greeted by the beautiful, smiling face that both calmed and excited him. His heart fluttered and his lips quivered as he replied, "Hello, Nga Nghin Do'i." This incredible woman had a mystical spell over him that his own fiancée never had.

She grabbed Val's list from Nghia Mau and said to Val, "Come to office." She started walking toward her office with Val following. She turned back to Val as she parted the curtains and laughed softly so Nghia Mau couldn't hear. "I don't know why she had list. She can't read English."

Val chuckled, but he was already in her spell. He would have followed her across a mine field at this point. When they got to her office, he sat down across from the her as she quickly scanned the list.

When she set it down, she looked at him and said, "I now know about your name. Valentine."

"Really? What about it?"

"'Valentine' mean 'love'—named after a holy man." Again she smiled. This was the most he'd seen her smile, and he was totally enraptured.

"Yes. There was a Saint Valentine a long time ago." Val blushed a little, flattered that this gorgeous woman was curious about him.

"He was beaten, then beheaded," she said sadly, the smile fleeing from her face.

Val was startled by the shift in her mood, and he felt a bit uncomfortable as he didn't know how to respond. "What a tragedy," he finally said.

Nga Nghin Do'i suddenly burst out laughing, "Oh, Captain. It was so long ago." Val smiled back at her and shook his head.

Then she turned her attention back to his list. "You lucky. I think we got everything." She then left to tell the girls in the warehouse and gave them the items they needed.

When she returned to the office, she sat across from Val, but a little closer than before. He noticed that she seemed less shy, looked him in the eye more often, and smiled more. Now she made more small talk, and business was almost an incidental detail of his visit. He began to feel even more relaxed around her, but he was still a little intimidated, and he couldn't figure why. There was still a hint of tension between them, as if each was holding back something that they really wanted to tell the other. Sometimes they just sat quietly and smiled at each other before breaking the silence with small talk or a joke.

Val was certain of only one thing—the lady across from him was unbelievable. She could fill any man's desires. What was even more amazing was that she was hidden away here in this store in a city most people never even heard of. He was elated that he'd not only actually gotten to meet her, but to talk with her and learn about her. He felt that she was truly a blessing, the best part of his stress-filled world away from home.

After a couple of hours, the girls had the trucks completely loaded. For Val and the rest of the Marines, this was definitely the hardest part of these trips—leaving the beautiful girls behind and going back to their dreary existence at Linh Thu. Val could sit in the sweltering heat of that tiny office and talk to Nga Nghin Do'i and never get his fill of her. As the trucks began to fire up, she came out to the docks and waved goodbye, saying, "Can't wait until next time, Captain!"

When she caught their eyes, all the other Marines gaped in awe at the beauty before them. The driver of Val's truck almost ran into a tree, and only slammed on his brakes when Val and Davis shouted at him.

"Goddamn, sir—who is that?" the sergeant said, his eyes wide disbelief on his face.

"That's one of the owners, Sergeant," Val answered.

"That's gotta be the most beautiful woman I've ever seen, and I never was a fan of Oriental women before I came down here." The sergeant wiped his mouth as he continued driving, catching one last glimpse of Nga Nghin Do'i in the rearview mirror.

"Watch the road, Sergeant!" Davis exclaimed as he pointed to a man walking beside a water buffalo.

"Oh my God!" the sergeant said as he nonchalantly swerved around the pedestrian and his animal and kept his gaze on the lovely image of Nga Nghin Do'i in the rearview mirror. "You can't keep hiding her from us, sir. Think she'd let us take a picture of her?"

"I doubt it...why?" Val asked with a smile.

"We could make a fortune selling pictures of her at the PX. She looks better in that dress than the *Playboy* Playmates do totally naked."

"Yeah. She's one in a million." Val sighed as he saw the last image of her walking back into her store. "One in a billion."

"She's better than that, sir. She's the only one like that in world...the only one."

§§§§§

They arrived back at Linh Thu and offloaded supplies in time for mail call. While the men were gathered, Papa told them what they believed happened to Baker and Charles. He fielded questions for a while, then sent them off to chow. He reminded them that they had to focus on their sortie that evening, so they needed to relax until briefing.

Val ran up in anticipation when his name was actually called during mail call, but his hope was dashed when he saw the letter was from an old college buddy. He was more than happy to get mail from home, of course, but he was understandably upset that he still hadn't heard from Virginia, despite the fact that he wrote her all the time.

Val joined his hooch mates at chow and saw their eyes moisten as they read their letters. Taken for granted at home, mail was never as important as it was to someone in combat a hemisphere away. Support and encouragement from home did more for morale than anything else. Val was always glad to hear from his parents and relatives, but they were blood, and their love came with the territory. But the love of a wife or a sweetheart was voluntary, fragile. Absence did not always make the heart grow fonder. He hadn't heard from the person he loved most in the whole world since his first week here. It weighed more and more on his mind with each passing day. He managed to keep his anxiety at bay during sorties, but anytime else it was eating at him.

§ § § § § §

It wasn't long before the Playboys were strapping themselves into their gear. The room was alive with the normal pre-mission chatter, but Val was silent. Nate looked over to his pilot and was concerned about where his pilot's mind was at. "Hey. You okay?"

"Yeah—I'm fine, Double-O."

"Well your big mouth is never this quiet before a sortie, so come on— what's up?"

"Nothing really—just some personal stuff."

Nate knew exactly what that meant. He knew that Val hadn't heard from Virginia for a long time and it was wearing him down. He sighed as he patted Val on the back as he headed out the door. "Hey, Man—take it easy. Let's just get back on the ground safely tonight, and if it helps, we can talk about it then. She's got a job that takes a lot of her. I'm sure she's just real busy. You'll hear from her soon." Nate knew Virginia too. He knew his words were thin, but he wanted to make sure his pilot wouldn't let them and the rest of the squadron down.

Val knew that Nate's words were a reminder to keep focused on the mission. He continued strapping on his gear in silence. When he finished and went to his locker for his helmet, his eyes fell on the large picture of him and

Virginia. Her arms were wrapped tightly around him, and they both had huge smiles on their faces as they snuggled against each other. Val knew something definitely wasn't right. He slowly closed his locker and headed outside. It wasn't long before he found himself in the dark cockpit of his jet, bathed in the gentle glow of the instrument panel. When he'd just finished starting his engines and was about to move on to the next checklist, those chilling images and all-too-familiar words overpowered his thoughts once again: *I love you, Val. Hurry back to me. I'll wait until the end of time for you if I have to. Just be careful and return home safely to me—I can't imagine life without you. I could never even think of loving anyone else but you.*

6

A COMMON BOND

"Get moving, boys!" Papa shouted to his aviators in the ready room as they hurriedly strapped on their gear and dashed out the door to their waiting jets. It had been a full week since Baker and Charles were shot down, and things had quieted down for the most part—except for today.

The Alert-5s were already in position on the runway, ready to throttle up and blast into the bright mid-afternoon sky. All the other flight crews of VMFA-2 rushed to their jets and were literally climbing over ground crews into the cockpits as their aircraft were being loaded with air-to-air ordnance. Engines were fired up just seconds after the pilot had strapped himself in and made sure all ground personnel were clear of the intakes and exhausts. Val and Nate looked overhead as the roar of the Alert-5s grabbing for altitude shook the ground. Time was precious as the even the Alert-5s wouldn't be able to hold their own for too long against the massive firepower that was headed southward from North Vietnam. A flight of thirty enemy aircraft was barreling down from several bases toward the flights of American aircraft returning to bases after their bombing runs. It was highly unusual for the North Vietnamese to send out that many aircraft at once.

Val voiced his concerns as he started his engines. "I got a really bad feeling about this, Double-O, like we saw this very thing just over a week ago."

"I totally agree with you, brother, but we've still got to run up the flagpole," Nate replied as he tested the warning lights on his panel. "All systems go."

"Good to go here, too. Let's see what these bastards are up to," Val said as he gave his plane captain the thumbs up and pushed the throttles forward.

Eight F-4s were taxiing at high speed to the runway, listening to the Alert-5s on frequency. Papa had committed nearly his entire squadron on this sortie, leaving only two F-4s with their crews behind to defend Linh Thu. For the first time since he could remember, he had no aircraft in the maintenance hangar, which was a stroke of good luck at a moment like this. The frequency was busily squawking with chatter between Panama and the Alert-5s, and it was apparent from the chatter that the enemy showed no intention of backing down. Just as Papa and Chappie were roaring down the runway, the squadron heard over frequency that nine aircraft had broken off from the main group, apparently preparing to engage the Americans after seeing the Alert-5s.

Under the strain of a high-g climb-out, Papa keyed up. "Put the coals to it, boys—this sounds really ugly!"

Soon the entire squadron was airborne and Papa kept everyone in afterburner longer than usual in order to catch up to the Alert-5s. Then he had the flight break into widely scattered loose-deuce formations at twenty-eight thousand feet in case of SAM launches. The crews had little time to prepare themselves for what might happen in just a few moments.

"Bowtie Flight, Panama. Multiple bogies are now at twelve o'clock, two-zero miles, southwest bound bearing three-five-zero in two groups. One group at angels two-four, another group at angels one-eight."

"Bowtie Flight, roger," Papa responded, then asked his flight, which now included the Alert-5s in its ranks, "Everyone got 'em?" Papa then took lead, tucking the Alert-5s to his right. "Let's go to angels thirty." Papa then directed his flight to thirty thousand feet so they'd be above their targets when it was time to engage.

"Holy shit! How could we not have them?" Nate said aloud to Val as he fixated on the mass of bright returns peppering the top of his APQ-120 radar scope.

The flight of Marines continued at high speed until Papa pulled back to seventy percent to save some fuel for when they engaged. Every aviator felt a bit anxious as they drew to within twenty miles of the enemy, who was still continuing along on their southeasterly course after breaking off their pursuit of the retreating American F-105s that were now well into Laos on their way back to bases in Thailand. The flight of MiGs began a slow left-sweeping turn to the east, when all of a sudden they broke into several directions heading back to the north at high-speed steep dives.

"What the hell?" Papa's RIO exclaimed as he looked over to Chappie's plane and asked his RIO, "You see what I'm seeing, Mason? I think they saw us!"

"Affirmative. They're gettin' the hell outta Dodge."

"I really don't think it's because they're scared of us this time. Everyone get ready to do some yank and bank!" Nate interjected.

"Care to tell me what exactly you mean, Robinson?" Papa demanded.

"The bogies are in full retreat exactly as they were when we lost Baker and Charles, sir. I suggest we get the hell out of here, sir. We're basically ducks on a pond."

"Say again, Robinson?"

"Sir. Remember what I said in our debrief after we lost Baker and Charles? I think Robinson's right," Val added.

"All right, cut the chatter, Dash 6." Papa then checked in with Panama to confirm that the MiGs were indeed in retreat. When Panama confirmed it, he had his flight immediately turn back to Linh Thu. When they'd completed their about-face, Val happened to look down to his right and see a white smoke trail closing in on the jet behind him. Before he could even key up to warn his fellow Marines, the trail exploded behind the jet.

The crew of Dash 7 was unaware of what was beneath them. They were simply flying along until their plane was suddenly and violently buffeted, the loud bang quickly followed by the distinct sound of a million BBs slamming into the side of the jet. "Shit—Dash 7 is hit," the pilot called out as his plane bounced around. "I'm hit in the number two engine and losing fuel! I'm shutting number two down!" The pilot fumbled around for a while but soon realized his aircraft was basically stable.

"Goddamnit!" Papa yelled. "Check him out, Dash 6!"

"Roger," Val answered as he rolled under his wingman. As he positioned himself below and behind Dash 7, he felt a cold sweat run down his spine as he realized he was now "All right Dash 7," Val said, "your number two engine is almost completely destroyed. I don't know how it's even staying in the fuselage. I don't see any other leaks or other signs of damage. Engine one looks fine."

"Roger. Guess I'm limping home," Dash 7 replied.

"Jordan. You stay with Dash 7 and make sure they get home okay," Papa ordered as his flight began to pull away from the two stragglers.

"Roger," Val replied, then looked into his right rearview mirror at Nate "Did you mark that one, Double-O?"

"Yeah. We were clearly out of Red Zone 1. I think they wised up to us now," Nate said as he was marking on the chart on his thigh.

"Those smartass bastards did it again! I fucking knew it!" Val fumed.

"We'll be the first ones to join you guys on your soapbox if we can get home in one piece without them taking another shot at us," Dash 7 said over frequency as he looked over to Val and Nate and could see they were having some sort of discussion.

"We'll be there in no time. At least your bird seems to be stable," Val said, then, "Tell me—what did it feel like taking a hit from that mystery weapon?"

"Well, it wasn't much different than what I read in your debrief after you took the hit from the SA-2. There was this bang, a large buffet, and this distinct sound, sort of like a million BBs falling off a table onto a hard floor—except the floor was my jet." Dash 7 then chuckled a little. "I think my panic buffeted the plane more than the weapon did!"

Val chuckled back and looked outside toward the runways of Linh Thu. "Well here we are—home at last. Looks like they got our typical welcoming party waiting for us." Val smiled as he broke off and saw the fire equipment standing by at the runway's edge, but all aircraft landed without incident.

As Dash 7's crew pulled into their barricade and shut down, they could see the astonished looks on the faces of the maintenance personnel. They hurriedly climbed out of their jet and parted the crowd gathered at their right engine, where they saw a sickening sight. The panels of the cowling were blown off and bent into sharp, ragged edges that had jutted into the jet's slipstream. The engine itself was burnt black, with the afterburner section torn open and exposed, and the entire engine held in place by only the forwardmost hoists deep inside the fuselage. They realized then and there just how dependable a plane the F-4J was. Few aircraft would have made it home safely with such damage.

"Wow! Thank God I didn't have BBs like that in my gun when I was a kid! I gotta write McDonnell-Douglas a letter of extreme gratitude!" the pilot said as he ran his hands over the damage.

Big John laughed as he looked at the wounded jet. "Goddamnit! You flyboys just can't stand the thought of us mechanics actually having a freakin' day off, can you!"

But Papa didn't share everyone's good humor. He sighed, then tapped Val and Nate on the shoulders and motioned for them to follow him. They looked at each other, figuring they'd said too much over frequency. They knew this meeting wouldn't be pleasant.

They followed Papa into his office, where he told them to sit down and be at ease. He wanted honest opinions without fear of repercussion. Nate showed Papa the mark he'd made on his chart, and both Marines shared their opinions with Papa once again.

"Relax, gents—I agree with you, but I still need rock-solid proof before I can bring it to the attention of my superiors," Papa said as he set his gear on his desk.

"Sir, how much more proof are we talking about here? Do we need to lose another crew?" Val asked, still fearful of talking to his CO in such a tone.

"No—absolutely not. I already planted the bug in General Petersen's ear down in Da Nang, but he doesn't want to do anything about it yet. Unfortunately we're gonna have to wait for at least one more attack against our aircraft, maybe even two. I just pray I don't lose any more guys in the process."

General Petersen was his CO and was in command of all Marine aviation units currently stationed in Vietnam, whether on land or on a carrier. He'd known of Papa since WWII and had met with him a few times in this war. He had the utmost respect for Papa and honestly believed Papa's theory on what was happening to his squadron, but he couldn't do much more for Papa because of neglect from his superiors back home. He knew his squadron was caught in the ultimate SNAFU—there had to be more disasters before anything would be done about it.

After talking with Val and Nate, Papa sent word that there was a mandatory meeting for both VMFA-2 and VMO-16 aircrews at 1600 in the Cannery. Later, when the men gathered, Papa saw that the Cannery was too small to hold everyone, he had them meet in on the hot-pad instead. That way even the Alert-5 crews could be present.

Papa made the briefing quick and to the point as he explained the theories he, Val, and Nate had developed. "I'm not gonna sugarcoat this, gents, so listen up. We're in the fight of our lives—not just with the enemy, but our superiors as well. Our enemies are setting a trap for us that we can't help but be caught in. They basically create a situation that we have to respond to, then wait until we do, and attack us with this new weapon that we haven't been able to do anything about yet. We've been lucky to have only lost two flight crews, though we've had a few aircraft damaged. My superiors don't believe me or at least don't want to, so they have no plans to help us. Unfortunately it'll probably take either the loss of several more aircraft or at least one more flight crew before they'll acknowledge the problem and even a couple more before they take action. So I just want all of you to be alert and protect yourselves. Don't be afraid to take evasive action in the air. Go over your survival training and be ready for the worst. Things may have to get worse before they get better. Good luck, gents. Let's stick together because we're all we got out here."

Papa didn't answer many questions after he dismissed the crews as he was feeling more stress than he had in months. He still had to prepare for the evening's sortie.

The night was still and beautiful as VMFA-2 headed north for another bombing run on a useless target—a small bamboo bridge somewhere in the darkness below, which would probably be rebuilt in less than twenty-four hours. The run was uneventful, as the bridge was in an area well away from AA guns or SAM sites. The Playboys also used only six jets on this sortie, as

Papa didn't want to risk damaging or losing another one—especially on a mission where he expected little resistance. The flight was once again approaching Linh Thu from the north and had purposely avoided Red Zone 1. The crews were accustomed to flying weaving patterns on RTB, but knew that if the base were IFR (Instrument Flight Rules), they'd be in danger of another attack since they'd be unable to "fly the weave," as the pilots called it. The flight approached a three-mile final, far beyond where previous attacks against them had occurred. Papa was in the lead and called out to the control tower that he was inside a three-mile final, which signaled that the runway lights needed to be turned on for landing. Just as the lights came on, he saw a small streak of light at his three o'clock rocketing toward him. His heart sped up as he suddenly broke to the right, toward the streak as he called out, "Heads up, gents! Take evasive action now!"

The streak narrowly passed behind him and continued on into the night. Chappie saw the streak but continued straight ahead and landed his jet, nearly overheating his brakes as he came in really hot. Dash 3 broke right and followed Papa while the other three broke left.

Papa looked up and saw where his squadron was and said, "Let's get down quick, fellas! Papa's got lead, Dash 3's in tow." With that Papa broke right into a low base turn, with Dash 3 not far behind. Papa turned a very short final at less than a quarter mile, and Dash 3 spaced himself just a quarter mile behind him. Val, who was flying the Dash 5 position following Notso, was focusing behind the tail of Dash 3 as he was nearing the end of his base turn. Suddenly another streak of light flared up from the darkness behind Dash 3.

"You got one on you, Dash 3, at your six!" Val said over frequency.

Dash 3 was just now at idle and boards and pulling into a sharp turn to final as Val's warning rang through his helmet. Val rubbed his eyes as the light seemed to hesitate for a split second, and he wondered if he was really seeing what he thought he was.

Papa was listening as he approached a hundred feet of the ground. The runway lights suddenly flickered and shut off in front of him, and the ground instantly turned black. He throttled up to go around, briefly stroking the burners, even though he feared it would reveal his position to the enemy. As his afterburners flared, the streak of light turned in the direction of the runway, but Dash 3 was between Papa and the mysterious light, and it slammed into the American jet but failed to explode as it impacted the tail.

Dash 3 immediately felt the collision and felt the rudder pedals suddenly go soft, indicating he'd most likely lost rudder control. "Tower, where's the lights?" the pilot called out, slightly panicked.

The reply was, "We're trying to get 'em back up."

Dash 3 concentrated on making his jet descend straight ahead at a steady rate, waiting for his landing lights to bathe the ground, which would be about fifty feet up. His RIO called out altitudes off the radar altimeter, and when they were approximately seventy-five feet above the ground, the lights suddenly flashed back on. Dash 3 could see he was still basically down the centerline and touched down without incident. He rolled out all the way to the end to give his fellow Marines all the room needed to get on the ground quickly. As he neared the end, he pressed hard on the pedals to see if the brakes were affected, and as expected they were.

Notso noticed what Val did and immediately pulled his throttles back as he turned a tight base and called out, "Dash 4, idle and boards, advise all other aircraft to do the same."

Val knew he had to keep the engines higher than idle for a little longer for proper spacing to land, as did each aircraft in succession. There were only two more jets behind him now—Dash 6 and Papa, and Val announced over frequency, "Dash 5 concurs, the enemy weapon really went after Papa when he hit the burners."

"Just get on the ground, fellas. We'll discuss this in debrief," Papa ordered.

Notso landed, with Val, Dash 6, and Papa just behind. Papa had just slowed down to make the turn at the end of the runway when another streak of light passed just over his canopy heading southbound into the trees. "Watch it, fellas—they're shooting at us on the ground. Turn off your taxi lights!"

The rest of the flight was on the parallel taxiway and had seen the streak pass over Papa's jet. Val, who had his canopy open, stuck his head out the right side and watched the streak continue on its southbound course, then fly erratically, suddenly flare up brightly enough to silhouette the jungle, and drop to the ground. "Papa, I think that thing crashed into the trees just beyond the perimeter fence line!"

"Roger, Dash 5—I saw it, too. We'll worry about it later. Just get to the barricades," Papa responded.

The lights shut down just as Papa unkeyed, and the follow-me trucks led the flight into their barricades on the northwest ramp. All the flight crews hurriedly climbed out of their jets and, except for Dash 3, piled into their waiting trucks. Dash 3 waited for Big John to inspect the damage to their jet. When Big John arrived at the ramp, he was accompanied by Little John and three other men. They could see the damaged tail before they even got up to it as the tail was taller than its barricades.

When Big John walked up under the tail of the wounded bird, he pulled off his hat and, in a fury, threw it on the ground as he exclaimed, "Goddamnit—you've got to be shitting me! Another fucking damaged plane? McDonnell-Douglas isn't going to be able to keep up with you all!" The crew thought the big man was directing his anger at them, but when he looked over and saw the fear in their eyes, he laughed and patted each of them on the back. "Just glad you boys are alive and safe!" The crew then scrambled for the truck that would take them to debrief.

§ § § § §

The debrief had less to do with the sortie than with the serious problem that faced any aircraft departing or arriving at Linh Thu. The men needed to know what they were dealing with if they were to successfully counter it. No one seemed to have any answers, and the men left the Cannery feeling rather melancholy.

Val immediately headed for his hooch. He wanted to write a letter to Virginia, but first he stopped by the post office to see if he'd received any mail because he hadn't checked in two days. He picked up three letters—one from a good friend, one from his parents, and one from a professor he'd had in college. Val had just about given up hope for receiving a letter from Virginia, so he was mentally prepared to find none each time he went to mail call or the post office. Still, it stung when he didn't get one.

When he got to his hooch, he sat down on his rack, pulled out his stationery, and began to write. He needed to hear from Virginia more than ever now that he and his comrades were facing even more danger than ever.

Val wrote about two paragraphs, then suddenly stopped and looked at the pictures of Virginia pinned to his locker. A torrent of emotions suddenly swept over him as he tore the letter up and threw it into the GI can. He took several deep breaths and closed his eyes to calm himself down and to clear his head. When he opened his eyes, he decided to try a new approach—he'd write her parents instead. It was a bold move on his part since her parents had some reservations about him. They liked him well enough, but they didn't like the fact that he was serving in a war they didn't approve of. They also had a problem with their daughter actually moving in with Val when he was at TBS (The Basic School) while they were unmarried. It was a changing world, and they felt some things were changing too fast.

Val had just about finished the letter when a sergeant came to his hooch. "Sir, are you Captain Jordan?"

"Yes, Sergeant."

"A couple of officers sent for you. Please come with me to sick bay if you will, sir."

Val was puzzled, "Sick bay? I'm not sick or injured, Sergeant."

"I know sir, but the officers who have sent for you are in sick bay."

"Okay," Val said, puzzled. No one he knew had been taken to sick bay.

Val followed the sergeant to sick bay, a large tent in the middle of Linh Thu's "business district"—basically the part of base that wasn't housing. Val entered the tent and was directed to cots against the wall at the far end of recovery. He headed in that direction, noticing that there were relatively few patients. Most were there because of ailments related to the climate—heat casualties, dysentery, fungal infections, and even some cases of malaria. When Val got to the recovery section, he looked around and noticed the cots he was directed to still had their privacy curtains around them. He slowly pulled them back and peeked in, and there he saw Captain Overstreet and Lieutenant Torres, their forearms and lower legs wrapped in gauze stained yellow from ointment. They were both sitting up reading magazines.

"Y'all sent for me?" Val asked softly.

Both men looked up and smiled as they answered in unison, "Yes—come in, Captain!"

Val pulled up a doctor's stool and sat between them at the foot of the bed. Torres pointed to the magazine he was reading and said, "Damn thing is freakin' ancient!" He smiled and continued sarcastically: "Did you know that the level of troop buildups is going to dramatically increase in South Vietnam, sir? And rumors are circulating that the Americans are going to be starting a massive air campaign called 'Rolling Thunder,' which is expected to commence within days?"

Val smirked, still wondering why he was sitting with these two men. "Well maybe I should resign my commission before it begins, Lieutenant."

Suddenly Overstreet spoke from behind his magazine. "I heard what's been going on the past few days, Captain. You boys are lucky your losses aren't any higher."

Val was both confused and angered by the intelligence officer's tone. "Thanks for being so concerned, Captain."

"Look, Captain"—Overstreet lowered his magazine to his lap and looked at Val—"I know no one on base cares a whole lot about me right now—in fact they probably hate me. I just want you to know we're on the same side here. I hate it when you guys risk your lives for nothing, and I don't want to see Americans die any more than you do."

"So why am I here, Captain? Do you want us to hang out at the pub and have some beers or something?" Val still wasn't sure what Overstreet was getting at.

"Captain, I know I'm not your favorite person, but you still risked your life to help me in that fire. I just want to thank you, and let you know that whatever you need from now on, you just say it. I'll do my best to help you."

"Me too, sir," Torres piped in. "You name it, I'll do it. Your squadron has a reputation for sticking your necks out for anyone who needs help. no matter what the risks. I'd like to do more than just say 'thank you'—I'd like to show my gratitude."

"I'm just doing what Marines do, gentlemen." Val warmed a little. "And Captain, we'd just like to know what we're up against, that's all."

"We're serious, Captain. Just name the task—we'll do it." Overstreet reaffirmed.

Val still wasn't sure about Overstreet, but knew Torres was solid. He'd have to see about Overstreet before he trusted him. He looked down at his watch and yawned as he said, "Listen, gents, I gotta get some sleep, I got an early flight and a long drive to Dong Hoi this week." He rose from the stool and nodded at both men as he said, "Y'all take care."

Val turned and was just about to walk away when Overstreet blurted out, "That so-called mystery weapon that's causing you so much grief is a new shoulder-mounted anti-aircraft missile launcher called the SA-7." Val stopped dead in his tracks, closed the curtains, and sat back down as Overstreet continued. "It can be fired by a foot soldier. It has a range of about a three to five miles and it's guided by an infrared filter that seeks out the heat from a jet engine. That is why it's nearly impossible to know that you're being tracked until it's almost too late. Your only defense is early detection, then either break the cone of vulnerability in time or get out of range. We have a similar weapon soon to be issued called the Stinger. I don't know who's using the SA-7s, but they apparently haven't had enough training, or else your losses would be much higher."

When Overstreet finished, Val said, "Well golly gee—lucky for us! Maybe by tomorrow they'll have had enough time to read the fucking manuals!"

"We will find them, Captain"—Overstreet raised his right hand—"because I want to get those bastards as badly as you do."

After a few more minutes of conversation, Val left sick bay and found Papa in the pub. Knowing he would most likely have had a few drinks and wouldn't be in the mood to talk shop, Val told his CO that he had to see him as early as possible in the morning because he had some very important news. Papa set the meeting for 0600.

§ § § § §

Papa was already waiting for Val in his office when he knocked on the door. "Come in, Captain," Papa said as he sipped his coffee and directed Val to the seat across from him. "What's so goddamned important that you had to disturb me in the pub last night?"

"Sir, I have really important news about our new problem."

"Is this another theory, or do you have actual facts?"

"Actual facts, sir."

"And what's your source?" Papa's stare told Val that he'd better have a good answer. When he hesitated, Papa said, "Go ahead, Jordan—tell me your source."

"Captain Overstreet, sir." The look on Papa's face told Val he had his attention.

"And why did Captain Overstreet talk to you first and not me?"

"I'm not sure, sir. Maybe he felt obligated because I pulled him out of that fire."

Papa sighed. "All right, then—go ahead."

Val told Papa what the intelligence officer had revealed to him, and what should have been a short briefing dragged out into an hour-long session. When Papa finally dismissed Val, he shouted at him, "Hey Jordan. Before I forget!"

Val stopped and turned back to his CO. "Yes, sir?"

"I reshuffled schedules around with so many aircraft in maintenance now, so you and Robinson are on Alert-5 duty, beginning at 1700."

"Does Robinson know that yet, sir?"

"He will when you tell him at chow—and spread the word that I want to have a meeting with all the flight crews of both squadrons at 1400 on the northwest ramp."

§ § § § §

Papa began his meeting a little early as always and continued with his tradition of telling his men exactly what was going on instead of blowing smoke. Every man was shocked—not by what Papa was telling them, but because had taken so long for them to find out, and that they weren't even actually supposed to know yet. Papa could feel the tension in the air, and he knew that morale had just dropped a few more notches. He knew it helped a bit that the men knew they could trust him and level with them when their lives depended on it. He also knew they were glad to know what they were up against—even if they had no countermeasures yet. As he dismissed the meeting, Papa looked out across the gathering and saw the hanging heads and long faces. He knew he'd better do something soon to help lift their spirits, or else he'd be facing even more losses.

§ § § § §

Val entered the Shack at 1700 with Nate and the other flight and ground crews on duty with them. They found the outbound crew relaxing in the air conditioning and as usual had to force them out. No one wanted to leave the nice, cool air of the Shack and return to regular duty. The new crews plopped themselves on the couches and racks and let out a sigh of relief, knowing that if the phone didn't ring for the next twenty-four hours, they'd basically have a day of liberty to relax.

At 2200 the phone rang and the alarm sounded. Everyone jumped to their feet, and as the ground crews ran outside, the flight crews hastily strapped on their gear. Val and the lead crew chief for the ground crews picked up the phone and got Panama's instructions. They hung up at the same time, and the crew chief ran outside with orders on what type of ordnance needed to be loaded. Val looked at the flight crews and said, "Well, I guess they finally had enough time to the read the SA-7's instructions. Here's the low-down..." He explained that a flight of six MiGs was headed after the Playboys, who were now either in the pattern and landing or were approaching the base and splitting into right and left patterns for the break.

The Alert-5s were taxiing within minutes and were loaded with air-to-air ordnance. They decided to taxi to runway 10 so they wouldn't get in the way of any of the Marines who were trying to land on runway 13. The control tower would have them "shoot the gap" between the aircraft already in the pattern for 13.

As the Alert-5s took position on runway 10, Val said to his wingman, "Barkley, let's keep out of afterburner as much as possible. Just use it until we're over the departure end, then shut them off in case those bastards are just trying to draw us out again."

"Roger, Dash 1," Barkley responded.

"Bowtie Flight, Linh Thu Tower. Runway one-zero cleared for takeoff. Wind calm."

"Bowtie Flight rolling," Val responded as he and his wingman throttled up to afterburner. The white-hot glow of all four engines in full afterburner shattered the darkness as the jets roared into the night sky. Papa had called ahead and had another two jets ready to launch, but had them hold on the ramp as he wanted to see if this was for real.

The Alert-5s pulled out of afterburner when they passed the departure end of runway 10 and went on military power for their climb-out to engage the MiGs. They began a left turn and headed north as both RIOs tried to get a solid lock on their targets. The MiGs continued straight toward Linh Thu, seemingly undeterred.

"All right, let's break left to get an angle on these bastards while we still can. I don't think they've seen us yet," Val ordered as both American jets broke high and left.

"Bandits are continuing toward us. They probably see us now because they'll be in range in about two minutes if they don't deviate from their present course," Nate told Val.

"Roger. Arm Sparrows. We have an angle of ninety, level at angels one-niner. We'll have them in thirty seconds."

"They're breaking off, Tibbs!" Nate said excitedly, using the shortened version of "El Tiburon," Val's call-sign. "They must be fucking geniuses! How the hell do they know when they're in range?" He knew that very soon they could be staring down a missile from an SA-7.

"Pursue them, dammit! Let's get as close as we can. Maybe the ground troops won't launch at us if we're too close to their aircraft. Full afterburner now!" Val ordered as he shoved his throttles to their full stops, hoping to close the distance and maybe even get a shot off. Val knew the F-4 was much faster than a MiG-17 or -21 at top speed, but he also knew their pilots might have timed their break so the Marines wouldn't be able to catch them when they saw the flames from their afterburners.

"They've got some balls showing us their positions like that," Barkley said as he watched them steadily keep just out of range.

"We're not going to catch them for a while, Tibbs. They're keeping a steady distance. By the time we did overtake them, we'd be deep into North Vietnam and low on fuel." Nate wanted to influence his pilot's decision.

Val hated that they were in the exact position he was trying to avoid, and he knew his RIO was right. "Okay, Bowties—pull back to fifty percent and start a steady right descending turn back to Linh Thu. Maybe we'll cut down on our heat signature."

Both pilots chopped their throttles and dove to the right, hoping not to draw a lot of attention. As they descended to ten thousand feet, Val had his flight level off.

"Why are we leveling off, Tibbs? Won't we be easier to spot?" Barkley asked.

"Well, they've been nailing us at low altitude on final. I want to try a high-key approach to runway 31, see if it'll throw 'em off. Once we're over the field, chop your throttles to idle. Maybe that'll keep a low-enough temperature so the weapon won't work."

"I hope you're right," Barkley said.

Val informed the tower of his intentions, then as his flight was over the base, he chopped his throttles and began the high-key approach. Barkley followed about a quarter mile in trail. The approach was going smoothly with only a few buffets as the altimeter rapidly wound down. It wasn't long before Val was short final. Barkley, not paying enough attention, allowed himself to gain too much energy and got too close to Val.

"Sorry, Tibbs—had my head up my ass. I'm right on your tail. I'm gonna just continue east downwind and land on 13. You should be clear of the runway in plenty of time."

"Roger. Avoid throttling up if you can," Val responded.

Barkley continued into the east downwind. When he was about mid-field, he felt a sudden jolt, and his number-one engine showered a stream of sparks, then suddenly shut down. "Shit! Tower, something just went through my left engine, maybe a bird. I'm gonna extend my downwind a hair." Barkley was still at idle, but the drag of the fodded-out engine caused him to lose a lot of airspeed and some directional control. He had to add some power to his number-two engine to gain the airspeed needed for a safe approach. Just as his hand pushed the throttle forward, an explosion rocked his jet, and in his rearview mirror he saw flames engulf his entire tail assembly.

Val looked up to see the telltale smoke column in the light of the flames and saw the piercing white glow of the rockets of the ejection seats fire off into the black sky. The jet suddenly banked right and exploded in the jungles east of the base. Papa was watching the whole thing unfold from the northwest ramp and immediately had rescue vehicles searching for parachutes in the sky with their spotlights.

Barkley and his RIO, Tromlison, were just being shaken loose of their seats as their personal parachutes blossomed in the still night air. Neither could believe how fast things had happened. Hot air billowing up from the fire beneath them briefly suspended their descent. They looked down and could see they were drifting toward the flames of the wreckage beneath them. They needed to be precise about where they landed. They knew that the base was surrounded by mine fields, and they certainly didn't want to land in the middle of them. But landing near the burning the wreckage wasn't an option either.

Their 'chutes had limited directional control, but they were still high enough to be able to direct their descent over the perimeter fence and onto the base somewhere. They pulled on the handles and managed to steer themselves over a runway. It wasn't long before spotlights were whiting out their vision as rescue vehicles waited for them to land. A solid thud and a grunt told rescue personnel that the flight crew had indeed landed and they rushed over to assist them. Both men were fighting their way free of the harness when the vehicles got to them. Luckily the injuries were slight: bruised noses, scratches on their faces, and slight ankle sprains.

Papa was relieved to see his two aviators sitting up in the back of the jeep as it pulled up. Val and Nate had just climbed out of their jet and were running over to the jeep. They saw Big John standing behind Papa, and they stood beside him as Papa walked off with his aviators and the medical personnel.

"Well, sir, at least one good thing'll come out of this," Val said to Big John with a smirk.

Big John knew a smart-alecky remark was coming. "And what's that, Captain?"

"At least you won't have to worry about fixing that plane," Val laughed as he nodded in the direction of the burning wreckage.

"You crack yourself up, don't you?" Big John smiled and walked away.

Val and Nate headed to the Shack to try to get some sleep, but they knew it would be impossible with the adrenaline coursing through their veins. They were relieved that their fellow aviators were safe, so that might help them calm down more quickly.

§ § § § § §

Morning came swiftly, and all aviators from both squadrons woke to a memo that told them to muster in front of the new HQ building at 0700. The memo didn't say why, but everyone expected it would be about what was going on just beyond the perimeter fence.

At 0700, everyone was gathered in front of Papa on the HQ steps. When he called the roll call to make sure every aviator was actually there, each man knew this meeting must be extremely important.

When Papa got down to business, he explained that they had to brainstorm and come up with a safe new procedure for them to fly into Linh Thu. "They're attacking us when we're on final—very smartly, I might add. They know the aircraft will be low, slow, and vulnerable—especially helicopters. It won't be long till they're launching on us as we're departing, which puts us in the same situation. So we need to find a solution—now!"

"Can we get some patrols going around the clock around the base?" a voice offered.

"We could, but it'd be like trying to find the proverbial needle in the haystack. These weapons have a decent range, so the launcher doesn't have to be close, plus it only takes one man to fire the thing. It makes for a large area for a patrol to secure. However, Lieutenant Torres is expected to be out of sick bay by the end of the week and he's going to lead his platoon to find the missile that crashed into the jungle south of the base the other night—if the Gooners haven't gotten it yet."

"Does DOD have any countermeasures available or in development?" another voice asked.

"They're researching some countermeasures now, but haven't found one they like yet that they can mass produce."

"So right now we're totally screwed," someone else shouted.

"Maybe. But we can cut our losses if we make sure our approaches get us on the ground fast and quiet. I believe all fixed-wing aircraft should do a low-overhead break with engines at idle as soon as the break is commenced. Helicopters need to keep it low and fast until over the run-up area on the north side, then use the run-up pad as a deceleration zone. By the time they reach the pad, they should be too low to be fired upon."

"What about bigger aircraft, like our COD flights?" another Marine asked.

"They're either going to have to do the break or do a rapid descent at idle from a high altitude, really close to the field. Another reason I want everyone to fly so close to the field is because of what we had last night. If an aircraft is attacked, the crew has a reasonable chance of making the field or landing very close to the field, even if they have to punch out." Papa then passed out a summary of his new policy on approaches to Linh Thu to each aviator, and informed the squadrons that the same information was being disseminated to all branches of the military. It was quiet as everyone read the material, then as they finished, the noise level started picking up again. Papa then added, "One last thing—everyone listen up." Papa waited until all eyes were back on him. "In order to avoid another incident like last night, we won't respond to MiGs that seem to be heading for Linh Thu." Papa knew everyone would want an explanation of a policy that seemed to contradict common sense. "I repeat: we will *not* respond to any MiGs that appear to be heading toward Linh Thu. We will, of course, continue to escort and defend American aircraft from MiGs, but not our base. Now I know I'm really rolling the dice here, but so far in the war, North Vietnamese MiGs have made any ground attacks. They primarily hit lines of bombers and attack aircraft and run back to their bases. So if they charge our base again, we'll simply let 'em. I'm thinking they'll stop coming at us if they know we won't respond because I believe they're trying to draw us out so they can fire these new rockets at us. If we don't come out to play, they won't be able to shoot any more of us down."

Val looked at Nate when Papa finished and smirked as he said, "I believe we've heard that suggestion before."

"Oh, well—at least he sounds like he agrees," Nate replied.

§ § § § §

Val was soon alone in his hooch with only his thoughts to keep him company, and it wasn't long before Virginia filled his head again. As he drifted into daydreams about her, his eyes focused on the picture on the wall by his rack. He took the picture off the wall and stared at it until it became the fuzzy background of his thoughts of their life together back home. Val was a man who truly lived in the moment. He remembered even minute details vividly because he craved the experience of the moment. The sounds in the background, the smells in the air, the clothes the person he was with was wearing, the colors of the scenery, all completed a perfect mosaic of where he was and what he was doing. It didn't matter what he was doing, whether he was alone or accompanied by someone, he simply appreciated being alive. Even if things didn't go the way he wanted, he still had the moment, and if things went better than expected; he had the moment to relive, and that completed him. He had countless moments with Virginia.

He remembered the first time he ever saw her, on the steps of the science building at college, and how he'd become oblivious to his surroundings when she returned his gaze—so much so that he almost ran into a trashcan alongside the walkway. Then there was the time he finally decided to ask her out, and he was shaking so bad that he barely had any control over his body when he walked up to her. He did his best to hide his tremors and his sweaty palms, and he had to make an effort to keep his voice from quavering. But as their lives began to intertwine, his confidence grew, until eventually she made him feel invincible whenever she was with him.

He thought of the first time they made love. He remembered how nervous but determined they were when they told her parents that they were moving in together even though they weren't married yet. There were difficult times mixed with the good, which would test their devotion to each other—like when they were separated because Val attended OCS, TBS, and flight school, or when she began her job as a stockbroker—a field traditionally dominated by men, where on top of the stress she had to work twice as hard, and occasionally fight off advances from her male colleagues.

No matter how rough life got, they always found a way to tough it out together. However, the war was clearly their biggest challenge. Val felt that if they could make it through this, every other bump in the road would seem insignificant. But the problem now was that he didn't know how they were doing because he hadn't heard from her since his first week here. He hadn't been this panicky since the first time he'd asked her out.

He wrote two letters—one to Virginia and another to her parents—pleading for word that everything was okay. He explained how he was depressed and losing sleep. On his way to the chow hall, he dropped the letters by the post office, believing they'd be in vain.

§ § § § §

Another week passed, this one quiet and almost devoid of action, as if the enemy no longer existed. There were no mortar or rocket attacks on the base, almost no calls for assistance from units in the field, and the skies were empty of enemy aircraft. Lieutenant Torres had recovered from his wounds and, true to his word, led his team into the jungles on the southern side of the base to look for the missile that had missed its target the week before. It was a dangerous job because, while the missile was located within three hours, it was in a mined wooded area, so the team had to be careful where they stepped.

The missile was stuck in branches about seventy feet up, and even from the ground they could see that it was burnt and damaged. After some discussion, one of the men volunteered to climb the tree and attempt to free the missile from the branches.

"Watch out for booby-traps, Sergeant," Torres warned him. He knew the NVA wouldn't have left the missile up there if they knew about it, so he was gambling that they didn't.

"Don't worry, sir—I used to work for Southern Bell, so I'm used to climbing. I'll have that thing down in under two minutes." The sergeant smiled as he tied support straps around the trunk of the massive tree and straddled it with his feet and hands.

"Just tell me when," Torres said.

"When what, sir?"

"To start timing you."

The sergeant chuckled and secured his footing, took a deep breath and said, "Now!" as he scrambled up the tree with amazing speed. The platoon watched in amazement as he reached the missile in less than twenty-six seconds.

"Goddamnit, Sergeant! Are you half orangutan or something?" Lieutenant Torres yelled.

"No," the sergeant yelled back. "Spider monkey actually."

"You mean howler monkey," another Marine piped in. "I heard you fucking that whore in Saigon from the street."

"Actually she was the one howling," the sergeant said as he scanned the missile for wires or other signs of booby-traps. The missile itself didn't look very impressive as he began to work it loose from the branches. Only about four feet long and very skinny, he didn't see how it could pack enough wallop to knock an aircraft out of the sky. After a brief struggle, the sergeant finally freed the weapon. Bearing in mind that it still had a live charge somewhere in it, he decided not to drop it. Instead he tucked it into his belt and carefully made his way back to the ground.

As soon as his feet hit the ground, Torres pushed a button on his watch and said, "One minute, thirty-nine seconds. Nice work, Sergeant."

"Thank you, sir. Guess I'd better be prepared for monkey jokes," the sergeant said as he carefully laid the missile across his backpack.

"Good idea, Sergeant," Torres said as he called for a helicopter to pick them up to avoid another trek through a minefield.

§ § § § §

Papa was waiting on the ramp for the helicopters to land once he got word that the lieutenant had the "package" in his possession. He was certainly curious about what this little terror looked like, and he'd have his first look soon enough. As soon as the helicopters landed, Papa and the platoon were driven to the HQ building, where Linh Thu's top brass got their first look at the weapon. As the sergeant unfolded the poncho he'd wrapped around it, the officers craned their necks for a glimpse. They'd seen the launcher that the platoon had recovered a couple weeks ago, and as the missile was unveiled, the officers' reaction was the same as the sergeant's who'd freed it from the tree. They were expecting something more ferocious than a simple tube with folding fins. This couldn't be the whole missile! How could this little thing bring down an aircraft?

Lieutenant Torres watched the officers' reactions and saw their doubts, so he pulled the magazine out of his M16 and picked out the top round. As he placed the round on the table in front of the other officers, he repeated an old saying: "Remember gentlemen—'dynamite comes in small packages.'" As the officers looked up at him, he pointed at the lone round on the table. "By itself, a bullet seems rather impotent." Then he picked it up, put it back in the magazine, shoved the magazine into his rifle, slammed the bolt home, and rapped the forward assist. "But put that bullet in a rifle, and you have a killing machine."

The officers looked at the lieutenant, admiring his cleverness. Among them was Captain Overstreet, who was still struggling for a little respect—although lately some were noticing that he seemed to be toning down his arrogance. After examining the weapon for a while without really gaining any insight, the officers turned it over to Overstreet so he could send it where it could be properly evaluated. After he left the room, the others sat in the silence, not really sure what their next move was. After a few minutes moments, all eyes fell on Papa. He straightened up, then looked everyone square in the eye. "Let's just continue the procedures I gave the flight crews. We'll keep doin' it until the Gooners change their tactics, then we'll have to adapt again, as we always do."

When the meeting ended and everyone else had gone, Papa stared out the window for a while, thinking of the chances he was taking and how so many lives depended on his decisions. Then he shook his head and said to himself, "Sometimes I think sitting home drawing unemployment doesn't sound too bad."

§ § § § § §

A few more days went by with little activity. The Playboys still had some night sorties and the Alert-5s went on a couple of scrambles to assist other aircraft and ground troops, but no losses were incurred and there were no SAM launches.

The flight crews enjoyed the peace while they could, knowing that it wouldn't last much longer. They followed Papa's edict for low-key approaches and adhered to his no-response policy if MiGs were heading for Linh Thu. But lately MiGs were nowhere to be found—almost as if they'd gotten word of Papa's plan and figured there was no point. None of the branches were reporting significant encounters with them in regular bombing missions over North Vietnam. In this case no news was usually good news, but Papa and the flight crews believed it was the calm before the storm.

They were proven correct the next week. North Vietnam implemented an aggressive air-defense policy during, launching twice and sometimes three times the normal number of aircraft against the Americans on their bombing runs. North Vietnamese pilots had never demonstrated such tenacity before as they inflicted a heavy toll on US attack aircraft and bombers and the fighters called in to protect them. The Alert-5s were being launched all hours of the day and night, and flight crews were no longer thinking it was cushy duty as they returned from skirmishes with damage to their aircraft and raw nerves. Even though the MiGs were keeping the flight crews busy over North Vietnam, they still never attempted to draw out a response from Linh Thu as they had in previous weeks—as if they'd forgotten how successful they'd been with the SA-7. The flight crews of Linh Thu operated on little sleep and lots of coffee that week, so in a way the MiGs were successful because they insured the crews weren't as sharp as they normally were.

§ § § § §

Everyone at Linh Thu figured that it was bound to happen sooner or later, and finally it did. It was early Friday evening and everyone not presently on duty was heading for the pub when the sirens sounded. Papa, who was just leaving his office, instantly ran back in and got on the phone to confirm his suspicions. He was right.

Panama had picked up strong paint deflections from about five unknown aircraft bearing down at high speed to Linh Thu. He called the Shack and told the Alert-5 crews to load their aircraft with air-to-air ordnance and to sit in their aircraft with engines running, but not to launch until his personal approval was confirmed on the phone or on frequency from the control tower. He told everyone to take cover in their hooches, but no one listened. They wouldn't miss the chance to catch a glimpse of a real MiG if they indeed came with visual range of the base. Everyone headed to the northwest ramp and took a seat in prime viewing area. Papa headed for the control tower, even though he knew there was a real danger that it would be a prime target if this was a real attack. When Papa got to the tower and saw practically the entire base over at the northwest ramp, he shook his head. The bogies were still not confirmed as bandits yet, but there was no doubt in their minds who they were and what they were doing. They were now just two minutes north.

The men on the northwest ramp actually had their personal cameras and movie cameras out, ready to capture the MiGs on film. The air was abuzz with chatter:

"What do we do if the MiGs actually attack?"

"I don't know—run like hell for cover I guess."

"Hey, does this look in focus to you?"

"Glad I'm not on Alert-5 duty today."

"These fuckers better give us a good show and not turn away again."

"By the way, where do you think the best cover is in case of an air raid?"

"Wherever the bombs and bullets aren't."

§ § § § § §

The lead MiG pilot was confused by the lack of response from the Americans. Why the hell weren't they airborne? Did they know that he was under strict orders not to fire on them? They were closing in on their decision mark. Were the Americans turning the tables and setting a trap for them? He looked back over escape routes they'd been briefed about if his squadron should come under attack from American ground fire. Safe return home was almost guaranteed. He looked back at the target growing ever larger in his windscreen, then back at his charts. Should he make his squadron proceed to the base, or should they turn back home at the mark? They were twelve kilometers from the base, and could clearly see the runways from here. There were still no signs of enemy aircraft attempting to launch.

He glanced at his clock. They were only two minutes from the base at their present speed. If they pushed it to full throttle, they could make three passes and still have enough fuel to get home, barring no encounters with enemy fighters on the way back. He then looked at his wingmen. They'd come this far—no reason to turn back now. If the Americans do finally launch, they'd met with a barrage of SAMs. He wanted to see his enemy up close and what they were really up to, for he was certainly not afraid of them.

He was Captain Tren Phan, and he was widely known and well respected throughout North Vietnam as the best fighter pilot in southeast Asia because he didn't employ the "hit and run" technique most North Vietnamese pilots did. He preferred to engage the Americans in a dogfight and would win or escape unscathed. Phan was intimately familiar with the violent side of human nature his whole life, through his family and his own experience. His grandfather had resisted the Japanese during WWII and was tortured and killed when he was taken captive. He witnessed the slaughter of his family and neighbors as a boy during the years of French occupation. He could trace his bloodline back through generations of war and struggle. Even so, he was a gentle and peaceful man; no one was more appropriately described as "cool under fire" than he was. He loved flying and was passionate about it, and when he was in the cockpit he revealed his aggressive side. He had traveled to Russia and learned all about the MiG-17, -19, and -21, and had shown he'd mastered them all. It wasn't long before he could outperform the instructors who'd taught him to fly, and was actually teaching them things they never knew their aircraft could do. Only one of his Russian instructors was his equal in his mind, and he was actually getting to train with him at home in a war against the Americans. That instructor's name was Colonel Tomb.

The Americans were learning of Tomb but had no idea he was a Russian advisor. Most thought he was Vietnamese. The pilot they usually thought was Colonel Tomb was actually Captain Phan, who was insulted to be mistaken for a pilot he considered to be a cowardly nuisance. He never showed his fear in air combat. He either came out victorious or managed to return home when his wingmen did not. What else would anyone expect from someone named Tren—which, loosely translated, meant "to be above; on top."

Phan looked at his fellow MiGs as he keyed up "*Nhanh len!*"—Faster!" as he shoved his throttle to its full stop, lighting the burner. "*Dung co so hai MY! Di vo'i tao!*"—Don't be scared of the Americans! Follow me!

His fellow pilots mimicked his actions as they flew in a modified echelon left formation after their leader pulled ahead. They knew exactly how far he wanted his formation spaced, and they flew with two hundred meters between each aircraft as they began the attack. Phan dove until he was only a couple of hundred feet off the ground, with his airspeed building at a tremendous rate. He wanted to be at the highest end of the attack envelope, which was the top airspeed for high-g maneuvering and weapons deployment of the MiG-21— somewhere around .9 mach. When he saw he was there, he adjusted his throttle accordingly to hold the airspeed and dove at the base that was now just off his nose. He streaked right down runway 13 about a hundred feet off the deck and noticed the people standing on the northwest ramp and the two F-4s that had engines running but were not moving. When he reached the departure end, he made a high-g left climbing turn and looked back to see the rest of his flight mimicking his flight path.

What was going on down there? he wondered. Was the enemy actually caught off guard? By now they must surely be aware of the danger. He kept the base in view as he swung his flight out to the northeast. After a few seconds without a reaction from the two jets idling on the ramp, he decided to turn back for another pass. "*Nua!*"—Again! he ordered over frequency and reminded his flight of the escape routes if they met with resistance. He turned his flight for another low pass over runway 13. This time he made sure he flew off centerline and closer to the jets and the group of people on the large ramp.

Back on the ground and in the control tower, the air was electric with excited conversation about the enemy's little air show.

"That was fucking cool!"

"Make sure you get me waving at them in the next shot if they come by again!"

The control tower personnel saw that the MiGs were indeed coming around for another pass, so the local controller said "Watch this! This should get an interesting response!" The controller grabbed the light gun and aimed it at the line of MiGs bearing down at them at an even lower altitude than before. He shined the steady green at them, which would indicate they were cleared to land.

Phan saw the light, and saw that the people on the ramp, including the crews sitting in the F-4s, were waving wildly at them—as if they were celebrities.

"*Nhin cai do kia!*"—Look at that there! he said in anger and amazement to his flight as he rocketed over the ramp and back into a climbing left turn. As he looked back to the base he caught a couple of his pilots even waving back, and he scolded them. He was still amazed that the enemy hadn't responded. He was also insulted by their arrogance.

He ordered one more pass at full throttle, hoping that a sonic boom might cause some damage, since he wasn't allowed to use his ordnance. This time he turned in sooner than on the previous two passes and dropped to fifty feet off the deck. He'd make sure the first part of his pass would be over buildings and the last part would catch the ramp and control tower and continue down the runway. Just as he over flew the perimeter fence, he passed mach 1. A thunderous, ground-shaking BOOM sounded overhead as the jet passed over the tents and then the crowd, who immediately plugged their ears. They looked up to see that the jet was firing its cannons down the length of the runway in the air, hitting nothing but the trees to the south. The sonic boom dug up dirt, blew over poorly secured tents, ripped through canvas, and cracked and shattered glass. The men on the ramp felt their bones rattle again and again as each jet passed. As Phan began his turn to the northeast, he ordered, "*Chung ta di di!*"—Let's get outta here! One by one, the silver jets roared by firing their guns before disappearing to the northeast, disgusted that they weren't taken seriously by their enemy. Even though they didn't succeed in luring any enemy jets to their destruction, Phan's flight still enjoyed flying low and fast over the base. Although the Americans were the enemy, it was still fun to see them wave and cheer at them, as if they were famous. Phan was the exception.

To him it was a personal insult, and he led his flight home burning for vengeance.

Papa and the CO of VMO-16 held meetings with their respective squadrons, where they expressed their displeasure with the men for how they'd gathered on the ramp while enemy aircraft were flying overhead, as if they were attending an air show. Even though he hadn't intended to send any aircraft to respond, he still expected them to understand that the North Vietnamese had the equipment and the ability to carry out a ground attack from their aircraft. He reminded them over and over that they were US Marines fighting a war against a very intelligent and resourceful enemy in their own backyard. If the MiGs came back, Papa reiterated that the base would once again stand down and not risk losing another aircraft to a SA-7. If the MiGs did indeed attack, the Alert-5s would engage them and respond to any further attacks the same way, but the base would need to find a solution to the Red Zone dilemma.

§ § § § § §

The air was thick with cigarette smoke and tension. In the middle of the ops room at Kep Field, near Hanoi, several officers stood in a semi-circle around an angry Captain Phan. Phan was humble before his superiors, but he made sure they knew he was serious about seeking results. He let them know how the enemy had to pay for the outrageous insult to him and the nation of North Vietnam during his last sortie. The other officers discussed it amongst themselves while Phan stood there. After listening to them talk about how the North Vietnamese Air Force had never carried out a ground attack against the Americans, how it would be a waste of time and resources, how the last attack in broad daylight was too risky, and how they did not want to provoke the Americans by giving them an actual reason to commence a large-scale attack on Hanoi, he finally burst out, *"Yeu tau, yeu tau!"*—Weaklings, weaklings!

The officer speaking stopped in mid-sentence and stared at Phan in disbelief. They searched his face for signs of an apology but got nothing but a fiery stare. The captain then tore into them about why they should attack the Americans, and soon. They should make the enemy not only respect but fear them. A real attack would assure that the enemy would respond to them not only when they headed for a base, but whenever they got confirmation of them heading south. This in turn would result in the downing of many enemy aircraft. Phan cut off any response from his superiors by pressing on. He whipped out a map. slapped it on the ground, and showed them how he'd attack and how he'd personally guarantee that he wouldn't lose any of his flight.

As Phan thundered away about his plan, they gave him their full attention. They could see the determination and passion in his eyes, and that he wouldn't take no for an answer. They knew of his skills and that he was probably the only one who could pull off such an attack. The officers drew in deep breaths and gave in to Phan. They told him it had to be done within the next twenty-four hours, or else it would not be allowed to happen. Then they began to list the men they wanted to go, but Phan once again cut them off. He firmly told them that he would be picking the men he wanted to go on this most important of missions. The officers tried to hold their ground, but quickly understood that since the aviators respected Phan so much, it was logical to let him have who he wanted. The officers finally gave in and told him that responsibility for this mission was his alone, and if he failed, he and his family would be forever disgraced.

Phan had no intention of failing, and he felt a little contempt for his superiors, who really did little but talk. As they talked about losing face, he shut them out and thought of his mission. his mind already in the cockpit on the way to attack as his superiors squabbled in the background. When his mind finally returned to the present moment, he watched and listened to the officers bicker. Hearing nothing of consequence, he took in a deep breath and said, *"Tot lam, anh phai di"*—Fine, I have to go. As he walked away, his superiors fell silent for a moment and he looked back at them. They began to question him and bicker once again among themselves. He just lifted his arm in disgust and waved as he shouted, *"Du'ng lam phien anh nu'a!"*—Stop bothering me! He continued walking away knowing he didn't have the time to waste—he had mission to plan.

§ § § § §

Val walked into the Shack to see Notso and Speedy eating dinner on the couch. "Dammit! I'm cursed with y'all again?" he exclaimed with a smile, but there was no other crew than he'd rather spend Alert-5 duty with than with Speedy and Notso.

Notso smiled back with a mouth full of chow. "Yeah, the brass informed us that they don't like you very much, Jordan, so they're gonna make you as miserable as possible."

"Well they must not like any of us much because they stationed us here," Speedy replied.

"No they actually like us a little. They send the people they really hate directly to Hanoi—or to Washington," Nate chimed in.

"All I know is that I must be stupid—otherwise I'd've joined the Air Force. I'd be stationed in Thailand, having liberty in Bangkok." Val smiled as he pictured it, then clenched his teeth and smacked himself on the forehead with his palm as he said, "Idiot!"

The men settled down and began to unwind for what they hoped would be a quiet tour of Alert-5 duty, even though they knew it was becoming rarer and rarer each day.

§ § § § § §

Seven men stared at a map on the table, each filled with fear and excitement as they anticipated what was to unfold that evening. They focused on each detail of the plan and knew that they were expected to perform exactly as required. Men who were accustomed to the climate of their own country began to sweat whenever they locked eyes with Captain Phan, who was a model of perfection to them. If they failed, they feared no one but him, for he'd personally selected them for this mission. Captain Phan repeatedly referred to this mission as "*Cuouc hanh-quan cao quan-trong*"—Operation of the Highest Importance. After a grueling and thorough briefing, the men donned their gear and headed off to the flight line. Once there, they noticed odd ordnance hanging from the pylons of their MiGs. It was air-to-ground ordnance—rockets and small bombs—but they'd even seen such armament, let along trained with them. Captain Phan allayed their doubt by convincing them they wouldn't fail if they did as they were told in the briefing. The men strapped themselves into their jets, fired them up, and followed him to the runway. Phan looked down at his watch—1924 local—so he lined his jet on the runway, stoked the burner, and roared into the evening sky with his flight in tow. It was only twenty minutes to their target at Linh Thu, and while the men in his flight wrestled with their nerves, Captain Phan was a rock of calm. At ten minutes into the flight, Phan again looked at his watch and ordered "*Di vo'i tao!*"—Follow me!—as he climbed to nineteen thousand feet and began a series of erratic climbing and descending turns, deliberately trying to get the attention of American radar. His men were afraid to advertise their presence, but they followed him without hesitation. After all, their captain had more American kills than anyone except Colonel Tomb.

§ § § § § §

Val looked intently at the people gathered around him at the table, then back at his cards. He let out sigh and said, "Shit. All right, then," and pushed his chips into the pot. Suddenly the siren sounded just as the crews were in the middle of the final bets of the rather large pot. Val grabbed the phone and spoke with Panama as the others scrambled for their gear. He hung up the phone, picked it back up, and dialed the plane captains and told them to arm the jets with air-to-air ordnance—Sidewinders and Sparrows, then began to quickly explain the mission to the other flight crews as he hastily strapped on his own gear. As they were running out the door, he passed the table where everyone was playing cards and overturned one of the hands on the table. He shouted as he ran out the door, "Goddamnit, Speedy—I knew you were bluffing!"

The Alert-5s were ordered to taxi to runway 13 and await Papa's green light to launch. He wanted them on 13 because, in case this was an actual attack, the enemy would most likely overfly to head for the fuel farm and flight line. For the Alert-5 crews waiting at the end of the runway, the tension was almost unbearable.

They heard Panama confirm eight unidentified targets heading toward Linh Thu. Then as they closed to about five minutes, Panama reported they were now showing only four. The flight crews were guessing that the MiGs had closed up their formation as they approached their target.

§ § § § § §

Linh Thu was in plain view of Captain Phan's flight of MiGs. Since he hadn't yet been intercepted, he knew the Americans were again just sitting back. A smile stretched across his face—it was time to show them what he was really about. He and his flight made a low pass almost identical to the one the day before, not firing any ordnance. As they streaked low overhead, Papa and anyone else watching could plainly see that the MiGs were indeed armed with more than just their guns. As the MiGs broke to the southeast, Papa almost ordered the Alert-5s to launch, but he waited. He counted four MiGs in that pass, then focused his attention on the ridgeline to the west, expecting the other four MiGs to make an approach and a possible attack from there. But it was eerily quiet.

Then four MiGs came out of nowhere from the south, firing at the flight line. Phan was filled with joy as he opened fire and saw the puffs of debris indicating a hit. The flight zipped over a line spread out in a tight echelon formation, making for a perfect moving curtain of cannon fire that swept across the line, causing mass hysteria to anyone near it. Still Papa held back an order to launch. The flight then turned east and performed a wing-over and opened fire with rockets and bombs on the flight line and on runway 10–28. When explosions started to rattle the entire base, Papa gave the Alert-5s the go when the MiGs were past them and ordered the backup crews to the Alert-5s to their jets.

The crews in the Alert-5s were both fearful and angered as the attack continued around them. They felt helpless as they sat in their jets and watched their base and other aircraft take hits as they awaited an order to launch, crew member cursing Papa for not ordering them up yet. As they sat, a low-flying

MiG made a pass over them, narrowly missing them with its cannon fire, but as he hit the afterburner in his pullout, the shockwave cracked Speedy's canopy.

"Shit!" Speedy looked at the rather large crack and then keyed up, "Bowtie 1, Bowtie 2 Bravo, my canopy just cracked from that last fly-by."

"Roger," Val answered. "You think she'll hold together if we get to launch?"

"I don't know, but I'll give it a go." Just as Speedy unkeyed, they heard the tail end of Papa's order to launch, and with daylight fading, the crews knew they'd be drawing all the attention and would be easy targets as they rolled onto the runway and began their takeoff rolls with full afterburners blazing.

"Break hard right and shut the burners down ten seconds after rotation, head for the ridge," Val ordered. "We gotta do this fellas—we're the only ones who can disperse these assholes. Everyone be vigilant for SA-7s, although they probably won't be launching any with the MiGs so close."

Phan and his wingman were lined up perfectly to destroy the departing enemy jets—it would almost be too easy and unsporting. The MiGs closed within gun range of the Americans and held their heading and altitude, waiting for the Americans to climb into the crosshairs of their gun sights. As the F-4s slid into the crosshairs, the MiG pilots squeezed their triggers, but the Americans suddenly did something weird—they shut off their afterburners low in the climb-out!

Val and Notso broke right as soon as they cut the afterburners, and the MiGs broke right to blindly follow when Phan realized what they were doing. The MiGs were now going too fast and would overshoot, and he immediately climbed and broke back to the left and was trying to order his wingman to do the same, but he was too late. His wingman heard the underside of his MiG thump with a spine-jarring jolt that made it snap toward the backside of the ridge. It exploded milliseconds later as he clipped the top of the ridgeline, careening into a spectacular cartwheeling fireball. Phan was angered that he lost a fellow pilot, but he was glad that he'd caught on to his enemy's plan in time. The Americans in the air were indeed clever. A burst of adrenaline flowed into his veins. The fight was on!

Val and Notso climbed back toward the base, which was lighting up with hits that seemed erratic and uncoordinated. Some ordnance hit the flight line and runways, but most were scattered around the base and even outside its boundaries. It was as if the MiGs had no idea what they were doing. The RIOs called out targets, but they were hard to lock on to.

Both pilots decided to switch to guns as most of the MiGs retreated after making a quick pass. Val and Notso saw two MiGs lining up for a run at the base from the east and began a right diving turn to swoop in behind them. As the MiGs passed underneath them, both pilots fired at them. The MiG pilots saw the Americans closing in and immediately retreated to the north in full afterburner as the RIOs attempted to lock on to them. Just as they were about to get a lock, Nate saw Phan's MiG pull in behind him. "MiG! MiG on our sixes!"

Notso immediately broke high and left and began a steep turn toward the MiG in order to scare him away. "Stay on those guys, Tibbs—I'll deal with this asshole!"

Phan saw the F-4 turning toward him firing its cannon, and broke off his attack in a climbing left turn toward Notso.

Just as Nate was about to get a lock onto one of the retreating MiGs, four other targets popped up to the west. "Shit! Do you see that, Tibbs?!"

Val looked down at the small radar scope on the lower right side of his cockpit. "Yeah, I see. Let's take them on instead." Val broke left to fly head-on into the flight of four MiGs coming from the west just as Panama came over frequency with warnings about them. As he rounded his turn, a MiG was in guns range right beneath him at twelve o'clock. "Hey look at that," Val said as he switched to his gun and opened fire.

Phan had broken left to cut inside of Notso. Just as the American jet streaked by, he began to turn left again to pull in behind him—and as he did, tracers streaked by his right wing. He looked over his shoulder to see the other F-4 firing at him. This pair knew how to cover each other! Finally he'd have someone to match wits against and wouldn't be an easy kill. Confident he'd be victorious, he pulled even harder into his turn, knowing the F-4 couldn't match his maneuverability. As he pulled in behind the F-4, it cut back to the left toward the other half of his flight. As he turned to follow, he saw the other sliding in behind him. He was neutralized and would be easy prey for the F-4! It was hopeless to fight these two without a wingman, so he broke to the right in retreat and would wait until they got closer to his flight. As he broke, he cursed the pair from his first flight that had retreated home. The cowards would be forever disgraced for abandoning him!

Notso pulled harder in his turn, knowing the MiG would be trying to get inside him. He caught a glimpse of Val firing at it, then saw the MiG breaking right. As he completed his turn, he saw Val turning toward the MiGs coming from the west and could see the first MiG sliding in behind Val. When Val turned left, it made the MiG, which was trying to maintain an outside and high position on Val, swing right into perfect firing position for him. Notso was about to fire when the MiG broke north in obvious retreat. Notso let him go, figuring the biggest danger was the four MiGs flying toward his base from the west.

The MiGs were beginning to descend for a run on Linh Thu when Panama announced over frequency that backup crews were joining Val and Notso. Phan saw the other two fighters closing on the first pair of F-4s and knew that it was best to call off the attack.

Just as the other four were about to get into missile range, mortar shells and rockets began to strike the ground around Linh Thu. The base was under ground attack now! The MiGs began their retreat north when Phan saw the ground fire and was furious that he didn't get to finish his attack. He figured that the sound of the air attacks must have enticed the bands of guerilla fighters to attack.

Bowtie flight saw the MiGs begin their retreat and then began to fear SA-7 launches. "Bowties, get as close as you can to the MiGs in case they start to launch on us," Val ordered. With that the F-4s closed in almost to guns range of the retreating MiGs. Each pilot even fired a stream or two as the RIOs began to try to lock onto a MiG.

In the jungles below, a soldier saw the Americans firing on their jets and pulled out his SA-7. He peeped through the sight, but he was having difficulty distinguishing a friendly from the enemy. He locked on to the strongest heat source and got the IR (infrared) squawk. The red light turned to green in his sights and he squeezed the trigger. His missile streaked toward its target. Another soldier saw his comrade launch and decided to do the same. He locked onto the strongest heat source and fired his missile into the now dark sky.

The Americans were about to let the MiGs go and head back to assist the base, and as they throttled back, they watched the MiGs begin to pull away from them. Suddenly a streak of light zipped out from under the nose of Val's jet and turned sharply toward the MiGs. Seconds later the trailing MiG exploded and crashed into the jungles below, just as Nate said he had a lock. Val selected a Sidewinder and called, "Fox 2!" as he squeezed the pickle and the missile streaked toward the MiG on the far left of the formation. As the missile closed in on the MiG, another streak of light appeared from the ground heading for the same MiG. It suddenly veered toward the Sidewinder and met it with a brilliant explosion. "Goddamnit! That was going to be my first air-to-air kill!" Val angrily said. He then realized what happened and said, "Get down and head for base, guys."

The soldiers on the ground realized what they'd done when they saw the trailing group of planes retreat toward Linh Thu. They agreed to put away the SA-7s until they could confirm it was an American aircraft they were locking on before they launched again.

Phan was furious! His own people had just shot down one of his wingmen, and he'd lost two aircraft on this sortie. All in all, the mission was a success and had accomplished what he and his superiors wanted—getting Americans to respond to their mock attacks so they could be shot down from the ground, which would demoralize them and make them afraid to fly. It was clear that the guerillas had to be trained better if this was going to work. They knew they'd caused some damage to the base and to the aircraft parked on the ground. He also learned that there were at least two reasonably good pilots stationed there. If his superiors tried to give him any flack about this mission, he'd put them in their place. He was confident that he would always be victorious.

As the Bowties approached Linh Thu, they felt they needed to do something to help their base, even if it meant being shot down by an SA-7. Val noticed the area from which most of the enemy fire seemed to be coming from and asked, "Is anyone armed with ground ordnance?" After everyone responded in the negative, Val knew it was up to him to come up with a quick plan to quell the attack on their base. He looked down at the base, and in his line of sight was one of his Sidewinders hanging on its pylon. He then recalled recently reading about how a Marine F-4 successfully destroyed an enemy boat on the Perfume River with a Sidewinder as it locked onto the heat from its engine. Val knew it was probably pure luck that it had worked, but it was worth a try. He looked at the ground again and decided he was going to fire a Sidewinder at the source of the heaviest concentration of fire. He had no idea if it would work, but maybe there'd be a strong enough heat signature from the artillery to get an IR squawk. Then he'd have the rest of his flight strafe the area with their cannons.

Val swung around to the north and saw heavy mortar fire coming from the northwest. He had Nate try to lock onto the area, but he had no luck. He swung back around a little closer as he observed the mortar fire light up again. Nate got a faint lock but lost it just as Val was about to fire. "Fox 2! Fuck it— what could it hurt?" Val said as he squeezed the pickle. The missile streaked forward and suddenly veered down into the jungle about twenty meters shy of the area Val was aiming for. It did make a fantastic explosion, which seemed to quiet the mortars. The rest of the flight rolled in and strafed the area, and the jungle finally grew quiet. Apparently the soldiers feared that enemy aircraft circling overhead could easily wipe them out if they pinpointed their position, and they had only a couple of SA-7s left until they got re-supplied.

After several minutes of silence, the Alert-5s landed. Just as Notso touched down, Speedy's face was slapped by a violent rush of air as his canopy broke loose and pulled itself off the hinges, shattering as it smashed into the vertical stabilizer. After they got back to the northwest ramp and shut down, he went to sick bay with bruises and a deep cut on his right cheek bone from his visor.

§ § § § §

When Captain Phan's flight landed back at Kep Field, his wingmen chat-tered excitedly about their mission and what a great success it was. Phan agreed it was a success in that it may have accomplished some psychological damage, but his pilots' ground attack skills left a lot to be desired. He knew that the physical damage to the base and the aircraft was light at best. Even so, he held his head high as he walked into ops, where his superiors were waiting, along with the two pilots who'd first fled the area once the Americans got air-borne. Even though he lost two of his wingmen when he'd promised he'd lose none, he knew he could shift their attention from that fact to another. First he explained that the two were not lost to the Americans, but because of their own comrades and one pilot's inadequate skills. Then he walked up to the trembling pilots and said to them, *"May nhin tao lam chi, yeu teo?"*—What are you looking at me for, you cowards? Then he cursed them as he insisted to his superiors that they should be forever dishonored for their cowardice. The superiors were stunned as Phan explained how they abandoned their wingmen on *cuoc hanh-quan cao quan-trong* when a couple of Americans began to resist. Phan railed against the men for almost ten minutes until a general shouted, *"Ho'i! Kha!"*—Enough! That's enough! He walked up to the pilots and looked them in the eye as he ripped off their wings. *"Di cho khac, yeu teo!"*—Get away from me, cowards! As the men hung their heads and turned toward the door, the general shouted, *"Tao canh cao may nghe chu'a! Du'ng co' lai day!"*—I'm warning you! Don't ever come here again!

As the men walked in disgrace out of the ops room, they passed by Captain Phan. One of them looked up at him with eyes full of pain and said, *"Tao khong hieu. May muon cai gi?"*—I don't understand. What did you really want from me?

Phan stared coldly at the man and replied, *"Tin-nhiem. Di cho khac, may dang bi danh ma!"*—Courage. Now get away from me, you deserve this!

Both men left the ops room knowing they'd most likely be assigned to something involving hard labor, if they were allowed to serve again at all, but that would pale in comparison to the shame of facing their families that they'd now disgraced. Even though they were merely reacting instinctively, they'd dishonored themselves.

§ § § § §

The morning light revealed just how lucky Linh Thu was. The bombs and rockets from the MiGs had been mostly concentrated on the east side of the base, both inside and outside of the perimeter fences. The bombs had missed all the runways and damaged only three taxiways. Taxiway Delta took the hardest hit, but it still left enough room for an aircraft to maneuver around the crater with little trouble if the ground on each side of the taxiway was dry. The MiGs' cannons left pock marks on the flight line, and had damaged nine aircraft, but damage was minor. The rocket and mortar hits from the guerillas had concentrated most of its damage in housing areas, leaving some roads with impact craters and some tents needing to be stitched up. The biggest damage was a direct hit to the chow hall's food storage shed and another direct hit on the general maintenance shop.

Val was ordered to Papa's office early that morning, and he knew it would probably be to discuss the damage to the base, since he'd already been debriefed about the MiGs. When he knocked on the door to Papa's office, Papa called him in. He went over the damage to the base and explained that a COD flight would arrive in a few days to restock the food that was lost in the attack, but would only bring a limited amount of building supplies for repairs. That meant another trip to Dong Hoi.

Val eagerly hopped into the cab with Davis as they started the trip to Dong Hoi. For Val, the chance to see Nga Nghin Do'i again mitigated the discomforts of the trips. As the trucks roared up the streets that led to Nghia Mau's store, they sensed something in the air, different from past visits. As they crossed the bridge into town, every man noticed the looks of distrust on the faces of pedestrians. They saw columns of smoke rising in the distance, and when the trucks turned onto to the alley that led up to the store, they noticed several damaged buildings on each side of the street. As the trucks drove closer to the store, each man was shocked to see stacks of merchandise in the parking lot under canvas tents. When they pulled into the lot, they saw a massive hole at the northeast corner of the building and much of the wall was missing.

Val immediately jumped out and ran up to Nghia Mau, who greeted him with her usual warm smile. He pointed to the missing wall and said, "*May co thay cai do khong?*"—Did you see what happened?

Nghia Mau's smile faded as she looked at the ground and said in a shaky voice, "*Chien-tranh. Chien-tranh*, Captain. *Tao khong muon thay no*"—War. War, Captain. And I don't want to see it anymore. He could see the pain in her eyes, and he smiled as she said, "*Lai day*"—Come—and took his hand. As they walked to the store, she explained how Dong Hoi had to endure a rash of attacks at night when people with conflicting views on the war clashed. The weapon most often employed was the bicycle bomb—a bike loaded with plastic explosives on a timer was left outside the building. Such bombs usually killed more than just their intended targets, as innocent people who happened to be nearby were often killed or maimed. More often than not the innocent victims were children playing in the streets and alleys. Nghia Mau was a victim of a bicycle bomb herself, as were some of the young women she employed. She'd lived with war her entire life, and this one seemed to be getting worse with each passing day. She was frightened that someone had now apparently mistakenly targeted someone at her store. She knew that she and her girls wanted nothing to do with this war—they all just wanted it to be over. Luckily, she explained, the bomb must have had a faulty timer, as no one was inside when it exploded. As she and Val sat down to discuss business, she looked at the damage and mumbled, *"Linh. Khi nao cac chung toi biet?"*— Soldiers. When will they ever learn?

After some small talk and business discussion, Val was directed to Nga Nghin Do'i's office. Before he went in, he went over the wall and examined the damage as he peered through. He tried to imagine the blast that could have done this to such a sturdy building. As he looked outside at Nghia Mau checking some of her goods under the canvas, Nga Nghin Do'i came out of her office. She snuck up behind him and said, *"Chao anh dep! May co den day thu'o'ng khong?*—Hi, handsome! You come here often?

Val was euphoric. He turned around and was rewarded with the breathtaking sight of Nga Nghin Do'i standing behind him with a smile that lit up the otherwise dismal corner of the store. He smiled back and managed to mutter "Hello."

"Why you here?" she asked.

Val took advantage of the opportunity to flirt. "I couldn't go another day without seeing you. It's been too long since our last conversation." Val then stepped towards the exit and smiled as he said, "Well now that I got that out of the way, I'll see ya later!"

Nga Nghin Do'i laughed and said "Bye" as she turned back towards her office. She then turned back to Val who was turning back toward her and added, "We could never have short visit, Captain. We like talking too much."

"No, I actually don't like to talking all that much; I just really like talking to you."

Blushing, she brushed her hair out of her face and replied, "Good, Captain." After they stared at each other for a few moments, she said "How can I help you?"

Val gave her his order, then they sat in her office and talked as the girls loaded the trucks. He noticed a new picture of an older man on her desk. As they talked, his eyes kept drifting to the picture. Finally he asked, "Isn't that your uncle?"

"Yes," she said.

"Val looked more closely at the picture. "I know this sounds cliché, but he looks really familiar. I think I've seen him before."

"Really? As I told you, he live in Hanoi," she said.

Nga Nghin Do'i seemed to withdraw a little after that, so Val steered the conversation in another direction. After the supplies were loaded, it was again time to part ways. When he got to his truck, he reached inside and pulled out two lilies he'd picked on the road just outside Linh Thu and gave one to Nghia Mau and one to Nga Nghin Do'i. Both women were taken aback and smiled as he said, "*Bao trong nhe*"—Take care of yourselves.

As the trucks drove off, the women smiled and waved, and Nghia Mau smiled and said, "*Linh. Khi nao cac chung toi biet?*"—Soldiers. When will they ever learn?

§ § § § §

Val checked in to find Papa very busy and not wanting to talk too much, so he left the office and headed for the flight line to check on the progress of Speedy's canopy repair. As he approached HQ, he noticed a group of men gathered on the road out front of the building. He made his way into the crowd and found Nate and asked him, "What's up?"

"We lost an OV-10 to an SA-7 early this afternoon. He was in his climb-out and was shot down about a mile off the departure end of 13. Both men ejected, but the AO was pretty banged up. The pilot carried him few hundred yards to a clearing, where they were rescued about forty-five minutes later. The AO was flown down to Da Nang or Saigon for treatment. The pilot was released from sick bay and is in debrief in the HQ building." Nate then switched subjects, "Anyway, how was Dong Hoi and the girls?"

"Dong Hoi has been hit by a rash of bombings. Lots of people have been hurt. Buildings have been damaged, including the store."

"Holy shit! Were any of the girls hurt?"

"Luckily, no, but they could get attacked again. I hope they'll be okay."

"So do I. Mainly because you promised to take me with you someday."

Val laughed. "Are you crazy? If I take you, none of us will ever stand a chance of getting a date with those girls."

§ § § § §

Two days later, a flight of four MiGs popped up on Panama's radar, seemingly headed toward South Vietnam. The Alert-5s were dispatched and were immediately met with SA-7s. One of the Alert-5s took serious damage to the empennage but managed to land safely back on base. Papa again pleaded with higher command for help, but was denied despite lives being in danger, mainly because he didn't apply through the proper channels and his paperwork was incomplete or not filled out properly. Papa announced that the Alert-5s wouldn't respond until the MiGs were within ten miles from Linh Thu. He also drew up new departure and arrival procedures to avoid SA-7 launches whenever aircraft departed or landed at Linh Thu. The situation was almost totally out of hand, and stress levels were higher than they'd ever been. Things were looking really bleak for the men of Linh Thu, and became even bleaker when the chow hall announced that if the COD flight didn't restock them in two days, the base would be out of food.

Papa again had to plead with the big brass for the bare necessities of life. His plea for food finally got some attention, and two C-130s were dispatched for Linh Thu that afternoon. A few supply officers turned in some favors and got the flights stocked with items that were otherwise almost impossible to obtain, so the men of Linh Thu anxiously waited on the northwest ramp for the C-130s and were more than happy to help unload the big birds of their precious cargo. As the men waited under the hot afternoon sun, someone in the control tower shouted, "Santa and his reindeer are on short final!"

The crowd erupted in cheers for the relief they were about to receive. The first C-130 touched down and rolled on to the taxiway, with the other a mile-and-a-half behind on short final. The men cheered even louder as the first C-130 taxied closer and its flight crew waved from the cockpit. The men watched as the second C-130 loomed large as it approached. Suddenly a streak of white smoke zipped out of the jungles and the flash and everyone on the ramp saw a large explosion on the right wing. The giant plane snapped to the left and exploded in a huge fireball as it slid to a violent stop after impacting in the grass on the east side of runway 13. All the men on the ramp were stunned and shouting helplessly as they ran toward the inferno behind the fire trucks. By the time the flames were extinguished, almost nothing remained of the massive plane, and the crew of the other C-130 were now afraid to depart back to Subic Bay.

Papa was quickly on a conference call with the brass, but it didn't help much that an admiral's nephew was the first officer of the C-130 that was shot out of the sky. The brass informed Papa and Linh Thu's other high-ranking officers that they were on their own until further notice as far as supplying themselves, except for food. They'd eventually get some help with the SA-7s, but it would probably be a few months, and from now on the arriving COD flights would be escorted by either VMFA-2 or VMO-16 planes. After the two-hour conference call finally ended, Papa excused the rest of the officers for chow. He plopped down in a chair and put his head in his hands and said, "Why didn't I just stay home and become a damned, dirty hippy?"

§ § § § §

Val finished his chow early and headed for Papa's office. He knew Papa had a full plate, but he wanted to talk to him about an idea he had.

Papa wanted to tell him to come by another time, but he never turned his men away when they had something important to talk about. "Spill it, son—I ain't got all day," he said.

"Well sir, the MiGs have basically been setting a trap for us the past few weeks—"

"Stop the fucking presses—Captain Jordan has a scoop!" Papa said sarcastically. "How many monkeys you got working on that one, son?"

Val waited as Papa went on for a bit before finally cutting him off, "sir—why don't we set a trap for them? Make 'em suck on their own cocks for once?"

Papa hesitated, then replied, "This oughta be good. Give birth to your brainchild, son."

"Well sir, if we can eliminate a good part of their fleet, they'll have no bait to sucker us out there to begin with. So we need to make sure all our aircraft are preloaded with at least a couple stations of air-to-air ordnance." Val grabbed several pens and placed them on Papa's desk to simulate F-4s. "Then we play along as usual, respond to their threat—but we *wait* until they send a shitload of MiGs like they did the first time they suckered us. We send about six or seven aircraft to respond"—he arranged the pens to simulate a group of MiGs and a separate group of F-4s—"then we take the rest of our jets and sneak them on the deck over the ridgeline heading north. The MiGs will break off their attack somewhere about here as they usually do"—he pointed—"but this time our other jets will have slipped in behind them unnoticed. Our first group will turn back toward base as normal, then make a wide break back toward the MiGs. They'll have spotted our 'sneaker group' and will make a hasty one-eighty to escape them. The MiGs will then be trapped in a double envelopment, and we should be able to take out a lot of them, if not all. If the SA-7s light up, they'll most likely take some of their own again. After they lose so many MiGs, it'll probably slow down or stop the mock attacks and save us some planes until we're equipped to properly deal with the SA-7s."

Papa was silent as he let the idea sink in. Then he looked back at Val and said, "Damn, that's a good idea!" He sipped some water from his canteen and set it back on his desk. "Your brainchild has balls bigger than this canteen. I like it. Suck on their own cocks—hah!" He slammed his palm on his desk, then smiled at Val and said, "We'd better bring down a lot of MiGs on this one, Captain, or else we'll all find ourselves in a court martial at Subic Bay trying to explain ourselves."

"We'll get those bastards, sir. You'll see." Then he smirked and said, "Twenty, sir."

"Twenty what, Captain?"

"Twenty monkeys, working 'round the clock on that idea, sir."

Papa laughed as he replied, "Why just twenty? I would've had sixty-nine. I always liked that...plus, the number's nice, too." Papa continued a smug smile as he envisioned pleasant thoughts of something completely different than Val's idea.

After a few seconds of silence Val started for to the door, waiting for Papa's dismissal. Papa then said, "Tell you what, Captain—if I go with idea of yours, I want you to lead the sneaker group while I lead the first response." Papa engaged his thousand-meter stare.

At first Val felt intimidated by the heavy responsibility he'd have to bear, but he was a Marine officer, and that meant he was a leader and expected to shoulder responsibility. He knew that if he led the sneaker group, lives would depend on him and men would be looking to him for answers. Val returned Papa's stare and hid his surprise as he said, "If you think I'm ready, I won't let you down, sir. I promise."

That was the response Papa was hoping for. "I know you won't, son— you're one of my best pilots." Papa patted Val on the shoulder and continued. "If you do let me down, you won't have to worry about the enemy—I'll personally kick your ass. Now you're gonna have a lot of questions to answer, and most of them will be your own. You're also gonna have a lot of stress and worries that you've never had before. All I can say to that is," he pointed to the papers on his desk and ran his fingers through his hair, drawing attention to the fact that they were gray from stress, "welcome to the burden of command."

7

Operation Cast Net

The sun baked Captain Phan and his wingmen as they awaited clearance from the tower to launch. His flight would sit on the runway until the timing was right for them to slide in behind the retreating American jets as they flew back from their sorties to Thailand, South Vietnam, or out to sea. The waiting tested their endurance as the temperature inside the cockpit heated surfaces enough to burn exposed flesh. Phan and his wingmen would wait, glance at their watch every now and then, and think of anything to take their minds off their discomfort. The only relief was the cool air flowing through their oxygen masks. Each man felt the usual jitters that precede a combat sortie. They knew as they got bolder with each mission, the Americans would get more aggressive and persistent in their attempts to shoot them down, sometimes following them almost to their base.

As the heat got nearly unbearable, the order to launch came and the men forgot their discomfort as they released their brakes and accelerated down the runway. Armed with 23mm cannons and Atoll missiles they were fully equipped to kill.

It was only a matter of minutes before they closed in on their targets—a line of F-105s heading back to Udorn or Ubon in Thailand. The tactic was simple: lock in on a target, shoot it down, and make a quick break for base to avoid engaging American fighters. They knew American technology was years ahead of theirs, and that the Americans could usually detect them early enough to avoid becoming targets. But in an actual dogfight, their MiG-21s could easily outmaneuver any American fighter except the F-5. They also had

143

an intangible equalizer—they were fighting to protect their homeland, and sometimes that motivation made all the difference.

Phan and his men closed to the range of their Atolls, armed them, locked on targets, and fired. As soon as the MiGs got a solid lock, the Americans broke formation in a frantic scramble. Phan knew it wouldn't be long until assistance was on the way, so they made quick work with the Atolls. Captain Phan's missile scored a direct hit that sent an F-105 plummeting into the jungles below. Other members of his flight scored hits, destroying another and damaging two more aircraft were so far. The damaged aircraft would easy prey as the MiGs switched to their cannons and began swooping strafes at the Americans. The MiGs' 23- and 30mm cannons were deadly—a single round could knock just about any aircraft out of the sky. Phan let a couple of his wingmen go before him and watched them successfully down wounded jets, and now it was time to try to get a couple of the stragglers that hadn't been damaged yet. Phan moved his throttle to afterburner to close in on the nearest F-105, then pulled back to seventy percent when he was above the jet and saw the pilot looking at him. Phan then started a shallow, diving roll that put the fighter right in his crosshairs. The American jet started to perform a high-g barrel roll to try to force Phan out front, but Phan was a few steps ahead of him, reversing his roll as he pulled back the power. For a brief moment the F-105 slipped out of the crosshairs but soon put itself directly into it. Captain Phan fired a steady stream at the jet, almost instantly causing chunks of it to shear off and causing smoke to belch out from several places. The American suddenly made an erratic right turn, and Phan swung out left to maintain an outside position so he'd be in the saddle for another stream of cannon fire. As he continued his turn, a shadow to the left caught his eye. He looked left and saw an American F-4 overshoot him in a diving right turn. Phan instinctively broke inside and rolled back to find himself outside the F-4, who was now trying to reverse the turn. *Yes! This American is trying to engage me! The fight is on!*

Adrenaline flowed through his veins—he lived for the thrill of the fight. As Phan kept his position through a series of rolls and high-g turns, he kept alert and constantly checked behind him. He knew American F-4s were almost always at least in pairs, and he knew his own wingmen had probably long since retreated, and would have no idea how to cover him anyway if they'd hung around. As he glanced over both shoulders, he saw nothing but clear sky, so he continued in pure pursuit of the adversary. The American then started to go vertical into a series of twisting climbs and dives called the "rolling scissors," but Phan was familiar with the maneuver and kept a safe distance in lag pursuit so he wouldn't overshoot. After a couple of series, the American became almost predictable. Phan could tell they were surprised that he was still on their tail. He switched to lead pursuit in an aggressive climb and was practically waiting for them as they completed their roll and he met them with cannons ablaze. After the F-4 took several direct hits, the pilot broke off in an Immelmann at the top of the next roll. He was seriously damaged and wouldn't survive the next series of rounds if they didn't get help to shake the MiG. Phan was considering backing off and swinging back around at a better angle when he caught sight of the American's wingman at his same altitude directly to his right. He knew the American would open fire, so he immediately started a steep climb. The American also pitched up in an effort to keep a solid lock on the MiG. The American pilots watched as the MiG began a quarter roll to the left, as if he was going to try to break left, so the pilot moved slightly left in his climb to keep his nose on the MiG.

Suddenly Phan reversed his roll until he was in a right knife-edge, then rolled ten more degrees to the right and yanked back hard on the stick. The MiG performed a high-g, diving right turn and slid under the American jet, who began to climb even higher in fear of a collision. Phan continued his turn but rolled his jet back to the left until it was almost wings-level and continued his back pressure on the stick. The jet pulled up into a shallow loop until Phan rolled over into an Immelmann and found himself directly behind the F-4, which was still climbing but had begun a break to the left.

Phan opened fire and hit the F-4 along its spine and empennage. As he closed in for the kill, he noticed he was getting low on fuel. Annoyed that his machine had less endurance than he had, he fired one last stream into the F-4 and sent it into the thick jungles below. He looked back at the first F-4 in time to see that the crew had decided to punch out. Phan saluted the crew as he over flew them in his turn back to the east, toward his base. He'd shot down three American jets and wounded two others, plus he got to engage the Americans in dogfight. A smile stretched across his face as he headed toward Kep Field. Today was a great day!

§ § § § § §

"Franks…Smith…Troy…Barnes…Rogers…Gonzales…Uh, Robinson."

What a shitty day, Val thought, again disappointed when he didn't hear his name at mail call. He'd been here for almost three month, and hadn't received a single piece of mail from Virginia since her first letter. Things that never seemed to bother him before got on his nerves all the time now. He found himself reflecting on things that he'd never usually think about. That just wasn't him, and now he worried that maybe this was who he really was and he just never really knew himself before. He was learning new things about himself with each passing day, but the thing he'd known long before he ever came to Vietnam was that he loved Virginia and he missed her constantly. It was his love for her that both inspired and tormented him every day during the highs and the lows of his life. He desperately needed to hear from her, but he had no idea how to make that clear to her.

Val wasn't the only one suffering rough times. The men at Linh Thu were now enduring constant rocket and mortar attacks, and overriding almost everything was the fear of a massive ground. Time didn't seem to exist in this war, and sporadic incidents of terror and combat now blurred together. Flight crews found themselves working fourteen-hour days, often waking up at 0300 and grabbing some chow—if it stayed down. Then a briefing for an hour, a mission, a debrief for another hour or longer. Alert-5s were being scrambled more than ever, and there was hardly any time left for sleep. The Seabees and combat engineers were constantly repairing damage to the base; the mechanics were constantly repairing aircraft, vehicles, tools, and equipment; and the support staff was constantly trying to make life livable for the personnel. Aircraft were still being shot at as they departed or arrived at Linh Thu, and help didn't seem to be on the way. The big question on everyone's mind—when would the war finally start to move north? It never seemed to even come up in Washington.

§ § § § §

The flight crews of VMFA-2 walked to their jets after Papa finished his briefing on that night's mission. It was more of the usual—another grove of trees out in the middle of nowhere—so the men were in no hurry to get airborne. Everything was such a blur of routine that the men hardly remembered starting their jets or taking off—and they all knew what a extremely dangerous state of mind that was.

Val stared out into the nothingness of a moonless night over the jungles as he and his squadron continued to the target area, the pale glow from the instrument panel the only source of light in the endless curtain of black. Val couldn't even see his own fingertips, much less his wingman. There wasn't even any light from the ground because they were flying over a rural area. It was like flying in a lifeless, endless black hole.

"Okay, boys, let's green 'em up and get to work," they heard Papa say in their helmets, called. his voice as soothing to each man as a parent's to a child waking a bad dream.

The squadron lined up in two parallel lines from which they would break and attack their target—a small bridge across a narrow river and a fuel farm— from opposite directions. The first line, led by Papa, broke away and swung out wide to make their approach from the south while the other line would attack from the north. Both lines would then pull out in opposite directions and return to the end of their own respective lines for a second run, if needed.

As the squadron got close to the target, AA opened up in thick lines in multiple directions. It was nice to have a source of light to challenge the dark, no matter what terrible consequences came from it. The darkness was a nuisance to both the flight crews and the men on the ground. It was also welcomed as a true friend, their only chance for cover, concealment, and survival.

Val watched as the ground lit up from the bombs of his wingmen and scanned the sky that was furiously flashing with bursts of AA. The jet ahead of him was beginning its run, so he took a deep breath, knowing he only had about ten seconds before he had to begin his attack. When he felt as relaxed as possible, he started to push the stick forward, knowing that relaxed feeling was about to evaporate. As he rolled his jet into a steep dive into the brilliant flashes, Virginia's voice resounded in his head: *I love you, Val. Hurry back to me. I'll wait until the end of time for you if I have to. Just be careful and return home safely to me—I can't imagine living without you. I could never even think of loving anyone else but you.*

"Dammit! Not now!" Val shouted aloud as he tried to focus on flying his.

"What's going on up there? We gotta move." Nate reminded his pilot that others were depending on him right now. "We're a little behind—we're gonna slow everyone up."

"I'm making up time now," Val said as he pushed his jet into a steeper dive into the heart of the AA. Tracers whizzed by in all directions and explosions flashed at higher altitudes as the F-4 built up tremendous momentum. Suddenly the brilliant flash from the bombs of the previous jet whited out his vision for a few seconds. When his vision returned, he could see the bridge was a raging inferno but hadn't collapsed yet. Small arms fire began to wink from the ground on each side of the bridge as he drew closer.

Armed with retarded Snake Eye bombs, Val put the bridge in the center of the pipper and basically guessed when to release. When he thought he'd have the right trajectory for the bombs to slide in a downward arch. As the AA grew thicker, Val S-turned a few times in an effort to throw the gunners off, but they were using radar-guided guns and recovered quickly. Val knew it wouldn't be long before he'd have to fly straight for a few seconds in order to release his weapons properly, and the gunners were waiting for that exact moment. Nate called out altitude and distance as they drew closer to the release point.

"I'm gonna release at 0300 and a quarter, Double-O."

"Roger. Keep her steady now on this heading. Niner hundred and one."

"Shit!" Val was sweating heavy as the tracers were now mere inches away. There was no way they wouldn't take a hit. "Feel lucky you don't have to look outside right now, Pal!"

"I know…seven hundred and a half." Explosions from another of his wing-men's hits rocked Val's jet and pushed the left wing up. Val was now fighting to keep his wings level in the turbulent air. Then a massive explosion brighter than the noonday sun swallowed up the night as one of his wingmen apparently bulls-eyed the fuel farm. The jet behind it aborted its run to avoid being engulfed in the fireball and shockwave that pushed Val's jet aside. Val couldn't even see his target anymore and put his eyes on his instruments. He rolled back ten degrees to the left, pushed the nose back down, and pointed the jet where he thought the bridge was. The darkness slowly took over again, and when he looked back outside, he could barely make out the burning bridge.

"We're too close—two hundred and an eighth," Nate told his pilot. "Our bombs will overshoot."

"Bullshit—we'll make it, because I don't want to have to dive through this shit again," Val said as he pushed his nose down steeper and pickled off four bombs at a hundred and fifty feet as his jet screamed over the bridge. He immediately pulled back up into the darkness.

Val's bombs cut through the air at incredible speed. The first fell short and exploded in the water. Two others slammed into the support stanchion in the middle of the river while the fourth overshot, skipped on the water, and exploded when it hit the shoreline. The bridge collapsed when Val's bombs destroyed the stanchion.

"Dash 6 aborting. Great run, Dash 5—the bridge is at the bottom of the river," Notso congratulated his fellow Marine.

Val laughed. "Amazing—I couldn't see a fucking thing!"

"Cut the chatter, Dash 5 and 6. I want to make sure we got this thing because rest assured we'll be out here bombing the same stupid bridge in a few weeks, whether we got it or not," Papa said over frequency, then added with a chuckle, "I don't think there's any doubt about the fuel farm."

The Playboys stayed in a high orbit north of the target area and out of range of the AA, whose gunners quit firing. Papa had confirmation that the targets were destroyed and was ready to RTB. In their orbit, several of the crews noticed a large convoy of trucks beneath them heading northbound on a desolate highway through the jungle.

"See that, Double-O?" Val asked as he looked down at the ribbon of lights below.

"Yeah, I see it. Wonder if we should check it out."

"Well I *am* gonna check it out," Val said as he dove low over the highway. He leveled off at three hundred feet above the treetops and slowed his massive jet as much as he could and passed off the right side of the convoy. The drivers couldn't see him in the pitch black sky, nor could they hear him over the loud grumbling roar of engines straining to pull such heavy loads. Val and Nate couldn't believe how much they could see as they flew by in the darkness above. The flatbed trucks were hauling SA-2s, AA guns, and large crates that were most likely full of ammunition and parts, possibly even SA-7s.

It was a perfect a target in perfect conditions. Each jet had at least two to four bombs left plus their guns, and the night environment favored them. They could completely wipe out the convoy before they knew what hit them. Val pulled up and rejoined his squadron.

"Dash 1! We've got to nail those trucks down there! They got SA-2s, AA guns, and maybe some SA-7s in the crates on the last two! With this cover, they won't even know we're here until it's too late!" Val announced to Papa. All the other aviators joined in and began to nag Papa like a child wanting a cookie to spoil their dinner.

"All right! All wings be quiet for a second, dammit!" Papa answered. "I'd love to hit those trucks, but the fact is that we can't. We aren't allowed into an Air Force Route Pack without their permission, just like they can't attack a target inside a Navy Route Pack. By the time we get permission, those trucks'll be almost to Hanoi."

"Can't we try to get a message to them? I'm sure they won't mind, considering these arms might be used against them someday." The entire squadron chimed in to agree. Then Val added, "Maybe they'd never find out if we destroyed them now."

"Dammit gents, forget the trucks! If we do attack them and someone *does* find out, you can bet your asses we'll all be sitting in the brig at Subic Bay awaiting our court martial. And believe me, they *will* court martial an entire squadron just to make an example." He hated having to tell them to stand down—it went against his every instinct. He knew the weapons would soon be used against Americans, but he wasn't in charge of the war.

The Playboys turned back toward Linh Thu in silence, each man looking back for one last look at the convoy. They knew that such an opportunity would probably never present itself again. It was like throwing away a winning lottery ticket. They wondered if all the branches were fighting the same enemy, or if they were competing against each other for recognition of individual accomplishments. They wondered if Washington realized that they wouldn't achieve victory this way. Soon they were approaching the base, and each jet scattered and made their approaches from all points of the compass in an effort to confuse anyone with a SA-7. Life at Linh Thu was just as confusing now, cloaked in fear and doubt, and each day each man felt more estranged from the rest of the world.

§ § § § §

Val took the long walk with the sentry who'd come for him to the only vehicle gate on the north side of the base. The sentry told him that he had a visitor who'd arrived earlier and was going through security screening at the gate. It was early morning, and the sky was mostly dark except for a few thin dusty streaks of pale pink on the east horizon. Val walked up to the heavily barricaded shack at the gate. As he entered the receiving area, he wondered who might be visiting him here and drew a blank. He guessed that it was most likely someone he knew from OCS, TBS, or flight school. As he waited by the desk he was thoroughly briefed on how he must escort his guest at all times, and how he was held responsible for their behavior. He then signed several forms and waited.

"It's been too long, Hotrod."

At first Val thought his mind was playing tricks on him. The voice made his heart stand still, and when he turned around, he saw the person he loved more than anyone. His voice quivered as he fought to hold back tears. "Virginia! What the hell are you doing here?" He ran to her and lifted her off the ground as he wrapped his arms tightly around her.

"I couldn't wait any longer, Val—I had to see you!" she said, tears sliding down her face.

Val realized that he was squeezing her hard and worried he might break her ribs, but he didn't want to let go. He kissed and passionately, then held her at arm's length so he could gaze into her eyes. She was the most wonderful thing he'd seen since he had been here. It was really her! She was really here in his arms! He stared deeply into her eyes and said, "I love you, baby! Is this why you didn't write?"

"Partly," Virginia replied with a big smile as tears glistened on her cheeks.

"This is the happiest moment of my entire life," Val said as he wiped a tear from her eye. Only our wedding will top it."

Virginia was so lost in the moment that she didn't realize she'd dropped her purse. "Oops!" she exclaimed when she saw it on the floor.

As Val bent over to pick up the purse, he clung to her hand, but when he glanced at the purse, he heard distinct popping sounds from every direction. All of a sudden he was showered by dust and fragments of cinderblock. Then he heard Virginia gasp as her grip on his hand loosened. When he looked up, he saw her a blossom of deep crimson on her chest. She looked down at him, disbelief and shock on her face. Her body quivered as she reached down toward Val, then she went limp and started to fall. He caught her in mid-fall as the sound of machine guns and explosions ripped the air. The cinderblock walls began to shake as a daylight attack was fully underway!

Val cradled her in his arms as he patted her face, trying to get a response. She looked at him with a blank stare as her body went limp. He pulled her to him and screamed in agony as his body started shaking violently.

Val suddenly became conscious of Nate as his Rio shook him. "Wake up, Val! Wake up, Buddy!" Val sat up abruptly and took in the familiar surroundings of his hooch.

"You were having one helluva nightmare, brother. You scared the shit out of us!" Nate smiled as he released Val's shoulders.

"What time is it?" Val asked.

"It's 0430. All of us were barely asleep when you started yelling."

"Sorry, fellas. I just had a dream worse than anything I see from the cockpit. I gotta see if Papa will let me make a phone call today."

"Can we get some sleep first?"

"You fellas can. I don't think I'll be able to for a while," Val said as he swung his legs over the edge of the bunk.

The others laid back down as Val sat in the darkness with his thoughts. He had a foreboding feeling that something terrible had happened.

§ § § § § §

At first light, Val headed to Papa's office, but when he got there he found out that Papa was at the Shack, so he made his way over there. As he got closer to the ramp, he noticed that it was busier than usual with helicopter traffic. Val entered the Shack to find Papa and the Alert-5 crews huddled over a map on the ops table, so he scooted up quietly behind them to see what was going on. Papa noticed Val's presence immediately and said as he looked up from the map, "Glad you're here, son—I was just about to send for you. Get your gear on. You, me, and a couple others are gonna take a little trip around base to see if we can't make those bastards hiding in the jungles lose some missiles."

Papa's manner struck Val as odd, but he went to the ready room to put his gear on. It seemed suicidal to dare the enemy to launch a weapon at them for which there was no countermeasure yet, Val was sure Washington probably didn't even know the weapon existed. Just as he did every time he strapped on his gear, Val mentally prepared himself for a dance with fate.

Meanwhile, Cowpoke Delta, an OV-10 from VMO-16 orbiting ten miles south of base, radioed in to Panama with desperation in his voice: "Panama, Cowpoke Delta, over."

"Cowpoke Delta, this is Panama, go ahead."

"Request immediate assistance. Need at least three sections of attack air. I'm on the Linh Thu one-seven-five at one-zero. Get help here ASAP."

"Roger."

While Val and several of his fellow aviators were hastily strapping on their flight gear in complete silence, Papa was about to leave the Shack when the red phone rang. When he answered, he said little but made notes and checked the map. When he hung up, he got on another phone and ordered several jets be loaded with air-to-ground ordnance. Then he ran to the ready room and shouted, "Chapman, Jordan, Wise, Mailer, Daniels. Grab your RIOs and get to your jets—we got some people who need us." Papa explained how two Navy jets had been shot down by SA-7s just south of base and the crews had bailed out and landed right in the middle of an ambush being set for the NVA by US Marines. When the aviators hit the ground, it gave up the ambush as they landed between the Marines and the NVA. The NVA troops had been joined by a Viet Cong unit that no one knew was in the area, and the combined forces now had the Marines caught in a double envelopment.

Panama was now assuring Cowpoke Delta that help was on the way. "Cowpoke Delta, Panama. Three sections of Fox-4s on the way from Linh Thu, they'll report to you on button red, call-sign Demon Flight. ETA eight minutes."

"Roger. They'd better haul ass or this'll be over in a hurry."

Minutes later, six F-4s were nearing the fix Cowpoke Delta had reported. Papa saw the action below and checked in. "Cowpoke Delta, Demon-flight Dash 1. Flight of six Fox-4s armed with nape-and-snake, twenty mike-mike, eight bombs per plane. We're at angels one-five right above you."

Cowpoke Delta's crew smiled as they heard Papa's smooth drawl, knowing the best air support in the world was orbiting above. "Roger, Demon-flight. What'll be your roll in?"

"Demon-flight will roll in at five thousand. We can pull out really low since the terrain is flat."

"Roger, Demon-flight, cleared for descent. Ready to copy?"

"Born ready, son. Give it to me."

"We have a platoon of Marines and two Navy wingers trapped in a double envelopment hiding behind the east berm of a rice paddy. They are taking heavy machine gun and sniper fire from the west berm and some hidden bunkers east of them. Both lines of enemy fire run north-south about two hundred meters and are approximately six hundred meters away from our friendlies. The best way is to split your flight into two sections of three and hit each line simultaneously from opposite directions."

"Roger. We'll have one group begin their run from the north and the other from the south. The north group will pull out to the west and the south group will pull out to the east," Papa replied. "Dash 2 and 3 are with me on the north; Dash 4, 5 and 6 will be the south group and will pull out to the east.

Wings split up and follow your leader. Two bombs per plane, five seconds between runs. Cowpoke Delta begin your marking runs."

"Roger."

"All right Demon-flight, pay extra attention to your surroundings. We will be dropping our ordnance really close to our boys down there and we will be in very close proximity of each other, so have your heads on a swivel."

Cowpoke Delta finished his marking runs and looked skyward to see Demon-flight splitting up just a few thousand feet above him. He waited until they'd lined up with their leaders and were about to turn inbound toward their attack runs when he announced, "Demon-flight is cleared hot. FACA will be ducking out to the northeast." Then he added with a smile that his voice gave away: "Give 'em hell!"

Simultaneously, Dash 1 and Dash 4—Papa and Val—checked in: "Dash 1 rolling in hot."

"Dash 4 rolling in hot."

Papa and Val were soon diving toward the deck at high speed. Each pilot looked at the rising smoke columns and then out over their nose to see the other jet closing rapidly head-on. Even though there was approximately twelve hundred meters between the jets, it seemed to each pilot that they were on a direct collision course. It was like watching the Blue Angels do their opposing solo pass at an air show. At less than fifteen hundred feet AGL, Papa and Val simultaneously pickled off two bombs.

"Looks on line fellas. All other jets keep walking your runs up your lines and we should get 'em all," Cowpoke Delta said.

Each following jet followed Cowpoke Delta's guidance, then the crews looked below to see the walls of flames as they rejoined the flight at five thousand feet. Before the last jets began their runs, Cowpoke Delta received an urgent message: "Danger—close! Danger—close!" The message was from one of the Marines below, warning Cowpoke Delta not to let any of the air strikes to get any closer.

Cowpoke Delta instantly keyed up. "Abort! Demon-flight, abort! Danger—close!"

"Shit!" Dash 6 cried under the strain of heavy g-forces. He'd already released his load, and the shockwave and flames rolled over the platoon. "Are they *okay*, Cowpoke Delta?"

Cowpoke Delta flew down the alley of clear air between the walls of fire to see if he could see anything at all, whether it was friendly or enemy. As he cleared the alley to the north, he keyed up, "Tiger Actual, do you copy Cowpoke Delta?" After a few seconds of silence, he tried again, "Tiger Actual, do you copy Cowpoke Delta?"

After a few more seconds of silence, a voice finally crackled in Cowpoke Delta's headset. "Cowpoke Delta, this is Echo 5 Tango"—which meant whoever was talking on the radio was a sergeant whose last name began with a "T."

"Go ahead Echo 5 Tango. Give me your status."

"We're all okay. The platoon commander is about to move us out to the north for extraction. Keep those fast movers around for cover in case Charlie is still around."

"Wilco." Cowpoke Delta then switched back to his air-to-air channel to update Demon-flight on the situation.

"We're not going anywhere until we're at bingo fuel," Papa replied to Cowpoke Delta.

It wasn't more than a few minutes until Panama informed all the aircraft that a flight of UH-1s had been dispatched from Linh Thu to pick up the platoon. As Demon-flight waited in their orbit, Panama announced that several MiGs were headed south toward them. All the RIOs picked up the echoes of the MiGs almost instantly. Val was instantly suspicious and started looking at the ground below them and as far north as was discernable. "Dash 1, this doesn't feel right."

"I know what you mean, Dash 4, but sit tight for a bit. I'm trying to formulate a plan. All pilots keep your eyes on the deck for now—something is definitely amiss. Cowpoke Delta, watch yourself as well—the Gooners could be setting us up for SA-7 attacks."

"Roger, Dash 1," Cowpoke Delta replied as he had his observer begin to scan the ground.

"What was your plan, Dash 1?" Val asked.

"Goddamnit, Dash 4—I'm still thinking!" Papa snapped back.

"No, sir—I meant before we were called out here to assist. What was the 'special op' we were about to do?"

"What's that got to do with anything, Jordan?"

"Just wondering if it could help us now sir."

Papa squinted as he realized what Val was getting at. "Genius, Jordan! You're a goddamned genius, son!"

"Well I already knew that sir. So what the hell's your plan?"

"I was going to have us fly the pattern at Linh Thu in pairs and see if we could attract some attention from SA-7 launches. As soon as they launch at us, the target jets break in opposite directions and go to idle and boards. The rest of you orbiting up high swoop in and blow 'em to hell! We're gonna do the same. Dash 5 and 6 act like they're responding to the MiGs. Dash 1 and 2 remain in a middle orbit at angels nine and attack when we see the area of the launch. Dash 3 and 4 stay even farther back and cover the rescue flight or assist the rest of us if ordered. I have a feeling they're not just targeting us jets today."

Dash 5 and 6 hit the burners and climbed toward the MiGs. Each crew knew they only had air-to-ground ordnance, with only their guns suitable for engaging with the MiGs.

"Mailer," Dash 5 called out to Dash 6.

"Go Daniels," Dash 6 responded.

"If the MiGs engage, don't forget to drop your bombs. We'll have enough trouble maneuvering without them. I can't imagine trying to dogfight with the extra load."

"Already thought of it. Just say when," Mailer replied.

Both pilots charged head-on into the flight of four MiGs, fully aware that the SA-7s would probably lock onto them. Despite the feeling of doom, they tried to get as close as possible to the MiGs, hoping to confuse any SA-7 operators on the ground.

Papa and Chappie lagged behind in their wide, sweeping orbit, trying to attract as little attention as possible, all the while scanning the ground. "I'm not gonna shit solid again while I'm here, Chappie. My nerves have been shot since the bastards started using those fucking things. I should be the targets for the launch, not those four young men," he said.

"They're gonna be fine, sir. I think we may get those bastards today," Chappie reassured his old friend and mentor.

"Don't worry about us, sir. We're happy to do it—especially if we get some of those bastards," Dash 5 replied.

"Glad to do it, sir," Dash 6 added as he glanced at his radar and the echoes of the MiGs.

As always, the MiGs broke away just outside of missile range, and Dash 5 and 6 weren't exactly sure if they should give chase or get ready to take evasive action. "Just lower your heat signature the best you can and standby," Papa instructed. "In a few seconds, act like you're gonna RTB. That's when most the attacks happen. We have you in sight and are watching for SA-7s."

Dash 5 and 6 were now heading back to Linh Thu and had no indication of being tracked. Papa and Chappie were watching the ground intently and dividing their scan to back up their fellow Marines, who were now rapidly approaching their positions.

"Demon-flight Dash 1, Cowpoke Delta. We are RTB."

"Roger," Papa replied in a shushing tone, not wanting to take his eyes off his immediate area. "Dash 3 and 4, keep 'em covered," he added.

Val and Notso—Dash 4 and 3—knew to keep quiet and not disturb Papa. They kept their scans on the ground around the flight of helicopters and Cowpoke Delta.

Dash 5 and 6 were now within Papa and Chappie's orbit and still hadn't been fired upon. Papa now wondered if the four of them were the possible targets. "Okay Dash 5 and 6—begin the plan I described earlier. Fly the pattern as if you're gonna land. If they launch on you, break in opposite directions and go to idle and boards. We'll get the bastards."

"Roger," was the reply from Dash 5 and 6.

Both aircraft performed repeated turns in the pattern without incident. The entire rescue flight was only ten miles to the east now, so Papa ordered Dash 5 and 6 to land. Papa and Chappie took their place in the pattern for a couple turns and had Val and Notso fly overhead cover. As the rescue flight drew to five miles, Papa and Chappie landed.

"I hope they don't launch when Dash 3 and 4 are the only aircraft in the air touching down on the runway. These bastards are pretty damn smart and seem to be a half step ahead of us every time," Papa said to Chappie.

Val caught the flash of smoke from the jungles below.

"All aircraft take evasive action—looks like we got a launch to the east!" Val called, then added, "Follow me, Notso—release two bombs on my mark!"

The last helicopter rocked and swerved around in a desperate effort to shake the missile, slamming around the occupants. The door gunner got a face full of missile as it passed, and he could have read the serial numbers if he'd cared to. He then got an eyeful of two Phantoms a mere twenty meters away in a diving turn, releasing bombs. The roar of the engines rattled his brain and deafened him as the heat from the explosions singed his face. "Goddamnit, I quit!" he yelled as he slammed the Huey's door shut. All aircraft landed without incident as Val and Notso's bombs seemed to have discouraged any further SA-7 launches.

Papa, watching from the taxiway, said to Chappie, "Sweet! It seems to have worked!"

"Let's congratulate ourselves when Dash 3 and 4 are down safe, sir." Chappie warned.

Val and Notso were smiling under their masks because Papa's plan seemed to have worked, so they turned for the base. As they entered a high downwind for 13, both Nate and Speedy's heartbeats momentarily sped up. Both alerted their pilots. "MiGs! MiGs—six miles north closing fast!"

"Shit! Break east and drop your load, Notso!" Val said.

"Wilco," Notso responded.

Val and Notso pickled off the rest of their bombs and turned north climbing as fast as they could. Within seconds three MiG-21s shot by heading south, then turned to engage.

"Holy shit! You still got 'em, Double-O?" Val asked as he broke into the MiGs to engage.

"Yeah. They're trying to stay outside us."

"Breaking high, Tibbs," Notso said, hoping to get some MiGs to follow.

"Gotcha. You got two on you. I'm rolling behind 'em now!" Val said under the strain of g-forces as he completed a high-g barrel roll. "Where's number three, Double-O?"

"He's trailing. Think he's waiting to see what we're gonna do. He's five o'clock high," Nate responded.

"Can't worry about him just yet. I'm gonna send a couple bursts into these two," Val said as he dove into the twisting formation of aircraft below him. One MiG slid into his pipper, and as he squeezed the trigger, tracers zipped around the jet and a couple of puffs indicated he may have hit the trailing MiG.

Both MiGs saw the tracers around them and began to panic. They broke off smartly in different directions, forcing Val to pick one to follow. He picked the one he thought he'd hit. "Your tail's clear for now," he told Notso. "Number three's trying to get on my six."

"Roger. Stay on the one you're chasing. Number One's bugging out, I think," Notso said as he watched the first MiG heading north. Notso began a steep climbing turn, almost a diagonal loop. At the top of the loop he saw the third MiG closing within missile range of Val. Knowing he had no air-to-air ordnance himself, he rolled right-side up and stoked the burners. The third MiG either didn't see him or was baiting him, but he nevertheless closed within guns range head-on above the MiG. Notso opened fire at the MiG just as it fired a missile at Val.

Val broke into a hard left turn and the missile curled behind him and continued flying away. The third MiG climbed and fired at Notso as the jets passed agonizingly close to each other. Val reversed his turn to pursue the MiG he was originally chasing, and caught a faint glimpse of it ducking behind the third MiG, who was in a fierce fur ball, the aviator's term for a dogfight, with Notso.

"This fucker's a steady stick, Tibbs! Help me out!" Notso said.

"I'm pulling in behind you now!" Val replied.

"Tibbs! That first MiG is back on our tail!" Nate told his pilot.

"Dammit! Where are the Alert-5s?" Val wondered aloud. He kept behind Notso and fired at the lagging MiG, who wasn't nearly as skilled as the one chasing Notso. The lagging MiG kept trying to shield the lead MiG from Val as the original MiG engaged was closing in on his tail. Val ignored the MiG behind him and tried to get at an angle to fire at the lead MiG to get him off Notso's tail.

"Break left, Notso! I can roll under the trailer and get a shot at the lead!" Val ordered.

Notso complied and Val rolled under and to the right of the trailer. The lead MiG, trying to maintain an outside position, slid perfectly into Val's pipper. Val was about to fire when suddenly the trailing MiG exploded. Val looked to the left to see a trail of white smoke just beneath where the MiG was.

"Shit! Watch out for SA-7s too!" Val called.

"Great! The MiGs weren't enough!" Notso said as he continued his turn.

Suddenly a massive explosion billowed up from the jungles below, and the MiG behind Val broke right under heavy tracer fire from above. "Stop wasting time chattering and get that bastard off Notso's tail, Jordan!" Papa's voice resounded in every headset. "Excellent run, Chappie!"

Val commenced fire on the MiG along with Papa, who had pulled above him. The MiG, seeing he was now outnumbered, fled to the north.

"Let's get home, fellas. Those jackasses won't be coming back. We shouldn't have to worry about another SA-7 launch—Chappie's got 'em pinned down."

Val and Notso were relieved and flushed with admiration for their CO and XO for helping them out. "What happened?" Val asked.

"Chappie and I heard and saw what was going on and launched before the Alert-5s. Those bastards are fucking smart! The ground guys with the SA-7s were gonna shoot you guys down after the rescue flight avoided getting nailed, so apparently they sent the MiGs back in to draw you out. They accidentally shot down one of their MiGs instead and Chappie dropped four bombs on 'em. I came up to cover you guys."

"We gotta find their communication system and break it down, sir. It's freaking deadly efficient," Val added.

"Who was that MiG pilot? He was incredible!" Notso observed.

"Yeah, he was. Maybe we can down him in our forthcoming secret op," Papa replied. "Let's just get on the ground, gents. We can talk about this in greater detail in the Cannery. I think we've set the bait for the trap. I think they believe we'll respond to MiGs heading for Linh Thu again. We just need to wait until they send enough of 'em that we can make an impression on them not to charge our base again."

§ § § § § §

Captain Phan was furious as he and his flight landed at Kep Field. His wingmen were simply not on a par with him in their dog fighting skills. There were some exceptions in the PRVAF (People's Republic of Vietnam Air Force), but he was unlucky enough to go on missions not only with those who were lacking in skills, but who had just completed flight training and were inexperienced. "*Tao se khung mat!*"—I'm going crazy! he said as he slammed his helmet down on the table in front of his superiors, waving his hands on each side of his head. He pointed to the other aviators, complaining that he was very displeased with their performance, then got down on his knees as if in meditation or prayer, lifted his hands and face towards the ceiling as if shouting to a deity, and shouted *"Cu'u toi vo'i!"*—Help! Captain Phan's superiors knew he would continue yelling, acting belligerent, and bugging them until he got what he wanted.

This was the first time in a while that the Americans had actually responded to his rushes at the *Bac Phi-Cang* (North Air Base), as he referred to Linh Thu, but they still weren't taking them seriously enough, and he took that as an insult. He needed to do something that they couldn't ignore, something that not only would cost them some aircraft from SA-7 launches, but that he could shoot some down himself.

But Phan knew he'd need help from his wingmen if he drew out the number of American fighters he wanted, and most of the ones he'd flown with so weren't dependable. He had to hand-pick the best pilots from Kep Field and other bases if he was going to be victorious. Victory, as he envisioned it, would not only be the destruction of many US jets, but make the Americans actually afraid to fly. He knew he had a lot of planning to do, so he went to the quietest place on Kep Field—a small, sun-soaked patch of grass that was sheltered from the noise of the runways.

§ § § § §

Val was sitting on his patch of grass with paper and pen and a picture of Virginia, wondering if he should even bother writing her a letter that she wouldn't respond to. He just hoped everything was all right. He decided to write Virginia's parents instead, to ask about her, if she was okay, to find out why she hadn't written in so long. Just as he finished his letter, Big John came walking by on his way to the Cannery, whistling a tune he'd just made up.

He saw Val's long face and said "Cheer up, young'un. How can problems at home be getting you down when you live in such splendor?" Val looked up to see Big John smile as he gestured around him, pointing to the dismal scenery that resembled a run-down prison.

Big John continued. "And think of all the lovely ladies we have around. Sure, they're over in the PX in the pages of some smut magazine, but if we didn't have them; we'd have to actually use our imaginations whenever we groom the poodle. Now that, my young friend, would be truly unbearable!

"No sir. Running out of Vaseline would be truly unbearable," Val added with a smile.

I'm supposed to bring you with me to the Cannery. The whole squadron will be there."

Val quickly stuffed his letter into his thigh pocket and followed the big man. As they walked along the muddy road, Big John continued singing his song:

"Mattress on the bottom,

Daddy on top,

Mama in the middle yelling

Give it to me Pop!

Yeah Baby!

Mama's now bent over

Daddy's hopped on top

Something's in the middle

Going Flop! Flop! Flop!

Yeah Baby!

Mama's now hollerin'

You'd better not stop!

Val burst into laughter as Big John danced and mimicked the moves described in the song. "Come on, young'un—sing it with me." Big John tapped Val on the shoulder. Val listened as Big John went through the song again, then joined in:

...Mattress on the bottom,

Daddy on top...

Everyone in the Cannery turned and stared at Val and Big John as they entered singing their new smash hit. After the men listened to the lyrics, they briefly joined for a laugh-filled chorus—a rare moment of happiness out here on the front lines. After the laughter died down, things got serious again. Papa placed an easel in the center of the front of the room. The words "Operation Cast Net" were written in bold letters on the first page.

"Gentlemen, welcome to the briefing on VMFA-2's exclusive special-op. As all of you are well aware, the enemy has been baiting us for quite some time. Right now, they're letting us get complacent. They'll wait until we're fat, dumb, and happy, and then—wham!" Papa slammed his fist into his other palm with a loud pop. "They'll blindside us when we least expect it, or when-ever we're the most vulnerable. Well, sometimes the best defense is a good offense, so now it's our turn to give it back."

Papa ripped off the first page of the easel, and everyone in the room cheered, "Hell, yes!"

When cries of "About damn time!" and "Time to kick some ass!" and "Let's do it!" died down, Papa continued. "I have to admit that I didn't come up with this idea on my own. Captain Jordan birthed this brainchild and I 'potty-trained' it a bit. Here's the basic plan: when I decide that the enemy has sent a large enough number of aircraft, we'll spring into action. We'll send the Alert-5s as always, along with six other aircraft. This group will be known as Alpha Group, which I'll lead. Another eight aircraft will depart and duck behind the ridgeline to the west. They'll fly low and fast trying to avoid detection and will pass behind the incoming MiGs. Once they're past them, they'll climb above the MiGs and call me. They'll be known as the Sneaker Group, and Jordan will be in the lead. Alpha Group will then speed up to close the gap with the MiGs. Once the MiGs turn to retreat they'll fly directly into the Sneaker Group, who will engage them. Alpha Group will engage from the rear, and we should have the MiGs trapped in a wagon wheel. We should down quite a few MiGs, and if the enemy tries to launch SA-7s, they risk shooting down their own. With so many jets in such close proximity, I believe the missiles will become confused and go after any random target of opportunity. If they do launch, I'll have six more aircraft standing by to carpet bomb the areas of the launches. They'll be known as Charlie Group, with Captain Mailer in the lead. Hopefully this operation will buy us breathing room from further MiG rushes and SA-7 launches for a while. I'm calling our little special op 'Operation Cast Net' because hopefully we'll catch a lot of MiGs and SA-7 launchers by surprise." Everyone nodded and cheered. Papa finished the briefing with the usual items: frequencies assigned, lost comm procedures, weapons used, speeds, altitudes, etc. He went over the basics of air-to-air combat to refresh the men's memories. They were much younger than he was and relied more on pure reaction, and they each knew what Papa lacked in youth he made up for tenfold in combat experience. Each of Papa's wars differed progressively in both tactics and machines. Though speed and technology altered some tactics, the basics of aerial combat remained the same.

When the men filed out of the Cannery, it was with a newfound sense of hope. As Val got up to leave, Papa grabbed his arm. "Stay for a couple minutes, Jordan. You too, Robinson."

"Aye, sir," Val and Nate responded almost simultaneously.

Papa, furiously scribbling on something, waited until just Chappie, himself, and Val and Nate remained before he looked up at them. Val said, "sir, do you think the enemy is focusing on strategy the way we are?"

"Slow down there, Aristotle—don't get too philosophical on me this late. I ain't even had my first beer yet." Papa laughed, but he knew exactly what his aviator was really asking. He handed Nate some papers and told him, "Run this to my office before you go to the pub. Dismissed."

"Aye, sir," Nate returned as he took the papers and left.

Papa took a deep breath as he pondered Val's question and looked outside into the black sky. "Warriors are warriors. Have been since the beginning of time. Tactics change and weapons may come and go, but warriors will always behave as warriors. Never forget that, son. The answer to your question is, yeah—they're putting the same effort into strategy, if not more. Remember that whether you agree with this war or not, we're the ones who are attacking them on their soil. We'll eventually leave one day, but they have to live with the end results, so they're fighting for their home. Sometimes that's all the strategy they need." Papa paused. "Now enough of this philosophical shit. The reason I had you stay is to ask you to pick up something to boost morale on your trip to Dong Hoi tomorrow besides just construction supplies."

Val smiled. "Aye, sir. I believe morale is on sale this week—while supplies last. While I'm there, I'm gonna pick up a life, too. You want one too, sir?"

Papa laughed as Val left, then muttered, "Goddamnit! I'd have to check that kid's pulse if he didn't make some smartass remark."

§ § § § § §

Many miles north of Linh Thu, Captain Phan stood in front of his superiors as they read the details of the operation he'd planned and his list of names. A general finally stood up and firmly said. *"Khong! Khong! Tao khong thich cai nai!"*—No! No! I don't like it!

"May noi cai gi ha?"—What are you talking about? Phan answered, surprised.

The general made it clear that he didn't like Phan's idea of sending several small raids with only a few aircraft, even if they had the most skilled pilots. He wanted to wipe out Linh Thu in one swoop with a single massive air strike, coordinating with ground forces in the area to launch SA-7s. Almost none of the pilots he requested would be on this mission, because they wanted to have them standing by to intercept American air strikes targeting Hanoi and the surrounding areas. He tried unsuccessfully to reassure Phan by letting him know that he was going to have two Soviet pilot instructors along to assist.

Phan was furious. He'd flown against a few of the pilots from Linh Thu and knew they were better than the average American fighter pilot. Even when he'd had them outnumbered, they'd usually managed to fight him and his wingmen off, even scaring away his inexperienced wingmen. He couldn't imagine what it would be like if they actually responded with large numbers of aircraft. He'd love the challenge, but he was smart enough to know he'd need skilled wingmen to achieve victory. He also knew SA-7 launches might be a bad idea if his pilots actually got caught in a fierce fur ball with the Americans. He didn't fully trust that the SA-7 operators SA-7s could guarantee their weapons would only down Americans. Phan thundered back at his superiors for insisting on such a foolish plan. They let him know that they wouldn't compromise on their decision—it was final. Phan stormed away, knowing that his superiors' stubbornness could cost a lot of pilots their lives. As he walked away he said under his breath, *"Do ngu, cung dau trau!"*—You stupid, stubborn buffaloes!

§§§§§

Val arrived at Dong Hoi to again find that the violence of war was not limited to the jungles and hills. Each time they came, he and his men saw even more civilian buildings collapsed, burned, smoking and otherwise reeling from some type of attack, whether by firearms or explosives. Dong Hoi had the misfortune to be almost in the middle of Vietnam, so forces from both sides crossed paths there daily. The danger to citizens was that they didn't necessarily have to claim loyalty to either side to be in harm's way. If one side merely suspected someone was supporting the other, or if they were caught in the wrong place at the wrong time, they could be killed. The days of easily distinguishable lines, fronts, personnel, and theaters of war were past. The world was changing indeed.

Val walked into the shop to see that it had endured another attack. Nghia Mau greeted him with her usual smile and warm welcome. He saw the damage was even greater than the last time and had been hastily repaired. Despite the damage and anxiety the attacks were causing, Nghia Mau and her staff all seemed in high spirits. Val and his men had nothing but admiration for their courage.

Val got the usual materials for the base and asked about Nga Nghin Do'i. *"No di roi"*—She's gone already, Nghia Mau said with a smile.

Val's face dropped in disappointment. He then mentioned Papa's request for something to boost the men's morale. He couldn't think of anything offhand, so he asked Nghia Mau if she had any ideas.

She thought about it for a moment. She wasn't sure if American men had the same tastes that Vietnamese men did, but she didn't think it would hurt to make a suggestion: *"Bia? Thuc-pham?"*—Beer? Food?

Val thought that sounded good, so he asked where he could get a lot of Vietnamese beer and food. He thought the men of Linh Thu would like a change from the offerings of the chow hall and pub.

Nghia Mau was pleasantly surprised that Americans weren't much different from the people she knew—maybe there was hope for this world after all. She responded that her friend owned the best restaurant in town and she would call and have them have lots of food ready when the trucks stopped by. As for the beer, she signaled to Val to follow her to a corner of her shop. She grabbed a crowbar and opened a huge crate, then watched Val's face to gauge his reaction when he saw several kegs and hundreds of bottles of beer. Her smile widened when she saw Val's face fill with happiness and gratitude.

Val gave Nghia Mau a powerful hug, kissed her on the cheek, and said with a smile, "*Chung ta hay cu'o'i nhau nhe!*"—Let's get married!

Nghia Mau smiled and blushed, knowing after talking with Nga Nghin Do'i that Val had a good sense of humor. She kissed him on the cheek and joked, "*Em can tho'i gian de suy nghi!*"—I'll need some time to think about it!

Nghia Mau gave Val directions to the restaurant, and he thanked her profusely as he left the shop. Just as he was about to climb into the truck to leave, a woman riding in on a bicycle caught his eye. She seemed to pedal faster when she saw the American trucks at the loading docks, and the Marines, suspicious, grabbed their rifles but kept them out of sight. When she pulled up in front of Val and removed the scarf concealing her face, men nearly swooned as she shook her hair out. Nga Nghin Do'i smiled as she approached Val. "Captain—good to see you!" She gave Val a hug—an unusually friendly gesture for a Vietnamese woman.

Val returned her hug with pleasure, thinking what a great day it was to be hugged by two beautiful women, one the most beautiful he'd ever seen. They talked for another half hour before he had to leave. By the time he climbed into the truck, he was in a warm daze that lasted until he hit the rack that night.

§ § § § §

Val went to mail call with low expectations, but when his name was called, he was shocked to find a letter from Virginia's parents. Wasting no time, he ran off to the patch to read it:

Dear Val,

I hope this letter finds you well and in good spirits. We know life is tough where you are, so keep hanging in there and return home safely to all of us soon. Let's put all your worries to rest now—nothing bad has happened. Virginia is fine as far as we know. We are as shocked as you are that she has not written you in so long. We went to talk to her, but every time we go over to her house or call her, she's not home. We know work has kept her very busy and she is working a whole lot of odd hours and shifts. We will keep trying to contact her and find out why she has not written you in a while. She is supposed to come over for her nephew's birthday in a couple of *weeks, so we can certainly talk to her then. We know you are under a great deal of stress, so we will promise to keep you informed no matter what she says. You are owed at the very least a honest explanation. Stay safe. You are in our thoughts and prayers.*

Yours truly,

Dave and Gail

Although he learned that Virginia was safe, the letter didn't really ease Val's mind—in fact it only worsened his state of mind. Why hadn't she written him? What could possibly be keeping her so busy that she couldn't take time to write the love of her life? All he could do now would be to wait for the next letter from her parents, or from Virginia herself. He left the patch and headed to the Cannery to brief for tonight's mission.

§ § § § §

A couple weeks had gone by with no activity from the PRVAF. Some pilots began to think that the enemy might have called off their feints toward the base again. Even SA-7 launches and rocket and mortar attacks had diminished. Had they scared them with the bombing tactics? Had the enemy run out of SA-7s? Maybe communication between the PRVAF and ground forces had been severed somehow. It was all a mystery.

A few still believed that the enemy would try again, that this was merely the calm before the storm. Washington somehow heard about Operation Cast Net and was displeased, saying it was an incredible waste of time and money, instead defending their way of running the war. It might take a few more blunders before higher command woke up and listened to those on the front lines.

§ § § § §

Inaction. It drove Phan crazy. He still got attack bombers retreating from Hanoi, but he still wanted to hit Linh Thu in a series of precision strikes. His superiors just sat around and talked and would then pat themselves on the back about what a great job they were doing. The new instructors from *Nga-So* (the Soviet Union) were as full of themselves as his superiors were. Their only positive was that they agreed with him about a series of strikes, instead of a single massive strike. Phan also knew that the longer they waited, the more time the enemy would have to prepare. The time to strike was slipping away. When were they finally going to attack? Why wouldn't his superiors listen to him and the Russians? Why won't they allow some of the better pilots to go on a mission of such critical importance? Was this their way of getting rid of him for his insubordination? Why were they such morons? He hated waiting for their orders—he knew how to achieve victory. Maybe it would take a few more blunders before the leaders would wake up and actually listen to those who were in the middle of the war.

§ § § § § §

A couple more weeks passed at Linh Thu with little activity from the enemy except for a few rocket and mortar attacks, which seemed to be the new normal. Enemy troops got inside the perimeter fences a few times to attack the flight line. They took heavy losses and rarely inflicted any major damage because the flight line was so heavily guarded. After a couple of failures, the enemy decided to switch tactics and attacked buildings instead. This was bad because a fire could easily spread over the entire base in minutes, since all the buildings were canvas or wood. When the enemy scorched the pub, the Marines took it personally. They retaliated by firing mortars and other artillery into the surrounding jungles at random times of the day and night, hoping to get lucky collapse a tunnel enemy troops might be hiding in. They were still trying to find out how the enemy were getting onto the base. If they solved that mystery, maybe they'd get some sleep.

Val still hadn't received any more word from back home about Virginia, and he had done well so far in disguising his severe disappointment and worry. So far he had not let it affect his flying and other duties; and he had to spend a few hours a day at the gym punching and kicking the heavy bag, speed bag, and double end ball to ensure his frustration remained out of the cockpit. He actually hoped that the PRVAF would send a major attack toward Linh Thu so he could take his anger out on the enemy, but even that seemed like it would never happen.

§ § § § § §

Captain Phan sat in his cockpit, stewing because he was third in command of his flights behind two Russian pilots. The last couple of flights against American bombers were more successful because his wingmen were now doing what he'd been trying to teach them for so long—except that they were listening to the foreigners in a way they hadn't listened to him, their own countryman. It was beyond frustrating. He looked at all the jets lining up behind him and took a deep breath, wondering how many of them would be returning with him to Kep Field. He then glanced at his watch and back at the pink haze on the horizon. *It will be dawn soon—a day neither side would forget.*

"*Di!*"—Launch!

§ § § § § §

One of the controllers at the DASC glanced sleepily at his radar scope as he sipped coffee. Suddenly it was nearly whited out by strong returns. "Captain!" he called for commander of the watch.

"Yes, Sergeant?"

The controller pointed at his scope as he tried to start tagging up his tracks.

"Good Lord!" the officer exclaimed as he quickly checked the flight schedules to ensure that he wasn't picking up American aircraft. "How many?"

"I count fourteen targets, sir, but I can guarantee that there are many more because some of them change size whenever the flight makes an erratic turn."

"They're bogies, all right. I'm gonna guess that there are at least twenty," the captain said as he picked up the red phone that was a direct line to the shack at Linh Thu.

The phone woke up the crews of the Alert-5 aircraft.

"Linh Thu, Panama. We got a major problem..."

The Alert-5 pilot listened and snapped his fingers to signal one of the ordnance techs to come to him. He wrote on a sheet of paper in large letters, GET PAPA OVER HERE NOW! The tech sprinted out the door to a pickup truck parked outside and sped off to Papa's hooch. When he got there, he charged inside and shook Papa to wake him. "Sir, it's time!" Just as the words sunk in, the base alarm sounded. Papa had the tech wake the entire squadron of VMFA-2 with a megaphone as he drove by each tent. Within minutes hundreds of men were sprinting to the flight line to arm and fuel aircraft, while the crews scrambled for their gear and then to their jets.

"This is it, gents—let's go to work!" Papa yelled at his men. He grabbed Val as he ran by and gave him a reassuring smile. "Make me proud, son!"

It was a sight to behold. Eighteen aircraft were quickly armed with Sidewinders and Sparrows, and ammo for their cannons, while the remaining six were armed with bombs, gun pods, and cannon ammo. Within minutes, Linh Thu was the noisiest it had ever been as forty-eight jet engines were fired up. Papa had decided to send every aircraft in the squadron to ensure that Operation Cast Net would work. Soon the squadron split up as Alpha Group lined up with Papa on runway 31, Sneaker Group lined up with Val on runway 28, and Charlie Group followed Captain Mailer to runway 31 behind Alpha.

"Time to get some!" Papa said on frequency as Alpha Group roared into the dark, still morning air. After Alpha was airborne, Charlie Group thundered down the runway and into the sky. "Mailer, make sure the MiGs see your group climbing above us into your orbit. It'll take their attention off the Sneaker Group."

"Doing it now, sir," Captain Mailer replied.

Val looked at Nate in his rearview mirror, then at Notso beside him. "Let's kick some MiG ass, Sneaker Group!" Val shoved the throttles forward and

Sneaker followed down runway 28 and leapt into the sky. "Stay low, guys. Clear the ridgeline by only two hundred feet or so." Sneaker Group roared over the ridgeline and soon Linh Thu was quiet again. "All right—let's dive to six hundred feet and stay there until you RIOs tell us we're behind the MiGs, then we'll climb above them. Stay fast—we've got the most ground to cover. Timing is everything." Sneaker Group was screaming over the terrain, flying map of the earth. The extreme groundspeed was readily apparent to anyone looking outside their canopy, the terrain just a green blur rushing by in the increasing light of dawn. All the RIOs had their radars tilted up as far as possible, scanning for the MiGs. It was soon obvious where they were as the scope lit up with returns, both from the MiGs and the rest of VMFA-2.

"MiGs are two o'clock and two-five miles at angels one-niner, Tibbs," Nate said.

Val looked at the small scope in the lower right side of his cockpit. "Got 'em, Double-O."

Papa, meanwhile, scanned the skies ahead of him in a mostly vain effort to get a visual on the large group of MiGs that were rapidly closing on his flight. "Keep it fast, fellas. We need to close the distance before any SA-7 operators can get a solid lock on anyone. As soon as we're in range, get a steady tone and fire." Then Papa added, "And pray that you don't have any duds on your rails."

§ § § § §

Phan looked at his radar and was shocked to see the response from Linh Thu. Something didn't feel right. They'd expected them to launch more than the usual two to four aircraft, but they'd launched more than ten—something they'd never done before. He warned his men to be vigilant because something suspicious was going on. He told the Russians that they might need to break off earlier than usual. The Americans were closing faster than ever before, and the whole operation might have to be cancelled if the Americans got too close because the SA-7s wouldn't be able to tell them apart and might shoot some of their own planes down, as they had done a couple times before. The lead Russian instructor shushed him, explaining that the Americans were clueless—and even if they got into a giant furball, their planes wouldn't be able to compete with the MiGs in a pure dogfight. Phan bit his lower lip to keep from tearing into the foreigner, who'd never been up against the pilots from Linh Thu. They'd show this Russian just who really was clueless.

§ § § § §

"We're now five miles past the MiGs and increasing, Tibbs," Nate told his pilot.

"Roger." Val then ordered over frequency, "Sneaker Group climb to angels two-four as fast as you can and turn south to circle behind the MiGs."

Sneaker Group pointed their jets skyward in a steep climbing right turn. Each altimeter wound up quickly as the F-4s rocketed through the sky. In a matter of minutes, the flight was at twenty-four thousand feet and headed south. The MiGs were just eight miles ahead and each flight crew had a visual on them. Val counted twenty-nine aircraft. Amazing! He'd never seen such a large formation of enemy aircraft. It was reminiscent of WWII films and the massive formations of bombers and fighters over the skies of Europe.

Val keyed up with pride to Papa. "Alpha Group, Sneaker Group is in position. Ooh-rah!"

"Nice work, son. We're about ten miles in front of the MiGs. We have visual. Be ready. They should break in about a minute when we're in missile range. All RIOs, get a steady tone as quickly as you can. All crews are cleared to fire at will. Make sure not to shoot any friendlies down. Let's get some!" Papa replied. Every Marine was pumped up and ready to fight. The jitters and butterflies were gone. The fight was on!

§§§§§

The Russian pilots looked at the massive formation of American fighters straight ahead, then looked at their radar. They were within missile range of the Americans, so it was time to run and leave them to the SA-7s. They ordered the MiGs to retreat just as loud tones sounded in their headsets. What? The Americans were engaging them instead of trying to chase them away? Just as the formation of MiGs completed their turn to the north, a terrifying sight met their eyes—more Americans, a huge formation of F-4s above them. Soon more tones sounded in their headset. Puffs of smoke could be seen streaming out from under a few of the jets. Missiles! The Russian pilots knew they were in trouble.

§§§§§

Papa watched as the MiGs broke to the north and announced, "There they go! Charlie Group, watch for SA-7s and prepare to attack! Sneaker Group, get ready to fire! Alpha Group fire at will!"

"Got a tone, Tibbs! Fire!" Nate said.

"Got 'em, Notso! Fire!" Speedy told his pilot.

"Fox 2!" announced Val and Notso as they released Sidewinders at the group of MiGs who were turning toward them.

§§§§§

Phan saw that his flight was trapped in a wagon wheel and knew that his fears were valid. He even admired his enemy a little for their well-designed trap. Within seconds his flight was surrounded, and aircraft were starting to fly around in erratic patterns as a fierce dogfight commenced. He could sense the panic and confusion sweeping through his formation, so he shouted "*Danh lon phai MY, do ngu!*"—Fight the Americans, you idiots!

Two missiles shot past Phan's MiG and he broke high. One missile curled skyward and went ballistic, the second exploded just two meters in front of a MiG, shattering its canopy, breaking off the radome, and killing its pilot, sending it into a steep dive. He picked an F-4 to close on, but he saw that each time he approached, there was always another behind him. Yes—it was time to fight, but because of the proximity of so many aircraft, getting missile locks would be a challenge. Good! That meant it would be settled with stick skills and guns—what he dreamed of. Phan closed on the F-4 and got a good angle on it. He knew that another would be closing in behind him, so he had to get his shot off quickly. The American was well out of guns range, but still too close for an Atoll missile to acquire. He had to either gain or lose distance, depending on the weapon he chose. He looked behind him to see another F-4 closing in. He pulled back and left on his stick to begin a barrel roll. Once he was at the top of the roll he pushed forward on the stick to load the wings with negative g-forces, slowing the roll and his airspeed and increasing the distance with the F-4. He finished the roll and put the F-4 in his pipper and squeezed the trigger. An Atoll rocketed toward the American fighter, then suddenly veered toward the ground. Dammit! He looked behind to see the American was lined up for a missile shot at him. He had to quickly make his second shot count. He got another solid tone after a few seconds of jockeying to put the F-4 back in the pipper. He fired a second missile, which screamed at the American. The missile closed in and exploded under the F-4's right wingtip as it dove left. The massive American fighter went into departure for a few seconds and then recovered, wounded yet still flyable. Phan broke hard right to shake the other F-4 on his tail. This was awesome—dogfighting with worthy adversaries!

§ § § § §

Papa pulled in behind a MiG and quickly got a lock on it. "Fox 2," he announced as he let a Sidewinder fly. The missile went straight to the MiG's tailpipe and blew it into pieces. He looked around and saw Chappie closing in on a MiG with another on his tail. Chappie rolled into a split-S and pulled out midway through the maneuver into a vertical dive. All three aircraft were in plain view directly ahead of Papa, and he pointed his nose just ahead of the MiG that was closing in on Chappie as he continued his steep dive. As he closed within fifteen hundred meters, Papa fired a cannon burst that the MiG flew into. As it started to smoke heavily, the MiG broke off from Chappie's tail and tried to run for Kep Field. Papa was about to pursue it until he saw another F-4 closing on it. The MiG pilot looked behind him to see two F-4s chasing him. Knowing that if he tried to run or fight he was surely staring death in the face, he punched out. "Dammit!" Papa said with disappointment. "I wanted that one."

Val closed on a MiG and was about to fire a missile at it when another dove between them just sixteen hundred meters ahead. Val was confused about why the MiG had made such a foolish move. Didn't the pilot see him? Was he trying to shield the other MiG? "Double-O, do you see any MiGs behind us?" He was wondering if another MiG had snuck behind them, using the MiG currently in front him as a distraction.

"Negative."

Val was angry that this MiG had cut off what would have been a sure kill, so he switched to his gun and sent several bursts into the MiG, which burst into flames. As it broke apart, it revealed the other MiG trying to escape to the north. Val went into lag pursuit and once again got a good angle. He got a solid tone and fired a Sidewinder. "Splash two!" he said.

Papa and Chappie were having an easy time locking on targets and shooting them down. Any MiG foolish enough to get behind either of them soon found out how quickly experienced combat pilots could shake and ultimately destroy their younger adversaries, despite the fact that the MiGs were far more maneuverable than the F-4s. The rest of VMFA-2 were stunned at how deadly and efficient their superior officers were and shuddered to imagine what they could do in an aircraft like the MiG. The F-4 was effective as long as its superior technology worked, and the pilots of VMFA-2 were among the best in the DOD, so for the most part they were able to cancel out the MiGs' maneuverability advantage. A couple of pilots already had kills, and Val and Notso had two apiece. Papa had three and Chappie had another three. The MiGs were wounding some of the F-4s, but for the most part they were trying to flee. But three of them that were proving to be a real handful.

On the ground, a group of SA-7 operators watched the skies above. The roar of jet engines and exploding ordnance was surprisingly loud despite how high the battle was taking place. It was obvious that the PRVAF was in trouble and losing a lot of aircraft. Should they try to help? The operators had a hard enough time even seeing an airplane, much less distinguishing friend from foe. Finally out of boredom or frustration, one of the men put his weapon to his shoulder and searched for any airplane he could find. One of his fellow operators pushed his launch tube down and shouted, *"Du'ng pha tao nghe chu'a!"*—Don't mess around!

The operator pushed his countryman away and shouted back, *"Di cho khac!"*—Get away from me! He continued to search the skies for an airplane to shoot at.

"Tao canh cao may nghe chu'a!"—I'm warning you, his fellow soldier pleaded with him, trying to explain that he might shoot down one of their own.

As soon as the soldier with the SA-7 found an aircraft, he locked on to it. The red light in the sight turned green and he squeezed the trigger, and a split second later a missile rocketed skyward, streaming a white column of smoke. *"Di xuong dia nguc di!"*—Go to hell! he said in disrespect for his fellow soldier.

"Do ngu! Chung giet!"—You idiot! We're dead! the soldier scolded his younger comrade and smacked him on the back of his head. Both watched to see if the missile hit anything.

Papa looked right and saw the smoke trail streaming from the jungles below and watched as the missile continued skyward. "Charlie Group!"

"We're already on it, sir!" Captain Mailer had his flight split up and were diving to begin their runs. The smoke trail led them directly to where the launch originated. They decided to launch two bombs per plane on this run and approach from different directions in order to confuse the SA-7 operators.

The men in the jungles below had no idea what was headed their way. They continued to search the skies for their missile and an explosion. The air grew still and soon a faint swishing sound could be heard over the noises from the jets above. A split second after they heard the sound, a massive bang accompanied by a fierce jolt pounded their bodies. The exact millisecond the jolt was felt, all hearing and feeling stopped and the bright day suddenly went black. It was a swift and merciful death—the best one can hope for.

§ § § § §

Phan saw his flight being decimated by the Americans while the SA-7 operators were most likely dead from bombs dropped by six other F-4s orbiting above. The only way to escape was to shoot their way out and run. He looked for a way out as F-4s flew around trapped MiGs like humpback whales bubble-netting a school of sardines into a ball.

There it was—the only break in the formation, to the northwest and low. It was a serious risk, since the Americans could still have the advantage of altitude, but it was the only way. Phan got a couple of his wingmen to follow as they throttled up and faked a right climbing turn, toward an F-4 turning eastbound. Just as he hoped, a trailer of the first F-4 followed, thinking the MiGs were going to engage the eastbound F-4. Phan ordered his men to stay in the climbing turn until he told them when to break. His pilots were nervous because they knew they were exposing their entire profile to the trailing F-4, making for an easy shot—and the F-4 pilot stared in disbelief as the MiGs gave him a ninety-degree aspect angle. But he wasn't going to complain— he'd take an easy kill if offered to him. Phan waited until he was sure the F-4 was about to shoot, then ordered his flight to reverse into a steep diving left turn into the F-4.

The F-4 pilot saw the MiGs break into him and had to maneuver not only to avoid a collision but to keep his targets in sight. He couldn't keep up with the MiGs in the rollout, but the pilot knew he could easily out-dive them if they were still in the descent. As he finished his turn, a huge blur shot by him— another F-4 orbiting at a higher altitude that had come to assist. Phan now had his wingmen at ninety-percent power and almost clear of the furball. Suddenly a missile streaked by on the right of his flight and began to curl back toward them. They were under attack again! Phan looked back to see an F-4 saddling up for another shot, and saw the first missile pass just under his flight and explode twenty meters to his left. The shockwave shook his jet a little but caused no damage, but he knew he and his wingmen probably wouldn't be so lucky again. He had to either shake this American or shoot him down. Phan stoked his burner and pulled into a loop, and ordered his wingmen to break into opposite directions. As he pulled into the loop, Phan kept his eyes on the F-4; his next move would depend on the American's reaction. The F-4 decided to chase him, at first in lead pursuit, firing rounds from his cannon just in front of his nose. Phan began to roll his jet, faking an Immelmann. The F-4 switched to lag pursuit, hoping for a missile shot as the MiG would overshoot in the Immelmann. Phan then performed another roll and pulled back into another half-loop the other direction, easily escaping the F-4. The Phantom looked ahead to see one of Phan's wingmen directly in front of him, so he switched targets to the one now in his sights. He opened fire and scored some hits, and the MiG shuddered when the rounds sliced through it. *"Cu'u toi vo'i!"*—Help! the pilot pleaded over frequency.

Phan had continued his half loop into a split-S and swooped in behind the F-4 shooting at his wingman. The energy from the maneuver brought him too close to the American for a missile shot, so he opened fire with his cannon. His rounds scored direct hits on the F-4's starboard engine, which now belched smoke. The American pilot shut down his starboard engine and broke away for the safety of his wingmen. *"Di di!"*—Let's go! Phan ordered his wingmen to break to the northwest, and they headed for Kep Field.

Papa looked below and saw one of his wingmen engaged in a fierce dogfight with a pair of MiGs. The MiG pilots seemed to be quite skilled, and Papa knew that his wingman wouldn't be able to hold off two pilots of this caliber for much longer. As Papa rolled in to assist, he noticed something very familiar about how the two MiGs were flying. He'd seen it somewhere before, but he couldn't quite place it yet. "Roll right, son," Papa called. "Help me get an angle on these bastards." The Marine complied and Papa soon was in the saddle for a shot with guns. When the MiG pilots looked over their shoulders, they saw another F-4 closing in on them. Papa fired and the MiGs broke off the F-4's tail. As he followed the left-breaking MiG, the other MiG stayed in its right break to assess the situation. Chappie saw what was going on and purposely trailed in the immediate background, hoping that the other MiG would reengage with Papa. The right-breaking MiG saw Chappie and knew it would be foolish to chase Papa's F-4; he instead went head on toward Chappie. Soon Papa and Chappie found themselves in the best dogfights they'd experienced since the Korean War. The MiGs they were engaged with were certainly steady sticks.

Despite the risks, Captain Phan was repeatedly going back to the fight to lead his wingmen out. He looked over to see the last two surviving MiGs engaged with two skilled Americans. He saw other F-4s jockeying for positions to guarantee that no matter where the MiGs went, they'd have another enemy jet on their tail. Phan climbed as high as he could and snuck over the top of the entire dogfight. As he looked down, he tried to decide whether he should even assist these MiGs, especially since they weren't Vietnamese. He finally chose the honorable thing—he'd make one attempt to help the Russian instructors he disliked—although he did have respect for the one who'd instructed him long ago in Russia. He waited until he could determine who was who, then stoked his burner and dove into the American fighters.

Below, Chappie closed in on his MiG and prepared to fire. It was apparent that the MiG pilot recognized the situation and decided to run instead of fight as he was getting worn out. The MiG pilot made a last-ditch attempt to shake Chappie, then stoked full burner to try to outrun the Americans. As he began his run, he looked to his right when the missile tone sounded and saw that another F-4 had snuck ahead and was waiting to intercept him in lead pursuit, and he saw the smoke trail of the missile it had fired. Just as he turned his head back to his instrument panel, the missile slammed broadside into his MiG.

Every time Papa tried to lock on to the other MiG, it was able to break the cone of vulnerability at the last split second. This pilot was good. Papa was patient and knew he'd get him in time. Finally the MiG pilot made the error of allowing Papa to get a solid tone on him, and the MiG pilot knew he was done for. Papa was about to squeeze the pickle when his wingmen shouted a warning about another MiG zooming in from above, firing its guns. Papa dove left to avoid a collision gunfire and saw the blur of a MiG-21 clearing a path for the other MiG. The other MiG rolled left and passed within feet of Papa's canopy. The two pilots managed a glance at one another at a closure rate of twelve hundred knots and both were shocked when they recognized each other by their helmet markings.

The MiG pilot stoked his burner as he followed Phan to safety. The Russian cringed in anger as he knew he'd tangled with the best of the best—the legendary Earl J. Driskell.

"Fucking Colonel Tomb! You bastard!" Papa was furious. "We'll meet again! And I *will* finish you next time, you cowardly piece of shit!" Papa shouted over frequency.

The rest of VMFA-2 was silent. They'd never heard their commander sound so vengeful and angry. How did Papa know Colonel Tomb? What happened the first time they'd met?

"Sorry gents." Papa looked around at his wingmen. "All groups RTB immediately, and of course let the wounded aircraft land first. Great job, boys! Incredible! I couldn't ask for a better group of flight crews. I knew only you fellas could pull this off!"

To the north, Phan and Tomb flew back to Kep Field in silence, Tomb knowing that Phan had saved most of the MiG pilots from certain death. When they landed, each surviving pilot ran up the captain and profusely thanked him for his incredible skills. As Phan passed his superior officers, he refused to make eye contact. He knew they'd never admit their errors and poor judgment, and he strained to keep from beating each to pulp.

To the south, each F-4 overflew Linh Thu and performed a few victory rolls as the men on the ground cheered. It was a total landslide—thirteen enemy aircraft shot down and another five wounded, with no F-4s lost and only four damaged, one severely. All the Phantoms landed safely, and as the final jet's tires screeched on the pavement, the rescue helicopters shut down on the hot-pad. Damaged jets pulled up behind the red-striped maintenance barricades while the others parked in their usual spots. The ground crews cheered the aviators as they headed to the Cannery for debrief. They doubled their cheers as they circled Papa's jet, proud of their leader who had the guts to stick his neck out and risk court martial to carry out this operation. When he stepped out of his jet, the ground crews carried him to the Cannery on their shoulders.

After the debrief, Val walked up to Big John, who always attended, and said, "Well, sir, you won't be playing poker for a while now with all the new repairs on your plate."

"I noticed. Thanks a lot, you jackasses." Big John smiled and held out his hand for Val to shake. "Excellent job, young'un. You're gonna be another Earl J. Driskell one day."

That was a compliment few if any others would ever get. Val returned the smile and said, "Thank you, sir, but God I hope I'm not still in the corps when I reach his age!"

"We'll see. You're just like him—you like nothing better than to be in the cockpit of a high-performance jet at full throttle. See ya at the pub, young'un."

§ § § § §

Val lay in his rack, his head spinning from the effects of the drinks at the pub. He didn't know how he should feel. He knew he was happy with the victory, but at the same time he felt uneasy. As his eyes drifted to the picture of Virginia taped over his rack, the feeling intensified. Even though it was dark inside the tent, he could always make out the details of the picture—he could see it with his heart and soul when he couldn't with his eyes. Now that combat offered no distraction—at least for the moment, his thoughts returned to the agony of not knowing what was going on with the love of his life.

The next morning, Val, Nate, Notso, and Speedy were stumbling toward Papa's office in the dim morning light, wondering why they'd been ordered to go there since Papa had promised the VMFA-2 crews he'd let them sleep in a little. The three officers lined up behind Val as he knocked on the door to Papa's office.

"Come in, gents," Papa replied without looking up from a stack of papers he was signing.

They walked in cautiously, still unsure why they were called out of their racks so early. They stared at Papa furiously scribbling on the papers, probably thinking how grizzled old Papa looked. He'd probably been drunker than any man in the pub last night, stayed longer than anyone else, yet was first up this morning without a hint of a hangover.

Papa finally looked up from the papers and handed each man a set. "I know you want to sleep a bit longer, and I also know you're too hung over to read the papers I just handed you, so I'll tell you what they are." Papa looked at the slumped Speedy, whose hands were shaking. "Easy there, son. Damn—you're a lightweight!"

The men glanced at the papers and strained to focus on what was written on them.

"Those papers are my way of boosting morale around here. They're passes so you can go have five days of liberty. I'm staggering liberty for each man in the squadron, and you four are the first to go. Normally you'd get a choice of where you'd like to go—Australia, Philippines, Bali, Japan, Thailand—but we're short of people and time, as you know, so I chose for you. You're going to Thailand—it's close, it's fun, and there are regular MAC flights there. Your flight leaves this morning at 1100, so be on the west ramp with your shit packed and your passes in hand. You exceeded my expectations yesterday, so congrats. Y'all are young bucks, hormones a-ragin,' haven't seen a woman in God knows when, plus you need to expand your repertoire when it comes to samplin' different flavors of women. Thailand is just the place to do that. The women are some of the most beautiful in the world and are very friendly, plus the countryside's nice, too. That's kinda a bonus. No need to say 'thanks'—I'm thanking you. Enjoy, fellas."

"Hey—what the hell just happened?" Speedy asked, confused. "I just dreamt that we were going to Thailand!"

"Don't worry, Buddy. What just happened was definitely a good thing! Believe me!" Notso placed his hand on Speedy's shoulder to steady him.

The men were barely across the muddy street when Papa came out and shouted "Hey, Double-O Eight! Come here a sec—I have a favor to ask of you." Papa had a peculiar grin on his face.

"Sir?" Nate staggered back to Papa and leaned over as the CO spoke. As Papa continued, a smile crossed Nate's face. "Aye, sir! You can count on me—I won't let you down!"

"You better not, son. If you do, it'll be the second sign of the apocalypse, and then we're all fucked!" Papa smiled as he sent Nate back to join his fellow aviators. "The first already happened when your buddy Jordan over there actually didn't give me a smartass remark before he left my office! Have a blast, fellas!"

8

THE REVELATIONS OF R&R

The tires of the massive C-130 Hercules smoked and chirped as they met the runway at Ubon Royal Thai Air Force Base in northeast Thailand. The climate was identical to Vietnam's—sweltering heat and humidity—but at least here they could have a little peace of mind. For the first time in four months, they wouldn't have to fear a rocket or mortar attack, and that would mean something else they hadn't had in a long while—sound sleep. On the ramp, the men decided to catch a nap, then see what trouble they could get into as the day progressed.

The Marines headed for their hotel, which was in the small town just outside the base. They'd stay there overnight, and in the morning make arrangements to hire a driver to take them to Bangkok if they didn't want to take a bus. As the others went to their rooms, Val stayed in the lobby and looked for a phone. As he waited for the desk clerk, he saw the clock on the wall and knew it would be an odd hour back home if he called Virginia, but he figured she'd be happy to hear his voice. When the clerk finally came back, he told Val that there was a pay phone in town he could use. Val thanked him and decided to just go up to his room and lie down. After all, he was here for fun, and he knew that there would be ample opportunities to call Virginia while on R&R.

Val walked into his room and noticed that it shared a tiny bathroom with the one next to his, which was Nate's, and he noticed it had a Japanese-style toilet instead of a western one, but at least this hotel had modern plumbing. The shower was basically a single spout in the wall of the room. Because the shower itself had no walls, the water simply ran into a drain in the middle of the bathroom floor. Val crashed onto his bed and dozed off. It was time to forget about what was going on just a few hundred miles east.

Three hours later, the Marines met in the lobby to check out the town. Since it was just under a half mile from the hotel, they decided to walk. As they followed the road, they took in the pungent smell of the drainage ditches that crisscrossed the surrounding countryside and talked about matters other than the war for the first time in months, as if they were back home again. They decided that while the world away from combat might be boring by comparison, there were enough thrills in everyday life to make it worth living. The afternoon heat wasn't even noticeable over the half-mile walk to town as their senses were distracted by the sounds, sights, and smells of the Thai civilization.

The small town was an eye-opener as they made their way down streets crowded with people going about their routines. They passed pagodas, markets, merchants, and small eateries. They were astounded when they found brand-name clothes at dirt-cheap prices. When they got to the residential district, they passed flats that housed large families, each with a tiny "house" just outside the door.

"What the hell are these for?" Speedy asked as he pointed at one.

"They're spirit houses," Val answered. "You give the spirits a good place to live and offer them small 'sacrifices' of food, incense, and such, and it keeps the bad spirits out of your home and away from your family."

"Oh," Speedy said as they walked back to a small shop. He noticed several beautiful girls walking by and pointed to them as they passed. "I'd go for that in a heartbeat."

"Careful about pointing, Speedy," Val replied. "And while we're at it, don't touch anyone on the head. It's the highest point of the body, sacred to Buddhists and Hindus. Oh, and watch out for small children—don't let them touch you. They're excellent pickpockets. In fact, keep your wallet in your front pocket." Val smiled. "If you think this little town is an eye-opener, wait'll we get to Bangkok!"

"Thanks, Mister Cruise Director—you're doing great!" Speedy said with his thumbs up.

The Marines bought some authentic low-priced clothes and jewelry to send home, and they felt a little guilty as they haggled over fractions of pennies with the merchants. They continued looking around until about 1900, then decided to have dinner. They found a small restaurant overlooking the Mekong River, where a small waterfall fell into it. Boats crowded the river close to town. Some were merchant vessels, but most were dwellings. The restaurant was open-air except for the kitchen, and lovely thick foliage surrounded the place. The smell of clove cigarettes, incense, and spicy food filled the air. A lovely lady led them to their table where a very large lazy Susan was the centerpiece. Notso spun the large metal dish several times before he asked, "We're not going to get individual plates?"

"Most Southeast Asian countries serve food from a communal dish. This makes it easier to pass the food around instead of picking up and passing a dish around and over people's personal space," Val explained.

"I hope they have forks. I don't how to use chopsticks," Speedy said.

"This is Thailand, not China or Japan, Speedy—they don't use chopsticks here," Val assured him. "Also, don't order any ice in beverages—or drink any water, for that matter. Besides, we don't have any interest in staying sober, do we?"

"Somehow, I think we're going to regret agreeing with you on that," Speedy replied.

"How do you know all this stuff, Tibbs?" Notso asked.

"I traveled a lot when I was a kid," Val replied.

"Have you been to Thailand before?" Nate asked.

"Yeah." Val smiled as his eyes glazed over. "A dancer in Bangkok taught me the secrets of the female body." He sighed. "GPAs everywhere would soar if there were more teachers like her."

Val's remarks sent three other imaginations into overdrive as each tried to picture what the next few days would bring. "Man I can't wait to get to Bangkok!" Speedy said as continued to spin the lazy Suzan in the middle of the table ever faster. "I might never come back! Hell the town may never survive the four of us!"

When the food arrived, only Val dug in right away. The others waited until they saw Val was relishing what he ate, then they cautiously began eating. Speedy started chewing a piece of meat he was unsure of, then all of a sudden spit it out onto his plate.

"What's wrong, Speedy?" Val asked.

Speedy leaned over and whispered, "Actually, so far everything's tasted good, but"—he lowered his voice and looked around—"I have noticed that there don't seem to be any stray dogs or cats. In fact I haven't seen any at all!"

The others chuckled nervously, but Val just laughed. "Dammit, Speedy— just eat the food and quit being a stupid American!"

"Okay, but if I start pissing on fire hydrants or dry-humping people's legs, I'm blaming you, Tibbs!" Speedy smiled as he put the meat back in his mouth and swallowed.

Before long the drinks were coming to the table with increasing frequency, and each man loosened up more than they had in a long while. Soon Nate was working his magic and before they knew it several beautiful girls were sitting at their table. One of them invited the Marines to the only dance club in town, which was opened for business mainly to entertain US Air Force personnel stationed at Udorn or Ubon whenever they had liberty. The Marines didn't need a lot of convincing as the paid the modest tab and stumbled over to the club with the girls, thinking that the Air Force guys had it made.

The club was packed, and the Marines danced into the early hours. Nate danced with every girl in the place, employees included, sometimes with two or three at a time. They finally left the club and stumbled back to their hotel rooms—and all but Val weren't sleeping alone for what remained of the night.

Val awoke to the sun peering through the blinds and the agony of a hangover. He reached across the nightstand into his bag and found a bottle of water, and drank the entire contents along with three aspirin. He stumbled to the shower and let the lukewarm water wash over his skin, using his head to prop himself against the wall. After getting dressed, he made his way into town and found the payphones.

The building where the phones were located was small, and all six booths were being used by Air Force personnel. Val plopped down on a couch that sat at the front of the room to wait for the first available phone. It seemed like an eternity before a phone finally freed up, but in reality it had probably only been fifteen minutes or so—and like Val, the Air Force officer who'd been using the phone had just wanted to speak to someone back home. Val pushed himself off the couch and stumbled over to the phone, feeling like he'd been run over by a truck. He dialed Virginia's number, but the phone just rang and rang. After losing count of how many times it rang, he finally hung up. He noticed he was still hearing a ringing in his ears, and looked around confused for a moment until he realized it was probably associated with his hangover. He left the booth knowing that someone else was probably waiting to use the phone, and when he returned to the lobby he saw that he was right. Outside, the bright morning sun penetrated his dark sunglasses and tormented his foggy brain. He looked back up the road to the hotel that now seemed light-years away and thought to himself, *Damn—I'd give my left nut for a bicycle right now.* Then he wondered who he was kidding. *I'm too hammered to ride a bike.*

When Val finally made it back to the hotel, one of the two girls in Nate's bed woke when she heard him stumble into the bathroom between the rooms. She raised her head up in curious amazement as she heard him take so long to urinate, then giggled and cuddled closer to Nate. Half an hour later, she woke up and looked at her watch, then reached across Nate and tapped the other girl on the shoulder. They both kissed Nate several times, then climbed out of bed and got dressed. Then they leaned over Nate, who was now awake, and kissed him several more times. They left him their contact information, told him how much they'd like to see him again, then quickly slipped out of the room.

Nate got up and put his boxers on and headed for the bathroom. When he heard Val rinsing his mouth with some water in the sink, he asked, "You okay, Buddy?"

"Yeah. I just excreted the last drop of water in my body. I'm a raisin now."

"You gonna make it?"

"Yeah. I went to town to call Virginia, but she wasn't home. I'll tell you about it later."

"Thank God you're gonna wait. Now unless you want me to fill your water bottle with piss, let me in there."

When the Marines sat down to breakfast, they looked like they were praying as their heads rested in their hands. The waitress finally came and was bombarded with orders for fruit juice, coffee, tea and fresh fruit—hangover antidotes. It was a quiet table as each man suffered in silence. Soon a young local man approached the table and asked with a huge, flashy smile, "Are any of you Captain Jordan?"

"I wish I wasn't right now," Val answered, and when the young man's smile weakened, he said, "Yes, I'm Captain Jordan."

"Hello. My name is Wyland. I am your driver. I take you to Bangkok today," the man said as his smile refreshed. He looked at the four men and added, "You look like you just come back from there."

The Marines chuckled, thinking if they got this wrecked at a local bar, what would four days in Bangkok do to them? Val said, "Yeah—sit down. Want breakfast? We'll buy."

Wyland's eyes lit up, and he seized on the chance for a free meal. "Sure—thank you!"

The drive to Bangkok was long and would have been tedious had Wyland not made it enjoyable by stopping at points of interest along the way. The Marines got to know quite a bit about him on the trip down. He loved showing off his country, and Americans usually paid him very well. Because he spoke English well, he was able to provide a better life for his wife and six children than most of his countrymen. To top it off, Americans always seemed to like his company and thought they were getting a real bargain by paying him five American dollars for a day of driving—which paid for almost four months of typical living expenses for him. He thought America must be a grand place, because every American he drove around seemed to be wealthy. Though some could be demanding and some were ignorant of or insensitive to his culture, he found that Americans were generally well-intentioned and good-natured people.

When they finally arrived in Bangkok, Wyland took the Marines to the hotel most of his American clients said they liked. Bangkok was so crowded that covering short distances in a car seemed to take forever. Wyland never wanted to stay overnight in Bangkok, so he always made the long drive home. When the Marines offered to pay for a room, he turned it down but gladly accepted an invitation to join them for lunch. After he gave the Americans sightseeing and nightlife suggestions, they paid him more than what they'd originally agreed on and asked him to pick them up at the hotel on Friday morning to take them back to Ubon. Before he left, Wyland asked Val if he could suggest a good American slogan for his taxi business. Val thought for a moment, then said, "How about 'Keep smilin'?"

Wyland smiled broadly and said, "I like that. See you Friday, gentlemen!"

The Marines then decided to take in some of the local tourist attractions before checking out the nightlife. They visited a number of Buddhist temples and were amazed by the Golden Buddha, the world's largest solid gold statue, in the temple Wat Traimit. The issue of dinner was solved by the good food offered by sidewalk vendors. When the sun started to set, they decided to head back to hotel to get ready for a night of fun.

Some of the places Wyland suggested weren't much from the outside, but inside they housed some of the most feral examples of human behavior they'd ever seen. In some cases their jaws just dropped while in others they felt it would be impossible to vomit enough to cleanse themselves of the images. They saw acts of bestiality that sickened them and watched women give exact change from their vaginas on demand. When the emcee introduced the Human Blow Gun, Val said, "Now what?"

Everyone clapped as two attractive women walked to opposite ends of the stage, standing about twenty-five feet apart. One woman opened a chest containing several balloons. With her arms extended out from her sides, she held a balloon in each hand. The other women opened a case containing tiny darts. She inserted a dart into her vagina, then swiveled and angled her hips until she was satisfied with her position. Then she grunted, and the balloon in the other woman's left hand burst. She repeated the stunt from different positions and distances.

The Marines looked at each other in amazement. "No fucking way—that's crazy!" said Notso, speaking for all of them.

After the show was over, the Marines made the rounds of clubs. They eventually ended up at a large, well-known nightclub called Dung co Mac co and stood outside staring up at the bright sign, which bore words in several languages. The place was crowded, and the line was longer than at any other club they'd passed, but it seemed to move pretty quickly. As they stood in line, a couple of American sailors came stumbling out, looking extremely happy.

One of them collapsed in the street, looked back up at his shipmate, and said with a huge smile on his face, "You know, I could die right now—I finally did it all!" His buddy pulled him up to his feet and they stumbled on down the street.

Val laughed. "I guess they took the sign literally."

"I guess so," Nate replied as he saw the English words on the sign: "Don't be shy!"

The Marines finally got to the door and went inside, and what they found was a dance club, strip club, sex club, restaurant, and good-old bar all rolled into one. Again they stared with mouths agape at what was happening on the stage. They watched for a bit, then proceeded to the dance floor next to the bar. There were gorgeous women, and Val warned his fellow Marines to double-check before they took one back to the hotel, because some of them were transvestites.

The air was thick with smoke that probably wasn't from just cloves or tobacco. People were smoking out of hookahs in a back room and doing other drugs in booths. The Marines pushed their way to the bar and ordered drinks. As they were orderings, a beautiful woman stopped them in mid-sentence. "Don't order that!"

Nate looked at her. "What should we order?" he asked.

"Let me handle it." The Thai woman leaned over to bartender and said, "Three lotus specials for us."

"There's five of us, you know," Nate replied.

The lady counted the Marines and said, "I see only four."

"Including you, there's five," Nate answered with a smile.

The woman smiled back. "Three will be enough. We share." She moved her arms motioning that the five were now a group. "I have friends at table over there. Follow me." She grabbed the drinks and led the Marines across the crowded room.

There were five other beautiful Thai women at the table. As they approached, Val whispered to the men, "We gotta be careful. Don't lose sight of your drinks. They could slip us a Mickey, then rob us blind at the hotel."

It wasn't long before everyone was having fun. The drinks tasted like some sort of sweet nectar with a slightly bitter aftertaste. Eventually Val began to notice that he could see the brilliantly-colored air molecules moving around. When he looked around, he saw dinosaurs serving drinks and other animals dancing, and the patterns in the carpet were now swirling like a kaleidoscope. He looked back at the table and where the girls once sat were now red foxes wearing sexy clothes. Speedy looked like Speedy Gonzales, Nate looked like a giant Roman sculpture, and Notso looked like donkey wearing a dunce hat. When he made each of the "paper, rock, scissors" hand gestures, his hand looked like paper, a rock and scissors in turn. "*Coool!*" he said with a glazed over look as he sank comfortably into his seat.

The others also seemed to be feeling the effects of the lotus special. Nate looked at the girls next to him and buried his face into their breasts. He only came up to put a straw in his mouth, like a snorkel. Speedy, freaking out, started shouting, "They're gonna kill us, Man," as he curled up in a fetal position in the corner of the couch, grabbing cushions to use as barricades. Notso looked to the dance floor as soon as the music paused between songs. The DJ looked like the devil, so Notso stood and shouted, "Hey! Hey! The levee ain't dry! The music can't die today!" Then Notso charged the booth and tackled the DJ, singing—practically shouting—"Bye-bye Miss American Pie!" Then he punched the DJ.

Several people pulled Notso off the DJ and threw him back to the table where his friends were. All the while he screamed, "I have exorcised the demon!" Nate thought one of the girls turned into a giant soft ice cream cone and proceeded to lick her. Speedy then switched his repetitious phrase to "They're gonna get us, man!" Finally Val spread his arms, which he thought looked like wings. "Grab on, everyone—I'll fly us outta here!" The nine formed a conga line and followed Val out the door.

Outside on the street, the conga line eventually ended up at a bar. Finally after another hour, the effects of the drink began to wear off and things began to clear up. "Where the hell are we and why do I feel like I just ran a marathon?" Val asked.

"You just experienced a lotus special," one of the girls answered.

"What the hell's in it?" Nate asked.

"Some local firewater, a touch of opium, and a couple sprinkles of acid."

"Let's get back to the hotel," Speedy said.

"Have we paid up here?" Notso asked, still reeling. "And why does my jaw hurt?" He didn't recall being punched in the face by someone pulling him off the DJ earlier.

Nate drew close to the others and said, "You want to sneak out?"

"No—you pay tab!" one of the girls said.

Nate again said, "No. You wanna sneak out?"

"No—you pay tab!" a different girl said.

Nate knew all the tricks. "Let's sneak out!" he said a third time. He knew the girls would agree after he asked a third time. The Marines stood up and started for the door.

One of the girls grabbed the others and said, "Okay," and they followed the Marines out the door and to their hotel. All but Val got a girl, so Nate wound up with three.

"Are you sure you don't want a girl?" Nate asked before he went into his room.

"Sure I want one, but I have a promise to keep to someone back home," Val said.

Nate winked at Val as he stood before his door and said, "I have a promise to keep too!"

Val could hear the noises from Nate's room through the wall as everything began to spin around. Later during the night, Val swore he heard some girls screaming "Papa! Give it to me! You bad boy! Earl is King!" Val blamed it on the lotus special.

§ § § § §

Val once again woke up with a pounding headache. The whole R&R was beginning to feel like one gigantic hangover, and for a split second he actually wished he was back at Linh Thu on duty. He concluded that if he couldn't beat this hangover he'd just join it by downing a warm beer backed by bottled water. He stumbled out the door and found the payphone in the lobby. No one was using it, so he flopped in front of it and dialed Virginia's number. The phone rang at her house and his heart beat with anticipation. When the phone was finally picked up, his heart fluttered wildly, but when he heard a man's voice, it sank.

"Hello?" the voice said groggily.

Val was too paralyzed to speak.

"Hello!" the voice said, more angrily now.

"Sorry—I have the wrong number," Val said and hung up. He stared at the phone for a little while, trying to collect his thoughts. In his foggy state he'd probably misdialed. As expensive as a call was, he figured he'd better get it right. When the same man answered, Val slammed the phone down and said, "What the fuck! Can't you fucking dial a phone?" He went back to his room, deciding to wait until he was sober before he tried again.

The Marines gathered again at the breakfast table looking like victims of a train wreck. Very few words were spoken until food and beverages arrived. "I love it here, but I don't know if I can handle two more days of this shit," Speedy groaned.

"Me neither. These gals can work you over," Notso added with his head cradled in his folded arms.

Nate was the only one apparently not in any pain. He sat and stared at his surroundings with a huge smile on his face, as if daydreaming. "Man! And to think all this time I thought a Singapore sling was just an alcoholic beverage!"

The Marines sat recuperating for a while, then decided to see what Bangkok did in the daytime. After walking around and looking at the sights, they bought more things to take back home with them, then went to rest and shower before having lunch. They found the restaurant that Wyland had recommended—a place some of his other American clients had praised. The Marines relaxed as they ate until they noticed a group of women at a nearby table. The women were distinctly European, and the men wondered what they were doing in Bangkok. They returned their attention to their food and idly chatted about what they'd do that night. It wasn't much later when they were interrupted by a female voice with a European accent. "Hello, gentlemen. Do you mind if we join you?"

When the Marines looked up, four gorgeous bronzed women stood over them—three brunettes and one blonde. Nate motioned for them to sit as they scrambled to grab chairs. Only Val didn't wonder why four beautiful women would make such a bold move in a foreign country, For as long as he'd known him, Nate had always been a magnet for good-looking females, but Val knew none of them were about to complain.

They weren't deep into their conversation before Nate started showing off his Italian and French, but the Marines did notice that the women were asking a lot of questions about their assignments and duty, where they were stationed, what kind of aircraft they flew—odd subjects for casual talk, which the avoided answering. By the same token, the women side-stepped most of the questions the Marines asked them. The women certainly weren't hurting for cash though and happily bought a few rounds of drinks. The Marines had no trouble talking them into making the rounds with them later. It seemed too easy.

Val was starting to feel a buzz and didn't want to spoil the rest of the evening by getting tipsy too early, so he asked what time it was. One woman, with green eyes, held out her wrist, and Val's eyes twitched when he saw her watch. Nate noticed from across the table, and when Val thanked her and excused himself to make a head-call, Nate excused himself as well and followed.

As they walked to the men's room, Nate asked, "What's up?" He and Val had flown together long enough for them to know each other like brothers, as if they could telepathically sense each other's emotions.

"The watch that green-eyes had"—Val's face creased with concern—"it was an Antonov Crystal."

"So? I see them all the time in shops here. What's the big d—" Nate suddenly put two and two together. "They're sure nosy about what we do. Do you think they're—?"

"Selkies? I'm not sure. They did ask a lot of questions and didn't answer ours, and they seem to have an endless supply of money. Remember Captain Overstreet's briefing?"

As they returned to the dining room, Nate looked at the women and whispered, "If you're wrong, we'll seriously kick your ass!" Then, more serious, he said, "What do we do?"

"Nothing. Let's just make sure we don't get too drunk. I don't think they'll try anything in public, but we need to lose 'em before we go back to our hotel. We can't let 'em know we're on to them."

Nate peered back at the table. "I'd better get back before those buzzed friends of ours tell them where we're staying."

Val waited a couple of moments before returning himself, He knew he needed to tell his wingmen, then violate their hormonal instincts and give the women the slip.

According to intel, Selkies were a group of elite female Russian spies. They were highly trained, and they were responsible for acquiring some very useful information for the Soviet Union. It was widely believed that only thirst and hunger were more powerful human drives than sex, so the Soviets decided to capitalize on that weakness as part of their espionage strategy. Selkies could easily seduce most men, and they thought nothing of using their sexuality to get information. It was a degree of patriotism that most American women never sought.

But these women were more than state-sponsored prostitute spooks. They were highly intelligent, well trained, and efficient assassins. The women were schooled in foreign languages and customs and were well versed in the use of a wide assortment of weapons and were martial arts experts. The women sitting with the Marines were dangerous and could easily slip them a Mickey, and the Marines could wake up to find themselves being interrogated in some unknown location.

Nate didn't know if Notso and Speedy suspected what was going on yet, so he looked out one of the windows and said, "Hey guys—come check out this fine piece of ass!"

The tipsy Marines jumped to their feet and quickly walked over to Nate, who put his arms around both of them and lowered his head and whispered, "Listen—don't get attached to these babes at the table. We think they're Russian Selkies, and if we don't give 'em the slip sometime tonight, we could end up in deep shit!"

"Russians? Dammit!" Speedy exclaimed in disbelief.

"Keep your voice down, Jackass!" Notso said as he reached over and smacked Speedy in the back of the head.

"Fine, then. How're you gonna let us know when and how to ditch these fine commie bitches?" Speedy asked.

"Okay. Whenever Val goes like this"—Nate scratched underneath his chin with a waving motion—"is when we sneak away, in a hurry. You haven't told 'em where we're staying, have you?"

"I haven't," Notso said.

"Neither have I," Speedy said.

"Good—" Nate was cut off by the green-eyed Selkie, who'd walked up beside them, curious to see what kind of girl would keep them looking out the window so long.

"Where's the girl?" she asked as she scanned the street. "Should I be jealous?"

"Maybe. She's out of sight now. We're still living in the moment. Man she was hot!" Nate pointed to a dimly lit alley over to the left.

"Hot?" she asked, confused.

"Yeah, hot. You know—beautiful, gorgeous, easy on the eyes."

"Oh," the woman said as she tried to make the connection between "hot" and "beautiful." Then she smiled. "Hotter than me?"

Nate knew her weakness then and there. She, like most women, was insecure when comparisons to other women were made, so he switched tactics. "Well, yeah. That woman could have tempted the devil himself!" He looked at his fellow Marines, hoping they'd get his drift. "We gotta look for her!"

"Really! You think she was prettier than me?" The Selkie seemed a little shocked, but Nate wondered if she knew what he was up to. Maybe the mind games were on.

"Oh, yeah. She was hotter than all four of you put together! I've never seen a woman so beautiful, and I've been to a lot of places. She could make me do anything she wanted." Nate knew that phrase would definitely get her attention.

All four women were dressed in hip American garb—short miniskirts and snug tops, and they had the bodies to make the outfits work for them. Nate knew he had to make sure they didn't see any hint of weakness. Green eyes was uncomfortably close, casually pressing against his arm. All of a sudden she wrapped her arms around his neck and stared into his eyes, holding the gaze like a snake charmer staring down a cobras. Nate's jugular vein pulsed as she ever so slowly slid her fingers up his neck to his cheeks, then behind his head where she held him as she kissed him on the lips. When she slipped her tongue into Nate's mouth, he gave in for a while, but in his mind he knew he had to maintain control of the situation. Eventually they pulled apart, giving the impression that it was a perfect kiss. "Was that hot?" she asked.

For her part, the woman was intrigued. She'd actually wanted to kiss him since she first locked eyes with him. Normally she used seduction to get something she wanted for someone else, but this time was different. *To hell with Mother Russia for one night!* the Selkie thought to herself as she and Nate embraced.

Not realizing what was going on inside the woman's mind, Nate saw this as a chance to get away. "Yes it was," he replied. Then he gave her a quick kiss and said, "Say, fellas, why don't we show these ladies a good time tonight?" He then gave Val a particular look, which Val picked up on immediately.

Val slammed his glass on the table. "Damn liquor's running through me like a bullet train! Excuse me, ladies." He stood up and headed for the rest-room.

As Val moved off, Nate followed him with his gaze, then feigned stretching a crick out of his neck. Notso and Speedy picked up on it, and Speedy said, "I gotta go too."

After a couple of minutes, Val and Speedy returned. Speedy sat down beside Notso and whispered something to him. Nate and the emerald-eyed beauty returned to the table and Val whispered into Nate's ear. When Nate nodded, the women looked at them with some doubt. To reassure them, Nate said, "We've been wearing these clothes all day—we want to change. Would you gals mind stopping by our place first before we go out?"

The women looked at each other, believing they had the Americans right where they wanted them. At the same time, they were a bit surprised that they'd snag them so easily. The green-eyed brunette, who seemed to speak for the others, said, "Sure. We'll walk with you. And don't worry about this"— she held up the check—"it's our pleasure!"

The four couples walked arm in arm down the street, talking and laughing as if a night of outrageous fun lay ahead, but the Marines were continuing to make eye-contact with one another so they wouldn't miss the signal to ditch their lovely temptresses. Eventually they approached a group of six local Thai women walking in their direction toward a bar. Val coughed, then scratched his throat to let the others know to follow his lead. He repeated the signal again to make sure his buddies saw him, then said, *"Duong, tay phai"*—The street on the right.

Val waited until the group of Thai girls passed, then pulled his arm loose and pointed. "That's her—the hot Thai chick!"

The women stopped and turned to look the Thai girls walking in the other direction. They couldn't see their faces, so they walked after them a few steps, trying to get a glimpse of the alleged enchantress. As they did, the Marines swiftly and silently slipped around the corner into another crowded street, ducking into a dark, crowded doorway and hunkering there until they saw the women walk in the direction they were originally heading. "Quick thinking, Tibbs," said Notso, patting Val on the shoulder. "I'm surprised I actually remembered the Vietnamese."

The Marines walked over to the next street to check out some clubs, looking over their shoulders all the while. They knew the women might still be lurking in the shadows or the crowds, and for a while it was hard to have fun. But as they got deeper into the drinking, their fears subsided. There was an abundance of western military personnel in Bangkok, so there were endless targets for foreign agents.

By the time the Marines hobbled back to their hotel rooms, Speedy and Notso had a girl on their arms, and Nate had two. As was his custom, Val was alone. It was their last night on R&R, so they had to make the most of it. Tomorrow they'd be taking the long drive back to Ubon, then flying the quick hop to Linh Thu and back to their reality.

§ § § § §

For the first time, Val woke without a pounding headache, but he still didn't feel a hundred percent as he went down to the phone in the lobby. He had a clearer head this time as he dialed Virginia's number and waited in anticipation as it rang. He looked at the clock and knew it should be after six in the evening the previous day. She should be home, and she should be thrilled to actually talk to her fiancé. The phone rang for some time, until it was answered by the same male voice.

When Val heard the voice, he paused, then said, "I'm sorry sir. I seem to keep dialing the wrong number. I'm trying to reach 555–555–5455."

"This is 555–555–5455. How can I help you?"

Val felt a sudden chill. "I'm trying to reach Virginia Lawson. Is, uh, she there?"

"Yeah, she is. She's in the kitchen."

Val tried to feel relieved, but why was a man answering her phone? "Well please put her on. This is her fiancé calling from Thailand."

The man paused for a second, then Val heard him yell, "Babe! Babe—it's *him!*"

Val was stunned, but the shock went deeper when he heard her say, "Dammit—I'm in the middle of fixing dinner. I don't want to deal with this now!"

The man came back on the phone. "She's coming, but I don't think she feels like talking right now. Can you call back tomorrow or something?"

Val flushed with rage, but tried to keep it under control. "Look. I'm halfway around the world, calling the States from a war zone isn't exactly easy, and I haven't heard from her in almost four months. At least she can say hello. And by the way, who the hell are you?"

"My name is David. I'm, uh—" Virginia cut him and grabbed the phone.

"Hi, Val—I'm here now. What do you want?"

Val was perplexed by her angry tone. "What do I *want?* Babe—it's me! What the hell is going on? Who's that guy? I've been worried. I haven't heard from you since I got here. I love you and miss you terribly. We're—"

Virginia cut him off. "Val—shut up for a second! Didn't you get my letter?"

"You sent me a letter? Well, no—I never got it." Val was still puzzled why Virginia was being so short with him.

"I sent it about twelve days ago. I was told it takes around two weeks, so maybe it didn't get there yet."

"Well I've been on R&R for four days now, so maybe it'll be waiting for me when I get back to base tomorrow. That'll be great!"

"Val, dammit—stop! Don't make this any harder than it already is!" Virginia's voice started quivering a little, as if she was holding back anger. "Dammit! I didn't want you to have to find out this way!"

"Find out what? If there's something wrong, tell me. You know I'd do anything for you. I love you. Tell me what the hell's going on."

"You don't need to worry about me anymore, Val, so stop it. You'll understand when you get back to your base and your stupid war."

"What do you mean? You're my fiancée, I'll always care about you. I love you and I'm worried about you. And what do you mean by 'your' stupid war? Believe me—I'd rather be home with you. I'm ready to marry you as soon as I step off the plane, but I'm starting to wonder. I'm a bit confused, so are you going to tell me what's going on?"

"Val, listen closely. I guess the only way to say this is to be blunt. You don't have to worry about me anymore. Things have changed—I've moved on."

Val's soul shattered like a glass goblet striking the ground.

Virginia continued. "I realized months ago that I don't love you, and I want you to stop loving me. I don't want your love. Val, dinner's burning, I'm tired, and I don't want to talk about this anymore. I don't want you to call or write. Just leave me alone!" She sounded angry and heartbroken, as if Val had done something to hurt her.

"Wait a minute. What did I do to deserve this? Everything was fine before I left. We were making wedding plans, for Christ's sake! I can't just stop loving you."

In California, Virginia shouted, "Dammit Val—it's over! Just leave me alone!" She slammed the phone down and leapt into David's arms on the couch.

David looked at her and said, "That seemed relatively painless."

"I feel so free now, like a weight has been lifted off my chest. Now we can concentrate on us." Virginia smirked as she snuggled into David.

David sniffed the air. "Great, but I think dinner's burning. You'd better go check on it."

In Bangkok, the abrupt end to the call was like a gunshot to Val's head, and his whole body went numb as his heart burst. When he finally got his leg muscles to work, he walked up to his room like a zombie, oblivious to his surroundings. His soul had been torn out of him, and he felt as if his reason for living had been stolen from him.

When he entered his room, he headed straight for the toilet and vomited. The dry heaves that followed were worse than he'd ever experienced. When he was finished, he rinsed his mouth with bottled water, then splashed some in his face. As he reached for a towel he caught a glimpse of himself in the mirror. His mouth was quivering, his eyes were red, and tears streamed down his cheeks. His mind kept replaying the telephone conversation. The coldness was almost inhuman. He recalled happy times, and he feared the contrast would drive him insane. Val sobbed. "Damn this fucking place! If I hadn't been ordered overseas, we'd be married now! What the hell am I doing here anyway? Now I have nothing to live for!"

§ § § § § §

When Val joined Nate for breakfast, his RIO sensed something was wrong, and it didn't take long for him to coax it out of his friend. Val told him how his day had begun, and Nate did his best to sympathize and comfort his friend. Nate knew how much Val loved Virginia—she was "the one," the only girl Val had ever seemed to love unconditionally. Nate had known both of them for quite a while, and he thought she'd felt the same way about Val. As a practical matter, Nate also worried that this heartbreak might affect Val's performance in the cockpit. Both their lives depended on his emotional health.

It wasn't much longer before Notso and Speedy stumbled to the breakfast table with their bags, both still groggy from hangovers. As they sat, they sensed a somber mood. "What's with you two?" Notso asked. "There's more than just a hangover in the air."

"Got nothing to do with a hangover," Val mumbled.

"Gotcha. We all scored, and Double-O slept with at least two women every night," Speedy joked. "In a place crawling with women, you were celibate."

"Here, Speedy," Nate said as he slid the salt shaker over to him.

"What's that for?"

"So you can rub more salt in Jordan's wounds," Nate said.

Wyland showed up right on time and the men regretfully climbed into his VW van, knowing that in a few hours they'd be back to work at Linh Thu. Wyland stopped and picked up a few more passengers, who turned out to be flight crews from the Air Force 366th Tactical Fighter Wing, known as the

Gunslingers. The airmen were impressed that they were sharing a ride with crews from the only F-4 squadron in the entire Navy that had guns on their aircraft. They were even more impressed when they learned that they worked for the legendary Lieutenant Colonel Earl J. Driskell, two-time double ace and almost an ace again in his third campaign. As the van drew closer to Ubon, the Marines prayed to every deity that their plane had broken down and they'd have to spend an extra day or two in Thailand. But the gods had their minds on other things as the C-130 was working fine.

As Wyland helping the Marines with their bags, he said to Val, "What's wrong, Captain? You quiet. You not have fun in my beautiful country?"

"I had a blast, Wyland. I just got some bad news from home this morning—and now I'm out of money."

"Don't let it bother you so much, Captain. Just heed some advice an American friend told me a few days ago"—Wyland shook Val's hand and gave him a business card—"keep smilin'!" Wyland grinned as he waved goodbye to his four new American friends.

"Never forget to KEEP SMILIN,' my friend. It will bring you greater fortune throughout your life than any money you will ever earn, borrow, beg, or steal. You can search the whole world over, but you will never find happiness inside of a wallet. But you can always KEEP SMILIN.'" Wyland smiled again as he waved goodbye to four new American friends.

9

WHEN A DOOR CLOSES...

The flight into Linh Thu was spine jarring as the C-130 absorbed the jolts of turbulent eddies in the hot, unstable air. With the high humidity, they expected a wicked storm later that day, and with the severe updrafts, such a storm would easily bring severe weather over Laos, canceling many flight operations from Thailand. Since the development of the mature storm was still several hours off, the flight to Linh Thu still bounced along. It wasn't long before the captain announced that they were twenty miles west of Linh Thu and were beginning the steep descent into the base. The ride was expected to get rougher as a fierce, steady westerly blew in from Laos, and because Linh Thu sat at the base of a high ridgeline, deadly rotor clouds washed down the peaks directly over the runways, which could force careless pilots and their aircraft onto their backs. Any approach into Linh Thu from the west was hair-raising at best and required the pilot's full attention even when the weather was VMC—but under IMC or high wind conditions, it was downright dangerous.

The C-130 was joined on each wing by two F-4s and covered from above by another pair for escort into the island of a base in a sea of enemy territory. The saddle was closing rapidly, and the F-4s squeezed in tighter for the closer quarters. Every pilot was growing equally nervous as the distance closed between aircraft in the rough air. Visibility wasn't an issue since it was VMC, but the bucking and jolting from the turbulence required extra concentration from everybody to avoid a collision.

197

"Get ready for the ride today, Frontier 1—it's definitely an E-Ticket," the lead pilot of the Alert-5 escort joked to the C-130, referring to the Disneyland package that included the better rides.

"Roger, Devil Dog," the Frontier 1 captain replied. "We're the only idiots stupid enough to be flying today."

"Yeah. I don't think we'll have to worry about SA-7 launches, because their operators won't believe anybody'd be flying today," the F-4 pilot replied.

The pilots could see the end of the saddle, with its plunge to flat land that continued to the South China Sea. Linh Thu was nestled just at the base of the ridgeline and sharply contrasted its surroundings. Just as the aircraft reached the edge of the saddle, a massive push sent each into a steep descent at a suicidal rate that tested the pilots' ability to counter the downdraft and currents. The downdraft and rolls suddenly ceased as the pilots found themselves only a few hundred feet over the treetops before suddenly beginning a high-performance climb as the momentarily still air swirled into a rolling updraft. Each pilot struggled with the flight controls and throttles, ready to perform the exact opposite maneuver with a few seconds as the wind sheared in different directions and speeds in an unpredictable manner. The formation then began their circle to the south with each aircraft fighting to maintain straight and level. The pilots watched as their groundspeed rocketed forward as they turned downwind, fluctuating with each gust that blew by.

"Frontier 1, Linh Thu tower, wind two-eight-zero at three-zero gusts four-eight. Wind direction variable one-niner-zero to three-zero-zero. Runway two-eight cleared to land, check gear down."

"Frontier 1, cleared to land runway two-eight. Gear's down. Here we go, Ooh-rah!" the pilot said as he turned his cargo plane to base leg, instantly crabbing into the wind to hold his ground track. The plane was still pushed eastward until it turned final, and the pilot set up for a long power-on approach in order to be ready for wind shear. In the cargo bay, the Playboys were bouncing around in their seats, disappointed to be returning to work.

"I knew we should've stayed in Thailand. This sucks!" Speedy said. "I'd've rather dealt with those commie broads!"

"Aw, calm down Speedy," Val said as he pulled a field devotional guide out his chest pocket. "Here—let me read you my favorite passage—"

"Hey! Don't do *that!*" Notso said as he tried to push the guide back into Val's pocket. "*You* reading that's blasphemy, Jordan!"

"Aw, don't worry," Val said as he began to flip through the book. But just as he picked something to read, a downdraft stronger than any of them had ever experienced dropped the massive plane close to a thousand feet in a matter of seconds, pushing everyone out of their seats and into their restraints as the wings curled under the strain of negative g-forces.

"Dammit, Jordan—I told you not to do that!" Notso yelled. "Now you pissed Him off!" The others were beginning to agree as they pressed into their harnesses.

The downdraft ended as suddenly as it began, slamming every occupant down into their seats. The aircraft was now at a mile final at only six hundred feet. As the plane steadied out, each passenger breathed a sigh of relief. The Playboys could feel the plane turn a bit to the right to get back on centerline, and soon after felt the tires greet the pavement and heard the engines groan under beta thrust as the huge plane slowed to taxi speed.

The plane taxied to the northwest ramp, where it kept two engines running until the GPU was plugged in. Then they were shut down and the rear cargo ramp was opened. The crew and passengers exited the forward hatch, and everyone was relieved to be on the ground. The Playboys looked around and saw smoke rising around the base, damaged buildings, and countless bullet holes and impact craters. Their hearts sank as they realized they were back to real life, and Linh Thu had apparently suffered an attack most likely to avenge Operation Cast Net—the reason they got to go on R&R in the first place.

The men sighed as their spirits now sagged as low as the roof over Papa's lanai, which had been apparently shaken loose during the attack. Val knocked on the door and Papa called them in. "Jordan, Wise, Sanders, and Robinson reporting back in, ready for duty, sir," Val said as they stood at attention in front of Papa's desk.

"Welcome back, gents. I hope you enjoyed yourselves." Papa then looked up from his papers at his aviators and said, "As you were. Relax."

"Looks like the base had her hands full while we were gone, sir," Notso said.

"Yeah, we had some real fun. Great to have you boys back. You're dismissed until 1930. We got a night hop tonight, so be at the ready room by 1900. Jordan, you're gonna be especially busy this week with supply detail, so I hope you're good and rested. Now if you'll excuse me, I have a lot of work to do until tonight. So go to your hooches, get some chow, or whatever you want until 1900."

As the men turned to leave, Nate waited until the others left, then turned to his CO and said, "Sir, I need to speak with you on a personal matter about one of your pilots."

"You're still here, Robinson?" Papa said as he looked up. "Is this matter so grave that you and the person you want to speak about can't work it out on your own?"

"It's not a problem between us, sir. It's more like…well, I'm concerned about Captain Jordan and our sortie tonight, sir."

Papa could see the concern on the lieutenant's face and knew it had to be serious indeed. "Continue, Lieutenant."

Nate hated talking about someone else—it made him feel like a gossip. "I don't know if I should be telling you this before Jordan has a chance to speak to you, but Val's fiancée dumped him for another man in a cold, inhumane way. He found out about while we were on R&R when he finally got her on the phone to find out if she was okay. He's broken-hearted, and I'm concerned about how it'll affect his performance in the cockpit. Sir, I've known Captain Jordan for a long time—since OCS—and he'll react to this in either of two ways."

"Which are?" Papa asked.

"Well sir, he's either gonna slip into depression and his performance will fall off, or he's gonna take unnecessary risks because he feels like he's got nothing to live for."

"And there's no way we're gonna know until we're up there in the shit, right, son?"

"Yes, sir, but—"

"However"—Papa pointed at Nate—"I fully understand your concern, being that it's your ass in the back seat with no way to fly the airplane. You did the right thing by bringing this to my attention, and I promise you I'll have a talk with Captain Jordan before our sortie tonight. If I feel he's unfit to fly, I'll ground him until I feel he's ready to fly again. Does that make you feel a little better, Lieutenant?"

"Yes, sir. Thank you."

"Anything else, Lieutenant?"

Nate digested the question for a few seconds, then replied, "Well actually, yes, sir."

"Well don't wait for me." Papa signaled for Nate to continue.

"Mission accomplished, sir."

"Pardon?"

"Your name is now known all over southeast Asia, not just Thailand. The ladies won't only ask for you by name, but will flock to you when they hear your name when you go on R&R, sir."

"You suave little Don Juan son of a bitch! You actually did what I asked!" Papa's eyes glowed with excitement.

"With pride and honor, sir! It was a privilege. Your reputation now precedes you, sir!"

"You either saved an old man's reputation—or ruined it, if I can't live up to the precedent you set. You know, one day I'm gonna invent a little pill that'll let an old man last all night, and the women of the world will hate me forever because it'll no longer matter if they have a headache and they'll never walk the same again. It'll be my billion-dollar idea so I can finally afford to retire! Maybe the ex-wife will finally leave me alone!" Papa chuckled as he stared off into space.

"You'll never retire, sir. Hell, you'll never even go on R&R. You love us too much!"

"Don't bet your love-tool on that, son!" Papa smiled, knowing in the back of his mind that his young aviator was probably right.

§ § § § §

Val walked into his hooch in a fog of melancholy. He was indeed depressed to be back to the grind, but that paled compared to the rough ending to his short vacation. He threw his bag on his rack, then stared in feverish revulsion at the small stack of letters bound with a rubber band sitting on his rack. He sat down between his bag and the letters and exhaled away some tension. When he thought he was prepared to be further depressed, he began to thumb through the stack—and his heart jumped a little when he found her letter. He felt something hard inside the envelope, but he couldn't imagine what it might be. He leaned back against a support post, next to the picture of Virginia taped there, and slowly tore open the envelope. He pulled out the one-page letter, and when he unfolded it some padding fell out. When he unwrapped it, he caught Virginia's engagement ring in the palm of his hand. It was like a knife in his already wounded heart. He remembered how he'd proposed to her that night so long ago. On her dinner plate was a note that contained a poem he'd written for her. When she unfolded the note, a ring fell into her hand—much as it did when she returned it. Val's eyes began to tear up as he started to read the letter:

§ § § § §

Dearest Val,

I know you've been writing for a few months now with no response, so to keep you from worrying anymore, it's only fair you know why. This is even harder to do since this is really the only word you've had from me since you left. I'll let you know right away that this is the last letter you will get from me.

I've changed, Val. Things have changed around here, too. I thought about my life every night for the first month you were gone, and I didn't like what I saw. I can't live like this anymore. I know now that even when you return in a year, I still won't like my life and could never be happy. Our life together has so many limitations, especially financially. I'm making great money at my company, but you don't *make even a quarter of my salary on government pay. I can't live in a house where I'm the breadwinner, and I don't see how you could possibly be satisfied with that arrangement either, being a man. So I've moved on.*

There's something else too. About a month after you left, I found comfort in someone else. He's here for me now, whereas you can't be because you're half a world away. He's in upper level management at my company and financially can provide for me in a way you can't. He's bought me things we could never have afforded on your pay, and he and I do whatever we want, whenever we want. I've never had that before. He loves me and has proven it by proposing with a diamond three times larger than your ring. I'd be old and gray before you could get me one as nice. We'll have a better life together than you could've ever given me. Don't get me wrong, Val. I know you love me. I've never doubted that, but the truth is, that no longer matters. I don't love you; I guess I never really did. You were just convenient at the time and always sweet to me. Don't try to call me, don't write me anymore. We're through, and it's not negotiable. You'll find someone else on your level in time, Val. You deserve it. Have a great life.

Goodbye forever and take care,

Virginia

P.S. Here's your ring. Don't worry about your things back here. I put them in storage and gave the address and billing information to your sister. She should be able to provide you with all the information about that.

Val tried to choke down his tears. He felt betrayed and confused, sad and angry. He folded the letter and dropped it on his rack, then felt the ring in his left hand and held it up for a closer look. The ring was simple—a single gold band with four latches shaped like oak leaves that grasped the corners of a three-eighths' carat diamond. As far as he was concerned, this simple ring symbolized unending, unconditional love every bit as profoundly as one three times its size.

Val looked at the ring a few moments longer before tucking it into his chest pocket. The sacrifices it represented as he'd saved up to buy it were meaningless now. He recalled that for as long as they were together, Virginia she seemed happy and content, and that she understood his obligation to the corps was temporary. He'd made it clear that difficult life would be for a while, and she was okay with it—in fact it seemed to draw them closer. Val wondered how she could have just stopped loving him, or if she meant it when she said she never really did to begin with. He decided he didn't know the woman who'd written the letter, and he wondered how he could have misjudged her for so long.

He read her letter one last time, then wadded it up and launched it across the room into a garbage can. He leaned back and closed his eyes, then opened them and decided to write her a letter. It was a jumble of emotions that he couldn't contain—anger, grief, confusion, despair. He pleaded his case, he told her he'd forgive her When he finished, he folded it and put it in an envelope. He was wiping away tears just as Speedy came in and told him that wanted him to report to his office immediately.

Val knocked on the open door of Papa's office and was immediately invited in. When he entered, he saw that the base chaplain was there as well. Papa told him to sit and said, "Relax, Jordan—you're not in trouble. I just need to get some things straight. Is there anything you'd like to discuss with me or Commander Yeary, son?"

"I don't think so, sir."

"Look, Captain—it's not my business to pry into the personal lives of my men, except when I believe something happened that might affect the lives of the entire squadron." Papa looked directly into Val's eyes. He wanted him talk about it on his own and get the emotional weight off his chest. "Now has anything happened recently that might affect your flying?"

Val lowered his head and mumbled, "Not really, sir."

Papa sighed, resigned to the fact that Val wasn't going share. "Okay, Captain. One of your fellow Marines told me about a certain event while you were on R&R. He only told me because he was worried for your safety and for the safety of your fellow aviators. All I need to know is that it's not going to hurt this squadron, and that men whose lives are dependent on each other aren't going to be affected, son. You may not be ready to talk about it right now, but I need to know if your head is where it should be before I send you flying into a hot target area. Now when you're ready to talk, feel free to speak with me or the commander here. Otherwise, I know you realize we still have a job to do here, and I want you to fly as good as I know you can. Am I clear, son? If you don't think it's safe for you to be up there tonight, let me know now so I can make other plans."

Val decided maybe he should get it off his chest instead of trying to keep it to himself. "Okay, sir. You apparently know that my fiancée dumped me for another man, and I found out about it while on R&R. I'm dealing with it the best way I can, and I promise you that it won't affect my performance in the air. I believe I'm able to carrying out tonight's mission without being a risk to myself, my crew, or anyone else, sir."

"That's exactly what I needed to hear from you, Captain. Now go rest up," Papa said.

"If you do need to speak with someone, please come see me, son," Yeary added.

"Actually sir, if I may, could I speak with you in your office now?" Val asked.

"Of course." The commander looked at Papa. "Sir, if you don't mind, could you have the chow hall send some chow to my office?"

"It's as good as done," Papa said as he picked up the phone and watched as the chaplain led Val out the door.

Commander Yeary was highly respected by all who knew him. He was well educated and had two PhDs from Duke University—one from their Seminary School and another in psychology, plus a master's degree in archaeology. He studied theology, philosophy, and mythology as well. Though he was trained as a Methodist minister, he didn't claim any denomination. He was familiar many non-Christian beliefs as well. He studied Islam, Buddhism, Hinduism, Judaism, Paganism, Voodoo, and many tribal religions from different regions of the world. He was fascinated by human nature and religion, and he didn't feel like he was in the business of conversion.

Even though he was a Navy officer, he loved the corps—so much that he wore Marine uniforms as often as possible. Most of the time he was seen in combat fatigues or a Marine "Charlie" uniform, his shoes and brass polished to a brilliant luster. He maintained Marine Corps fitness standards, and when he was a chaplain at OCS in Quantico, Virginia, he would regularly be seen doing PT beside the candidates, always motivating them with words of encouragement. His six-four frame towered over most men, but he always had a warm, friendly air about him. Men knew he would always bend over backwards to help someone in need.

"Tell me, Captain—what's going on through that head of yours?" Commander Yeary said as he opened the conversation.

As Val told the commander the whole story, the chaplain listened and took mental notes. Val even showed him the letter he'd written earlier, and he sat patiently as Yeary read it.

Yeary finished the letter and looked over at Val. "Good letter. You got your point across well. Now do yourself and Ms. Lawson a favor and tear it up. I know you're hurting and angry, but this isn't going to help—in fact it'll only prolong bad feelings for both of you."

"I should just give up on the love of my life, sir?"

"Absolutely not, son, but let's get a couple of things clear. Is she truly the love of your life, and are you hers?"

Val paused for a few seconds, but was cut off before he could an answer. "You hesitate. If she *was* the love of your life, shouldn't you have answered immediately? If she's the love of your life, of course you shouldn't give up on her. But are you the love of *her* life? It does take two, you know.

"Maybe you need a time apart emotionally before you determine that you belong together. You may come to realize that she is *not* the person you should spend the rest of your life with. From what you told me about her letter, you may not have known her as well as you thought you did. Someone more suitable may still be out there. People sometimes have impossible expectations of each other. Even when they get married, people seem to forget that it's two individuals sharing their lives, not two people becoming one entity.

"Don't be afraid to let go of what was never meant to be, son. When you let go, you'll actually regain control and find peace rather than lose control and be torn apart by the negative energy of bad feelings. By not sending that letter, you are by no means giving up—you're letting go. It's when you hold on to such feelings that you cause yourself and others harm."

"Sir, that's easier said than done. I can't help but feel I failed in some way, and that maybe if I hadn't come down here, we'd still be together."

"I never said letting go would be easy, son. And there you go creating something that probably wasn't there at all. Going by what you told me she said on the phone and what she wrote in her letter, it wouldn't have made a difference if you were still home. She seemed to be going through a transition. She works at a major financial company that deals with making money out of money. She works with that man whether you're here or there, and she probably was probably dazzled by thoughts of material things the moment she set foot in the door offices. She probably would've fallen for the guy whether you were there or not. Is that who you think you'd want to spend the rest of your life with? Is that what would make you happy? Son, she may discover that money can't buy happiness or love, but she'll have to come by that on her own."

"I don't understand why she had to be so cruel, sir."

"Let me tell you a quick story. Back in the time of the Buddha, a woman came to his door crying and cursing her life because she lost a child to disease for the second time. She complained that her life was cursed and she was being singled out and punished for something she must have done. The Buddha asked her what would make her the happiest and most content, and she replied that her children be brought back to her and that they live long, healthy lives. The Buddha agreed and said her wish would be granted if she would take a cup and get a mustard seed from at least one house where a life was not cut short or touched by tragedy. So the woman set off on her quest, calling on every house in her village, knocking on every door, making sure no one was missed. No one could qualify to give her the seed because every house she went to had suffered loss and hardship. She returned to the Buddha and told him that he had given her an impossible task, that he too must be picking on her. The Buddha then said to her, 'Is it not obvious to you now? Everywhere you went, you could not find a person whose life was not touched by tragedy or loss. Hardships are as much a part of life as joy. So you should not scold either, but learn from both. Embrace both, to experience each is to mean you are alive. Through your joys you are thankful and appreciative to be alive. Through your tragedies you appreciate happiness and joyous times even more. Do not cling to the reasons that caused your tragedies, appreciate them, learn from them, let go of them and live in the present moment. The tragedies of the past are in your past and can no longer affect the present moment. Learn to embrace and let go. Tragedies also remind us that we are truly not in control of all around us and what happens to us. Appreciate that. Do you really want to be in control of everything? No one can truly handle such a burden, and besides surprises in life make life's experiences deeper and richer if you learn to appreciate them. Learn to let go.' The woman never again thought she was being singled out.

"Never forget that, son. You're certainly not the only one who's gone through what you're going through now. Things will get better. Learn and let go."

Val looked up at the clock, which said 1855. He got up to leave and said, "Thank you, sir, I do feel better. I'll be back to talk a little more later. I have a sortie to fly."

"Don't be afraid to ask for help every now and then, son. Don't try to do everything on your own. Even Jesus had twelve disciples to help him spread the good word." The chaplain rose to escort Val out of his office with his hand on Val's shoulder.

"Oh—I almost forgot, sir!"

"What, Captain?"

"Could you destroy this letter for me?" Val asked as he handed over his letter to Virginia.

"With pleasure, son—with pleasure."

Val double-timed the short distance to the ready room and entered for the first time in over a week. It was almost like the first time he'd ever seen it. He walked over to his locker, which was next to Nate's, and began to put on his gear. Still taped to the door was a picture of him and Virginia, her arms wrapped tightly around him. He looked at it for a couple of seconds, sighed, then shut the locker. Val looked over at Nate, who was studying him carefully. "What is it, brother?"

"Nothing. You all right?" Nate still had doubts, but he hoped Val wouldn't do anything rash that would endanger them both.

"Fine. Why shouldn't I be?"

"No reason. Maybe this'll be a short one tonight and we'll get a good night's rest."

Val knew what was on Nate's mind, so he reassured him. "You don't have to make small-talk and tap dance around your concern. I'll fly as I always do. I promise you, brother—we'll get back to base safe and sound."

Nate finished with his gear, grabbed his helmet, and held his hands up as he headed for the Cannery. "I know…I know."

Val grabbed his helmet and followed him, and both took seats in the last row. The lights dimmed and Papa began briefing them about their mission. Tonight they were to bomb a railroad bridge, then provide an A-6 squadron from Yankee Station whatever cover they needed until they were safely out to sea. Both missions were close to each other—only forty miles apart—and that would probably invite a response from anti-aircraft guns, SA-2s, SA-7s, and MiGs. The AA fire and SA-2 launches were expected to be intense since this was the northernmost mission for either squadron thus far. Even the glow from Hanoi could be visible tonight if the air was clear enough.

When the briefing concluded, the men shuffled out the door to their aircraft. Each jet was loaded rather lightly, with four Mk 82s on the centerline station and a pair of Sidewinders on each inboard wing station, plus their guns. The target was expected to collapse after just a couple of direct hits, and the light loading would allow for a greater combat range and would improve maneuverability if they encountered some MiGs while covering the A-6s. Papa didn't have a lot of aircraft going on this sortie. Four men were on R&R, four stayed back for Alert-5 duty, so it was only himself, Chapman, Jordan, Wise, Mailer, Gordie, and Freeman. He privately called this group of six crews his "Varsity Squad"—in his opinion the best in his squadron. He knew this lineup should get the mission accomplished quickly. The quicker it was done, the quicker he could get to his whiskey and sleep. The men climbed into their birds and took off into the eerily dark night.

The night was black as high clouds had moved in and covered the stars. To their left, the men saw the brilliant flashes of a distant thunderstorm. The sheer size of the storm was apparent as lightning forked high into the atmosphere, illuminating the massive layers of moisture that had been lifted to over fifty-nine thousand feet over several hours. The power and driving energy of this storm was more powerful than any weapon man had ever even devised. The crews of the aircraft knew that the weapons their planes delivered were feeble compared to the forces of nature.

On climb-out after departure, the storm practically whited out the edge of the RIOs' scopes until their jets turned to a northerly heading. They were warned about the severe weather in their preflight briefing, so they wanted a short time on target in order to beat the storm back to Linh Thu. Hopefully the A-6s would also hit their marks quickly and the North Vietnamese would choose to stay home tonight and not challenge the Playboys or Mother Nature tonight. Flying in such weather was truly suicidal.

The audible tone from the Fan Song radar indicated to the Playboys that they were being tracked long before they acquired their target. The guns lit up early and helped the F-4s locate the bridge. The whole flight en route to the bridge was heavily barricaded by AA fire, so each crew member knew it wouldn't be long before they'd also have to keep vigilant for SA-2 launches.

"All right, fellas, let's get this over with so we don't have to tangle with Mother Nature tonight," Papa said as he saw another brilliant flash. Lightning made tracers harder to see, especially if they came from the west. He nosed his jet over into a steep dive, flying right through the mix of tracers that sprang up from seemingly every direction around him, some whizzing by closer than his comfort level preferred. Each aviator knew that for each tracer they saw, there were at least six or eight rounds they couldn't see.

"Hi-ho, hi-ho! Here we go—bombing another useless target, but at least it makes for a good show," Val said to Nate on the ICS as he watched Papa and Chappie dive in front of him.

The attack was a basic hi-lo-hi pattern, all from the same direction. The Marines were expecting the mission to be a quick one, and though they antic- ipated heavy resistance as usual en route to target, they were surprised by the amount of defenses present at the target. Maybe this was actually an important target to the enemy. The tracers swarming the sky would momentarily disap- pear with each bright flash of lightning, so because the Playboys wouldn't be changing flight paths, they expected to take some hits.

Papa leveled off for a split second before releasing his load and beginning his ascent. As his jet pointed back at the black sky, he could again see streaks of tracers climbing into the air faster than his jet was. Just then a blinding flash of lightning whited out his vision, though he kept silent about his dilemma. He flew by the seat of his pants as he could feel the push of his bombs exploding behind him. He closed his eyes and examined the stick and throttle with his grip. He'd been a pilot for so long that he knew what his air- craft was doing even if he couldn't see—as if the plane was an extension of him. He steadied his climb and made a sharp left turn in an effort to throw off the AA gunners, and when he felt he was back at orbiting altitude he leveled off, still blinded. He opened his eyes to see the pale glow of his instrument panel and his vision slowly returning. He saw out of the corners of his vision the flickers from other bomb blast beneath him, and the flashes of lightning and tracers above and around him, like he was flying in a confusing layer of strobe lights. No matter where he looked, flashes of light were constantly streaking by. He looked at his altimeter and saw that he was only a hundred and fifty feet above the orbit altitude. Not bad for a temporarily blind old man! He banked back to the right to view the target area far beneath him and flew a wide orbit. In his headset he heard, "Muffdiver 1, Muffdiver 5. Target destroyed, shall I abort?"

"Affirmative. Abort. Abort. All wings climb to angels one-eight to join up. We need to check the status of those BUFFs," Papa ordered as his flight joined up with him and he called Panama, now also known as Strike, to check on the status of the A-6s. "Strike, Muffdiver 1."

"Muffdiver 1, Strike. Go ahead."

"Target AZ-five–one-six destroyed. Need status on Flamin' Hookers."

"Roger, Muffdiver 1. Standby."

As the Playboys continued south toward Linh Thu above the cloud deck, another AA battery opened up and burst through the clouds to their left, reminding them that even though the enemy could not see them, they could still shoot them down because their guns were radar guided. They were also reminded that this wasn't a great place to be because it shortened the time that they could visually detect SA-2s or SA-7s. Papa reminded them of just that as he said, "We're not safe yet, fellas. Keep your eyes and ears peeled for MiGs, SAMs, and tracers. We're still vulnerable."

Linh Thu DASC—Panama or Strike, as they were known to the aircrews—interrupted Papa's warning with news on the Flamin' Hookers, the A-6 squadron they were supposed to provide cover for. "Muffdiver 1, Strike."

"This is Muffdiver 1, go ahead, Strike."

"Flaming Hooker's flight leader said they are feet wet, going home."

Papa smiled as he couldn't believe that he might actually be back on base at a decent hour without any damage to any of his squadron, but he knew not to get too cozy yet and jinx anything. "Roger, Strike. Muffdivers are RTB."

The storm was now more clearly visible to the west—a long string of a squall line that looked like a massive wall of destruction, resembling a pyroclastic cloud from a volcano. There was going to be some fierce weather later on tonight, so Papa had his flight add a touch more power to the throttles.

About nineteen miles north of Linh Thu, DASC called back. "Muffdiver 1, Strike. Say position and stores."

Papa sighed, knowing his night wasn't over yet. "Muffdiver 1 and flight are on the Linh Thu zero-two-zero at one-niner, angels one-niner. Three jets have full load, which is four mark 82s, four jets have half load. All have Sidewinders and twenty mike-mike."

"Roger Muffdiver 1. Change to button blue, a platoon needs immediate attack air assistance, call-sign Night Wolf. They are twenty-five southeast of your position."

"Wilco." Papa was unhappy that his night wasn't over yet, but someone needed their help, and he certainly wasn't going to refuse some young kid on the ground who was staring death in the face. After all, that's why his squadron was stationed so far north in dangerous territory. "You heard Strike, fellas. Button blue now!"

All pilots switched frequencies and listened in as Papa reached out to the platoon. "Night Wolf, Muffdiver 1." The frequency was silent except for a few crackles and chirps. "Night Wolf, Muffdiver 1, over."

The radio finally sounded in each man's ear with the pleas of a desperate voice accompanied by loud sounds of gunfire and mortars. "Muffdiver 1, Night Wolf Echo 5 Tango. Army platoon at Delta Zulu three-five. Under heavy fire from the northwest, just over five hundred meters, over."

It didn't matter that it wasn't a platoon of Marines. The job of an air unit was to support and assist their fellow Americans however they could. Papa and his aviators could tell that the sergeant talking to them had probably never spoken on a ground-to-air radio before, and had absolutely no idea how to coordinate an air attack. That would present a major challenge, made more difficult by the blackness of night over unfamiliar terrain. With the enemy so close to friendlies, it was going to be hard to tell them apart.

Papa tried to make his radio calls as simple and straight forward as possible. "Roger Night Wolf. ETA five minutes, stay down. We'll be dropping thousand-pounders."

The jets turned eastbound toward Delta Zulu three-five, penetrated the cloud deck, and flew just under it. They could now have a visual on the ground and target area, try to determine who was who when they overflew it, and make a quick plan for their attack. Papa knew he needed more information as his flight drew closer, finally catching the flashes of mortars and the winks of small-arms fire.

"Night Wolf, Muffdiver 1. One-zero miles northwest of your position, have visual on target area. Are you on the east or west side of the fight? Be sure before you answer, we've got some heavy ordnance."

"Muffdiver 1, Night Wolf Actual. We are on the northwest side of the area. Charlie is now about five meters to the south and east, possibly in our perimeter as well. Understand you have thousand-pounders?"

"Affirmative. Do you have smoke or flash grenades?"

"Negative. We do have field candles, though."

"Roger. Put the field candles over Charlie's position. Have your men lay low and do not look at Charlie when I say 'target hot,' over."

"Roger."

Papa knew the flash from the thousand-pounders could cause permanent blindness at night. He also knew the shockwaves would be devastating at such a close range, so having the troops lie low and as flat as possible would pro-tect them. He had his flight fly a wide orbit above the firefight on the ground, waiting to see the field candles.

"All right gents. Once we see the candles, we'll approach from the south and work our way northeast. Dash 5, 6 and 7 will begin, since they have full loads. Everyone else will adjust their runs accordingly. Two bombs per run, five seconds between runs. Right-hand pullout, orbit at angels five. Call roll-ing in hot and rolling out of target. Make adjustments as you see them. Under-stand?"

"Roger!" the pilots answered as they continued their scan for field candles.

"Field candles are away!" the platoon commander announced over the fre-quency.

Soon Papa caught sight of three projectiles soaring skywards, showering sparks until reaching their apex, then bursting into a fiercely bright ball of light that hovered above the ground, pouring light in all directions and illumi-nating the ground. The light remained suspended in the air because of the gases billowing upward into the parachute. Field candles were commonly used in night engagements with the enemy to aid in determining their position for both artillery and the troops on the ground. Their disadvantage was that since they lit up the surrounding terrain so well for about eight minutes, the enemy got to see you if you were in close proximity of each other. Troops on both sides were trained to take cover and remain as still as possible until the flare sank to the ground and faded.

Under the bright glow of the candles, the Playboys could see the enemy scrambling for cover, so each aircraft quickly rolled in and spaced themselves appropriately for the attack. "Target hot! Target hot!" Papa announced to the platoon commander as his squadron began their approach, hoping the young lieutenant had passed the word to his platoon to lay low and not look at the enemy's position. Papa knew that the troops would instinctively want to look in the direction from which they were receiving fire. They'd have to find the discipline to trust their platoon commander and their fellow Americans, invis-ible to them in the black sky above.

"Muffdiver 5, rolling in hot," the pilot announced as he lowered his visor to shield his eyes from the light of the field candle, in case he looked in its direc-tion. He dove down to treetop level and stayed there for about two seconds until he felt he was over the target. He had to fly by an instinct that had been instilled in him in training, one that he'd have to use in the absence of assis-tance from a forward air controller. He pickled off his two bombs just as he heard, "Muffdiver 6, rolling in hot."

"Muffdiver 5, rolling off target, two away."

The whole jungle was now as bright as day as his bombs exploded simultaneously with a brilliant flash, swallowing the intense light of the field candles.

"Dash 6 adjusting right...two away, rolling off target." Once again the thunderous blast brightened the black of night.

"Dash 7 rolling in hot, adjusting left...two away, rolling off target." Another brilliant flash followed his bombing run.

"Okay, let's all adjust right to make the dogleg northeast." Papa looked up and saw the field candles were spent, tangled in the trees, and one had been blown far west by the bomb blasts. The fires still burned from the bombing runs, so it would help with the next series of runs, but Papa wanted to be sure he had the enemy's position pinpointed as best as they could. "Lone Wolf, Muffdiver 1. Launch a couple more field candles if you have any to mark the enemy positions to the northeast of the ones we just hit. We'll nail 'em and hang around and strafe anything we missed."

"Roger."

"Jordan, stay behind. Chappie. Wise and me'll make this run. You'll be cleanup."

"Roger, Dash 1," Val replied, but he was upset because he thought Papa was worried about his mental state.

Two candles soon blazed over the enemy's position, and Papa called the target hot as he began the run with Chappie and Notso. All three jets made their runs without incident, and silence now accompanied the fires from the bombing runs. Papa called the platoon commander and said it appeared the enemy had been eliminated, so the Playboys orbited for a few minutes before deciding to check in with DASC and fly home to Linh Thu. They moved their orbit directly over the platoon at angels ten as they awaited a response from DASC, and it was right then that intense small-arms fire suddenly erupted close to the platoon. Dash 6 was beginning his turn southbound in the orbit when a small flash of light streaked toward him, suddenly breaking as he turned south. It continued streaking into the vast blackness above, but soon another one streaked toward Dash 7, again missing but not by much. Hell was suddenly breaking loose beneath them.

"Muffdiver 1, Night Wolf Actual. Gooners in our immediate perimeter. You got any bombs left?"

Papa had his flight fly an irregular pattern over the platoon and spread farther apart. He knew he'd seen two near misses, and he knew immediately what they were. "Muffdivers spread out, it looks like they got sevens!" he ordered anxiously. When he saw that his squadron was okay for the moment, he replied to the platoon commander. "Affirmative. One aircraft has two bombs left, but you're much too close for us to drop 'em, unless you want us to send you off with the Gooners! We can do some strafing runs, but we gotta watch those bastards with the tubes!"

The fight intensified before their very eyes, and the Playboys felt helpless to assist the platoon as each time they got close, ground fire flew up at them, and they knew an SA-7 might be hidden amongst it. Val, finally tired of standing by and watching while hearing the desperate pleas from the platoon commander mixed with sounds of terror in the background, called, "Fuck this! Dash 3's going in!"

"*What?*" both Papa and Nate said, stunned.

Val dove straight down above the main fight and performed a half roll to put his canopy facing east in vertical dive so he'd round out straight into the enemy's face.

"Man, I want to help them as bad as you do, but let's not be suicidal!" Nate pleaded.

"Don't worry—it's still me, brother, I'm just doing my damn job," Val said, focusing on the area where the heaviest concentration of enemy fire seemed to be coming from.

"Goddamnit, Dash 3! Watch your ass! I will not be writing obituary letters tomorrow!" Papa said, and for the first time since he'd known him, he worried about his stability.

Val continued the dive, set his gunsights on the enemy position, and called out the sweetest words the platoon commander had heard during the firefight. "Target hot!"

The platoon commander launched a field candle in the general direction of the enemy, and the enemy quit firing toward the platoon when they saw it light up. Instead they concentrated all their resources to the black sky as Val neared them from above.

Val gasped as the enemy fire stopped, as it made it harder to gauge his run. The candle surprised him as its light flared over the trees, momentarily hiding the ground fire that suddenly opened up from every direction, for the enemy had no idea which direction Val was coming from. Val let his finger slip down to the trigger and waited a second before squeezing, rattling off cannon rounds in support of the platoon's own fire. The enemy troops now knew where Val was and peppered the sky toward the west as they ducked for cover. The Phantom's roar drowned out the gunfire as Val passed overhead, and the enemy again fired blindly into the air toward the whine of the jet engines.

"Damn! That didn't help much, except to give the platoon a few seconds of relief drawing enemy fire!" Val said during his climb. He looked back toward the west to see Papa and a couple of other Playboys make a quick strafing pass, then saw one aircraft duck under a streak that continued skywards.

"Shit! Boys, get the hell outta here!" Papa ordered as he told the platoon commander to shoot a few more candles over enemy positions, which he hoped would silence their fire long enough for them to begin a retreat. When the platoon commander got a moment, Papa asked if they wanted an immediate extraction by helicopter. If they did, Papa promised he'd call it in and cover them until they were safely out of the area. The platoon commander refused Papa's offer and began to launch some of their field candles as they continued their retreat. Val and his fellow aviators remained in a wide orbit as they saw the candles blossom up over the enemy from an ever increasing distance.

"They're far enough apart now, Dash 1. I can make a quick run," Val said to his CO.

"Dammit, Dash 3! There may still be sevens down there! We're lucky that they're bad shots, so let's not push our luck!" Just as Papa unkeyed, fierce mortar and rocket fire ripped toward the platoon, which could wipe them out if they didn't get help soon. Papa sighed as he saw the fire intensify, then reluctantly keyed up again. "Okay Dash 3, you are cleared hot! Fly in from the east and hit 'em on the backside. That should also give you the best distance from the platoon. Fly a simple, direct hi-lo approach, nothing fancy. Release with enough room to run fast from return fire."

"Roger!" Val replied as he broke off from the rest of his flight. Papa called the target area hot for the platoon and had the rest of his flight move in closer to try to confuse SA-7 launchers on the ground. But instead of a high approach, Val screamed in at low level from the east. The enemy suddenly intensified its fire at the platoon, then quit as abruptly. The jungle was once again still and dark, lit up only by field candles and scattered fire from the Americans farther to the northwest.

"I got a bad feeling," Nate said as he lowered the angle of his radar.

Papa could make out movement on the ground in the flickering light of the candles and previous bomb runs and knew that the enemy was changing something as they scurried frantically to the east. He looked over to the east and knew Val was in serious trouble. "Abort Dash 3! Abort! Abort! They're about to throw the kitchen sink at you!"

Intense fire broke out from the ground, and just as Val started to break off high left, tracers zipped by close enough to touch. Soon tracers raced up toward the rest of the flight, forcing them to scatter. Explosions flared up around the jets as the enemy set high ranges on their small artillery and mortars. Val's jet, surrounded by explosions, and he knew he wouldn't get out of this mess unless he took quick action. He reversed his break and rolled inverted for a split second as he forced his jet into a high-g rolling turn into the heart of the enemy's fire.

"What the fuck are you doing, Val? You're gonna kill us for sure!" Nate exclaimed. He'd never been so scared in his entire life or ever doubted his pilot until now, as tracers actually skipped off their jet and explosions went off just meters from the aircraft.

Val didn't have time to answer as he concentrated on weaving his way through a deadly web. He started a steeper climb and continued his rolling turn. He heard his fellow aviators announce that they were taking hits, so he knew it was up to him to end this and help not only the platoon but also his fellow Marines. Val saw that he was now in a seventy-degree bank, fifty-degree climb, so he rolled back to the right and pushed down on the left rudder pedal. The jet broke into a steep descending turn, and he was now looking toward the ground in time to see the flash trail of an SA-7 heading straight at him! He pulled back on the stick to tighten his turn, which was actually a super-tight graveyard spiral that could easily go into a spin if he let his jet go into an accelerated stall. The missile passed by within a few meters and didn't explode, but Val knew that it could quickly turn back on him. The missile did just that—a sharp, four to five g turn back toward Val's jet, with Nate keeping his eyes on it as he worried about his pilot's mental state. Val continued the diving turn toward the east until he was fifty feet over the heart of the enemy fire, then released his bombs and began a sharp breakaway to the west with the missile drawing ever closer despite Val's evasive maneuvers. Even as he struggled to elude the missile, he had to avoid hitting the terrain, since he was so low.

"Still on us, Tibbs! I'm going to punch us out if it gets much closer!" Nate announced.

"Negative! We'll still be killed by the explosion, or we'll end up in enemy hands! I'm hoping it'll track the heat from our bombs instead of us!" Val said as he looked to the sky, deciding that there was more room to maneuver in the blackness above. He kept a series of twists, turns, breaks, rolls, climbs, and dives going, trying to shake the closing weapon, but nothing seemed to fool it. Val kept thinking, *Damn! This thing's gotta run out of fuel sometime—it's not that big!* He looked ahead and felt the rush of adrenaline as he saw two field candles close enough to be sucked into his port air intake. He dropped the right wing into knife edge flight and pushed the stick forward to perform a negative-g push around the first, then immediately pulled back on the stick to break right around the second, rolled to left knife edge, and began a steep climbing left turn. As his jet soared skyward, he looked over his shoulder to where the missile should be, but it was gone. He leveled the wings and pushed over into a shallow negative-g dive to find it, when he caught an explosion out of the corner of his eye—the SA-7 exploding beside the last field candle. Val breathed a sigh of relief and joined up with the rest of his flight. They headed back to Linh Thu in silence, Val and Nate traded glances in the mirrors as both thought about the close call.

Val had barely climbed out of his jet when Papa grabbed him by the collar and pulled him behind the concrete barricades. As Papa jerked him away, Val looked to Nate and said with a rue smile, "Guess I'll catch up with you later."

Papa slammed Val against the barricade and released his collar, then spread his arms out. "Well?" Papa then pointed northeast, from where they'd just returned. *"Well?"*

"Well what, sir?" Val was taken aback by Papa's anger.

"What the hell was that all about?" Papa said, staring Val down. Val remained still, but he was ready to defend himself in case Papa tried to strike him—which for the first time since he'd met his CO he thought he might actually do. Papa took one step back and calmed himself, which he could do quicker than most people. He tone still stern, though, he continued: "You promised me that you were gonna just fly like you usually do, keep your sensibility, not do anything unnecessary! Now dammit, Captain, you'd better be straight with me. Are you feeling okay?!"

Val was still bewildered by Papa's displeasure—after all, he'd saved the platoon and kept the flight from taking further hits losing a jet. "I'm fine, sir. I was doing what I thought was best, and I'd probably do it again if faced with a similar scenario, sir."

"Getting yourself killed is not what's best for everyone, son! You're a damn good pilot, Jordan, a real asset to the corps, but it only takes one lapse of judgment for even the best pilot to bite the big one. That was definitely not an example of your usual good judgment, so promise me you won't pull that shit again! I know how bad you want to help everyone, but just be smart about how you do it. I know that this is a difficult time for you, but going back in a box won't solve your problems at home. Put those problems aside until you're back on the ground. Clear?"

Val stood still, ingesting Papa's words, then hung his head as he said, "Yes sir."

Papa could see his young Marine sag, so with concern he asked, "Is there anything you'd like to share with me, Captain? As you know, the second priority of a Marine officer is the welfare of his men. That's why we're having this little discussion in the first place."

Val sighed, and then raised his head. "There is one thing I'd like to make clear, sir."

"What's that, son?"

"Well, to see if you can understand where I'm coming from, may I ask a rather personal question, sir?"

"Of course."

"Besides your ex-wife, did you have a lot of girlfriends or other relationships, sir?"

Papa felt Val was setting him up, but sometimes he couldn't be sure, the way he could look so serious. Val hadn't been acting the same since R&R, so he had to take him seriously. "Well, yeah. I'd say I ruled the roosts I romped in."

"I see," Val said as he looked at the sky. When he looked back at Papa he said, "I guess you ruled the roosts over in Thailand, sir. Not a night went by that I didn't hear your name screamed out." Val suddenly started humping the air and waving his hands. "Oh Papa! Give it to me! Earl! Earl!" Val then settled down and smiled. "You must be God over there, sir! You set such a standard that everyone had to be compared to you—even Robinson!"

Papa eyed Val with a smirk. He couldn't believe his young pilot got him again! He laughed as he said, "Dammit, Jordan! It's good to have you back! I know you're okay! Go get some sleep after my debrief!" As Val walked away, Papa chuckled and shook his head. "How in the hell does he do that?" he mumbled.

It wasn't much later that night when a great crash shook the ground, forcing the men to the floor of their hooches, weapons in hand, as fears of another mortar attack welled up. The fears abated when they realized the booms were from the thunderstorm in the skies above, but that raised other concerns as their flimsy housing threatened to blow away at any moment. For the moment, the forces of Mother Nature brought the war to a standstill and reminding everyone on both sides of the conflict who was really in control.

10

ANOTHER OPENS ELSEWHERE

The calm morning was in stark contrast to the stormy, black night before, and just like mornings after a mortar attack, Linh Thu was in a state of disarray. Roofs were missing, tents were ripped, trash was scattered about, and the Seabees now had to contend with mess from the storm on top of the damage from last week's mortar attacks. Val made his way over to the flight line as he usually did in the morning, along the muddy road's huge puddles, some almost knee deep. As Val stood at the edge of the flight line, he heard heavy footsteps behind him. He glanced over his shoulder to see Little John walking up.

"Looks like someone else besides us will be busy this week for a change, huh sir?" Little John said. Despite his size, he was usually quiet and introverted.

"Yeah. No one can blame us flyboys for this one," Val replied.

"Yep," Little John agreed and quickly walked away.

"Just wait!" Val called after him. "One of these you and I'll have a real conversation!" Val laughed as he shouted to the maintenance officer's back.

"You don't want that, young'un." The voice of Big John came from behind Val. "Then he won't shut up, just like a teenage girl. Believe me. That's why us mechanics try not to discuss anything else but what's required in the line of duty."

"Dammit, sir—for such a big man you sure can sneak up on people." Val laughed.

"I don't sneak up on people—people just choose to ignore me!" Big John laughed as he walked closer to the flight line. He looked back at Val and said, "Hey, Captain—let's make a deal."

"A deal?"

Big John smiled. "Yeah. You boys don't fuck up any more aircraft this week, and we'll have young Torres and his boys get those bastards hiding in the woods so you won't have to keep going on those long-ass trips to Dong Hoi."

When Big John mentioned Dong Hoi, Val thought about Nga Nghin Do'i for the first time in a while. His heart skipped a beat as he replied, "I actually enjoy going there, sir."

"Oh yeah." Big John's smiled widened. "I forgot—the girls. They're already a legend around here."

"You can find girls anywhere on the planet, sir. In Dong Hoi your dreams come true."

"Really? Who'd'a thunk it? All this time I thought you had to go to Holly-wood or the Playboy Mansion to make that happen, and now I find out that all I had to do was go to war in some dinky little country and look in some ware-house in a fishing village. What's this world coming to?" Hands on his hips, Big John smiled and shook his head.

"I don't know, but I think the yellow brick road leads to Dong Hoi!" Val joked as they turned to head toward Papa's office, where Val was to meet Lieutenant Davis.

The sky was busy with the steady beat of rotors as scores of helicopters flew in and out of the base like a beehive. Most of them were just stopping for fuel, a sign that something was amiss elsewhere. Before long the chaplain walked up behind them. "Morning, gents. That was some storm we had, wasn't it?"

"Yes sir, it was." Val changed the subject. "What's all the commotion this morning?"

"As far as we know, sometime near the end of that storm, the NVA made a huge push south of us somewhere and practically wiped out the South Viet-namese Seventh Regiment. That basically leaves nothing between the NVA and some of our strongholds south of here. See the South Vietnamese Hueys buzzing around?" Commander Yeary said, pointing to three UH-1s that bore the South Vietnamese insignia.

"Looks like if they actually find the NVA positions, you flyboys might get to bomb a target that actually matters, young'un," Big John.

Their attention was suddenly drawn to one Huey flying erratically, as if the pilot was taking his first lesson on a rotorcraft. The chopper ceased its uncoor-dinated motions as it neared the ground, stopping to hover five feet above the pad at the fuel farm, then gently set down. When the engines quit whining, a young Vietnamese man wearing a US battle fatigue blouse over black shorts and sandaled feet jumped out of the pilot's seat. He looked at the three officers standing thirty yards from him and smiled as he gave them a half wave, half salute. He popped open the fuel cap to his bird and inserted the nozzle of the pump. He then lit a cigarette as he began pumping fuel into his aircraft, oblivious to the fumes and the fact his bird wasn't grounded with a bonding cable. The Marine officers stood in utter astonishment at the young man's disregard for safety and were about to shout a warning when the fuel spouted out of the helicopter like a geyser. It continued for a couple of seconds until the pilot finally noticed when Jet A spilled on his feet and soaked his blouse.

The young man, either ignorant or unfazed by his actions, nonchalantly turned off the pump, put the nozzle away, and replaced the fuel cap, all the while with the lit cigarette in his mouth. He smiled and waved once more at the three officers who stood open-mouthed, then climbed into the hot cockpit of his helicopter with his clothes soaked in Jet A that would slowly evaporate into explosive fumes, and still with his lit cigarette fired the helicopter up and flew away. The three officers agreed as they went their separate ways to keep a distance between themselves and the fuel farm.

Davis caught up to Val on the road on the way to Papa's office. "How was R&R, sir?"

"Good and bad. Mostly good—a good week overall. How're things around here?"

Davis smiled grimly. "Bad and good. Mostly bad. Only one thing good actually happened. It's going to suck hard again this week."

"Jeez! What was the good thing?"

"That the weather ruined the Gooners evening last night. What was your bad thing, sir?"

"My fiancée dumped me for another man and I found out about it when I called her. Oh, and some Selkies latched onto us, but we gave 'em the slip."

"Sounds like we're even, then."

"Yeah—guess you can say that." Soon they were on Papa's lanai, and Val knocked.

Papa called them in, and the first thing that aught Val's eyes was a legal pad filled with notes that must have been a shopping list for their trip to Dong Hoi. Val had a question for Papa that he really didn't want to ask because Papa might not send him to Dong Hoi, but he figured he'd better ask so Papa would know it was on his mind.

"Sir, should I leave base today when there's a chance they'd need us to assist forces to the south of us?"

Papa was glad to hear that his pilot was concerned, but he'd made his plans as soon as he was apprised of the morning's events. "Don't worry about it, son. I've got four aircraft on Alert-5 duty, and we've got enough other crews to handle any situation that comes up. Thanks for the concern, though." Papa looked over to Lieutenant Davis. "Better get going—you've got a long day ahead."

"Do we have extra firefighters on standby, sir?"

"No—why?" Papa knew Val was about to make a smart-aleck remark, but he thought the question was really odd.

"You'll need 'em if any more South Vietnamese pilots fuel up with a cigarette burning in their mouths again, because this place'll flare up like a Buddhist monk!" Val smiled as he ducked out the door to the trucks waiting outside.

§ § § § §

As the convoy neared Dong Hoi, Val could feel his heartbeat pick up a bit. He always got a little excited when he came up here, but now it seemed different. As they went around the switchback to Nghia Mau's store, his breathing increased too. He reached for his canteen and took a good swallow, then splashed a little water on his face. As the trucks backed up to the loading dock, several of the girls ran out to greet them. Nghia Mau herself came out and smiled as Val and the lieutenant stepped out of their truck, then gestured at the store to point out the new paint job—light blue. Val figured it was to spruce the place up after more attacks.

"*Tao rat la thich cai nai*"—I really like it, he said as he returned her greeting. He bowed to Nghia Mau, and Lieutenant Davis mimicked Val as she bowed and waved them into the store for tea. As she poured them each a cup, Val told her that she'd be pleased to know that he had a huge order and whatever they had in stock they'd take now and come back for whatever needed to be shipped in. After they made casual conversation for a while, Nghia Mau sent Val into Nga Nghin Do'i's office, where he sat for a good ten minutes before he heard the soft shuffle of feet that he knew belonged to Nga Nghin Do'i. He heard some whispering outside the door recognized her soft voice. Val felt a wave of heat rush through his body, and he thought to himself, *What power does this woman have over me?* Nga Nghin Do'i stirred feelings in him that even Virginia never did.

The door creaked as she opened it, and she said, "*Chao buoi sang,* Captain Jordan*, tao khong thay may lau roi! Bail au nay may o dau?*"—Good morning, Captain Jordan, I haven't seen you in a long time! Where have you been?

At first Val fumbled for words and looked down at his feet. Then he said, "*U lau roi. Tao ban lam di choi Linh Thu*"—Yeah, it's been long. I'm busy hanging out at Linh Thu.

She saw how he looked at his feet and took quick, darting glances at her, which she found odd. She switched to English and, sensing he was under some strain, asked, "What's wrong, Captain?" She then uncharacteristically placed two fingers under his chin and lifted gently until he was looking directly into her eyes. "Is it so hard to look at a friend?"

As Val stared into her deep brown eyes, he was overwhelmed by a feeling of tranquility. He forgot all his troubles, both home and here, and lost all sense of time. His looked deep into her, beneath her physical beauty, and knew he was seeing a beautiful soul as well. Under his breath he said, *"Ep dep lam."*—You are so beautiful. When Nga Nghin Do'i smiled coyly and flushed as she pulled back, Val realized she'd heard him. "I'm sorry. I meant that as a compliment. You just have this effect on me."

Nga Nghin Do'i smiled, realizing this was a chance to tease Val a little. "Really? What effect is that, Captain?"

"I don't know—it's hard to explain. I get both nervous and calm whenever I see you. Strange, huh?"

"You get that way around all women?"

"No—just you," Val said with a sheepish smile as he took a deep breath.

Nga Nghin Do'i laughed. "It is not so strange. I get comfortable around me, too."

Val laughed with her and sighed. "Not the way I do."

"Well then, give me your list." She held out her hand, and when Val playfully tugged at it as she grabbed for it, they both giggled. After a moment he let her have it, and she smiled at their little game, them examined the list. She tucked her long black hair behind her ear as she read it, asking Val to translate anything she didn't understand. As she read, Val looked at her in awe, and every so often she sensed him gazing at her and glanced at him with a smile. Though she was very reserved and seemed to have her emotions under control, Val sometimes thought she showed signs of nervousness—especially after she stole a look in his direction.

As they got to know one another, they became comfortable enough to talk more about themselves, like two young friends anywhere. He was fascinated by this brilliant woman, who seemed to have a profound understanding of herself and the world she lived in. Nga Nghin Do'i was in turn charmed and intrigued by Val, who made her feel comfortable enough to speak her views on any subject they chose to talk about. He was nothing like the arrogant stereotype so often portrayed to people here, the first man who saw beyond her looks and showed an interest in what she had to say. He seemed to have a genuine and earnest respect for all people, even the ones he was sent here to fight against. He didn't fit the image that most of her countrymen had of American pilots—cold and ruthless as they dropped bombs on innocents who had nothing to do with the war. She always wanted to ask Val how the Americans could do such things, but she always ended up putting it off until they knew one another better. For his part, Val understood that Nga Nghin Do'i surely had other things going on in her life besides the store, but he didn't want to pry either.

Val and Nga Nghin Do'i talked for almost another hour before he looked at the time and realized he had to get the supplies back to Linh Thu. As Val left the store, Nga Nghin Do'i, Nghia Mau, and the other girls followed him to the loading docks to send off the Americans in their usual joyful manner. The Marines waved to the girls until they were out of sight, then sat tight for the long journey to base, ever alert for signs of trouble.

As Val looked out over the flat terrain west of the Nhat Le River, tall watchtowers in the distance always caught his eye. They were actually built to be storage towers for grain, similar to silos in America, constructed of mud, wood, and limestone—natural materials widely available throughout Vietnam. During the numerous conflicts that had engulfed Vietnam since its existence, the two-story towers had served as lookout posts, and when modern firearms came along, they made perfect locations for snipers, grenade launchers, small mortars, and machine guns. Since there were towers at the edge of almost every large paddy, they could be linked up by phone line to coordinate their defense. On the flipside, they were easy targets for air strikes or artillery, and destroying one meant that some village or group of villages had no grain storage facility. Val shook his head as he pondered the destructiveness of war, and how it was always the poor innocents who suffered the most. He shook off the thoughts and let his mind dwell on Nga Nghin Do'i.

Before he knew it, they were driving through the gates into Linh Thu and Val's reverie was shattered by the ear-piercing roar of the Alert-5s launching toward the south, heavily loaded with both air and ground ordnance. *Something bad's happening down there,* he thought. The trucks stopped at Papa's office, but Lieutenant Davis came back out when he found out Papa wasn't inside.

"Papa must be at the Cannery or the shack, Captain."

"Let's send the trucks to the Seabees holding area, then go find him to tell him what we procured," Val replied as he watched his fellow aviators disappear into the hazy sky. As the trucks took off, they slogged down the muddy road toward the shack. Before long they ran into Papa making his way back to his office.

"Afternoon, sir!" Both men exclaimed without a salute.

"Afternoon, gents. How'd it go in Dong Hoi?"

"Here, sir." Davis handed Papa the invoice.

Papa read it over as the three men continued toward his office. "Good work, gents. Looks like you not only got everything we asked for, but Captain Jordan picked up some morale boosters at bargain prices." Papa flipped the list over a couple times before saying, "Dammit—you forgot the one thing I ask for every time you go up there, gents!"

Val and Davis looked at each other, wondering what they'd forgotten. Finally Val asked, "What was that, sir?"

Papa chuckled. He was finally going to have the last laugh. "Our god-damned tickets out of this shit-hole!" He looked at Val. "Gotcha, Captain."

Val watched Papa do a little jig before he said, "Actually we got them weeks ago, sir, but we had to sell them on the black market to cover your late alimony payments."

Papa stopped laughing and glared at Val as if he'd crossed the line. Val saw the look and flushed. Papa looked like he was about to let Val have it, then burst out laughing. "Goddamnit Jordan! Either you're extremely confident, extremely foolish, or you just don't give a shit!" Papa laughed as they walked up to his office.

A few minutes later a Seabee knocked on Papa's door. "Come in, Chief." Papa called.

"Sir, Lieutenant Torres sent me. You need to come with me to the holding area. We discovered something you definitely need to see!"

"Lead the way, Chief!" Papa looked at Val and Davis and said, "Come along, gents."

When they arrived at the holding area, they saw crowd gathered around something on the ground. The chief pushed a gap through the crowd so Papa and the two officers could see Lieutenant Torres and several of his Marines peering into a large drainpipe with a flashlight.

"What's going on, Lieutenant?" Papa asked.

Torres looked up at Papa and snapped to attention. "Sir! I think we solved one of our problems with the restless locals." He pointed at the drain and handed Papa the flashlight. "Take a look for yourself, sir."

Papa grabbed the flashlight, then crouched down and peered into the pipe. As his light cut the darkness, he noticed a hatch cut into the bottom of it about five feet away. Papa leaned back up and said, "What the hell! Where does that go?"

"A couple of my men followed it for almost a mile. It connects into a tunnel just west of the base that connects into tunnels the Gooners use to move men and supplies. This is how they're getting onto the base during night raids, sir."

"How did you boys find it?"

"One of the Seabees was digging a cache for us to hide weapons in, sir."

"Now that we know about this, Lieutenant, what do we plan to do?" Papa asked, "How can we use it to our advantage?"

"On it, sir. We plan to do some green ops in the tunnels and see if we can break down the communication system with the SA-7 launches and the attacks on this base. Who knows—we may eventually be able to find weapons, prevent attacks, maybe get some real intelligence on troop and supply movements and other tactical information, sir."

"Excellent, Lieutenant. Too bad Washington has absolutely no interest in that kind of information," Papa said. "And if we can't get anything useful...?"

"We already booby-trapped it and rigged it for destruction," he said, then gestured around and added, "We'll post a few Marines every night to keep tabs on enemy movement during raids—and kill them of course." Torres pointed to three hidden machine gun and sniper blinds that surrounded the drain from three different directions.

"Perfect! Carry on, Lieutenant!" Papa said as he signaled Val to follow him.

As Val and Papa walked back toward his office, Val asked, "Sir, was it real busy here with the things going on down south?"

"Yeah son, it was. We don't actually have a scheduled sortie tonight, but that doesn't mean we got it easy. We're all basically on Alert-5 duty tonight, plus I got a bad feeling about a major attack on us. We could be easily overrun in less than forty-five minutes if the Gooners properly coordinated an. I hope our recon boys can get us some useful information." When they got to the office, Captain Overstreet was waiting for them.

"Sir, I need to speak to your squadron. I have some information that might save some lives from SA-7s."

"What the hell's going on? Did I miss a memo?" Papa said as he stared at the intelligence officer. He sighed, then said, "All right, Captain, whatcha got for us?"

"Well, Captain Jordan's last encounter with the SA-7 may have revealed a practical defense against the weapon. Could I brief both squadrons ASAP?"

Papa picked up his phone and barked orders. "How about thirty minutes, Captain?"

"Perfect. See you at the Cannery in thirty." As Overstreet turned to the door, the sound of the Alert-5s overhead in the break-to-land filled everyone's ears. "I know you're leery, but trust me this time, sir." He stepped outside to watch the final Phantom in its tight turn swooping down to the runway—a beautiful and elegant sight. Overstreet was happy just knowing that he'd be helping them survive.

Half an hour later, the Cannery was packed with aviators from both VMFA-2 and VMO-16, everyone buzzing with theories about what Captain Overstreet had to say. "Silence, gents! Quiet please!" Papa yelled to quell the murmuring as he stepped to the front with Overstreet. As soon as it was quiet, he continued: "This has been one helluva day! First Lieutenant Torres and his boys discover how enemy troops have been getting on base during night raids. Then they figure out that they might have a way stay a step ahead of them if they find their tunnel network. Now Captain Overstreet has some information that might save lives. Give him your full attention, gents! Captain, they're all yours."

"Thank you, sir. By show of hands, how many of you were there during the last attack on the bridge the night of the thunderstorm?" Only the Varsity Squad raised their hands, and everyone turned to look at them.

"Okay. How many of you who were there saw how Captain Jordan avoided the SA-7?" About half the men who'd just raised their hands raised them again.

Overstreet walked up to Val and said, "Tell us how you did it, Captain."

Val wasn't really sure what happened since it all went so fast, but he gave it his best shot. "Okay—I vaguely remember the launch and how I tried to draw the SAM into the explosion from the bomb, but it stayed with me. I looked up and saw some field candles about to sucked into my air intake, so I maneuvered to avoid them, and when I looked back I saw the missile had exploded and taken out one of the candles I missed."

"That's the key," Overstreet said. "We know these missiles lock onto your heat signature, but they can be fooled. We understood that they'll track a heat source equal to or hotter than yours, and Captain Jordan verified that for us. Field candles burn hotter than jet exhaust—even when in full afterburner. Two other things saved Captain Jordan that flight—there was more than one field candle to confuse the missile, and he flew a zigzag pattern, then broke away from the field candle and missile."

"Great! Now we just need ground troops to launch field candles wherever we fly," yelled one pilot.

"Not exactly. You do have to zigzag and break away from the missile and the countermeasures."

"What countermeasures?" someone else called out.

"I'm getting to that. Next week Major Darryl and his boys will be busy fitting your aircraft with flares and chaff." Overstreet ignored the ripple of sarcastic remarks and continued. "'Flares and chaff' are what your countermeasures are called. Both will be activated by pushing a button on the control stick. 'Chaff' is little strips of metal designed to fool radar-guided missiles. Flares are burning pieces of magnesium, designed to fool heat-seeking missiles. You'll use 'em just like Captain Jordan did with the candles. You break one way as you release your countermeasures, then break the other way. A missile should track the countermeasures. Even if they don't, they'll take longer to reacquire you, so you should have time to avoid them by breaking the cone of vulnerability with precision maneuvering." Overstreet then showed the aviators some classified footage from the manufacturers of the countermeasures during flight tests back in the States.

When the briefing ended, the aviators were optimistic about the counter-measures, but they knew that nothing was foolproof. The missiles they used in combat didn't work all the time, so they couldn't expect the flares and chaff would work all the time either. Each aviator took the time to shake Over-street's hand and thank him.

But before he knew it, Big John approached him, his face a mask of fury. "Dammit, Captain, you can't stand the thought of us mechanics having a god-damned day off?"

"But, sir—" Overstreet shrank back, certain the big man was going to squash him.

"Relax, Captain—I'm kidding. We'll be happy to install the countermea-sures if they save lives. In the long run we'll have our days off if more planes come back undamaged."

§ § § § §

The evening started off quiet, as it normally did at Linh Thu. As the sun disappeared and the sky turned darker, deep thuds and pops could be heard in the distance somewhere south of the base. Most of the time they ignored these noises, but occasionally a massive thud caused the men to stop whatever they were doing and southward. Brilliant flashes accompanied the thuds and briefly lit up the sky, like distant lightning. A huge firefight was obviously taking place somewhere down there, and each VMFA-2 aviator knew they could expect the Alert-5s to launch soon. Soon the phone did ring, and within minutes the Alert-5s roared into the sky, afterburners aglow. Papa had a sneaking suspicion more assistance would be needed, so he summoned the Varsity Squad.

The crews had barely walked into the shack when the phone rang again. Papa answered and signaled to his men to get their gear on fast. Chappie grabbed the other phone and ordered the ordnance techs to arm the squad's aircraft with air-to-air ordnance and four bombs on the centerline station. Both officers hung up and Papa yelled over the screech of brakes from a pickup truck outside, "Come on, gents—I'll explain on the way!"

Each man ran out the door and piled into the bed of the truck, all still fum-bling with their flight gear and looking at Papa in the front. Papa finished with his own gear and began to brief his Marines. "All right, gents—the South Vietnamese are engaged in a huge skirmish over some area that the NVA doesn't want to give up for some reason. The target is so crucial to the enemy that those jets you heard overhead was a flight of six MiGs going in to shoot down our Alert-5s and any other American or South Vietnamese aircraft. We're going to engage those aircraft and shoot them down. We've also been loaded with four light bombs to assist the Alert-5s with helping the South Vietnamese on the ground. Just listen to me and we'll all be coming back later for drinks, got it? Any questions?" It was one of the shortest, least detailed briefings he'd ever given, but they didn't have the luxury of time. The truck screeched to another stop and the aviators piled out and scrambled to their jets, which had already been preflighted. It was go time!

Within minutes the seven jets were climbing through the flight levels with the RIOs busily scanning for enemy aircraft—elusive at the moment as the sky quickly darkened. Except for Papa and Chappie, none of the men had actually been in a night dogfight Radar and missiles helped, but the blackness outside the canopy greatly increased the chance of vertigo and spatial disorientation. It took every bit of a pilot's discipline to trust his instruments when he got disorientated, since his senses would be telling him something different from what he perceived. If there was no moon or starlight, it was hard to tell if the aircraft was even flying straight and level, much less performing the erratic maneuvers of a dogfight. The aviators tried to push any doubts and fears to the back of their minds as they closed on the area of the firefight on the ground, and the only question that mattered at the moment was, where were the MiGs?

Papa keyed up to check the status of the Alert-5s. "Bowtie 1, Varsity 1."

"Varsity 1, this is Bowtie 1, go ahead."

"What's your status? You boys okay?"

"Yes sir. We also have a couple South Vietnamese Skyraiders with us."

"We're orbiting at angels two-zero. There's seven of us. We have about forty-five minutes of playtime. We all have 500-pounders if you need assistance helping the boys on the ground. Have you seen any MiGs?"

"Not yet, sir. We got a strong echo about seven minutes ago, but we don't know what it was from. We'll keep our eyes peeled."

"Roger. Carry on," Papa replied, then spoke to the Marines orbiting with him. "Everyone keep scanning. Strike confirmed a flight of at least four unidentified aircraft in this vicinity about niner minutes ago."

The Varsity Squad kept in a wide, circular orbit so that a RIO always had a scope facing every direction at any one time. As Val rounded the turn to the southeast, he picked up a brief flash below him.

Nate immediately keyed up the same time Val saw the flash. "Tally ho! Contact one-zero miles southeast of our position, unidentified aircraft heading northwest bound." Strike was sounding in the pilot's headsets at the same time with the same warning.

Val was still looking in the same direction and caught another glimmer that strongly resembled the shimmer of the smooth polished metal surface of a MiG in the sunlight, except it was much fainter as it caught a moon beam. "I got visual on at least two bogies eleven o'clock low."

Papa gave the order. "All right. Jordan, Wise, Mailer—identify them. Call if you need any assistance."

All at once the three Phantoms dove into a steep split-S to sweep in behind the two aircraft that had now disappeared in the darkness. The RIOs and pilots still had the aircraft on their scopes, and as the Marines closed in the aircrafts' faint silhouettes began to take shape below and ahead of them. The Marines continued to silently pursue the aircraft, trying to identify them. About the time the one on the right flew above a cloud and his characteristic shape of a MiG-21 was clearly distinguishable, they locked onto one of the Alert-5s, leaving no doubt who they were now.

"I hope at least one of you RIOs has a solid tone," Val said.

All three RIOs replied affirmatively. As the pilots moved their fingers to their triggers, Mailer glanced over his right shoulder and his heart thudded as he saw three other MiGs so close that he could see the glow from the lead aircraft's instrument panel against its own canopy glass.

"Shit—three MiGs on our six. Varsity 1, I need immediate assistance." Mailer said. "I'm breaking off to see if I can draw them off you two," he told Val and Notso.

Captain Phan just watched Mailer's F-4 break right, telling his flight to let him go and keep their scan up for more American fighters. He and his wingmen closed in for the kill as Val and Notso closed in for the kill of the MiGs they were following.

"Guess we're all gonna get it!" Speedy said, referring to the two MiGs they were about to shoot down and that his and Val's jets faced the same fate.

Mailer was continuing in his break to pull in behind the MiGs when, at Phan's command, the right wingman broke to engage him. Mailer held his course for a split second, trying to guess what the enemy he couldn't actually see was doing, and he knew that the radar had a half-second lag in acquiring targets. On the scope, he saw the MiG break high right, so he pulled into a barrel roll to slow his jet to fall in behind the MiG.

"Stay there, Dash 7!" Papa ordered as he and the rest of Varsity Flight descended behind them. "Dash 3 and 4, what're you waiting on? Splash those bastards! We got your six!"

Phan saw what was going on. His suspicions were validated—he knew more Americans were lurking around in the darkness somewhere. Not wanting to give his exact position away yet, he waited until the F-4s were closing into firing range, then stoked his burners and fired his cannon, blasting his way between the Americans ahead, forcing them to break for cover. Phan then disappeared from visual range. All aircraft's radars were pinging with returns as the furball ensued in the blackness, only pale moonlight against clouds reminded the pilots that they actually had a sense of sight. The fight was on!

"Stay with yours—I'll keep on mine, Notso!" Val said.

"Watch out! I hear these guys will fly at each other trying to force us to collide!" Notso reminded Val.

"Mailer, get your guy now! These guys are breaking different directions!" Papa ordered. "Watch your sixes, boys—they're trying to do to us what we did to them a month ago!"

Phan looked beneath him and saw two Skyraiders making their bombing runs. He knew he was on someone's radar, but he was sure he could get at least one good shot at the South Vietnamese planes and pull out of missile range from anyone following him. He rolled inverted and pulled into a fast, steep dive behind the Skyraiders, then closed the distance, got the angle, and got a solid tone. He fired an Atoll, which immediately went ballistic. Frustrated, but knowing he still had a solid tone and time to spare before an American got on his tail, he fired another missile that streaked toward the Skyraider and exploded right behind it, tearing off its empennage and sending it into a spin. His shot on the second Skyraider had the same result. Chappie, who descended behind Phan when he got the lock on the Skyraiders, was closing the gap on Phan and ripple-fired two Sidewinders at him. The first missile seemed to lock on, but Phan turned into it before it could acquire. The second curled behind him and Phan performed some crazy high-g Derry turn to force it to overshoot and forced Chappie off his tail.

"Damn—this guy's good!" Chappie said over the ICS to his RIO.

"I got two 'chutes! Those boys are drifting north!" Chappie's RIO called out. "I'm switching frequencies to get a rescue flight for 'em!"

Chappie and Phan, with equal skills, began an intense dogfight that remained even and taxed them both. "I'm gonna need help down here with this one," Chappie called out over frequency.

"On my way," Papa called out, barely able to make out what was going on beneath him as he tried to make sure his flight crew was okay. As he closed in on the fight, he could still see the men's 'chutes in the pale moonlight. To his horror, a stream of tracers from the southeast streaked toward them. "What the hell! Who's shooting at those boys?" Papa squinted when he thought he saw a shimmer of light reflecting off an aircraft. Soon he could make out a MiG-21's silhouette against the scattered cloud layer. His pulse soared with rage— he knew only one pilot dishonorable enough to fire on helpless men in 'chutes. "Colonel Tomb, you bastard!" It was an unwritten rule among fighter pilots everywhere not to shoot at men who'd bailed out, and bad karma usually caught up to those who did fairly quickly. Papa broke off from Chappie and flew straight toward the silhouette. "Sorry, Chappie—those boys are in serious trouble. Get me a solid lock now, Simms!" Papa ordered his RIO.

Val and Notso quickly closed on their respective MiGs and wounded them with missile shots, but they both seemed to disappear. "You got 'em, Speedy?" Nate asked.

"Nope. I think they dropped to the deck and are buggin' out."

"Anyone need any help?" Notso and Val asked over frequency.

"Dash 2 does. Fightin' a steady stick here," Chappie said under the strain of g-forces.

Both pilots saw the fight against the backdrop of the firefight on the ground. "We're on our way. How're you doin,' Mailer?" Val asked as he and Notso dove to assist Chappie.

"About to splash this guy," Mailer replied as he ripple-fired two Sidewinders. Whenever a missile ignited or a cannon was fired or a burner was stoked, it was like looking into the rising sun after climbing out of a dark cave—it lit up the sky around it and briefly whited out one's vision. Even more spectacular was the explosion from one of Mailer's missiles as it found its mark on the MiG. "Yeah! Splash one!"

Just as Val and Notso closed in behind Chappie and Phan, the brilliant explosion of one the MiGs that one of them had wounded lit up the horizon as it crashed. "Guess we'll have to split credit for that one," Val said over frequency.

Phan knew all his help had run for home. As he looked back and saw that six F-4s were about to surround him, he knew it was time for him to run too. He knew that only one could be on his six at any one time, but with them all around him, no matter where he flew he'd be in someone's sights. He immediately broke into another high-g Derry turn and combined it with an Immelmann, and flew head on toward the Americans. When he knew he was head on with them, he let all his missiles fly and fired all his guns to scatter them as he stoked the burner and screamed toward the north.

Papa, meanwhile, closed in on the MiG and opened fire with his cannon, still furious. He scored a few hits along the left wing root and fuselage, and as Papa passed the MiG, he cranked his jet into such a hard turn that both he and his RIO started to black out. Finally he relaxed his inputs on the control stick, and when vision returned Tomb was twelve o'clock low as expected. Papa and his RIO were amazed that the Phantom completed such a maneuver without going into departure, but they weren't the only ones amazed. Tomb was shocked to see the Phantom on his tail only two miles behind now. He looked high left and saw six other Phantoms closing in, and low right he saw two more—the Alert-5s, closing in to assist. Time to go! He performed the same maneuver that Phan had just executed, but Papa wasn't fooled. He armed his Sparrows, ready for a long shot. When he had a solid tone, he ripple-fired his missiles, which streaked toward the MiG. Only one acquired, and Tomb was still hoping he could get out of range, but he saw the missile was closing too fast. He had to be patient, which took nerves of steel. When the missile closed to within three hundred yards or so, he performed a high-g barrel roll, which broke the cone of vulnerability as the missile stayed on its course. The missile finally overshot and went over the top of the MiG and exploded in front and above him, close enough for him to actually hear the explosion. The shock-wave cracked the canopy enough that Tomb feared it might not last all the way back to Kep Field. It would certainly be a reminder of yet another entanglement with Colonel Earl J. Driskell, the best of the best.

"Goddamnit! Damn that bastard's luck's gotta run out sometime!" Papa shouted angrily over frequency, furious at Tomb.

A South Vietnamese UH-1 announced that they'd picked up the crew of the Alert-5 jet and was headed for Linh Thu, and when the firefight below seemed to quiet down, the Playboys headed back to base in silence.

"Good job tonight, fellas. We lost one aircraft, but at least our boys are okay and going home safely," Papa said to his squadron.

Val laughed on frequency. "They'll be safe as long as the chopper pilot doesn't light up and try to fuel the aircraft while they're in it!"

Everyone got a good laugh and Papa chuckled back, "Dammit Jordan! We're not in my office! Save the smartass remarks till we're on the ground!"

11

AROUND THE BEND

Although war is terrifying and deadly, life in a war zone can at times seem as routine as normal life. The difference is that in a war zone, complacency can be fatal. For the men of VMFA-2, it was the deadly routine of escort, close air support, and bombing missions mixed with regular attacks on their base. Val was making more frequent trips to Dong Hoi now since COD flights had been scaled back in order to provide other support functions. Papa was extremely angry with upper level management and their decision to scale back the COD flights to Linh Thu. His base was so isolated from all other friendly territory that it was impossible for them to get the daily essentials of life otherwise. The brass had no sympathy for Papa's arguments and basically blew them off, as if the men at Linh Thu were disposable whiners. Finally, after even more protests from Papa, they decided to send a high-ranking officer to Linh Thu to see if the base really needed such flights, and if Linh Thu was even serving a purpose. Papa was insulted, feeling that the brass thought he was making things up about the living conditions there and how much value the base was to the war effort by providing the fastest close air, intercepting, and escort support for ground and Air Forces. Linh Thu also provided damaged aircraft not based there a place to make emergency landings. Papa had also pointed out that if the Americans abandoned Linh Thu, the enemy would surely find it a perfect base from which to launch MiGs to intercept American bombing attacks on the North, and possibly serve as a springboard for attacks against the South.

Papa got word that Marine Major General Deegan, second in command of all Marine Air Wings in Vietnam, was to arrive at Linh Thu just after noon the next day. Papa, Chappie, and the COs from VMO-16 and the support units held a meeting at the HQ building to discuss how to convince Washington that Linh Thu was a vital asset and how it badly needed more COD flights to sustain itself. The meeting lasted almost all day, and when Papa went back to his office, he sent for Val.

Val, Nate, Notso, and Speedy were playing cards at the chow hall when Papa's assistant approached their table. "Captain Jordan?" the young corporal said.

"Hold on a second, Corporal," Val replied as he concentrated on his cards.

Speedy smiled. "Your call, Tibbs—in or out?"

Val stared at his cards, knowing that Speedy had to be bluffing again. "Dammit—I'm not sure." He then looked back to the corporal standing behind him, showed him his cards and asked, "What do think, Corporal—should I call?"

The corporal smiled as he looked at Val's hand, then over to Speedy. "Most definitely, Sir. Lieutenant Sanders bluffs a lot!"

"Hey! Don't give away my secrets, Corporal!" Speedy said with a laugh.

"It's no secret, sir—the word's out." The corporal looked back at Val and said, "I took forty bucks off the lieutenant last week, sir."

"You're right, Corporal!" Val smiled back at Speedy. "Sorry, Speedy, but I gotta call!"

"Dammit!" Speedy cursed as he laid down a pair of threes.

"That's it?" Val laughed. "That's what you bluffed with? Hell I can beat that without showing my full hand," he said as he set down as pair of tens, followed by three queens for a full house.

Speedy laughed. "Dammit, Corporal—you're no longer allowed to poker night!"

"Don't listen to him, corporal—he's just a sore loser!" Val said as he pulled the pile of singles to his side of the table. "Come to papa!" He counted thirty-five of them.

"Speaking of Papa, sir" the corporal said. "The colonel wants you at his office ASAP."

"Okay." Val stood up and looked at his friends. "I'm going to Papa's office"—Val handed the corporal ten dollars—"and the good corporal here will take my place and finish kicking Speedy's broke ass!" Val leaned over the corporal as he sat down. "Make sure to get the pink slip to his Charger by the time I get back."

As he walked away, Val heard the corporal say, "All right, gents—time to separate you from your money, Lieutenant Sanders, just ante up the keys to your Charger, because I know your checks bounce more than a ball at a Knicks' game!"

Val was soon knocking on Papa's door, and as he awaited permission to enter, he overheard Papa chewing someone out on the phone. When Papa called him in, Val noticed how red Papa's face was. "Jordan—just the man I need to see," Papa said as he looked up from his paperwork.

"Hope that conversation on the phone wasn't about me, sir," Val remarked.

"Nope. That was a real idiot—some general from the Pentagon who called from Subic Bay trying to tell me how to run my base, because after all he would know best, being cozy in some office in Washington. Anyways, Captain, you are about to be an extremely busy man for a long time."

"Great," Val said. "So I'm back to doing busy work, sir?"

"Hardly. Starting in two days, you will be making trips to Dong Hoi at least twice a week. Our COD flights have been severely cut back, and the only things they'll be delivering is what you won't be able to pick up in Dong Hoi—fuel, weapons, aircraft parts, some food, some medical supplies, et cetera. You'll be picking up basic supplies for maintenance and reconstruction, office supplies, food, medical supplies, and the like."

Val couldn't contain the smile that grew across his face. He sighed as said, "If I must, I'll make the sacrifice. It's a cross I'll just have to bear."

Papa caught on right away. "You son of a bitch! You better thank the gods that you're the only one who speaks Vietnamese, or else *I'd* be going—and maybe not coming back. Those chicks would either have a new employee or be expecting babies."

"Too late, sir! I already put in my application, and my paycheck's already signed over to support the kids I'm about to have!"

"Smartass!" Papa laughed, then became thoughtful as he had an idea. "Since you're so cocky and have a plum assignment, it's time for you to get some karma back, Captain."

"What do you mean, sir?" Val asked, thinking something bad was about to happen.

"General Deegan's arriving from Da Nang tomorrow after he visits Khe Sanh. He'll need an escort at all times—"

"Don't do it, sir!" Val pleaded.

"Yep! You're going to babysit him tomorrow during his visit."

"What did I do to deserve this?"

"You said it earlier, Captain—busywork."

"But why me, sir? Come on! There must be someone else more qualified for this duty! I'm with Vietnamese women with brass, sir!"

Papa laughed until it hurt, then folded his hands. "Yes! Finally I get the last laugh!"

"Sir, I'll do anything if you pick someone else," Val said in desperation.

"Nope—my mind's made up. All you gotta do is be honest if he asks you any questions, Captain. Be on the flight line at 1145 tomorrow."

Val looked heavenward and said, "Thank you for teaching me humility." Then he walked out of the office looking like someone who'd just lost a winning lottery ticket.

§ § § § §

The next morning Val found himself standing on the northwest ramp waiting for a C-130 with a general aboard. It wasn't long before the racket of the escort F-4s and the C-130 was heard as they approached from the south. The C-130 lumbered along as it turned a long final to runway 31. When it finally centered up, small artillery and rifle fire opened up from the jungle all around the massive aircraft. What was supposed to be a nice easy, approach into the base was now becoming a stomach-churning, white-knuckle flight through a downpour of ordnance. The C-130 had to do some wild maneuvering to avoid taking hits, and all the men watching from the ramp gasped in disbelief at the giant plane's impossible contortions. The only one not gasping was Papa, who was pleased with the greeting even though he was naturally concerned for the safety of the 130's occupants. The general would now find out firsthand how dangerous it was to live at Linh Thu and that there should be no excuse for reducing COD flights for the brave Marines stationed here. Soon the ground fire got even heavier, and the F-4s decided they had to take action to draw some of the heat from the cargo plane. Both F-4s rolled beneath the Hercules and blindly opened fire into the jungles, ever vigilant for SA-7s. They knew the large plane was basically a sitting duck for a launch unless they were in position to draw the missile off the C-130 and onto them. It wasn't much longer before the enemy did exactly that and launched a SA-7 at the cargo plane.

"Shit—we got a SAM launch!" the flight leader called out over frequency. "I'm going to draw it off! Break hard right, PAT 1!" he ordered the C-130 as he cut left under its left wing, between it and the missile, then broke left once he was sure he had it on him.

"Dash 2 rolling in hot!" the wingman called out as he dove in low and dropped four 500-pound bombs in the vicinity of the source of the ground fire and the SA-7 launch.

The flight leader saw the missile closing in and waited until it was within 250 yards before performing a high-g barrel roll, which confused the missile as it continued on straight ahead. "Watch it, guys—that missile's still live! It could curl back on any of us!"

All the pilots watched as the missile suddenly broke low and exploded on taxiway bravo, possibly drawn by the heat that radiated off its surface.

"The bombs seemed to have silenced the guys on the ground, PAT 1. Continue on your approach—we got you covered," Dash 2 said to the C-130 pilot, who had to make a hard turn to get back on centerline. Dash 2 added, "When are you guys gonna believe the memo about short approaches from close in? Long, straight-in approaches are too risky!"

"I'm a believer now," the 130 pilot replied, trying to catch his breath.

"Make sure you pass the word to anyone else headed our way," Dash 1 added.

"Don't worry—I will," the pilot said as he finally touched down and saw the fire crew extinguishing the flames of the missile that nearly brought him down.

Soon the Hercules rolled up to the northwest ramp, and men who would normally be at attention for a VIP scattered. Papa didn't want to make the general a target for anyone looking at the base through a rifle scope, so the only ones awaiting the general were Papa and Val. Crews still swarmed the plane to offload its cargo, but no one had been ordered to greet the general.

When the door swung open and Major General Deegan stepped onto the ramp, Papa and Val snapped to and, without saluting, said, "Morning, sir!"

Squinting, Deegan looked out over the ramp, apparently disappointed by the absence of the pomp that normally greeted a man of his rank. And when he received no salute from a mere light colonel and captain, he snapped in anger. "What kind of undisciplined operation are you running here, Colonel?"

Papa was a little stunned by the general's tone, but not totally surprised. He knew most high-ranking officers were used to having their asses kissed. "What do you mean, sir?"

"No one salutes a superior officer on this base?"

"Not unless they want to send them home in a body bag, sir," Papa replied with a smirk as he gestured toward the jungle. "I figured your ride in here might have tipped you off to that, sir. Everyone stationed here is equal in rank when in the view of the enemy, sir."

The general was taken aback by Papa's bluntness. He was used to people cowering to him. Papa simply treated people with the same respect they paid him, no matter who they were or what rank they were. Deegan turned to Val. "Who is this?"

"This is Captain Jordan, sir. He'll be your escort while on base today."

"Welcome to hell, sir," Val said as Papa tried to stifle a chuckled.

The general sensed that any man based here had seen too many close calls to be intimidated by rank. "So tell me, Colonel, why exactly am I here?"

Papa was confused. "Sorry, sir—do you mean you don't know?"

The general had been here only a few minutes and had already been insulted twice. He was clearly unaccustomed to that and was growing angry.

To imply that a member of the general staff didn't know what was going on, even when they clearly didn't, was disrespectful. "Is everyone a smartass here, Colonel? Of course I know why I'm here—I'm checking to see if you know!"

Papa, not afraid of anyone, simply turned the question back to the general. "Of course I know why you're here, sir. The brave men of this base will convince you and anyone above you that your idea was not only bad, but horribly wrong. Now I'm sure you're used to having everyone agree with you and kiss your ass, but out here, surrounded by people who are nightly trying to kill us, the only thing that matters to us is that we stick together and watch each other's backs. You've only been here a few minutes and all you've done is remind us you're the brass. You act like we're just peons out here on the tip of the spear, an inconvenience and a waste of your time. Now you can threaten any of us with office hours or even a court martial, and you'll see that none of your bureaucratic bullshit scares us. In fact, it would be a welcome relief from this place. If you don't believe me, stay the night if you have the balls to. After one mortar attack or flying one mission with our boys into the middle of AA or having to dodge SAMs when just trying to land back at base, I promise you'll see it our way.

"Now I've got a lot of work to do, so if you don't have any questions for me, I leave you in the capable hands of one of my best pilots, Captain Jordan, here. He'll take you anywhere you need to go. I'll meet you at this afternoon with the other COs and XOs in the HQ building's conference room. So if you don't mind, sir, I bid you adieu for now!" Papa stormed off shaking his head, thinking some of these high-ranking officers got where they were because they knew someone, not because they deserved a promotion.

Deegan, his mouth agape, stood there trembling. Papa's passion and honesty was obvious. He couldn't remember ever having anyone speak to him that way. He noticed that several men had stopped their activities and stared when Papa was chewing him out. He sensed that these men would side with Papa without him ever asking them to. That was true loyalty. He wondered how to inspire such devotion in the people who worked under him. He shouted out after Papa, "Sorry, Colonel—I was out of line. I'll see you later at HQ." The general then looked at Val, who was still tensed up and ready to spring to the defense of his CO. The general was impressed. "So Captain, I apologize again," he said. "What exactly would you like to show me?"

Val pointed to a jeep that was waiting in front of the C-130. "Climb in, sir. There's much to see, many to hear, and much to be learned today, sir."

As the two officers drove around the base to survey the damage from night attacks and raids, the general noticed how the men were all working hard, yet seemed to be smiling and joking a lot. Val showed the general the tunnel entrance, the damaged buildings, living quarters, chow hall, and cramped ready room and sick bay. He showed the general the fleet of trucks that was one of the lifelines of the base and how they had to be driven a great distance for the essentials needed to keep the base alive. Val gave the general every opportunity to speak with the men as they made their way around the base, and everyone he spoke seemed equally dedicated. The general was still impressed, but he wasn't sure he could admit he was wrong to his colleagues and superiors back home. As far as general officers were concerned, arrogance went with the territory, and it was going to take some convincing to make him care about anyone other than himself.

The general was surprised when Val drove up to the flight line to several men awaiting them with flight gear in front of an F-4 hooked up to a start-cart. The general asked Val, "What's going on, Captain?"

"You've seen this base from the perspective of those on the ground, now you get to see what us wingers have to deal with," Val replied. The term "wingers" applied to anyone whose job entailed aviation—particularly flight crews.

As the general climbed out of the jeep, he was hesitant as men strapped a g-harness and survival gear to his body, then strapped a helmet to his head. Val pointed to the rear cockpit. "Listen to the plane captains and climb in, sir."

The plane captains briefed Deegan on how to arm his ejection seat, ejection sequences, how to open and close the canopy, basic survival tips, and other basic information about his flight in the back seat. Deegan was still feeling overwhelmed and unsure if he should go on this flight—after all, he was nearly killed by the enemy coming in here.

Soon Val had the jet fired up and peered at the terrified general in the rear-view mirror. "Relax, sir—everything's gonna be fine!"

"Where are we going, Captain?"

"Just a short little flight around the area, let you see what we're up against every day."

"Look, Captain—I saw how busy the flight line was today. This really isn't necessary!"

"Yes sir, it is—it absolutely is," Val said as he snapped on his oxygen mask and stoked the burners as he was cleared for takeoff on runway 10.

The plane jolted forward and the general felt the g-forces pin him against the back of his seat. Soon everything outside was rushing by in a blur, and suddenly the plane pitched up to where the only thing he could see was the blue sky. He looked over his shoulder and saw the ground literally falling away from below him. "Holy shit!" he exclaimed.

"You haven't seen anything that will make you shit your pants yet, sir. Wait until we get a little farther north," Val said as he cranked his jet into a hard high-g left break. He then performed a couple of aileron rolls for fun.

"That's enough of that, Captain," the general said, nerves evident in his voice.

Val flew the general around the general area of Linh Thu and pointed out the areas farther north where the enemy was located and most of the action occurred. After ten minutes he got as close as he possibly could to North Vietnam's SAM umbrella without penetrating it, then headed east for the coast. As they crossed the coastline over the South China Sea, Val dropped down to below a hundred and fifty feet above the water to give the general a good view and the exhilaration from the sense of speed that low altitude provided. As Val flew along, his radar scope showed several strong returns about ten miles ahead that kept disappearing and reemerging at different places on the scope. Curious, he proceeded directly to the source of the echoes. As the distance rapidly closed, Val could see smoke rising from the shoreline and saw the definite shape of an OV-10 in full planform view against the hazy sky as it performed a wingover for strafing runs. Val pulled his stick right and swooped around the scene in a wide orbit as he slowed his jet down. He looked down to see a lone US serviceman, either Marine or Army, running for his life along the beach from several enemy units trying to close in on him. The man was unarmed and in serious trouble if someone didn't come to his rescue soon. Val switched frequencies to Button Red, and heard the OV-10 crew trying to relay their distress call to Strike. Val immediately knew his jet was unarmed, but out of habit he checked his stores anyway and was pleasantly surprised to find he had a fully loaded cannon. He knew it would be risky to take the general on a combat sortie, but the man on the beach needed help now.

"Strike, Showbunny 1," Val keyed up.

"Showbunny 1, Strike, go ahead."

"Showbunny 1 is a single Fox-4 on scene at the beach with the OV-10 that is speaking to you, armed only with twenty mike-mike, can assist until Alert-5s and rescue flight arrive from Linh Thu."

"Roger Showbunny 1. Contact FACA on this frequency, call-sign Guard Dog 4."

"Showbunny 1 Wilco."

"Captain—we don't have time for this," the general said.

"Sir, we have to make time. That GI down on the beach doesn't have any!"

"Captain—all this for one man? Do I need to remind you that you have a high-ranking general on board?"

"What are you saying, sir, that your life is more valuable than his? I bet his family would disagree!" Angry, Val cranked his jet into a hard left breaking dive to shut the general up.

"Turn back to Linh Thu now, Captain—that's an order!" the general moaned under the strain of g-forces.

"Duly noted, sir. This conversation is over for now. Someone down there needs our help! I'm sure you'd expect us to do the same for you if you were in his position," Val said as he leveled out, then checked in with the FACA. "Guard Dog 4, this is Showbunny 1, single Fox-4 with twenty mike-mike setting up for a strafing run from the north, can you give me any guidance?"

"Affirmative Showbunny 1. Thank God you're here! Follow my smoke columns, they'll be right on the enemy positions." Guard Dog 4's pilot led the way, firing a series of Willie Petes along the enemy's line. As he peeled off, he called out, "Showbunny 1, you are cleared hot!" The pride was evident in his voice.

"Showbunny 1's rolling in hot," Val replied as he lined himself on the rising smoke columns. He flew just below a hundred feet off the deck and placed the smoke columns in the pipper and squeezed the trigger. The cannon growled as rounds spewed out its muzzle and tore up the ground, sending sand flying everywhere, some even higher than Val's present altitude. Enemy troops were being sliced to pieces by the explosive-tipped rounds. Some body parts flew up past the canopy, and the general noticed when a piece of bloody uniform slapped his canopy. He was starting to get a taste of the reality of war. Suddenly a loud bang shook the jet just off the left side of his canopy.

"What's going on, Captain?"

"Relax sir—the enemy's just firing some small artillery at us," Val said nonchalantly as if it were an everyday occurrence—and for Val and his fellow aviators, it was.

"We can't stay here much longer, Captain! They might kill us!"

"That's quite possible, sir, but we're not leaving until our relief arrives."

"Goddamnit! This is crazy! I don't want to die here!"

"That GI down there doesn't want to die either, if he doesn't have to. Anyway, this is what we do every day. It's our job. A Marine knows that when he signs up."

That stung. The general was beginning to feel that maybe he wasn't so superior to people beneath his rank as he looked down at the man on the beach, practically dead from exhaustion but still joyous that the jet above him was trying to save his life.

Val speaking to the FACA pierced his thoughts. "Guard Dog 4, we're reversing course for another pass from the south. Do you still see any enemy around?"

"Affirmative, Showbunny 1. They're moving to the west, trying to get under some cover or trying to sneak up to our guy from another angle. Do you need me to mark 'em?"

Val looked ahead and to his left and still had the enemy troops in sight. "Negative, Guard Dog 4—I'll splinter 'em." Val dropped down again and charged on as he was met by heavy ground fire, the enemy unwisely revealing their position. As tracers and explosions swarmed around the jet, the general cowered lower into his seat.

"Showbunny 1, you are cleared hot! Kick ass, my friend!" Guard Dog 4 added as he saw Val lining up for the kill.

Val opened fire and began to decimate the southern end of the enemy line, which was closer to the man on the beach, who began to run for the cover of the coastal grasses.

As Val continued spraying bullets along the length of the enemy's line, the Alert-5s checked on. They announced they saw Val making his strafing run and lined up for a couple of passes to drop some thousandpounders. Val climbed out of their way into a wide, high orbit to ensure the man was still okay. Soon the enemy was engulfed in flames and silenced as a UH-1 swooped in and picked up the exhausted but relieved GI. Val and the other air-craft were now heading for Linh Thu when the enemy missile siren sounded in all headsets.

"What's that, Captain?" the general asked, knowing it couldn't be good news.

"Looks like the Gooners are launching SAMs, sir. I need you to just scan the ground for white smoke trails heading at us. If you see one, let me know where it is," Val replied.

"What? Shit! What can we do?"

"Well, seeing the missile is crucial in me being able to avoid it, sir, so look for it!"

Just then the lead Alert-5 called out. "Got 'em! Looks like three SAMs heading our way from three-o'clock high. Let's see who they're tracking."

With that all three jets broke in different directions, their crews keeping all eyes on the missiles. The missiles appeared to be locked on to Val's jet. "Looks like Showbunny 1's the lucky one!" Val called out.

When the general realized that he was in Showbunny 1, he said, "Holy shit! How are we going to get away, Captain?"

"We're not, sir—we're going to sit tight right here for a couple minutes."

The general grasped one of the ejection handles. "Just let me know when we're going to bail out and I'll pull the handle, Captain."

"We're *not* bailing out, sir! Get your hand off the handle now!"

"Why?"

"I don't need you accidentally pulling the handle when I try to outmaneuver these things. Believe me sir, you *don't* want to eject unless it's absolutely necessary—and *I'll* let you know when to do it! Take your hands off the handle *now!* I'm in command of this aircraft, and *that's* an order!" Val wanted to let the general know he was very serious.

Deegan reluctantly acknowledged that he wasn't in charge of the plane and took his hand off the ejection handle. The pilot seemed to know what he was doing. "Okay, Captain."

"Thank you. Now sit tight—we're gonna pull some g-forces here shortly." Val waited as the missiles closed with less than an eighth of a mile as the general sweated in the seat behind him. Val then pulled up into a high-g barrel roll followed by a Derry turn in the opposite direction of his roll. He looked back to see the missiles arc past him and go ballistic. Val pointed out the smoke rings they made in the stratosphere as they exploded.

"How often you men have to deal with those?" the shaken but relieved general asked.

"Every day. We wouldn't have to if Washington would let us attack the facilities where they're store, but I guess you know what's best for us half a world away," Val said sarcastically, hoping the general would now bring up the matter at the Pentagon.

Soon Val touched down at Linh Thu and pulled his jet into his barricade. The ramp was noisy as an OV-10 pulled into its barricade and the Alert-5s taxied to their barricades. A Huey was thumping somewhere in the distance to the southeast. After the general shed his flight gear, he ran up to Val, who was talking to his plane captain. Deegan grabbed Val's shoulder and pulled, and Val turned around to face him.

"Why did you put me in danger back there, Captain?" the general shouted angrily.

Val didn't answer but instead stared at the UH-1 now touching down behind him.

"Answer me, Captain!" the general shouted. Val continued to ignore him, keeping his attention on the Huey as it shut down and its occupants climbed out. "Goddamnit, Captain, you'd better answer me!" the general shouted so loud that everyone around them stopped and stared at him and Val.

In a moment a young man barely eighteen, his torn, blood-stained fatigues visible beneath a blanket, was escorted up to them by corpsmen. He was a soldier who'd gotten separated from his platoon the night before during patrol and had spent a terrifying night trying to locate his platoon, only to run directly into an enemy platoon attracted by his whispers for help in English. He spent the rest of a sleepless night trying to evade death or capture at the hands of the enemy platoon. He spent most of the night running for his life, especially when he ran out of ammunition and was nearly captured twice; only the darkness aided his escape.

His platoon knew not to risk looking for him until daylight, and had spent most of the morning trying to evade the overwhelming numbers of enemy forces themselves. When they extracted, they sent the word to Strike to look for him, but expected the worst since the young man had no radio. By pure luck, Guard Dog 4 happened to be flying over the area when an enemy platoon flushed him out, dehydrated and totally exhausted, and began chase. They had nearly captured him as they pressed on toward him in clear defiance of Guard Dog 4's strafing runs. Then Val's jet roared overhead and made them take cover.

The young man walked over to Val and gave him a tight bear hug as he thanked him profusely with tear swollen eyes and told him how he ran out of ammunition and was sure the enemy was going to kill him. As he excused himself to thank the Alert-5 crews before being taken to sick bay, Val stared at the general and answered his question. "He's why I put you in danger today, sir," Val said, pointing to the soldier from Alabama. "Why don't you catch up to him and tell him you were prepared to leave him there to die? Sir! You know what, *sir?* Even after this, I'd still put my life on the line to save you, *sir!*" Val walked away in disgust, then looked back and added, "You're probably expected at the HQ building now, sir. Your afternoon meeting will be after lunch"

§ § § § §

Val stepped into his hooch to see Speedy gently rapping his head against one of the support beams. He smiled. "Let me guess—you lost your Charger to the corporal."

"Nope—to Notso when he drew to an inside straight." Speedy looked up to ceiling and added, "Who's that lucky?"

"Maybe you should ease up on the bluffing."

"I know. I still have a chance to win it back Saturday on Alert-5 duty."

"That's if he antes it up."

The look of panic in Speedy's eyes grew. Obviously he hadn't considered that Notso might not ante it back up. "He will—he's got to, right?"

"I don't know. It's a pretty sweet ride! I was hoping to take it off your hands on one of these games!"

"Then you'd sell it back to me, right?"

Val looked away as he said, "*Riiiiight!*"

§ § § § §

The afternoon passed quickly, and with the waning sun at twilight the massive C-130 fired up on the northwest ramp to fly Major General Deegan back to Da Nang. As the plane taxied to runway 13, most of the men of Linh Thu were happy to see him leave. As the Hercules lifted off and finally disappeared over the horizon, Papa took his hands off his hips and turned back toward his office with Big John, Chappie, and Commander Yeary in tow.

"Well that was painful. Good riddance," Papa growled.

"Did anyone notice that he smelled bad?" the chaplain asked.

Papa laughed. "Yeah! What was that?"

"I always heard Pentagon generals and politicians were full of bull," said Big John. "I think Captain Jordan scared the shit out of him during his flight—literally."

§§§§§§

Early the next morning, Val found himself in Papa's office with orders to go to Dong Hoi for just a few items. Papa told him that he'd be making a lot of small trips with one truck, either alone or one other person, practically every day until they got word about the COD flights. Val couldn't be happier. It was the best news he'd gotten since he arrived in Vietnam. Now he could see Nga Nghin Do'i almost every day if she was at the store.

Papa handed him a list and told him to be back in time for tonight's briefing. Val moved faster than he had in a long time and raced to the truck parked outside. He fired up the truck and sped away to Dong Hoi.

Before he knew it, he was crossing the bridge over the Nhat Le River into Dong Hoi. Val drove the confusing, twisting streets to Nghia Mau's store. As he rounded the final turn, he was shocked to see smoke rising from the front of the store. When he screeched to a halt, he saw that the fire seemed to be out, but there was no sign of any of the women. He ran into the store, shouting, "Nghia Mau! Nga Nghin Do'i! Is everyone okay?"

When he entered the main warehouse, he found all the girls in a circle on the floor comforting Nghia Mau. Val rushed over to them and bowed, then knelt down in front of Nghia Mau. "*Khoe khong ha?*"—Are you okay? He noticed a lot of rope on the floor, and as he saw the looks of helplessness on their faces, he knew something was wrong.

"*Toi khoe, cam o'n,*"—I'm fine, thank you, Nghia Mau replied, tears streaming down her face as she grabbed Val's hand and squeezed.

"*Nga Nghin Do'i sao roi?*"—How is Nga Nghin Do'i? Val asked.

Nghia Mau finally looked at Val, terror in her eyes and nodded toward Nga Nghin Do'i's office.

Sensing that whatever danger the women had faced was still present, Val gently loosened his grip on Nghia Mau's hand and crept toward the office. He noticed that the door to the office, practically always open, was closed. He twisted the knob, but the door was locked. Val could hear muffled sounds being filtered through the door, and the soft sounds of crying and moaning. His body throbbed in pain as he made out a male voice and then the sound of a loud slap and the shriek of pain from Nga Nghin Do'i.

Rage flushed Val's entire body as he heard the sound of tearing fabric. Without a second thought, Val kicked the door down. As the door slammed down, it slammed into the back of a Vietnamese man that was trying to force Nga Nghin Do'i onto her desk. The familiar sound of a rifle hitting the ground echoed throughout the office at the same time the door struck the back of the Vietnamese man. Val's eyes focused on the shattered look of fear and hopelessness on Nga Nghin Do'i's bruised face, and the stream of blood that trickled down onto her dress, torn from her shoulders to the small of her back, exposing her bare back and upper torso.

The man, still stunned by the hard impact of the door against his head and spine, groaned as he began to gather himself. He wore some sort of military uniform, but it was distinctly not NVA. His belt was unbuckled and his pants around his ankles. The rage within Val erupted and he grabbed the man by his windpipe and punched him square in the face, sending blood flying everywhere and sending the man across the room and slammed him into the wall.

Val then charged him and sent a side thrust kick into his knee, which snapped his leg like a twig. As the man doubled over in pain, unable to support any weight on a broken leg, Val caught his chin with a vicious uppercut punch with his left hand. As the man's body flew upward from the force of the impact, Val landed another solid cross directly on the man's face. The man's head ricocheted off the wall and, as it began to fold into his upper torso, Val snapped the man's neck at the Atlas vertebrae when he landed a solid knife hand strike to the base of the skull.

The man collapsed to the ground and Val kicked him in the ribs a few times before ending the man's life with a stomp kick to the head. Val continued to stomp the man's face in an uncontrollable eruption of violence. Val leaned over and picked up the man's AK-47 and raised it over his head to smash the man with the butt of the weapon.

Just as Val was about to strike him, Nga Nghin Do'i pulled him back, shouting, tears in her eyes, that the man was clearly dead. Suddenly the blur of rage came into focus and Val found himself standing in the middle of Nga Nhin Do'i's office, gasping from physical exertion. He looked at the dead man and then at Nga Nghin Do'i, who was trying to tie her dress back up around her shoulders through her sobs of shock and disbelief.

Val couldn't believe he had attacked the man in such an uncontrollable rage. It was so fast and so fierce that he lost all control of his actions, as if he were a wild animal. Val gathered himself and walked to Nga Nghin Do'i and embraced her. She returned the embrace and continued to sob as Val attempted to comfort her with his voice and usual gentle manner.

Sensing that whatever danger the women had faced was still present, Val gently loosened his grip of Nghia Mau's hand and crept toward the office. He noticed that the door to the office, practically always open, was closed. He twisted the knob, but the door was locked. He could hear muffled sounds through the door—crying and moaning, and Nghia Mau and the other women walked in and thanked Val and hugged him. After he helped bandage the small cut on Nga Nghin Do'i's forehead, they all sat in the waiting area sipping tea in silence, everyone staring blankly off into space. When Val thought enough time had passed, he asked Nga Nghin Do'i what had happened.

She explained that some men threw some Molotov cocktails into the shop, which luckily burned out quickly. As the women were dousing the flames, one of the men came in wielding an assault rifle and ordered all of them into the warehouse, threatening to kill them one by one if they didn't do as he said. He then tied them all up, and when he came across Nga Nghin Do'i, he separated her from the others and decided to rape her. He forced her into her office and ordered her to undress, and when she resisted he struck her on the back of her head with his rifle just hard enough to stun her. Even dazed she tried to resist, so he struck her again on the forehead. He then tore her dress and attempted to undress her as he forced her over her desk. When she fought, he slapped her viciously. The women outside had managed to untie themselves and were trying to figure out how to help Nga Nghin Do'i when Val arrived.

The soldier had just about taken the fight out of Nga Nghin Do'i and was about to completely remove her dress when Val kicked down the door and put a swift end to the problem for them.

Val asked, as he always had previously whenever Nghia Mau's store was attacked, why they were being targeted and who the attackers were.

As usual, the women wouldn't answer, and Val wondered what they were trying to hide. He decided not to press it too much, but he was a little angry that they would still ignore the question even after Nga Nghin Do'i had narrowly escaped being raped.

Val helped the women clean up the mess and Nghia Mau gave Val the supplies he wanted for free, but Val insisted on paying anyway. He finished loading his supplies and helped Nga Nghin Do'i fix her office door. Val asked what they were going to do with the body of the soldier, and the women had no immediate answer. Nghia Mau closed the store for the rest of the day and sat at her desk for a while, then walked out to Val and the girls in the warehouse. She made everyone swear that they would never speak of today in public, and if the soldiers came back looking for their friend, they would all say that he left after he stole some merchandise and they didn't know where he went. Then she walked over to a space where broken-down boxes were kept and pulled out a very large one. She had her girls put the body into the box, then had the girls load the box into Val's truck. Val protested, knowing he couldn't have the body of a Vietnamese citizen in his truck. Nghia Mau cut him off and explained her plan. She felt that Nga Nghin Do'i needed to leave the office for the day, considering what had happened, and she'd probably be better off if she wasn't alone tonight. She explained that Val could take her and the rest of the girls to a village called *Bac Lang* (North Village) just out-side of Dong Hoi on his way back to his base. The village, which was where they lived, was one of two known as the *Hai Lan Langs* (Twin Villages) that were separated by a field with two huge stone incinerators—one for preparing food and other household purposes, and the other for various industrial and agricultural purposes. They'd keep the elders and other villagers preoccupied while Val and Nga Nghin Do'i placed the body in the box in the industrial incinerator. Val wasn't sure if he liked the idea, but he agreed, knowing that the girls would be in a lot of trouble if anyone found out.

The girls loaded the body and piled into the truck bed. Most of them had never ridden in a car or truck before—they either walked or rode a bike. Nghia Mau and Nga Nghin Do'i climbed into the cab with Val, and he fired it up and drove toward the Twin Villages. The girls knew that the villagers would be suspicious about a US military truck driving into their villages, but they knew that their minds would be eased once they got to meet and talk to Val—an American who knew how to speak their own language.

When they arrived, Val waited by the truck as the women spoke to the elders. Kids playing nearby were overcome by curiosity and ran up to the huge vehicle sitting outside their village with a white man leaning against it. They'd never seen a truck up close nor an American man at all, and when Nghia Mau called Val, the children thought he was a giant. The elders feared that allowing an American into their village would come back to haunt them and weren't afraid to express their fears—even in Val's presence. To their sur-prise, Val spoke to them in their native language, telling them that he was hon-ored to be able to help the ladies from their villages and would never again come unless properly invited. He explained that he would help anyone in any way he could, no matter where they were from. Val couldn't help but notice that for such poor people, they seemed to be well dressed. Every villager, no matter their age or gender, wore high-quality garments.

When the villagers finally went about their business, they kept a wary eye on the American. Val and Nga Nghin Do'i unloaded the box and carried it to the incinerator. Val was surprised just how heavy such a small man was as he and Nga Nghin Do'i struggled to lift the box into the incinerator. Soon the box was inside and engulfed in flames. The chimney belched a thick black smoke, and that same horrible smell that Val was familiar with after attacks on Linh Thu settled around the oven. One of the villagers asked what the horrible smell was from, and Nga Nghin Do'i replied "Rotten animal fur."

Their lives were forever changed by the day's events, and there now was a new bond between them and the girls at the store. They'd all face a death sentence if word leaked out, and Val would surely face a court martial and imprisonment, maybe a death sentence as well. Soon Val and Nga Nghin Do'i covered their faces with cloths and shoveled the ashes out of the incinerator, then spread them around a partially flooded rice paddy.

After they were done, Nga Nghin Do'i walked him around both villages, pointing out various houses and buildings and introducing him to some of her neighbors. They walked into the north village to a dwelling and she invited him in. When Val stepped inside he saw many garments and bolts of fabric lying around and hanging on the walls. There was something covered by a cloth sitting on a table in the middle of the room, and she uncovered it to reveal a treadle-powered sewing machine. He was surprised by its excellent condition, considering its age, but it was clearly used often. She smiled at Val, then went behind a screen to change. Within a few moments she came out from behind the divider in another dress, carrying the torn one to the sewing machine. She smiled again and pointed to the machine as if she was showing it off and asked, "You like?"

Val smiled back and replied. "Yes. Whose is it?"

"It is mine. See?" She pulled off the needle guide plate and handed it to Val. He looked at it, confused. She grabbed his hand gently in hers and said with a coy smile, "Turn it over. See?" He flipped the plate over and saw the letters "N. N." engraved in the corner of the plate. "My uncle found the machine in England. He got the store to engrave it with my initials."

Val smiled. "Your uncle sounds like a good man. I'd love to meet him some day."

"You will. He comes down here every now and then." Nga Nghin Do'i noticed that she was still holding Val's hand. She gently released her grip and returned the guide plate to her machine. She sat down and began to work on the dress that had been so brutally torn, and by the time she was done, the dress looked like it had never been damaged.

"What do you do with all the fabric?" Val asked, gesturing around the room.

"I buy the fabric and make clothes for people in the villages."

"Do the elders require you to do that?"

"No." Nga Nghin Do'i looked up and her eyes got misty. "I love doing it. It makes everyone so happy. Our home is full enough with pain from this war, but I can still bring a smile to people's faces with my 'joy machine'!" Nga Nghin Do'i tapped her sewing. "I also bring them food and amenities to help them in their daily lives. I get pleasure from the look on their faces when they receive something they need but never asked for."

A soccer ball bounced into the hut, and the children were afraid to come inside because a tall American was standing inside. "*Lai day! Lai day! Du'ng co so hai!*"—Come! Come! Don't be frightened! Nga Nghin Do'i called.

The youngest child cautiously entered, and Val bent over and handed him the ball and said with a smile, "*Anh khong lam em dau dau.*"—I won't hurt you. The child smiled and took the ball from Val, then ran back outside. When the he regrouped with his friends, he told them about his adventure, how he bravely took the ball from the giant American. The other children looked at him in awe, then one of the others kicked the ball back into the hut and they all ran to the door and peeked in as the same boy walked in and again took the ball from the big white man. When they got the ball back, they kicked it into the hut again, and this time Val picked it up and walked to the door where the children were peeking in. Grinning, he jumped around and playfully growled at them, and the children screamed with glee and ran away laughing. When they were a safe distance away, they turned around and kicked the ball back to Val. He kicked it back to them, and for a while they made a game of it. When Nga Nghin Do'i finished sewing, she covered her sewing machine and snuck up behind Val to intercept the ball on its way to him. She kicked it back to them, and before they knew it they had a soccer match going—she and Val against a small mob of children.

Val and Nga Nghin Do'i were having more fun with the kids than either of them had had in a while as the events of this morning and of the daily grind melted away. Soon the game drew a large crowd as villagers stopped what they were doing and watched. Val motioned for several of the adults to join in, and soon members of both villages were either watching or playing along. When the game finally ended, a little girl came up to Val and handed him a flower she'd been hiding in a rice baskets.

Then Nghia Mau invited him for a quick meal before he had to leave, and he found himself the guest of honor of people he knew didn't fully trust him. Nevertheless, each person wanted to make sure he had enough to eat and drink, and despite their suspicion of him, everyone was having a good time.

Val didn't want to leave, but when he looked at his watch he saw that it was time to go. He heartily thanked everyone and Nga Nghin Do'i walked him to his truck and stood with him at the door alone. The sun was low in the sky, and it highlighted her beautiful face. Awash in the moment, he reached behind him in the cab. "I don't know if this is a good idea, but I want the best for you and your friends." He handed her the AK-47 rifle he'd taken from her attacker. "Use it only as a last resort."

"Thank you." Nga Nghin Do'i took the rifle and set it on the ground beside her feet. "I'll never be able to thank you enough for this morning."

"You already have," Val said as he pointed to the villages. "I think about you all the time, Nga Nghin Do'i. I care deeply for you and everyone at your store"—he handed her the flower the girl had given him earlier—"but especially you."

She felt a rush of heat sweep through her body, then hugged him tightly and gave him a kiss on his cheek. She backed slowly away and smiled at Val as he fired up the engine and drove into the evening sun.

Val drove the whole way to Linh Thu in a dream state, thinking only of the woman he knew he was falling for. He arrived back at Linh Thu and dropped off the supplies, and as he walked by HQ, Papa ran outside and called him in. Val walked in to see Lieutenant Torres giving a briefing to Captain Overstreet and all the COs and XOs. Papa interrupted Torres and said to Val, "You're pretty familiar with the Dong Hoi area, right, Captain?"

"Yes, sir."

"Does the Nhat Le River have a large bend just northeast of the city?"

Val grabbed a map and pointed on it. "Yes, sir—right here. It's about six or seven klicks northeast of the town. Why?"

Torres said, "Well, sir, my scouts have been exploring the tunnel system we found. One tunnel ends on the river. My scouts weren't too sure where they were when they came out, so they actually snuck into the city at night and found out. I believe the enemy is sending supplies down the river, then enters the tunnel system at that point. This is a chance to intercept and cut off enemy supplies."

Papa laughed as he reemphasized his previous point. "As I tried to explain, Lieutenant, Washington doesn't give a shit. You met the general. It's obvious those idiots don't want to win this war, or else we'd fight like we wanted to win. But don't think I'm raining on your parade—this discovery of yours could still be useful to us when the time comes." Papa looked at Val. "Did you get everything, Captain?"

"Yes, sir."

"You look like someone just walked over your grandpa's grave. You okay?"

"Yes, sir."

"Very well. You got Alert-5 duty starting at 1900, so go rest up at the shack."

"Sir? Ah, never mind," Val said as he continued out the door.

Val walked into the shack and noticed a technician was working on the air conditioner. "What the hell's going on?" he asked

"During last night's raid, the AC caught some stray rounds," the technician answered.

"Those bastards! That's definitely crossing the line!"

The technician laughed. "I know. We should try them for war crimes. This has to be against the Geneva Convention."

"How long until you think you can get it fixed?"

"I'm not sure. No one has parts for something like this around here, and wasn't it you who pissed the general off? Looks like we're screwed!"

Val thought of the general when the technician brought it up. "Oh. It was worth it then!" He smiled and sat down on the couch. Despite the heat, his discomfort eased as he thought about Nga Nghin Do'i and the lovely people he'd met in the Twin Villages.

12

THE GRASS ISN'T GREENER

Except for a scramble that was called off shortly after he was airborne, Val's night in the shack was noteworthy only because of the heat. All the scramble accomplished was to ensure the men wouldn't be able to sleep for what was left of the night. Alert-5 duty was truly a double-edged sword—while it was relaxing and allowed the men to enjoy the air conditioning when it worked, it could also wreck a person's sleep cycle.

Val heard that Papa and the rest of the Varsity Squad had run into Colonel Tomb again on their sortie earlier, and Tomb had successfully shot down an Air Force F-105 and a Navy A-6 earlier that day. Papa had cursed the Russian as reports kept coming in that he was growing ever more cowardly, only attacking unescorted targets or targets he knew couldn't successfully fight back. He would streak for Kep Field at the first sign of American fighters so he wouldn't have to risk a dog fight. Unlike the Americans, whose rules and regulations practically neutralized any advantage that they had in the war, Tomb had no rules to follow.

Unknown to Papa and the American pilots who'd ever encountered the colonel, they weren't the only ones to despise him. He'd made many enemies in the North Vietnamese Air Force as well, and Captain Phan hated the Russian nuisance so much that he'd been tempted to shoot him down himself. Tomb had a habit of swooping in from out of nowhere to take an easy kill on a jet that Phan had spent considerable time wearing down and wounding. This infuriated Phan, but he was patient—knew the opportunity would present itself for him to settle with Colonel Tomb soon enough. He also believed that karma might take care of Tomb for him.

Val sat outside watching the sun rise in the morning light, absorbed by thoughts of Nga Nghin Do'i. Even though it was too hot inside the shack to sleep, he barely noticed. She was affecting him in ways he couldn't explain, and he knew that his interest in her was beyond physical. He was changing, and she was responsible.

At the same time, Val felt a weight on his chest over the killing of the soldier who'd attempted to rape Nga Nghin Do'i. It wasn't that he felt remorse for killing the man—he got exactly what he deserved—he just knew that there could be consequences for killing him. He knew keeping silent would stress him out, so he had to tell somebody—but whom? Who wouldn't turn him in to the Vietnamese authorities, who'd love nothing more than to make an example of an American killing a countryman? He knew the blame was his, and he wanted to protect Nga Nghin Do'i, Nghia Mau, and the other girls. Sweat dripped down his forehead as he sat with his eyes closed.

His eyes snapped open when the answer struck him—the chaplain. Val glanced down at his watch, knowing his relief would be coming soon and he'd be off Alert-5 duty. He'd stop by to see if the commander had time to see him. Just then he heard the door behind him open and close, and when he looked back he saw Nate in the morning light.

"Morning, brother," Nate said as he stretched. "I think I get better sleep in my hooch, even without air conditioning."

"Well neither did we last night, brother," Val replied.

"I know—thanks a lot. That's what you get for pissing off the general. You better find a replacement part on one of your trips to Dong Hoi." Nate laughed, but when he saw Val's expression change. He knew Val had something on his mind. "You all right, Man?"

Val and Nate knew each too well. Val knew he couldn't hide what happened long without Nate knowing something was wrong. "Buddy, I need your help this morning. What are you doing after we get off?"

"Whatever you need me to do, Buddy. What's up?"

"I gotta go to see Commander Yeary and get something off my chest. Can you come with me? I'd rather if I only have to tell it once."

Nate looked at his best friend and knew it had to be something really serious. "You know you can count on me, Man. I'll be there." Nate patted Val on his shoulder as he went inside to grab his stuff as he saw the next Alert-5 crew walking up the road to the shack.

Val and Nate walked in silence to Commander Yeary's office, Nate feeling the weight of whatever Val was carrying inside him. They got to the chaplain's lanai just as Yeary was unlocking the door. Val and Nate snapped to as they said in unison, "Morning, sir."

"Morning, boys!" the commander replied with a smile, even though he could tell that the officers weren't making a social call. "Would you gents like to come in? I've got fresh coffee to brew and you're welcome to some."

Val said, "Yes, sir. I need your counsel if you have the time. I asked Lieutenant Robinson along because we go back a ways."

"Of course, Captain! I always have time for any of you—you know that!"

Once inside, the commander made coffee and poured three cups, then set them on his desk. "Sit down—have some coffee."

Val preferred tea, but since the chaplain had gone to the trouble, he sipped at it gratefully.

Yeary sat down and when he felt everyone was relaxed he said, "So how can I help you this morning, Captain?"

"Sir, it's difficult for me to talk about, but I got myself into pickle yesterday in Dong Hoi, and I'm not sure what to do." Val looked at the commander, but he just told him to go on.

"I went to get supplies as I always do, except this time when I arrived at the store, it had smoke pouring out of it. So I went inside to see what was going on and found all the girls in the middle of the floor untying themselves." He looked at the chaplain.

"Continue, Captain."

"One of the girls was missing, and the manager told me she was in her office. She was terrified. So I checked the door and it was locked, but I heard the sounds of a struggle and some crying, so I kicked the door down and a soldier trying to rape the other girl. He was wearing a uniform and had an AK-47, but I didn't recognize his uniform as either North or South Vietnamese. He crawled out from under the door and I…" Val hesitated.

"Go ahead, Captain," Yeary urged.

"Well sir, I…I beat him to death," Val said, sounding both resigned and relieved.

"You mean literally to death, Captain?"

"Yes, sir."

"I see." Yeary settled back in his chair, absorbing what Val had just told him. "What happened to his body? Did you turn it in to the authorities?"

"No, sir." Val sighed, knowing the commander would probably be really disappointed when he told him the rest. "The girls and I loaded his body into my truck and took it to the village where most of them live. We cremated his body in a huge incinerator. Then we spread his ashes over a partially flooded rice paddy."

"Damn, Dude!" Nate let slip, then covered his mouth.

"So nobody except those of us in this room and the girls at the store know about this? Was the soldier alone? He didn't have any other soldiers with him?" Yeary asked.

"The girls said a few of them attacked the store, but he stayed behind after they left. That's when he tied them up and tried to rape one of them. So far as I know we're the only ones who know," Val replied.

"Is there a remote chance that his friends will come back looking for him? Wonder why they were attacking the store in the first place." The commander thought for a second. "The girls could be in danger—and you could be in a lot of trouble if anyone finds out."

"I know, sir—I'm sorry. I just reacted. I saw a woman in trouble and I just…reacted. I never meant to kill him." Val lowered his head and rested it in his hands.

"Do you feel remorse for the soldier, or for the trouble you might get into, Captain?"

"I don't feel bad for killing the man—he was violating an innocent girl, so he got what he deserved. Yes I am concerned for what could happen to me, sir, but more worried about the girls. Most likely I've made things worse for them."

"Good! You shouldn't feel bad for what happened to the soldier. You were defending the girls, and if this came to light, you'd have enough witnesses to support that you were defending a helpless girl against an armed man. Now should we tell anyone? I'm not sure. You said the body was cremated, so there's no body to recover. If anyone looks for him, the girls will know what to say.

"But now I'm in a pickle, Captain—a moral dilemma, if you will. We're in the middle of a terrible war, and we kill people all the time—with your bombs and cannons, and with small arms when the enemy sneaks onto our base during night raids. But that can't be an excuse. You're a good man, Captain. You're not violent, and it took an extremely violent incident to make you do what you did. You didn't go to the store planning to kill someone, but you had to react to save that girl. You can say he brought it upon himself."

Val was shocked to hear a man of the cloth say such a thing, but he knew he wasn't getting off the hook that easily. He knew he was in a lot of trouble, and for a second he wished that he'd kept his mouth shut.

Yeary continued: "As a martial artist, I understand what you did and why you don't feel you did anything wrong when you killed the man. But as an officer in the United States Navy, I know we can't just sweep this under the rug. Your error was disposing of the body without informing the authorities. However, if this goes up the chain of command their investigation might putting those girls' lives in danger, maybe get them killed. So here's what we're gonna do." Yeary looked both Val and Nate in the eye. "I'm going to bring this up to Papa and Captain Overstreet. The only reason I'll involve Overstreet is because he'll know how the other side is handling the situation if they have knowledge of it. I want you to relax and try not to worry about it—and most importantly, say nothing to anybody. Papa's a reasonable man. I'm sure he'll see this as I do. Go to your hooches. Papa will probably send for you later. Is there anything else you'd like to say, Captain?"

"No, sir." Val swallowed the lump in his throat.

"Then you're both dismissed." As Val and Nate rose to leave, the commander added, "Relax, Captain. Papa's got connections—he can help resolve this quietly."

"Don't forget, sir—I did piss off a general."

"I doubt it'll go that high, son. You're gonna be fine. It's good that you were honest enough to tell me about it now instead of our finding out later."

"Sir, I just want to reiterate that I'm more concerned for those girls than myself," Val said as he and Nate were about to step out the door. They walk to their hooch in silence awhile before Val finally said. "I fucked up really bad, didn't I?"

"No!" Nate was frustrated to hear Val even say such a thing. "Any of us would have done the same thing."

"I just wonder why I didn't stop before I killed him," Val said morosely.

"Brother, you can't think like that! It's easy for anyone who hasn't been in that situation to say you should've stopped. None of know how we're going to react until we're in the middle of it! You weren't consciously thinking of killing him—you were defending the girl's life, and your own life. Don't you think he'd have killed you if he had the chance? He could've easily grabbed his rifle if you'd let up. Anyway, fuck him. Rapists are just a notch above child molesters." Nate said.

"Thanks for being here for me, brother," Val said as he slapped Nate on the back.

§ § § § § §

"Goddamnit! What the fuck do we do about this?" Papa said as he held his head in his hands. Papa then looked up at Yeary and Overstreet. "Captain, have you heard anything about this over any of your intel networks?"

"No, sir. We probably won't for a while. Unfortunately the next time we hear about it is if they take their revenge on the store. But really, who knows? They may not even care that this guy's gone missing."

"Who do you think the soldier worked for, based on the uniform description?" Papa said.

"Sounds like a member of the Political Bureau Guard, sir."

"Who?"

"Guards assigned to members of the communist party, sir."

"So there was a member of the bureau in Dong Hoi a couple days ago?"

"Well, maybe not officially—most likely some guards on liberty, sir."

"So why do you think no one will care if the man went missing, considering his job?"

"Well sir, a lot of these guys hang out at places within the NVA and the PRVAF, sort of like the KGB of Russia. They're feared and therefore hated by many enemy troops. I intercept messages about these guys disappearing, and I've had reports of their bodies turning up. So it's likely that his superiors will think he's just another statistic, sir."

Papa looked up at Yeary. "What do you think, Commander—should we take this up the chain or handle it ourselves? I think I can make it disappear if we handle it. I think I can minimize it even if it goes up the chain, but I don't know how they'd handle it if the press got wind of it."

"Captain Jordan is quite concerned for the girls at the store, sir. He feels guilty about this enough already, and I've personally seen far worse than this—premeditated murder even—get swept under the rug. But it's ultimately your decision."

Papa leaned back and sighed. "How many people know about this?"

"So far only the three of us and Captain Jordan and Lieutenant Robinson," Yeary said.

"You think you can keep this away from prying eyes if something comes across the boards?" Papa asked Overstreet.

"Absolutely, sir," the captain replied. He was definitely willing to help the man who'd saved his life.

"All right." Papa then shouted out to his assistant. "Corporal, get in here!"

"Yes, sir?" the corporal asked as he opened the door.

"Go get Captain Jordan and Lieutenant Robinson and bring 'em here. They should be in their hooch."

"Aye, sir."

When Val and Nate arrived and found themselves standing in front of the three other officers at attention, they felt as if they were in a court martial.

"At ease, gents—take a seat," Papa ordered. "I'll get right to the point. The three of us have been mulling over this all morning, and after listening to all the facts I've decided on a course of action." Val took a deep breath and swallowed the lump in his throat again. "Captain Jordan, you are suspended from flight duty until further notice. You are also suspended from trips to Dong Hoi for one week. I'd take you off that duty for good, but you're still the best man for the job. Besides, the base would die if those runs were suspended for much longer than a week. You'll continue supply runs to Dong Hoi after the week is up, but try to use different sources if possible, to avoid drawing attention to the girls you're so concerned about. I'll reinstate your flight status after your next review, and this goes on your fitness report. Besides, your tour is almost over, so there are some decisions to be made. This has been a tragic turn of events, and I believe what you told Commander Yeary. Just don't let me find out that even a fraction of your story was fabricated, or else further disciplinary action will result. Do you understand, Captain?"

"Yes, sir." Val couldn't look Papa in the eye. He knew his CO was disappointed in him.

"Lieutenant Robinson, you will not tell another soul about this. If the brass hears about it, careers could be destroyed, and those girls could pay with their lives. You and everyone in this room better watch their tongues at the pub, understood?" Papa gave everyone a look that said they'd answer to him personally if word got out.

"Yes, sir!" was everyone's response. They knew Papa was really sticking his neck out for his men by not informing his superior officers, so respect and admiration for the aviation legend grew even more by the men in the room.

"Do you have anything to add, Captain Jordan?" Papa was fishing to see if Val was trying to keep anything else inside.

"No sir."

"Were you about to tell me about this when you got back from Dong Hoi, son?"

"Yes, sir."

"Well dammit—next time, don't wait to talk to me about anything. Yes, I am your CO, but I'm concerned about the welfare of my Marines. Don't keep secrets; we can deal with just about any problem right here without it having it go up the chain of command. Captain Overstreet, Commander Yeary, do either of you have anything else to add?"

"No, sir," they replied in unison.

Papa looked back to Val and Nate. "Both you and the Lieutenant are dismissed."

"Wait for me outside, boys," Yeary ordered.

"Aye, sir." Val replied.

Val and Nate stood on Papa's lanai, feeling relieved but disappointed that they wouldn't be flying for a while. Soon the door opened and Commander Yeary joined them. "Walk with me," he said.

As they walked slowly down the road, Yeary said, "I told you Papa was a reasonable man, Captain. He just went above and beyond for you without batting an eyelash. Make sure you return the favor by continuing to be the best flight crew you can be when you get back in the air."

"We will, sir—I promise," Val answered.

"Just because right now you got off rather easy doesn't mean this is over. This still has a good chance of coming back to haunt us, whether directly to us or the girls in Dong Hoi."

"Is there anything we can do for them, sir?" Val asked.

"Not really. The only way they're guaranteed safety is if no one finds out about this or they get some protection from the Vietnamese government. Also remember that even though you don't feel guilty about killing that man and even have a good reason not to, it doesn't mean that killing another human being is something to celebrate."

Val was a little offended. "Sir—I don't feel like I was anything but humiliated by the whole event. I don't feel proud of what I did, and if I gave that impression, I apologize. I feel shitty about it all and I lost sleep over it. I appreciate that so far I've gotten off rather easy, but I still feel horrible."

The chaplain let Val go on until he was finished, then said, "Relax, Captain—I'm on your side. I just was making sure your feelings didn't change just because you didn't get stiffer punishment. I know that for you not being able to fly is punishment enough. Both of you are fine officers and a great team—a real asset to the corps. Please feel free to talk to me whenever you want. In fact, I'd appreciate it if you'd join me at the pub."

Nate looked at his watch and laughed. "It's only one o'clock! Hell—it works for me!"

Val laughed. "Sorry for venting, sir. I could really use a beer right now."

"That's all right, son. I knew you needed to vent a little. So now I'm gonna buy you guys a couple of beers."

"And we'll let you, sir," Val added with smile.

§ § § § §

After a week finally passed, Val was allowed to continue his supply runs to Dong Hoi. With no way to find out what was happening to his friends at the store, especially Nga Nghin Do'i, the week had dragged by. During the week, he'd checked with Captain Overstreet to see if there'd been any reports of the store being attacked, but so far there'd been nothing. Now, Val drove the big truck as fast as it could go over the dirt road, but he slowed down as he finally approached Dong Hoi. On the west side of the Nhat Le River, he looked to the north and could barely distinguish the Twin Villages from the numerous watchtowers in the hazy air over the steamy rice paddies. Traffic had picked up a bit, and he had to weave through the bicycles, pedestrians, vehicles, ox carts, and beasts of burden. Finally Val pulled up to the store and was relieved to see no new damage. He jumped out of the truck and sprinted inside.

As Val entered, he was greeted by Nghia Mau and Nga Nghin Do'i, both sporting huge smiles. "Thought you never be back!" Nga Nghin Do'i said in English.

"It's been too long! I've been worried sick about all of you"—Val embraced Nga Nghin Do'i and whispered in her ear—"especially you!"

Nga Nghin Do'i felt her heart beat faster for a couple of seconds and returned the embrace even tighter and whispered, "I missed you, too."

They embraced for almost a minute, and when they pulled apart, their faces were a mere inch apart. Their eyes met with a new purpose, and they trembled as they felt something different in the air. Their lips were almost touching, and they could feel the other's breath and heartbeat. They held the gaze for another few seconds, moved closer, then separated at the last moment when they felt all the eyes upon them. Nghia Mau stood there with a warm, soft smile that clearly her approval of her friends' growing closeness.

Nga Nghin Do'i smiled coyly and blushed as she looked at Nghia Mau, who nodded to her. "Come—bring list," she said as she took Val's hand and led him to her office. He could feel the gentle strength in her grip from years of sewing and working with her hands. Val gripped her hand a bit tighter, to see how she'd react, and to his delight, she squeezed his hand, then let their fingers intertwine. He suddenly felt light headed, and he felt like he was floating. They walked into her office and sat together behind her desk. As she began to go over the list she was about to reach for a pen when she realized they were still holding hands. Her right hand was still snuggly in Val's grip. She flushed and laughed softly. "Can I have my hand back?"

Val chuckled. "Nope. I like it where it is."

She knew that Val was flirting with her. "How can I write?" she said with a smile.

"I'll write for you. You just tell me what you want me to put down."

At first she thought she would protest, but then she decided to go along with him. "Okay—but you have to write in Vietnamese."

"I'll do my best," he replied.

They began to go over his list, and as she called out each item, she'd tell him if it was in stock and how much it cost—holding hands all the while. Every once in a while or the other would give a gentle squeeze, which was immediately returned. Occasionally they found themselves tracing the inside of the other's palm with their thumb, and as they did they looked deeply into each other's eyes. Something was clearly evolving between them.

Nga Nghin Do'i continued down the list, mentally converting the local currency into dollars. Her prices were the most reasonable anywhere he could have found, and when she said, "Condenser for air conditioner. In stock. Twenty dollars,"

"Okay—got it," he said, amazed that she actually had such a thing in stock. She explained that she had several old air conditioners that were actually from American military bases in Saigon. Val asked how she'd acquired such appliances, but she seemed to dodge the question. When Val saw it made her uncomfortable, he decided not to press the issue, but it lingered in the back of his mind. There was still so much he wanted to know—not only about the store and its employees, but about Nga Nghin Do'i, for reasons that had nothing to do with business.

"Nine planed one-by-eight boards, five feet long. In stock. Nine dollars."

"Got it," he said. She'd barely look up as she mentally went through her store's inventory, which she knew so well. She'd never missed an item he asked for and never misquoted a price.

"One twenty-pound box of eight-penny common nails. In stock. Two dollars."

"Got it." Her prices were so fair that he never felt the need to haggle.

"Twenty reams of typing paper. In stock. Two dollars."

"Got it."

"One hug because we finished. In stock. Free."

Val wasn't sure if he heard correctly. Vietnamese women weren't usually so forward—and when he looked up at her, she was blushing, as if she was shocked that she'd said such a thing. He smiled. "I definitely got that!" They stood and tightly embraced.

As they embraced, she asked, "Do you have some time after we load the truck?"

"Yes. Why?"

"Come to village with me. I want you to meet someone."

"Absolutely." Val jumped at the chance because he didn't think he'd be welcome there again. When she started to step back, Val pulled her in tighter, and she let herself fall back into his embrace, now holding him even tighter than before. She sighed softly, and in a moment they synchronized their breathing.

Neither wanted to part, but they knew they still had work to do. When they ended the embrace, Nga Nghin Do'i leaned in and gave him a kiss on his cheek. It was more than just a peck, and he felt it was a message. He returned the kiss, then as they backed away from each other, their eyes locked. In their gaze was an acknowledgement of their desire for each other, and the realization that for now anything more wasn't possible. As they gazed at each other, they heard soft footsteps approaching them from the warehouse. As one of the girls came in, she handed her the list of items to get. The girl smiled as she sensed the romantic tension in the air. Then she disappeared back into the warehouse.

Both Nga Nghin Do'i and Val were a little flustered as they smiled sheepishly. "Well, I, uh...I should help get things, uh...loaded," he stammered. "Yeah." She giggled as they made to move in opposite directions and wound up bumping into each other. As they danced around each other, Val dropped his hands to her waist and she raised her hands to his shoulders. Again their eyes met as they quickly backed away with a smile.

It wasn't long before the girls had everything loaded and Val and paid the bill. Nghia Mau and Val chatted until Nga Nghin Do'i interrupted them by saying goodbye and waving. As she walked outside to climb into the cab of the truck, Val looked at Nghia Mau, but before he could speak again, she smiled and gestured toward the truck. She knew what was developing between this American and her dear friend. "*Xin loi! Toi day de lam gi vay?*"—Sorry! What are you still doing here? She then added, "*Du'ng co lo, den do chi! Tao heiu!*—Don't worry about me, go to her! I understand!

Val looked at the truck and saw Nga Nghin Do'i running her fingers through her long black hair. He looked back at Nghia Mau and blushed face. He thanked her, bowed and gave her a hug, then ran toward his truck.

She smiled at him as he climbed into the cab and fired up the engine, and within moments the truck was in gear and heading toward the Twin Villages. The drive through town took awhile, but once they were out in the countryside and on the west bank of the river, there was almost no traffic, and in seven or eight minutes they reached the villages. Just as on his previous visit, Val's truck drew a lot of attention as it lumbered along.

Nga Nghin Do'i had Val park just south of the *Bac Lang* (North Village), and she jumped out and signaled for him to walk with her into the village. She led him into the village center and then to the row of huts on the west side, then she turned left and made her way to the hut at the southwest corner of the village, people shouting greetings to her the whole way. When they arrived, she told him to wait outside while she went in. After a few moments, he could hear her approaching the door, speaking with a man. They were speaking loudly at first, and Val sensed that she'd told the man that the American waiting outside the door could understand Vietnamese.

After a few more moments, she emerged from the hut and signaled for Val to come closer. "Come—I want you to meet someone!" She wore a look of pride.

Soon an elderly Vietnamese gentleman came out from the hut wearing western-style casual clothes. He gave a gentle smile, but there was a look of wariness on his face. "Val, this is my uncle, Nhiem-vu Phuc-Nguyen." She held her smile as she gestured at the man. Then for her uncle's benefit, she pointed at Val and said, "Captain Valentine Jordan."

Val bowed to show respect, but the man stopped him and held out his hand to shake. Val shook the man's hand, and each noticed that the other's grip was firm. As they shook, Val realized that the man's name meant "a duty to reconstruct." That was interesting. Val asked Nga Nghin Do'i, "Is this the uncle who worked at the embassy?"

"Yes, I am," Nhiem-vu Phuc-Nguyen said sternly.

"Yes—and he taught you English too!" Val smiled at the man, who was clearly still studying him. "Pleasure to meet you, sir. What did you do at the embassy, sir?"

"I studied the American lifestyle, so to speak."

"I take that to mean you were in clandestine operations," Val said matter-of-factly.

Nhiem-vu Phuc-Nguyen was surprised that the American didn't seem judgmental or intimidated. "That would be more or less correct."

Val surprised the gentleman with his directness again. "You've been to the Soviet Union, you speak English well, you must command respect among the people here, so you don't have to answer if you don't want to, but I'm guessing you're some kind of representative for this region in the Hanoi government since you live up there."

"Correct again. I am a member of the Communist Party." Nhiem-vu Phuc-Nguyen waited for the American's reaction. "Does that bother you?"

"Why would it?"

Nhiem-vu Phuc-Nguyen was surprised again. "You're an American serviceman. Aren't you trained to hate Communists?"

"I disagree with communism, sir, but I don't hate everyone who's a Communist. I dislike the system we're supposedly here fighting against, but not the people we're fighting. I try not to hate, sir, but yes—I do disagree with people from time to time."

"That's shocking, Captain, but in a good way." Nhiem-vu Phuc-Nguyen had traveled the world and, like Val, had learned to appreciate other cultures, and Val impressed him. "I think you Americans are going to lose this war." He wasn't sure if his remark was intended to test or provoke Val.

"We've already lost, because our government doesn't care if we win or not. They just want to make a quick buck at the expense of people's lives. Our leadership won't let us fight the way we need to fight in order to win, so I won't disagree with you on that."

"What will your country do if the Communist Party takes over?" Nhiem-vu Phuc-Nguyen had been to the US and seen firsthand the power the country could marshal, He knew the American was right.

"We can't be here forever, sir. The people of this country will ultimately decide what they want for themselves, and if that's communism, so be it. They may regret it down the line, but that's for them to find out. I can't and don't want to change how people think."

Nhiem-vu Phuc-Nguyen knew the American was a good, honest man, so he lowered the wall he'd put up. He gestured at the village and said, "Come, Captain—let's walk. Stay for dinner if you can, I would be honored."

Val now knew that he was almost obliged to stay, so he looked at his watch, which showed 1145. "I can stay for dinner, but I have to be back at base by sunset."

Nhiem-vu Phuc-Nguyen understood. "That's plenty of time, Captain."

After walking in silence for a bit, Val said, "You have two lovely villages here, sir. It's so peaceful. I've enjoyed meeting the villagers and I greatly appreciate their hospitality."

Nhiem-vu Phuc-Nguyen looked around and smiled. "Yes. I grew up here, as did Nga Nghin Do'i. It has not always been so peaceful here, Captain. Many people in these very villages over many generations have suffered greatly in the many conflicts that have torn our land apart over the centuries. However, you are correct—the people have retained their generous and hospitable spirit despite the immense suffering. All we have is hope—hope that one day our land will finally be at peace and the suffering will come to an end. Whenever we think we have achieved that, another foreign army comes into our land and tries to tell us how to run our lives." He looked hard at Val for his reaction.

Val understood the purpose of the last remark, but he didn't totally disagree. Of course he was loyal to his country and the corps, but he knew that the US had been in the wrong before in its short history. "I'm not here to tell anyone how to run their life, sir. I'm here because I was ordered here by my government, who is my employer. There are many Americans who don't agree with this war, and despite the general perception of us, we are not all rich. Many Americans understand suffering, just as you do. We're not to blame for all the suffering in this land, sir. Many of your own countrymen cause much pain to their fellow citizens, sir. I've seen it firsthand." Val glanced at Nga Nghin Do'i, who was playing with some children in the middle of the village.

Nhiem-vu Phuc-Nguyen noticed that as Val looked over at his niece, he was struggling with his emotions. "What do you mean by that, Captain? I know how cruel and inhumane the opposing sides of this war are to each other, but what have you seen?"

"You know Nghia Mau, sir?"

"Of course I know Nghia Mau. She lives in this village and she and my niece own a store together that I helped them acquire." Nhiem-vu Phuc-

Nguyen was revealing a personal side to Val. "You could say that Nghia Mau and I are very fond of each other, Captain."

"So you care about Nghia Mau, sir?"

"Very much so."

"So why is her store being attacked regularly by violent vandals—and who are they to begin with?" Val deliberately kept silent about Nga Nghin Do'i attempted rape.

"Her store is being attacked?" Nhiem-vu Phuc-Nguyen asked, astonished.

"Yes, sir. I don't ask for much from anybody, sir, but please, can you get the attacks to stop? I worry about the women who work there. Maybe they're afraid to ask you. I care a lot for them—and especially your niece."

Nhiem-vu Phuc-Nguyen added concern to his tone of anger as he looked over at Nga Nghin Do'i. "You are fond of my niece. I can tell she's fond of you because her eyes light up whenever she speaks of you. You seem like an honest man, Captain. I will find out who is attacking the store and put a stop to it." Nhiem-vu Phuc-Nguyen leaned into Val. "Understand one thing, Captain. It will be impossible for you and my niece to ever have more than a business association, especially with this war going on. You Americans think everything will have a happy ending, but life is not always that way. Besides, you would have to lose so much in order to make it work, and you Americans cannot seem to let go of too many material things. After all, you may think you care for her, but the truth is that she's really an exotic curiosity you wish to indulge in."

"You've never been more wrong, sir. I wouldn't bring up the attacks to you if I didn't care. I wouldn't help them if I didn't care. I'm willing to give up everything for people I care about—my country, my so-called possessions, my livelihood, my freedom, my life. I may have done that already in a way you don't know. You don't know me yet, sir; so don't be quick to judge. As for your niece, she's an incredible person, not an exotic curiosity, and I love the person she is!" Val was startled to hear himself utter the word "love" with such conviction.

Nhiem-vu Phuc-Nguyen realized he'd struck a nerve and decided not to insult something the American was so passionate about again. "Forgive me, Captain—I have overstepped my bounds. Tell me more about yourself and where you come from."

They continued to talk as they walked around, and Nhiem-vu Phuc-Nguyen introduced him to almost everyone, giving Val a history lesson along the way. Nhiem-vu Phuc-Nguyen revealed how he'd personally witnessed members of his own village being shot right in front of him or being locked inside a hut that set was ablaze. He remembered their screams as they were either asphyxiated or burned to death. He remembered cries of women being raped or the agony of parents when their children perished.

At some point he decided to do something to end the suffering. He began by working under a leader in the resistance against the French, eventually taking command of a unit. He made friends with a visionary resistance leader named Nguyen Tat Thanh, a man with many aliases over his long career. The two men became good friends, and when Nguyen Tat Thanh moved to London, he invited Nhiem-vu Phuc-Nguyen to come along. Both learned many languages and served in various political posts, and it was in London where they began to publish papers about Indochinese independence. They asked President Truman and later President Eisenhower for US help to get foreign militaries out of their country, and in return the US would get unlimited trade and access to ports in Indochina. Somehow, Nguyen Tat Thanh angered Truman and later Eisenhower after he told them that they were wasting their time in Korea and that Vietnam was a more important fight. It would be an easy victory for the United States to kick the French out, since he and his resistance had already successfully pushed the Japanese out in 1945. He angered Truman even more when he appealed to several members of Congress and actually almost had Congress interested. The president felt that this Indochinese revolutionary had now overstepped his bounds; so in order to persuade Congress not to stray, he did the one thing that would guarantee American antipathy—label the revolutionary a Communist.

When Nguyen Tat Thanh got word about what happened, he and Nhiem-vu Phuc-Nguyen began flirting with communism. Because the response from the West was so slow, they realized the West wouldn't help them kick out the French and gain independence, so they formed the Vietnamese Communist Party and sought help from the world's most powerful Communist country—the Soviet Union. Somewhere along the line, Nguyen Tat Thanh got a new alias—Ho Chi Minh, the "bringer of light." Most of his supporters affectionately called him *Bac Ho* (Uncle Ho). He then changed Nhiem-vu Phuc-Nguyen to the name he actually went by—Dat Tren Nguyen, his real name. However, Nhiem-vu Phuc-Nguyen—"a duty to reconstruct"—was much more appropriate for their cause.

Val was mostly curious about Nga Nghin Do'i's history, and her uncle divulged a lot about her past without getting too personal. He told the story of how she got her name on the day she was born, when every villager stopped by to see the most beautiful baby anyone had ever seen. She'd smiled and seemed happy no matter who was cradling her in their arms, so her name seemed to suit her perfectly. He told Nghia Mau's story and how her gentle spirit allowed her to take in orphaned children and how she extended the same kindness to every person she met. He didn't leave out the dark stories of the tragedy of constant war and foreign armies attacking the villages, and how the women had to hide in the jungles far to the west to avoid being raped. He described how Nghia Mau lost her ability to have children, and how the village also coped with devastating storms that all but wiped out their rice paddies.

Each tragic story was a testimony to the resiliency of the people in these villages, and Val knew this was true for people all over Vietnam. He saw how these people knew how to be happy even though they owned practically nothing of material value. He saw how loyal spouses were to each other and how tight family units were. Through them he could see how shallow many Americans were, and how Americans often cared about things that meant nothing in the grand scheme of things. His life back in America seemed devoid of meaning by comparison. Back home, people were generally rude and untrusting, but here as he interacted with the villagers, he began to feel as if he was part of the village. He knew they had good reasons to be wary, but they seemed to be good judges of character and welcomed him, even though he represented the foreign enemy. Val still didn't know how to feel about Nga Nghin Do'i's uncle, who represented the very system he was sent here to battle, but since he was in this tranquil place he suspended his warrior role.

Time seemed to fly as Val enjoyed the company and food, but eventually it was time to go leave. Many of the villagers followed him outside to bid him goodbye, and Nhiem-vu Phuc-Nguyen and Nga Nghin Do'i escorted him back to his truck.

"It was an honor to finally meet you, sir, and I hope to see you again," Val said as he shook hands with Nga Nghin Do'i's uncle.

"I'm sure we will meet again, Captain. We will probably see each other several times if you come back to our villages again." Nhiem-vu Phuc-Nguyen smiled and took a step back, then nodded at Nga Nghin Do'i as if he were giving her permission for something.

Nga Nghin Do'i then took Val by the arm and led him around the truck to the driver's side, where they stood by the door looking deep into each other's eyes, hands interlocked. "Thank you for coming with me back to the villages," she said with a smile.

Val smiled back at the Vietnamese beauty. "The pleasure is always mine. I like it here." But as much as he would have liked to remain, Val knew he had to go, or else stranded on a dark road deep in enemy territory. He also knew he might be disciplined if he was too late. "I have to go," he said. "I'll be back very soon." He saw that Nhiem-vu Phuc-Nguyen was no longer standing on the other side of the truck.

As Val began to climb into the can, she pulled him into her arms and embraced him tightly. "Thank you for all your kindness, Val." She then gently grasped Val's face in her hands and gave him a lingering kiss on the lips, a kiss filled with passion.

That left Val in a love-struck daze. She'd never called him by his first name, nor had she ever kissed him on the lips. He had no recollection of starting the truck and driving home.

§§§§§

Even though Val and Nate wouldn't be flying the night's mission, they attended the briefing because it was important to show support for the other crews. Val might not be flying tonight, but he'd achieved hero status because he'd found the part needed to fix the air conditioner in the shack. Papa was pleased to see them in the Cannery sweating it out with the others, and after the briefing he went over and shook their hands and said that the suspension should end soon. For Val and Nate it felt like an eternity, though it had only been two-and-a-half weeks. They expected it might be another two weeks or so, but if someone was shot down…well, who knew. They didn't want to contemplate that.

The other crews knew that Val was on suspension but didn't know why. Most came up to him and said how lucky he was to have a two-week paid vacation. Val would tell them that it was no fun and he'd rather be up there flying. They'd hustle to the control tower during a mission to count the jets as they returned, and they'd be relieved when every jet made it back, even if one or two limped in wounded. This went on for another three weeks, and Val was so guilt-ridden that he apologized to Nate nightly for keeping him out of the air—and since there was no other jet to put Nate in, he'd have to wait until Val's suspension was lifted.

After the last sortie, Papa told Val to report to his office at 0700 the following morning, and Val was there promptly, knocking on the door. When he entered, he saw Papa and Commander Yeary looking over some files on Papa's desk, and Papa was making some notes. He looked up. "At ease, Captain—sit down." Papa continued writing for a few more minutes, then finally stopped writing and looked up. "I'm tired of lying, Captain."

"Sir?"

"People want to know why one of our best pilots was grounded, and I had to lie because I couldn't reveal the real reason. So when people ask you, it was because of issues back home that you needed time to straighten out. Got it?"

"Yes, sir."

"Now, Captain"—Papa flipped through Val's fitness report—"you have an outstanding record of service with the corps. I'm going to reinstate your flight status effective immediately. However"—Papa shut the file and picked up a stack of papers—"you have some decisions to make. Do you know what these papers are?"

"No, sir."

"Your tour here is over at the end of the month. You can either go home and finish your tour with the corps there"—Papa looked deeper into Val's eyes— "or you can reenlist for another tour here, where pilots like you are badly needed. If you do decide to go home, I'd like to recommend you for combat instructor so you can get new pilots as prepared as possible before they're shipped here. It's your choice, Captain, but I need your decision before the end of the day." Papa turned to Yeary. "Anything to add, Chaplain?"

"Yes, sir." Yeary looked directly at Val. "Captain, you've had one helluva tour over here. No one will fault you, no matter what you decide. Just think it over carefully."

Val didn't hesitate as he reached for the papers, thoughts of going home all but gone as he recalled Nga Nghin Do'i's embrace. "Where do I sign, sir?"

Both officers were surprised that Val decided so quickly. "Now I know you're crazy, Captain," Papa said with a hearty laugh.

"What made you sign so quickly, son?" Yeary asked.

"There's nothing to go home to, but good things are happening here," Val said, smiling.

"Well glad to have you back, son—and your luck continues, because you got Alert-5 duty with Notso and Speedy. Enjoy the air-conditioning!"

For the first time, Val left the office without making a wisecrack on the way out. He went straight to his hooch, grabbed his gear, and walked to the shack where Nate, Notso, and Speedy were already settled in. As he walked in, he shouted, "So who's got the pink slip to the Charger right now? I want it!"

His friends jumped up and shook his hand, and asked if everything was okay back home. and Val said that it was. Before long the cards came out and another poker game began.

§ § § § §

It was 0500, the dead calm of early morning, when the red phone rang and the alarm sounded to wake the crews in the shack. Val grabbed the phone along with an ordnance technician and listened to the situation as everyone else put their gear on and ran to ready the jets. A line of B-52s and A-6s were returning from an early morning raid on Hanoi when six MiGs jumped them. One A-6 was badly wounded and another was already down. One of the B-52s was seriously wounded and probably wouldn't make it back to base. Both flights were over the South China Sea headed southbound. It would only take a few minutes for the Alert-5s to intercept the flight and drive the MiGs away. The ordnance tech ordered his men to load the jets with air-to-air armaments and only two bombs in case they were needed later. Val quickly briefed the rest of the flight crews as they ran to their jets and strapped in. Moments later the quiet of pre-dawn was shattered as they blasted off into the sky, streaking northeast. The sky was still dark but beginning to lighten as the Alert-5s approached the line of American jets. It was a sight to behold—the giant American bombers streaking contrails in the early morning air. One of them was trailing thick black smoke as well, and every once in a while a flame would light up the trailing edge of its left wing. The RIOs began to search for the MiGs on their scopes and it wasn't long before they picked up several strong returns from the northwest.

"Tally ho! We got five blue bandits eleven o'clock about four miles, still heading toward us. I don't think they see us yet!" Notso said as he could barely make out the outlines of five MiG-21s streaking toward the formation of retreating bombers.

"All right—they'll probably try to target the wounded bird, so let's hide here on the left of the formation and we'll have a straight shot at 'em," Val said. "Where are the A-6s?"

"Strike said they're landing at Yankee Station and are safe," Speedy answered.

"All right, so all we have to do is protect these BUFFs," Nate added. "Let's kick ass!"

"Here they come! They'll be in range of their missiles soon, so let's lock 'em up!" Val ordered as he watched the formation of MiGs line up behind the wounded bomber.

"Got a solid tone," both Nate and Speedy announced as they locked up a pair of MiGs.

"Fox 2!" Notso and Val called as they ripple-fired a pair of Sidewinders each. Notso scored a direct hit and the MiG exploded into a ball of fire. Val's missiles exploded under a MiG's nose and sent it into a flat spin as the nose burst into flames and bent back over the fuselage, not allowing the pilot the chance to eject—if he was still alive.

"Splash one!" each pilot shouted with glee. "Lock up another one before they run!"

The MiGs suddenly saw the two F-4s and broke in different directions for a hasty retreat. The F-4s passed behind the formation of bombers and continued toward the retreating MiGs. They continued trying to close the distance to get another shot when a pilot's panicked voice shrieked in their headsets, "God damn—he's killing us! *Help!*"

All four heads turned to see a MiG firing another missile into the massive wounded bomber and beginning strafing runs with its cannon. At once they recognized the fighting style of the MiG's pilot—Colonel Tomb!

"Keep on these guys, Tibbs! I'll deal with this asshole!" Notso shouted as he pulled into an Immelmann and streaked toward the MiG still pouring rounds into the helpless bomber. "Get a solid lock on this asshole, Speedy! I don't want him getting any more chances to come back at the bomber or us!"

"Almost got him!" Speedy said as he frantically worked his scope. "Got him! Fire!"

Notso ripple-fired two more Sidewinders. The first one streaked toward the MiG but suddenly veered left at the last moment and went ballistic. The second switched targets and began to lock onto the burning bomber. Luckily it exploded well short of the B-52 and didn't add more damage to the struggling aircraft. "Shit! You still got him, Speedy?"

"Affirmative. Get him!"

Notso fired two more missiles. "That's my last Sidewinder—we got two Sparrows left!"

The first missile exploded over the spine of the MiG and caught Tomb's attention. The second exploded under his starboard wing and broke off the outer tip.

"We got him now! Switching to guns!" Notso announced.

Tomb fired another missile into the B-52, which caused it roll over. The crew recovered and considered bailing out, but the rear gunner saw the MiG begin to dive away to the northwest in a split-S with a Marine F-4 on its tail, and the crew decided to ride it out all the way home.

"Damn! The MiG is still maneuverable even though it's missing part of its right wing!" Notso said.

Tomb saw Val's jet closing within firing range of another MiG and knew he probably couldn't hold off two F-4s for long with a wounded aircraft, so he aimed at Val's tail.

"Tibbs—watch your six! We're chasing a bandit that's aiming right for you. He's basically Winchester except for guns!" Notso warned Val.

Nate looked over his shoulder just in time to see that the MiG appeared to be trying to ram them. "Break left, Tibbs—this guy's gonna hit us!"

Val broke left and saw the blur of the MiG and Notso zip by in the corner of his eye. He then gave up on the MiG he was chasing and rolled in to assist Notso. "Watch him, Notso—he'll try to make us collide, so I'll stay behind in lag pursuit."

"This bastard isn't getting away today!" Notso shouted.

Tomb stoked his burners, then did something crazy—he rolled into high-g barrel roll, pulled his engine to idle, and dropped all high-lift devices even though he was well above their operating speed. Suddenly Notso found himself shooting by the MiG despite trying to slow down. Tomb knew he'd only have a split-second window in order to make his maneuver work before the second F-4 had him dead to rights. He finished the roll to see the first F-4 climbing into a loop. He pushed the throttle to the firewall as he pitched up and squeezed off a stream of machine gun and cannon fire, then pushed over and began to run toward the northwest. Tomb's rounds buried themselves in Notso's starboard engine, which began to smoke and belch fire.

"We're hit, Notso!" Speedy shouted. "Looks like the number-two engine!"

"I'm shutting it off! We're okay—all other systems are go!" But Notso knew that his performance would be limited on just one engine, so he had to hope they wouldn't encounter any more MiGs.

"I'm above you at your four o'clock, Notso. You look okay!" Val called, then mimicked Papa: "Dammit, Colonel Tomb—you'll get yours soon enough!"

"The bombers are safe now, guys. We each got a kill, so let's call it a good morning and go home," Nate said as he looked toward the south and the breaking dawn.

"Notso, I'm gonna fly a lazy trail about a mile and a half behind you in case you have any more problems with your jet," Val said. "Let's swing around to northeast of Linh Thu to sweep the area of any remaining MiGs."

The flight approached to twenty miles of Linh Thu, and both crews were quiet as they looked around in the growing morning light. Suddenly Val caught a glimmer off of polished metal, and Nate saw a target briefly appear on his scope. "Tibbs!" he called, not sure if it was a false target or not.

"I see it!" Val responded and shouted a warning to his wingman. "Watch your six, Notso! I think there's still a MiG around here, but I can't tell for sure." Val then looked to verify his position. They were twenty miles northeast of Linh Thu—in enemy airspace, but in an area almost always clear of enemy traffic, somewhere between Dong Hoi and Linh Thu. "You still got him, Double-O?"

"No—I don't know where he went!" Nate replied.

Val began to scan the sky around his jet, and suddenly another glimmer appeared in front of Notso's jet. Val wasn't sure if it was an aircraft or sunlight reflecting off water on the ground—but it was better to be safe than sorry. "Break right, Notso! He's right in front of you! I'll have a clean shot!"

Notso immediately broke high and right and continued his turn heading north away from Linh Thu. The enemy jet was nowhere to be found—either visually or on radar. What was going on? Val then broke right to join up with Notso, and as soon as he rolled his jet, something caught his eye—a flash of silver directly under him. The MiG was hiding beneath him! When Val rolled inverted, the MiG streaked forward out from under him, and as it passed by his canopy Val saw it was missing its right wingtip. "Colonel Tomb," he hissed. "How did he sneak back around?"

Tomb streaked toward Notso, still completing his turn back toward the south in full knife-edge flight, giving him full planform view for a target. He opened fire with all his guns and his cannon, and Notso's jet absorbed multiple direct hits before the stress of a high-g turn began to force the frame to crunch under the strain. Smoke and fire belched from places all over the jet, and the frame began to warp under pressure. Tomb pitched up into a climb, rolled into a split–S, and again fired into the wounded F-4 when it slipped into his pipper before he broke into a right turn and zipped away.

"Notso, Speedy—get out of there *now!*" Val screamed to his wingmen.

Then an explosion broke the jet into two pieces as it began a flat spin right in front of their eyes. The pieces continued to spiral down through the atmosphere with no signs of life, and Val and Nate could do nothing except shout to get out of the aircraft. Finally they saw the explosion of the ejection sequence as the crew's seats rocketed out of the jet.

"I got one, make that two 'chutes! They're out!" Nate shouted as he watched helplessly.

"Strike, Bowtie 1. Mayday! Mayday! *Mayday!*" Val called out to Strike as he gave them their location. "We got both crew members down! Need immediate rescue air! We're on the Linh Thu zero–one-zero for twenty miles! Move it! Move it!"

Val began an orbit above the parachutes and watched them slam into an open rice paddy bordered by thick jungle to the west. Neither man appeared to be moving or tried to make radio contact. As he orbited, Val knew he'd soon be at bingo fuel. Finally he could see both men crawl toward each other, and it seemed that they were injured. Strike said that a UH-1 and an AH-1 were on their way with an ETA of fifteen minutes, and Val breathed easier. But then he heard Nate in his headset, "Tibbs, look—we gotta do somethin'!"

Val looked down to see a platoon of enemy troops emerging from the jungle with a light armored truck behind them. The troops fired some rounds toward his wingmen. "No! *No!*" Val rolled his jet over and switched to his gun. He had to swing out in order to get a clean shot at the enemy troops and not hit his wingmen.

Nate kept his eyes on his friends as Val turned the jet as quickly as he could. "Hurry, Tibbs—they're almost on them!"

"I'm getting there!" Val strained under the heavy g-forces as he finally rolled out and began a strafing run from the north to the south. He could see one of friends take a hit from an enemy round. "No!" Val opened fire and the cannon dropped several troops, but there were many more behind them. He knew it was going to take a long time between runs; he needed that AH-1 here to assist right now! "Where are you, Chariot Flight?" Val called out to the rescue flight.

"ETA nine minutes."

"This is gonna be over in five. Move your asses!"

Val set up for another run, but the enemy troops were rapidly closing the distance, so he cut in early on this run. His cannon roared, dropping a few more troops as they returned fire at him with their rifles. Soon he was over-shooting them and would have to turn around. The enemy troops picked up their pace to get to the Americans before the jet could swing around for another pass. Val set up for a perfect run, but to his horror he saw it was too late! The enemy had surrounded Notso and Speedy and were viciously beat-ing them with their rifle butts. Even at this altitude and speed he could make out the blood on their flight suits faces. He couldn't fire without hitting them. He'd never felt so helpless in his life! "No-no-no—this isn't happening!" he shouted as he watched helpless from above, unable to assist. He watched as they were dragged to a truck, being beaten and kicked every so often until they were thrown inside. Just as the truck began to disappear into the thick vegetation of the jungle, his jet's low–fuel warning echoed through his head-set. "Nooo!" Val choked back tears, knowing he had to leave, unable to help or even find out if they were okay.

The rescue flight arrived just as Val began to climb away for his return to Linh Thu. With a quivering voice he let Strike know what had happened and that the rescue mission had to be scrapped. As Val and Nate flew back in hor-rid disbelief, they didn't speak. The only sound in the cockpit was the occa-sional choked-back sob. Five miles out, Vietnamese voices came over frequency and spoke for about forty-five seconds. Obviously the enemy troops had found Notso and Speedy's search-and-rescue radios, adding insult to injury.

What was supposed to a triumphant return to flying and reenlisting for another tour ended up being the darkest day of Val's tour in Vietnam.

13

THERE BUT FOR FORTUNE

They tasted blood. It ran down their faces and flowed from their noses. It filled their nasal cavities, making breathing almost impossible. It was salty and metallic, almost like soy sauce. Speedy and Notso tried to open their eyes, but realized there was no point as they were blindfolded. The pain was indescribable, and the bumpy road made it worse.

They had a natural urge to wipe the blood from their faces, but they couldn't move their hands or feet without choking themselves because their hands were tied behind their backs and connected to their feet by a single rope that was knotted around their throats. If they tried to move their arms or straighten out their legs, they'd put pressure on their own windpipes and strangle themselves. There wasn't going to be any relief for a long time—not until the truck reached Hanoi.

Val and Nate landed and climbed out in total silence, their faces flushed with anger and streaked with tears. Their minds had just now begun to absorb what they'd just witnessed. They wiped their tears as they walked into the ready room and removed their gear, knowing Papa would soon be debriefing them. They looked over at Speedy and Notso's lockers, absent of flight gear. It was sinking in—their friends were really gone, possibly dead. Both men sat in silence, staring at the empty lockers.

Soon enough they were ordered to report to HQ, and when they walked into the conference room, they saw Papa, Chappie, Big John, Commander Yeary, Captain Overstreet, and Lieutenant Torres sitting on the other side of the table, legal pads and pens before them. They each wore the same shattered look that Val and Nate wore.

"Sit down, gents," Papa said.

Chappie poured Val and Nate each a glass of water and set it in front of them. "Here you go, men. I know this is hard, but we need to debrief now, while it's fresh in your minds."

"Take your time. Whenever either of you are ready, just go ahead and speak," the chaplain added reassuringly.

"Sorry about your friends, young'uns—we gotta know what happened," Big John added.

After a bit of uncomfortable silence, Papa decided to get some of the other information he needed first, then he'd just ask Val and Nate some yes–and-no questions. He looked at Overstreet and said, "Captain, have you heard anything about my boys on any enemy lines of communication yet?"

"No sir, but I expect to soon. My personal belief is that they are going to the Hanoi Hilton, where NVA takes most aircrews and high-profile POWs."

"Lieutenant Torres," Papa said as he turned toward him. "do you know what route the NVA usually used to move POWs? Might we have a chance to intercept them?"

"Sorry, sir, their routes are varied, and by now they're too close to Hanoi. The rescue flight Captain Jordan called out to assist lost sight of them in the jungles."

Papa sighed. At least four members of his squadron were now in POW camps somewhere in North Vietnam, and there was nothing he could do about it. "How was a MiG able to catch them so easily?" he said.

Val spoke up and the entire room got quiet. "The MiG faked us out. We thought he'd run home, but apparently he dropped to the deck and snuck up behind us. Notso'd lost his number-two engine." A tear began well up in Val's eye and stream down his cheek. "We saw a glint ahead of us that I thought was a MiG, but apparently it was just the sun reflecting off water on the ground. I told Notso to break so I could cover him—that was a mistake that might have cost them their lives. When Notso did break, he was easy prey for the MiG that snuck up under me. It happened so fast—the MiG shot him down before I could get into a position to assist. I could have got a shot off as the MiG ran away, but I was more concerned for my wingmen."

Papa shook his head. "Sounds like the chickenshit Colonel Tomb. Was it him?"

Val wiped the tear from his cheek and replied, "Yes, sir." He slammed his right fist into his left palm and added, "I wanna kill that son of a bitch, sir! I *will* kill him, even if I have to break the Rules of Engagement to do so, sir!"

Every man in the room felt Val's rage. "We understand your anger, Captain, but don't get yourself a court martial. That won't help Notso and Speedy," Chappie said.

Val and Nate were in no mood to debate the rules that Washington had burdened them with. Uncharacteristically, Nate blurted out angrily, "No more bullshit! How do you know Colonel Tomb, Papa? How can we stop him?"

No one knew how to react to what amounted to insubordination, but Papa dropped his head for a second, then sighed. He knew he should come clean—especially to his best flight crew. "His name's not really Tomb—it's Victor Makarov, a prominent Soviet family. His grandfather founded what's now the largest handgun maker in Russia. My first of many run-ins with Makarov was in the skies above Korea. He shot down a lot of B-29s in his MiG-15 before we even had an operational jet fighter in theater—and our first straight-wing jets were no match for the MiG. Finally the F-86 and its naval version came online, and Makarov found it harder to get kills. His only easy kills were new pilots as experienced flyers seldom did worse than score a draw with him. So he developed sneaky tactics, like ambushing aircraft, and it brought his kill ratio back up. Then he started picking on wounded aircraft." They could hear the disgust in Papa's voice.

"I flew several sorties against him, and he and I would have to break it off after long battles because our fuel got low." Now Papa became angry. "Then he started pretending he was out of fuel early and would leave the area, only to sneak back and shoot down aircraft as they were headed back to base or to their carriers. Then he'd shoot at pilots that had ejected as they floated helpless in their 'chutes. That's how he got the name 'Colonel Tomb,' because even if he shot you down, he'd make sure you were dead by killing you in your 'chute if you bailed out. His chickenshit style pissed me off and I'd try to track him down to kill him, but he always got lucky and either escaped or wasn't where I happened to be flying. He's a capable combat pilot and a slightly better than average dogfighter, but he prefers to pick on planes that can't fight back and will do everything to avoid a straight-up, head-on dogfight.

"I hate him. I've seen him murder men hanging in their 'chutes. I've seen him finish off wounded planes, and I've watched him run from me. He knows me, knows I'd love to cut him to pieces, but he's too chickenshit to engage me. We only had the two engagements when he jumped us after a sortie going back to the carrier and were low on fuel and ammo. I wore him down both times, but he ran and I couldn't chase him. We will get him gents—it's just a matter of time; so be patient. What's more important here is that we make sure he doesn't get any more cheap kills on any more of our boys." The pain and anger about Tomb and the loss of his flight crew was apparent in his eyes.

After a moment, Val said, "I don't know how we can keep it from happening again, considering his tactics. He won't get involved in a dogfight when we're in large numbers or know he's there. Every time we surprise him, he flees to the north."

"It's logistically impossible to have more than four aircraft on Alert-5 duty at one time," Papa said. "We just have to carry on as we have so far, but anytime any of our boys gets wounded, we have to cover them better than we have been." Papa sighed as he looked around the room. "You know this is what comes with the territory as fighter pilots. We still have old problems we haven't fixed yet—the SAM attacks, night raids, rocket and mortar attacks, COD flights almost totally eliminated, budget cuts, no replacements for flight crews whose tours end or are killed in action or captured. We haven't hit the panic button yet, and we won't now. All we can do is stick together." Papa looked directly at Val and Nate. "I promise you and all the crews—we *will* get Colonel Tomb, even if I have to look the other way or sweep something under the rug to get it done." Everyone in the room knew Papa would risk just about everything to help his men.

He looked around again before continuing. "Captain Overstreet, Lieutenant Torres, keep digging up all the intelligence you can. I want to solve most of these problems before the end of the next quarter. Jordan, Robinson, get out of your gear and relax the best you can—we'll finish the debrief tomorrow morning. For now get some chow, have a drink at the pub, whatever. The rest of you, carry on. Dismissed."

"Aye, sir!" everyone said as they slowly got up and filed out of the room. Chappie stayed behind and spoke with Papa for a while on some subject no one was able to discern.

§ § § § §

Colonel Tomb walked to his locker and stuffed his gear in it, feeling as confident as ever. A small crowd of PRVAF aviators crowded around him as he pulled out a small poster of a MiG-21 in full afterburner, its guns and cannon blazing. Also on the poster were small stickers of the American flag covering the upper half. Tomb then pulled from the back of the locker a page of small stickers of the American flag. He looked proudly at this poster and drew a smile across his face—he'd had this poster since he graduated flight school in Russia, and it reflected almost two decades of his personal history. He knew he most likely hadn't shot down the B-52 in the sortie he'd just completed, just wounded it, but he did shoot down an F-4. The aviators around him watched as he pressed another American flag to his poster, then cheered and patted him on the back. Tomb gloated as he told his story, not at all shy about embellishing it to make himself seem more heroic.

Captain Phan heard the cheers as he was approaching the ready room. When he turned the corner, he saw the crowd gathered around Tomb. "*Ta di di!"*—Get out of here! he shouted in disgust at his fellow aviators. He wasn't sure if he was more angry at them for not preparing for their sortie, or because they were so easily sucked in by Tomb's lies. When the men began to scatter, Tomb looked angrily at the captain. Phan ignored the Russian for a while as he strapped on his gear, but he could feel the weight of Tomb's stare. Finally he looked hard at Tomb, without fear. *"Cai gi cho!"*—What is it!?

Tomb replied that he was tired of Phan's jealousy and that he was a better pilot than anyone in the PRVAF or Soviet Air Force, and better than any American. Phan had to show more respect to his rank and superior flying skills. Tomb went on to say how Phan was disgracing his country and insulting the USSR with his disdain for the colonel.

Normally Phan ignored Tomb, but this time he the colonel had gone too far. He stepped up to Tomb and shouted, *"Noi lai lan nu'a coi!"*—Say that again! When Tomb repeated his insults, he assumed a combative stance.

Phan looked into the Russian's eyes without fear. This time it was his turn! For anyone to hear, he exposed Tomb for what he was—an arrogant liar and a dishonorable coward, a man who boasted about his kills when he was only brave enough to finish off a wounded aircraft—a man who would kill a pilot hanging helplessly from his parachute.

As Phan turned to leave, it dawned on him that any conversation with the colonel was a colossal waste of time, and angry that he'd even paid any attention to the Russian, he looked over his shoulder and shouted, *"Do so lam! Do ngu so lam! Di xuong dia nguc di!"*—You coward! You idiotic coward! Go to hell!

As the words sank in, Tomb realized that the captain knew the truth—and it was often hard to hear the truth. Even though he had little respect for most of the PRVAF pilots and other personnel, he knew that Phan was a far better pilot than he was. He could either accept things as they were, or get Phan out of his life simply by returning home. But he knew he'd be bored at home, consigned to teaching in a classroom instead of flying. He knew that Phan had something he'd never had—even back home in the Soviet Union—and that was the loyalty, respect, and fear of everyone who served with him.

He knew Phan could embarrass him if he embellished his stories too much. For the most part, he and Phan stayed away from each—and that was Phan's choice. When they had flown together, Phan had actually saved his life a few times. The captain didn't have quite as many kills as he had, but he'd earned almost all of them in honest combat.

§ § § § §

The truck had finally come to a stop, but the bleeding and pain continued. Speedy and Notso lay quietly on the floor, listening to heavy footsteps outside. Soon someone was shouting at them in a language they couldn't understand, and they felt someone rolling them over and heard the sound of a knife being drawn out of its scabbard. Unable to see, they were more scared and helpless than they'd ever been in their entire lives. They had to trust that these people, their enemies, knew that it was wrong to murder them and were responsible for their humane treatment. After all, as far as they knew, North Vietnam were signatories of the Geneva Convention.

They felt the blade cut most of the ropes that bound them, and again someone began shouting at them in Vietnamese, but they had no way of knowing what they were expected to do. Soon they were being pulled toward the back of the truck, and it was now clear that a guard wanted them to get out, but their legs were numb from being bound for so long and they tumbled to the ground when they tried to stand. Their guard kept yelling at them and kicked them each several times. Both weak from loss of blood, when they tried to get up, they were dizzy and unsteady. When blood again flowed through their legs, they sank to the ground again, which earned them more shouting and kicks. After a moment or two, they struggled to their feet and felt a rifle butt nudge them in the kidneys. After they stumbled forward for a bit, their guard suddenly stopped them and viciously tore off their blindfolds, pulling away dried blood and ripping off scabs.

Now they could see the armed NVA soldiers flanking them, shouting and gesturing at a door in a drab building surrounded by concertina wire. The guards pushed them through the door and led them to an office, where they were unsympathetically greeted by an NVA officer seated behind a desk.

"Names?" the officer said. When neither Marine answered, he pointed at Notso. "Give me your name and rank now!"

When Notso refused to answer again, the soldier behind him struck him hard in his left kidney with his rifle butt, knocking him to the ground.

"You make this harder than it should," the officer said. "Now get up!" The officer then looked at Speedy. "Perhaps you got brains! Give me your name and rank now!"

Before Speedy even had a chance to speak, the soldier behind him drove his rifle butt into Speedy's spine. The officer looked at both men. "This is going to be long day! Make it short! Give me name and rank now!"

Speedy finally got up and stood beside Notso, and the soldiers behind them cut their hands free. Notso finally answered for both of them. "Captain Frank Wise, Lieutenant Jamie Sanders."

After writing for a while, the officer handed them some forms and said, "Sign last page."

Notso was amazed that the man had spelled their names correctly, but otherwise neither he nor Speedy could read anything on the papers because

everything was in Vietnamese. When they hesitated to sign, the officer nodded at the soldiers behind them. Immediately both Speedy and Notso felt the
sharp point of a bayonet against the bases of their skulls. The officer pointed
at the papers and said, "Sign!"

Both men signed and wrote in large capitals after their signatures "NBF-
WBBF."

The officer looked at what they'd written and said, "What is this?"

"It's code for our titles and positions," Speedy answered.

The officer was suspicious, but he recalled that almost every American
POW wrote something similar when they signed. Then he spotted a drop of
blood on the page and became angry. "You nearly ruin this! Be neater!"

Speedy and Notso leaned over and said, "Where?"

"Here!" the officer shouted as he pointed to the smudges of blood.

"Where?"

"Here! You blind?"

Speedy and Notso looked at each other, then spit blood on the papers and
the officer's hand. "Is that better?" Speedy said, knowing they'd most likely
take a beating for it.

Which they did as the soldiers struck and kicked them. The officer tossed
two leaflets at them on the ground. "These are rules! You learn rest as you
go!" Then he shouted to the soldiers, "Get these pigs out of here!" He looked
at the letters by their signatures again. He knew that since almost all POWs
put something like it by their signatures, it must be some kind of code. He
didn't care because here he was king and the POWs were at his mercy. Eventually it'd force the answer out of someone.

§ § § § §

The sortie that evening was short as the Playboys landed safely at Linh Thu
without incident. Only one SA-7 was fired at them, but the missile's rocket
motor malfunctioned and burned out at a thousand feet, and the missile
crashed close to where it was launched from. As Val and Nate pulled into their
bunker, they looked over to where Notso and Speedy used to park, and the
emptiness there was still a raw wound. It just wasn't the same without them,
and no matter where they went the emptiness was evident—whether it was in
the sky, in the pub or chow hall—or in their own tent.

Val and Nate walked back to their hooch after having a couple drinks, and
the two empty bunks across from them made them feel like parents who'd lost
their children. It made it hard to sleep, but as often happened, once they did
drift off the thuds of mortars woke them up. Another night raid—a fact of life
at Linh Thu.

§ § § § §

The next morning revealed that the sniper stationed to cover the drainpipe that the commandos were using to enter the base had a busy and successful night as at least ten bodies were being taken away in the bucket of a front loader. Val knew he had some busy days ahead—later today for instance he'd be going to Dong Hoi after a CAP flight to cover A-6s, A-7s, and A-4s returning to Yankee and Dixie stations from a sortie.

Val and Nate were originally supposed to go with another varsity squad crew, but instead they were assigned to fly with the newest crew on their first sortie since arriving in Vietnam. It reminded Val and Nate of their first flight in Vietnam—a CAS flight to help a recon team trapped on the mountainside. The newbies' names were First Lieutenant James "Roostercomb" Cesco, and his RIO, Second Lieutenant Ronald "Never" Wright.

As Papa dismissed the crews after their briefing in the ready room, he pulled the new flyers aside. "Listen, fella"—he pointed to Val and Nate, who were just about out of sight now—"do whatever those boys tell you and you'll do fine. They have loads of experience and will never steer you wrong." Papa smirked. "After all, they learned from me!"

"Aye sir!" Both men smiled back and ran out to the waiting pickup. As Cesco hurried away, Papa mumbled to himself, "Damn, that kid looks familiar! I just don't know where I've seen him before!"

On the ramp, the senior crew looked at the newbies and knew they had to be above average to be assigned to VMFA-2, but they still had no experience. Val and Nate felt personally responsible for them and realized how Papa and Chappie must feel about everyone under them.

Soon the two jets were holding short of runway 31 waiting for the return of Alert-5s from a quick CAS flight. Val and Nate at the other jet staggered behind them on their right wing, then looked at each other in the rearview mirrors. Soon the Alert-5s zipped by and scooted clear of the runway, and the tower gave them their takeoff clearance. "Rhino Flight, Linh Thu Tower, runway three-one cleared for takeoff. Wind light and variable."

"Here we go, brother," Val said.

"Let's break these FNGs in," Nate replied as Val answered the tower.

Val shoved the throttles forward and stoked the burners as his jet roared down the runway in the thick tropical air. Soon Lieutenant Cesco mimicked Val's actions and closed the gap as he joined up to Val's wing.

Val checked in with Panama. "Strike, Rhino 1, CAP flight airborne off Linh Thu will be on station in niner minutes to assist Alpha Strike Four-Zero."

"Strike copies Rhino 1. Alpha Strike Four-Zero should be RTB in one-two minutes. Area clear of bogies for now."

"Roger. Rhino Flight will be standing by on button black."

"We just wait, sir?" Cesco asked Val.

"Affirmative Rhino 2. Level off at angels two-zero for a left hand orbit on the Linh Thu zero-four-zero at two-five," Val replied, adding, "Keep chatter down, the call could come at any second and we need to hear every detail."

The Phantoms continued their orbits for over fifteen minutes and would get the returns of American aircraft returning to their carriers on their scopes, but no MiGs. It seemed like it was going to be a quiet CAP flight, which would be strange because there were always MiGs during Alpha Strikes. Most of the time they just made their presence known and made a few passes and retreated, but lately the pilots were growing bolder and actually engaging the escorting fighters, with little to moderate success. All Val could think of was getting the chance to shoot down the Russian. He actually hoped for Strike to call about some bogies to engage. After ten more minutes, it seemed that the MiGs weren't going to show up, but finally Panama called for them. "Rhino 1, Strike."

"Go ahead, Strike, this is Rhino 1." MiGs? Val's heart was racing, He was almost licking his chops as he pictured blowing Colonel Tomb out of the sky.

"MiGs airborne. Three-zero miles northwest of your position at angels one-niner, four targets heading southeast bound. Fly heading three-two-zero and climb to angels two-five, vector for intercept."

"Rhino 1, Wilco," Val said with a smile, then said to Cesco as he began his climbing turn, "Rhino 2, fall back and trail me by at least one and three-quarter miles. You have to cover my tail, and our loose deuce will prevent us from being downed from any SA-2s."

"Roger, Dash 1." Cesco remembered Papa's advice and did what Val told him.

Panama kept updating the MiGs' position to Rhino Flight, and when they were about fifteen miles from the MiGs, they were nearly in range for the RIOs to get a lock for missile launches. The distance between the MiGs and the F-4s shrank rapidly as they closed at over twelve hundred knots.

"They're turning, Tibbs—I think they've seen us," Nate told Val. "Break right and we can still get the angle."

Val looked up and saw three MiG-21s in a left turn heading back north. "I got 'em, Double-O! One's coming head-on at us. He may try to fire at us!"

The charging MiG zipped over the canopy, then made a sudden but steady left turn back toward the other three. Val and Nate strained to look over their shoulders to track the MiG and saw their wingman suddenly pull in behind it.

"No, Dash 2—break off now! He's baiting you!" Val ordered his eager new flight crew.

"There's the trailer overhead now!" Nate informed Val.

Val looked directly overhead to see another MiG pulling into a hard left break to slide in behind his new wingmen. "Shit! MiG on your six, Dash 2!"

Cesco looked behind him to see a MiG-21 rapidly closing on his tail. He was amazed at how fast the Russian-built jet maneuvered. Wright shouted to his pilot, "Watch out Rooster—we're in a lot of trouble here!"

"I lost him, Never—where'd he go?"

"Shit—he's about got us! Forget the MiG you're chasing! Get outta here!" Wright's heart fluttered wildly as he saw the MiG's cannon winking at them. "He's firing and falling back! He's gonna get us locked up for a missile shot if you don't lose him!"

Val saw the MiG firing but had to wait until it was a little farther ahead so he could match its turn rate. If he broke now he'd overshoot it and end up in front of it. Val knew that his new wingmen didn't have that luxury of time— he had to do something now! Val pulled into a high-g barrel roll in an effort to bleed off some energy and slip in behind the MiG. The MiG kept its tight turn, which inadvertently helped Val by setting him up for the high yo-yo maneuver. He dove in behind his adversary and found the MiG sliding into his pipper dead ahead. It was too close for a missile shot, so he switched to his gun.

"Get him, Tibbs!" Nate gleefully cheered.

Val squeezed the trigger, and the Gatling spewed rounds toward the MiG. Some overshot, but enough found their marks as the MiG shuddered under the explosive-tipped rounds that shredded the airframe and power plant. The pilot immediately stoked the burner and ducked away in a supersonic split-S. "Tail's clear, Dash 2! Watch yourself and don't get over-eager! Now get back and cover my six right this second!" Val ordered his wingman.

"Yes, sir—sorry!"

"Don't be sorry—just watch yourself! We gotta depend on each other out here!" Val then asked Nate, "Got me a tone on any bandits yet, brother?"

"Just one more second and I'll have it," Nate replied. "Got it—fire!"

Val ripple-fired two Sidewinders, and neither tracked their target. The MiG pilots knew that the American strike force was already in safe territory, so it was time to bug out. Val sensed from his experience up here that it was time to leave before the SAM sites began to track them. "Rhino Flight, let's go home—low and fast to avoid SAM launches, keep the loose deuce." Val began a steep diving turn to the south with Cesco in trail.

As they approached Linh Thu, the tower informed them that they had to circle to the south and land on runway three-one as a wounded A-6 was inbound and of course it had priority. Rhino flight complied and orbited twenty miles south while the bomber limped in. Val and Cesco stayed in a low orbit at five thousand feet, awaiting clearance to land. In the orbit, Val looked down and saw a POW camp that the Americans and South Vietnamese used to hold NVA and Viet Cong prisoners. He could clearly see that the prisoners were just lounging, some smoking, some walking around the yard. He wished his friends were getting that kind of treatment, but he knew they weren't—if they were alive.

Before long Linh Thu tower cleared Rhino Flight to land on any runway they wanted, since the winds were light and variable. Val had his flight perform a low overhead break to throw off any SAM launches and landed on runway 31. As both aircraft taxied up to their barricades, Val and Nate felt pangs of sadness when the new guys pulled into the slot for Notso and Speedy's jet. It was going to take some getting used to. As soon as the jets spooled down, the new crew climbed out of their jet and over to Val and Nate's.

"Sir! Can you show us more about flying against these MiGs? I hear that there are two really great MiG pilots that frequent the areas we fly our sorties." Cesco asked.

"Sure—that's why we're here," Nate answered for Val as he hopped down.

"On one condition," Val said as he followed Nate.

"What's that, sir?" Wright asked.

Val pointed to Cesco and said, "Tell me why they call you 'Roostercomb.'"

"You know, sir, I'm quite sure," Lieutenant Cesco said as he removed his helmet. His red locks of hair had pinched up high on the crest of his head, forming a small but short Mohawk that flopped over on one side.

"Never mind. I think I figured it out." Val said as he began to chuckle with Nate and Lieutenant Wright as the four men made their way to the ready room.

"Gotcha," Val said, chuckling. The four men made their way to the ready room.

§ § § § §

Notso and Speedy were thrown into adjoining cells so small that even a small native man would have been cramped. With hardly any light to see by, they tried to get comfortable possible without aggravating the many injuries they'd suffered. Notso reached over to his left shoulder and felt that the wound from the round that had grazed him had finally stopped bleeding, but he knew he was at risk for infection in this damp, dirty setting. There was only a single thin beam of light coming from the crack of a window that had been sealed over. In their separate cells, Speedy and Notso strained to read the pamphlets they'd been given with the prison rules written in bad English.

§ § § § §

RULES FOR POWS

- Bow to all Vietnamese persons when you are in presence
- No talk to other prisoners ever

- Do what you are told by Vietnamese official
- No talk until told
- No food or mail in cell
- No complain
- Prisoners who brake rules will beaten

§ § § § §

Despite his pain, Notso chuckled. *Brake!* He and Speedy could hear another prisoner moaning in pain and then being reprimanded by the guards when he failed to quiet down. In the light from the open doorway to the guard's quarters, they saw him being yanked out of his cell and beaten for five minutes or so before being tossed back into his cell. It was then they really understood how grave their situation was.

§ § § § §

Val climbed into his truck and roared toward Dong Hoi, thinking of Nga Nghin Do'i the whole time. When he got to the store, he was pleased to find out from Nghia Mau that they hadn't suffered an attack in almost five days. She also proudly showed off the new sprinkler system she'd personally installed to protect the store in case it was set on fire when no one was there. Val asked if they'd ever been attacked when no one was there, and after thinking about it for a while, she was stunned to realize that it had only been attacked when they were there. Again he asked if she knew who was attacking the store, and again she parried the question by giving Val a beautiful white lily and told him to give it to Nga Nghin Do'i when she arrived because it was her favorite flower. Val asked, *"Nga Nghin Do'i o' dau?"*—Where is Nga Nghin Do'i?

"Bac. No dang den khoang mu'o'i gio."—Up north. She's coming here about ten o'clock.

Val sat down to tea with Nghia Mau and the girls. Soon the room lit up as she walked in and flashed her radiant smile. She ran up to Val and embraced him and, forgetting the others were there, kissed him on the lips. The girls giggled and whistled, and Nga Nghin Do'i blushed bright red as she took his hand and led him to her office. As they cleared the curtain to the warehouse Val saw a number of huge crates that he'd never seen before.

"Gi thay cai?"—What's that thing? he asked.

She answered in English: "We had a large shipment come in yesterday."

"Shipment of what and for whom?" Val continued, surprised by the volume of crates.

"Gosh you're, uh…" Nga Nghin Do'i was searching for the word in English. "um, *nosy* today!" She smiled as she looked at him, knowing he'd probably keep asking until she gave him a real answer. "It's parts for a machine for one of our other clients."

Val sensed she didn't want to say more, so he didn't press the issue. Instead he sat down next to her.

Nga Nghin Do'i grabbed his list and began to go over the items. As she was scanning it, she asked, "How is the air conditioner working?"

Val smiled as he replied, "Great! We haven't been hot since we got the parts."

"Oh what a shame," she said, dropping her eyes.

Unaware that she was setting him up, he asked, "Why is it a shame?"

"Because me and the girls were hoping that your base would send us more hot men!" Then she giggled and blushed, unable to believe she'd said such a thing.

Val flushed himself as he returned her smile and gently squeezed her hand. "I'm the only hot man you'll ever need, my dear."

She looked deep into his eyes and said, "You are right about that."

Val and Nga Nghin Do'i went about their business as usual, except that now they flirted more. It was all too soon that the girls finished loading Val's truck, and he and Nga Nghin Do'i found themselves again standing on the dock not wanting to say goodbye. Finally they locked in a tight embrace that ended with a long, deep kiss. As they finally pulled apart, their eyes remained locked together. They knew they were falling in love, and at the same time they recognized the obstacles that would keep them apart. As Val climbed into the cab of the truck, she put her arm on the door to prevent him from closing it. "Come to my village tomorrow," she politely demanded with a smile.

Val leaned over and kissed her again, and she gently placed her hand on his face to prolong the kiss. When they finally pulled apart, he smiled and said, "I'm already there!" As he drove away, he watched her waving at him in the rearview mirror until she was out of sight—and when he looked forward again he saw that he was about to drive into a building. He slammed on the brakes, backed up and reoriented the truck. When he was finally rolling in the right direction, he smiled and muttered aloud, "I must be in love!"

§ § § § § §

The briefing for the night's sortie was almost a carbon copy of previous sorties—attack a useless target and risk getting shot down, then try to squeak back into Linh Thu before the SAM operators locked up on you. Just before the briefing broke, Captain Overstreet ran in with some papers and herded Papa and Chappie in a corner. Everyone could see Papa and Chappie shaking their heads and pointing to one sheet of paper or another, and soon everyone was buzzing about what was going on. Finally Chappie went to the briefing podium and said "Quiet down, gents—quiet down!"

When the room grew silent, Chappie said, "Seems we've had a change of plans. Papa and Captain Overstreet will now conduct a new briefing, so give them your full attention."

Papa approached the podium and added, "Actually, gents, I won't be giving this briefing at all—Captain Overstreet will. Go ahead, Captain."

Overstreet set up an overhead projector, then began. "Thank you, sir. Men, your sortie has changed because another Alpha Strike changed their target tonight. You'll be leading the strike by attacking this building here"—he pointed to a projected photo—"believed to be a storage facility for flak guns. The purpose of your attack will be twofold: one, to destroy some AA and make all your lives easier; and two, to divert attention from the main attack of the Alpha Strike." The room began to rumble as the target actually seemed to have tactical value, which was unheard of. "As you can see, you'll be very close to Hanoi—only fifteen miles south—so expect heavy resistance either from AA, SAMs, or MiGs, or a combination. Each of you will be lightly loaded with two 500-pounders apiece, because after you attack you'll fly cover for the Alpha Strike. For that you'll be heavily armed with air-to-air ordnance. Colonel Driskell or Major Chapman will finish the briefing on TOT, fuel, lost comm, and RTB procedures. Men." Overstreet motioned to the COs, and they took over the briefing as he made a quick exit.

Chappie did most of the briefing, but Papa finished up when he saw see the looks of confusion around the room. "Well shit gents! I don't know what else to say! I've been down here for over six years and I never gave a briefing for a sortie that actually had military value, except for CAS and CAP flights to help our brothers in arms. I'm just as confused as you are, but you can bet your ass this probably isn't because Washington had a recent change of heart and actually wants to try to win this war. There must be some political explanation. Anyways, go put on your gear and get to your jets." As everyone got up to leave, the chatter got louder.

Chappie hollered to Val and Nate across the room. "Jordan, Robinson—c'mere, please!" When they made their way to the front, he said, "Normally you guys would be in the number-three slot, but since we're most likely gonna get heavy AA, I want to stay with the newbies and make sure they get back alive. Understand?"

"Yes, sir," Val said. "Shouldn't we move them from the back since the last guy is most likely to get tracked?"

"Already done, Captain. They'll be in the middle, in the number-four slot. You'll be in the fifth slot, but your call-sign will still be Dash 3. After the bombing run, you'll move to slot three and they'll be your cover in slot four for the CAP flight. Keep them outta trouble! Questions?"

"Yes sir," Val replied.

"Go ahead, Captain."

"Have you seen the new kid's hair? He looks like he escaped from a Bangkok cockfight!" Val broke into laughter.

Chappie busted out laughing too, then replied, "I'm not Papa, Captain. Save your smartass remarks for him. Dismissed!"

Papa looked over at Chappie shaking his head and laughing and saw Val and Nate leaving the room, so he slid up behind Chappie and said, "He got you, didn't he."

"Yes, sir."

Papa sighed. "Welcome to my world! See the shit I have to put up with every day?"

Val and Nate looked over to the new guys as they finished their preflight and began to climb into their jet. Nate saw could see the concern on Val's face in his mirror, so he keyed up. "Relax, brother—they'll be fine. It's our job to make sure they will. Let's wake our girl up and finish this so we can go to the pub."

Val looked back at Nate in the rearview mirror. "You're right." He looked at his plane captain outside and shouted as he gave the engine-start hand signal. "Number one!" Soon both engines were running and all BITs were done, and the entire flight was taxiing to runway 31. It wasn't long before they were all airborne and headed north, and when Val looked to the east he saw the glow from Dong Hoi and wondered how Nga Nghin Do'i was doing. He shook his head and began to concentrate on the task at hand.

Twenty miles from the target, Papa ordered his flight to "green 'em up," and the flight descended and split up for a low attack from different directions. As they approached the target, the sky lit up with AA, thicker than anyone had ever seen before. The new guys were terrified—they knew this was the real deal and not a practice exercise back in the States. Papa, Chappie, and Mailer made their runs without incident, and now Val, Cesco, and Parker were up. after them would be Johnson and Planer to clean up.

Val keyed up to Lieutenant Parker, "Dash 6, Dash 3, cover Dash 4 real good, let them know if they're not on line or doing something wrong. Dash 4, watch me and do exactly as I do and you'll be fine."

Wright and Cesco both answered with a confirming, "Aye, sir."

Val dove low through the flak and began a swooping turn from the south and pickled off his bombs right on the already damaged target. He then began his climb out to the east and strained to look over his shoulder to see that Roostercomb doing what he was supposed to. The newest flight crew dove through the AA, following Val's exact flight path and dropping their bombs right on the target. On the climb-out Val saw their jet shudder from the explosion of some AA just behind and to the right of their jet, but the well-built F-4 shrugged off the insult and joined up on Val's wing. Soon all the jets had finished their runs, obliterating the target in the process. Each man wanted to ensure that this target was destroyed since it contained AA weapons, which were bringing down more American aircraft than MiGs or missiles.

Papa's voice soon filled every headset. "Good job, gents, but we're not done yet. The Alpha Strike has begun, so all RIOs keep looking for MiGs. We're gonna orbit right here and be ready to take action when we're called, so keep the chatter down."

The silence continued as MiGs were launched from Kep Field and other bases, but as soon as they approached the Alpha Strike and picked up the returns from the Playboys circling above and diving to intercept, they bugged out and headed back for the safety of their base. The Rules of Engagement prevented the Playboys from following the MiGs back to the base and either shooting them down or strafing them parked on the airfield. The rules also prevented any bombing strikes on the enemy bases. It ticked the pilots off as they knew the MiGs and their bases could be wiped out in a single major strike.

"You still got 'em, Double-O?" Val asked as he charged down behind one persistent MiG that weaved his way through the Alpha Strike, occasionally firing his guns and cannon. Val was hoping the pest was Colonel Tomb as he rushed in madly through the middle of the strike with Cesco in tow.

"Yeah, but hold your fire. We've got too many friendlies between him and us. If you can get closer, maybe we can get him with guns."

"Where's he at?"

"One o'clock, four miles at angels one-seven. Two friendlies between him and us."

Val looked at his small scope on the lower right of his panel. "All right—I got him. I'm gonna climb high and swoop in behind him."

"Watch the bombers!" Nate said as he saw two shadows zip by above him. "And don't forget the new guys are trying to keep up with us back there."

Val pitched up high above the fight and briefly stoked the burners, but shut them down after only a few seconds so as not to give away his position to any other MiGs. He then rolled inverted and saw his MiG way below him heading northwest. He cut the power and pulled into a steep dive, performing a couple of energy bleeding S-turns to slow down and to avoid other aircraft that were retreating from their bombing runs.

Cesco was using all his concentration just to keep up with Val as he dodged friendly aircraft and strained to see what his wingman was chasing. He knew that the longer he followed him, the farther they got from the safety of the other F-4s and the friendlier skies over the Alpha Strike target, but he had blind faith in his wingman's abilities. As two bombers zipped by close, he said out loud over the ICS, "Holy shit! This is crazy!"

Val quietly slid in behind the MiG. He'd soon be in perfect position for a missile launch; most likely the MiG had no idea that two enemy jets were close behind. "Let me know, brother," he said to Nate, awaiting a solid tone.

"Almost," Nate replied.

Suddenly the MiG performed a crazy wingover maneuver, and as it began to slow and dive back down, it gained precious distance but was still in missile range. The MiG suddenly broke right in a high-speed diving turn, apparently spotting his pursuers.

"Shit! I think he's seen us! Looks like he's running for home!" Val said, then added, "What was the purpose of that crazy maneuver he just did?"

"I think he was checking his six. He must've had a suspicion he was being followed," Nate answered. "Let's catch him before he gets home! We're only ten miles from Kep!"

Val closed rapidly on the retreating MiG and doggedly pursued the poor pilot as he tried everything he knew to throw Val off his tail. The pilot was growing physically tired and knew he couldn't keep it up for much longer; it would only be matter of time before the American would have him dead to rights. He had have to do something!

It wasn't long before Nate got a solid tone and told Val to fire. Just as Val squeezed the trigger, a bright flash shot out from the MiG, now a mere mile-and-a-half from its base, and quickly burned out. The pilot had ejected out of fright! As Val's missiles streaked into the vast blackness, one of them tried to track the ejection seat, but when it burned out went after the other missile. Val and Cesco looked at Kep Field below and knew this wasn't a good place to be alone. They began a rapid climbing turn to the southeast just as Papa came on frequency, scolding them to do exactly what they were doing.

Val looked back to Nate in the rearview mirror. "Does that count as a kill?"

"I don't know, brother. We have to ask Papa when we get back to Linh Thu."

Soon Alpha Strike was returning to their carriers or bases, and the Playboys rushed to Linh Thu. For the most part they were safe from SAM launches this evening as two Iron Hand missions had taken out several SAM sites even before the Playboys struck their weapons depot. The flight back was happily boring for the first time in almost a year.

After the debrief, everyone headed for the pub. Lieutenants Cesco and Wright followed Val and Nate into the pub, and Papa called them over to his table, where he, Big John, and Little John were cutting up. Seeing them called over reminded Val and Nate of the time Papa called them over after they'd taken the SA-2 hit. As the newbies approached the table, the scene went into slow motion for Val. It was déjà vu—Papa and Big John were laughing and making a ruckus. All eyes were on them, and Val knew all too well that the new guys were wondering if they'd be able to measure up as they sat at a table ruled by a man idolized by nearly every fighter pilot in the world. The new crew sat down, and Papa went still as he looked at Cesco with an expression of confusion. The chatter dropped to a murmur as the newbies met their CO socially for the first time.

"Boy, what the hell is up with your hair?" Papa laughed aloud and the whole bar erupted in laughter with him. The pub then quieted down to hear the new guy's response.

"I was really unlucky with the genes, sir," Cesco answered.

"I'll say," Papa said with a smirk.

Cesco could feel he was tense, and he knew he had to make a good showing in order to win some respect from this crowd. "So, Colonel, sir, I hear you can out-drink anyone under your command, sir."

Big John smirked as he sensed some sort of challenge in the young man's voice. "That's a fact, young'un."

"Until   now,   sir."   Cesco   smiled   as   everyone   went "Oooooooooooooooooooooo!"

Papa smiled back. "Are you saying you can throw down with the old man, my foolish young rooster—or should I say 'cock'?" Again everyone went "Oooooooooooooooooooo!"

"That's what I'm saying, sir—I challenge thee to a duel!" Cesco replied as he   air-slapped   Papa's   face   with   an   imaginary   glove.   Another "Oooooooooooooooooooo rose up."

"Let's do this! The kid wants to die outside of combat—pretty smart if you ask me!" Papa smiled and the entire bar shouted "Yeaaaaaaaaaaaaahhhhhh!"

Little John nodded at the bartender and shouted "You know what to do!"

Soon Little John set three beers and three shots in front of Papa and Cesco. Big John stood up and explained the rules for the new guy. "All right, young'un. You have to finish the *first* round here before you can move on, and the one who finishes first chooses the weapon for the second round. First to get through three rounds wins." Big John looked at Papa, and then at the new guy. "You sure you want to do this, young'un? You haven't lived a full life yet."

"Just be ready with the next round—I'll be ready in less than seventy-five seconds," Cesco replied to a round of cheers.

Papa laughed. "Cocky little fuck, you are." Then he said to the crowd, "All right—let's put some hair on this kid's balls!"

"On my mark"—Little John looked at his watch—"Go!"

The room resounded with cheers, but Cesco just watched as Papa finished his first beer and shot and began on his second. "You'd better get started, Kid!" Val yelled into the lieutenant's ear.

"Not yet! I gotta give the colonel a fighting chance. Kind of even the odds so he can't say I cheated!" Cesco answered.

As Papa picked up his second shot, everyone looked at Cesco, some thinking he'd given up already. Only Lieutenant Wright smiled as he watched and shook his head. As Papa lifted the third beer to his lips, Wright yelled, "Now, Rooster!"

Cesco grabbed his first beer in one hand and first shot in his other and downed them both in under three seconds. Then he went down the line, and Papa looked astonished as the young man downed all his beers and shots before he did. "Next round!" the lieutenant exclaimed as he slammed his last glass down and saw Papa wasn't finished. "Waiting on you, sir!" Everyone was now cheering.

"You want more beer?" Little John asked.

"Naw—let's step it up. Six shots of whiskey apiece!" Cesco yelled.

Papa looked at the small pilot. "Six shots? We're supposed to go down each round!"

"The major said it, sir—winner calls the next round."

"Our rules don't call for six shots."

"Maybe it's time for some new rules, sir!"

Papa looked at the young man again with a smile. "All right—bring it! But this time you start with me!"

"It's your funeral, sir—however you like to be humiliated!"

"You cocky little bastard!" Papa smiled, knowing he liked the new kid.

The new drinks were set down, and Lieutenant Cesco finished all six shots in less than a minute, while Papa still had one more to go. "Next round!"

"What now—rattlesnake venom?" Big John asked with a smile.

"No sir. Let's do eight more shots, but this time we do them straight up, shot for shot."

"Got it!" Little John said as he poured out sixteen shots.

Papa looked like he'd just jumped into a pit of vipers. "Do you not like me, son?"

"Yes sir—I like you."

"Then why're you trying to kill me? Did I fuck your girlfriend or something?"

"No sir. I just thought you said you could hold your liquor!"

Papa looked up at Little John and smiled. "All right—let's do this!"

"On my count gents," Little John said. "One!"

Both men grabbed their shots and the lieutenant beat Papa handedly.

"Two!"

Same result. After the third shot produced the same result Papa winked at Big John and said, "All right—play time's over! Time for my A-game!"

"Four!"

This time Papa handedly beat the lieutenant.

"Five!"

Same result, and then Papa beat Cesco easily the rest of the way. Someone shouted, "Papa was just setting the kid up!" After the last shot, Papa shouted, "Bonus round—three beers and three shots!"

Cesco was blown away. Papa had set him up and hustled him like a pool shark. The bonus round concluded with Papa finishing all his beers and shots before the newbie halfway through his second. Papa looked up the crowd. "All right—lay 'em down! Payday!" Papa then looked at Cesco, who was bewildered. "Can you believe there are still people who actually bet against me?" Papa said. "Easy money!" Papa threw Cesco part of his take and put his arm around the lieutenant's neck. "Don't sweat it, Kid—no one beats the old man! I'm proud of you for hanging in though! You may be my new protégé! Where'd you learn to drink like that?"

"I'm Irish, sir. I had whiskey in my baby bottle!" Then he said, "By the way—you didn't fuck my girlfriend, sir!"

Papa looked confused. "I know, son—don't take it personally. I was just joking."

"You fucked my mother instead, sir!" Cesco continued, and when he had Papa's full attention he added, "I'm your son."

Papa's brow furrowed as he searched his memories, and Cesco said, "You know Anne Tullamore?"

Papa's eyes lit up. "Yes!"

"She's my mother." The lieutenant waited for it to sink. Papa was speechless, and it was apparent by the look on his face that he didn't know how to react to the bomb had been dropped in his lap. Papa was about to spill his guts, but Cesco laughed and cut him off. "Just kidding, sir—at least about me being your son. But you did have a relationship with my mother before you met your wife."

"Goddamnit, son—you scared my balls into my throat! I just gained ten years of age!" Papa grinned at his newest pilot. "No wonder you looked familiar—you have some of your mother's facial features, and take that in a good way! You can out-drink everyone but me, just like your mom. I knew you couldn't be my son though—my loins couldn't produce something so ugly! Hell, I like you, Kid. Welcome to my squadron."

§ § § § § §

The morning for Speedy and Notso began abruptly when their cell doors slammed open and they were greeted by men shouting in Vietnamese, who dragged off the thin blanket that was their bed. The guards then forced them outside and herded them toward another part of the prison. They found just being outside oddly comforting. but they knew it wouldn't be for long. As the door to their destination was opened, they were shoved inside and led to a small, dark room with a floor crusted over with some type of dried black liquid. Soon they heard footsteps approach from behind them, and then a figure moved in front of them. It was the officer who'd processed them into the prison their first day. The officer opened some blinds part way, and in the sunlight Notso and Speedy could see that the crust on the floor was dried blood. They knew immediately that they were going to be tortured. Each man could feel their hearts race, but they knew they had to resist whatever was thrown at them. They'd agreed on the drive to the prison not to only divulge false information if they felt they were about to break.

The officer had Notso and Speedy forced onto their backs across a large drum, then their arms were bound with rope and pulled down toward the floor through a pulley and back toward their heads. Their feet were also bound with ropes and pulled to the floor and toward their heads through another pulley. The pain was excruciating as nerve bundles were squeezed and distorted. Another rope was then bound around their necks near the base of the skull and pulled through a pulley on the floor. It created a choking sensation and made each Marine feel as if his head was being separated from his necks. The pain was so intense that they prayed they'd pass out, but their captors had years of experience and knew when to slack off to keep them conscious.

Speedy and Notso remained silent and tried to focus instead on some other mental image. Soon they started to lose feeling in their extremities because of the restricted blood flow. They thought the numbness would relieve the pain, but when their captors eased the tension on the ropes, the restored blood flow allowed the pain to resurge. The guards also knew how to put tension on tendons and ligaments, then ease up at just the right moment to avoid real injuries—although they didn't really care if injuries occurred.

This all went on for almost three hours, when finally each Marine broke their silence and finally gasped their first words, giving out false information that might have sounded technical but had no intelligence value. The Vietnamese officer was wise to this too, however, since years of interrogation had taught him that any information he received was either out of date or made up. Still he kept the torture going in the mostly false hope that he might one day extract something useful. His orders were very straightforward: each prisoner was to be interrogated and he was free to use any means to get information.

After four hours without receiving any useful information, the officer decided to return the Marines to their cells. When the ropes were loosened, each man collapsed to the floor. The guards ordered them to get up, but they were unable to move as they were weak and their limbs were numb. Only after they were kicked and beaten did they find the strength to stand. They were again forced outside into the welcome sunlight as they were marched back toward their cells. Along the way, Speedy and Notso passed several other American prisoners going the other way. They scanned their faces and saw blank, empty looks in their eyes. Then suddenly they saw two faces that looked familiar, but all too quickly they were tossed back into their cells—which ironically was somewhat of a relief.

§ § § § §

Val found himself singing aloud in the cab of his truck as he bounced along the poorly maintained road to Dong Hoi. It wasn't long before he lumbered into store's parking lot. He ran into the receiving area and gave Nghia Mau and Nga Nghin Do'i each a large white flower that he knew they liked. He embraced Nga Nghin Do'i and kissed her for a long time before they scampered off to her office hand-in-hand like a couple of love-struck teenagers. As they entered the warehouse, Val saw that there were twice as many large crates as there'd been the previous day. He laughed and said, "Wow—are they reproducing?"

"Yes. The first shipment was destroyed in an attack last night," she said matter-of-factly.

He could tell that she didn't want to talk much about the crates and he wanted to respect that, but his curiosity was piqued. Some were destroyed in an attack last night? Where—here? What was in the crates? Val felt that the only way he'd find out without seeming nosy was to take a peek when she was preoccupied with something else. All of a sudden she kissed him and said, "Hey—you awake?"

"Sorry," he answered with a smile.

Nga Nghin Do'i was very intuitive and knew what Val was thinking about. "Forget the crates, Val—stay with me. Soon we go to village." She dealt with Val's relatively short list and finished in less than twenty minutes, then shouted the order to the girls. As they got to work, Val and Nga Nghin Do'i continued to talk and flirt in the privacy of her office. Before long their conversation subsided, and their feverish gazes gave way to kisses—tentative at first, then deep. They were so lost in their passion that they failed to notice one of the girls waiting patiently at the door to tell them that the truck was loaded. When they finally did notice, they flushed with embarrassment as Val said, "Sorry—she had something in her eye and I had to get a closer look."

The girl didn't understand English, so she just gave an approving smile and after Nga Nghin Do'i excused her she left the room. Nga Nghin Do'i looked back at Val with a smile as she fixed her hair and stood. "Come—we're going to village." She sent Val to the truck and let Nghia Mau know she was leaving.

Val took in the sights of the countryside along the way, slowed down as he drove past a watchtower to get a better look. "Are there people inside of these?" he asked.

"Not in any of these. They are"—she stumbled for the English word— "unstable. Too unstable to use as a lookout. We just keep rice or livestock in them now."

"Okay," Val said. "Bet you can see a long way from up there." The towers stood at least fifty feet tall.

"Yes. On a clear day you can see the ocean." Nga Nghin Do'i chuckled as she continued. "As a little girl, I used to sneak up there at night and look at the moon and the stars. I used to believe I would float up to the sky and sleep on the clouds. After a while the people from the villages would come look for me and my uncle would always find me up there and carry me home. It was so peaceful." Her face was suddenly overtaken by the recollection of pain. "I believed I could escape the world up there." She recalled the images of friends and family members being beaten, raped, tortured, and murdered right in front of her not only by French soldiers but by Vietnamese who were paid by the French to inflict terror in across the countryside to retain control through fear. After a few minutes she returned her attention to Val, who was looking at her with sympathetic eyes. "Sorry—let's go to the village," she said with a forced smile.

The villagers heard the familiar sound of the engine, and the children swarmed the truck and ran alongside as it lumbered into its usual parking spot near the incinerators. After Val shut the engine down, he let the children climb into the cab where he let them grip the steering wheel and showed them the horn. After playing with them for fifteen minutes, he looked for Nga Nghin Do'i and found her at her sewing machine, patching up clothes for villagers. "The children love the truck," she said. "It's their biggest toy!"

"Then they'd really love my jet!" Val said with a laugh.

She returned his smile, knowing he meant that innocently, but she knew most Vietnamese hated American planes and pilots, believing that they indiscriminately killed innocent people. She knew most of her countrymen never got to meet Americans and learn their side of things. She knew that most Americans never got to meet Vietnamese and hear their view of the war. It was sad. She felt that if the two sides ever got to meet outside of the hell of the combat zone, the war would probably end today. They'd let the politicians and the rich who profited from the war duke it out while the rest went on with their lives.

Nga Nghin Do'i shook off the deep thoughts and smiled again. "Here—I have a surprise for you!" She walked behind the room divider in back of her sewing machine. When she returned, she was carrying something wrapped in newspaper and a fancy blue silk bow. She handed Val the package and said, "Open this—it's for you."

Val smiled as he accepted the package. He untied the bow and removed the paper to reveal some newly made traditional Vietnamese clothes.

Nga Nghin Do'i watched as he examined his gift. "Do you like? I made them for you to wear when you visit." She motioned to the divider. "Try them on!"

Val smiled as he thanked her and stepped behind the divider. As soon as he slipped the clothes on, he realized how unusually comfortable they were. He also noticed that they fit perfectly and allowed for freedom of movement. When he came out from behind the divider, Nga Nghin Do'i's eyes lit up with pride. He walked up to her and kissed her, then said, "You're amazing! How'd you know my size without measuring me?"

Nga Nghin Do'i smiled. "I see how tall you are when you stand in front of me, I feel how big you are when we hug. I have measured you in many ways." They kissed again for a while before they walked outside to have lunch with the villagers.

Val was again the center of attention at lunch as everyone from both villages gathered to greet him. He spoke to many of them and was learning some of their names and their stories. Most had similar backgrounds—simple but deep and rich in history and tradition. All gave the impression they were content and happy, unless the war was mentioned. All had lost relatives and friends, and many had had their lives dramatically changed by the wars they'd lived through. He heard many village elders say the same in one way or another, whenever the war was mentioned: "It is tragic—Vietnamese killing Vietnamese. This war has torn not just a country apart, but has divided families because of where they live on some map." Yet despite the tragedies, most managed to find happiness.

Val wondered if Americans would be able to do the same under similar circumstances. Each time he came to the Twin Villages, he realized how trivial things Americans considered problems really were. That's not to say some folks back home didn't have genuine problems, but many things Americans worried about were miniscule compared to what these people faced on a daily basis. Val noticed how friendly everyone was and how they all seemed concerned for his welfare and comfort. When lunch ended, people went about routines, and Val and Nga Nghin Do'i took a long walk.

The strolled north along a narrow path by the Nhat Le River, waiting until they were out of sight of the villages before moving closer together and holding hands. It was a beautiful setting—water lilies blooming in the shallows at the river's edge as huge trees sheltered them from the intense heat and sun. Some small merchant and fishing vessels trolled along the river, and Dong Hoi could be seen in the distance toward the east.

Nga Nghin Do'i smiled. "I love this place at sunset or moonrise. You can see the city lights shimmering in the distance against the darkening sky. It's beautiful."

"I bet it is," Val replied as he pulled her closer to him and stared into her eyes. "But I'm looking at the most beautiful sight I've ever seen. I'm truly blessed to share this moment. If my life were about to end right now, I'd feel content. I think of you all the time, Nga Nghin Do'i. I don't care whatever else is going on in my life—I know for sure that I want to spend every moment with you." Val pulled her into him tighter and kissed her.

All too soon it was time for Val to return to Linh Thu. He changed back into his uniform and climbed into the cab of his truck, then placed his gift on the seat beside him. Then he drove away to the west, knowing he'd cherish his memories of his wonderful day.

§ § § § §

Each time Speedy and Notso marched to and from their torture sessions, they saw the two prisoners who seemed familiar. Within a week they'd learned how to communicate with other prisoners, since talking was forbidden—tapping with a stick on the floors, walls, or bars of the cell in a combination of Morse code and a kind of prison shorthand. The guards never caught on, perhaps thinking that the sounds they heard were caused by insects or small rodents—and even if they did catch on, they wouldn't know the codes or passwords the prisoners had devised.

Once they got the hang of the code, Speedy and Notso decided to try to reach out to the two prisoners. It turned out that the other two were already curious about Speedy and Notso and tried to contact them first. In their first exchange, Speedy and Notso learned that these men were the highest ranking prisoners there until Notso arrived. When the others asked them their names and unit, Notso tapped back that they were Marine aviators with VMFA-2 in Linh Thu, and Notso and Speedy heard back that the other two were as well. Finally they learned that the other aviators were Lieutenants Baker and Charles, a crew shot down almost a year ago by a SAM.

They chatted this way into the night, Notso and Speedy answering what questions they could about how people were doing and how the war was progressing. Despite being imprisoned in this unimaginably horrible environment, they found comfort in knowing that there were friends among them, and that bond that would help them survive.

§ § § § §

On every visit to the store over the week, Val could see from the scars that attacks had escalated. Unable to take it anymore, he pulled Nghia Mau and Nga Nghin Do'i into the office and demanded to know more about them. "I don't think you're being totally honest with me. I care deeply about all of you, so who's attacking you like this, and why?"

Nga Nghin Do'i and Nghia Mau looked at each other, knowing they couldn't keep it from Val longer. They could see the concern and fear in his eyes, and they knew he was an honorable man. When they hesitated, he said, "Please stop stalling! I'm not leaving until you tell me the truth." He could see that Nga Nghin Do'i was about to open up, but then she changed her mind. "Come on! I care about all of you. I can handle the truth. Please!"

She finally drew in a deep breath and, pained, looked into his eyes. She took his hand in hers and led him out of the office and into the warehouse. Val could see that her eyes were beginning to well up with tears, and it bothered him that he'd upset her.

"Where are we going?" he asked, his tone gentler now.

"You want answers? I'm giving them to you!" she said sharply as a tear slid down her cheek and her grip on Val's hand tightened. She led him to the back of the warehouse and came to a halt in front of the crates he'd been asking her about, now covered with tarps. "The attacks started shortly after your first visit to our store. I never wanted you to find out this way, but it's best you know the truth sooner than later." Nga Nghin Do'i choked down tears as she pointed to the crates. "Go ahead—see for yourself." When Val hesitated, she said, "Look, damn you!"

He lifted the tarp and folded it back over a corner of one of the crates, and there he saw words printed in the Russian alphabet, which he couldn't read. But he also saw the words "*Phao cao-xa.*" Because it wasn't an everyday Vietnamese word, it took a few moments for him to figure it out, but when he did, he was paralyzed by confusion. "*Phao cao-xa*—anti-aircraft gun?" As he looked over the crates, he saw some were marked "SA-7" on the sides. There were crates of parts for mortars, rockets, and small artillery, along with crates of AK-47s and ammunition. Farther back he saw components for SAMs.

Shocked, he looked at Nga Nghin Do'i and saw that she was sobbing now. "What are these doing here?" he asked "Why do you have all these weapons?"

"You know why! You know who my uncle is! Who do you think I support in this war?"

"You supply the North Vietnamese with weapons? The people we're here to protect you from?" Val's eyes began to tear up. "Then why do you help me if I'm your enemy?"

"*You* are not my enemy, Val—no American citizen is! It's your *government* that's my enemy—and every Vietnamese citizen's. And who are you protecting us from? Ourselves? We never asked for your help after your government turned us down the first time—your government just came over and forced themselves on us! And by the way, I never helped any Americans before—not until you!"

Val suddenly realized that he was the one who'd put the store and its employees in danger. "So your store is being attacked because you aid the enemy—me?"

"Apparently so."

"But why these things?" Val kicked one of the crates. "They've killed many good men—some of them good friends of mine! Even the ones who survived are in prison being tortured. But mostly these things just kill!" Tears began to run down his cheeks.

"As do your bombs, Val!" Nga Nghin Do'i said with passion. "What do you think happens when your bombs fall from your jets? People die! Sometimes even good people, innocent people, old people, children. It doesn't matter—they all die! Every time a bomb explodes or a bullet finds its mark, someone becomes an orphan, a widow, a widower. Your country has brought yet another war to my homeland. We have Vietnamese killing Vietnamese, not just Americans. If you think your countrymen are the only ones who suffer over here, you need to open your eyes. My people have suffered through many centuries of war, and we're tired it. Why can't everyone just leave us alone? We never attacked anyone! We asked for your help to get the French out, and your country said no. We didn't ask you to occupy our country. Now we fight each other. Now Vietnamese soldiers come through our villages and steal our food, and leave us with nothing!"

Val was torn between a woman he was sure he loved and his loyalties to his country and friends. "But why weapons? Why do you have to supply my enemies with weapons?"

"Do you really think I like distributing tools of death? How well do you really know me, Val? I want to go back to selling dresses, clothes, fishing equipment, hardware, and building supplies, but now the only way I can make money to support the people in my village and help buy them food is sell weapons to soldiers like you."

Val raised his voice. "Do I seem like someone who *wants* to hurt anyone, Nga Nghin Do'i? How dare you group me with people like that!"

She realized that she'd hurt Val with her last remark, which was not her intention at all. "No, Val—I know you're not like them. Please forgive me for saying that. I know you have lost friends to these weapons, and I'm sorry, but I have lost many friends and family to weapons from all the wars of our past, and from Americans in this one, too!"

"Why do you help me?" he asked. "Why do you risk your safety and that of Nghia Mau and the other girls? Why would you still want to have anything to do with me?"

Still crying, she said in a shaky voice, "First of all, you don't come asking for weapons—you come for materials to fix things or make people's lives easier. And two…" Her tears got the better of her and she looked away. After a taking a deep breath, she pulled herself together and walked up to Val, stared into his eyes and wiped a tear off his cheek. Then she cupped his face in her hands and finished: "… because I love you, Val! Because I love you!" She kissed him on the lips and walked to her office, leaving Val standing speechless in the middle of the warehouse surrounded by his enemy's weapons.

§§§§§

Before he knew it, he was back at the base. The ride had passed quickly as his mind was preoccupied by inner conflict, and when he almost backed the truck over Lieutenant Davis in the receiving bay, it was clear his mind was elsewhere. After a couple of close calls, Davis asked Val if he was drunk and told another Marine to take the wheel.

Val barely remembered the sortie into Laos that evening—something he should have remembered, since it wasn't over Vietnam. He barely said anything to Nate or anyone else that wasn't related to duty, which was out of character. He had a few drinks in the pub and spoke only to the bartender, passing on every invitation to sit with someone.

Val didn't stay long, and when he walked outside he stared into the glorious star-filled night sky as he made his way to his hooch. He stopped at the patch and stretched out on one of the chairs, alone at last with his thoughts. What a day! No matter what else he wrestled with, his thoughts always returned Nga Nghin Do'i, whose beauty couldn't be marred by tears. He thought about everything she'd said and tried to put himself in her shoes. He knew he was over here fighting against her people. He eventually concluded that it didn't matter much that she was working with his enemy—his relationship with her was on a purer, more basic level and had nothing to do with his duty or patriotism. He knew that he loved her, and that was more important than this ridiculous war.

Just then Val's thoughts were interrupted by an explosion. It could only mean one thing—Linh Thu was under attack again! He raced to his hooch to grab his combat gear. He met Nate, then Cesco and Wright, at their hooch as the new aviators filled the bunks previously occupied by Speedo and Notso. When everyone had their gear, they ran to their combat station—a sandbagged bunker dug in preparation for attacks like this. The explosions soon became more frequent, and the men sensed this was going to be a longer attack than they'd previously experienced. Soon the explosions were joined by the rattle of small-arms fire, and the radio was alive with calls for help at the post near the drainpipe as large numbers of the enemy were crawling out. Shortly afterwards they saw two groups of men sneaking down the road they were covering.

"Wait until you know you can drop 'em before you open fire," Val whispered to his team. "Remember your fields of fire." He had the lieutenants hold their fire and to watch down the street the other way as he recalled the commandos used a lot of diversion tactics.

"Popping a frag on 'em!" Nate said as he and Val opened fire on the two groups and he fired a fragmentation grenade. The grenade landed right between the groups, and it exploded on impact and brought down at least five men. The others scattered for the cover of the shadows just as the lights on the base flashed out, and the blackness was broken only by muzzle flashes and light artillery explosions. Soon the noise became overwhelming as Linh Thu opened up its artillery at the hills where the enemy fire was originating. Val and his comrades were shaken whenever the enemy shells landed nearby in what seemed to be the fiercest artillery battle they'd ever experienced.

Soon the enemy added rockets to the mix, and the skies were lit up by the artillery and rocket explosions from both sides. Val looked down the street whenever the area was lit up from an explosion to check for enemy movement. In the light of the most recent explosions, Val saw the five men Nate had dropped still lying on the ground, but when the next round hit, he noticed there were only four bodies and no sign of their comrades. He waited for the next explosion to verify that he hadn't miscounted

"Guys, we got a problem! Keep your scan up! Those bastards are sneaking around somewhere near us, trying to flank us!" Val pointed to the four bodies on the road.

Every subsequent explosion revealed nothing but emptiness around their position, but that didn't mean they could breathe easier—in fact, it only made them more nervous. During the next explosion, Never heard a plop right beside his left ear. He looked over to see a grenade rolling toward them! "Grenade—cover!" he shouted as they hunkered down. The grenade exploded with an ear-piercing blast, and clumps of earth rained down on top of them. Rooster opened his eyes and slowly stuck his head up to check their surroundings. Just as he raised his head, he heard a scream from his right side and looked over to see a VC charging him. He was temporarily frozen—he'd never had a man charge him with the intention of killing him. Val looked over and opened fire as he shouted, "Shoot the bastard, Rooster!"

Roostercomb snapped out of it and fired two rounds into the charging enemy and saw him drop right at the edge of their position. Val pumped two more rounds into the man to make sure he was dead. "Behind you!" Never shouted as he opened fire on another man charging with a hand grenade in his hand. Never dropped the guerilla just as he attempted to lob his grenade. "Grenade!" Never shouted, and each man ducked down again as it exploded and again rained chunks of earth down on them.

"Goddamnit!" the lieutenants yelled in unison. Just then Val and Nate opened fire at five guerillas charging up the street. Just as Roostercomb and Never joined in, Rooster stumbled back against the bunker wall when he tripped over a box at his feet. When he was sure his fellow Marines were holding off the enemy, he ducked down to investigate and pulled up a heavy crate that contained an M-60 machine gun and two cases of ammo. "Guys—look what I found!" he shouted as Never helped him load it and unfolded the bipod. Rooster set the machine gun on a sandbag and opened fire, dropping the charging guerillas in their tracks. "Come on and get some! Get some! You commie bastards! Get some!" he shouted as his fire cut the men down within a few seconds, in a single swoop.

All four cheered and patted Rooster on the back, but as they were celebrating, a grenade dropped among them. They looked at each other, then rolled over the sandbags in four different directions as the hole collapsed in on itself after the explosion. The shockwave hammered their internal organs, leaving them curled up in pain for a few seconds.

"Everybody okay?" Val shouted as he and the other Marines patted themselves down. All except Roostercomb responded in the affirmative, and after waiting to hear from him a few seconds, he called out, "Rooster? You okay?" Still no response. "Rooster?"

Finally Val some movement over the collapsed roof of the bunker. Rooster peered up and shouted. "Hey guys—I still got the '60!"

"Let's get out of the open and into the drainage ditch, fellas!" Val urged.

They sat in darkness lit up by the fierce artillery. Suddenly they crouched down when Nate pointed out two men running down the street toward them. Rooster set the M-60 on the lip of the ditch and slid his finger on the trigger, ready to shoot. "Hold your fire, Rooster—they look like friendlies," Nate whispered.

Through the deafening booms, the aviators heard Papa and Chappie's voices. "Captain Jordan," Papa said, breathlessly. "Are you boys okay?"

As the aviators stood up and waved, Papa and Chappie ran to them, glad to see they were in one piece. "Dammit, boys! I saw that grenade explode over here and I thought the worst!" Then Papa's eyes cut over to Rooster holding an M-60, ammo belts and his M16 slung over his shoulder. "Damn, son— where'd you get the heavy hardware?"

"Found it in the bunker, sir!"

Papa turned to Chappie. "That explains the M-60 that was reported missing earlier this week. Those boys in Saigon were right—they actually did ship it to us." Papa quickly changed subjects. "The flight line is well covered, and so are all the buildings—except for sick bay. The medics are reporting that they're having to drop more and more enemy troops and that they're running out of ammo. We're going to assist them, fellas!" Papa again looked at Rooster. "Especially since our redheaded stepchild now has a machine gun. Move out!" They men spread out in a skirmish line and headed toward sick bay.

Sick bay was on fire when they got there, and the medical staff and fire-fighters were trying to evacuate patients and defend against guerillas at the same time. "Goddamnit!" Papa was furious. He ran up to the fire commander. "How many more are in there?"

"Six. We could get them out quicker if you can create a perimeter around us, sir."

"Done! Just get those people out now!"

"Yes, sir!"

"Chappie! Get our boys in a defensive perimeter along the road. Put the '60 at the tip point where he has the greatest field of fire! Give me your radio!"

"Aye, sir!" Chappie set up the men and gave Papa his radio as he took cover beside him.

"This is getting out of hand! We gotta get some air support! I think we can sneak the Alert-5s off! I got a large detachment around them for security!" Papa said as he changed to another frequency.

"I agree, sir. Our base can't take much more of a pounding!" Chappie said just as Rooster and the others opened fire.

"Shack, Oscar Five Delta, over!" Papa shouted into the radio.

After twenty seconds of silence, the radio crackled. "Oscar Five Delta, this the Shack, go ahead."

"Have your maintenance men do a dark, quick runway sweep of 13. If it's clear, launch the Alert 5s loaded as full as possible with air-to-ground. We need the guns on the hill silenced now!" Papa ordered.

"Thought you'd never ask, sir!"

"Oscar Five Delta, out. Call me only if you can't launch—otherwise kick some ass!" Papa set the radio down and began to join the fight, but Chappie had already ordered a cease fire since the enemy troops were dead.

At the shack, maintenance men jumped into jeeps with armed Marines for protection and sped off toward the runways to check for damage. Ordnance techs began to load the Alert-5s with all the armament they could carry, and plane captains preflighted the aircraft while their aircrews planned their attack inside. Soon the crews rushed outside and climbed into their jets to await the return of the jeeps with the okay for launch. Finally only one crowded jeep returned. "Where's the other jeep?" a plane captain asked.

"An artillery shell exploded near us and flipped it. We're all okay and the runway's fine. We pushed the jeep off the runway with this one—it's just off the right side about halfway down. Let the pilots know," a sergeant said as he climbed out of the jeep. The plane captain ran and told both flight crews as they fired up their jets and kept all lights off. Soon both jets were performing a high-speed taxi to the runway and quickly lined up. Night was again day as four afterburners lit up the runway and the jets roared into the air. "Yeah— kick ass!" the ground crews shouted as they watched the jets get airborne.

The fire was out in sickbay, but Papa and his men were in the middle of a firefight out front, and everyone paused when the Alert-5s roared overhead. Papa shouted, "Give 'em hell, fellas!"

When the enemy artillery operators saw the jets take off, they began to argue among themselves about whether to continue shelling the base, know- ing death was in the skies above. It wasn't long before all hell broke loose, followed by an eerie calm.

After the Alert-5s were finished, the shelling ceased and now the dominant sounds were the small-arms fire around the base as skirmishes with enemy troops wound down. The F-4s landed and taxied back to the shack, and Papa and his team headed there.

As the men walked down the road, they could tell even in the darkness that their base was reeling from the unusual fury of the attack. "Goddamn! Who pissed in their Cheerios this morning?" Papa said as he paused to overturn an enemy body with his toe.

"Don't know, sir," Chappie replied, "but I have a suspicion that we weren't the only base hit like this tonight. We may even be hit again, so we'd better keep our guard up."

"I don't disagree," Papa said as he entered the ready room of the shack with his Marines.

"Colonel's on deck!" a sergeant shouted and all men snapped to attention.

"At ease, son," Papa said as he went to the flight crews. "You boys think you got 'em all? Think they may try to attack again tonight?"

"Yes, sir. I doubt they'll try again, but if they do, we'll hit 'em again," a captain replied.

"Sir!" A corporal came in from the radio room. "Reports are coming in from all over South Vietnam and Laos. All bases and large field base camps have been hit in a massive coordinated attack—just like Tet in '68 and post Tet in '69, sir!"

"Does anyone need any air support, Corporal?" Papa asked.

"No, sir—all the attacks were successfully repelled."

"Good. Spread the word that everyone needs to sleep at their combat stations in case those bastards try again." When Papa saw the corporal still standing there, he said, "Well Corporal—get to it!"

"Aye sir!" The corporal snapped to and sent the message out, then jumped in a truck to drive around the base and tell every battle station to stand fast.

§ § § § §

The morning found every man at Linh Thu groggy from a night at combat stations with little sleep. Smoke rose almost vertically in the still morning air from a few places around the base, and the morning light revealed more damage than the base had ever absorbed. Val surveyed the damage as he walked to his hooch and then to Papa's office, where he knew the list of items to get in Dong Hoi would be long. After Papa gave him the list, he climbed into his truck and drove off, uncertain about how he'd be received by Nga Nghin Do'i and the girls after what had transpired the day before. He hoped that all would be forgiven and things would go on as they had before he'd learned that Nga Nghin Do'i was helping to supply the enemy he was here to fight. All too soon, the familiar sight of the store filled his windshield.

Inside the store, the girls were gathered around Nghia Mau and Nga Nghin Do'i. All the girls knew what had happened between Val and Nga Nghin Do'i yesterday and didn't know exactly how they should feel about the matter. When they heard the familiar rumble of Val's engine, they looked at each other and wondered what would happen today. The girls bowed to Nga Nghin Do'i and excused themselves to the warehouse. She knew she had their support, no matter what happened.

When the engine shut down, the brief quiet was interrupted by Val's footsteps and the creaking of the door as he entered. As soon as he and Nga Nghin Do'i made eye contact, they knew they had things to say to each other. Val bowed to Nghia Mau and gave her a hug, and she smiled and passed him over to Nga Nghin Do'i, knowing it as well.

Val and Nga Nghin Do'i made their way to her office in a heartrending, tension filled silence. As soon as the door shut, they looked at each other, wondering who'd speak first. The girls watched them disappear behind the closed door and began whispering.

All of a sudden, they both began to speak at once, and then just as suddenly ceased and found themselves again staring at each other in silence. Val waited for a moment, then began again. "I'm sorry for my outburst yesterday. I want you to know that I was disappointed that my suspicions were true, not angry at you. I completely understand your side of the situation. At first it was difficult to know where my loyalties should lie." Val approached her and pulled her into an embrace, then looked into her eyes. "Now I know. I'll be forever loyal to you. To hell with the war. Please forgive me."

"I forgave you the moment I kissed you. I know that it is hard for a warrior to go against his duty. And I meant it when I said that I loved you. I do love you, Val." They leaned in and locked into a passionate kiss, and everything that had happened yesterday faded like a forgotten dream.

Eventually they got to Val's list, and when the truck was loaded, Nga Nghin Do'i asked, "How long do you have before you have to be back?"

"I have to leave in time to get back before sundown."

"Come with me to the villages. My uncle should be there and he'd like to see you again."

"Let's go," he said as he motioned to the truck and changed into the clothes she'd made for him. They hopped in and were quickly on their way to the Twin Villages. Val again looked at the watchtowers as they drove along the muddy road, and it wasn't long before the children were swarming the truck as it pulled up to its regular parking place. Val had just shut down the engine when he noticed Nhiem-vu Phuc-Nguyen step out of a small hut. He'd heard the large truck pull up and the children laughing. He was glad Val was here. Even though he was the "enemy," he liked him. Val was open-minded and listened to his adversary's opinions, and he seemed to like people in general and not judge them. He walked up to the truck just as Val and Nga Nghin Do'i were stepping out.

"Captain Jordan! It's our pleasure to see you again!" Nhiem-vu Phuc-Nguyen smiled as he swept his arm around. He wondered how an American obtained local clothes, but he was glad to see that Val was accepting the local culture and trying to fit in.

"Morning, sir. The pleasure is mine." Val bowed, then they shook hands.

"Walk with me, Captain," Nhiem-vu Phuc-Nguyen said. "How are things at Linh Thu?"

Val knew that he was fully aware of the attack of last night, so Val just downplayed it. "Fine—busy as usual, sir." The old man was about to speak again, but Val cut him off. "Sir, may I trouble you with another plea?"

"Certainly, Captain."

"I know you have a lot of power, sir. I beg you to stop the attacks on Nghia Mau's store." Val sighed as he continued. "I know that certain people are angry that they're helping the enemy, namely me, but I'm not acquiring any weapons or military materiel from them. There's no reason to terrorize the innocent people who work there. I fear for their lives. You could find out who is doing it and order them to stop. Please do it before they hurt or kill Nghia Mau or your niece or the other girls."

Nhiem-vu Phuc-Nguyen mentally digested Val's request, knowing Val was sincere in his concern. "Has anyone been hurt?"

"Does it matter, sir? The fact is, they *could* get hurt or killed. Those terrorists—and I do mean terrorists, because warriors do not target innocent civilians—only attack the store while the girls are there." Nhiem-vu Phuc-Nguyen knew that Val was angry because he didn't seem too concerned. Val sighed again. "Loo...I know that the store supplies your army with weapons. So that's even more reason for these cowards not to attack. They're helping your cause, sir! Stop them! Please!"

"Do you have any proof that they are just attacking when the girls are there?"

"Yes! The girls have said so. Besides, there's never an attack at night." Val decided to play his trump card. "Sir, I witnessed one of your cowards trying to rape your niece! I had to kill him to stop him. Stop these attacks before another goon gets the same idea!"

When Val said that, Nhiem-vu Phuc-Nguyen recalled that a few Communist Party guards mentioned how one of their comrades went missing after a trip to Dong Hoi. Could it be the same person? He was furious that such a man might have tried to rape his niece—who was more like a daughter to him. While he wasn't happy that Val had killed a Vietnamese citizen, under the circumstances he understood. "I give you my word Captain—the attacks on the store will stop."

Val and Nhiem-vu Phuc-Nguyen strolled around for over an hour talking about the war, their homes, their lives—bonding even though on opposing sides. Once again, they talked about Nga Nghin Do'i. When her uncle, a high-ranking Communist Party member, learned that a US Marine Corps fighter pilot was in love with his niece—and vice versa—he didn't know how to handle it. He knew there was really nothing he could do about it, and that their relationship certainly wasn't hurting anyone at the moment. He felt that as soon as the war ended, Val would be shipped home a hemisphere away and his niece would marry a nice Vietnamese man—and that would be that.

The two men joined the villagers for lunch, and afterward Nga Nghin Do'i and Val took a long walk. He explained what was happening at his base and how he'd recently lost two good friends and didn't know if they were even alive, or where they were imprisoned if they were alive. Val told her about how Virginia had dumped him, and how the saddest event in his life was actually a blessing because it allowed him to get closer to her. When they came to Nga Nghin Do'i's sewing hut, she worked on some clothes for her friends as they talked. Before long, Val knew he needed to head back to the base so the Seabees could get to work. They walked to his truck, where he changed back into his coveralls, and Nga Nghin Do'i asked, "What were your friends' names who were shot down?"

Val told her, thinking what could it matter. He tossed the clothes in the truck and climbed into the cab when she said, "You know it's only fortune that we are still here."

"What do you mean?"

"Your friends, my parents, my friends, the soldiers on both sides of this war, the innocent civilians—it's only by pure fortune that we aren't like them, either dead or in misery. We could easily be like them, but for some reason, we got lucky. You thought your fiancée's cheating was a tragedy, but you said it ended up being the best thing that ever happened to you. Once again, you could have been in misery, but because of fortune you aren't. Maybe this war and all its tragedies will have some fortunate effects in time."

"I know I'm a fortunate man."

"Because you weren't shot down?"

"No—because I am loved by you"—he hugged her tight—"and because I love you." He kissed her, then climbed into his truck and drove off.

It wasn't long before Nhiem-vu Phuc-Nguyen walked up to her. "*Co' khoe khong?*"—Are you okay?

"*Toi khoe. Toi rat khoe.*"—I'm fine. I'm really fine. "*Bac? Tao co ah-hue. Khi nao thi may lam viec do?*"—Uncle? I have a favor. When can you do it?" She paused, as if trying to remember, then said, "Captain Frank Wise, Lieutenant Jamie Sanders…"

§ § § § §

Val finished unloading his supplies and found out he was on Alert-5 duty. He grabbed his gear and went to the shack, where he was surprised to find that he'd gotten there ahead of everyone else. Alone, he turned on the radio and read some old magazines that he'd probably read before. Suddenly a song came on that caught his attention. "Show me the prison, show me the jail, show me the prisoner whose life has gone stale..." He stood up and gazed outside at the activity around the base and the evening's sortie blasting off into the darkness. "...Show me the country where the bombs had to fall. Show me the ruins of the buildings once so tall..." As he watched afterburners light up and then shut off, he was amazed that he could still hear Joan Baez's cover of Phil Ochs' song over the roar of the engines. "...and I'll show you young man, with so many reasons why...it's there but for fortune go you and I, go you and I."

14

LOVE NEVER DIES

"Tibbs—I got at least three bogies, three o'clock and thirty miles, closing at close to six hundred hundred knots. Bearing zero-two-zero." Nate told his pilot as the targets lit up his scope.

Val looked over at his little scope. Strike came over frequency shortly after Nate finished talking. "Bowtie 1, Strike. Multiple bogies three o'clock and thirty miles, bearing zero-two-zero at six hundred hundred knots. Targets are inbound to your position."

"Roger Strike. Bowties are looking," Val replied and then looked over at Roostercomb's jet off his right wing. "Rooster, let's turn head-on with 'em and climb above 'em. Stay at least two miles in trail. When I pass 'em I'll swoop at 'em and see if I can get a couple to engage, then you swing in behind and nail 'em. Give 'em a taste of their own tactics."

Rooster smiled. "Roger, Dash 1—let's get some!"

As Val and Rooster broke into their oncoming enemies' flight paths, Val got the same feeling he got when he last met Colonel Tomb, when his friends were shot down. He had an inexplicable sense that Tomb was among the bogies flying head-on at them. "Climb higher than me, Rooster!" Val ordered as he intently scanned the skies ahead, hoping to catch a glimpse of his enemy before they saw him, in order to gain the edge.

Rooster climbed almost three thousand feet above Val, and when he leveled off he saw a glimmer way ahead and below him that could only be off the smooth skin of a MiG. "I got a visual on the bogies, Dash 1! I count four."

"Roger. Stay with our plan," Val told his wingman.

317

As the distance closed at a rate of twelve hundred knots, Rooster noticed what appeared to be another aircraft trailing the four MiGs a mile or so behind. "Dash 1—looks like there's another bandit a mile in trail of these four. He must be trying to set the same trap!"

"Roger, Dash 2." Val frowned in disgust under his mask. "All right, Dash 2—listen carefully. Go with the original plan except after you swoop in behind us, stay there for only five seconds to sucker the other MiG in after you, then break out into a loop and take him out. Don't worry about us—we'll shake our guys."

"Wilco, Dash 1."

Val looked out to his adversaries, who were in visual range. "Here we go— Ooh-rah!"

He flew past his enemies and pulled into a split-S to engage the last MiG in the formation so that it was between him and the trailer MiG—that way Rooster would only have one MiG to deal with. Rooster watched from above and took a last look at the fifth MiG, took a deep breath, and rolled into a split-S to swoop in behind the fourth, which was closing in on Val. He completed his maneuver to see the fourth MiG a perfect target directly in front of him. He called to his RIO, "Get a quick lock on that guy before we break away!"

"Done—fire!" Never said, excited.

"Fox 2!" Roostercomb ripple-fired two Sidewinders and looked over his shoulder to see the fifth MiG closing rapidly. Without waiting to see if his missiles hit their mark, he pulled into a high-g tight loop, hoping to catch the last MiG off guard. At the top of the loop, Never looked back and saw a MiG spinning toward the ground trailing smoke.

"Splash One, Rooster! You got the first guy!" Never cheered. "Let's make it two!"

Roostercomb continued his loop and swooped in behind the fifth MiG. As soon as he got directly behind, it broke into a split-S, then into a loop, knowing the Americans was carrying too much energy and would overshoot. Before Rooster could react to the break, he found himself turning defensive in a furious furball with the more maneuverable MiG.

Val looked over his shoulder when he heard the explosion of the fourth MiG. "Damn—Rooster actually shot that guy down!" He laughed as the three MiGs in front of him broke in different directions and picked the one that crossed from his right to left to chase. The MiG was just six hundred yards off his nose, so he switched to pure pursuit and to his guns. "Let's keep an eye out for his buddies, Double-O," Val said, reminding both of them that there were still at least four other MiGs out there.

"I am," Nate reassured his pilot.

Val chased the MiG for a while longer through a series of turns until it broke into a steep right turn, then he climbed high into a half barrel roll to the outside of his adversary's turn. He was now above his prey and saw that he was still in the break. Val, who now had almost the entire planform view of the MiG, pointed his nose just ahead of the MiG in its turn and squeezed the trigger in short bursts. The M161A1 Gatling spit rounds just ahead of the MiG that worked their way backward as Val changed the angle with rudder pressure. Eventually the rounds began to slice through and chew up the radome and cockpit and scored hits all along the fuselage. The MiG pilot somehow avoided being struck by the rounds that tore through his cockpit and immediately decided he'd quit pressing his luck. From above and behind, Val and Nate watched as the MiG shuddered under the stress of the hits and saw the explosive discharge of the canopy and the pilot as he punched out. "All *right!* You scared him out of his jet, Tibbs!" Nate exclaimed in glee.

Val smiled but knew that there were at least three other MiGs out there and he needed to know how his wingman was doing. He looked around and couldn't see any other MiGs, and his scope was clear, so he figured the other two that had broken away earlier had probably made a run for it. Val pulled his jet into an Immelmann, knowing his wingman was somewhere behind him, and he'd have a better chance to see him if he was heading back toward him. Val again glanced at his scope to catch the echo of his wingman, then checked with his RIO. "Where's Rooster, Double-O?"

"He's toward our one o'clock high about five miles, looks like he's got company," Nate answered as he discerned a larger than normal return on his scope, an indication of two aircraft in close proximity to each other.

Val looked ahead and right and caught a glint of sunlight reflecting off a metal surface, which told him a MiG was there! He then saw the large familiar shape of an F-4 behind it—Rooster getting the angle for another kill, it looked like. Val saw that for the moment his new wingman was safe and in control, so he slowed down and closed in quietly from behind, wanting to witness the new guy's second kill from a good vantage point. All of a sudden he felt like he'd been here before, and just as a flash caught his eyes from below him, Nate called out that another aircraft was overtaking them all from below. Val's heart began to pound angrily as he knew it could only be one person—Tomb! He rolled into a high barrel roll, and while he was inverted he got a visual on his adversary—a lone MiG-21 eerily similar to one of the ones that broke away from the fight a few moments earlier. As Val began the downward portion of the barrel roll, he strained to se and could finally make out that the right wingtip had recently been repaired. It *was* Tomb! The desire for vengeance coursed through his body and took control of his mind. He knew he had to control the emotions so he could think and react clearly in order to survive and win.

"It's fucking Colonel Tomb, Double-O. Make sure he's not setting us up for an ambush," Val said, and Nate could hear the restraint in his voice.

Nate knew his pilot better than anyone. "No problem, brother. Just make sure you don't let your emotions get the best of you. Keep level-headed and use the judgment that's kept us alive so far!"

"Don't worry, brother—I wanna get this guy in a straight-up dogfight, not chickenshit like he does," Val replied as he completed his roll and slid in behind Tomb. "Rooster, Stay on your MiG. I got the guy behind you. He won't stay behind you long—he doesn't want a kill that doesn't come easily." Val then queried his RIO about getting a lock. "How're we doing, Double-O?"

"Almost. This angle looks good. I should have it here in a coupla seconds." Nate worked frantically to get a lock on the now wildly maneuvering target.

Colonel Tomb saw the other F-4 rapidly closing on him and knew that he might have been too eager to try to jump the first one. He thought he was alone since his wingmen were supposed to have kept the one behind him busy. He knew it wouldn't be long before the big American jet would have a missile lock on him, and he needed to take evasive action. He began a right break, then rolled over into a Derry turn to escape back to the left, knowing the big F-4 couldn't match the maneuver, but he needed to get out of missile range quickly because it wouldn't take long for the technologically superior F-4 to compensate for its lack of maneuverability once there was adequate space between them.

When Val saw the colonel begin his break, he knew it would be foolish to purely pursue the MiG in such close quarters—it was after all the MiG's specialty. He began a gentle break right, then saw the MiG quickly swap directions in the Derry. Val actually let his jet slow down to increase distance from the MiG, then reversed his turn gently to the left. When he saw the MiG go into a split-S at the end of the Derry turn, he rolled inverted but didn't pull through yet into a split-S, knowing that would most likely put him in front of the MiG when it completed the maneuver. He planned to wait until the MiG was directly under him before he pulled through.

Colonel Tomb looked up to see that the F-4 wasn't biting and was waiting for him to get farther away. He then pulled into a loop that put him on a direct collision course with the F-4. He was counting on the fact that the pilot was paying close attention to him and knew if he didn't move, they'd all be killed in a midair collision.

Val looked at the MiG that was now closing straight at him at a rate of twelve hundred knots. He'd seen Tomb pull this tactic before and knew that the colonel was counting on him to move, and that the colonel would either escape or close in for the kill after his adversary reacted to avoid a collision. He was in this fight to the bitter end, so he held fast, intent on making Tomb make the first move. "Be ready, Double–O—if Tomb doesn't move or makes the wrong move, we might not make it."

"I'm with you, brother." Nate had faith that Tomb didn't want to die in a collision.

In his cockpit, Tomb broke out in a cold sweat as he saw the inverted F-4 rapidly fill his view. What was wrong with this crazy American! Did he want to die? Finally he couldn't stand it anymore and fired his guns and cannon blindly as he pushed the stick gently left, then hard forward as he rolled around the F-4 so close he could almost make out rivets. Once clear, he pulled hard into a high-g split-S, making his vision gray out.

The MiG passed by the F-4 so close that Val and Nate could actually see the panicked colonel in his own cockpit. Val immediately rolled right-side-up and began to pull into a climb to follow the colonel, only to see him diving again close by. "Dammit!" Val shouted as he saw the shockwave and felt the thunderous boom of the colonel breaking the sound barrier and bugging out to the north.

"We can still close on him, Tibbs! We're a helluva lot faster, and we're still in safe territory for another one-five miles or so."

To Nate's surprise, Val declined. "There'll be another time. By the time we catch him, we'll be too deep into enemy airspace, and we're close to bingo fuel as it is." He looked around and saw that Roostercomb was now alone. "Did you get him, Rooster?"

"Technically no. He punched out when I got a lock. The missiles destroyed an empty jet."

"How's your stores?"

"Minus four Sidewinders, full twenty mike-mike and getting close to bingo fuel."

"Roger. Let's go home." Val led his new wingman back to Linh Thu.

§ § § § § §

There was no quality sleep that night as Val replayed the dogfight with the Russian over and over in his mind. He only relaxed enough to sleep when he thought of his drive to Dong Hoi the next day. Finally the morning arrived and Val grabbed the daily shopping list that was now tacked onto Papa's door frame. Val got a kick out of how guys would pencil in their personal requests at the bottom of the page—beer, porn, women, etc.

Val was almost walking on air as he climbed into his truck and began the drive to Dong Hoi. When he was almost five miles out, he noticed two men in local civilian clothes walking along the road, and for some reason they seemed suspicious. It was odd because Linh Thu was so far out in the middle of nowhere. As he passed them, he continued to surreptitiously observe them in his rearview mirror. When one of the men nonchalantly snapped a picture of him, Val picked up the microphone to his radio and reported the men to base ops and suggested that Lieutenant Torres and a team check them out.

Soon Val was in Dong Hoi, as usual fighting the traffic. After twenty minutes, he finally made the final turn to the store. As he approached the parking lot, he noticed another man among the pedestrian traffic pull a small camera and quickly snap a picture of him. This time he stopped the truck and watched as the man who took the picture picked up his pace and hurried away down the street, not even noticing that Val had stopped. Val made a note of where the man went, then continued to the store. After backing up to the loading docks, he shut the truck down and ran up the street to the building the man had entered.

Nga Nghin Do'i smiled as she heard Val's truck back up to the docks and her heart sped up a little. She walked outside and shouted her greetings to him as he shut down his truck and stepped out, but when he smiled and blew a kiss, then took off running down the street, she was confused. When she noticed Val enter a building, she immediately made her way up the street to investigate.

Val opened the door of what was a dark, crowded pub. He looked around to see if he could spot the man who'd taken his picture. As the door shut behind him, every pair of eyes turned his way to see an American serviceman in flight coveralls standing at the entrance. The room fell silent and the jukebox could now be heard in the background, playing American rock music. A local man opened the door behind Val and seemed confused when he saw the American standing there. He quietly slipped around Val and made his way to the bar and sat down. Val quietly stepped into the room and walked toward the right corner, where a man resembling the one who took his picture was sitting. Val approached him and asked, *"Tao co the' ngoi day du'o'c khong? Tao co the' mo'I may uong cai gi khong? Bia?"*—Is it okay to sit here? Can I get you a drink? Beer?

Shocked that an American knew his language, the man didn't know what to make of the situation. Val knew that he wouldn't want to be seen with an American, so he grabbed two beers, paid the bartender and gave him a hefty tip, and sat down with the man. After a couple of minutes, the man took a few sips of beer as Val continued to smile at him from across the table. After looking at them for a while, the patrons lost interest and went back to their own business, still keeping an occasional suspicious eye on Val.

Finally Val let the man know why he was there. *"May hinh. Dau may hinh?"*—Camera. Where's the camera? Terrified, the man shook his head to suggest that he wasn't sure what Val was talking about. Val didn't buy it—he asked again as he held out his hand, *"Dau may hinh?"*—Where's the camera?

The man pleaded that he hadn't stolen his camera. Val explained that wasn't looking for a stolen camera—he just wanted to know why the man took his picture. Just as the man was about to speak, another man, younger but wearing similar clothes, came out from a back room and bumped into Val's table, then began to fish something out of the older man's pants pocket. Val said, *"Chao. Ngoi xuong di!"*—Hi. Have a seat! The man looked Val in the eyes and dropped what he'd found on the floor. When Val looked down and saw a camera, the young man quickly bent and grabbed it and threw it into the back room and locked the door. Then they both charged out of the pub down the street. Now all the patrons focused on Val again and he sensed he was no longer welcome. He smiled as he slowly got up and made his way to the door, and apologizing to everyone on the way. Just as he got to the door, Nga Nghin Do'i walked in. The men who were menacing him stopped when they saw her.

Nga Nghin Do'i quickly diffused the situation and grabbed him by his arm Once they were outside, she began to scold him. "What the hell were you thinking? You could have gotten yourself killed! Why did you run in there in the first place?"

"A man took my picture when I left Linh Thu and then another took my picture when I turned on your street. I just wanted to find out who he was and why he took my picture."

"Your father must be proud you never follow his footsteps and became a spy! That was not the way to find out what you want to know!"

"Who do you think they were?"

"How would I know? Anybody thinks it strange to see an American in Dong Hoi. They probably scared!" She laughed. "Even more now! Big scary American who speaks Vietnamese, asking for cameras and buying beers."

"Hey—I left a very good tip!" Val said, laughing too.

Back at the store, she kissed him and said, "You're crazy—but I can live with it!"

Val replied with a laugh, "Glad you can overlook my flaws!" After necking awhile longer, they made their way inside to gather the items on Val's daily list. After everything was loaded, Val sat down to tea with all the women. Nghia Mau turned on an old radio behind her desk and tuned in Armed Forces Radio, and again American pop music filled the room. Val stood up and held out his hand. *"May co the' nhay vo'i tao du'o'c khong?"*—You wanna dance with me?

She smiled and turned her head away, as if bashful, and said, *"Tao khong the' nhay dieu nay."*—I can't dance to this stuff.

"*Lai day!*"—Come! Val said as he pulled her to her feet and over to an open space. Nghia Mau and the other girls cheered and encouraged her to dance. As Val pulled her close, he could tell she was shy about dancing in front of everyone. Val looked into her eyes and smiled. "*Du'ng co' lo! Du'ng co' lo!*"— Don't worry! Don't worry! All of a sudden she just let go and moved to the music with Val. As they danced, the other girls laughed and giggled, and soon he went over to them and got all of them, including Nghia Mau, to get up and join in. They danced for another twenty minutes or so until Nghia Mau noticed another customer standing at the door, watching with curiosity and mild disbelief. She flushed with embarrassment as she went to turn down the volume on the radio. Val stopped her and walked over to the man and, with the girls' help, persuaded him to join in. After dancing for another ten minutes, everyone laughed and sat down to tea. Finally the man picked up the fishing net he'd ordered and left. By then it was time for Val to head back to base, so he bid everyone goodbye and walked outside with Nga Nghin Do'i.

Outside on the docks, Val and Nga Nghin Do'i held each other and kissed for a long while, neither wanting to let the other go. As he pulled away, he said, "I hope it won't be long before we don't have to go our separate ways." After a final kiss, he added, "I love you, Nga Nghin Do'i. Soon we will be together for the rest of our lives." He then fired up his truck and left her standing on the dock repeatedly mulling over his last remark.

§ § § § §

Nighttime at the Twin Villages was an ambivalent mixture of calm and anxiety. Most of the time it was quiet and peaceful, but sometimes the distant rumble of bombs or artillery fire or the rattle of small-arms fire filled the air. And then there were the occasional troops that wreaked havoc as they passed through, as had happened many times in the past. Many villagers sat outside and looked up at the stars before going to bed; however, tonight there was more to see. The whine of jet engines could be heard above, and when they looked north toward Hanoi, the flashes they saw were quickly followed by thuds that they could actually feel. The distant fireworks show carried on for over an hour before things got quiet. Thirty minutes after everything had finally settled down, the villagers were asleep in their beds When, around three a.m., they found themselves being forced out of bed at gunpoint by shouting NVA soldiers. Women, children, men—it didn't matter—all were rounded up and forced to sit in the middle of the villages, many of the beaten to make them go. Some women were groped and even taken into huts and raped as the soldiers finally corralled everyone in the open space. They found the village elder and dragged him out in front of everyone and forced him to his knees with the butt of an AK-47 to his head. When he was on his knees, the platoon commander kicked him, then grabbed him by his throat. The elder looked into the eyes of his assailant and asked, *"May muon cai gi?"*—What do you want from me?

The platoon commander smiled, then punched him in the temple. As the man regained his senses, the commander motioned to his men surrounding the terrified villagers. *"Chung ta muon an!"*—We want to eat! he said. Then he slapped the man again, pulled out a Makarov 9mm pistol, and forced it into the old man's mouth. *"Dau lua?"*—Where's the rice? In the background, a woman being raped in a hut was screaming.

When the terrified elder nodded, the platoon commander withdrew his pistol and the man pointed to a hut. The commander gestured to one of his men to investigate, and the soldier went inside the hut and opened several baskets. When saw that they were full of rice, he went back outside and shook his head. Furious, the commander fired a round beside the elder's thigh. He screamed that his platoon didn't want the "crap" rice the villagers ate—he wanted the good rice that they took to market. The village elder was hesitant, since that was the villages' only source of income. The commander walked over to a pig in a small corral next to the villagers and fired two rounds into it. Then he went back to the elder and said, *"Dau lua?"*—Where's the rice?

The elder was going to tell him, but he wasn't quick enough. The platoon commander nodded to two other soldiers, who dashed off. After about a minute, the woman's screams ceased, and after a moment of silence she began sobbing and moaning, and sounded like she was coming closer. Soon the two soldiers reappeared, carrying the woman who'd been screaming up to the front of the villagers where the elder was on his knees. Two soldiers propped her up naked against a food-drying rack with her legs spread. The elder pleaded for them to let her go—he would tell them where the rice was. The commander ignored the pleas and ordered one his soldiers to hand him his rifle. The terrified woman cried as the commander approached her with a rifle. Then he forced the muzzle into the woman's vagina up to the front sight post, looked back at the elder on the ground, and said, *"Dau lua?"*—Where is the rice?

The elder was sobbing in anger and pain as he pointed to a hut and explained that there was an underground room beneath the workbench inside, where the rice was stored. Two soldiers immediately ran to inspect the hut as the platoon commander held the terrified woman. As he waited, he pawed her face and breasts to remind her that her fate was in his hands. When the soldiers returned to confirm what the elder had said, the commander sent more men to gather up the rice. When they returned, he had them gather the rice that the villagers used for their own sustenance as well. When the elder pleaded that he let them go now that he had what he wanted, the commander slapped him one more time. Then as the soldiers began to drift out of the villages, the commander removed the rifle from the woman and ordered his soldiers to take her with them. She began to scream as the elder begged for her life. When he realized that she might hamper their movement, the commander groped the woman one more time and told her that he'd be back.

§ § § § §

Nga Nghin Do'i rode her bicycle to the Twin Villages the following morning when one of her best employees didn't report to work. She'd spent the night with a friend in Dong Hoi and knew nothing about what had happened the night before. She entered the villages to find a funereal atmosphere. She saw that the village elder, a good friend of her uncle's, was limping badly and had clearly been beaten, and she learned that her employee had been repeatedly raped, beaten, and tortured. The villagers told her that the soldiers had stolen every grain of rice, not just what they took to market. They asked her what to do, since the next rice harvest was weeks off and the soldiers had burned the seed stocks they needed for the next cycle. The thought of starvation hit home when Nga Nghin Do'i heard babies crying in the background.

She walked around the villages and saw the pain and destruction, and felt the same familiar anger and helplessness brought about by war that she'd known her whole life. As calmly as she could, she reviewed her options. She knew she'd need massive amounts of relief aid quickly, but where could she get such help? She knew her uncle wasn't available—he was hidden in some secret place in Hanoi. Soon she approached the hut where her employee was recovering from her ordeal the night before. When she entered, the sight of her friend lying on a cot naked, bruised, wounded, and shattered was heart-wrenching. As she knelt next to her friend, her eyes came across the shredded, blood-stained clothes wadded up next to her bed. She grabbed the girl's hand as tears began to stream down her face. *"Toi xin loi. Toi xin loi. Du'ng may dang bi danh mi!"*—Sorry. Sorry! You don't deserve this!

As Nga Nghin Do'i began to pull away, the girl squeezed her hand tighter and said weakly, *"O' them mot chut nu'a di."*—Stay a little longer.

Nga Nghin Do'i took a deep breath and said, *"Tao khong the.' Tao phai di ngay."*—I can't. I have to go now. The girl looked at her as she always did, with the confidence that Nga Nghin Do'i would take care of everything. Nga Nghin Do'i brushed the girl's forehead, leaned down and kissed her, then stood and gave her a look of reassurance. Nga Nghin Do'i knew exactly what the girl wanted and what the villagers needed. She said, *"Du'ng co lo, de tao lam cho!"*—Don't worry, I'll do it!

Nga Nghin Do'i returned to the store and went to her office. Practically all her employees and Nghia Mau either lived in or spent time in the villages, so everyone knew what had happened the night before. She began to feel survivor's guilt, thinking that she should have been there to help, although she knew there was nothing she could have done, and she might have been a victim herself. She looked at the AK-47 hidden behind some rolled blueprints in the corner of her office and briefly fantasized about killing the soldiers who'd raped her friend and terrorized the villages. It wasn't more violence that she wanted, but she *was* human. *Damn the war. Dam all the wars!* she thought.

She knew she had to forget her anger and focus on a solution for the villages because there would soon be a lot of hungry mouths to feed. But how could she obtain and deliver such large amounts of aid in short order? She didn't have the means to move supplies in such quantities—and even if she did, she didn't have the money to cover the cost of such goods. She knew she needed some serious help from someone, but who? Just then she heard Val's truck backing to the docks, and all at once her thoughts coalesced.

When Val entered the store, he knew instantly that something was wrong from the forced smiles of Nghia Mau and the girls. *"Khoe khong ha?"*—You okay? At that moment, Nga Nghin Do'i came out, bowed to Nghia Mau, took Val's hand, and led him back to her office. He knew something was terribly wrong, and when they sat down she squeezed his hand and told him what happened.

"I give you what is on your list for free today, but I desperately need a favor," she said.

"Sure. What do you need?"

"I need the money you use to pay for the supplies to buy food, seeds, medical supplies, material to make clothes." She squeezed his hand, and before he could respond, she said, "I also need your truck to take the supplies to Twin Villages—today."

He gave her a look of reassurance. "You got it. How else can I help?"

She practically leapt off her seat into Val's arms and kissed him as tears began to stream down her face. "I knew I could count on you. It's one of the things I love about you." After a few moments, she sprang out her office and divided Val's money among a few of the girls and sent them after the supplies. Nghia Mau was overcome with joy and ran to hug Val as tears streamed down her face. Here was a man who was supposed to be their enemy, yet he was so willing to help her people when they were in need.

Within a couple hours all the girls returned and loaded the truck with the supplies. Nghia Mau closed the store and the girls jumped in the back while she and Nga Nghin Do'i climbed in the cab with Val and drove to the villages. The noise of the engine announced their arrival, and Nghia Mau told Val to honk the horn to summon everyone. When the villagers saw the American truck, they weren't sure what to think. Still traumatized by what had happened the night before, the last thing they wanted to see was a military vehicle driving into their village—even if it was someone they knew as a friend.

Val drove up to the open area between the villages and shut down the engine. Val, Nga Nghin Do'i, Nghia Mau, and the girls formed a line from the truck to empty it of the supplies and organize them. They then had the villagers distribute everything. When the village elder saw what the American had brought, he was overtaken by joy. The vehicle of war had became a chariot of mercy, delivering enough food to last until the next harvest, enough medical supplies for their wounds, enough material for Nga Nghin Do'i to make clothes, and even new seeds to plant rice. He thanked everyone profusely.

After the supplies were distributed, Nga Nghin Do'i made her way to the injured girl's hut with some salve for her wounds and the fabric she would use to make her a couple of new outfits. The girl smiled and thanked her, and told her that she had no doubts that Nga Nghin Do'i would save the villages. Nga Nghin Do'i told her she'd have her uncle find the soldiers who'd done this and they'd be punished. Finally it was time to find Val and see how everything was going. She leaned over and kissed the girl again and said, "*Bao trong nhe.*"—Take care of yourself.

"*Khong. Bao trong nhe!*"—No. You take care of yourself! The girl forced a weak smile, and Nga Nghin Do'i smiled back, then went back to the truck was—only to find the area deserted. When she didn't see Val anywhere, she stopped a villager and asked, "*May co' thay Captain Jordan khong?*"—Did you see Captain Jordan? The villager pointed to the largest hut at the northern edge of the villages. Nga Nghin Do'i thanked him and went to the hut. As she got closer, she saw a large crowd gathered around it, the people erupting in laughter from time to time. She could also hear faint, sporadic burst of off-key music. She pushed her way through the crowd and saw Val and some children inside, playing traditional instruments. Val was clueless, and when it was his turn to play it turned out off key, which sent everyone into a fit of laughter. She laughed along with everyone else whenever he messed up. As their eyes finally met, they flashed each other a loving smile.

After entertaining the villagers for a while, Val got up to join Nga Nghin Do'i on a walk along the river. When they reached the hut where she kept her sewing machine, they got so lost in the passion of their kisses that Val failed to notice it was getting dark. He knew he had to leave, but he didn't want to. After another half hour he finally tore himself away and found himself in the dangerous situation of driving to Linh Thu in darkness.

Val knew he was in trouble—not only with Papa, but by risking his life like this. The danger was not only from the enemy, but from his fellow American aviators who might mistake him for a North Vietnamese vehicle from overhead and attack him. He'd have no chance of avoiding such an attack and slim chance of surviving as he'd never even know he was being targeted. He kept his foot on the accelerator and tried to think of something pleasant, but as he drove, his thoughts were interrupted from time to time when he saw lights in the sky. Momentarily panicked, he'd crane his neck and try to track whatever he saw, but they'd be quickly lost beyond the trees of the jungles near Linh Thu. As he took his eyes off the road to follow the lights of another aircraft, he failed to see the large buffalo standing in the middle of the road. When he finally saw it, he instantly realized that he had no room to swerve—especially when a second buffalo materialized from behind the first and blocked entire road. "*Shittttt!*" Val shouted as he laid on the horn, slammed on the brakes, and downshifted. He watched helplessly as the truck skidded, then suddenly the buffalo bolted into the jungle just before the truck slid to a stop. The sudden stop caused a crate in the bed to crash into the rear window of the cab, shattering it and showering him with broken glass.

Val took a deep breath and brushed off the glass. As he restarted his engine and was about to put the truck into gear, a movement in the brush down the road caught his eye. Thinking it might be NVA troops, he grabbed his M16, but he thought enemy troops would have opened fire by now. His heart pounded as the bushes by the road began to part, and he rested his weapon on the door with his finger curled around the trigger. Suddenly a great tiger stole out from the brush and paused to stare at the truck idling in the road. It raised its head to sniff the air, then dropped it to the ground, hoping to catch the scent of its prey—the buffalo. But when it caught the scent of blood on Val from the small cuts he'd received from the broken glass, he took a few steps toward the truck. "Not tonight, kitty—go away!" he shouted at the big cat. The tiger stopped in its tracks when it heard a human's voice, and Val aimed his rifle just in front of the cat's feet. If he needed to, he'd fire a couple rounds near the tiger to scare it off. The cat pondered the situation with feline curiosity, then let out a snarl and went back to find the buffalos' scent again. Within a few seconds, the cat melted into the jungle. Val shook his head as he put the truck in gear and drove away. *What a beautiful animal. A perfect killer, but it only kills when it has to,* he thought.

Soon Val arrived at the main gate at Linh Thu, and as the guard checked his ID he was on the phone. Val knew it could only be with Papa. Sure enough—the sergeant came out of the fortified booth and walked up to Val's window. "Evening, Captain. Glad to see you're safe. The colonel wants to see you ASAP." The sergeant smiled and winked as he waved Val through. "Good luck, sir—he sounds really pissed."

When Val pulled up at the CO's office, Papa was waiting for him on his lanai with his hands on his hips and an angry look on his face. The engine spooling down and the hiss of the air brakes couldn't conceal the anger in

Papa's voice. "Goddamnit, Jordan—where the hell have you been? I just about polished off a whole bottle of Rolaids worrying about you. I'm fifty fucking years old with no kids, yet here I am babysitting halfway around the world!"

"Sorry, sir—I had to investigate something," Val said as he grabbed his war belt and M16 out of the cab.

"Oh really? I suppose your little 'investigation' led you inside some girl's panties."

"Sorry to disappoint, sir—I'm not Lieutenant Robinson. Some guy took my picture when I got to town, I chased him into a bar, went to some villages, distributed supplies, nearly hit two buffalo, nearly got eaten a tiger—"

"Oh never mind—just don't do this shit again! I don't have to remind how dangerous it is off base at night!" As Val started to walk toward his hooch, Papa yelled, "Well?"

"Well what, sir?"

"You mean you show up two-and-half-hours late, have me choking down antacids, and you don't have the courtesy to make a smartass remark?"

Val thought for a moment, then said, "Sorry sir, I don't have one tonight. However…" He reached into Papa's chest pocket and pulled out the list for tomorrow's supply run, then took a pen from his own pocket and wrote something on the list. "You can add this to tomorrow's list because we will—I mean, *I* will need it." Val then put the list back into Papa's pocket and walked away.

Papa pulled out the list and read what Val had added: "Rear window for truck, new skivvies for me." Puzzled, he walked to Val's truck, and when he opened the door he saw the broken glass. "What the hell?" Then he began to laugh and shouted down the street after Val. "Now I can get some sleep after spending several hours in the head shitting out a whole bottle of Rolaids."

"See you in preflight sir!" Val yelled back as he headed to his hooch.

§ § § § § §

Dong Hoi was relatively safe compared to other towns and cities in Vietnam. The Of course the locals felt the war, but not nearly as much as Saigon or Hanoi. Its proximity to the seventeenth parallel made it a crossroads for both sides. The communist North had a huge presence in the city, and so did the freedom fighters from the South. They crossed paths in a clandestine intertwined web that wasn't apparent to an outsider. Intelligence gathering was a major industry in Dong Hoi.

In a dark room in the back of a pub in Dong Hoi, two men stood over three trays as they developed photos, the smells of the chemicals blending with their clove cigarettes and beer. One man took a swallow of beer as the other agitated the developer tray. As the images appeared, it was apparent that the quality wasn't the best, but what could they expect considering the conditions. As each photo came out of the fixing bath and went into the wash, they could see that the images were decent enough, and when the prints were finished they were hung on a line with clothes pins.

As the men compared older photos to the newer ones, they saw the same American military truck periodically arriving at the large store on the western side of the city. The truck had only one occupant—an American dressed in flight coveralls. It was hard to tell from the photos if it was the one who spoke Vietnamese and who'd chased one of them into the pub a couple of days ago. They kept moving chronologically along the line of photos until they came to the newer ones taken over the last two days. The older ones all showed the American military truck and its single occupant, which appeared to be the same man. The men were stunned when they finally looked at the newest photos, which were taken much closer to the store because one of them had hidden in the shrubs near the loading docks. What shocked them was that this American was being kissed by a beautiful local woman, the same one who'd came into the pub a couple days ago and retrieved the American. It was clear that theirs was more than a business relationship, and that made the men angry. Not only was the American in their country uninvited, possibly killing Vietnamese, but he was taking advantage of local women! The men knew that the photos would be the proof they'd need to get approval for action from their superiors.

The men took the photos down from the line when they were dry and stuffed them into a folder to be sent to their superiors. They went to the back of the room they were in and moved a desk, then removed several floorboards and climbed down the short ladder hidden under the floor to a small, cramped room crammed full of radio equipment. They radioed to their bosses that they had an urgent package that needed their review and that they'd await orders once they had time to make a decision.

§ § § § §

The night was busier than usual for Captain Phan. The Americans had been hammering Hanoi all night from different directions. He'd already lost three fellow aviators, but he'd evened the score on his last sortie. When his jet touched down at Kep Field, he quickly taxied over to get refueled and rearmed. He sat in the cockpit with the canopy open and downed two canteens of water that a plane captain handed him. He looked above as he heard the whine of jet engines above and actually caught a fleeting glimpse of an American jet streaking by in the darkness above. He then looked to his ordnance techs and shouted angrily, "*May chuan bi chu'a? Mat bao lau?*"—Are you ready yet? How much longer? He then pointed to his watch and to the sky above as the sound of enemy aircraft grew louder. *"Nhanh len! Nhanh len! Giac lai ra'i tam gia-dinh!"*—Hurry up! Hurry up! Enemy pilots are carpet-bombing our home! Finally the techs gave him a thumbs-up and Phan fired up his MiG-21 and taxied so quickly to the runway that his ground crew thought he was going to rotate on the taxiway. Just as he pulled up to the runway, he heard the tower clear him and his friend for takeoff.

"Cung ban?"—And friend? Phan keyed up in surprise. He then caught movement out of the corner of his eye and saw another MiG-21 pulling up behind on his right wing. He was disappointed to see that it was Colonel Tomb taking to his wing, probably figuring he'd get some easy kills by sticking close to Phan. Furious, Phan keyed up and rebuked the colonel. *"O' lai day di! Du'ng theo anh nu'a! Du'ng lam phien anh nu'a! Tao mu'on di thu gi-dinh!"*—Stay here! Stop following me! Stop bothering me! I want to defend my home! Phan was furious and insulted that the colonel would latch onto him at a time like this. He stoked his burner and his MiG leapt into the night sky, and as he looked behind he could see that the colonel was right there on his wing. He knew Tomb would never assist him in fending off Americans, yet he'd expect him to cover the his own wing and protect him from the Americans. Phan decided to ignore Tomb and just do his job and defend his homeland. He knew he could easily lose the colonel in a dogfight, or he could simply out-fly the colonel and leave him alone. One way or another he could rid himself of the pest.

Phan scanned the darkened skies for signs of enemy aircraft. As he did, he'd occasionally pick up the image of Tomb tucked in just behind and above his right wing. This angered him even more because he knew the colonel wasn't scanning for Americans, he was just waiting for Phan to do all the work and then pounce on an easy kill perhaps wounded by the captain. Finally Phan caught a glimpse of a line of American attack aircraft at two o'clock low. He tried to shake Tomb by suddenly breaking left, hoping the colonel would follow. If he did, he'd perform some actual combat maneuvers that he'd use to shake an American off his six in order to separate himself from Tomb. He looked back and was surprised to see that Tomb didn't bite on his fake-out but instead actually started into a gentle right turn *toward* the Americans. Even better! Now he could drop back and let Tomb deal with the Americans alone.

Tomb slid in behind the formation of F-105s and locked onto the one bringing up the rear. Just as he got a lock, the formation broke into pairs heading in three directions. He followed the pair that broke right, and just as he turned to pursue, he saw the lead aircraft in the pair that broke left explode in a fireball that forced him to look away. He knew that Phan had just scored his first kill and that the wingman was going to be his next victim.

Phan was now in guns range of the wingman as he continued his high-left break into an Immelmann. He switched to lead pursuit and sent rounds just ahead of the doomed American as the pilot flew into the rounds. As fire ripped through the American jet, it took direct hits from the guns and the cannon. Phan poured more rounds into the jet and it soon burst apart in a furious explosion—kill number five for the night so far!

Phan began to look for another victim. As he did, he saw Tomb score an actual missile strike and was pleased to see the colonel get a valid kill. He knew he'd better be ready for the CAP cover to be approaching soon, so he needed to work fast to get more kills before the ensuing furball begun with the F-4s. He quickly check behind him and caught the glow of afterburners about five miles high behind. The F-4s would be here soon! Phan ignored the attack aircraft now and began to trail way behind Colonel Tomb. He wasn't going to cover the colonel—he was going to bait the Americans inbound in hot pursuit.

Tomb got a lock on the wingman he was trailing and let an Atoll missile fly. As it destroyed the strike bomber seconds later, an F-4 rolled in behind the him. Phan waited until he saw the F-4's wingman close in above and behind the first one on Tomb's tail, then barrel rolled above the wingman before the RIO could know what was going on. Phan got a solid lock and sent an Atoll up the F-4's tailpipe, which tore the large jet into small pieces when it exploded. The F-4 trailing Tomb broke out immediately from behind the colonel as its crew screamed for help from their wingmen that another MiG was around. As the F-4 broke, it flew right where Phan wanted it to and was almost instantly in the center of his pipper. Phan sent another Atoll airborne and it flew a direct line into the other F-4's right wing, shearing it off and sending the jet snap rolling to the ground. Seconds later the bright burst of light from the rockets on the ejection seats filled up some of the black voids of the night sky.

Tomb immediately dove to shoot the helpless crew as they hung in their 'chutes. "*Khong! Khong Colonel Makarov!*"—No! No Colonel Makarov! Phan keyed up furiously. He despised the colonel for such cold-blooded, cowardly acts, but he watched Tomb open fire at the men hanging helpless in their parachutes. "*Anh han em Colonel! Anh han em!*"—I hate you Colonel! I hate you! Phan shouted at him over frequency, hoping that if the colonel ever bailed out, someone would give him the same treatment. Phan knew that he and the colonel would soon be outnumbered and low on fuel and ordnance, so they had to bug out. Phan turned back toward Kep Field only to be greeted by the sight of an F-4 blocking his path halfway through his turn. The F-4 had a good angle and distance and would easily be able to track him for a missile shot. Time to fight! Phan immediately reversed his turn in a climbing yo-yo and forced the F-4 to the inside of his turn and directly into an overshoot. The F-4 crew watched as they were now suddenly in front of the MiG whose pilot was very skilled! Phan looked at his fuel levels and knew that he couldn't survive a long drawn-out fight, so he either had to continue his RTB or make quick work of this American. He knew that more F-4s would soon be bearing down on him so he got a quick lock, fired an Atoll, downed the enemy jet, scolded Tomb to leave the crew alone as they bailed out, and dropped down low as he zipped for Kep Field. Eight kills—not a bad night's work!

§ § § § §

Val climbed into his truck to find that the rear window had been replaced with clear plastic duct-taped to the frame. He shook his head as he shouted to Papa before he left "What the hell? Are we back home in the South? What kind of redneck, jury-rigged operation are we running here?"

"Dammit, Jordan! Now you're starting the day being a smartass? Now get your ass going and make sure you leave early enough to get back on time!"

"Aye, sir! See you earlier this afternoon—I promise."

"You bet your ass you'll be back earlier! I'm not shitting out any more Rolaids! Those things hurt just as bad going out as they taste going in!"

Papa laughed as he waved Val toward the gate.

Soon enough Val was backing up to the loading dock at the store and was being welcomed by the girls smiling and waving to him. As he climbed out of the truck, the girls tried out their best English: "Hello, Cap-tan Jordan!"

Val bowed and smiled. "Morning, ladies!" He noticed something different about the way they were acting and asked, *"Co' chuyen gi mo'i khong?"*—Anything new?

They smiled and explained that it was Nghia Mau's birthday today, so he should be extra kind to her, which was not a problem for Val. He quickly scurried to the empty lot behind where there were always lilies and wildflowers. He picked a bouquet for Nghia Mau, and as he ran to the docks he said to the girls, *"Tao san-sang bay gio"*—I'm ready now!

When Nghia Mau greeted him, he bowed, then hugged her and kissed her on the cheek as he presented her with the flowers. She knew instantly that he'd picked them from the lot behind the store, but she was still pleased by his gracious gesture. She studied the various flowers in the bouquet and smiled as she picked through them. Val had just turned toward Nga Nghin Do'i's office when she said that something smelled really bad—then added that it looked tasty.

Val turned around to see her holding a dead mouse by its tail. Then she tipped her head back as if she were going to drop the mouse into her open mouth. She then looked at Val and laughed. *"Tao cau noi dua! Yy, xau! May nen thu mon thit meo xao ca-ri!"*—I'm joking! That's awful! Though you should try some curried cat meat!

Val laughed—she got him good. He smiled as he walked away, *"Cam on, tao an chay hom nay duy-nhut!"*—No thanks, I'm vegetarian for today only! She laughed and left him to go speak with Nga Nghin Do'i in her office.

Nga Nghin Do'i heard most of the conversation and smiled as Val entered her office. "Nghia Mau has some zingers every now and then!"

"Yep. I thought she was really gonna eat that dead mouse."

"Why did you put dead mouse in her flowers?"

"I didn't, though I was going to put in some curried cat meat."

Nga Nghin Do'i looked at Val in bewilderment, unable to understand how he came up with such a remark. But she let it go and they moved on to business. After about an hour, the girls had everything loaded and she asked him to escort her to the villages. She explained that she wanted him to follow as she rode her bicycle because she'd installed new brakes and wanted to try them out. As Val started the truck and hopped back out, she went to get her bicycle. She returned in a moment with her bike and a frown on her face.

When he glanced at the bicycle, he could see why—the rear tire was flat. "My spare inner tube is at villages. Can I ride with you?" she asked with sympathetic eyes.

"Nope," Val said, expecting her to look shocked. When she did, he added, "I'll ride with you." He opened the driver's-side door and motioned for her to climb in.

"No—I can't! Are you crazy? I've never even driven a car before!" she protested.

"Well, it's time you learned." Val smiled as he lifted her bicycle into the bed and climbed into the passenger's side. "Come on—I'll be right beside you."

She hesitantly climbed into the cab and sat on the seat, then looked around the cab and wondered how she was going to handle the big machine. She looked in the rearview mirror when she heard the cheers from the girls on the dock and felt as if she was under pressure to come through.

"Don't think about who's watching you," Val said. "You've seen me drive many times, so I'll talk you through it!" He smiled and explained the pedals, the air brake release and the gearshift, and made sure that he was as clear and thorough as possible since she'd soon be driving through crowded streets. With great deliberation, Nga Nghin Do'i put the truck in gear and let out the clutch as she began to press on the accelerator. Suddenly the truck suddenly lurched forward and stalled. Val explained that she'd let the clutch out too fast and told her how to restart the engine. When the same thing happened, Val thought she'd give up and demand that he drive, but she stubbornly tried again. She concentrated extra hard and when the truck began to move forward she let out a cry. "I'm doing it!" She stopped just shy of the end of the parking lot because she wanted to try getting the truck going from a dead stop again. This time she gave it a lot more gas and the truck lurched forward but didn't stall as she managed the clutch just right. When she saw the look on Val's face, she laughed and said, "I got the hang of it now, no?" and pulled onto the crowded streets of Dong Hoi.

Val felt a little panic when she failed to turn loose of the wheel after she completed a turn so it would return and quickly explained that she needed to do that—and like amateur driving instructors everywhere, he even found himself pressing a nonexistent brake pedal. But he kept his cool, and it wasn't long before they left the crowded streets of Dong Hoi behind and were cruising along the country road to the villages.

Nga Nghin Do'i laughed the whole time, unconcerned about the close calls back in Dong Hoi. She was simply enjoying herself more than she had in a long time. She looked at Val, who was finally regaining his normal color. "What's wrong—don't trust me?"

"I trust you—I just have to learn to trust your driving," Val said nervously.

"No worries—I got it now," she said with conviction as she honked the horn.

Val shook his head and laughed. "Oh good—we're here," he said as they approached the villages. But when they went on by, he said, "Whoa—where are we going?"

"I'm having fun! We'll come back in little while!" She looked at Val. "Relax—just another few minutes, okay?"

"All right. But no wheelies!"

She didn't understand know what a wheelies was, but she forgot about it and soon turned back to the villages and honked the horn when she got there. The villagers were surprised when they saw her driving the truck and beamed with pride. As she climbed out, they made her tell the story of how she came to be operating such a large machine.

Val stayed for lunch and decided that he had to leave shortly after. She took him to her sewing hut, where they kissed for a while before Val knew he had to leave. She walked him to his truck and showered him with kisses, hugs, and gratitude for letting her have more fun than she'd had in a long time driving the truck. He told her that he'd be counting the seconds until he saw her again as he fired up the truck and drove away.

Back at Linh Thu, Val drove through the gate and dropped off his truck at the supply depot, then headed for Papa's office to check in. When he saw that Papa wasn't there, he assumed from the disarray in the normally spotless office that he'd left in a hurry. He pulled a chair out onto the lanai and decided to wait. He was back earlier than usual and had time to kill before the briefing for tonight's sortie. After twenty minutes, he heard the roar of an F-4 in a low overhead break, so he stepped down off the lanai to investigate. Val quickly recognized Papa's jet in the break, and it wasn't long before his eardrums were again punched as Chappie's jet began his break, followed by Mailer's jet, then Roostercomb's. In less than a minute all four jets were on the ground taxiing to their barricades on the northwest ramp. Val was going to walk to the ramp but decided that the man who probably got no sleep would be back to his office soon enough. After another twenty minutes, a pickup pulled up in front of the office with the man himself riding in the bed, still in his flight gear. Papa climbed out, thanked the men in the truck, and saw Val before even taking a step. Papa looked at his watch, then pinched himself to make sure that he was awake. "What the hell! Is this a sign of the apocalypse? What in the hell are you doing back so early, Jordan? Were the girls on vacation?"

"No, sir—just got a quickie today. They had other things to do." Soon the sound of helicopters filled the air and Val switched subjects. "What was the scramble about, sir?"

"Just the normal shit. The Alert-5s are up north right now—well, they should be returning about now from CAP cover for a bombing raid. Some MiGs jumped the strike force before they began their runs. Just as they left, we got another call about an Army platoon being swarmed in an ambush. We had to hurry to get them out of the shit. Wounded are coming in now." He pointed toward the barely visible choppers on the southern horizon. "Mailer got shot at by a SA-7, barely juked away from it when it exploded behind his number-two engine. They're okay and his jet has minimal damage, but damn it's been a while since we saw one of those things. We gotta remember they're still out there."

"I thought maybe they'd run out of them. I guess they've been restocked," Val said nervously as he wondered if the woman he loved might be responsible for the return of the deadly weapon. Just then the roar of the Alert-5s in the break filled his ears and drowned out the sound of the approaching helicopters.

Papa looked up and was relieved when he saw his men turning above him. "Thank God they're back." He looked at Val. "Come on in, Captain." Val followed as Papa set his helmet on his desk and unhooked his g-harness. "Whatcha got for me, Jordan?"

"Well, today's supplies actually cost less than usual because the ladies cut me a deal, and as usual I got a few things that weren't on the list."

Papa chuckled as he sat down at his desk to examine the receipts. "How in the hell are you getting such good deals? I mean really—are you fucking one of the owners?"

"Soon I hope," he said under his breath, then aloud, "They just love me, sir."

"I know you usually get stuff that's not on the list, but they're usually comfort things. What I want to know is"—Papa looked up from the receipts—"why do you have that fucking smug look on your face?"

Val was about to answer when Lieutenant Davis rushed in all excited and out of breath. "Sorry, sir," he apologized, then looked at Val. "Captain, how in the heck did you get the window fixed so quickly?"

Val smiled. "I know some people, Lieutenant."

"Okay, Jordan—these girls may have every item the world would need to rebuild itself after a nuclear holocaust, but you mean to tell me that they're expert mechanics as well?" Papa smiled and shook his head. "Damn—I gotta marry one of 'em."

"Well, yes, to be quite frank, sir." Val laughed, then looked at Davis. "Lieutenant, tell the mechanics at the motor pool and all the Seabees that they're fired." Val looked back at Papa. "Maybe you should break the bad news to Big John and the mechanics, sir."

"Dammit, Jordan—you're dismissed. Smart ass!" Papa laughed, then added, "And for your information, that'd be good news for anyone based on this hellhole."

§ § § § § §

The flight crews knew that something was up when they learned Captain Overstreet would be giving the briefing on that night's sortie. When the overhead projector was turned on, they saw that the target was once again in Laos instead of Vietnam. What was going on? There were more and more raids going into Laos these days. Wasn't the war supposed to be against North Vietnam? In one sense it was better for them because there wasn't as much of an air defense over Laos as there was over Vietnam, but there was the occasional AA fire or SAM launch. Most of the aircrews thought these sorties were a waste of resources and time. Why were they picking on Laos? It was bad enough to make enemies in one country, but now the US government was making enemies all around Southeast Asia. These sorties were just as bad as the worthless ones over Vietnam—there was simply no gain for the effort. Even the politicians publicly denied such operations were going on outside Vietnam—they just didn't help the American cause. The alleged reason for the attacks in Laos was suppression of the Pathet Lao—supposedly Laotian communist guerillas—but agents operating in Laos almost never encountered them. The only good thing was, these sorties were usually an easy night's work.

Before Val knew it, he was zooming west through the darkness with ten aircraft from his squadron. Somewhere below was Laos and their target—a couple of thatched huts that were supposedly a staging area and planning center for the Pathet Lao. If there were any people down there, they had no idea how swiftly they were about to meet their death. Val thought about how a swift, painless death was the best anyone could ever hope for.

"All right, gents—let's green 'em up, destroy this useless target, and go home to the pub." Papa broke the silence. "Varsity squad line up on me, single file, four seconds in trail. This should be easy. Left-hand pullout at one thousand. Clean your racks. Bring nothing home except your Sidewinders and twenty mike-mike."

Since little or no resistance was expected, the F-4s were lightly loaded to begin with—only four 500-pounders, two Sidewinders in case they ran into MiGs, and a fully loaded cannon. Papa and his squadron spread out in a long single-file line and began their run from the east to the west, and the crews knew that it would probably take no more than four jets to obliterate the target—the rest were there in case somebody was off target. Papa rolled left to start everyone's run now from the southeast to northwest, with a southbound pullout. As soon as he positioned himself where he wanted the squadron to commence attack, he rolled right into a steep dive toward the target. He gave each jet only twenty-second's distance to adjust their run, and it seemed like less than that before everyone was over the target and releasing both racks. By the time the last jet pickled off its load, the crew could no longer see the ground where the target once stood in the flames—they just released their bombs into the inferno. As they pulled away to rejoin the squadron, they were thinking "overkill."

"Good job, gents—let's go home," Papa said, thinking it went too easy. He'd never known a sortie to go off without a hitch.

It wasn't long before Linh Thu was in sight and Papa had the flight break up into sections of two to come in for the break. Papa had Val and Mailer fall to the rear to watch for any trouble. Just as the last two aircraft before Mailer began their break, the telltale streak of a SAM zipped up from the jungle toward one, then another raced up toward his wingman.

"Idle and boards, Dash 9 and 10—you've got SAMs headed toward you!" Val keyed up trying to keep panic out of his voice. He watched as the missiles continued streaking skywards. He knew that he and Mailer were still too far away from Linh Thu to close the throttles and still make the field. "Mailman, keep your eyes on the missiles—they could track us now!" Val quickly looked in one a rearview mirror at Nate. "Double-O?" He knew that his RIO was on top of things and had already where the launches came from.

"I got it, Tibbs, but we only have Sidewinders. If we had a Sparrow, I think I could get a lock on 'em and take 'em out," Nate replied, knowing Val wanted to attack the attackers.

Val thought for a moment as he watched the SAMs fizzle out as they ran out of fuel and plummet to the earth. He recalled how Papa suckered enemy ground forces into revealing their position when they had to cover a downed aircrew awaiting a rescue flight home and knew it might work again. "Mailman—fly over the runway, reverse your course, and fire your cannon into the jungles at the approach end of runway one-three. Make a right pullout to the east—I'll sweep in from the north and see if I can't wipe out those bastards—or at least make 'em keep their heads down until we're on the ground."

Mailer knew exactly what was on Val's mind and was more than happy to comply. "Roger, Tibbs. I have another idea that might help you even more. You'll see it right before I pull out to the east." Mailer began his run over the runway and Val made a wide three-sixty to buy time and scan for enemy activity. Mailer briefly stoked his burners, hoping to catch the attention of any SA-7 operators. When he was halfway down the runway, he broke right to reverse his course. Once he was pointed back the opposite way, he switched to his cannon and blindly opened fire into the jungles.

Papa watched what was happening as he was taxiing back to the barricades. "What the hell are those guys doing now?" He shook his head.

In the jungles outside the base, the enemy began to scramble for cover when they saw the flashes of the Gatling cannon being fired at them. One SAM operator boldly stood up in the hail of incendiary rounds and put the sights of his weapon on Mailer's jet. Just as Mailer was practically on top of them, he squeezed the trigger and the missile launched. As soon as the missile cleared the tube, the operator saw the American jet do something he'd never seen before.

Mailer knew he was at the end of his sucker run and broke right. As he began his break, he released a couple of the new magnesium flares that were being tested as a SAM countermeasure. He knew that he was so low that the flare would fall into the jungles within a few seconds, which would help Val get a Sidewinder lock if an enemy did bite.

Val watched from a short distance away as Mailer began his break and was pleasantly surprised to see the two flares zip out from behind his jet as he broke away. He saw a light streak squirt up from the jungle and immediately track the flares falling back to the ground almost on top of where the missile was launched. "Mailer, you fucking genius!" Val said as keyed up then spoke to Nate on the ICS. "Double-O?"

"Let's see if this'll work. I hope it'll track something on the ground," Nate said as he locked up the flares and the SAM that had exploded on the ground. "Got it—fire!"

Val squeezed off both Sidewinders and watched as they actually performed as designed for once and tracked the heat from the ground and exploded on target. Mailer snuck in from behind and fired his two Sidewinders into the heat rising from the flames, and the SA-7 operator and his comrades met a swift, surprise death from above.

As Mailer and Val pulled into their barricades, they could see that Papa was waiting for them. After they shut down their jets and climbed down the ladders onto solid ground, Papa motioned all four men over to him. They approached and Papa shouted, "You jackasses really like to waste ordnance, don't you?"

"Sorry, sir—we're just trying to prevent any more launches," Val answered.

"I know what you were trying to do, Captain—relax. What I really want to know is, did it work? Did you get the Sidewinder to lock onto a ground target?"

"Yes, sir," all four men answered in unison.

"So in theory all the target has to do is give off enough heat, huh?" Papa then looked at Mailer. "By the way, how well do you think those magnesium flares are gonna work to against infrared missiles, since you're the first to use 'em?"

"It seemed to work this time, sir—in fact I'd have to say it saved my ass back there. Plus it helped Captain Jordan lock onto them," Mailer answered.

"Good—maybe we have a way to avoid losing any more people. It looks to me that the key to this is early detection that you're being tracked, or keeping up with the missile once it's launched. There's possibilities here, gents!" Papa patted them all on the back and directed them to the Cannery. "Let's get this debrief over with and hit the pub! Maybe those bastards won't shoot at us tonight after your display of genius!"

§ § § § §

Val returned from his trip to Dong Hoi at a more normal time, and when he checked in with Papa, he was sent to the HQ building after a quick meeting. When he walked into HQ, a clerk directed him to Captain Overstreet's office. Wondering what was going on, he approached Overstreet's office, knocked on the open door, and stepped in. Overstreet was poring over a stack of papers in the center of his cluttered desk, sweat streaming down his face. When he heard Val knock, he looked up and said, "Come on in, Captain."

"I'm in, Captain. What's going on?" Val said. The DIA officer looked like he was trying to figure out how to tell him something.

"Captain, I have to ask you some questions about Dong Hoi. Do you have time?"

Val wasn't sure what to think, but had Papa ordered him to give any help and information he could to Captain Overstreet. "Papa says I do," he said with a smile.

"All right. You go to this store every day, correct?" Overstreet held up a picture.

Val's heart began to flutter as he wondered if the DIA found out who Nga Nghin Do'i was and that she was supplying the NVA. "Yeah."

"Good. Are these two women the owners—the ones you deal with?" Overstreet held up photos of both Nghia Mau and Nga Nghin Do'i.

"Uh-huh."

Overstreet set down the photo of Nghia Mau but continued to hold up the one of Nga Nghin Do'i. "Are you aware of this woman's connection with the leadership in North Vietnam?"

Val hesitated, then realized it was best to tell the truth. "I am."

Overstreet could see that Val was under some stress. "Relax, Captain— you're not in any trouble. I called you in for a different reason."

Val was relieved but confused. "Really? Why?"

"Look. I know that you have feelings for this woman—that's why I called you in. She's clearly playing both sides. She supplies the NVA because her uncle basically forces her to, and of course she helps us with stuff we badly need."

"So? Get to the point, Captain."

"Sorry, my friend. I came across this message this morning." Overstreet handed Val a teletype containing a decoded intercepted message from various NVA commands:

All units in Zone 3: level 5 threat in Dong Hoi. level 5 threat in Dong Hoi. possible traitor operating in store in western quadrant of city. has been positively identified as helping American soldier at store. detain for questioning and terminate immediately. repeat. detain for questioning and terminate immediately. identification photo follows this transcript …

Overstreet gave Val time to digest the message. "Your friend's in danger. You have to warn her, see if she has a place to lay low. This message is clearly *not* a decoy. They sent it out over every one of their frequencies in a code that's not hard to break. They're serious. I'd like to go with you tomorrow when you leave for Dong Hoi. If anything, I can be an extra gun if we run into any of these operatives. Believe me, I want to help you." Overstreet saw the panic in Val's face, then saw Papa's tall frame fill the doorway.

"Don't sweat it, son. I know all about it. The captain will go with you tomorrow." Papa patted Val on the shoulder.

"Why are you guys so willing to help?" Val asked.

"This lady has made our lives a lot easier out here, and she took a risk doin' it. It doesn't matter who she's related to. No one gets to choose their kin, son," Papa said.

Overstreet added, "You saved my life once, Captain, and you give up all your free time to make these supply runs. The least I can do is help her."

Val looked at his CO. "Sir, to be honest, I'm not in the best frame of mind to be flying. I won't be able to relax down until I get to Dong Hoi tomorrow."

"No worries, son. Take the night off and get all the rest you can. We're flying into Laos again anyway. You and the captain here have a busy day tomorrow." Papa patted Val's shoulder again and left for his office.

Val tossed and turned in his rack all night as he was consumed by worry for Nga Nghin Do'i life. He knew one thing for sure—he loved her and would do anything to keep her safe. He tried to calm himself and convince himself that Nga Nghin Do'i was okay, and that there was nothing he could do until first light anyway. But images of enemy soldiers torturing, raping, and killing the love of his life kept stabbing his brain, eliminating any chance of peace. He tried to tell himself he'd do Nga Nghin Do'i no good if he didn't get some rest for tomorrow.

§§§§§

When first light finally came, Val was already at his truck, and it wasn't long before Overstreet joined him, carrying his battle gear. "I knew you'd be waiting, so I came early," he said as he placed his gear into the floor of the cab, handed Val a steaming cup of tea, and climbed in. "Let's go, Captain—we've got work to do."

Val fired up the engine, and soon the officers were roaring along the road to Dong Hoi. He had the accelerator almost to the floor the whole trip, yet the truck didn't seem to go fast enough. Once in the city, Val sped down the narrow streets, scattering pedestrians. Overstreet couldn't find enough things to hold onto as the truck careened around corners. "Jeez, Captain!" he said in a vain attempt to get Val to slow down.

When Val made the last turn, his eyes were filled with the terrifying sight of smoke billowing from the store, thinking the worst had already happened. He brought the truck to a screeching halt out front and he and Overstreet grabbed their battle gear and ran to the door. When Val kicked it down, smoke poured out. He looked to the shed at the right of the store, where he knew the girls kept a fire hose and a pump that drew water from a nearby canal. Val grabbed the hose and Overstreet turned on the pump and opened the valve. Val ran inside and found the source of the smoke to be some agricultural chemicals that were ablaze. He noticed that some volatile fertilizers were piled next to the chemicals and knew he had less than a minute to prevent an explosion. Val doused the flames with water for fifteen minutes, then put out a couple of smaller fires around the warehouse. When he finished, he turned the hose off and walked outside. "Captain—shut the pump off!" he yelled to Overstreet.

Overstreet shut off the valve and the pump and both men began to roll the hose up. "No one was inside I hope," he said.

"Nope." Val looked at his watch. "They should be here already, though. I hope they're just running late this morning." Overstreet then nodded his head toward a point beyond Val's shoulder. When Val turned around, the girls were just arriving on their bicycles.

Nga Nghin Do'i ran up to the two Americans and shouted, "What happened!"

As she approached, Overstreet got a good look at her and saw how truly beautiful she. "Your store was attacked by NVA operatives, ma'am." Overstreet replied.

As she hugged Val, she looked over at the American she'd never met. Val said, "Nga Nghin Do'i, meet Captain Overstreet. We *have* to talk to you about something *extremely* important, right now!"

"NVA? This is just another attack by locals," she said, trying to convince herself.

"No—this is not another local attack. You're in real danger! You have to listen to us," Val said. "Read this!" He handed her the intercepted message and picture of her. As she read, her eyes welled up with tears—especially when she came across the picture of her and Val kissing. "You can't stay here anymore—you *have* to come with us! We can protect you! Please—I'm begging you! Come with us!"

"Come with you *where?* This is my home—this is my life!" she said, tears now streaming down her face as she look at her store, still smoldering from the extinguished fire.

"Ma'am—these people *will* kill you!" Overstreet said. "They won't stop until they do. Please listen to Captain Jordan. They will kill you! Please come with us!"

"What about my employees? If I'm not here, they will torture them to find me then. I can't just leave them!" she said between sobs. "My uncle can put a stop to this!"

"That's if you can contact him. You haven't been able to for almost three weeks!" Val replied. "We can take all of you! Please—come with us!"

"No! This is my home! No one is going to bully me out of it!"

"These people will not just bully you, ma'am—they'll torture and kill you if they find you! Believe me—they already know where to look!" Overstreet pointed to the smoldering store. "They may be watching us right now!"

"Please, Nga Nghin Do'i—I love you! I love you, and I love Nghia Mau, the girls, the people in the Hai Lan Langs. Let's prevent a disaster! Come with us! Please!" Val pleaded as his eyes began to well up with tears, hoping that she'd listen to reason.

Nga Nghin Do'i and Val embraced for a long time, and when they separated, she said, "I love you, Val, but I can solve this without running away. I know you're only concerned for my well being, and I respect that enough to promise that I won't stay here. I'll leave for Hanoi this morning to find my uncle and put an end to all this! My girls and Nghia Mau will stay at the village." She looked at Overstreet. "How long do you think it will be before they forget about us?"

"I don't know, ma'am." Overstreet knew there was the very real possibility that they'd never back down. "If your store isn't attacked for a month, then maybe they've given up. However, it depends on how important it is to them. If you can get to your uncle and he orders them to back down, then you might be safe." Overstreet looked at Val. "Going to Hanoi might not be such a bad idea." He thought Val and Nga Nghin Do'i needed some time alone, so he went back to the truck and stood with Nghia Mau and the other girls, who'd just come back out of the store.

After Val and Nga Nghin Do'i held each other for a few more minutes, she spoke up. "Here's what we'll do." She pulled back so she could look Val in the eyes. "I'll go to my uncle—that should take three days. His orders would go out immediately. I'll return after he issues the orders. All in all, I'll be gone for maybe a week and a half. The store will be open at odd hours for the next few weeks. I'll give you the schedule so you can still get the supplies you need. Don't worry, my love—I can fix this quickly."

Val was somewhat relieved that she was at least taking their advice about not staying in Dong Hoi. He was also amazed that she'd be in Hanoi in less than a day on a bicycle. Val embraced her again and said, "Please leave today! Go back to the villages and pack up. Don't waste time! We'll drop you off there right now!"

When Nga Nghin Do'i wiped away her tears, Val could see that her eyes were filled with more resolve than he'd ever seen in her before. He was confident that she wouldn't be stopped and would return with everything resolved. She let go of him and walked over to Nghia Mau. After talking for a long time, they hugged, apparently in accord on whatever they were talking about. As Nga Nghin Do'i turned back to Val and Overstreet, Nghia Mau spoke to the girls. Nga Nghin Do'i walked up to Val and handed him his list, and it was then that Val didn't even realize she'd taken it. "All your supplies are free today. Thank you, gentlemen—you saved my store and possibly my employee's lives." As the girls loaded the truck, she held onto Val while the four of them had tea. It wasn't much longer before the girls had the truck loaded, and when they were finished they set to work on the store. Nghia Mau hugged Val and Nga Nghin Do'i and wished her well on her journey to Hanoi, then handed her the new hours of the store to give to Val. Overstreet hopped in the truck beside the Vietnamese beauty, who sat in the middle. Like everyone who saw her, Overstreet was overwhelmed by her beauty.

Val dropped Nga Nghin Do'i off at her village and wouldn't leave until he saw that she was on her way to Hanoi. He watched as she began to pedal northward, and realized that things were truly out of his control. As she disappeared from view, he knew while he could exist without her, that wouldn't be truly living.

§ § § § §

It was hard to know if the delirium experienced in this awful place was from the pain of torture, malnourishment, or fever from an infection caused by the constant beatings. Notso and Speedy had to keep their spirits up in this hell, where the only hope was the end of the war. Unlike the infamous Hanoi Hilton, this tiny prison was subject to almost no scrutiny committed more violations of the Geneva Convention than its larger, more famous counterpart just fifteen miles north. It was hell even when they weren't the ones being beaten or tortured because they could hear the shrieks of the other prisoners from their tiny cells. All that kept their spirits up was the simple communication system the prisoners had devised. For some reason today, the guards were on edge. They made sure their uniforms were sharp, and they had the prisoners clean areas of the prison that they weren't normally allowed to enter. When they were cleaning the guards' quarters, the prisoners saw they'd hoarded Red Cross parcels that prisoners were to have received. They even saw personal items that had been confiscated from prisoners—watches and jewelry, even pictures from prisoners' wallets. All these items were now moved out of plain view, so something clearly was going on. The prisoners were being drilled about how to bow properly and not make eye contact with any Vietnamese person. At night the cells were alive with rumors that someone of obvious importance must be coming to the prison soon. When the beatings diminished and the prisoners were being drilled on how to answer questions, the rumors were confirmed.

A couple of days later, all the prisoners were abruptly herded out of their cells early in the morning and made to stand at attention near the guards in the tiny prison courtyard. Within a few minutes, a black car drove into the prison's receiving area and stopped just outside the courtyard. The prison commandant was hopping around like a lost puppy as someone stepped out from the car. It was obvious the commandant was sucking up to this dignitary. It wasn't long before the two men made their way into the courtyard.

The newcomer was a short gray-haired Vietnamese man who looked very displeased with the commandant and his men. He walked down the line of guards looking unimpressed, then made his way to the line of prisoners. The man gave each American a good looking-over and continued until he stood in front of Notso, then stopped to look at Speedy, then went on for a few steps before returning to the two Marine aviators. He looked at them intently for another few moments, then said in perfect English, "What are your names?"

Notso and Speedy were shocked by the man's English and weren't sure what to make of it. When neither replied, the old man asked again. "You two—what are your names?"

Notso finally spoke up. "Why does it matter?" The commandant flew into a rage and began to strike Notso and curse him in Vietnamese about respect. Notso stood tall and absorbed the beating until the commandant kicked him in the testicles, which forced him bend over in pain. As the commandant was about to strike Notso on his now-exposed spine, his hand was effortlessly intercepted by the old man. *"Hoi! Ngu'ng!"*—Enough! Stop! the man said before sending the commandant to a corner.

Humiliated, the commandant bowed and backed to the corner. The old man reached out and helped Notso stand. "Sorry—the commandant is a mental midget. He will not touch you again today." As Notso stood back up, the old man pointed to both Notso and Speedy. "Now tell me your names. I can go find out from the records in the office, but it is more cordial to get them directly from you."

Notso answered for both of them: "Frank Wise and Jamie Sanders."

The old man said, "Ah, yes—I have heard of your names. You are pilots from Linh Thu."

Speedy and Notso didn't know what to make of this. They were indeed wondering why some old man knew their names and where they were from.

The old man knew the men must have many questions, so he decided to ease their minds. "Relax, gentlemen—you are not in trouble. I personally know one of your fellow pilots. He is a good man. Things will be changing around here. Soon we will win this war and all of you will be going home." As the old man started away, all the prisoners wondered what to make of the man who had the guards and commandant cowering.

"Who are you, sir?" Speedy said as the man was walking away.

The old man smiled at him and bowed then said, "You Americans have a saying—'friends in high places.' That's who I am—a friend in a high place." The old man turned toward the commandant and his guards and began to admonish them. Several of the guards and the commandant began to frantically scurry around as the old man continued his visit. Soon enough, the Americans found themselves alone in the courtyard, enjoying the fresh air and sunshine, guarded only by snipers in the watchtowers.

§ § § § §

Phan sat in a small room at Kep Field, thumbing through documents. He finally came across a file about Linh Thu. There wasn't much in the thin file except for some notes about what went on there. He came across some long-distance photos of some of the people stationed there and didn't think much of them until he came across three particular photos. One showed an F-4 on the taxiway with peculiar writing on side of the nose. He knew little English and the word was unfamiliar to him: BETELGEUSE II. What did that mean? He was sure he'd seen that plane before, but where? The next photo was of a tall older man, but it wasn't the image that struck him—it was the caption: Earl Driskell, who he knew to be the legendary two-time double ace. It was interesting enough to see what the legend looked like, but what fascinated him more was that he was based at Linh Thu. But when Phan saw a photo of Driskell climbing out of the plane with the peculiar writing, it hit him. He *had* seen this plane before—in the great battle nearly a year ago, where the Americans had trapped his squadron and shot down many of his comrades.

Phan smacked the file so loudly that it drew a look from Colonel Tomb, who was sitting a few seats over. Phan shot Tomb a sneer, but that didn't deter the colonel from coming over to see what upset the captain. When Tomb saw the photos of Papa, he laughed. He explained to Phan that he knew Driskell and had flown against him in Korea several times, and had barely escaped being shot down by the American legend. He told Captain Phan all the stories he knew about Papa, which took almost an hour. He explained that no one pilot could ever hope of taking the American legend alone—you'd have to have at least three wingmen. Phan laughed to himself, thinking this might be the only time in his life that he'd listen to what Tomb had to say.

When Tomb was finished, Phan turned away and studied the pictures some more. Tomb laughed and patted him on the shoulder, pointed at Papa's picture, and said in broken English just to irritate Phan a little more, "You fly against this man, you meet death!" As he left the room, he added, "Even with your great skills, Captain!"

§ § § § §

The night's sortie took the men of VMFA-2 back over Laos again for a mostly uneventful evening. But when the squadron landed back at Linh Thu, the crews were shocked to find out their night wasn't over yet. All the F-4s were reloaded with air-to-air ordnance, and the flight crews were ordered to wait in their aircraft for a call they expected within the hour. Apparently the Air Force and Navy would be commencing a huge bombing campaign and the Playboys would be flying CAP to cover for them and deal with MiGs. It was odd to expect MiGs over Laos because they usually confined their patrols to North Vietnam. Why would MiGs bother attacking lines of American aircraft over Laos? Was someone of importance to North Vietnam in Laos tonight? If so, why was the US attacking them, because that might actually make sense, and US policy hadn't made much sense so far.

Soon enough the call came and the Playboys were blasting off again to Laos. The orders had them orbiting north of the actual target area in order to intercept any MiGs, which would most likely be coming from that direction anyway. It was amazing to see the number of aircraft being utilized for this attack. Whatever was down there, the US wanted it destroyed, and maybe the North Vietnamese wanted to prevent that so much that they were willing to send MiGs to protect it.

The Playboys orbited over their assigned fix in silence, listening to the chatter from the actual attack. Val would occasionally glance in his rearview mirrors to see Nate looking as bored as he was. Val looked toward the target area, which was now aglow from the tons and tons of ordnance being dropped on it, when he saw a fast-moving shadow moving westbound along the ground, silhouetted from the light from the target area. His adrenaline surged as he said to Nate, "Double-O, tilt your radar down as far as you can. I think we got some bandits in the area!"

Nate tilted his radar down and instantly picked up multiple returns. He keyed up so the entire squadron could hear. "Contact—at least six bogies! Bearing two-five-zero, heading westbound toward target area at angels two. I don't know if they're aware of us yet!" All RIOs pointed their radars in the same area and Papa ordered his squadron to identify, then destroy if they were confirmed enemy aircraft.

Papa said to Val, "Split up, Dash 3. You lead the second group. Take Dash 5, 6, and 8. I'll take Dash 4, 7 and 2 with me."

"Roger Dash 1," Val replied.

The Playboys split into two groups to spring a trap for the MiGs, with Val's group directly behind them for a lock to spook them into Papa's group. As Val closed his group to within Sidewinder range of the MiGs, which they'd now clearly identified, all the RIOs locked on. As soon as the MiG pilots heard the warning that they were being tracked, they did as predicted and broke to the

L. ERIK FLEMING

northeast. Val's group pursued them and warned Papa's group to prepare to
lock them up and take them out. The MiG pilots saw that Val's group was still
pursuing them, but not as aggressively as Americans usually did, so they
knew something was fishy.

One of the MiG pilots suddenly called out a warning as he saw Papa's
group above and directly ahead in missile range with nearly perfect angles. At
once one MiG broke away from his group and Val's heart fluttered as he knew
it could only be Colonel Tomb bugging out early, possibly to return for an
ambush later. Val wanted to break from his group, but Papa made him stay
and ordered Nate to track him while the rest of the squadron took out the rest
of the MiGs. It wasn't long before the black night skies were lit up from brilliant flashes of igniting missiles and exploding MiGs. Three MiGs were
downed and the two remaining ones broke for North Vietnam. Papa ordered
everyone to return to the orbit area in case they tried to come back, and then
asked Nate where Tomb was.

"Roger, Dash 1. It appears he dropped to the deck to try to avoid detection.
He appears to be orbiting about twenty miles northeast of us, probably waiting
for us and the strike force to RTB so he can ambush someone," Nate said.

"Roger. Okay, gents—the Air Force bombers should be safe as they'll go to
Thailand or South Vietnam. We just have to watch the Navy boys. I'll have
them break to the south to go home to avoid the colonel and his friends. We'll
also break south, then swing around the colonel in a wide orbit to the northeast and come in behind him from the northwest. Whoever has the shot—just
take it! We're only gonna get one shot at this because we'll be at bingo fuel
soon. Let's get this bastard!" Papa switched frequencies and let the leader of
the Navy strike force know how to RTB, then came back to the Playboys' frequency.

Soon enough the Navy strike force turned a huge sweep southbound,
knowing they should be safe especially after they crossed the coastline. The
Playboys performed the same wide sweep that they knew any MiGs in the
area would notice. Nate told the squadron that Tomb was still in the same
place and gave everyone his location. As soon as Papa was sure that Tomb
would be fooled, he had the squadron drop to the deck and speed up as they
turned northbound in a huge sweep around the area where Tomb was. They
kept the turn going until they were northwest of the colonel's position, and
when they turned back eastbound, it was time to climb and engage him!

Tomb watched the show from a safe distance, eagerly waiting for the group
to RTB so he could sneak in behind and ambush them. He waited about
twenty minutes more until the strike force surprised him by turning south.
What were they doing? They had F-4 cover! Why were they going south? Did
they know he was waiting for them? He saw on his radar that the F-4s had

also bugged out to the south, and then suddenly disappear off his scope! What was going on? He had a bad feeling—something wasn't right. It was time to head back for Kep. Just as he turned northbound, he heard the audible warning that his jet was being tracked. He looked behind him and saw the unmistakable shapes of eight F-4s diving on him. He was in big trouble!

"Got him locked up, sir!" Mailer called out.

"Take the lead then, Dash 4—we'll cover you!" Papa ordered. "Fire, goddamnit—fire!"

"Fox 2!" Mailer called out as he ripple-fired two Sidewinders at the Russian.

Tomb saw that two missiles had been launched at him, but he still had time to break the cone of vulnerability. He also knew that he might have to do this several times if the Americans were properly lined up on him. Only one could be on his six at a time, but how many missiles did each have? His best bet was to outrun them. Everyone, himself included, was low on fuel and couldn't perform combat maneuvers for much longer before they had to RTB. He waited until the missiles got within ten seconds of impact, then performed a high-g Derry turn mixed in with a barrel roll to force the overshoot. He timed it perfectly and the missiles streaked on by, one exploding a quarter mile ahead and to the right of him, the other continuing on until it ran out of fuel. As soon as the first missile exploded, he went full military power, remaining out of afterburner. He knew the F-4s were faster, but they also had two huge engines guzzling great quantities of fuel and had already used most of it in the CAP flight and brief engagement with his comrades.

"He's running, sir!" Mailer called out. "Shall we pursue?"

Papa responded, disappointment obvious in his voice as the missiles missed their mark. "Negative. We'll be at bingo fuel soon. Remember I warned that we'd only have one shot. Looks like the colonel lucked out again! Let's go home, Playboys." They landed at Linh Thu without incident, and after the debrief went straight to the pub for a while before turning in to get some sleep and purge the alcohol from their systems.

About three in the morning everyone was awakened by the alarm sounding in response to a mortar barrage. The Marines' discovery of the drainpipe had discouraged the enemy from using it to infiltrate the base, but between flashes of exploding ordnance a guard in one of the watchtowers observed enemy troops carrying something into the tunnel that led to the drain pipe. Papa figured they must be stuffing the tunnel with explosives—not only to damage the base but to keep the Marines from using it to access the tunnel system that snaked under North and South Vietnam. Papa called the machine gun posts covering the drainpipe and ordered them to blow the charges Lieutenant Torres's men had wired. After confirming the order, the Marines complied, and in seconds a massive explosion rocked the base, and the watchtower that first reported the enemy activity swore they saw flames shoot up randomly in the surrounding jungle beyond. As soon as the charges went off, the mortar attacks and other enemy activity ceased, and an eerie silence descended. They couldn't see the ditches that suddenly formed around the base as tunnels collapsed.

"Is that what it takes to shut those bastards up?" Papa said as he climbed out of his bunker. "Shit—we should've done that a long time ago!" All the men at Linh Thu remained at their battle stations for another half hour, then finally made their way back to their racks.

§ § § § §

The trip to Hanoi was fraught with danger for Nga Nghin Do'i. Even though she was a local, there were many hidden perils along the long way. Any country at war was a dangerous place, and a civil war set citizens against one another. You never knew who you could trust. There were enough people she trusted that she could stay with along the way, but there were stretches in between that could be dangerous for someone whose face was familiar to North Vietnam intelligence as a possible traitor. She knew many shortcuts and hidden routes along the way to her uncle's place, but she didn't allow herself to be complacent as she made her way north.

Hanoi was a bustling place, extremely crowded—and dangerous, as the Americans were not as reluctant to bomb the city as they used to be. Her uncle had many hideouts in the city and all over North Vietnam. He often spent time in the caves in the Haiphong area, where lakes and rivers carved out grottoes deep into the limestone rocks, some so large that the North Vietnamese had actually used it as their second-largest command post, accessible only by boat. He also spent time in secret places below the streets of Hanoi, and hideouts in the northwestern countryside. She knew where each hiding place was, but she hoped he was in one close by.

It wasn't long before she saw the skyline of the city on the horizon. She paused for a minute for a few deep breaths before pressing on into the stress of the city. Before she knew it, she was riding her bicycle down along busy streets, heading for the first place she thought he might be. She turned down an alley behind a large block of buildings where there were stairs that descended to the basements. She rapped on a door with a particular series of knocks and soon someone opened a peephole. She uttered a few key words and was admitted into a small room. To verify her identity, the man who answered the door asked several questions. She looked at the shadows to her right and saw a man with an AK-47. She was then allowed into another room, where she stood before a desk.

"May di gap Nhiem-vu Phuc-Nguyen phai khong?"—Are you going to meet Nhiem-vu Phuc-Nguyen? a heavyset asked, already knowing the answer. When she said she was, the man said, *"No di roi. O' lai day di."*—He's gone already. Stay here.

Nga Nghin Do'i waited as another man with an AK-47 watched over her shoulder. She knew that everyone here knew who she was, but no one was taking any chances when it was impossible to know who to trust. After a five-minute absence, the man returned and motioned to her. *"Di vo'i tao."*—Come with me. She got up and followed him down along some passages to a tunnel that led to one of the many command centers that the Communist Party elite used in an effort to maintain secrecy. Eventually she reached the room her uncle was in and they embraced as she walked into the door. He nodded at the receptionist to leave them alone.

"To'i day de lam gi vay?"—What are you doing here? he asked, surprised to see her.

"Nhin cai nay kia!"—Look at this here! She handed her uncle the intercepted intelligence transmission with her picture and explained what was going on in the villages and at her store. They talked about the war, Val, the attacks on the store and the villages, and how they *must* stop. She explained how Val had saved the Twin Villages from a tragic outcome by helping them get supplies and told him that a girl was brutally raped and the elder—his close friend—was severely beaten by NVA troops. She told him that her own life was now in serious danger from spies who didn't know what was really going on at the store and expressed concern for her employees lives—including her uncle's own love interest, Nghia Mau. All the while she cried, lamenting how the war was threatening people she loved. She even voiced concern for Val's friends languishing in a prison somewhere in North Vietnam.

Nhiem-vu Phuc-Nguyen couldn't stand to see his niece cry. She was a sweet, caring soul who thought of others before herself and knew that her concerns were genuine and required action. He was quite angry about what happened at *his* home and that his own forces were now targeting *his* niece, who had nothing to do with this war. It was more than an insult or insubordination—it was an outrage! He also felt guilty that he'd forced her into the war by using her store to move supplies and weapons for the communist North. She didn't care if her country was democratic or communist—she didn't even care about power or politics. She only hoped that North and South Vietnam would become one country again and that all foreigners went home and left her people alone.

He took a deep breath as he held his niece his arms and dried some of her tears, then said soothingly, *"Du'ng khoc nu'a. Tao hieu. Du'ng co lo, de tao lam cho ngay!"*—Don't cry. I understand. Don't worry, I'll do it right away!

He picked up the intelligence intercept and told her that he'd put his orders to cease and desist to all commands as soon as she was finished with her visit. As they talked, he pulled out a thick packet of papers and photographs. He explained that he'd just gotten back from a quick trip to a prison on the south side of Hanoi. Then he switched to English to confuse unwanted eavesdroppers. "Don't get caught with that packet. Burn it if you come in contact with NVA troops that you feel will search you. When you get home, give it to Captain Jordan—he'll make good use of it. Both you and he have my word that everything will soon be taken of."

She looked at the package. She had an idea what was in it, but knew not to ask here. "Thank you, Uncle. Everyone at the store and villages will thank you, and I know Val—er, Captain Jordan—will thank you." She stood up, wiped her cheeks dry, and hugged him once. "Thank you, Uncle. I love you! See you at dinner tonight!" She left the office and walked down the maze of tunnels to the reception desk. The receptionist was infatuated with his boss's beautiful niece, and she graced him with a smile as she passed his desk and casually tucked the packet into her pack. Once outside, she grabbed her bicycle and rode to one of her uncle's many apartments. She would have dinner with her uncle, then leave in the morning for her long ride home.

In his office, Nhiem-vu Phuc-Nguyen sent out a cease and desist order to all commands not to bother the Twin Villages, the store at Dong Hoi, and his niece. He explained that the case had been investigated at the highest level and that everyone in these places, especially his niece, were not traitors and supported the Communist Party and North Vietnam in their resistance against America. Anyone who ignored these orders or took matters into their own hands without consulting him would be punished.

§ § § § §

Ten days without seeing Nga Nghin Do'i were painful for Val, who had no idea if she was okay, but today he'd be driving to Dong Hoi, following the new schedule she'd given him before she left for Hanoi. Before Val left, he checked in with Captain Overstreet, as he'd done every day for the past week-and-a-half, to see if he'd intercepted any more messages about Nga Nghin Do'i. "Relax, Buddy," Overstreet said and handed Val an oversized envelope with a pornographic magazine inside. "I meant to give that to you last night, but I got too busy."

Val opened the envelope and slid out the magazine, then looked back at Overstreet. "So this is what you DIA boys do all day!"

Overstreet looked at what Val was thumbing through and said, "Oops. Sorry, Captain—I meant to give you this one."

"Well don't get me wrong, Captain—I don't mind this one." Val smiled as he took the other envelope and opened it.

Overstreet watched Val as he read the message Nhiem-vu Phuc-Nguyen had sent out, then smiled as Val's expression changed. "Looks like your girl accomplishes what she sets her mind to."

Val was relieved that she was safe and flushed with pride at Overstreet's compliment. "Yeah—she's one incredible woman. She's got more grit than most of us Marines ever dreamed of." He handed the message back to Overstreet, then ran to his truck with a grin on his face. As Val climbed into the cab, Overstreet shouted so loudly that two Marines passing by whooped: "Hey Captain—bring back that skin magazine!"

Val shouted back, "If you don't mind, I'd like to keep it for a while—I want to play a joke on Papa!" Then he took off for Dong Hoi, and before he knew it he was backing up to the dock at the store.

Nga Nghin Do'i's heart raced when she heard Val's truck. She jumped up from her desk and ran outside. When Val saw her reflection in the rearview mirror, he killed the engine and leapt from the cab into her arms. They embraced and kissed as if they hadn't seen each other in ages. Then they raced into the store, where Val gave Nghia Mau a long hug before disappearing with Nga Nghin Do'i into her office.

"I'm so glad you're safe. I worried every night you were gone," Val said between kisses.

"I'm happy just to see you again," she replied.

"I saw the message from your uncle. You *are* amazing, Nga Nghin Do'i!" Val said as he hugged her, and she was happy to return Val's affection. "I don't want to ever be apart for that long again—I want you by my side for the rest of my life," Val went on. "If that means I stay behind in Vietnam or if you come to America, so be it."

"Are you saying what I think you are?" she asked.

"I sure am. I was hoping for a better setting to say this, but I can't contain it any longer." Val pulled back just enough to look her in the eyes. "I love you, Nga Nghin Do'i. I can't imagine living without you. I want to marry you. I'll give up everything for you. I'd gladly stay in Vietnam with you. If you wanted to go to America, I'd make that happen."

She wasn't sure how to react. She loved Val, but she wanted to be sure Val knew what he was saying. "Are you sure? Do you really know what you're asking for?"

"I've never been more sure of anything in my life. I'd give up the world for you," he said.

"I love you, Val. I want the same thing you want, but I'd have to get my uncle's blessing. I'm sure he will give it."

"I know he will," Val answered.

"Right now, let's just enjoy this moment," she said as she snuggled into him.

They spent the next couple of hours getting the order together, with frequent breaks to make out. Eventually it was time for Val to leave again, but when they were alone on the docks, they had a hard time tearing away from each other. But Val couldn't put it off any longer, so he finally climber into the cab and shut the door. All of a sudden, Nga Nghin Do'i remembered something. "Wait—I have something for you and Captain Overstreet."

"What is it?" he asked as she ran back into the store.

A few moments later she came out with a large packet, which she handed to Val with a kiss. "Don't open until you're back on Linh Thu," she said as she stepped back.

He set the packet on the passenger's seat and pulled away from the dock. Soon he was out of the city and heading through the countryside to Linh Thu with only the thoughts of the woman he loved. When he finally got back to Linh Thu and checked in, he and Papa and Val had their usual conversation about the trip, the entire time Papa eyeing the packet Val had set on his desk without a word about it.

Finally Papa's curiosity got the best of him. "What the hell is that?"

Val looked at it. "I'm not really sure, sir—I have several theories. Maybe we should open it at the HQ building."

"Who's it from?"

"It's from Nga Nghin Do'i's uncle, sir—a member of the Politburo. She said Captain Overstreet would be interested in it." Val shifted in his seat and continued. "I suggest that you, me, Captain Overstreet, Lieutenant Torres, Major Chapman, Major Darryl, and Commander Yeary go through it before tonight's briefing, sir."

Papa pondered what Val said, then picked up the packet and noticed how heavy it was. "Well, if she said it's meant for the intelligence officer, then that's what we'll do." He set the packet down, then picked up the phone and arranged for everyone to meet the HQ conference. "Be there in thirty minutes, Captain—and don't forget that package."

Before Val got up, he pulled out the porn magazine he'd gotten from Overstreet that morning and tossed it at his CO. "Here, sir—this is special delivery for you!"

The magazine landed on Papa's desk and bounced open to an explicit picture of a naked woman spread-eagled on a bed. "Goddamnit, Jordan—you're getting bolder!" Papa laughed, then glanced at the picture. "Better make that meeting in forty-five minutes!"

Within a half hour, the seven officers sat around the conference table looking at the mysterious packet that Val had brought back from Dong Hoi, waiting for Val to open it. Finally Papa said, "Well, open the damn thing, Captain."

"Aye, sir." Val broke the seal on the packet and slid the contents onto the table. A cover letter slid out first—more like a set of instructions on how to use the information in the package. He read the letter aloud:

"Captain Jordan: I hope you have received this package and my niece was not caught delivering it to you. She has convinced me to help you and your friends. She has never even met them, so I'm not sure why she is so concerned for their welfare, but I know she cares deeply for all people and even more so for you. I have located your friends. There are four of your squadron mates being held in the same facility. They are being detained at the Lam Khuat Prison on the southwestern border of Hanoi. You could never hope to find them on your own because the facility is very well disguised and the occupants are sometimes moved to an alternate facility northwest of the regular one from time to time. I have decided to help you rescue your friends and all the other prisoners at the facility. Why? I hate the man who runs the facility, I am convinced he killed several friends of mine years ago and was involved in a recent attack on the Hai Lan Langs where many people were tortured and had their very livelihoods stolen from them. You have helped the people in the villages and the girls in my niece's store so many times, the very least I can do is help you at least once. In the packet you will find all you will need for a coordinated attack on the facility. I can guarantee the safety of all the prisoners because of an exercise I have ordered on the date mentioned in the plans. You will have what you need to know—precision accurate charts, diagrams, schedules, etc. Please do not delay on your attack and rescue—it will only work with the precise timing in the schedules I have provided and planned. I know that your superiors will be skeptical of this, but you know me and you have my word. Good luck, help your friends.—NVPN."

The officers absorbed what they'd just heard, unsure what to think yet. Val slid out the rest of the contents of the package, and everything that Nhiem-vu Phuc-Nguyen promised was there. He briefly studied the plan and realized that Nga Nghin Do'i's uncle had put a lot of effort at great personal risk into the plans he'd given to his enemies. Val went through the photos and names of the Americans being detained at the prison—twenty altogether, with four were from Linh Thu—and his heart skipped when he saw the image of a battered Notso and Speedy. He also was shocked and relieved to learn that Baker and Charles were there, and he briefly flashed back to the night they were shot down.

"What's the look for, young'un?" Big John asked as he saw Val's expression change.

"Pictures of Speedy and Notso and Baker and Charles." Val choked up a little. "These guys were my *wing men!* Sorry, sir."

"Shake it off, son." Commander Yeary said. "The real issue here is, can trust this man and pull off this rescue?"

"We have the resources needed to do so, sir," Lieutenant Torres chimed in. "My major concern is the timing of the whole thing. This could be a trap."

Chappie looked up. "The only person who's ever met this man is Captain Jordan. What do you think, Jordan—can we trust this man?"

Val set down the photos and looked around the table at everyone in turn. He took a deep breath and said, "Yes we can trust this man, sir. I have no doubt about his sincerity."

"You seem pretty confident, Jordan. You'd better be damn sure and not let your feelings for his niece cloud your judgment. We need to know for sure. So once again, Captain—can we trust this man? Can we get our boys back without losing anyone?" Papa said.

"Well sir, I can't guarantee that we won't lose anyone, but I can honestly tell you that we can trust the man. He doesn't hate Americans. He wants us out of his country for sure, but he doesn't hate us. He kept his word to me before by ordering an immediate halt to the attacks on the store, so I have no reason to doubt him on this."

"You understand the risk we're taking if we decide to go through with it." Papa looked at the calendar on the wall. "According to our source in Hanoi, we have to commence this operation in exactly ten days. If we're going to commit the resources to this, we need to make a firm decision soon. Captain Overstreet, keep this package in a place where the officers here can have access to it for the next three days. We'll all meet again in three days for a final decision. Dismissed."

"I'd like to state my opinion now, sir—we need to get our people back," Val said.

"Son, we all want them back, but let's be smart about this and not rush blindly into anything that already has about a million pitfalls," Papa replied. "We'll decide in three days, which will give us a week to prepare if we decide to green light this op."

§§§§§§

The next morning Val woke up optimistic for the first time in a long while. He'd actually gotten a decent night's sleep and stretched out as he watched the sun rise over the trees to the east. He walked swiftly to Papa's office to pick up the day's list of supplies, only to see it wasn't taped to the door sill as it usually was. He felt a little panic seep and immediately set off to find Papa. As he walked along the muddy roads, he bumped into Papa coming out of the HQ building. "Slow down, Captain," Papa said as he pulled a piece of paper out of his breast pocket. "Here's today's list."

"Thank you, sir." Val said as he put the paper in his pocket.

Papa studied Val for a little bit and said, "You okay, son?"

"Yes sir, Why?"

"You're not on edge as you usually are. Got anything you'd like to share?"

"No sir. I'm fine—really." As Val started to turn away to head to the motor pool, Papa grabbed his arm and turned him back around.

"Be careful, Jordan. I'm worried that you're letting your feelings for this local gal cloud your otherwise good judgment."

Val thought the comment was more about the rescue operation. "sir, I'll be fine. I'm gonna get our supplies, and in a few days we'll have our mates safely back here!"

"Good. Have a safe trip, Captain," Papa said, picking up on Val's confidence.

"Thank you, sir—see you this afternoon," Val said as Papa released his arm and he went off to pick up his truck.

Val was soon on the way to Dong Hoi, thinking both of Nga Nghin Do'i and how relieved he was to know that his friends were at least alive. Just as he entered the parking lot, he saw Nga Nghin Do'i climbing off her bicycle and his heart came alive. She looked to where the familiar noise was coming from and flashed her brilliant smile and waved. Grinning, Val leaned out of his window and waved back, almost hitting his head on a lamppost. Nga Nghin Do'i laughed and watched as he backed the truck up to the loading dock. When Val stepped out, he rubbed his head and checked himself in the mirror.

Laughing, Nga Nghin Do'i approached him and said, "You shouldn't show off, Val—it's not your thing."

Val smiled back. "Can't disagree with you there." After they hugged and kissed, she tugged on his arm and pulled him inside the store.

"Come on—we have work to do," she said through her giggles. They quickly found themselves in her office looking over Val's list, which was considerably shorter than most trips. When the girls got to the store, it didn't take them long to load Val's truck, and soon Val and Nga Nghin Do'i found themselves with more free time than usual. As they used the opportunity to express their ardor for one another, Val thought she was unusually affectionate today. He wasn't sure what had gotten into her, but he knew he really liked it.

Around the noon hour, Val shared lunch with Nga Nghin Do'i and the others, and afterward Nga Nghin Do'i took the rest of the day off. Before he knew what was happening, she was driving his truck to the villages, and Val was once again stepping on his imaginary brake pedal. She giggled almost the whole way, and her laughter only subsided when the engine shut down after they arrived.

Val went into Nga Nghin Do'i's sewing hut to change into the clothes she'd made him while she checked around to see if anyone needed any garments repaired. As soon as he emerged from the hut, children swarmed around him to play. Nga Nghin Do'i left him in their hands as she set to work. The children quickly organized a soccer game in the space between the villages, and Val quickly found it hard to keep track of which of them were even on his team. When one child passed him the ball one time, then tried to steal it from him another, he said, "*Cho mot chut!*"—Wait a minute! When he explained to the boy that he couldn't play both sides, the child said, "Why not?" in his native tongue. "That way I win no matter what happens." Val, finding the logic indisputable, bowed his head and said, "*Hoc-gia!*"—Genius!

After a couple of hours of exhausting play, Val looked over to see Nga Nghin Do'i walking up to him. "You look like a man in need of rescue." She laughed as she looked at his sweaty clothes. "Come with me." She grabbed his hand and led him away with the children chanting "Val and Nga Nghin Do'i sitting in a tree…"—their version of a Vietnamese children's rhyme. As they walked toward the Nhat Le River, she said, "Stay for dinner. I promise to get you home before dark. We would be honored"—she paused, then looked into his eyes—"and I want to spend every second I can with you. I wish you didn't have to leave. I hate it when we're apart."

Val gripped her hand. "Not as much as I do. Soon I won't have to leave."

The walk was over all too soon and the hours flew by. Before they knew it, dinner was over and Val would be leaving. Suddenly a young man came running screaming at the top of his lungs to the villagers and Val: "*Linh! Linh! Dan viet linh! Bac! Di! Di!*"—Soldiers! Soldiers! Vietnamese soldiers! From the North! Go! Go!

Startled, Nga Nghin Do'i was gripped by fear as she knew Val would either be killed or tortured if he was taken captive by the approaching NVA, but she also feared for the villagers, knowing what happened last time soldiers came. The village elder shouted to Val and Nga Nghin Do'i to leave because the villagers could handle themselves. She grabbed Val by his wrist and took off running to his truck. Just as they darted out from the cover of the huts of the village, the silhouettes of the troops could be distinguished in the growing darkness. She gripped his wrist tighter and pulled him to the ground. "Stay low! It will be harder for them to see us!" She ducked in a hut and came out with a field hat. "Put this on. It will disguise you from a distance!" Already dressed in local clothes, the hat would help complete the effect, although there was no concealing his stature. But maybe if he hunkered over…

Val and Nga Nghin Do'i kept a low profile as they made their way toward his truck, which was parked on the southern edge of the southern village. They looked back to see the NVA platoon entering the north village and talking to the elder. They didn't want to dash to the truck lest they be noticed and give the impression that they were running away. They ducked in and out of the shadows finally sprinted across the open space to the truck. When they looked back, they saw that the platoon had split into several groups, and the team that was headed their way was wasting no time. He had to get moving now!

When they got to the truck, Nga Nghin Do'i shoved Val inside. "Go now, my love—I'll be fine! Just go! They'll kill you if they find you here!" Val didn't want to leave and was about to resist until she added, "They'll kill us both if they find you here!"

Val's suddenly pictured the girl who'd been raped the last time an NVA platoon came through. He reached out and grabbed Nga Nghin Do'i's wrist. "No—you come with me!"

"No! I will not leave my people!" She choked up. "Don't argue—we don't have time!" She looked at the soldiers making their way to the northern tip of the southern village.

"I'm not leaving without you!"

"Stop being bullheaded! Let go—they're coming! Please go!"

"They've already seen us—now get in here!" he pleaded.

"No! Start the truck! Go!"

Just then a round struck the cab as a soldier fired off a few shots and charged a vehicle that clearly didn't belong in the villages. Val felt unfamiliar strength as he grabbed her by the wrist and yanked her into the cab as the engine finally roared to life after. Val slid over to the passenger side, and as another round smacked the cab, he shouted, "Let's go!" He pulled his M16 to his side, but he wanted to avoid having to use it at all costs.

As another round hit the cab, she slammed the truck in gear and mashed the accelerator. The truck lurched forward and stalled as she popped the clutch. More rounds were now hitting the truck, and she began to panic as she tried to restart it. Then she felt Val's hand on hers as he spoke calmly while rounds pinged off the truck. "Just relax. You can do it. Just start the truck and let's go." He then slid his M16 onto the window rail, ready to fire.

Energized, she finally got the engine to start, got the truck in gear, and mashed the gas pedal down. This time the truck lurched forward and kicked up mud on the rapidly approaching soldier. As they began to speed away in the darkness toward Dong Hoi, she began to cry and pounded the steering wheel in anger. "My friends! They will surely be killed now!" She began to sob as she drove. "What have I done? I left my friends when they needed me the most!" Just then they heard a loud bang on the right side of the truck, which immediately began to slew.

"Don't lose control," Val urged, but Nga Nghin Do'i seemed to instinctively know what to do, and as they slowed down he heard the familiar clump-clump-clump of flat tires.

"What's that noise?" she asked the steering got heavier.

"Flat tires. The soldier might have shot out a couple."

"What does that mean? Can we not get to Dong Hoi?"

"No—we have to pull over. I only have one spare. We have to find a place to hide the truck until I can call for help," Val replied.

"We've only gone a few kilometers. They can still find us if they keep heading this way."

Val took a deep breath. "Do you know where we can hide until I call my base?"

"No—" Nga Nghin Do'i said, then she saw the silhouette of a watchtower in the distance. "Actually, yes. There." She pointed, then carefully turned the truck off the road and onto a divider between two large rice paddies. "*Thap canh*—uh, watchtower?"

"We can hide a truck in the watchtower?"

"No, but we can hide it beside it under some palm leaves. It will look like a waste pile."

"Won't the soldiers check the tower?"

"No. Most are near collapsing. The ones that are still good are filled with animals and grain. The Japanese and French never found my relatives or me in these towers, so my own countrymen should overlook them as well." She shut the headlights off as she approached the tower and pulled the truck behind it, then shut the engine down. She looked at Val as she climbed out of the cab. "Come on—we need to hurry."

Val jumped out and together they gathered huge palm leaves that had fallen from the trees lining the borders of the paddies. He was amazed at how easily she could shinny up trees to grab leaves that were still hanging but about to drop. After an hour, they had enough leaves to conceal the truck and he was about to grab the radio from the cab when she suddenly grabbed him. "Come on—the soldiers are just a few hundred meters away!" She led him up a ladder to a room at the top that was dimly lit by light coming in through the small windows. As Nga Nghin Do'i pulled up the ladder, Val looked around and saw bags of rice stacked against the walls. He peered out one of the small windows to check on the enemy platoon and saw that it was on the road trying to follow the tracks of his truck but gave up when the tracks disappeared off the road. The platoon continued south up the road and eventually faded from sight. They both breathed a sigh of relief, and Val reached over and squeezed her hand. "It looked like the entire platoon, so they didn't hang around in the villages long enough to hurt anyone."

Nga Nghin Do'i squeezed Val's hand in return, relieved and exhilarated at the same time. "I'm glad you made me come with you."

"Why's that?"

"Well, you were right. They probably would've killed me. But more importantly"—she leaned into him and wrapped her arms around him and pressed her body tightly against his—"it gives us a chance to be alone and finally share a night together."

With that she pulled Val's hat off and kissed him passionately. She then pulled off his shirt and ran her hands over his muscled torso. She continued to kiss him, running her hands over his muscled body, feeling the warmth of his skin. Before long they collapsed into each other's arms on a makeshift bed of rice bags. As their passion escalated, Val carefully slipped her top off and ran his hands over her silky smooth skin from her face down along her torso. As his hands cupped her breasts and slid down the flat plain of her stomach, she shuddered and let out a sigh of surrender. Val's lips began to follow after his fingers as she found the ties on the front of his pants. She carefully untied them and slipped his pants off as Val did the same with hers. Naked now, their heat became intense as they felt each other's bodies with every pore.

Eventually their bodies became one, and the outside world and all its problems ceased to exist in that moment when two lovers erupt in their own perfect union. And as the night dissolved into morning, the sun burst through the small windows onto Val and Nga Nghin Do'i as they cuddled. When she rolled over to face him, who was just beginning to wake, she said as she gently stroked his face, "*Em yeu anh. Anh la tat ca. Em muon thanh vo anh.*"—I love you. You are everything to me. I want to be your wife.

"*Luc nao anh cung nghi ve may. Em la do'i anh. Anh yeau anh. Em muon anh cu'o'i em.*"—I think about you all the time. You are my life. I love you. I want you to marry me. He gently stroked her long shiny hair and continued down the back of her neck and down her spine, continuing along her firm buttocks and thighs. They felt happier than they had in a long time, and made love again before finally getting dressed.

Yawning, Val headed down to the truck and called Linh Thu on his radio. He explained what had happened and was informed that a helicopter would be there in twenty minutes and would air hoist the truck back to Linh Thu. He knew Papa would give him hell for not calling earlier, but would probably forgive him when he learned that Val was trying to avoid detection by the NVA. Nga Nghin Do'i soon left to check on her village, and they parted under the steady beat of rotor blades of a CH-46 Sea Knight from VMO-16.

§ § § § §

Looking through a small window, Val could see his CO's tall frame waiting on the ramp with his hands on his hips. The big CH-46 had just dropped the truck off at the motor pool and was bringing him to the northwest ramp, where it would land and taxi into its barricade. When he exited the chopper, Val was still dressed in his local Vietnamese attire and carrying his flight coveralls in over arm.

"Goddamnit, Jordan—I'd give you office hours or some other punishment for your little AWOL episode last night, but you'd just enjoy the break too much!" Papa shouted when the helicopter engines quieted down enough to be heard. When he got a good look at Val's outfit, he nearly fell over from laughing so hard. "What the hell? You make one ugly Vietnamese dude! You'd better change before some hung-over, trigger-happy Marine shoots you. Then come to my office immediately!"

"Aye, sir. Glad to see you handling this so well," Val said.

"Who said I'm handling this well?" Papa said. "Because of you the MCX is out of Rolaids *and* Tums."

"You sure have an odd way of saying you worry about the men under your command, sir," Val said with a chuckle as he went to change into his flight fatigues.

"Yeah, well you assholes have been trying to kill me for years now, but I'm still here!" Papa shot back.

When Val was back in uniform, he waited for Papa in his office. Papa came in and ordered Val to sit down, then asked about last night's events.

"Well sir, I'd picked up our supplies and the store owners invited me to their village. It was still early in the afternoon and I had plenty of time, so I went. Just as I was about to leave, a platoon of NVA troops was spotted heading to the village. One of the women helped me escape and get to my truck. When I got to the truck, the enemy troops had gotten close enough to open fire. I sped away as quickly as I could but had a blowout only a couple klicks down the road. I found a place to hide the truck, but as I was about to call on the radio, a team from the platoon was patrolling nearby and I had to hide a watchtower. I concealed the truck with palm leaves and waited out the night until it was safe enough for me to call base."

Papa thought for a few moments. "Maybe I shouldn't send you on any more of these little excursions. The risks are too great."

Val protested. "No sir—the risks are actually small. This has never happened before, and it most likely won't happen again!"

Papa was surprised by how unwilling Val was to give up the trips to Dong Hoi. "Relax, Captain—keep your bearing! Don't let your feelings for the local honey cloud your judgment. I'll let you continue the trips, but you have to leave the store for the base in the early afternoon from now on. If you're delayed because of a large order or traffic or anything else, you'd better get on the horn right away and let us know! I'm not going to spend another sleepless night wondering if I just sent one of my men to be captured or killed—got it?"

Val calmed down and said, "Yes sir."

"You're dismissed, Captain. Oh, you're on Alert-5 duty tonight with Lieutenant Cesco. Report to the shack at 1900."

"Sir, I have one other issue to bring up, if you don't mind."

Papa sighed. A smart-aleck remark was forthcoming, he was sure. "Go ahead, son."

"Is cockfighting illegal on base, sir?"

Papa rolled his eyes, knowing he was being set up. "What do you mean, Jordan?"

"Well sir, Lieutenant Cesco was supposed to be helping the cooks at the chow hall clean a live rooster for dinner one night, but the rooster got loose and tore him up. It wasn't long before everyone was demanding a rematch and placing bets. The rematch tonight, but if the lieutenant has Alert-5 duty, there's gonna be a lot of upset fight fans."

The image of Roostercomb tussling with a rooster made Papa laugh. "Goddamnit, Jordan, that's lame! Have a better one for me next time!"

Val grabbed his gear and reported to the shack, where he saw Cesco, now sporting a standard Marine haircut, playing a game of poker with Nate, Lieutenant Wright, and several of the ground crew. He flashed back to Speedy and Notso absorbed in a serious poker game. Val threw his stuff on his rack and looked over the new guys' cards as he went around the table. He leaned over and whispered to both the new aviators, "Don't bluff—it never works here!" Both men looked up at him in awe, wondering how he guessed that they were bluffing. "By the way, Rooster, where's all your hair?" Once Val got his gear ready in case of a scramble, he sat down to join in on the game.

The poker game went on late into the night until everyone got tired and hit the racks. The night was interrupted by another raid, but while not as serious as previous ones, no one got much sleep afterward because they feared another one. But there was none.

No one minded hanging out in the shack, since it was the closest thing to a vacation on Linh Thu. The night went by without a scramble for the men on Alert-5 duty, but they still had the dayshift to go through. When everyone woke in the morning, they weren't greeted by the usual bright sun—today the skies were sullen, with a strange low overcast stratus layer that masked the summits of the peaks to the west. At 0800 Captain Overstreet stopped by the shack to share some intel with the crews inside. "You guys mind if I speak to you a few moments?"

Since Val was the highest ranking officer there, he spoke for everyone. "No, Captain—what's up?"

"Well there's a massive push by the NVA sweeping south of Hanoi. We do have ground troops, mostly Spec Ops forces, in the regions, and they seem to moving toward." He knew they were wondering how that affected them, so he answered their questions before they were asked. "You can probably expect several scrambles within the next few hours—especially if they find our boys out in the field."

"So if we get called it will be mostly CAS missions? You don't expect we'll be needed to cover any air strikes scheduled today?" Val asked.

"As far as I know, there are no air strikes scheduled outside the daily sorties. My concern for the CAS flights is that the enemy may be resupplied with SAMs. The Navy reported from Yankee Station that a dozen overloaded small fast boats went directly to the docks at Haiphong. When a patrol boat got a peek at them, they were unloading weapons into trucks that most likely dispatched all over North Vietnam. Just be careful out there, use your flares, stick to the avoidance tactics you've been taught, use your brains and don't take unnecessary chances. If you're shot down and manage to bail out, you have about an eighty percent or higher chance of being captured today. Just be careful."

"Roger, Captain—thanks for the heads-up. What're the chances of being called out?"

"Pretty high—maybe eighty-five percent. I'll be surprised if you go two more hours without a call. Be careful today, gents." Overstreet smiled and left.

Val looked around and said, "Try not to dwell on it, gents. Relax and think about naked women." He grabbed a *Playboy* off the coffee table and flipped open to the centerfold. "Like how many positions you'd nail *her* in if you had an hour with her."

Just as Overstreet had said it might, the phone rang within an hour—and just as he'd predicted, it was a Spec Op platoon needing close air support as they had engaged a large, enemy regiment. Val plotted out the coordinates on a map and handed a waiting ordnance tech the list of ordnance to load. As Val spoke on the phone, Nate, Cesco, and Wright crowded around him. When Val hung up he gave them the particulars and realized that the target area was close to Dong Hoi, but he didn't have time to think about that.

"All right, guys—this is our target area." He pointed to the charts so the pilots and RIOs could mark it on their personal charts. "There's an overcast layer at twenty-seven hundred feet, so be careful. That'll make for an extremely low pullout, close to release altitude. We have a platoon trapped here by an entire NVA regiment. We are to drop within their perimeter, so be damn sure you don't hit our guys. There's an OV-10 from here arriving on scene right now, so that should be a big help directing our runs. We'll get the rest on scene. Let's move!" Val pointed to the jets that were now ready to go.

The crews jumped into their cockpits and strapped in as the pilots fired up the engines. They performed their BITs and checklists on the taxi to runway 31, and before they reached the end of the runway, pilots and RIOs heard the order from the control tower. "Bowtie 1, Linh Thu Tower. Wind calm, runway three-one cleared for takeoff. Change to departure."

"Roger. Bowtie 1 cleared for takeoff runway three-one. Switching," Val replied as he switched to button blue for Strike, pushed full throttle, and stoked the burners with Cesco in tow. Within seconds, the green jungles were blanketed by the clouds as the jets penetrated the overcast layer at twenty-six hundred feet. Within another few seconds, they left the blur of the clouds for sunny blue skies as they punched through the top of the layer. Val checked in with Panama. "Strike, Bowtie 1. Flight of two Fox-4s on the Linh Thu three-one-zero at one-five. Climbing to angels one-niner. We're on button blue loaded with six thousand-pounders, twenty mike-mike, and two Sidewinders each. Proceeding to target area west of Dong Hoi for CAS flight."

"Bowtie Flight, Strike. Roger. Proceed as requested. No enemy traffic observed between you and target area. Contact the FACA on button brown, call-sign Maestro 1 Charlie."

"Roger. Bowtie 1 switching." Val switched frequencies and called up the OV-10 that would now be overflying the target area. "Maestro 1 Charlie, Bowtie 1."

"Bowtie 1, Maestro 1 Charlie. You must be my CAS flight. Give me your stores and fuel status."

"Bowtie 1 is a flight of two Fox-4s loaded with six thousand-pounders, twenty mike-mike, and two Sidewinders each. We have approximately five-five minutes of playtime. Will be on target in eight minutes at angels one-niner."

"Roger Bowtie 1. I'm at angels two. The base of the overcast layer is at two-eight-zero-zero. Gooners are everywhere! I'll be marking hotspots with Willie Petes. Run in from one-eight-zero. Have a right-hand pullout zero-niner-zero at whatever altitude you want. It's all going to be low-low-low today with the weather. One bomb per run. Ten seconds between runs. We'll work in a circle starting on the east side working counterclockwise. Read back."

Val read the mission back and had his flight descend to four thousand feet AGL. The angles were going to be really shallow on this mission; luckily there was no high terrain to contend with on the coastal plain, so the jets could fly and release really low and have a relatively safe pullout. He put his flight into a counterclockwise orbit as they awaited the FACA's orders to commence attack. He looked back at Nate in his rearview, then said over the ICS, "Hey brother—does this remind you of our first flight here, minus the mountains?"

"Yeah. It's like déjà vu. Be careful, just because there's no terrain doesn't mean that we're out of danger."

"I know. Let's just hope this is a quick one."

The flight circled considerably longer than they were used to before hearing orders to attack, so Val checked in to make sure everything was okay under the clouds. "Maestro 1 Charlie, Bowtie 1. What's the status?"

"Bowtie 1, Maestro 1 Charlie. Sorry. I was telling our troops to take cover and I'm dealing with a lot of ground fire. I've got the first two targets marked. I'll clear you as soon as I know our boys are clear."

Val listened to the explanation from the FACA, then looked at the chart on his lap. There was something peculiar about this location, but he couldn't figure it out yet. Just as he was about to give it some more thought, the order came. "Bowtie Flight, Maestro 1 Charlie, you are cleared hot. Call roll-in."

Val finished his orbit and began his northbound turn and keyed up. "Bowtie 1 rolling in hot." He pushed the stick forward and took deep breaths as his jet touched the cloud deck in a shallow dive at thirty-four hundred feet. He knew the bases of the layer were around twenty-eight hundred feet, so he wouldn't be in the clouds for too long. Suddenly the gray flashed deep green as he punched through the bottom of the layer over open rice paddies and began to scan for the smoke from the FACA's marking run.

"I have you in sight, Dash 1. Move right and you will be on line. Cleared hot," Maestro 1 Charlie said.

Val looked to his right and saw the rising smoke column and greened up his first rack. He could see that Dong Hoi was pretty close to the target area—only ten miles or less to the east—and the paddies were sprinkled with several small villages. He was closing fast to the first smoke column, and put his jet into a shallow dive. Trying to estimate the correct angle for a good on target release, he maneuvered his jet for the best position. Nate counted down the seconds as Val released when he thought the bomb should hit the mark.

"I have one away, Dash 1," Maestro 1 Charlie said. As the bomb hit close to the mark, he continued. "On target Dash 1. Dash 2 cleared hot. Call roll in."

"Roger. Dash 2 rolling in hot," Rooster called.

"Make your drop right at Dash 1's drop and that should eliminate that target," Maestro 1 Charlie instructed.

As Val pulled up, he felt the shockwaves off the single bomb and he thought about what a powerful weapon it was. If he could feel its energy in his jet, speeding away at altitude, he could only imagine what it must feel like on the ground near its detonation. Rooster performed his run flawlessly and both jets returned to their orbit to await Maestro 1 Charlie to make his next marking run.

Maestro 1 Charlie flew over the target area and saw that the enemy troops were heading north. The friendlies immediately turned south to gain some distance. It was weird that the enemy regiment was retreating after just two runs. They could be trying to get to the entrance of a tunnel to take cover, but they could also be setting a trap for the US troops. Nevertheless, they could wreak havoc on any extraction flight coming in to pick up the Spec Ops platoon. Maestro 1 Charlie turned westbound to see if he could spot any more enemy troops south of the friendly platoon, to see if there might be a trap, but only saw movement to the west and north. He couldn't just ignore them, especially since he had the firepower available to eliminate any possible problems, so he decided to set up for another marking run. He lined up and fired a Willie Pete into the heaviest concentration of troops, which were following a rice paddy heading north toward a village. "Dash 1 you are cleared hot. Call roll in. Drop two bombs on this run. Drop directly on my smoke."

Val mimicked his earlier actions and began the northbound turn in his orbit and called, "Dash 1 rolling in hot." He again put his jet into a shallow dive to punch through the cloud deck that was now beginning to annoy him. He watched both his altimeter and his radar altimeter as the continued through the veil of clouds that was masking his view of the target area below. He said to Nate over the ICS, "Looks like the layer is thicker right here. We're at twenty-six hundred feet and haven't broken out yet. You got Maestro on radar?"

"Affirmative. He ducked out to the west like last time. He's eleven o'clock, two miles." Nate then saw something odd on his radar—Maestro 1 Charlie apparently heading back *toward* them! "Hey Tibbs…"

Val looked at his scope. "I see!" He fumbled with the weapons select with his left hand as he watched the scope. He selected his weapons just as he punched through the cloud layer and focused on the smoke. He noticed something strange about the scenery that greeted him—they were much closer to both Dong Hoi and the Nhat Le River, and for some reason it seemed familiar. He thought he could make out a village beyond the smoke, so he wanted to be sure to avoid it. He started his release dive and keyed up as he was again distracted by the FACA heading toward him and he worried that he was getting too close. "Maestro 1 Charlie, say intentions."

"I'm about to turn back west—" But just as Maestro 1 Charlie finished speaking, he saw a white streak heading for him and immediately recognized it as a SAM launch! He began evasive maneuvers and, uncharacteristically panicky, yelled over the frequency, "Danger—SA-7! Abort! Abort! Abort!"

Val shuddered as he heard the panic in his FACA's voice. As he began to pull up, his hand slipped when the jet was buffeted by something and accidentally hit the release button on his stick. His climb had changed the angle of his drop, and his heart lurched when an entire rack of five bombs slid off the pylons and soared over the smoke to drop into the middle of what he now clearly saw was two villages! He looked at his selection panel and noticed that while he was distracted by his FACA, he'd accidentally selected the whole rack. He realized that the jolt he'd felt was from the SAM that missed the OV-10 and exploded between it and his F-4 when its tracking sensors got confused.

When Val leveled off and looked down, he saw the villages completely disappear in a massive ball of fire. *"Shit! Oh shit! Oh fuck! No! Noooo!"* he screamed as he put his jet in a tight high-g orbit. As the flames stopped began to settle down, he saw the only thing still standing was a tall smokestack. From what he could see, parts of the villages seemed to have survived the initial blast, but then the smokestack exploded with such force that the shockwave actually shook his jet. It must have contained a highly explosive material, like fertilizer. *Oh, shit!* Val suddenly broke out into a cold sweat and his heart stopped when he realized what he had just done. He now knew why this area was so familiar—the smokestack was the centerpiece of the Twin Villages! *You just destroyed the Hai Lan Langs! You just killed your friends!* he screamed in his mind, and then he screamed for real as tears began to flow down his face into his oxygen mask. He ripped off the mask and flipped up his visor to verify what he knew was true. *"Noooo! Fuck noooo! This can't be happening! Oh my God no! Oh shit! What the fuck did I just do?"*

When Val began to punch the top of his instrument panel, Nate tried to calm his pilot down. "Hey! What's going on up there? Calm down! I don't like it either, but it *was* an accident! You didn't try to hit those villages. I'll testify to that to the end, brother!" Val was still flying tight orbits around the bomb site that was still engulfed in heavy smoke and fire, all the while presenting an easy target to nearby enemy troops.

Val tried to get Nate to understand why he was so distraught. "Those aren't just *any* villages—they're the Hai Lan Langs!" When Nate still didn't understand, Val screamed, *"Where Nga Nghin Do'i and Nghia Mau and the girls from the store live! I just killed them. All the children, all the innocent people! They weren't soldiers, they were just farmers, and I just killed them all! Goddamnit—I just killed them all!"*

Nate finally understood the gravity of the situation. He keyed up to ask if the platoon they were called in protect had been extracted. Maestro 1 Charlie told him that the rescue flight was inbound and was expected within the next ten minutes. Believing their situation to be extremely grave, Nate said to the

FACA, "Maestro, Dash 1. We've got some big problems and we need to RTB. Dash 2 will provide air support until those boys are safely headed for Linh Thu. We need to leave now." Nate paused then said, "Did you copy, Dash 2? This is Dash 1 Bravo. You will provide air cover until the rescue flight is headed home and then you will RTB. Got it?"

"Roger Dash 1 Bravo," Rooster replied.

Nate looked at Val and said over the ICS, "Look—I know you may not want to leave yet, but let's go home, brother! We can deal with this better on the ground. Who knows, maybe most of the girls weren't there. They should have been at the store."

Val stoked the burners and screamed to Linh Thu, sobbing as he flew. Disregarding the SAM avoidance approach procedure after he broke through the cloud deck on approach, he just landed straight ahead without flying an overhead pattern. He taxied to the shack before getting clearance and shut down his jet quicker than he should, ignoring most of the shutdown checklist. He jumped out of his jet, ripped off his gear, and sprinted to the motor pool, where he jumped in a truck and sped off to Dong Hoi without authorization, almost driving through the closed gate despite the protests of the sentries. Papa was furious when he learned that Val had just driven off and ran to the shack to see if Nate knew something. They met on the road just as Rooster roared in and touched down.

"Goddamnit! Where the fuck did Jordan go?" Papa shouted as the Rooster taxied by. When Nate explained what happened, Papa became worried on top of his anger. "Doesn't he realize that area is crawling with enemy troops? He's just going to drive down there in an American military truck and think he won't be noticed?"

"I don't think he's worrying about that right now, sir."

"We've got one of those trucks lightly armored, right?"

"Yes, sir. I think I saw one e like that. We use it during night raids."

"All right. Go grab your web gear. I'll put Mailer on Alert-5 duty and get a team of Marines to go with us to get Jordan. Do you know how to get to the store?"

"No, sir, but Captain Overstreet does," Nate said.

"Right. He'll be coming with us. Meet me in front of my office in five minutes. We need to find him and get him back here before dark."

"Aye sir!" Nate replied as he ran for his hooch to get his gear.

§§§§§§

Val roared down the road, still choked up and filled with pain as he kept the accelerator to the floor. Even over the engine noise, he could hear the rescue helicopters carrying the platoon he'd just covered flying above the cloud deck on their way to Linh Thu. Val didn't even bother stopping at the village—he just headed for the store. He nearly ran down several pedestrians as he sped along the overcrowded streets. When he finally pulled up to the store, he jumped out of the truck and sprinted to the store, noticing as he ran that Nga Nghin Do'i's bicycle was absent from the rack. When he got to the doors, he found them locked with a note in Nghia Mau's hand taped to one saying that the store was closed due to a disaster at home. He hoped that meant they were all still alive.

He jumped in his truck and took off through the crowded streets of Dong Hoi again, heading for the thick black smoke in the distance. Soon he pulled up as close as he could to the edge of the villages without being scorched by the intense heat still radiating from the burning debris. As he jumped out of the truck, his chest tightened when he saw there was nothing left—nothing! No huts, no buildings of any kind, no signs that people ever lived here, just a huge burning crater and a widely scattered debris field.

Val staggered around the crater sobbing, hoping for a miracle, some sign of life. As he stumbled along, he saw someone on the other side. When he was sure it wasn't a mirage, he hurried around the crater and found Nghia Mau sitting there sobbing hysterically. When he approached, she looked up and saw him there in his flight fatigues, his face streaked with tears. He knelt down beside her and they embraced, and she sobbed into his chest. Within moments he was sobbing again too. When he pulled back, he looked into her eyes and asked, *"Nga Nghin Do'i o dau?"*—Where's Nga Nghin Do'i?

She dropped her gaze and began to sob again, gripping his hand and then holding him as she sobbed. *"O dau? O dau?"*—Where? Where? Val asked desperately.

Nghia Mau couldn't even bare to say it, so she simply pointed a shaky finger to the billowing smoke and flames. Val suddenly yelled out in agony and pain, *"Noooo! Why! This can't be happening! God no! Please noooo!"* He felt a pain like none he'd ever felt. His sobs were so violent that he thought his ribs would break. He'd killed the woman he would have gladly died for! As he sobbed, Nghia Mau comforted and embraced him.

§ § § § §

Nate met Papa at his office with his combat gear. "Change of plans, son" Papa said. "We're gonna take a helicopter out there. That way we'll have the Marines to help cover from the air. The CH-46 can airlift the truck home and we can all get out of there quickly." Papa looked at the ten Marines waiting in front of his office. "Let's go, gents—we leave now!" Papa led them to the waiting CH-46 on the northwest ramp.

§ § § § §

Val and Nghia Mau cried for another forty-five minutes, then she pulled away and told him that Nga Nghin Do'i had come back to the villages to pick up lunch for the store. All the girls had come with her to help her carry some bolts of fabric to her sewing hut. Then she said, *"Tao phai din gay."*—I have to go now."

"O dau?"—Where? he asked. Then he grabbed her hand. *"Cho!"*—Wait!" He wiped his face and looked this gentle woman directly in her eyes. Then he said in a quivering voice as he pointed to the plumes of thick black smoke, *"Toan bo la loi cua anh! Viec ngau-nhien khung khiep! Toan bo la loi cua anh! Lam on du'ng han toi!"*—It's all my fault. A terrible accident! It's all my fault! Please don't hate me!"

"Ha noi. Tao that su khong muon di."—Hanoi. I really don't want to go, she said. She looked back at what was the Hai Lan Langs—her home, then she looked back to Dong Hoi—her work. She wiped her tears with a shaky hand and hugged him hard, kissed him on the cheek, then touched his chest over his heart and said, *"Tao phai di. Em khong bao gio quen anh. Em se luon-luon nghi ve anh. Bao trong nhe."*—I have to go now. I'll never forget you. I'll always think of you. Take care of yourself.

Val was stunned when she showed only sympathy and no anger or hatred toward him after he'd confessed to murdering all her friends and family. He returned her farewell, then watched in tears as she climbed on her bicycle and rode away. He thought about all the lives he'd destroyed in an instant, all the people who'd been his friends that were now just memories. The woman who'd made him the happiest he'd ever been was now gone forever—because of him! As he walked up to his truck, he turned for one last look at what had become one of his favorite places to visit, relax, and have fun. He dropped to his knees and cried again for what he had done. As he knelt, it began to rain, and when he looked up he thought he heard the familiar beat of a CH-46's rotor blades.

Within a couple of minutes, the big chopper was circling above him and then setting down behind him. Nate and Papa jumped out and ran over to Val, who was still kneeling a few paces from his truck. Several Marines ran out and starting hooking a harness around it. Val was expecting Papa to chew him out, but he didn't care about the disciplinary action that was sure to follow. It wouldn't compare to the pain and punishment he was already suffering. But when Papa ran up to him, he placed a surprisingly sympathetic hand on Val's shoulder and said under the noise of the helicopter, "Glad to see you're alive, son! Now let's go home—this place is crawling with the enemy!" Ten minutes later they were flying toward Linh Thu with the truck dangling underneath the chopper. Halfway home, fighting tears, Val said, "Sir, we'll never be able to get supplies from the store again. The owner lost everyone who worked there and just fled to Hanoi."

"We'll deal with it later, Jordan!" Papa said, realizing that Val was a little numb. "Let's just get home without being shot down." Papa patted Val on the shoulder again. "Let's not make a bad day even worse. When we land either go to your hooch or Commander Yeary's office. We'll worry about everything tomorrow."

Val withdrew into himself. As thoughts of his mistake resurfaced, he no longer tried to hide his tears from his fellow Marines. He didn't care if they saw him cry—he didn't care about much of anything now, He was overtaken by a hollow feeling, a longing he'd never felt before and couldn't explain. He suddenly felt as if he no longer cared about doing anything or talking to anyone. or what happened in his life. He even wondered if life was worth living. How would he ever get over what he'd done? Who would ever forgive him for what he did?

When they got back to Linh Thu, Val quickly found himself standing in front of the chaplain's office, knowing that Papa would be happy that this was his first stop. The commander was talking to someone else just then and stuck his head out the door to tell Val that it would be another fifteen minutes or so. Val stood up and walked outside, and when he stepped around the corner of the building, he saw Little John standing behind Big John, talking about something. Big John laughed, then walked toward the flight line, and Little John turned and walked in Val's direction. "Don't keep a good joke a secret, Little John," Val said.

Little John stopped. "It wasn't a joke, sir—just a silly observation." Val turned away, figuring Little John would keep it short as he always did. But Little John continued to speak. "I know what happened, sir. I'm sorry. I hear she was one of a kind."

Val turned back and said, "What?"

"You lost your special lady, sir. I know how you feel."

Val said, the bitterness clear in his voice, "How can you know how I feel?"

"I lost my fiancée and my unborn daughter almost two years ago in an automobile accident, sir." Val was stunned to hear this. "She was supposed to pick me up from work. We had a huge fight that morning, probably about something stupid. The thing is, we had a small tiff the day before that, about me being selfish and too focused on my career. I told her she was overreacting; then insisted that she come pick me up from work, even though she'd told me she wasn't feeling well, being eight months pregnant. I could've gotten someone else to drop me off on their way home, but I was being stubborn, telling her I didn't want to bother anyone and that she had to come get me. So she did, except she never made it. A truck in the opposite lane lost its brakes and couldn't stop. It hit a car in front of it, sending it out of control into her lane. They met head-on at fifty miles an hour. The driver of the other car was killed, as was my fiancée and unborn daughter.

I lost everything in one split second. I was devastated. I thought I'd never get over it. I never thought I could forgive myself because it was my fault. I didn't even care if lived. I was sure I'd never be able to forgive myself. I thought I had the worst story in the world until one night I was drowning my sorrows in a bar. That night I met someone with a sadder story. Turned out he nearly lost his wife and kids to his drinking after he lost his job—and he lost his job because one day the brakes in the truck he was driving gave out, and he caused an accident that killed three innocent people. He said he'd never forgive himself. I didn't know what to say. After wrestling with my emotions for a while I realized that he'd been living in agony for something that was beyond his control, just as I was. I finally grabbed his shoulder and explained who I was and said, 'It wasn't your fault—I forgive you.' He and I made a pact to stop feeling sorry for ourselves and to accept that things are always going to happen that are beyond our control. It's a really good thing that things are beyond our control. I don't want to be the one responsible for things that I'd probably just fuck up anyway, so it's best that the universe is in someone else's hands. He eventually patched things up with his wife, and I have a fiancée waiting for me back home. She'll never replace my other fiancée, nor do I want her to. It doesn't mean my current relationship with her is better or worse—I don't love her any more or less. It's just different, and that's a beautiful thing." Little John smiled and was about to walk on when he stopped and turned back to Val, who stood there stunned. "You see, sir—I learned that love never dies; it only changes its form."

Val, sobered by what Little John had told him, still felt as if nothing anyone could say could help him deal with his feelings right now. But he wanted Little John to know that he appreciated his desire to comfort him. "I knew I was right about one thing."

"What's that?" Little John asked.

"I knew you were a great conversationalist," Val said. "I knew you and I would have a long, great conversation one day instead of the sentence or two we usually exchange. You should open up more with people, Little John. I think people would love what you have to say." Even though he was glad for Little John's words, he still felt hollow in side.

The door to the chaplain's office suddenly flung open and Commander Yeary smiled. "Captain Jordan—please come in."

Val turned around and replied, "You know, sir—I don't believe I need to anymore. I got help from a pleasantly unexpected source." He wasn't sure that anything the chaplain told him would actually help yet, as he still felt awful inside—worse than he'd ever felt in his life...hollow, helpless, as if he was beyond healing and always would be.

"That's one of life's greatest secrets, son. If we're willing to open our hearts, our eyes and our ears, we can find help and answers sometimes even before we ask for them."

15

REDEMPTION IS ONLY TEMPORARY

Val lay in his rack in the still of an unusually calm night undisturbed by enemy mortars, rockets, or small-arms fire. The dark, quiet void left him with only his thoughts and the images of Nga Nghin Do'i that played in his mind's eye. He thought about the wonderful people in the villages and joyous times he'd had there. Then his thoughts shifted to Nghia Mau and her gentle, yet strong manner. Though he didn't want to, he couldn't help but replay the rush of events that caused the tragedy. He recalled the fierce bump and the horror of feeling his finger slide down to the release button and the terrifying sight of five thousand-pounders falling toward their unintended target. He remembered his horror when he realized just which villages he'd destroyed in the blink of an eye. He recalled how he felt empty and wasted when he went to the ruins and saw the damage close-up and realized that virtually all of what he loved on this earth had been vaporized in the sweet Vietnamese countryside by his hand.

He sat up in his rack and placed his head in his hands, then grabbed a towel that was hanging within reach and wiped his face. Then he went outside and walked around the base in the silence of the early hours, trying to clear his head, wondering if there was any way he'd ever be able to heal the vicious wounds in his heart and soul. He knew there was no use thinking about how he could make up for what he'd done—he certainly couldn't undo it. But he couldn't help asking why it had to happen. What had they done to deserve what he'd done to them?

Eventually he found himself walking along the barricades at the flight line and came to his jet. It was resting in her protective enclosure, ready if needed to spring into action and carry out a deadly mission. He walked over and ran his hands along the trailing edge of the left wing, then walked around his jet, almost as if he was performing a preflight inspection. He eventually came up to the radome, then stepped back and looked at the his amazing multi-purpose aircraft. She was sleek and beautiful, a work of modern art wrought from steel, aluminum, and titanium. Even on the ground she looked as if it were zooming through the skies. He thought of how she roared to let those on the ground know she was here to dominate her enemies and reassure her friends.

Then he thought about the reason for his jet's existence. It was to kill, pure and simple. It even looked like it was meant to kill, an aerial predator that carried out its deadly purpose with deadly efficiency whenever called upon. Even though he knew all along what her job was, it never truly hit home until now. He loved flying her, he loved the thrill of her speed and power and how she demanded his attention to make her perform properly and get him safely home again. It was because of his inattention that he suffered now. He never dreamed that she'd actually kill anyone close to him, all because of his failure.

Tears began to fall again as he leaned forward against his jet near the left wing root. She supported his weight with ease and kept him from falling over, as if she were trying to comfort him and remind him of how she had saved his life many times by performing exactly as she was designed to. He wiped his face and leaned over the wing of his jet, trying to regain control over his emotions when he realized he was now bathed in a light from behind. "Hey—what are you doing? Back away from the jet!" he heard.

Val looked up to see a truck driven by sentries on their nightly rounds shining a spotlight on him. He knew that behind the blinding light was an intimidating .50 caliber machine gun. He cautiously raised his hands and said as he carefully stepped away from his jet, "Captain Jordan, gentlemen—this is my jet."

"Come closer, slowly, keep your hands where we can see 'em!" the man ordered. Once Val got close enough, a sentry approached him with a M16 at the ready. He could read Val's ID patch on his chest and signaled to another sentry in the truck to turn off the spotlight. "Morning, sir. What are you doing out here at this hour?"

"I couldn't sleep, Sergeant, so I just took a long walk and ended up here at my jet."

The sergeant noticed that Val wore his flight fatigues and wasn't carrying any web gear. "Be careful, sir. If you take a walk at night, you should always carry your gear in case we get attacked from the jungles or the hills." The sergeant walked back to the truck and signaled to the driver to drive off.

Val said before they drove away, "Thanks for looking after us every night."

"Glad to do it, sir. It's our job!" the sergeant said as the truck drove away.

Val walked back to his jet and patted the turkey feathers on her monstrous engines and said, "Night, girl—get some rest. We'll have a busy enough time tomorrow night." He took one last look at her before he made his way back to his hooch.

§§§§§§

Not surprisingly, Val slept in later than usual, and when he did get up he was greeted with a message to meet Papa and the other officers at the HQ building to discuss a mission. He quickly dressed and made his way to HQ and walked in to see the same officers that had reviewed Nhiem-vu Phuc-Nguyen's letter. The contents of the package were spread on the table, and the officers were standing around it sorting through the material and talking amongst themselves. Papa paused when he saw Val at the door. "Come join us, Captain—we're about to begin."

"Aye, sir," Val said as he approached, though he'd made up his mind days ago that he wanted to go ahead with the operation.

Papa looked around the table at Chappie, Big John, Overstreet, Torres, Yeary, and Val. "All right, gents—take a seat. Let's make a decision before we leave here today." When everyone was seated, he began: "I trust you all looked over this information over the past few days." When everyone responded in the affirmative, he continued: "All right then. I'm gonna start this meeting a little different than usual. Let's just begin by voicing a go/no-go opinion, then we'll go over the particulars. We'll start from my right and work around the table." Papa looked to Chappie, who was seated to his immediate right.

Chappie looked around the table and made eye contact with every other officer before he returned his attention to Papa. "I say we green light it, sir. If all this information is accurate, then it should be relatively easy. I want to get our boys back, sir."

Papa nodded and looked at the next man. "Major Darryl?"

"I agree with Major Chapman, sir. Let's go for it. We have a low risk of casualties if it goes as planned. I think we have the resources available to handle any problems in case it doesn't, which would actually be the norm. On a personal note, I miss our boys. We have a chance to bring them home, let's do it!"

Papa nodded again. "Thank you, Major. Commander Yeary?"

"Sir, I can't disagree. We have a crack recon team under the capable command of Lieutenant Torres, and we have all the aircraft and firepower we need to help them handle any trouble that might arise. Let's bring our boys home, sir."

Papa smiled at Torres as he continued. "Thank you, Commander. How about it, Lieutenant? It's gonna be you and your boys on the ground taking most of the risks. How to do you feel about the whole thing?"

"Sir, I'm a hundred percent in favor of it. My platoon is ready and just as enthusiastic as I am. Let's do it! Let's get those men out of that hellhole and bring 'em back home!"

Papa smiled again and then turned to Val. "Captain Jordan, I think I already know how you feel about it, but let's hear it for the record."

"Yes sir, you're right—let's do this! I'm more than happy and willing to provide close air support. Let's bring our friends home!"

Papa nodded. "Okay then—now it's my turn. I'm fully committed to this operation and I'll commit any resources required to ensure a positive result. I agree with everyone—let's bring our boys home! The Varsity Squad will provide all CAS and CAP support needed, VMO-16 will provide any OV-10s and helicopters needed to make it work."

He took a deep breath as he looked around. "Now that we're a go, let's review every detail. We need to cover everything since there are a million things that can go wrong." They went over the schedule provided by Nhiem-vu Phuc-Nguyen. It was extremely detailed, and things needed to happen with precision. They had to figure out how to build in some "screw-up" time, in case there were unforeseen delays. The op was to commence in six days, when the prisoners at several camps and prisons would be transferred to other facilities in an effort to confuse American intelligence. The operation would occur at a transfer facility where they'd be awaiting transport to another facility. They'd be out of their cells and would be lightly guarded. The recon team would have to take the lightly armed and manned facility in less than ten minutes, then get the prisoners to their extraction point before the heavily manned and armed prisoner transfer truck pulled up to the facility, which was a window of only seventeen minutes if it wasn't running early.

Nhiem-vu Phuc-Nguyen assured them that it wouldn't be, that he'd make every effort to ensure that it was keeping to its schedule or running late. Since he didn't want any more of his fellow countrymen to die at the hands of a foreign enemy, he'd given assurances that the only men guarding the prisoners when the recon team was to strike would be the commanding officer and a few of the guards from the facility where the POWs were being held. All were men Nhiem-vu Phuc-Nguyen believed to be involved in the murder of a communist party central committee member anyway, and also involved in a night raid on the Hai Lan Langs in which villagers were beaten and raped and robbed of their rice and livestock, so he'd feel no remorse if these men were killed by Americans—he just wanted them punished.

The officers planned the operation down to the minute. Torres's recon team would be in the field the night before. A flight of two OV-10s would depart an hour before the op to scout the area for unexpected enemy activity and would be the comm link for all units involved. The Varsity Squad would depart Linh

Thu half an hour before the operation commenced and orbit just north of Linh Thu, loaded with drop tanks for extra playtime and armed with both air-to-air and air-to-ground ordnance and would be listening and ready to assist whenever called upon. Four UH-1 and one CH-46 extraction helicopters and two AH-1 escorts would depart just after the Varsity Squad was airborne. They would orbit several miles south of the extraction point ready to land when the recon team arrived with the POWs. When the recon team seized the facility, they'd lead the POWs to a tunnel no longer used by the NVA and keep them underground and out of sight until they got to the extraction point, which was some eight miles south of their prison. They'd be bringing food, water, and several stretchers for the POWs, since they'd probably be injured and weak. They'd continue down the tunnel and climb out near a prominent bend in the Nhat Le River, where the helicopters would land and extract all hands to Linh Thu.

Once they were safely back at Linh Thu, the other aircraft would land. Timing was critical, and everyone knew that the most time-consuming part of the operation would be moving weak, injured prisoners through cramped tunnels—the biggest question mark of the mission since no one knew how long it would take. The meeting lasted most of the day by the time it ended everyone knew their roles and knew how to brief the members of their teams, who had no idea what had just transpired. Everyone else involved would now attend daily meetings starting tomorrow and continuing until the operation began.

Val felt hopeful for the first time in a while, even though he knew so many things could go wrong on the operation. Getting his friends back was now the only thing he had to look forward to, thanks to the events of the past couple of years and especially two days ago. As he walked to his hooch alone with his thoughts, the gravity of the recent events still held a stranglehold on his soul despite his fresh outlook. Getting his friends back safely would only provide a temporary distraction from the tragedy that consumed him.

Val had barely gotten to his hooch when a corporal caught up to him and told him that Papa wanted to see him in his office ASAP. Val walked with the corporal to Papa's office, and Papa called him in. Val walked in and Papa motioned for him to sit in the chair opposite his desk without looking up from his paperwork. When he looked up, he said, "We've still got a major issue to deal with, Captain."

"What's that, sir?"

"Where are we going to get supplies now that the store is closed? Our COD flights have been cut to even more."

"There are other suppliers in Dong Hoi, sir. The question is, will they do business with an American."

"I'm sure when you flash money in their faces they will. I just worry if you might have made some enemies there over the past few months, with the men taking your picture, the attacks on the old store and such. Do you think it's safe for you to try?"

"Well maybe not alone. If I show up with a small detail of Marines, they may be less likely to try something."

"Okay—we'll try it after our little op is done. I want us to concentrate on the mission until we get those men back here. I think we have enough supplies to last us a week, unless there's an attack. We'll discuss this again in a week. Stay focused and sharp, Jordan. We need everyone to be at their peak on this mission. If you have any problems arising from your recent trauma, please see Commander Yeary, or come see me."

"I will, sir."

"Okay—dismissed. Normally I'd want you to just leave without giving some smartass remark, but if you've got one, let 'er rip!"

"I don't really have a remark, sir." Val stood up to leave. "Just be sure to ask the chow hall for the 'Jordan Special' at lunch today, sir."

"You trying to poison me, son?"

"No, *sir!* You'll understand when you go to lunch."

A few hours later, when Papa was in the chow line, he said to a private with a serving spoon, "Someone suggested I try the 'Jordan Special.'"

The young man smiled and replied, "Yes, sir—one moment. Take a seat somewhere and I'll bring it out to you, sir!" And the young man disappeared into the kitchen somewhere. Papa sat down at a table, and when the entire mess hall got quiet and looked his way, he became suspicious. The young man finally came up behind him carrying a tray with a plate covered by a stainless steel dome. Papa stared at his reflection in the polished cover and shook his head, wondering Val was up to now. "Go ahead, son—the anticipation is killing me!" Papa laughed. The private removed the cover to reveal a roast chicken, and there was a card at the back of the tray. Papa laughed as he opened the card and read:

Dear Papa,

You always worry about getting a Big Chicken Dinner (military slang for a Bad Conduct Discharge) so here it is! Roostercomb beat the rooster, so if you come across a red hair, Rooster would like it back! Hopefully the cooks found them all. Now you can finally get a decent night's sleep even though the base lost its best alarm clock. Enjoy!

The chow hall erupted with laughter along with Papa as he thought about the effort Val put into this joke. "Goddamnit! That man has *waay* too much time on his hands!" Papa then cut the chicken up and offered pieces to everyone in the chow hall.

§ § § § §

The lights of Hanoi finally came into full view. It had been a long trip, and an exhausted Nghia Mau rested a bit before entering the crowded streets of the capital city on her bike. She made her way along the same narrow backstreets and alleys that Nga Nghin Do'i had trekked through several weeks earlier. She knew that this was the best place to start looking for Nhiem-vu Phuc-Nguyen. She knew all the codes and taps for admission to all but the most secret places. She was allowed inside the first hiding place and held at the reception area as she noticed the soldier with the AK-47 in the shadows. Eventually a heavyset man walked into the reception area and signaled for her to follow him. The man smiled as she stepped into the light. She was a very attractive woman who didn't look her age, and not even mud, sweat, and rain-soaked clothes diminished her beauty. When the man gave her the once-over, Nghia Mau felt violated. He finally resumed eye contact with her and bowed, then had her to follow him through the tunnel that led to one of the planning rooms for the North Vietnamese Communist Party. Finally they emerged into a brightly lit office, where Nhiem-vu Phuc-Nguyen was sitting behind a desk going over papers. He looked up and couldn't believe his eyes when he saw his lover behind the receptionist. "*Tao yeu! To'i day de lam gi vay?*"—My love! What are you doing here? He nodded to the receptionist, who left. He saw that she was exhausted, so he let her sit at his desk and poured her some tea, then put some dumplings on a plate for her.

When the receptionist was gone, Nghia Mau allowed herself to cry. "*Di! Di! Chung di!*"—Gone! Gone! They're all gone!

Nhiem-vu Phuc-Nguyen could see his lover was more than slightly distressed, she was genuinely devastated about something. "*Tao khong hieu. Nguoi nao di?*"—I don't understand. Who's gone?

"*Hai Lan Langs chung di!*"—The Hai Lan Langs are all gone!

"*Hai Lan Langs di? Sao?*" The Hai Lan Langs gone? How?

Nghia Mau sobbed as she demonstrated with shaky hands above the desk. "*Tiem kich! Ra'i tham!*"—Fighter jet! Carpet bombing! As her body shook with sobs, she dropped her head onto her folded arms on the desk.

Nhiem-vu Phuc-Nguyen was devastated and furious! The Americans had destroyed *his* villages? The place he grew up? His people all gone? This would not go unanswered! Someone *would* suffer! He began to cry as images of the villagers flashed through his mind—lifelong friends, innocent children, the girls that Nghia Mau had adopted over the years...and his niece? With a shaky voice he asked, "Nga Nghin Do'i?"

With a heavy sob, Nghia Mau just said that she was gone.

Nhiem-vu Phuc-Nguyen raised his fists in anger and screamed toward the ceiling at the enemy pilot. Nghia Mau gently grabbed his hands and looked into his eyes. "*Captain Jordan—khun-khiep tai-nan!*"—It was Captain Jordan—a horrible accident!

Nhiem-vu Phuc-Nguyen was even more shocked. He said in English, "Captain Jordan? That cannot be! Why?? I will never forgive him for such an atrocious act! He gained our trust and this is how he repays us? I will never forgive him!"

Nghia Mau tugged at his hands and pleaded Val's case, repeating how it was an accident and how Val was just as devastated as they were, even begging her for forgiveness when he'd admitted to her what had happened. She then accused Nhiem-vu Phuc-Nguyen of being just as much at fault as Val was, for forcing the women to get involved in the war by sneaking weapons and supplies through the store to the communist forces. He'd placed them in danger of guerilla attacks and never put a stop to them—even after *Val* had pleaded with him to stop the attacks. It was *Val* who helped the villages when they were attacked by *North Vietnamese* forces. She explained that Val had not targeted the Hai Lan Langs, merely performing his duty trying to suppress enemy forces that *Nhiem-vu Phuc-Nguyen* could have kept out of the area. She explained that the pain they were experiencing was no deeper than what Val was feeling. She knew that Val would never forgive himself and that he needed comfort from close friends just as much as they did. It wasn't all Val's fault—it was because of politicians and rich men who couldn't control their lust for power. She then took a deep breath and pointed to him with a steady finger and said in English, "Not just Captain Jordan—people like *you!*"

Nhiem-vu Phuc-Nguyen was in a state of shock. No one had ever spoken to him like that. He loved this woman more than anything, and she had put him in his place like no one else could. He stood up, wiped the tears from his face, and bowed to her elegant logic. He looked at a picture of his niece on his desk, then thought of all the others from the villages. He dropped to one knee, buried his head into Nghia Mau's chest, and embraced her as he began to sob. She cradled his head in her arms and wept with him.

§ § § § §

Time for the mission was rapidly approaching. While everyone involved had small doubts in the backs of their minds, they were willing to risk anything to rescue their friends. Val knew that Nghia Mau had probably made it to Hanoi by now, and even he began to have second thoughts about what

Nhiem-vu Phuc-Nguyen might do when he found out his home had been destroyed by American bombs, perhaps even dropped by Val. Would he devise a trap for the rescue team? He went to see Captain Overstreet and explained his concerns and urged him to carefully monitor all enemy communications. If anything abnormal appeared to going on, the officers might have to meet to reconsider green lighting the operation.

Two days before the operation was to commence, Overstreet did verify some unusual enemy activity near where the operation was to take place. An entire regiment of NVA forces were camped out less than ten miles from the site and showed no signs of moving. It was certainly going to present a problem if they didn't move on. Reconnaissance flights were now dispatched around the clock to the area to keep an eye on the troop movements, and the officers would have to make a last-minute go/no-go decision. Two hours before the recon team was to be dropped in, the regiment finally moved off to the southwest. The operation was on!

Within moments, three UH-1s were lifting off the northwest ramp heading north to begin observation and eventually to take their positions for the raid. Torres looked at his men in his chopper as they touched up their camouflage and checked their weapons and gear. They'd be very deep into enemy territory with no way to be quickly extracted, but that's what they were trained for. As daylight faded, the Hueys shut off all exterior lights to hide from trigger-happy enemy ground troops. The trip seemed to take forever, but soon enough the choppers reached the proper coordinates and hovered just above the trees.

The facility where the exchange was to take place was still ten miles away. It was in flat, treeless terrain, except for a line of trees on its eastern and northern edges. Camouflage and concealment would be crucial to avoid early detection by the enemy, but the platoon had proven time and again that they could perform their duty flawlessly. They expected nothing less from each other as they slid down the ropes from the helicopters. As each man touched the ground, he took up a predetermined position. Each focused his eyes on the darkness for signs of movement. After the last man touched the ground, the thud of the ropes hitting the trees signaled the helicopters would be departing momentarily. The last man crept over to Torres and tapped him on the right shoulder as he took position on his right flank. With that Torres gave the hand signal to begin the long hike to the target area. The sky quieted down as the helicopters slipped away to the southwest, and the nighttime jungle noises resumed and filled their ears, making it hard to notice enemy movement. The team couldn't afford to waste any time—they needed to be in position before daybreak. They'd be exposed unless they were in their camouflaged positions just outside the transfer facility, which was supposed to be empty by the time they got there.

At Linh Thu, Papa watched the returning Hueys set down on the northwest ramp. There was still so much that could go wrong with the operation, and if they failed, men would most likely die, and those who survived and weren't taken prisoner would surely be court-martialed. Papa looked at his watch. The recon team would be lying still in the open grass for almost twelve hours before the operation even began. Hopefully they wouldn't be discovered.

In the jungle, the walk took a few exhausting hours, but soon enough the recon team found themselves at the edge of the clearing, with the transfer facility in plain sight several hundred yards away. The team knew they now had to change their camouflage from broad, thick leaves to thin blades of grass. This would require frequent replacement as the grasses quickly died after being plucked from the ground. After the camo adjustment, the men spread out to their predetermined positions to observe enemy movement and spring into action when the time came.

Back at Linh Thu, Papa led his squadron on two quick bombing runs, one into Laos and one near Hanoi. The scuttlebutt around the base was that peace talks with North Vietnam had been stalled once again. Rumors were flying about a huge aerial operation that was to begin shortly, concentrating on pre- viously off-limits targets in and around Hanoi to force the North Vietnamese back to the negotiation table. Papa did his best to quash the rumors so his men would concentrate on the task at hand. After both sorties finished, the ground crews grew curious as Papa ordered five jets pulled aside and had each armed with an assortment of ordnance along with several drop tanks to increase their range and time aloft. The ground crews noticed the jets belonged to the Var- sity Squad, so something was about to happen. It was strange that the jets weren't added to the next night's availability list for raids and were off-limits for Alert-5 duty. Rumors began to fly once again.

Day broke and the recon team noticed that a small platoon of twenty-three NVA soldiers had camped in the transfer facility overnight. They were not supposed to be there, and they showed little sign that they'd be leaving any- time soon. Torres glanced at his watch. The prisoners should be on their way to this facility shortly; hopefully the platoon would have moved on by then. They continued to lie motionless in the grass, just a hundred meters from the facility, invisible to everyone.

In their prison, Notso and Speedy and the other POWs were awakened when their cell doors were flung open and guards shouted at them in Vietnam- ese. Then they were forced to stand and walk outside to the courtyard, where a large truck was waiting. The prisoners were crammed into the cargo bed of the truck with ten guards. Two more guards climbed into the cab with the prison's commanding officer and the driver. Soon the truck drove off and headed southwest, the prisoners wondering where they were bound.

In the grass, the recon team heard the rumble of a distant truck, and suddenly two large trucks pulled up to the transfer facility. Who were they? What were they doing here? Were the prisoners arriving early? The team observed an NVA officer shouting at everyone angrily as he jumped out of the first truck, and soon the platoon came outside. After a few moments of arguing, every one of the twenty-three soldiers climbed into the trucks, which fired up and drove off. As the team members breathed a sigh of relief, they heard the familiar noise of the reconnaissance OV-10s somewhere overhead. Things were about to happen!

Back at Linh Thu, two fully armed OV-10s had left the base headed directly north twenty minutes earlier. Right now a flight of seven helicopters was sitting on the northwest ramp, all fueled, fully armed and preflighted—two AH-1s, four UH-1s, and one CH-46. Meanwhile, Papa had pulled five of his best F-4 crews and their jets off normal duties. Everyone on the base knew something was up and tried to pry info out of everyone else, but no one seemed to know for sure what was going on. Just as breakfast was being served, the helicopters fired up and flew to the north, in the same direction as the OV-10s had. People lost interest after they were out of earshot, but when flight crews began to preflight the F-4s, the decibel level of the chatter in the chow hall rose dramatically. Within twenty more minutes, the bellow of the F-4s starting engines drew all men on base out of the chow hall to the ramp to see if they could guess what was going on. The departure of all the aircraft seemed to be precisely choreographed.

The crews of the helicopters continued to their extraction point, checking comms and weapons along the way. All the crews felt honored to be a part of this mission, but they were anxious—they wanted everything to go as smoothly as possible. Hopefully within two hours they'd be bringing home some American POWs.

Val gave his plane captain the engine-start signal as the turbines spooled up and his war-bird came to life. He performed all his BITs and looked at Nate in the rearview mirror, who gave him a thumbs up. "All right, Double-O—let's bring our other brothers home."

"We will, brother—we will," Nate replied.

Papa's voice came on frequency and each crew confirmed that they were all systems go. Ground control cleared them for taxi to runway 31, and the flight streamed out to the runway. They would take off in a section departure of three, then two—Papa, Chappie, and Val in the first, and Mailer and Rooster in the second. Papa got his flight to the end of the runway and held short as he glanced at his watch. When the minute hand touched six, it would be go time! One minute prior, Papa called the tower for clearance and got it. He taxied his section into position, and when the minute hand slid to six on his watch, he announced depart as he and his section stoked the burners and roared down the runway. Then Mailer and Rooster taxied into position and mimicked the first section, departing with afterburners aglow.

In the grass near the transfer facility, Torres looked at his watch. The truck with the prisoners should already be here. What was the delay? Just then his radio man gave him a thumbs-up when the OV-10s called to announce that the truck was only a half mile away. Soon enough they could hear the engine, then finally the truck drove into view and into the facility. It was shocking to see their comrades battered and beaten as they were being forced out of the truck. They had to wait until the truck was gone before they attacked.

When the truck stopped, the guards shouted and forced the POWs to get out. Notso and Speedy stood with the others in the middle of the courtyard and noticed that there were only thirteen guards, including the commanding officer. Normally there were at many more around them at all times. They also saw that there were no guards in the watchtower or at any other high point. What was going on? Were they going to be executed? And now the truck that brought them was leaving! Something wasn't right!

When the recon team members saw that the truck was clear, they knew they had to move quickly before the gate was shut. The radio man checked in with the OV-10s. "Maestro 1, Rattler Echo 4 Whiskey. You on frequency?"

Those were the words the OV-10 crews were waiting on. "Affirmative Rattler Echo 4. Waiting on Chariot Flight and Guardian flight to check in."

Instantly the leader of the extraction flight chimed in. "Chariot flight is on frequency."

Papa checked in with Panama and was told to switch to button brown to check in with the FACA. Everyone felt relief when they heard Papa's smooth southern accent. "Guardian Flight is on button brown. Let's start the party!"

With that, the OV-10s split up. Dash 1 engaged the truck that had just delivered the prisoners and destroyed it with rockets and cannon fire, causing it partially block the road. The explosion alarmed the guards in the transfer facility, and just as one of them began to walk to the north wall, the three guards who were trying to close the gate dropped to the ground, dead. Suddenly the ground just outside the south and west side of the prison came alive as the grass began to rise and charge. Small arms fire broke out from several directions, and the guard turned around to see two more of his comrades now dead on the ground. His commander ordered him to close the gate as he went for the radio, but as the guard got to the gate he was met by the terrifying sight of several large men covered in grass charging him only yards away. Before he could shoulder his weapon, he felt pain exploding in his abdomen and chest as he fell to the ground.

Unsure of what was going on, Notso urged the other POWs to move away from the remaining guards, but when they noticed the guards' commander trying to flee, the prisoners quickly tackled him and pinned him to the ground, making sure that if anyone escaped this attack it wouldn't be him.

The recon team was now pouring into the facility, and the prisoners were cheered by how quickly they finished off the last of the guards. The team surrounded the elated POWs, and approached the terrified commander, who was still pinned under two Marine aviators. Torres found the keys for the restraints, then had two Marines restrain the commander officer as he freed the last two POWs.

"He speaks English!" Notso said as he threw his restraints into the commander's face.

"Great!" Torres said as he had his platoon gather the other POWs for a quick withdrawal. "Well, Mister Officer, should we kill you quickly or let your prisoners tear you apart?"

The officer looked horrified, unable to believe what had happened. "You will all die! You never get home! Troops be here soon!"

Torres checked his watch. As usual the Force Recon Marines worked so efficiently they were ahead of schedule. "We still have over twelve minutes." He then turned to his radio man. "Check with Maestro to see where the enemy transports are."

"Aye, sir." The radio man checked in with the OV-10s and they confirmed that the enemy transports were almost fifteen minutes away, slightly behind schedule.

"Sorry. We'd love to chat, but we've got to be going!" Torres said, looking at the officer. "And *you* are a security risk. No one can know what happened here! Sorry." With that a few Marines dragged him to a post that was obviously used for executions. One Marine struck him hard in the kidneys with a rifle butt to subdue him as they walked away.

As soon as his men were clear. Torres grabbed the radio and said, "Angel of death." Suddenly the back side of the officer's head burst into a pink mist as a single shot from the platoon's sniper still hiding somewhere in the grass found its mark. The POWs weren't sure what to think as they watched the enemy officer executed as he knelt helpless in front of them. He certainly wasn't a good man, so maybe he deserved it.

"We have to leave now, men—we have a long walk ahead of us. Any of you unable to walk or needs help?" Torres asked as he explained what they were facing. The trek was still fraught with danger as they were deep in enemy territory. They'd be exposed for almost a mile until they got to the jungle, then be exposed in the jungle for another mile. Then they'd make their way through an old enemy tunnel, where it was still possible to running into enemy forces with not much room to fight.

With renewed energy, none of the POWs asked for assistance. After giving them a chance to have some water and energy bars, the platoon flanked the POWs and lead them away. Lieutenant Torres checked in with all the aircraft on the radio, "Rattler Oscar 2 Tango actual. On the move with cargo. Keep your eyes open for trouble! No casualties." The aircrews felt a rush of relief, and Val found himself thinking this might even work!

§ § § § §

A North Vietnamese radar operator who was normally afraid to turn on his radar at night because of Wild Weasel aircraft was more inclined to turn it on for brief periods during the day. The radio had been squawking nonstop that morning by a prisoner transfer unit that they were being overflown at low level by American aircraft about twenty miles southwest of Hanoi. The operator finally had his equipment spool up and it instantly lit up like a Christmas tree with returns. Several of the returns appeared to be orbiting around two distinct points about thirty-five miles south of Hanoi. The operator called his commanding officer over and showed him the display and discussed options on what to do about it. The CO got on the horn and called out to any SAM stations in the area, but most had been destroyed or disabled from the increasing frequency of Wild Weasel missions. After almost twenty minutes without results, there was only one option left—get some MiGs airborne to investigate. He called over to Kep Field and explained what was going on, and the officer at Kep Field agreed to dispatch some MiGs.

Captain Phan was trying to get some rest as the increased frequency and intensity of American attacks in the Hanoi area lately had been keeping him in the air a great deal. He'd barely gotten to sleep when a knock at his door woke him up. "*Gi!*"—What! he asked in a tone that made clear he didn't want to be bothered.

"*Tiem kich! Giac Lai! Lam toi Ha noi! Linh lam khuat!*"—Fighter jets! Enemy pilots! Encroaching farther to Hanoi! Soldiers hiding nearby!

During the day? How bold these Americans are becoming. How dare they! He suddenly sprang up from his bed and ordered that his jet be ready for combat and that he have some brave wingman accompany him. They must be ready to defend their home! Within a few minutes Phan was outside on the ramp with five other pilots and Colonel Tomb. He cursed Tomb in disgust and told him to stay behind and let him and his countrymen handle this, but the colonel insisted on going. Phan agreed to let him go, but told him to keep his distance. In a few moments the pilots were strapping themselves in.

§ § § § §

Surprisingly, the POWs were covering ground more quickly than the Marines anticipated. They were about to leave the open grassy bald and melt into the jungle, leaving them only about a mile to cover before they reached the tunnel. They had to find the tunnel in a timely manner, then make sure it was still usable. As they approached the cover of the jungle, the POWs looked forward to be out of the open. When a POW accidentally dropped an energy bar wrapper, not a single Marine noticed as they were busy scanning their surroundings for signs of the enemy. Now they were entering the dark, thick jungle.

Above, Maestro Flight watched from a careful distance as the transfer trucks finally approached the prison. As they made the turn around the walls to the gate, the lead truck slammed on its brakes so suddenly that the trailing truck nearly rear-ended him. The driver of the second truck cursed loudly until he saw what caused the first truck to stop—the body of a guard in front of the gate. Otherwise, they were greeted with only stillness. When they cautiously walked into the prison, they saw no prisoners, just the bodies of the rest of the guards lying, all obviously shot. But who shot them? None were in defensive positions—it was as if they were suddenly caught off guard. Who could strike so efficiently? And where were the prisoners? Was it Americans who hit this facility? If so, who were they? And how did they know the prisoners would be here? How could their timing be so precise? The officer in charge looked at his eleven-man detachment and quickly checked inside to see if there were any survivors. When he got to the radio room, he noticed the radio had been destroyed. He sprinted outside and used a truck radio to call for assistance and instructions, then he had his men search the area for clues. The enemy couldn't have gotten very far—they were only three minutes behind schedule!

Above, Maestro Flight informed all aircraft and the platoon that the transfer trucks had reached the facility and had discovered what had happened and were now fanning out and searching the area around the facility.

Below, the radio transfer truck radio barked that a platoon of NVA soldiers should be there to help search within a half hour; meanwhile the guards should continue to search for clues about where the enemy might have gone.

In the air, Papa and his flight continued their orbit southwest of the target area, listening to updates from Maestro Flight about the mission's progress. So far things were going smoothly—maybe too smoothly. Mission glitches were almost SOP, and he feared what one might actually entail. He checked his fuel stores and saw that they still had almost ninety minutes of playtime—as long as they didn't have to drop tanks and engage.

Near the transfer facility, the guards were joined by an NVA platoon just twenty minutes into their search. Most of them were concentrating on the areas immediately around the facility, which caused the platoon's commander to shake his head in frustration because the attack obviously originated some distance away. He ordered his platoon to begin searching the area beyond the grassy bald, and after ten minutes a rifleman shouted that he'd found something. The officer approached and saw that his rifleman was holding a foil wrapper of some kind. He held the wrapper close to his nose and sniffed the telltale aroma of sweetness. Just as he began to turn away, something caught his eye—a trail in the grass that had almost returned to its original state. It was impossible to tell how large the enemy force was that liberated the POWs, since they'd proceeded almost single file, but clearly they were heading toward the jungle, perhaps to an extraction point. The Americans performed daytime extractions, but generally not this far north unless they had enough firepower to suppress any effort to interfere with the extraction. He shouted to his platoon to line up—they were going to find the enemy. The prison guard commander asked what they should do, and the platoon commander said he didn't care—his platoon had work to do. Just then he heard the sound of turboprops overhead, which meant that they were probably being watched by the Americans.

From its orbit, Maestro 1 saw that the enemy platoon was now entering the jungle near where the recon team had, and soon it would be impossible to see the enemy "Rattler 1, Maestro Flight. You have an enemy platoon entering the jungle where you went in right now! Call us right now if you want any help before they become invisible to me!"

Deep in the jungle, the recon team was in the area of the tunnel entrance, and it wasn't long before a POW stumbled into it. The team checked for booby traps and then proceeded inside with the POWs—and just as they were inside the tunnel, the radio crackled. The team was now underground and the radio would be useless until they reemerged on the banks of the Nhat Le River some eight miles away.

Maestro 1 tried again to reach the platoon to no avail. He guessed that they must now be underground, and he was glad that they were making such good time—but now they were unaware that an enemy platoon might be sneaking up on their six. Maestro 1 announced the events on frequency so all aircraft would be ready to strike if needed. Just as Maestro 1 finished his call, Panama came on guard channel to warn all aircraft that they had contact with a flight of MiGs off Kep Field heading their way. Maestro Flight dropped their altitude close to the canopy of the trees to avoid detection by the MiGs, and Chariot Flight did the same. It was up to Guardian Flight to fend the MiGs off.

Papa had his flight climb to angels twenty and had the RIOs tag up the MiGs and track them. "Okay, gents—let's not let these bastards ruin our day. Drop tanks. We should still be able to hang with these guys even with our light ground ordnance load. We should be able to take 'em out from farther away, so let's be smart about how we engage 'em!"

Some distance away, Phan was leading his flight southbound, scanning his tactical radar for signs of the enemy. He couldn't see smoke from any type of aerial attack, but the targets were still on the radar operator's scope just before they launched. If they weren't covering an attack, what were they doing out here? He kept his flight speeding toward the area where the enemy was first reported orbiting, still seeing no signs of the Americans.

Nate tagged up the targets on his scope and announced over frequency: "Tally ho! Radar contact! Six bogies bearing zero-one-zero at three-zero miles. Indicating six hundred knots at angels one-eight-zero. Still heading for us, don't think they detected us yet," At once all pilots checked with their RIOs to make sure they were also getting the returns tagged up.

"All right, we'll split into two sections. Chappie and Rooster will go with me. Mailer will join Jordan's wing. We'll overfly them and split them up from behind. Stay with your target," Papa ordered over frequency.

The distance between the opposing flights was closing at a rate of about twelve hundred knots. Just as they closed to three miles, the North Vietnamese pilots spotted the telltale smoke billowing from the F-4s as they kicked in afterburner and suddenly shot by overhead and dove into a split-S behind the formation of MiGs. Phan had his jets break off singly in multiple directions. He looked behind and saw that three F-4s were flying loose trail behind a MiG and two others were doing the same behind another MiG. Why were these Americans here? Where was the strike force? Were they just out hunting MiGs?

The MiG with three Americans behind him needed the most help, so Phan ordered one of his wingmen to assist—otherwise the MiG would be shot down. As he rolled toward the Americans, he ordered two more MiGs to assist the one being chased by two F-4s. Phan saw the Americans were setting a perfect pursuit and defense of their wingmen. If he tried to get behind the lead enemy to engage, the wingmen would simply roll in behind him and his wingman—a perfect trail. The Americans knew what they were doing!

Papa urged his RIO to lock up the MiG in front of him, which he finally did. "Fox 2!" he called out as the missile streaked toward the MiG. Phan watched helplessly from a distance as the MiG exploded and noticed how quickly that lead aircraft made short work of his wingman. Phan knew his best chance of getting kills and to survive was to resort to Tomb's "gun and run" tactics. He looked for a chance to close in behind the last F-4 in trail of either section.

"Got him, Double-O?" Val asked when he knew he had the perfect angle for the kill.

"Fire!" Nate ordered.

"Fox 2!" Val squeezed the trigger and a Sidewinder surprisingly performed flawlessly and tracked directly to the target and broke it in two.

"Tibbs—I got a coupla MiGs trying to get behind me. I'm gonna take 'em high and you should be able to get behind 'em," Mailer announced. He climbed high to try to get the jet into a rolling scissors or a high yo-yo. Val looked behind him and saw that both MiGs had followed Mailer. He rolled into a split-S that he continued into a loop to end up above and behind the trailing MiG. Mailer watched Val arc high and pull in behind the trailing MiG, which immediately broke high before Val could complete his maneuver. Val saw the MiG and immediately dove low under the climbing MiG, trying to sucker him to reengage. The MiG saw Val beneath and took the bait, rolling inverted into a dive to try to get behind Val. Val pulled high into a slow barrel roll to bleed energy and slow down. The MiG overshot and ended up in front of Mailer, trying to break right.

"There he is, Mailman! Nail him!" Val called out.

Mailer looked ahead and right to see a MiG below him breaking right, and immediately switched to lead pursuit with his gun, scoring at least three hits. The MiG was wounded but still turning so Mailer positioned his F-4 to where the trailing edge of the MiG's left wing appeared to blend in with vertical stabilizer, with no space in between. He matched the MiG's turn and switched back to pure pursuit as he locked him up and sent a Sidewinder directly up the tailpipe, destroying it in a ball of fire.

Phan watched as the furball unfolded in front of him. He looked down and off to the north and saw Tomb keeping his distance, which filled him with a rage. Only half his flight remained now and he'd probably have to run because the Americans were very skilled and would probably finish them all off quickly. Suddenly tracers streaking across his canopy brought his focus back to the fight. As he looked around, he had to dive away from an F-4 that was nearly going to collide with him from left and take his nose off! He ducked under the big jet, and as it streaked by he noticed writing just behind its radome. As he broke away in the opposite direction, he realized it was what he'd seen in the pictures of Lieutenant Colonel Driskell—BETEL-GEUSE II! He was in another furball with the legend! As his wingman closed in on his wing pleading for help, Phan had an idea.

After over an hour of searching in the jungle, the NVA platoon finally found the entrance to an old tunnel that had been breached and resealed. The enemy must have gone in the tunnel. It would be useless to try to follow them because there was no room to engage or outflank them, plus there were connecting tunnels and it was nearly impossible to know where they went. It was ironic that the enemy was now using *their* tunnels. Did they know where they led? How would they know if there were no NVA or VC somewhere inside? It seemed a risky thing for the Americans to try.

The commander pulled out his charts to see if he could figure out where the enemy might go. The tunnels were far from friendly territory, and it seemed unlikely that they'd follow them to South Vietnam. They must be trying to reach an extraction point without being spotted. The commander felt this whole operation had been pretty well thought out, something the Americans were doing more of as the war went on. Studying the map, he saw that the closest tunnel exit was just shy of eight miles south of here, near a prominent bend in the Nhat Le River where supplies shipped by boat were often offloaded. Maybe the Americans had a boat waiting there—and maybe just the spot to set a trap. He got on the radio and informed his command what he thought was going on, and they agreed to commit a small force to that location, to arrive within a half hour. The officer glanced at his watch. The Americans should be about six miles into the tunnel, considering their head start and that this tunnel was large enough for even an American to stand in. Based on that, they'd be less than a half hour from the exit, so the timing should be perfect!

Above, Phan used hand signals to communicate with his wingman, who then followed him as they flew north and joined up with Tomb. The colonel wondered if they were all going to make a break for Kep Field, and Phan explained that they were indeed going to make a run for home but first they had to throw the Americans off their trail. They'd hit full throttle, break to the east, get the Americans to commit, then suddenly slow down, force an overshoot, and break to the north as quickly as possible and get out of range and safely home. Tomb agreed to the plan, wishing he'd thought of it first.

Val and Mailer joined up with Papa's group in loose trail, ready to split up again if the MiGs broke up again when they engaged them from behind. As the F-4s began to close on the remaining MiGs, Val spotted something about the wingtip of the MiG on the far right. That could only mean one thing—Colonel Tomb! "Dash 1, Dash 3," Val called.

"Go ahead, Dash 3," Papa answered.

"I want that MiG on the far right—it's Colonel Tomb!"

Papa strained as he looked at the MiG they were closing in on and could faintly make out the damaged right wingtip. He replied, "Relax Jordan—we *will* get him this time! No one do anything stupid or without my permission, got it?"

All the crews agreed to Papa's terms as they began to close in on the MiGs.

Above the Nhat Le River, Chariot Flight knew it was almost time. They began their approach to the extraction point on its banks, hoping to be heading for Linh Thu within twenty minutes with the recon team and POWs. The AH-

1s swept the extraction point to check for enemy activity, but so far it looked desolate and quiet—perfect. They let the other helicopters know that it was okay for them to land and they'd continue to patrol for enemy activity. The other choppers quickly descended on the LZ and touched down, feeling like sitting ducks if they had to stay there too long.

In the tunnel, the recon team and POWs were anxious as they drew within a mile of the extraction point. Torres still had a feeling that things were going too smoothly, but he was thankful for the absence of surprises so far. He whispered loudly to encourage the POWs, "Doing great, guys! Only about ten minutes until we get to our ride home." The men kept pushing through the muddy tunnel on their way to the waiting helicopters.

A mile away, one of the Chariot Flight crew chiefs ran to the tunnel opening and checked for booby traps. He knew the recon team would have to check from their side before letting the POWs through. The outside was clear, so he gave a thumbs up for all helicopters to see and ran back to his Huey.

The AH-1s were now joined by Maestro Flight in their surveillance of the area. They made wide orbits low to the canopy to avoid the attention of any nearby SA-7 operators. As one of the Cobras turned along the river, he saw speeding six boats armed with large-caliber machine guns, grenade launchers, and at least a dozen fully armed troops apiece. He called Maestro Flight to get some help immediately from the fast-movers; this could get really ugly in a hurry! Just as he looked back at the boats, he was greeted by machine gun fire that tore into his tail rotor. His bird was badly wounded and he needed to RTB immediately or else crash into the jungles below. Maestro Flight ordered him to RTB, and explained that help was on the way from Guardian Flight.

The MiGs, meanwhile, seemed to be waiting for the Americans, which was strange since they usually ran the first chance they got. Papa was about to bark out an order when the radio crackled with pleas for help from Maestro Flight. "Guardian 1, Maestro 1 Tango. We need immediate attack air assistance. There are six gunboats on the river heading to the extraction point, all heavily armed. They wounded one of the AH-1s and are in a heavy engagement with us and the other AH-1."

Val was pissed to think that Tomb might get away yet again! Dammit! Just then Papa's voice sounded in everyone's headset. "We're on our way, Maestro 1 Tango!" Papa looked around at his flight, now within range of the MiGs. *Shit!* He knew the POWs were why they were up here to begin with. but he sure didn't want Tomb to get away again. He hated the man as much as Val did. All of a sudden the MiGs broke east, which was the direction his flight had to go in order to assist the extraction. For some reason he couldn't explain, he decided to hang with the MiGs a few seconds longer.

To the east, Phan looked around his formation. After staying in the break and seeing the Americans were continuing to pursue as he wanted, he looked to his wingman on his left. He nodded his head, and both jets stealthily broke north, leaving Tomb alone with the Americans still in the easterly break. He didn't notice until they were miles away, too far to assist him and too far for him to even hope of catching them. The colonel looked back and to his horror saw a flight of F-4s on his six.

Papa was shocked! Two MiGs broke away to bug out for home, leaving Tomb alone. What luck! He looked around at his flight for a moment before he said, "Chappie, take the rest of the flight to the extraction point! I'll join you shortly—I'll handle this myself!"

"Aye, sir. Let's go, Guardian Flight!" Chappie ordered.

"I want to stay with you, sir!" Val pleaded.

"No, Jordan—go help our boys on the ground!" Papa ordered. "Now!"

Val again found himself in a difficult place. He wanted to make sure Tomb got what he deserved, but he also wanted to make sure his friends got home safely. After wrestling with his emotions, he finally broke off from Papa and joined Chappie's wing along with the rest of the flight. He looked back in the rearview mirror and saw Nate staring at him. He explained to his RIO over the ICS, "I'm not going to lose them again, brother!"

"We won't. Let's get some!" Nate replied.

Tomb suddenly saw that he was now alone with only one F-4 on his tail, but the American was a steady stick and was not going to be shaken easily. He keyed up and cursed Phan for leaving him, pleading for help and asking why he was left alone.

Phan keyed up and replied in English, just to drive the point home. "You said it yourself, Colonel. You meet that man, you meet death—even for someone with your skills, Colonel! So now meet death. His name is Colonel Earl Driskell, United States Marine Corps!" Phan smiled as he and his wingman headed for Kep Field. He knew that when he arrived, his commanding officers would ask where Colonel Tomb was, and it would be his sad duty to report that the colonel would never return again."

Tomb did fear for his life. He was now going to face the man he'd fled from for so long, from way back in MiG alley over Korea until now. He knew he was going to have to fly better than he ever had in order to escape. He looked back and saw Papa's jet on the outside of his break, just outside guns range, but inside missile range. He had to keep Papa there because it nullified his weapons, but how? He could see that Papa was slowing down in order to increase the distance for a missile lock. He reversed his turn, then reversed it again. Papa was still there. He tried the double reversal again and added a Derry turn at the end of the second reversal in a desperate attempt to throw

Papa, but Papa was having none of it. With each second that he didn't shake Papa, he realized that Papa was gaining distance for the missile lock. Time to go vertical. Tomb pulled back on the stick and performed some half rolls to try to make Papa bite on one of them, but again to no avail. Papa barrel rolled to keep his energy low and to keep the MiG in front of him. Tomb was running out of airspeed and was nearing stall. He was going to have to break off the climb, but Papa had managed to stay way behind him, so he was going to have to react quickly once he got some speed.

Papa was waiting in anticipation as he knew Tomb was running out of speed. He sat back as Tomb's MiG began to lower its nose to get out of the climb. Then Tomb fell directly into the pipper, and Papa squeezed off a Sidewinder that began to track Tomb before suddenly veering groundward. "Dammit!' Papa yelled as he checked his air-to-air stores. He only had two Sidewinders left. If he ripple-fired them on the next lock, he'd be out of air-to-air ordnance, but it might be his only chance considering their unreliability.

Tomb broke left in a diving turn to gain energy. He was hoping that Papa would bite and aggressively dive too fast and overshoot, but he realized he was dreaming as he looked back and saw Papa still hanging at the perfect distance, patiently waiting to get a good angle and solid lock. He quickly pulled out of the break, then broke back into the original break, hoping the hesitation would fool Papa, but Papa rolled in a tight barrel roll and held steady. Just as Tomb began to pull out of the dive, Papa ripple-fired his remaining Sidewinders. The first one went ballistic, but the second tracked directly at the MiG. It was then Tomb showed impressive stick skills by breaking the cone of vulnerability, causing the missile to overshoot.

"All right—time to do this the old fashioned way, Comrade!" Papa smiled as he switched to his gun and closed the distance while Tomb was still trying to get away from the missile. Tomb saw tracers zipping by and felt his jet shudder as it took several hits, but so far in places that didn't seem to affect its performance. He suddenly pulled down into a split-S and saw Papa streak by, so he immediately rolled out of the split-S, expecting to see Papa directly in front of him in guns range. But as he completed his roll, no Papa! In fact, wherever he looked; he saw nothing but sky! He realized Papa must've pulled into a split-S and ducked under him. Tomb immediately rolled inverted to scan for Papa, but when he rolled, still no Papa! All of a sudden tracers began to streak by from above, and he realized Papa had somehow gotten above and behind him. He rolled right-side-up and began a right break. Papa must have continued into a loop, staying on the underside of the MiG to shield himself from sight. Brilliant! When Papa saw the MiG break right, he just performed a left barrel roll to keep the MiG inside of him. Then Tomb began a descent in order to get Papa into a rolling scissors, but Papa rolled left into a climb. What was he doing? Tomb thought he could finally escape now—Papa would be out of guns range and he could get some distance between them. Tomb pulled hard into a split-S, expecting to see Papa zip by and disappear way behind him, heading in the wrong direction.

"Sorry for this, Buddy—just bear with me!" Papa said to his RIO as he suddenly pushed forward on the stick and forced the jet into an outside loop. When Papa had the colonel in his sights, he rolled right-side-up but continued the steep dive. Papa now gained back all his separation and immediately went to lead pursuit as he opened fire with his cannon. "Goodbye, Comrade!" he said as he continued firing.

The colonel saw the tracers rip the air in front of him as Papa fired at a shallow angle from above. Then the rounds began to shred his jet, and he felt excruciating pain as a 20mm explosive-tipped round splintered his right leg while another severed his left hand from his wrist as others tore the cockpit apart. He felt his spine shatter as his jet violently exploded into two pieces that began to tumble wildly toward the earth. He was pinned in his seat, unable to move, unable to eject. His eyes began to roll into his skull as the buildup of g-forces continued for what seemed like eternity. The pain and discomfort paled in comparison to the fear of not knowing when it would all end. Suddenly a force like a massive punch jolted his body and as all his bones shattered and his organs were crushed, everything went black.

Papa watched as his opponent broke up and fell from the sky, and briefly orbited the helpless jet to ensure that the colonel did not eject. Once the pieces impacted the earth, he said nothing—he just exhaled and turned east to help his squadron help the POWs. But Papa's RIO cheered and keyed up over frequency to announce to his squadron mates, "Comrade Colonel is finally in his tomb and we're inbound to assist!"

The other Playboys cheered briefly, but quickly focused on the task at hand as they approached the extraction point. The boats were in plain sight and the OV-10s and the remaining AH-1 were making runs at them, causing serious damage, but one good run from the F-4s would put a quick and decisive end to the melee. Chappie checked in. "Maestro 1, Guardian Flight is overhead. Five Fox-4s with four 500-pounders, four Sidewinders each and twenty mike-mike. Give us a mission."

"Roger Guardian Flight. You think a Sidewinder will work on a ground target?"

Chappie smiled. "They barely work on an air target, but we'll give it a try."

"We'll duck out to the west. Approach from multiple run-ins, use whatever ordnance you want, give yourselves eight seconds between runs."

"Roger." Chappie then directed his men to break up and go in numerical order and try Sidewinders and 500-pounders or make strafing runs—whatever it took to destroy the enemy or make them retreat.

"Dash 2 rolling in hot," Chappie announced. He had his RIO attempt to get a lock off the heat signature of the boat's engine. "Fox 2!" Chappie ripple-fired two Sidewinders. The first hit the water and exploded, sending water flying and nearly causing one of the boats to hit another one as the shockwave of the water hit it. The second Sidewinder actually struck its target and ripped the boat into pieces. Chappie called out, "Dash 3, bat cleanup. I want you guys to stay back—that way we'll see what's working or not."

"Roger, Dash 2," Val responded.

"Dash 4 rolling in hot!" Mailer called out as he approached from the east. He armed his first rack of bombs and still had his RIO get a lock onto one of the boats. "Fox 2!" His Sidewinders hit the water, so he released his first rack when he thought he'd hit some of the boats. One bomb exploded on impact with the water, which destroyed the boat near it, the other hit the riverbank and exploded.

When the tunnel was rocked by an explosion, Torres worried that it might collapse if there was another close hit. He didn't know what was going on up on above ground, but it couldn't be good. The exit was only about a hundred yards away, so he halted the POWs as he and another Marine checked the hatch for booby traps. Once it was declared safe, he carefully opened the door and saw the battle a few hundred yards downriver. He signaled to the men behind him to move quickly as some of his men formed a ring around the POWs and the others escorted them to the choppers.

Rooster rolled in hot and managed to sink another boat, leaving only two. The POWs were being hurried to helicopters that were now beginning to take fire. The AH-1 popped up from behind the waiting helicopters and fired on the closest boat in order to suppress their fire. Val saw that the POWs, the recon platoon, and the helicopter crews were in trouble, and as the boats were distracted by the Cobra and others shooting at them, he snuck up behind them. He flew north around the bend in the river, turned back south, and dropped to just above the water. He knew the choppers were too close to try a missile, so he armed his cannon and greened up both racks of bombs. "Dash 2 rolling in hot."

He roared so low that he actually kicked up a rooster tail and zipped around the bends of the river lower than the trees along its banks. The gunners on the boats were intent on the west bank, and when one of them stopped to reload and dropped his spent magazine on the deck, he glanced aft and was shocked by what greeted his eyes—a fighter jet coming right at them! The jet then seemed to wink as cannon fire suddenly erupted from its nose.

When Val targeted the boats, he squeezed the trigger and his Gatling growled as it spit out rounds that drew a line right up to the second boat and began to shred it. Some of the explosive-tipped rounds cut through the fuel tank, and the boat exploded. He then released both racks of bombs, and they all soared forward. All but one exploded on the bank or on the river, but one nailed the last boat. As the last boat exploded, the recon platoon and the POWs cheered. Notso and Speedy, just now reaching the helicopter, looked up at the jet that was now roaring skyward. They knew it could only be Val and shouted, "Val, you crazy bastard—see you back at base!"

Finally the helicopters were lifting off and heading southwest to Linh Thu just as Papa called his flight to join up on his wing. When they were gathered around him, he sounded like he was holding back tears as he said, "I've been down here for many years, gents, but this was the *only* sortie worth flying since I've been here—and it only happened because one of our own Marines made friends with the enemy we came halfway around the world to fight. Let's always remember this day."

The first AH-1 made it to Linh Thu without further incident. Guardian Flight landed next, followed by Maestro and finally Chariot Flight. Val and Nate ran over to the helicopters as they shut down on the ramp, and Papa rushed over to join them. Every member of VMFA-2 joined up on the ramp, hoping to greet four of their missing comrades. Finally the CH-46's cargo door opened and most of the POWs and the recon team emerged, with. several other POWs jumping out of Hueys. The POWs were directed to waiting pick-ups that would take them to sick bay, and almost all of them were in tears as they set foot on friendly soil and some even kissed the ramp. As they walked to their trucks, they hugged Torres and his team and the flight crews who'd risked their lives for them.

Baker and Charles made their way through the crowd to find their old CO, who was smiling as tears welled up in his eyes. Papa opened his arms and hugged them both. "Damn I'm glad to have you boys back! Let's get you cleaned and healed up and send you home!" Then he looked around for his other squadron mates and finally caught sight of them across the ramp. He was stunned to see how badly they appeared to have been beaten during their relatively short time in enemy hands. He shouted, "Notso, Speedy—get your asses over here! I had to do a lot of paperwork because of you!"

Notso and Speedy grinned and ran to Papa and nearly tackled him. "Damn, I'm glad to see you boys! The poker games haven't been the same!"

When Notso and Speedy released Papa, Notso said, "Rumor has it that you took care of Colonel Tomb for us and finally gave him a little payback!"

"Can't say he didn't have it coming!"

"How did this all happen, sir? Was this operation your idea? How did you know where we'd be?" Speedy asked.

"You actually need to thank our enemy for that, gents. A member of the communist party literally handed us the entire plans for the operation."

"*What?*" Speedy and Notso asked.

Papa smiled. "You'd better ask Captain Jordan about that. He has a way with people."

"Where is Val?" they asked.

Papa pointed at the line. "He and Robinson are probably waiting for you by the trucks."

Notso and Speedy continued down the line of old squadron mates, shaking hands and hugging old friends. Finally they approached the trucks and saw Val and Nate waiting. "As usual! Dragging your asses at the end of the line!" Notso shouted.

Val and Nate whooped in joy when they saw their old friends and pulled them into a group hug. "Damn good to see you guys!" Val said with a smile.

"Nice job," Notso said.

"On what?"

Speedy laughed. "That last jet *had* to be you guys!"

"I understand this was all your doing." Notso smiled. "Did it have anything to do with your influence on a sweet local gal?"

"It was all her doing. She was a strong woman."

"What do you mean *was?*" Speedy asked.

Val sighed. "I accidentally dropped five thousand-pounders on the villages where they lived. She and most of the girls from the store were there at the time."

"Oh, shit," was all Notso could manage.

"Look—I don't want to spoil the moment by feeling sorry for myself," Val replied, then reached into his pocket and handed Speedy an envelope.

"What's this?" Speedy asked as he began to open the envelope.

"We promised we'd keep it safe for you," Val said as Nate nodded. When Speedy pulled out the pink slip to his Charger, Val added, "I want to separate that from you fair and square—in a good poker game!"

"Oh hell no—*I'm* gonna take it off your hands!" Notso laughed. The men embraced one more time, then Notso and Speedy got into the truck.

§ § § § §

The POWs were from all the branches, and most would be flown to Saigon and then home once they'd been declared fit for travel. Most were ecstatic to be going home, but all would leave Vietnam feeling empty in way. Their wounds would heal, but many had scars that would remind them that their past wasn't so far behind. Many would have mental problems that would haunt them the rest of their lives. The exuberance on the ramp at Linh Thu would fade, to be replaced with feelings of estrangement.

Notso and Speedy tried to stay with squadron in Linh Thu, but the DOD wouldn't allow it. They were stationed back in the US and would remain there until VMFA-2 was finally allowed to leave Vietnam, wouldn't be anytime soon. They were ordered to go to Miramar, where they'd serve as instructors at the new Fighter Weapons School, which was designed to teach dogfighting skills. Eventually it would become known as "Top Gun." They continued to write Val, Nate, and Papa, begging all the men of VMFA-2 to come be instructors at Miramar rather than leave the corps and take their knowledge and experience with them.

§ § § § §

Strangely, Val felt more alone than ever before. He'd gotten his friends back, but now they were gone again. Every night he was haunted by flashbacks of the villages in flames. He dreamed of Nga Nghin Do'i every night, his longing often manifesting itself as physical pain. The healing process would be long and might never be complete. He still took walks at night out to the flight line, which was now becoming increasingly busy. The earlier rumors actually ended up being the truth: North Vietnam had walked away from the peace talks in Paris and refused to come back. President Nixon decided to show his trump card and force them back to table by beginning a bombing campaign that actually hit targets of tactical and strategic value around Hanoi. Operation Linebacker would show North Vietnam that America had been holding back and fighting a limited war. The US would now show what she could really do if she committed herself. Val was flying up to five sorties a day now. The first Operation Linebacker certainly got the attention of North Vietnam, but it wasn't until Operation Linebacker II that they realized they'd better get back to the table if they ever wanted to get America out of their country.

16

SOMEDAY NEVER COMES

The base seemed strangely empty to Val now. The glow and optimism from a few weeks ago faded as soon as the POWs were on a plane bound for Saigon. He'd lost someone he loved through his own actions, and his friends were now gone and on their way home. It was weird—they'd been absent from the base for months, enduring the hell of a POW camp, and then he had them back for a few days, only to lose them again. He thought about the hundreds of other POWs somewhere in North Vietnam, and how he wished he could bring them home as he had the twenty others a few weeks ago.

The war was changing: bombings had been escalated in both Laos and in the Hanoi area, the Navy was now mining North Vietnamese ports, and the new decade was only a couple of years old. Val hadn't been home since he was sent over here. Many of his fellow aviators stayed in Linh Thu as well. The brass rank had put the pinch on Linh Thu by cutting COD flights in half, and Val had failed to find another supplier in Dong Hoi. It was now too risky for him to leave base, as the war was reaching a feverish pitch and the North Vietnamese were now constantly pressing southward, waiting for the moment to pounce and move in for the kill. SA-7 attacks had been on the rise for a short period, but as supply routes were now finally being attacked, they were beginning to decline again.

It was late in the year, and the North Vietnamese once again walked away from the peace talks, so President Nixon ordered another series of vicious attacks on the Hanoi area. It seemed to work the last time, so maybe this would finally drive the point home. The attacks would be called Operation

Linebacker II, after the first operation of the same name earlier that spring that had eliminated the MiG threat. Only a few MiGs dared to get airborne off the badly damaged airfields to challenge the Americans anymore.

§ § § § § §

Captain Phan was stressed as he sat in the ready room. His homeland was under steady attack, with no end in sight. The Americans seemed to have an endless supply of aircraft, bombs, and pilots. He'd been flying so many sorties that he was beginning to get sloppy from fatigue. He needed some relief and encouragement, but he had no idea when and where it would come from. The PRVAF was running out of missiles and very few aircraft were armed with them unless there was an extraordinary reason to do so. More and more the MiG pilots were finding themselves trapped while trying to engage the Americans with guns only. The problem now was that the American missiles that had been so faulty were now much more reliable, which meant they could destroy the MiGs before they could get close enough to employ their guns. As he sat quietly in the empty ready room, he could hear his commanding officers rushing around in the hallway. He could hear footsteps approaching and the voices of the other officers kissing up to someone. As they approached, one of the officers called the ready room to attention. Curious, Phan got to his feet and was shocked to see one the central committee members of the communist party standing there. Nhiem-vu Phuc-Nguyen approached the young pilot and told him to relax and walk with him for a few minutes. As Phan walked beside the political leader, Nhiem-vu Phuc-Nguyen rolled his eyes as he heard the shuffle of feet behind them. *"Dung theo anh nua!"*—Stop following me! he said sternly.

Nhiem-vu Phuc-Nguyen despised most of the officers, feeling they were incompetent and wanted to do as little as possible, expecting recognition for completing simple tasks—just like most officers and people in management he'd met during his life. He realized that were still a few who actually knew what they were doing and did their job well, and expected no praise for simply doing their jobs. He'd grown up as a simple farmer and had risen to power because of his vision and the willingness to work hard to give life to his vision, not because of who he knew. He knew that Captain Phan was like him in that way. He asked the pilot what he thought he needed to win this war. Phan explained they needed more equipment, weapons, and brave men. Nhiem-vu Phuc-Nguyen smiled and explained to his eager pilot that the Americans *will* lose the war because they were still not committed to winning, even though they'd escalated bombings of tactical targets. He explained that America had not committed full resources to any war since World War II. He urged Phan to be patient—the communists would win this war through persistence. He knew the Americans would eventually tire of the war and would begin withdrawing troops when they saw that were gaining no ground the way they were fighting it and with the dwindling support at home. Phan said he was willing to fight to the end and would take on the Americans with a hang glider if it came down to it. Nhiem-vu Phuc-Nguyen smiled and patted the pilot on the back.

Back in the ready room, he stood before the other officers with Captain Phan and told them he had an important announcement: Captain Phan was being promoted to general and would command the entire People's Republic of Vietnam Air Force. He was pleased to see the shock and dismay on their faces as one officer asked why. *"May linh! Du'ng lam cho so hai con gai!"*— He's a warrior! Not a cowardly schoolgirl! Nhiem-vu Phuc-Nguyen smiled and bowed to Phan, and explained to him how he could get in touch with him and the high command. He left the building for his waiting car.

Phan smiled and waited until the political leader left the base. As soon as the security arm came to rest at the main gate, he turned his renewed passion to finding ways to protect his homeland. He was a man of action, not bickering about things that might or might not happen. He lived in the moment and made decisions based on the current situation. The other officers now cowered before him as he issued orders with a kind of authority they weren't accustomed to. Things definitely weren't going to be the same around here!

§ § § § § §

Linh Thu was on high alert. The commanding officers of aviation operations in Southeast Asia for the Marine Corps and the Navy were both arriving in Linh Thu within the hour. Some pressing issue needed to be discussed with the COs of the three squadrons, the Seabees, and the medical and logistic units stationed there. Rumors were again flying about what might be going on—a three-star general and an admiral would be arriving shortly, and the base was still reeling from a barrage of mortar and rocket fire the night before. It wasn't long before the C-130 landed at Linh Thu and the brass drove to HQ to meet with Papa and the other top officers. Introductions were brief, and all the men sat down at the table to discuss whatever issue brought these officers there.

"It's an honor to meet you, Colonel Driskell. You've run your squadron and this base as smoothly as you fly combat jets," the general said as he broke the ice. "We have two issues to cover. First, you're being promoted to full colonel effective immediately." The general held up a plaque and shook hands as he pinned the eagles to Papa's collar amidst rousing applause. After the ten minutes of congratulations for Papa, the general went on. "However, I'm afraid my other news might not be so good." He now had their undivided attention.

"Effective this week, Linh Thu will be officially closed and dug up, and all personnel will be moved to Da Nang. Everyone will be gone by Friday. This is a sad occasion as this base has saved countless lives with quick responses and been a refuge for distressed aircraft needing a place to land. But it's been determined that it's too risky to keep this place operational. You're too deep into enemy territory and too difficult to keep supplied. Intelligence believes that the NVA has targeted this facility for a major push within the month, which would easily overrun it. We expected by now we'd have gained more ground than we have and that this area would be under South Vietnamese control, but alas that hasn't happened.

"The squadrons stationed here will continue to carry out their current missions from Da Nang. There will be a major operation beginning later this month that will entail nonstop bombing of Hanoi for a week around the clock, and you'll be participating in that from Da Nang. The orders for all your commands to begin their respective withdrawals are in the folders in front of you. VMFA-2 will be the last to leave so it can protect the entire withdrawal operation, which must be done by air since there are no friendly roads from here. Please review your orders and have your questions ready before I leave at 1600. It's up to you how you inform your men and get underway; however, the last C-130 will leave here on the date and time in your orders, and any stragglers will be SOL! You've got a busy week ahead, gentlemen. Dismissed."

The general was surprised when everyone in the room cheered and applauded. For some reason he expected everyone to be disappointed. When Papa saw the look on the general's face, he said, "Shit, sir—you honestly thought we'd be upset? That's the best news we've heard in years! No more getting up in the dead of night to repel bad guys who shell the base? Hell, what'll we ever do with our combat gear? No more knots in the pits of our stomachs because of SAM launches whenever we approach base? That'll suck! Where's the fun in that?"

"You gentlemen have no sentimental attachment to this place?" the admiral asked.

"No, sir. The only positive aspect about this base was that because we were so deep into enemy territory, top brass like yourselves seldom came to visit, so we just did our own thing and carried out our mission without adult supervision." Papa laughed, unconcerned that he might have insulted his superior officers.

"Well then, I guess we actually had good news, Colonel," the general said with a grin.

The brass wasted no time leaving the dangers of Linh Thu and left before their scheduled departure time of 1600. As Papa and the others watched the C-

130 fade into the distance, they were filled with optimism for the time in a long while. Papa decided he'd tell his squadron during the briefing for the nightly sortie, and he'd tell the Alert-5 crews before then. But right now he and the others had to go over the details of the withdrawal.

§ § § § § §

Val, Nate, Rooster, and Never were on Alert-5 duty that night and were playing cards with the enlisted men on duty with them when Papa walked into the shack. As the men began to stand, Papa said, "As you were, gents—relax. I have some interesting new for you." When he saw that he had everyone's attention, he continued: "Great news, boys—Linh Thu will be officially closing this week. The entire base will be relocated to Da Nang, and we'll be the last to withdraw. Down there we should be able to finally get a decent night's sleep, and not have to worry much about SAM launches. The withdrawal begins tomorrow morning at first light when the transports start arriving to haul things away. We'll be gone by Friday at first light. Our personal supplies will be loaded the night before, and most of our squadron will be gone by Thursday except for the Varsity Squad. We'll leave on Friday morning in our jets—and we actually have orders to destroy the runways with runway buster bombs and carpet bomb the rest of the base so it won't be usable to the enemy. Enjoy your card game. Hopefully you won't get called out tonight. The other good news is that we won't be involved in any more nightly sorties until we're completely moved to Da Nang. Your last mission here might be to wipe Linh Thu from the map. Night gents!" Then Papa went to go brief the rest of his squadron.

As soon as Papa cleared the building, the men sat in silence for a while. They had mixed feelings—glad on the one hand to finally be moving somewhere safer, but regretful that things wouldn't be as relaxed once they were under the watchful eye of the brass. Still, the air was filled with cheers as the men not on Alert-5 duty celebrated at the pub, trying to use up the alcohol because they knew they wouldn't be taking it to Da Nang.

Val walked outside to the lanai, again unable to keep from replaying the horrible accident that killed his friends and his lover. He still felt a dull ache in his chest and his eyes still filled with tears when he thought about it. If it hadn't been for the supply runs he'd had to make for Linh Thu, he'd never even have med her, and now he was leaving that place.

The peace he'd sought on the lanai was shattered when the phone in the shack rang. He immediately ran to answer it because it meant that someone need his help. When he picked up, he wrote down the mission as Rooster listened in on one extension and the ordnance tech listened on another. Rooster and Val began to plot out the coordinates on the chart, then hung up as the ordnance techs and plane captains prepared the birds for action. Val went over the mission with Rooster and their RIOs as they hastily strapped on their gear and sprinted out the door to their jets. The plane captains gave each flight crew a thumbs-up as they helped the crews strap in and the pilots fired up their engines. A bombing raid had been jumped by MiGs, which had managed to shoot down two jets. The crews had bailed out and were being extracted when they were ambushed by an enemy platoon that shot down one of the rescue choppers. MiGs were still patrolling the area, waiting for the next extraction attempt so they could shoot them down. The Alert-5s were armed with both air-to-air and air-to-ground ordnance and ready for any situation that presented itself. Within minutes, Val and Rooster were roaring into the night sky.

"Strike, Bowtie Flight airborne on the Linh Thu zero-two-zero at one-zero at angels one- eight for angels two-zero. Heading to assist extraction at target area alpha one-three-foxtrot."

"Roger, Bowtie Flight. There are two bogies orbiting the target area at angels one-seven bearing zero-one-five at twenty-five at your eleven o'clock and twenty-five miles orbiting. The extraction flight is inbound from Yankee Station ETA two-zero minutes, call-sign Kingfisher 1 currently four-zero miles offshore at angels five on button green."

Val and Rooster didn't even have to speak as their RIOs immediately went to work tagging up targets. When their RIOs looked up to them, Val continued with Panama: "Roger Strike, Bowtie Flight is tallyho on all targets."

"Roger Bowtie Flight. Go get 'em!"

"Roger Strike, Bowtie Flight will report back on frequency, switching to button green. We're going to get some payback and kick a little ass. Ooh-Rah!" Val responded as both he and Rooster switched to button green and continued to track the MiGs.

On the ground, the downed aircrews could hear the MiGs orbiting above them, waiting to pounce on their next ride to safety. The engine noise made it hard to hear enemy ground activity as the MiGs occasionally dove low to see if they could pick up signs of rescue helicopters on their radar that might be slipping under them at higher altitudes.

"Let me know when, Double-O," Val said as they got within ten miles of the MiGs.

"Roger. Should have him in a couple seconds," Nate replied as he frantically worked to lock up a target that was diving rapidly. "Got him—fire!"

"Fox 2!" Val announced as he ripple-fired two Sidewinders at the lead MiG, which was in a steep dive over the area of the aircrews on the ground.

The downed aircrews, lying as low as they could as a MiG screamed a couple of hundred feet over their heads, looked up, and just as the MiG passed by, two streaks zipped in behind it and the black sky was suddenly lit up. That meant friendlies were up there!

"Splash one," Nate cheered as he and Never knew the second MiG would bug out unless they tagged him first.

"I already got him! Fire!" Never called out to Rooster.

"Fox 2!" Rooster called as he mimicked Val's actions and ripple-fired two Sidewinders. The missiles screamed into the retreating MiG and destroyed it. "Splash two!" Rooster said as the RIOs checked the rescue flight's position and kept scanning for other MiGs.

The downed aircrews now heard the roar of the F-4s above and knew that the skies would be clear of the enemy. They wanted to cheer but knew they had to lay low until their rescue flight arrived in case enemy ground troops were close. Val checked on with the downed aircrews on the radio. "Vulture flight, this is Bowtie 1, anyone listening?"

"This is Vulture 7 Alpha—go ahead, Bowtie 1."

"Bowtie Flight is a flight of two Marine Fox-4s over your position. Your rescue flight is about two-zero miles offshore, ETA one-zero minutes, call-sign Kingfisher 1. We'll be up here until you are headed safely home. Give us a call if you have any problems with enemy activity."

"Roger Bowtie Flight."

Within ten minutes the CH-53 was overhead extracting the downed air-crews. Things were going smoothly until a 20mm heavy machine gun opened fire on the big chopper from the west. The helicopter pilot frantically called out on frequency, "Bowtie Flight!"

The Playboys were watching from above and saw the gun open fire. Val cut the chopper pilot off in mid-sentence and said, "This is Bowtie 1—we're on it, Kingfisher!"

Val led Rooster into a steep dive to make their runs from north to south directly over the area the gun was firing from. "We'll drop two of our 500s, Rooster. Stay ten, repeat ten, seconds in trail. Right-hand pullout, then into left orbit low at angels six so we can quickly engage again."

"Roger, Dash 1," Rooster said as he S-turned to give himself the delay behind Val.

Val dropped low and released a rack of bombs on the area where the gun-fire was coming from, and the ground was now aglow from the burning ord-nance. Rooster could now see the exact position of the guns and pickled off his bombs directly on target, completely destroying them. As he climbed out and pulled in behind Val's wing in the orbit, he called out. "We won't a need a second run, Dash 1. I nailed 'em!"

Val hoped his wingman was right as they continued to orbit and observe the progress of the rescue. Within another five minutes, the CH-53 called to say that he was outbound with everyone accounted for. Val waited until he saw them over the ocean, then climbed to return to base. When he checked in with Panama to inform them that his flight was now back inbound to Linh Thu, the controller said something that made Val feel a little sad. "I guess this'll be the last we hear from you boys on the frontier. We're sure gonna miss you off Linh Thu because of your quick response time, but I know it'll be safer for you in Da Nang. You boys deserve some sort of honor for staying out there in the middle of the shit for so long without ever missing a beat! Thank, boys—good luck in Da Nang!"

"Thanks, Strike. You boys do a helluva job too. If you don't, we'd lose even more crews. Let's have a beer when the war is over."

"Roger Bowtie Flight. First round's on me!"

Val landed and found Papa waiting for them at the shack. When they got out of their gear, they went to the lounge to see what their legendary CO wanted and found him at the table with several bottles of beer. They were surprised to see him there, especially with beer, until he said, "I heard your conversation with Strike, Captain. It got to me. I never thought I'd miss this hellhole, but maybe we all will a little. After all, we've spent a good chunk of our lives here, and this place has made us brothers in a way nothing else can. We may have seen more than our share of risk because we're stationed here, but we were free from the usual GI bullshit that the brass thrives on. Since you didn't get to party at the pub, I didn't want you to feel left out. I know this is illegal and goes against regs, but fuck it—have a beer...one apiece anyway. Enjoy fellas!" Papa opened up a bottle and held it high as they toasted each other and the base they'd called home for so long.

§ § § § §

Each morning as the week flew by, Linh Thu looked more empty and abandoned. When they returned from a mission, Lieutenant Torres and his men rigged the base with explosives. They also made sure the mines that surrounded the base were rigged in with the other charges that were scattered about. After that task was complete, Torres handed Papa the remote control switch, then his platoon caught the last helicopter to Da Nang. Now only the Playboys were left, their jets having been fueled and armed with as many heavy bombs as they could carry earlier that morning.

As late afternoon began to surrender to twilight, Papa gathered his flight crews on the northwest ramp for the last time on the frontier. "Change is inevitable, boys. We'll continue to carry on with our mission from a new base, but this place is what helped shape and define us. Now we have to make sure that the enemy can't use her against us." He paused and choked back a lump in his throat. "We'll fly low patterns, orbiting to the south. We'll have twenty seconds between runs. Release a full rack on each run. Target any part of the base that hasn't been hit or damaged by previous runs. Keep going until you exhaust *all* your ordnance—except your gun of course. Once we are Winchester, you'll join up on my wing and we'll fly southeast to Da Nang and land at our new home for the remainder of this war. Questions?" There were none.

Soon the Playboys were airborne and joined up with Papa in a huge low-level orbit south of the base. Papa waited until everyone was orbiting in numerical order, then with some regret opened the cover on the switch Lieutenant Torres had given him and pressed the button. That set off a massive explosion around the base, starting in the northwest and working its way southeast. Smoke and debris soared skyward, and the Playboys had to wait until the dust and smoke settled before they began their runs in their nearly overloaded jets. Papa turned his northward leg in the orbit and said with a hitch in his voice, "Dash 1 rolling in hot." He flew down runway 31 until he was at the center of the base where the runways intersected, and was shocked to see that almost none of the buildings were standing and most of the base was unrecognizable. He then pushed the button on his control stick and pickled off his first load. "Four away."

He listened for almost twenty minutes as each pilot mimicked his calls on all five of their runs until the last jet was finished. Then he led his squadron on one last overflight of the base, and each man looked down at the huge smoking crater that was once the place they called home. Papa then keyed up— "Mission complete. Target destroyed." He turned to the southeast and led his flight to their new home.

§ § § § §

Da Nang was nice in that it was relatively safer than Linh Thu, but it didn't feel the same. At first Da Nang personnel asked the men from Linh Thu what it was like to be stationed in such a dangerous place, and they'd reply that it was s strangely comfortable—maybe because it was a friendly island in a sea of enemy land. The rumors again proved to be true as President Nixon ordered Operation Linebacker II to commence in mid-December. The Playboys found themselves flying around the clock for a week as they attacked the Hanoi area and targets in Laos. They also flew CAP and CAS missions for other bombing raids and various ground operations, and there were still Alert-5 duties. The targets in Hanoi actually seemed to have military value, and the North Vietnamese were caught off guard and were now reeling from the destruction the Americans showed they could rain down on them. MiGs were almost nonexistent as most of their airfields were damaged.

§ § § § §

General Phan was furious, but at the same time troubled and feeling defeated. He went through the alley in the early morning hours and into the secret entrance to Nhiem-vu Phuc-Nguyen's offices and was greeted by the heavy-set receptionist. Phan was directed down a corridor to the political leader's office and entered to find the communist party leader practicing Sho-tokan Karate katas and techniques, which he'd learned on a trip to Okinawa many years ago. Phan bowed, and the leader acknowledged the pilot with a nod as he continued with his kata. When he finished, he bowed to the general and offered him some tea. Phan was furious and refused the tea. Nhiem-vu Phuc-Nguyen smiled and asked why the young general was so upset.

The general said in Vietnamese, "I heard you returned us to the peace talks in Paris after the bombings this week."

Nhiem-vu Phuc-Nguyen sipped his tea and simply replied, "Yes."

"Why? Are we giving up? We can defeat these invaders just as we've defeated every invader throughout history."

"You are correct. We can and we will defeat these invaders." He watered a plant on his desk. "And to answer your question, General—we are not giving up."

"Then why do we return to the talks? To barter our dignity and our country over some table halfway around the world with the very enemy we must defeat?"

Nhiem-vu Phuc-Nguyen could see Phan was very upset, and he sighed as he sat down and looked him in the eyes. "And how would you win this war, General?"

"I need more planes, more pilots, more anti-aircraft guns and missiles, more precision strikes from ground forces!"

The political leader sighed, then stood up and approached the young general and placed a hand on his shoulder. "General Phan, you are a true warrior, but we cannot defeat the United States by trying to fight their fight and going toe to toe with them. That would be useless—it would be suicide. We can never match their supply of weapons or personnel. When we beat them on the battlefield, it was because we made them fight our fight." The communist leader paused as he looked his young general in the eyes. "More importantly, we have defeated them from within—not on the battlefield, but at home." When Phan looked puzzled, Nhiem-vu Phuc-Nguyen continued: "There is an old Shotokan axiom about winning by losing. Do you know what that means, General?" Phan shook his head. "By going back to the peace talks, we appear to be surrendering, but we will be doing the very opposite. If it appears to them that we are backing down, they will pull their troops out of our country. Remember I said that we will not defeat them on the battlefield, but from within? Just as Sun Tzu wrote long ago in the ancient manuscript *The Art of*

War. He also said that to win without fighting is best. Most of the people of the United States hate this war and want to see it end—they are putting pressure on their government to withdraw. So—we will win. We will beat them from within—without more fighting! If we look like we're backing down, they will pull out their forces. When they pull out, we will move south and unify our country. They will be gone. There will be nothing they can do. We will achieve what we wanted all along, General—a unified Vietnam with no foreign army on our soil telling us what to do. We win! Do you see now? Patience, my friend, and we will achieve total victory."

Phan bowed to the political leader. "You are very wise, sir. I would like to defeat them in battle, but you know much more than I do. I can see that we won't have to fight much longer with your way. Please forgive my insubordination."

Nhiem-vu Phuc-Nguyen smiled. "Of course, General. Stay safe and strong. I will need you when we make our final push south."

Phan bowed again and left the political leader's office. Nhiem-vu Phuc-Nguyen smiled as he looked at a picture of his good friend that had been dead for several years now, Ho Chi Minh. He held up the picture and said, "Soon my old friend, our dream will be lived by every person in Vietnam. I wish you were still here to see it!"

§ § § § §

The war finally did end. The US did just as Nhiem-vu Phuc-Nguyen predicted and began a steady, guarded retreat. When they finally pulled out and left the defense of South Vietnam to the South Vietnamese, the North Vietnamese simply rolled through with almost no resistance. Papa and his squadron found themselves back at Miramar, and as they left Vietnamese airspace, most of them found themselves crying tears of joy and tears of pain. They felt they'd left something unfinished, something their country had done only once before—in Korea. Most of the men went their separate ways once they got back to the US. Practically all who'd achieved ace status were denied the honor because their base supposedly didn't exist, and many of the operations they'd carried out were either classified or considered illegal, and the government simply was no longer interested in rewarding achievement. The men still had to expend the effort, but in the end were not recognized. Many were simply ignored as soon as they were discharged—including those who were wounded in action.

Papa was offered another job at the Pentagon, but when he turned it down he was denied his ace status in retribution. He would have been America's only three-time double ace, and was actually a triple ace in World War II. But the pen is always mightier than the sword. The politicians who sent him over there didn't want to recognize his talent and achievements—they were more concerned showing Papa who was really in charge, even though Papa couldn't have cared less about who was in charge. He was the last of a dying breed of officers in the military, for he was not focused on his own career as most new officers were. He simply enjoyed flying jets and was more concerned about the mission and the welfare of his troops.

At first Val flew with a group of smuggler pilots out of McAllen, Texas, smuggling electronic goods to Mexico during their economic collapse. After a few years he was hired by the CIA to fly secret missions in obscure places around the world, but he remained in the Marine Corps Reserves and still flew high-performance jets. He dreamed of Nga Nghin Do'i practically every night, and she always looked as beautiful as he remembered. He hated waking up and having to return to the heartache of reality. He often thought about the people of the Hai Lan Langs and how about it took them awhile to accept him, but when they did it was like he became part of a family. He imagined what it would have been like to have children with Nga Nghin Do'i, and pictured them living a happy, simple life running a store that sold hardware and fishing tackle.

He was in the middle of a particularly vivid dream, Nga Nghin Do'i sitting next to him on the banks of the Nhat Le River where lilies bloomed in brilliant colors, when he woke up in a cold sweat and sat up in bed breathing heavily. In the morning he was heading off to Washington, DC, for the dedication of a new memorial to the Vietnam War. Many of his old squadron mates were going to be there, along with countless other vets.

§ § § § §

Val couldn't believe it. He was actually standing alongside Papa, Chappie, Big John, Little John and his new wife, Commander Yeary, Rooster, Never, Nate, Notso, Speedy, Mailer, Baker, Charles, Captain Overstreet, Lieutenant Davis, Lieutenant Torres, and practically everyone he'd known during the war—and they were all in their dress blues! They hugged and told stories and just chewed the fat, almost as if they'd been transported back in time back to Linh Thu. The dedication ceremony was beautiful, and the polished wall with 58,226 names (at the time) was gorgeous as it reflected the American flag in the early morning light. The crowd was huge, but Val finally made his way to the wall and ran his fingers over the polished black, granite-like surface. The wall had a sobering effect on anyone who drew near to it. While the surrounding area was a busy and noisy, right by the wall it was total silence. Even children grew quiet as they closed in on the wall. As Val reverently ran his fingers along the surface, he wondered if Vietnam had ever done something like this for their fallen soldiers.

His reverie was interrupted by the crying of a woman crouched nearby, a boy of about eight or nine between her and Val. *Must be her son,* he thought as he eavesdropped on their conversation. She was making an impression of a name on the monument with a crayon and a piece of paper as her son traced the name with his fingers.

"This is Daddy, Mama?"

"Yes, Sweetie," she replied as she wiped away a tear.

"I wish he wasn't dead."

"I know, Honey—I wish that too. You were still in my tummy when he died." She knew it wouldn't be easy to explain to her son why his daddy's name was on this wall, even though he'd been told that his father had died serving his country. It was a concept impossible for a child to understand, and Val knew that.

"What was Daddy like?" the boy asked.

The woman's tears flowed steadily now as she was clearly not expecting questions like this here. She leaned in and kissed her son on his cheek, then said in a shaky voice, "He was a brave man and good man, Sweetie. You'll be just like him when you grow up You're already a lot like he was. He loved fishing and playing football, just like you."

"How come he had to die, Mommy? Why do we have to have wars?" The boy could see that his mother was upset.

Again her tears flowed. "I don't know, Honey. That's even hard for a grownup to understand. Maybe someday you will understand."

Val felt a tear roll down his cheek as he listened and wondered how many similar conversations had taken place not only here but all over the world wherever a child lost a parent in a war. He wiped his tear and leaned down to the young child. "Young man, I never knew you father, but I know what kind of man he was. He was brave, strong—and *unselfish!* I hope that you will grow up to be just like him, young man. I hope that you and everyone else your age will never have to go away like he did for the same reasons he did. Maybe there's a reason to all this, but maybe we're not meant to know why yet. If you do ever understand 'why,' son, don't keep it a secret, but I'm here to tell you now, young man, 'someday' never comes."

Mother and son looked at the Marine crouching over them and smiled through their tears. They could see was moved. She said, "Thank you, sir— you described my husband perfectly. And I thank you for your wishes."

"I'm honored to have had the chance to meet you both," Val said as he stood and walked away smiling. He had a reunion dinner to attend, something he was looking forward to.

§ § § § §

The time with his old friends flew by, and before he knew it he was walk-ing back to his hotel. As he passed the front desk, a heavyset Vietnamese man in a business suit approached him and asked, "Are you Valentine Jordan?"

"Yes."

"I have been ordered to give this to you. It's from an old friend who was here looking for you earlier today, but he had to catch his flight and regretfully could not meet you in person." The Vietnamese man handed him a thick enve-lope.

"Thank you," Val replied as the man turned and walked away. When the man was out of sight, he went up to his room and opened the letter. At the bot-tom of the second page was a familiar name—Nhiem-vu Phuc-Nguyen. He thought about what the messenger had said and wished he could've gotten to see the Vietnamese leader—especially since he'd apparently come to the US for the dedication ceremony. Val sat on his bed and read the letter and was shocked by what he found tucked in the folds of the pages—plane tickets. Again tears began to fall on what was already a day filled with tears and mixed emotions.

17

LOVE IS STRONGER THAN ENMITY

The miles of red tape the US government presented in a vain effort to prevent Val from traveling to Vietnam was mind-boggling. Why should the government care? Vietnam was clearly not now—nor ever was—a threat to the US in any way. Did the US have a bruised ego? The embargo against travel and commerce with the country made no sense. It took a few months to finally get approval, and to make matters worse, the flight was long and uncomfortable. But he could hardly believe it when he looked outside his window and saw the familiar view of the pristine ocean and beaches below. Feelings he'd buried for what seemed like an eternity were suddenly resurfacing, both positive and negative. It was hard to believe, but he was really here again!

Val was surprised to see a man holding a sign up with his name on it when he walked out of the jetway in Hanoi—the same man who'd handed him the letter in Washington. Val approached the man and said, "You're looking for me, I see."

The man replied in his accented English, "Good afternoon, Mister Jordan. I'm Ban Viec Phuc-Vu. I will be escorting you during your visit—wherever you wish to go." Val smiled to cover up his rush of emotions. "We have a car waiting outside. Please come!" Val followed the man as he walked up to the "Diplomats Only" section of customs and had him rushed through with almost no questions or delays. Before he knew it, he was settling into the back seat of a luxury sedan that quickly drove away from the airport and into the city. Ban Viec Phuc-Vu looked at his passenger in the rearview mirror and said, "Your host is very busy, but he will meet you in two days. In the meantime, feel free to take in the sights of our great city. If you need anything, I am at your service."

Val looked at his driver and said, "I thought you never left your boss's side. Won't he be needing you?"

As they reached Val's hotel, he said, "He told me that my job the next couple of weeks is to make sure you have the most pleasant stay possible. He will spend more time with you in two days."

When Val got to his room, he sat on the bed and listened to the noise of the busy city outside. As his eyes closed, it hit him again, and the emotions he'd been suppressing for a long time surfaced again. He began to recall the events that led to his lover's demise, and as always he felt numb, hollow, and helpless. Strangely, the feelings were comforting to him now, after the years he'd spent trying to deal with them. He hadn't allowed himself to get close to anyone since Nga Nghin Do'i's death, and he'd thought that maybe he was meant to be alone in life, considering his relationship with Virginia had failed. He'd be here in Hanoi for only a couple days before returning to places he was familiar with and visiting new places. Rather than have dinner, he remained on his bed with his thoughts and eventually fell asleep.

§ § § § §

All of sudden it was morning, and Val had breakfast and walked around a bit before Ban Viec Phuc-Vu came to pick him up. He drove Val to several sites from the war with America, including the Hanoi Hilton, buildings that had been damaged by American bombs but although condemned were still standing, and finally Lam Khuat Prison, where Baker, Charles, Notso, and Speedy had been imprisoned. He was struck by the damage that was considered beyond repair—more terrifying evidence of how destructive their weapons were. He was amazed by how many bomb craters there still were too. The numbers of bombs that had been dropped on this place was staggering.

Val felt weird as he walked around the ruins of Lam Khuat, of which only the foundation was visible through the tall grass. As he stepped into what had once been a large room, he saw stains in what remained of the floor. He knelt down to examine them and realized they must be human blood and was stunned that not even a few years of weather could remove the evidence of suffering. Val looked at his driver, who was gauging his reaction.

"This is not a place we are proud of, Mister Jordan. That's why it has been torn down."

Val sighed and replied softly, "I know. It's something you try to prepare yourself for, but you never know how it'll strike you until you actually experience it."

"Perhaps we should leave this terrible place, sir."

"Not yet. I asked you to bring me here, so I bear you no ill will. I just need a few more minutes, then we'll leave."

"As you wish, Mister Jordan," he said, staying well behind now.

The place had Val all twisted up inside. As he took in the surroundings, he didn't want to imagine what his friends had endured here. He thought about the mental strength it must have required to make it through each day, and how his friends were clearly tougher than he'd ever given them credit for. As he walked along, he found some concertina wire that at first glance looked rusty, but then he realized that it was also stained with blood. He recalled something Notso and Speedy had told him about a prisoner who'd tried to escape and ended up getting tangled in the wire. They left him to suffer awhile in his trap of sharp metal edges before finally finishing him off with a round from an AK-47. They left his body in the wire as a warning to the other prisoners until the smell got too bad.

Finally he had enough of the images of suffering and he signaled to Ban Viec Phuc-Vu that it was time to leave. The next stop was the transfer facility, from where the POWs were rescued. As Val looked around, he was stunned to find the shell casing from a 5.56mm round that had to be from a recon team M16.

When they were on the road again, Ban Viec Phuc-Vu said, "The last place we will visit today will be Kep Field, Mister Jordan. Your host would like you to meet someone there." Because of the traffic, the drive took awhile, but soon enough they were being waved through the main gate. As they pulled up to a building, an officer stepped out and PRVAF personnel in the vicinity snapped to attention and saluted. When the car came to a stop, Ban Viec Phuc-Vu climbed out and motioned for Val to follow him. As they approached the officer, Val saw five stars on his shoulder boards—the equivalent of a rank not held since Omar Bradley had the honor in the US military. The general and Val's driver then exchanged salutes, and they spoke softly for a few moments before Ban Viec-Phuc-Vu smiled and motioned Val closer. "Mister Jordan, please meet General Tren Phan, commander of the People's Republic of Vietnam Air Force."

Val and Phan shook hands, then the general motioned for them to follow him. "Welcome back to Vietnam, Mister Jordan," Phan said in his best English. "I understand you were a fighter pilot like me. Tell about your tour of duty over here, if you don't mind."

"I flew F-4s for VMFA-2. In fact I still fly for the Marine Corps Reserves," Val replied, thinking that the details would mean little to the general.

"VMFA-2? Really? The squadron that was stationed on the base in the middle of the jungle? I believe you called it Linh Thu?"

Val was surprised that the general knew anything about his squadron or the base. "You know of Linh Thu and VMFA-2, sir?"

"Yes! Your squadron was commanded by the legendary Colonel Earl Driskell. I personally flew against you a few times. Luckily I never tangled with the master himself, but I was in a couple of battles while he was there. One in particular was when he set us up in a perfect ambush by having part of his squadron sneak behind us and trap us in a double envelopment. Brilliant!"

Val smiled. It had been his idea, but he wasn't going to steal Papa's thunder. "I was there, too. I led the group that snuck in from behind."

"Really? Amazing! You were the best we ever went up against—our most worthy opponents. What is your rank now?"

"I'm a major now." Val changed the subject. "Did you ever fly with a Russian named Colonel Makarov, call-sign Colonel Tomb?"

Phan took a deep breath. "I did. I hated the man. He was not an honorable warrior. I was extremely happy when Colonel Driskell shot him down. To be honest, I made sure he would be alone to fight Colonel Driskell. I knew that he would not return from the fight. He was a bad man, Major."

Val smiled. He liked this man! "I'm glad to hear you say that, General. I hated the man too. I remember how he shot my friends down. I was hoping I'd get him alone and shoot him down, but I can't complain about how things worked out. Pap—uh, Colonel Driskell—deserved to shoot him down because he'd faced him in Korea.

"How many kills did you have, General?" Val asked to gage his former enemy's reaction.

General Phan sighed and looked his former enemy directly in the eyes. "I will not lie to you, Major. I shot down and killed many of your countrymen throughout the war. I believe I shot down around thirty-four total by the war's end." General Phan smiled.

The two former enemies talked for hours about flying and the war, and about how the Marine aviators from Linh Thu had not been accorded the respect they deserved by their government after the war ended. Val and Phan found that their personalities were a lot alike, and as the afternoon wore on, the general took Val to the flight line. Val was shocked to see how badly American air power had decimated the PRVAF—there were barely enough MiGs left to make two squadrons. The field itself had been bombed many times toward the end of the war, and hastily repaired just as many times.

The general walked Val over to a hardened shelter where a gorgeous black two-seat MiG-21 was kept. The aircraft was immaculate and looked brand new. Phan pointed to the jet with pride and smiled. "This is my jet, Major. We both love to fly. Let's go for a ride!"

Val was ecstatic. "Fantastic—I get to fly in a MiG!"

"Once we get up to altitude, I'll let you fly her, Major. We'll go fly over your old base and anywhere else close by you'd like to see." Phan handed Val some flight gear and went over the MiG's emergency systems and procedures. The general actually let Val sit in the front because the two cockpits were identical since it was used for training.

Soon the noise of a spooling Russian turbine filled the covered shelter as Phan performed his preflight ground checks. Val felt like he was flying in Air Force One as all traffic was cleared out of the general's path, no matter what phase of flight they were in. The takeoff was quite impressive—similar to the F-4, but lacking the raw power of his old American Phantom. Once airborne, the MiG was surprisingly light on the controls and simple and reliable to fly. It was much more maneuverable than the giant F-4, but light years behind the technology of the new generation of American jets, and not nearly as maneuverable as the newest American war-birds. But the MiG was a joy to fly as it let the pilot feel like he was in charge of his destiny without having to rely on a computer to tell him what he could do, like the Tomcats, Eagles, and the brand-new F-18 Hornet.

The weather was perfect, and it wasn't long before the former enemies reached Linh Thu. Val could barely recognize it. He'd flown near it many times after he'd been moved to Da Nang, but time had totally overtaken it now. The crater was now simply a large depression that the jungle had reclaimed. The trees still had not grown as tall as the ones around it yet, but they were getting close. Val dove down low to fly a low and slow pass over the place that was his home for a few years. As he flew over, he could barely make out the last twenty feet and the bottoms of the numbers for runway 31. Val felt a mix of emotions sweep over him in a wave as he stoked the burner and began to climb out to the northeast. They flew along the coast back to Kep Field and joined up with a few other MiGs for the overhead back into Kep Field. Before he knew it, the flight was over, and when they were on the ground, the general invited Val to have dinner with him and his family, and when the evening ended they exchanged contact information.

Back in his dark hotel room, Val was again alone with his thoughts. His dream of Nga Nghin Do'i was more intense than ever. He could feel her breath, and smell the scent and feel the texture of her smooth skin, and hear her soothing voice. He found himself back on the banks of the Nhat Le River, standing on the shore looking out over brilliant lilies—and suddenly she appeared, crouching down to smell the flowers, gently picking one and putting it in her glistening hair.

She turned to Val and said, "Hello my love."

"Hello," he said, choking up

She looked at Val with her immaculate smile, then stood and approached him. "Why that shattered look, my love? Aren't you happy to see me?"

Val was still choked up, even though he dreamed of his long deceased lover every night. "Happier than I am when I'm awake." He looked into her eyes as tears welled up in his. "I miss you so much, and I love you. I'm such a coward that I can never find the proper way to say 'I'm sorry.' I can never forgive myself and I don't know how anyone can forgive me for what I did. Now that I'm down here again, I can barely stand it."

"Stop it, Val. People will understand. People have already understood. You will see soon enough if some phases of it haven't been revealed to you already."

"Why?" Val felt tears stream down his face. "Why did this have to happen to all those good, innocent people, to you? And why me? I'm the last person to want that to happen!"

"'Why' doesn't matter," she said as she gently embraced her lover. "How you deal with the aftermath is what matters. You are down here to make peace with it and continue on with your life and make what you can right. The people who brought you down here are doing the same. You are all good people. Learn from every experience and be in every moment." She gently propped Val's face in her hands, wiped away a tear with a finger, and said as she looked into his eyes, "*You* are a good person, Val. I fell in love with you because of it. You have nothing to be sorry for, because what you did was not in malice, it was simply a terrible accident. Forgive yourself and continue being who you are."

"I wish all of you, but especially you, were still here," Val replied. "I love you, I still love you, I will never stop loving you."

"I know, my love. I will always love you." She looked toward the sky, which suddenly became brighter, then looked back to her lover. "You need to go now, my love."

Val embraced her even tighter as he looked into her beautiful dark eyes, just as brilliant as he always remembered them. "I don't want to go. I want to stay right here. Can't we be here for a while longer?"

Nga Nghin Do'i looked at him with tenderness and love in her eyes, then leaned in and kissed him on the lips. As she pulled away, she smiled and said, "No, we cannot. You need to go. You have a big day today. You will soon be closer to me than you have been in years. Go, my love. I love you."

With that Nga Nghin Do'i walked back into the lily field and melted into it as the sky got brighter and brighter. Val suddenly woke to find himself professing his love for her aloud with the sun shining directly into his eyes through a narrow gap between the curtains on a window across the room. Disoriented at first, Val quickly got up and walked to the sink to splash his face with water. He tried to shake off the vivid dream, but it only became more intense. A knock at the door soon interrupted his thoughts. When he opened it, there stood a smiling Bac-Viec Phuc-Vu. "We have a long drive today, sir. Could you be packed and ready in thirty minutes? Your host should meet us at our destination today."

Val nodded and smiled. "Absolutely. You want me to meet you in the lobby?"

The heavyset Vietnamese man smiled back. "That would fine, Mister Jordan."

Val met Bac-Viec Phuc-Vu in the lobby with his bag and followed him out to the car. He motioned grabbed Val's bag motioned him into the car, then put the bag into the trunk. Soon they were driving south out of the city. After twenty minutes, Val finally asked, "Where are we going today, my friend?"

"Dong Hoi, Mister Jordan—we are going to Dong Hoi." Bac-Viec Phuc-Vu glanced at his passenger in the rearview mirror to see Val's reaction. When he saw Val's blank, emotionless expression, he added, "I have family there. It will be nice because I get to visit them while you meet your gracious host and see the sights."

"How long will it take us to get there?"

"About four hours. We should get there around eleven."

The rest of the ride was rather quiet as Val kept to his thoughts. Val took in scenery and noticed that the watchtowers that used to dot the landscape were now all gone. The rice paddies were pock marked and bordered with large fish ponds in many places—obvious bomb craters. The hills and jungles were barely visible on the western horizon in the thick tropical air. Even the simple villages with their simple people were showing the effects of time. The villages were being replaced with what seemed like subdivisions. There was evidence that modern technology was making inroads. The simple existence was still there, but it was different than Val remembered. Nothing was left untouched by time. Soon the city of Dong Hoi loomed in the distance, and before long they were entering a city now much busier than Val remembered. As they slowly drove along, Bac-Viec Phuc-Vu made his way along streets that were crowded with more cars than Val ever saw there. "Where are we going?" Val asked.

"To my relatives' house, Mister Jordan. I would like you to meet them. Your host will meet you at their house later today."

"I would be honored to meet your family," Val said with a smile, glad to delay the pain he knew he'd feel when he revisited places from his past.

Soon Val was being greeted by Bac-Viec Phuc-Vu's family, and was invited inside for tea and lunch. He enjoyed spending time with them, and of course they were curious about this tall white man who knew their language. The children were just like those of the Hai Lan Langs many years ago—curious, giggling among themselves as they played with this American. After another hour, Bac-Viec Phuc-Vu received a call that Val's host was running late, which he told Val and asked if there was anything he'd like to see while he waited. "Yes," Val answered. "Could you take me to the *Tong-Hop*—Department Store?" Val was referring to Nghia Mau's store on the northwest corner of town.

Bac-Viec Phuc-Vu agreed and led Val to the car and drove him there. Val's heart began to speed up as they approached the familiar switchback, this time from the opposite direction. When he caught sight of the store for the first time, he was shocked to see that it was crumbling to the ground. When the car stopped, Val asked before he got out, "Didn't anyone want this property after Nghia Mau left?"

"Nhiem-vu Phuc-Nguyen would not allow it for a while. When he finally did put it up for sale, it was in too damaged a state for anyone to be interested in it."

Val looked at the store and glanced at the loading docks under the collapsed roof. As he grabbed the door handle to get out, he muttered, "I really destroyed a lot of lives that day—even the ones who didn't die in the blast." He got out and walked toward the store.

Bac-Viec Phuc-Vu climbed out almost as soon as Val had shut his door. "Mister Jordan. You didn't destroy the lives of those who survived. In the end, you only made them stronger and better"—he paused and took in a deep breath—"and you made yourself stronger and better, whether you realize it or not." He looked Val directly in his eyes. "Perhaps it's time you *do* realize it. You'll see by the end of this day, I hope." Suddenly the phone in the car rang, and Bac-Viec Phuc-Vu nodded his head and said, "Excuse me for a moment, Mister Jordan." He slid back inside the car to answer the phone as Val continued to look around. He walked up to the docks and memories flooded his mind of Nga Nghin Do'i, Nghia Mau, and the girls. He began to choke up as everything came rushing back. His reverie was interrupted by Bac-Viec Phuc-Vu's shout. "Mister Jordan—I have to pick up your host at my family's house. Would you like to come or will you be all right here for a while?"

Val choked back his tears and said, "I'll be here for a while, then I may go up the road."

"Fine, sir—I shall return shortly. I'll find you no matter where you go."

Val continued to explore the store. He knew it might be dangerous, but he wanted to see what, if anything, was still inside. The walls contained evidence of fires, and the only living things were bugs, spiders, rats, lizards, and snakes. The reception area was barely intact, and Nga Nghin Do'i's office had collapsed in on itself. He walked through a cobweb into the warehouse area and swiped at what clung to his face. The warehouse was empty, bereft of the life and goods it used to contain.

As he turned to leave, something caught his eye on the floor near where the entrance to Nga Nghin Do'i's office used to be. He crouched down, and after digging it free from the soot and ash, he saw it was an old photograph, damaged by the elements and time. He wiped it as clean as he could and was shocked to see that it was a picture of Nga Nghin Do'i and him embracing on the loading dock, perhaps one taken by the spies who'd been shadowing him during the war. Val stumbled outside and fell to the ground in the bright afternoon sun as he looked at the picture and felt the emotions rushing through his heart. As tears began to fall, he lost all sense of time there on the ground in front of her store.

"*Dung khoc nu a!*"—Don't cry! said a little voice from behind him. When he felt a small hand on his shoulder, he quickly dried his face and turned to see a young boy of about eight. He smiled and nodded at the young boy.

"*Tai sao buon?*"—Why are you sad? the boy asked with genuine concern as he looked into the eyes of this giant American who'd stood and was now towering over him.

Val smiled and handed the boy the picture and said. "*Cua toi vo. *"—My wife.

The boy, surprised that this big white man knew his language, looked at the damaged picture and could tell it was very old. "*Dep! Dep!*"—She's beautiful! Beautiful!

Val told the boy a brief story about the beautiful woman in the picture and himself. The boy seemed curious and listened intently. After talking for a while, the boy told Val that he was from a village northwest of town down on old dirt road. Val told the boy that the woman in the picture lived in two villages that used to exist near where he lived now. The boy's eyes lit up and he yelled, "*Ca ou—ca ou!*"—Fish pond—fish pond!

At first Val took the boy literally and started to explain that the woman didn't live in a fish pond but used to live in a pair of villages near his village—but before he finished he realized what the boy actually meant. He was referring to the crater that was once the Hai Lan Langs and must now be filled with water and was being used as a fishpond. "*Tao muon ca ou!*"—I want to go to the fish pond! Val held up an American dollar and explained that he would make it worth the boy's while.

"*Di di!*"—Let's go! the boy said with excitement and he waved at Val to follow.

§§§§§

Val opened his eyes as he looked down at the needle guide plate to Nga Nghin Do'i's old sewing machine. He looked at his hand and watched as his blood dripped into the soil at the edge of the pond. He could hardly believe that he was actually here again, almost in the exact place that he and Nghia Mau had hugged as they comforted each other near the inferno caused by Val's bombs. He glanced at his watch and noticed he'd been there almost an hour reminiscing about his experiences in Vietnam. His attention was drawn to the south side of the pond when he heard a car door slam shut. He looked up to see Bac-Viec Phuc-Vu getting out from behind the wheel. There were passengers visible inside the car, but he only thought he knew the identity of one. He turned back to the pond in silent meditation when he heard another door slam shut. He tried to dry the tears from his face as he heard footsteps approaching behind him, then he felt a gentle hand on his right shoulder as a woman's voice said in accented English, "My aunt told you she would never forget you, Valentine Jordan."

Val's heart nearly stopped. He stood and turned to see a young Vietnamese woman flashing a familiar smile. "Who are you? Who is your aunt?" It suddenly struck him—Nghia Mau! She'd mentioned a sister in Hanoi once.

"Though this is the first time we've met, I feel that I've known you forever. She always spoke of you; she said that you were a beautiful person. If she were here now, she would say, 'How are you, dear friend?'"

Val smiled as he wiped away yet another tear. Looking at this young woman was like looking at a young Nghia Mau. "How did you learn English?"

"Years of living with a political leader teaches you many things, my new friend. My name is Hien-Lanh Trung-Tram." She offered her hand to shake, then offered an embrace. Val mentally translated her name and realized it meant "gentle heart."

As he accepted the embrace from the stranger who felt oddly familiar, he said, "I will always remember your aunt's kindness—all the girls she helped. I now hear that you help orphans in and around Hanoi, just like she would do. Her kindness had guided me in my life. I'm inspired to be more like her." He looked at the pond again and paused to collect himself. "Even after all these years, all I can say is 'I'm sorry.' I hope you can forgive me— although I don't see how anyone be forgiving for what I did."

As she embraced her new friend, she replied, "Of course I forgive you. Nghia Mau forgave you the moment you told her that it was you who dropped the bombs, because she knew that you'd never deliberately hurt a friend. You never tried to hide it. You took full responsibility and had to live with the overwhelming burden for so long. She knew you loved the villagers, and you have paid a higher price than all of us. You are a braver and stronger person than I could ever be."

Her words came as a surprise. "No I'm not, Hien-Lanh Trung-Tram, and I realize that even more now. Nghia Mau was always the pillar of strength and kindness. She had the power to find peace and soften even the most stubborn soul." Val looked at the car and his host as he spoke.

"You are too kind." She leaned up and kissed him on the cheek as she wiped his tears. "My aunt said that your strength was your kindness to everyone, and Nga Nghin Do'i knew that too. You were always human first, a warrior second." She looked at the men approaching from behind. "Val, please give your host some time now. I will see you every day through the remainder of your time in Vietnam." She paused for a second, then added, "Vietnam. It feels good to be able to say that instead of 'North' from 'South' anymore. It's now just Vietnam. That's the way it should be."

"Major Jordan. Walk with me a moment." Val turned to see his host, Nhiem-Vu Phuc-Nguyen, walking up to him. "Stay here a few moments, Dear," he said to Hien-Lanh Trung-Tram.

Val walked with the political leader until they were out of earshot of everyone else. When they stopped, the communist faced Val at the edge of the pond. "For years I hated you. I blamed you for the death of my friends and family. I blamed all the problems I had during the war on you—maybe because you were the only enemy I had personal contact with. Do you remember how I would try to antagonize you whenever we talked at these villages? I arrogantly waited for years for you to come crawling back and begging for my forgiveness, as if I was high and mighty and you were beneath me. But after a strong woman you know talked some sense into me, I realized how wrong I had been. The fact is, I'm the one who owes the apology, Major."

Val was stunned. "*What?* I *did* kill your friends and your niece, sir! And you think you owe me an apology? What for?"

"I was never more wrong, my friend. I learned more from you during the war and even after this terrible accident than any other time in my life. You showed me more about courage and love than any meditation session or books ever did."

"I don't understand, sir. I've wanted to ask for your forgiveness since the bombs slid off my jet. In fact, one of the reasons I came down here was to make amends, to finally tell you in person how sorry I am."

"You loved my niece with all your heart—even *after* you found out that she was helping your enemy, an enemy that had caused some of your friends much pain and suffering. You still loved her and all the villagers, my friends and family. I learned more about the power of love and compassion and the power of the courage to stand up to your superiors who did not approve of getting help from your enemy. People are supposed to hate their enemies, but I never saw that in you. You hated the war, you saw the suffering it caused to everyone all both sides. I wanted to meet you in Washington a few months ago to personally thank you."

"I wish I could have met you in Washington at the ceremony, sir. There were many of my squadron mates who wanted to thank you for helping us get our friends back."

"That was an impressive ceremony. Maybe one day Vietnam will have a place dedicated to all who suffered during our war with America. We lost close to two million of our countrymen during that war. Brothers killing brothers, families torn apart, depending on what side they supported. It was horrible. I forced my lover and my niece into this war by making them move supplies for me. They did, but they hated it, just like they hated the war. They were like you—they never hated people, just the war. I wish they were both here to see the peace today. As far as your friends go, you don't need to thank me, Major. They were suffering at the hands of a horrible man, and I was glad to help you. It is I who still wants to thank you, Major Jordan."

"Why thank me? I would still hate me if I were you."

"No you wouldn't. You don't know how to keep hate inside you. That is what makes you strong, Major. Anyone can hate. It's easy and lazy. It takes more strength to love and be kind. No matter if someone was your enemy, you still cared about them as a person, you hated the situation that made you become enemies. Your love was stronger than your hate. You loved my family, you loved my friends, you gave me only respect—even though I tried to antagonize you whenever we met. So I ask your forgiveness. Your actions, were never out of anger or deviance—you were doing your duty. And *this*"—he waved is arm—"was a terrible accident. You still never hated your enemy. You cared for everyone, and you have suffered greatly for your kindness. You lost the woman you loved because of your actions, and you have had to live with that fact every day since, yet instead of being angry, begging for sympathy or being full of vengeance, you still show kindness. I want to thank you because you taught me through your splendid example that love is always, and always will be, exponentially stronger than enmity.

He sighed, then went on. "I realized that when I lost Nghia Mau in the bombings of Hanoi during the last days of the war. I'd sent her to the area of Hanoi that was attacked as I forced her to run messages for me. When I lost her, I was again angry at Americans, and my anger for you resurfaced—but like you, I had to face the facts that it was because of me and no one else that the love of my life was dead. It was my fault all along. I decided at that moment since we now shared a common yet tragic experience to be more like you and not hate my enemy and blame them for all my problems—especially the ones I was responsible for. Again, you taught me that love is stronger than enmity." He put his arm around Val and pulled him into an embrace. "Thank you, old friend. Thank you, and please forgive me for my anger. We may never be totally at ease with each other, but we do have something in common now that we did not have before."

Val embraced his old enemy and replied, "I accept your apology sir, although you never have to apologize to me. Thank you for helping my friends and keeping an open mind and giving me the chance to come down here again. My condolences for your loss of Nghia Mau. I loved her. I think about her and Nga Nghin Do'i every day." Val reached in his pocket and handed Nhiem-Vu Phuc-Nguyen the guide plate to Nga Nghin Do'i's sewing machine that had her initials engraved on it. He knew that the political leader had given it to his niece as a gift and that it would mean a great deal to him. Tears again ran down Val's face as he said, "I just found this near the pond. She loved you dearly, and she was an talented seamstress and gifted in so many ways. You gave it to her years ago, now I get the chance to give it back to you. I finally get to say what I've wanted to say for years to you in person—I'm so, so terribly sorry!"

The political leader looked down at the plate and tears began to stream down his face as well. "I know you are sorry, Major. You don't have to apologize anymore. Everyone knows it wasn't on purpose." Nhiem-Vu Phuc-Nguyen released his embrace and looked at his new friend and Nghia Mau's niece and his loyal assistant standing at the car. "Come—let's have some dinner."

"Sure. Just give me one more moment at the pond, sir."

"Of course." Nhiem-Vu Phuc-Nguyen turned toward the car and the two people waiting. He wiped his face and when he reached his companion and his new niece, he showed them the guide plate. Hien-Lanh Trung-Tram watched as Val walked to the pond's edge, and she shouted, "Val, they're here—all of them. They're all around all of us every day, no matter where we are—Nghia Mau, Nga Nghin Do'i, and all the villagers. They didn't *go anywhere,* you know!"

Val looked back and smiled. "I know. I now know." He looked up at the sky and at the surrounding countryside. He reached into another pocket and pulled out the photograph he found in the store in Dong Hoi, along with a single lily, a piece of incense, and a piece of paper that had a poem he'd written for this moment. The poem read:

I'm here after many a year

I'm here after shedding many a tear

I'm here not because someone told me so

I'm here because there are still so many things I need to know

I'm here because not even time can change how I feel

I'm here because I need to know what's false and what's real

I'm here because I have wounds that need to finally heal

I'm here because I couldn't change so many things

I'm here because there is so much onto which my heart still clings

I'm here again to finally end the fall after all this time

I'm here again to finally begin the long overdue climb

*I'm here because I finally realize how many moments with you I
wouldn't want changed*

*I'm here because I finally realize how perfectly each moment was
actually arranged*

*I'm here because I now know that even if I could've foreseen that
devastating day*

I'm here because I know that I would've loved you anyway

I'm here because another moment with you time will eventually grant

I'm here simply because I can be and because of me you can't.

As he set everything down, he lit the incense and watched the smoke rise in the still air. He wiped his tears and looked around again. His eyes briefly stopped on the village a mile north, where the boy that led him here was from. Then looked back at the pond. "My love, you were right. You've made me a better, stronger person. I *will* see you again. You were right—you were always right. I do feel closer to you now." As he walked to the car and his waiting friends, he took a last look at the pond and his surroundings, and all of a sudden a gentle breeze made ripples across the water and gently stoked the petals of the lily, flexed the edges of the photograph, and stirred the incense smoke. Val bowed to all three of his hosts, and then they all got in the car and slowly drove away to Dong Hoi.

CPSIA information can be obtained at www.ICGtesting.com
Printed in the USA
LVOW061702290612

288240LV00003B/136/P

9 781618 970473